BEAUTIFUL TERROR

A DARK STALKER ROMANCE

BURN IT ALL DOWN DUET
BOOK 2

HEIDI STARK

Beautiful Terror
Heidi Stark

FOREWORD

Your soul was not designed to carry the burden of someone else's refusal to grow.

—Anonymous

Everyone else rests.

And I just keep fucking walking.

—Lhakpha Sherpa

IMPORTANT NOTE

This is book 2 of a pitch-black romance duet with very triggering situations involving graphic descriptions of domestic violence and other violent situations. Please take this warning seriously.

Adoption
    Alcoholism
    Attempted murder
    Attempted suicide
    BDSM
    Blackmail
    Bullying
    Captivity and confinement
    Cheating
    Child abuse (mention)
    Coercive control
    Daddy/praise kink
    Death of a friend
    Dissociation and dissociative episodes
    Drink spiking
    Drug and alcohol addiction and recovery
    Drugging

Drug use
Dubcon
Emotional abuse
Financial abuse
Forced drug use
Gore
Grievous bodily harm
Homelessness
Infertility
Intrusive thoughts
Kidnapping
Mental health issues
Mention of past sexual assault
Murder
Narcissistic abuse
Non-consensual sex
Paranoia
Pedophilia allegations
Period sex
PTSD
Physical abuse causing serious injury
Poverty
Public sexual activity
Racism
References to pregnancy
Revenge pornography
Schizophrenia
Self-harm
Self-loathing
Sexism and misogyny
Sexual coercion
Sexual assault
Sexually explicit scenes
Sleep disorders
Slut shaming
Somnophilia
Squirting
Stalking

Suicidal ideation
Threats of violence
Torture
Toxic relationships

SUPPORT

If you or anyone you know is experiencing domestic violence and needs support, please call 1-800-799-7233, or if you are unable to speak safely, you can log onto thehotline.org or text LOVEIS to 1-866-331-9474.

PLAYLIST

Killer - Valerie Broussard
Angels & Demons - jxdn
Peter Pan - Kelsea Ballerini
I Ain't A Bitch - Alaura Lynne]
You Should Be Sad - Halsey
Vampire by Rumor - TX2
Mind Games - Sickick
Gangsta - Kehlani
Play With Fire - Sam Tinnesz
Miss Me More - Kelsea Ballerini

Bad Decisions - Bobi Andonov
Make Hate to Me - Citizen Soldier
I Feel Like I'm Drowning - Two Feet
Demons - Bryce Savage
Sick Like Me - In This Moment
The Devil In I - Nikki Idol
Figure You Out - VOILA
Bad Liar - Imagine Dragons
Monster - Willyecho

Love is a Bitch - Two Feet

How Villains Are Made - Madalen Duke
Who Do You Want - Ex Habit
Sugar - Sleep Token
The High - Bryce Savage
Traitor - Olivia Rodrigo
Gravity - Matt Hansen
Blossom - Røry
gfy - Blackbear, MGK
Human - Rag'n'Bone Man

The Emptiness Machine - Linkin Park
Joke's On You - Charlotte Lawrence
Over Each Other - Linkin Park
Needles - Seether
Death of Peace of Mind - Bad Omens
Lady, Touch Yourself - Nikki Idol
Bad Things - Nation Haven

Bad Things - Camila Cabello, MGK
Please - Omido, Ex Habit
Cravin' - Stiletto, Kendyle Paige
Daddy - Ramsey
On Your Knees - Ex Habit
Fuck Away The Pain - Divide The Day
RUNRUNRUN - Dutch Melrose

JOIN ME!

Love exclusive content, early access, and all the behind-the-scenes chaos? Then you belong in my world.

Hang out in my Reader Group – Where we obsess over morally gray men, scream about cliffhangers, and share the kind of bookish chaos you won't find anywhere else.

Get my Newsletter – Exclusive teasers, giveaways, bonus scenes, and secrets I don't share anywhere else, along with early opportunities to join my ARC team for upcoming releases. If you love surprises (and trust me, you do), you don't want to miss this.

Welcome to the dark side. You're going to love it here.

CHAPTER 1
IMPOSTER SYNDROME

MARGAUX

feel him leaning down next to me, his breath hot and shallow as he presses his ear close to my mouth and nose. My heart pounds as I realize what he's doing—checking my pulse. His trembling hand lingers near my neck for a moment too long, as though he's weighing something darker in his mind.

"Oh my god, I'm so sorry," he whispers, his voice cracking with something that might almost sound like remorse. Almost.

I stay limp, forcing my breathing to remain steady as his arms slide under me. "I'm so sorry," he repeats as he lifts me, as if I weigh nothing, cradling me like a child, and carries me across the room. My disorientation makes it hard to gauge where he's taking me, but when he lays me down on the bed, I feel the softness beneath me.

His hands withdraw, and I squint just enough to see that he's stepped back. A surge of adrenaline jolts through me. Without a second thought, I scream—loud, piercing, primal. My voice bounces off the walls, filling the room with a cacophony of desperation.

I lunge for the nightstand where I left my keys, my heart pounding so loudly it drowns out the chaos around me. My hands shake as I snatch them up and, in my panic, I glance around for my phone. It's nowhere in sight. A fresh wave of terror grips me—I can't waste time looking for it.

I make a break for the door. His hand shoots out, catching mine with a vise-like grip. He yanks at the keys, and I hold on with a ferocity that surprises even me. The jagged metal digs into my palm, sending a sharp sting up my arm. But it's nothing compared to the chaos screaming inside my head.

Somehow, I pull free, stumbling into the outdoor hallway and slamming the door behind me. I don't stop. My bare feet pound against the pavement as I race toward the security shack, each step fueled by the primal need to escape. The humid night air clings to my skin, heavy and suffocating, but I don't care.

I see the flashing blue and red lights before I hear the commanding voices. Relief floods through me, tangling with the adrenaline coursing through my veins. Someone must have heard my screams—a neighbor, maybe—and called for help. They ask me questions—too many questions— but my words tumble out like jagged stones.

"He hit me," I stammer, my voice trembling. "He smacked me in the face."

"What started it?" the officer asks, his tone detached, procedural. The words hit me like a slap.

What started it? What kind of question is that? I glance at the floor, biting back the bile rising in my throat.

"I was listening to a song," I manage. "By Machine Gun Kelly." My laugh is bitter and jagged. "He hit me because I was listening to a Machine Gun Kelly song."

The officer's eyebrows twitch, his expression unreadable, but he nods and takes down my words. They take pictures of my injuries—my swollen lip, my black eyes, my bruised arms, the red marks around my neck.

"Is he still in the apartment?" he asks.

I nod, though my body trembles uncontrollably. "He's... he's back there," I manage, my voice barely above a whisper.

The officers exchange a glance, then spring into action, moving swiftly toward my apartment. I collapse onto the small bench outside the shack, my breaths coming in shallow gasps. My words tumble out like jagged stones as another officer kneels beside me, asking more questions.

I glance back toward the flashing lights, my heart still racing. Relief and fear war within me, each battling for dominance as the weight of what just happened settles heavily on my chest.

"He jumped the fence," one officer pants as he returns to the group. "He's on the run."

Of course he is. Nothing motivates Timmy more than avoiding consequences.

They escort me back to the apartment, and we take a brief look around. Money is spilling out of the safe in the back room.

"Does anything seem to be missing?" one of the officers asks.

I take a quick look. "Some cash, I think," I say. "And my phone." And then I notice what else isn't there. My diamond and platinum engagement ring from my second marriage, which I designed myself, as well as the matching platinum wedding band. "And some jewelry."

Why the hell did he take those?

"Anything else?" he asks, his tone patient.

I shake my head. "No, not that I can tell. I'll take another look in a bit, though."

"Do you want to press charges?" another officer asks.

I hesitate, the words sticking in my throat. "No," I whisper. "Just… make him stop."

———

The next two days pass in a haze. The physical pain is nothing compared to the emotional weight pressing down on me. The mirror is a cruel enemy, reflecting back the swollen lip, the purple shadows around my eyes, the finger-shaped bruises on my arms. Each time I glance at my reflection, I feel more like a caricature of myself—a battered, broken version of the woman I used to be.

I call the domestic abuse hotline at the number listed on the card the police officers once again gave me, the little yellow rectangle a reminder of what I endured. A woman with a calm, soothing voice answers, and I share what I can remember of the other evening.

"This is serious, and you should consider leaving," she implores me. "Men who strangle their partners are seven hundred and fifty times more likely to kill them. There's a real chance he could come back and end your life."

I feel simultaneously terrified and numb at her words. The statistic is shocking. But Timmy wouldn't really try to kill me, would he? This was another aberration, a result of drinking too much and misunderstanding my laughter at a stupid song. Still, her words prickle at the edges of my mind. *Seven hundred and fifty times more likely to kill their partner.*

I google strangulation, and am upset to learn that when someone does try to strangle you, there's a risk that down the line—weeks or months or possibly years—it could lead to you having a stroke. Timmy's actions have potential long-term health consequences for me, and his penance is a couple of measly nights in jail. It doesn't seem right. But I'm too defeated to even think about going through the court process again. It's too much.

As a small respite, I drive over to the side of the island where my friend Rebecca lives with her boyfriend, Jetson.

We hop into her car and drive further to the part of the shore where people hang out around bonfires. She's sympathetic and supportive as I share my experience, and as a small act of warped defiance we blare Machine Gun Kelly songs through her speakers, singing them as loudly as we can.

We meet up with Jetson, who is hanging out with some of his friends over that way. The mood is relaxed, a stark departure from what I've just been through.

Later in the evening, the three of us sit on fold-out chairs down on the sand.

"You know, he's actually crazy," says Jetson, his tone grim. "He's likely to hurt you again. I know it's hard, and that you care about him, but I think you need to leave him."

"I agree," says Rebecca, her tone nonjudgmental. "Being with him is going to be a constant roller coaster of highs and lows. I know some people are into that, and if that's what you want, that's fine," she shrugs, "but he's dangerous, and I personally don't want to have anything to do with him ever again."

"Same," Jetson nods.

I sleep on the couch at their place, and for once I don't feel afraid. I don't fear the sound of the door beeping and swooshing open. He doesn't know where I am, and he can't access me because he's locked up.

I feel a sliver of freedom and, for the first time in a long time, I sleep well. But I know it won't last.

The next morning, I enjoy the long drive back to the apartment, listening to music and podcasts that I enjoy, that Timmy would only have negative things to say about.

For once, I feel like I've regained a tiny semblance of control over my life.

CHAPTER 2
GUESS WHO'S BACK, BACK AGAIN?

MARGAUX

And then he's back.

Timmy walks into the apartment, his face a mask of contrition. He moves toward me, slow and careful, as though I might shatter if he touches me too abruptly.

"I'm so, so sorry," he whispers, his voice thick with emotion, a tear running down his cheek. He pulls me into his arms, and I collapse against him, the tears spilling over before I can stop them.

He pulls something from his pocket and hands it to me. It's actually two things, the diamond and platinum rings. "I didn't mean to take these, I swear. I grabbed money for ice cream, and I guess they got tangled up in the bills somehow when they were in the safe."

I quirk a brow. "What?"

"Yeah, and I didn't want the cops to steal them, because I know they're important to you. So I shoved them up my ass and hid them there for a while. But then one of the other guys in the cell told me you can get dysentery from shoving things up your ass, so I took them back out."

I'm speechless.

"Don't worry," he continues. "I washed them really well."

I'm frozen, still unsure how to respond.

"I really didn't mean to hurt you," he murmurs, stroking my hair. "I just... I panicked. I'm so sorry, Margaux. I love you so much."

I cry harder, and he holds me tighter. For a moment, I let myself believe him. I let myself sink into the warmth of his embrace, desperate for comfort, for safety—even if it's from the very man who caused my pain.

———

The next day, I bring it up, unable to let it rest. "I still can't believe you hit me over a song," I say, my voice trembling.

Timmy frowns, his lips curving into a slight pout. "Well, you were smirking at me," he says. "And you laughed. I thought you were mocking me."

My jaw drops. "Timmy, that's no excuse. Even if I was—which I wasn't— that's no reason to hit someone. Don't you understand that?"

He shrugs, his expression almost childlike. "I don't know. I panicked. And then you said you were going to call the cops. I hate going to jail, Margaux. You know that."

My blood runs cold. "So you tried to *kill me*? To *avoid jail*? Do you even hear yourself?"

He shrugs again, his face devoid of the gravity of the situation. "I didn't mean to hurt you that badly. You're blowing this out of proportion."

I stare at him, my heart sinking as he dismisses my pain like it's a minor inconvenience. "You *strangled* me, Timmy. You smashed my head against the ground. I could have *died*. Look—I have two black eyes, a fat lip, and I'm covered in bruises... caused by you."

He rolls his eyes. "Your eyes aren't even really black eyes. Stop being so dramatic." He pauses, and then casually adds, "Oh my god, so the cop caught me outside the 7-Eleven where I was eating an ice cream."

It's as if the whole situation is a comedy in his eyes, a situation generating a repertoire of anecdotes to entertain others with, including me.

———

Later, as I stare into the mirror, his words echo in my mind. Maybe he's right. Maybe I am being dramatic. The bruises are fading now, turning a sickly yellow-brown. My lip isn't as swollen and lopsided.

Maybe this really *was* just a mistake.

Maybe it wasn't that bad.

I don't look like the photos of women who've had the shit beaten out of them by their partners, where their eye sockets are completely black and their fat lip reaches their nose. My face isn't covered in blood and scratches.

Maybe he did just really mean to knock the headphones off my ears and he missed slightly.

And then he panicked.

He didn't mean to smash my head on the floor, surely.

Especially not a hard concrete tile floor like this. He just wanted to stun me so I'd calm down and he could apologize for hitting me in the face.

Maybe it's not such a big deal, after all.

I'm embarrassed for calling them black eyes now.

Because they're nothing compared to what other people are subjected to by their partners on a daily basis.

I'm sorry I ever used that term for them.

The cops seemed to take it seriously, but they take everything seriously.

I bite my lip, the pain grounding me..

This was all just a misunderstanding, because I laughed, after all.

CHAPTER 3
SUNDAY SCARIES

MARGAUX

've had the Sunday Scaries before—back in my corporate life, when Mondays loomed like a guillotine. But this? This is something else entirely. The Scaries have reached Code Red. 911. *Nuclear.*

Again and again, it goes. The cycle, unrelenting. Sunday isn't a day anymore—it's a countdown, a pressure cooker—a trap.

90 Day Fiancé. It's just a reality show, a wildly popular one at that. I know people judge it, but I love it. For me, it's harmless escapism—mindless entertainment that fills the gaps in my chaotic life with other people's, usually sillier, drama. But for Timmy, it's something else entirely.

The show has become a battlefield, the arena for his unpredictable moods

A few hours before it airs, Timmy starts acting twitchy, the energy in the apartment shifting like storm clouds gathering on the horizon.

His movements are sharper, his tone clipped. It's as if he knows what's coming, what I'll inevitably want to do, and he's already preparing to fight it.

Every word, every action is a potential landmine. If we make it to the show without incident, he'll sit beside me, watching intently.

At first, it feels almost sweet—like he's taking an interest in something I enjoy.

But I know that's not how things will play out. These days, my stomach knots as the clock ticks closer to showtime.

If I press play? It's like pulling a pin on a grenade.

And today is no outlier.

"I hate this show," he declares, pacing the room. "It makes me really upset, seeing people fight like that on TV. It's toxic. It makes me emotional."

I raise an eyebrow, my voice incredulous. "Timmy, you watch horror movies where people are dismembered, tortured, and mutilated—where they cut off other people's body parts and torture animals—and *this* is what upsets you?"

"It's different," he snaps. "This is real. It's people hurting each other for entertainment."

I don't get it. I really don't. How can a trivial reality show provoke this kind of reaction when the messed-up stuff he willingly consumes barely seems to faze him? But I don't say that. I've learned not to poke the bear.

Still, the mere existence of the show is enough to set him off.

But then he starts talking. And talking. And talking. He analyzes every couple, repeating himself, interrupting the dialogue on screen. When I pause the show to hear him out, he'll monologue for twenty minutes.

If I disagree with his assessment of a couple or their choices, the tension spikes. That's the trigger. The powder keg explodes.

Sometimes it boils over. He storms off, slamming doors and muttering about how stupid the show is, how stupid I am for liking it.

He stomps out, slamming the door behind him, off to drink with the transient crowd on the beach. He comes back hours later reeking of cigarettes and cheap booze, his mood volatile, his words sharper than broken glass.

"You have an illness," he tells me, sneering. "For watching trash like that."

My chest tightens. "It's a show, Timmy. A stupid show."

"And you drink too much," he retorts, his slurred voice dripping with accusation. "You're no better than those idiots on TV."

I don't drink too much. Not really. Not like this. *Not like him.*

At least when I drink, I'm silly and fun and maybe a bit sloppy, not mean or cruel like you.

My inside voice has grown stronger since knowing Timmy. There's no point sharing my thoughts out loud—I know that.

I can just watch the show and enjoy it and move along with my life, but you can't.

And yet, some Sundays, he's different. He'll sidle up to me around showtime, his tone almost conciliatory. "You've worked really hard this week. Why don't you watch your show? I promise I won't complain."

Like he's granting me permission to enjoy my own life. Like I'm a child he's indulging with a treat.

I feel like I'm going insane.

The irony isn't lost on me—he's turned our real-life relationship into a drama more intense and damaging than anything playing out on screen.

————

Lately, Timmy has developed an obsession with back rubs. It started innocently enough—an act of intimacy, a way to relax together. But it's grown into something else entirely.

"Tickle me," he demands, handing me the tweezers. "Pull the hairs out of my back."

It's not sexual, but it feels invasive, a chore I never signed up for. And he reciprocates, but even that feels transactional, a reminder of the strings attached to his every gesture of kindness.

At the same time, his savory broths—once a source of comfort—have turned into another tool of control. I can't even enjoy a simple bowl of soup without it becoming a power play.

Whether he wants to offer the broth to me or not is indicative of his moods, which directly impact the energy in our apartment. *Off, off, off.*

If I have a sip, it tastes good. But I know it's just a game now. A weird tool. Imagine having broth as your tool to manipulate another human being. *Will I share it with you or won't I?*

And then he'll mention what a nice person he is, going out of his way to accommodate my preferences.

"See, I made it extra spicy, just the way you like it," he says, his tone saccharine.

"I made the onions just slightly cooked so they're crunchy for you."

"I made it super spicy, just the way you like it."

"I didn't put the crunchy things in that you don't like."

Always the gentleman and yet also never the gentleman.

So thoughtful, but the thought nearly always turns out to be grounded in manipulation.

Or, worse, he eats it in front of me with a smirk, refusing to share.

It's broth, not a dick, Timmy. Stop taking it so hard.

The games never end. Something as simple as soup has become a test, a manipulation, a reflection of his mood. And I hate it. I hate that he's tainted so many things I used to love.

There's no more spoon-feeding—which I'm fine with because that's annoying, although he does keep warning me it's hot. It's just a stark contrast from how he behaved when we first met, when he pretended to put effort in for anyone's benefit but his own.

I'm so tired.

I'm so exhausted.

There's literally nothing that Timmy can't find a way to ruin.

I don't know how that's even possible.

I didn't ask for this, Timmy.

I love your broths, but I wish that's all they were about.

I hate that something so deep of flavor, so rich, so resonant, can be made by someone like you. Someone fake deep. So into themselves and their shallow representation.

Something that used to make my stomach flutter now makes it flip like a wild storm.

Something that gave me peace now gives me panic.

Like you.

You were my life raft and now you're my murderous anchor, pulling me down into the murky depths.

I hate it.

I hate you.

But I also love you.

And I feel like I'm drowning.

CHAPTER 4
OOPS! HE DID IT AGAIN

He fucking hit her again.

That piece of walking human garbage dared to lay a hand on *my* Margaux.

My fingers curl into fists, the urge to fly over there and drive them straight through his pathetic face—to castrate him—is nearly overwhelming. The thought of Timmy's bloodied, broken form sprawled out beneath me is almost soothing.

But I can't intervene—not yet. Not now.

I know she won't accept it.

I pace the length of my office, replaying what I've read in their messages, their emails. The way he's wormed his way back in with those manipulative, sugary apologies. "I'm so sorry, baby. I'll change. I promise. I love you." Reminding her that he doesn't deserve her—he's right about that. Making her promises he never intends to keep. It's all so fucking predictable, like he's ripped a page out of *How to Gaslight and Manipulate 101: A Textbook for Abusive Boyfriends*. It makes me gag.

She's so damn smart—way too smart to fall for his bullshit—but when it comes to him, all logic flies out the fucking window.

She wants to believe his lies, and so she does.

And I can't blame her. It's not her fault. I know what she's been through.

I know how she's been conditioned to believe that scraps of affection are worth clinging to.

He's aging, he's balding, but he sweeps his long hair over his receding hairline and always wears a cap. I can see through it, though. The way his scalp flakes all over his black T-shirts.

His medical records speak for themselves. Toe fungus, staph infections, an STD here and there. They speak to someone who doesn't take good care of themselves, and puts themselves in avoidable situations.

She deserves so much more than him, but he's already poisoned her self-worth so thoroughly that she can't see it. Can't see that she's so much better than him. Can't see she's so much better *without* him.

Without him, she probably feels like she has nothing. And he knows it. That's his ace, the thing that keeps her tethered to him, no matter how much he hurts her.

Pair that with her stubborn Taurus nature, with sunk cost fallacy kicking in strong—she's already invested so much in this human dumpster fire—and she's toast.

I sit down, but the chair feels like it's on fire. I can't sit still. I slam my hands on the desk, then push up, pacing again.

I know how this ends. 'Men' like Timmy don't change. He'll drain her, suck the life out of her, until she's a shell of the vibrant, strong woman she was. And if I don't stop him, he'll destroy her.

But here's the problem—she doesn't see him as a threat. To her, he's still her hero, the man who 'loves' her—he's got her convinced they're soulmates, meant to be, that he cares about her more than anything. He's made her feel sure he's just misunderstood, and only she can help to fix his tormented mind. He *needs* her.

In reality, he doesn't care about anything but himself.

He's so much like her brother. The same slimy charm, the same knack for turning a room in his favor. It's probably why he's still breathing despite all the people he's screwed over. But unlike her brother, Timmy has no one watching his back. No one but his enabler of a father, and even that won't be enough to save him when the time comes.

"Dex. Are you in there, bro?" My workmate, Jordan, taps me on the shoulder, and I almost jump out of my skin.

"Fuck, you scared me, man."

"I was talking away to you, telling you all about my date last night. And then I just made up a bunch of bullshit. You didn't bat an eyelash at the stripping pizza dancers. That's when I realized you weren't listening to me."

"Stripping pizza dancers?" I'm so confused.

Jordan shakes his head. "Never mind, man. I'm just messing with you. You had your head in the clouds."

"Uh, yeah. Sorry…"

"Hey, it's not a problem. Are you still thinking about that girl? What's her name? Mary?"

"Margaux."

"That's the one."

"Yeah… she's going through something and I'm trying to figure out what to do about it."

"How so?"

"Dating some douchebag who's no good to her. He's smacking her around physically, but to be honest, I'm as worried about the mental damage."

"Narc tendencies?" Jordan quirks a brow.

"Absolutely," I nod and frown. "Very controlling and jealous. But also demeaning, and mixes it up with splashes of kindness. Just to fuck her all the way up."

"Good luck, man," he shakes his head. "It's really hard for people to realize they're in that situation. And then it's even harder for them to get out. My sister dated someone a lot like that for about eight months. That was three years ago and her mind's still all fucked up over the guy. Left her with a shattered sense of self-worth. She still cries over him at family dinners."

"Jesus. Yeah, that's what I'm worried about." My brow furrows, and I press my lips into a firm line. "I know she's going to wise up and get this guy out of her life. But I'm worried about the damage he'll do in the meantime. It looks like he's already pushed her friends away, and she has a tiny family. He's become like her entire world, and it's a dangerous world."

"That's how guys like him operate," says Jordan. "My sister's narc had her living in another town. Said they needed to move for—in his words—a fresh start. Promised her the world. But in reality, it was just his way of isolating her, and of moving her away from her support system."

"Wow, these guys are textbook shitheads aren't they?" I scowl. "This guy's done the same thing to Margaux. A real predator. Sunk his claws in on day one when she moved to a new location, and then got her kicked out of her place. Then suggested they move to this really remote part of the island where she can't even walk around because it's surrounded by tweakers. And then he leaves her alone for hours at a time after berating her."

Jordan lets out a low whistle. "Fuck, that's no way to live."

"I know, right? He's really dimming her glow. I hate to see it."

"So… what are you going to do about it?"

"I'm figuring it out," I sigh. "I don't want to risk pushing her away. Obviously, I want to go running in there to rescue her, but I have a feeling it'd just have the opposite effect. So I'm gathering all the information I can, and I'm waiting for the right time. I just hope I don't leave it until it's too late."

"Damn," he shakes his head. "Good luck man. That's some heavy shit."

"Lucky I'm strong." I flex my bicep and instantly feel stupid.

Jordan rolls his eyes and laughs. "Don't… ever do that around Margaux."

I laugh back. "No worries there."

If I step in now, if I go over there and rip him limb from limb like I want to, she won't thank me—won't see me as some kind of gallant white knight. No, she'll see me as the bad guy, the monster who took her 'true love' away from her.

My jaw clenches so hard it feels like my teeth might crack. It's a sick, twisted fucking reality. He hits her. He manipulates her. He degrades her. But somehow, I'm the one who'd look like the villain if I stopped him. I know how this type of relationship works.

I glance at the corner of my desk where her photo sits. She doesn't even know I took it. She was laughing, her red hair tousled by the wind, her blue eyes sparkling in the sunlight. That's the Margaux I fell for. That's the Margaux I'll protect with everything I have, even if it means walking this tightrope for a little longer.

I'll fix it soon enough—this isn't about *if* I'll act—it's *when.* Because one thing is certain: Timmy's days are numbered. He just doesn't know it yet.

I pull out my phone and open the encrypted app I use to monitor their messages. Yes, I know it's crossing a line, but fuck it. Desperate times call for desperate measures. If keeping tabs on him gives me an edge, then so be it. I'd rather cross a line than stand by while she's being systematically destroyed.

Soon, I'll have my moment. Soon, Timmy will get what's coming to him. But not yet. Not until Margaux sees him for what he truly is.

Because the only thing worse than losing her to him would be losing her trust. And without that, I'll have no way to save her—I'll lose all access and push her further toward that talking sewage leak.

And I *have* to save her.

Even if it's the last thing I do.

CHAPTER 5
THE EROSION OF SELF

MARGAUX

The days pass in a haze of dull pain and quiet dread. My head still throbs from the impact, the egg-shaped bump on the back of my skull refusing to fade, a constant reminder of that night.

The bruises around my eyes shift from purple to sickly yellow-green, a grotesque gradient that makes me avoid mirrors.

My throat aches, the lingering soreness a cruel echo of his hands around my neck. Every time I touch it, the words of the domestic violence advocate play on a loop in my mind: *Seven hundred and fifty times more likely to kill their partner.*

I haven't left the apartment. I can't. I'm too ashamed of the marks on my face, the ones that snake across my arms and legs where I hit the floor and where he gripped me like I was an object.

The physical wounds are bad, but it's the invisible ones that are worse. I feel as though I'm losing pieces of myself, slipping into an abyss where reality blurs and my thoughts betray me. I tell myself to hold on, but to what? He's been calm for the last few days—apologetic even—but it doesn't feel like peace.

It feels like a predator circling its prey, waiting for the right moment to strike again.

———

A FEW DAYS LATER

It starts small, like it always does. A comment, a look, an irritation in his voice that builds into something monstrous. By the time Timmy is screaming, I'm bracing myself, mentally checking out—but then, abruptly, he stops.

The silence is worse than the yelling. His scowl stays, his lips pressed so tightly together they turn white, and his eyes... those eyes. There's no apology in them—only menace.

He's hoping I'll drink enough to not remember. And that's fine by me, because I want to escape, too. I want to drink until this entire nightmare becomes a blur. And he knows it. Every time I leave the room to use the bathroom or grab something from the back room, I come back to find my glass refilled. At first, I thought it was kindness, a small gesture to ease the tension. But now, I'm not so sure.

The alcohol doesn't feel like an escape anymore—it feels like a trap. It's pulling me further into his world, his control, numbing me enough to dull my defenses.

And that's what he wants. For me to forget. To forget the bruises, the screaming, the manipulation. To forget my own sanity. Because if I can't trust my memory, how can I trust my judgment?

I know I'm slipping. I feel it in the way my thoughts tangle, in the way I hesitate before every word I say, afraid of how he might twist it against me. I'm unraveling, and I don't have the energy to stop it.

And so I go along with it, consuming cup after cup of cheap vodka. Because remembering would feel even more like madness.

And feeling anything is the last thing I can handle right now.

———

A week later, I see it. The reason for his recent calm.

It's a video, innocuous at first, appearing in the shared cloud we use for photos and files. I almost don't click on it, but curiosity gets the better of me because it's a video of me that I don't remember him taking. And then I'm watching it, my stomach twisting into knots as the scene unfolds.

I see myself sitting on the kitchen floor, mascara streaking down my face. My shoulders are hunched, my body language screaming defeat. My posture is off, like I'm trying to hold myself as still as possible so I don't accidentally provoke him any further.

The TV hums in the background, a jarring contrast to the tension in the room.

Timmy's voice is calm, too calm. "Can you just say it, Margaux? Just one more time? Can you just say it?" His tone is laced with mockery, his words slow and deliberate, like he's speaking to a child.

I don't respond. I can see the misery etched across my face, the way I'm trying to hold myself together. The shock in my eyes is evident, even on the small screen. He continues, his voice pushing, needling, prying. "It'd make it so much easier for everyone if you just say what you said."

I've stopped engaging, but that only seems to spur him on.

He sets the phone down, but the recording doesn't stop, the video now aimed at the ceiling. Suddenly, his voice explodes. "Stop hitting me! Stop pushing me!"

My voice, trembling and strained, cuts through his yelling. "I don't know what you're talking about. I'm sitting on the floor in the kitchen, and you're over on the other side of the room by the bed."

He's slurring his words now, sounding drunk, sounding dangerous.

My own voice carries a note of fear but also something sharper—defiance. I try to hold him accountable, pointing out the inconsistencies in his story, even though I know he's recording me.

I know he wants to twist this, to use it as evidence of something, but what?

The realization hits me like a blow. He's creating a narrative, crafting a version of events where he's the victim and I'm the aggressor.

He's not just trying to gaslight me in the moment—he's archiving his lies, collecting 'proof' to use against me. For what purpose, I don't know. Maybe to convince others. Maybe to convince himself. *Maybe to destroy me.*

All I'm doing in the video is speaking my truth, standing up for myself and correcting his lies. Holding him accountable for his changing stories. And yet he's making me out to be the one with the problem. I should feel angry, but all I feel is hollow.

I don't know if this is the first video he's taken like this, or if there are more that just haven't synced to the cloud. But it doesn't matter, really. The energy it would take to fight back is energy I don't have.

I've spent so long trying to defend myself from his words, his hands, his manipulation. Now it feels like I'm fighting a war I've already lost.

So the video stays out there somewhere, lingering in the cloud, waiting to be used against me. A shadow that will follow me, just like him.

For what purpose, I have no idea.

But I know it isn't good.

CHAPTER 6
DIGGING MYSELF DOWN DEEPER

MARGAUX

can't take it anymore. I really think I've reached my limit. My hands tremble as I type out an email for work, my mind unable to focus.

Something inside me has snapped, a fragile thread pulled too taut, finally breaking under the strain.

Every word I write feels like an impossible effort, every keystroke weighed down by the relentless cycle of chaos Timmy has put me through.

Every time I try to relax, my mind betrays me, pulling up maddening memories like a relentless slideshow of pain and indignity.

The smirking emojis and affectionate banter he exchanged with that ugly girl—her, of all people—are etched into my brain like a scar.

The bruises on my body that never seem to completely fade, a testament to his outbursts and the violence and general roughness that has become a part of my daily existence.

And his constant criticism, picking apart my words, my actions, everything that makes me *me*, until I feel like a hollow shell of who I once was.

He always has an excuse, of course. His star sign. His alleged mood disorder. Anything but personal accountability.

And he gets away with it, every single time.

Because every time I try to hold him accountable, he makes me regret it, so it's just easier to say nothing. To let things slide. To let him roll over me like a bulldozer.

It's the Timmy show and my co-starring role has warped to the point I'm now an extra making a cameo here and there.

But now, as I glance over at him lounging on the bed, watching another dumb movie, I feel the familiar tide of resentment rise within me. There he is, not making any attempt to be a productive member of society, while I'm here holding everything together—emotionally, financially, mentally. He knows that if he upsets me, it affects my ability to write, and sometimes renders me unproductive for the remainder of the day—so he upsets me a *lot*.

My fingers hover over my laptop keyboard as I force myself to stay calm, to keep the words from spilling out. But they're pressing against my chest, clawing to be free.

"You don't care about me at all. Just what I can buy for you," I say finally, my voice trembling but determined.

His eyes flicker toward me, disinterested. "K."

That one syllable. That dismissive, infuriating syllable. My heart pounds, blood rushing to my temples. "You don't actually care about me," I say, louder this time, anger cracking my voice like a whip.

"K."

The one-letter word feels like gasoline poured on an open flame, and I erupt. "I'm done with everything. I'm so done. You wasted months of my life. We are *done*. You never loved me. *You piece of shit!*" The words pour out of me, each one louder than the last, my voice shaking the air between us. My body is trembling now, too, humming with a sick energy. I'm mortified by my loss of control.

He finally looks at me, his expression a mixture of boredom and disdain. "Okay, fuck you," he says, his tone even, unaffected.

"Fuck you!" I scream, my voice raw and desperate, the sound of it ricocheting off the walls.

Without another word, Timmy stands and slides open the screen door. I watch as he walks off, his silhouette disappearing in the direction of the meth tents nearby. I sink back into my chair, feeling the adrenaline drain from my body, leaving me hollow and defeated.

What have I become?

I turn on one of my reality TV shows, my attempt at normalcy as I stare blankly at the screen. But it doesn't help. The shame is relentless, gnawing at me from the inside.

I could have said nothing. I should have said nothing. But how could I?

His apathy, his refusal to contribute anything of value to this relationship or his life, his constant provocations—it's like he's deliberately pushing me to the edge, testing how far I'll go before I break. And I hate that *I've* become the one starting arguments now—that *I'm* the one who yells and screams.

It's not who I am.

At least, it didn't used to be.

A few hours later, my phone buzzes. It's a text from Timmy.

TIMMY:

I left because I'm scared of you.

I stare at the message, my vision blurring with anger and confusion as I read it over and over. I mean, I was kind of being a bitch. I *did* yell at him. And technically, I *did* pick the fight. But I'm not letting him off that easily.

ME:

No. You want to fuck that ugly bitch.

And blame me.

That's what you want.

It's so gross.

As soon as I hit send, I feel a wave of shame crash over me. Who am I? Who is this bitter, angry woman sending hateful texts? I can no longer stop myself.

I've never been like this with anyone before, let alone a romantic partner. But now, with Timmy, it feels like all I do is lash out, whether in person or via texts—just like nearly every other text exchange with every other person on his phone.

I'm becoming the very thing I despise—he's shaping me into a monster, and I'm ashamed because I'm letting myself be driven there.

I hate myself for letting him drag me down to his level.

I'm becoming the problem, or at least part of it.

It's not who I am at my core, although maybe it is now. And I don't like what I'm seeing in the mirror.

———

Three days later, the pendulum swings.

Timmy stands in the kitchen, meticulously weaving ti leaves into a lei. His hands are careful, deliberate, as he threads hibiscus and plumeria into the green braid. "Margaux," he says softly, his voice full of reverence. "You're so beautiful. You deserve the world. I've picked flowers that match your gorgeous red hair and your freckles. I wanted to make you something to show you how much I love you."

The warmth in his tone wraps around me like a blanket, soothing the raw edges of my soul. For a moment, it feels like the start of our relationship again—those intoxicating early days when he made me feel special, cherished, adored.

"I love it," I whisper, my voice trembling. *And I do.* I love the lei, the gesture, the way he's looking at me with such tenderness. But more than that, I love the feeling of being seen, of being cared for, even if it's fleeting.

I let myself sink into the illusion, clinging to the hope that maybe this time he'll actually change. I'm holding out hope that this version of Timmy, the gentle and thoughtful one, is who he really is.

But deep down, a small voice whispers a truth I'm not ready to face: *that version of him was never real.*

As I lay my head on his shoulder, inhaling the sweet scent of the flowers he picked just for me, I feel the weight of my own transformation.

I've always been someone who uplifts, who loves deeply and forgives easily. But now, I'm unkind. I'm mean.

I'm losing myself, piece by piece, and I don't know if I'll ever find my way back.

I don't know if I'll survive this.

CHAPTER 7

THE AGONIZINGLY SLOW WHEELS OF JUSTICE

DEX

I lean back in my chair, stirring the coffee I don't really want, as I chat with my friend. Cynthia works in the domestic violence division of a social justice organization.

"How have things been going?" she asks, peering over her cappuccino.

"Pretty good," I say. "But I'm worried for a friend of mine, and I'm hoping I might draw on your expertise. Domestic violence isn't something I'm well-versed in, and I think she might be in trouble. But I don't know the ins and outs of it."

"Fire away," she says. "Anything to help you."

"Okay, so this tool-knob she's been dating—well, apparently they're engaged—" I roll my eyes. "Anyway, I did a little digging, and he has at least six separate restraining orders filed against him. But it looks like most of them didn't turn into anything. Something to do with dissolution after the hearing."

She nods and puts her coffee down. "So, this is actually really common," she explains. "Basically, it's a huge deal for a victim of domestic violence to actually get up the courage to go to the courthouse and file for a temporary restraining order. You have to go within court hours, and there are other people sitting around you while you fill out the form. The form itself is very long—pages and pages—and you have to be as descriptive as possible. An advocate might come and sit with you and help you to fill it out, but it's hit or miss as to whether the person you end up getting is helpful or not—it's a volunteer position after all."

"I see. That all sounds intimidating."

"Yep," says Cynthia, taking another sip of her coffee. "And then when you've completed the form, you hand it in and need to go through it again with a person representing the court. They make sure that it's filled in correctly before it goes to the judge. So they'll walk through it with you and ask additional questions. Then you need to leave the courthouse—for a few hours generally—and come back to collect the restraining order, and that's if the judge even signs it off."

"Then what happens?"

"Well, depending on the court, the victim may have to drive to the police station and hand in the restraining order to the cops. In some cases, the courts will email it directly to the police station, which makes it a bit easier."

"And then what? It gets served and that's it?"

"No," Cynthia shakes her head and frowns. "Then the victim has to come back to court and face the accused. The abuser gets to defend themselves and tell their side of the story. And then the judge decides whether to make the order permanent for a set period of time, or to dissolve it. That can be another point at which people dip out, because in a sense, it means they relive the incidents driving the restraining order."

I frown. "Jesus."

Cynthia's words are still bouncing around my skull like a ricochet. "It's like the system is set up to keep victims silent," I mutter.

Cynthia nods, her expression solemn. "It often feels that way. I've seen so many people walk out halfway through the process, defeated before they even get the temporary restraining order. The system is supposed to protect them, but it's built in a way that makes them relive their trauma at every step."

I let out a low breath, my jaw tightening. "And the abuser? They just… get to fight it? Counter-file and make themselves out to be the victim? That's just—" I can't even finish the sentence. My fists clench under the table.

"That's one of the hardest parts," Cynthia says softly. "It turns the entire process into a battle of credibility. And abusers often have the upper hand because they know exactly how to manipulate the narrative. They come in prepared, armed with whatever they think will make them look good and the victim look unstable."

I grind my teeth. "So Margaux would have to sit in the same room as that bastard, while he lies through his teeth and tries to make her look like the bad guy?"

Cynthia nods. "Exactly. That's why so many victims don't show up to the hearing. It's just too much. And without the victim there to testify, the restraining order usually gets dissolved."

The thought of Margaux, standing alone in a courtroom, facing Timmy's smirking face as he twists reality to suit his narrative, makes my blood boil. She would be retraumatized over and over again, and for what? A piece of paper that might not even keep him away?

I think back to ten or so years ago when Margaux went to trial for being sexually assaulted. I remember the agony it put her through. I know how badly it affected her, how it ripped her apart and revictimized her—maybe even more than the actual rape. I can't even imagine how retraumatizing it must be to go through this process and file at all. Judges and courthouses and police stations and cruel counter-accusations—all the things I know she's tried desperately to avoid and push from her mind for the past decade.

"Jesus Christ," I say, running a hand through my hair. "Can they make it any more difficult for the victims? No wonder she was too scared to press charges. I can't imagine her going through that again, not after..." My voice trails off.

Cynthia reaches across the table and squeezes my hand. "I'm sorry," she says, her voice gentle. "I know it's hard to hear all of this, but knowledge is power. If you're going to help her, you need to understand the hurdles she's facing."

I nod, swallowing hard. "I just... I can't believe this is how it works. The system is supposed to protect people like Margaux, but it's like it's designed to break them even more. How the hell is that justice?"

Cynthia's eyes are sad but resolute. "It's not justice. Not yet. But that's why we fight. It's why I do what I do. And it's why people like you need to step up, too."

I sit in silence for a moment, my coffee growing cold in front of me. Cynthia's words sink in, but so does the reality of the uphill battle Margaux has faced—and will likely continue to face. She's strong, but even the strongest people have their limits.

As I walk out of the coffee house, the brisk air hits me like a slap in the face. My thoughts are heavy, my mind racing with everything Cynthia said. It feels like the system is rigged, like it's designed to grind victims down until they give up. To make them feel worse and to discourage them from coming forward.

And Margaux is a smart cookie, but the whole process just sounds... confusing and overwhelming, in a situation where I'm sure the victims of these crimes are already confused and overwhelmed.

Margaux doesn't deserve that. She deserves peace, safety, and the chance to heal without the constant shadow of fear. And if the system won't give her that, I will. Whatever it takes.

I clench my fists as I walk to my bike, determination settling like a stone in my chest. Margaux doesn't need to face this alone. Not anymore.

Because while the system might be broken, I'm not.

And I'll do whatever it takes to keep her safe—no matter what lines I have to cross.

CHAPTER 8
I'M SO EXTRA

MARGAUX

A few days later, we're sitting on the bed. Timmy is immersed in some sci-fi movie while I'm trying to read a book for work to understand a few tropes I'm less familiar with. The contrast couldn't be starker —him, absorbed in fiction purely for fun, and me, fighting to stay focused on a work task I genuinely need to get through.

At first, his running commentary is just background noise. A comment here, a question there. But as the movie progresses, his words start coming faster and louder, like a child unable to watch quietly. He's narrating every scene, asking my opinion about characters and plot points he knows I'm not paying attention to. He *knows* I detest this type of sci-fi, too—the kind with aliens and spaceships—I respect that other people enjoy it, but it's just not my thing.

"Timmy, please," I say, trying to keep my tone calm but firm. "I need to read this, and you're slowing me down."

His head snaps toward me, his expression morphing from casual to wounded in an instant. "You're such a bitch! I can't believe you're so mean and cruel to me. I was just including you in what I was doing."

I take a deep breath, counting to three in my head. "I'm not being cruel. I'm just asking for a little peace and quiet so I can concentrate."

"You should really stop drinking," he snaps, his tone laced with disdain. "It turns you into a complete asshole."

My stomach twists. I've barely touched my drink. It's not alcohol fueling my frustration—it's his constant disregard for my boundaries, my work, my time.

"For fuck's sake, Timmy," I finally snap, my voice rising despite my efforts to stay composed. "I just want to sit here and read. Can't we do separate activities side by side? Must we do exactly the same thing at all times? I love you, but for fuck's sake."

He huffs and turns his attention back to the movie, sulking like a scolded child. I try to refocus on my book, but my motivation for reading has evaporated, replaced by a simmering frustration that refuses to let me settle.

Shifting gears, I grab my laptop and open a document. Writing has always been my escape, and I hope the shift will help me channel some of this energy into something productive. My motivation to write usually dries up the moment Timmy starts acting like this, but today feels different, so I go with it.

For a moment, it works. Words flow freely, and I start to feel a glimmer of accomplishment. But it doesn't last long.

The movie ends, and Timmy switches to playing Mario Kart.

I brace myself, hoping he'll get absorbed enough in the game to leave me in peace. But it's not long before his voice rises again.

"*Stupid fucking game!*" he yells, slamming the Switch down on the bed. "It's so *rigged!* The computer is *against me!*"

"Timmy, it's only a game," I say, trying to keep my voice steady. "Just try again. Please, I'm trying to write."

He glares at me as if I'm the source of his frustration, his anger at the game spilling over onto me. "Don't tell me to be quiet in my own house," he growls. "Fuck you."

I swallow hard, willing myself not to react. The tension in the room is suffocating.

He picks up the Switch again, but I can feel his agitation radiating off him in waves. It's only a matter of time before it boils over again.

Sure enough, after coming third in a race, he throws another tantrum, muttering and cursing loudly under his breath.

"Timmy, *please!*" I snap, my voice breaking. "I can't handle constant narration about a film when I'm reading, and I can't handle tantrums over video games while I'm writing."

He stares at me for a long moment, his eyes cold and accusing. "You're awful, Margaux. You know that? Just *awful*."

I sigh, my shoulders slumping under the weight of his words. "You're right. I know. I must be so extra."

"You are," he says, his voice sharp and cutting. "You really are."

The words hang in the air like a noxious cloud, choking me. I sit, staring at the screen, my fingers frozen over the keyboard. The words I was so eager to write have vanished, replaced by a hollow emptiness that settles deep in my chest.

I know I'm not awful. I know I'm not 'extra' for asking him to respect my need to get work done. But the constant drip of his dismissive, biting comments wears me down, chipping away at my confidence and my sense of self.

And the worst part is, I can feel myself continuing to change—becoming angrier, more reactive, less like the person I used to be.

————

Later in the evening, he starts pushing my buttons again, over nothing, and then locks himself in the back room.

I try to follow him in there to have a conversation, but then I hear the unmistakable sound of him drilling the door shut.

"Are you fucking kidding me?" I scream, louder now. "You just *drilled* the *door shut*?"

It's very Timmy of him to make a hole in the perfectly good door. I'm beyond infuriated.

"You're such a fucking piece of shit loser! You have no friends!" The words coming out of my mouth are vile, the resentment that's been building up now spewing freely. But I can't stop the torrent. "Well, you have *two* friends but neither of them wants to spend much time with you! You wear people down and nobody can take you in anything more than tiny doses!" My words are mean, but they're also accurate.

I'm shrieking now, my voice loud enough to ring in my ears.

Suddenly, there's a knock at the door.

I peer out the peephole, and a member of the security team is standing outside.

Fuck.

I sigh and open the door.

"Margaux, we need you to lower your voice," says the guard, her face grim. "It's quiet hours, and you're being very loud."

I'm mortified. "I'm so sorry," I say, my cheeks burning. "I'll stop."

She nods and then leaves, and I stand in the doorway for a moment, mortified.

Half an hour later, I'm even more embarrassed when I check my email and see the write-up come through, with my landlord cc'd on the email. "Margaux was yelling during quiet hours." In the scheme of things, not an egregious charge, but still embarrassing.

Fucking fuck.

And the irony that Timmy is now smirking at me, the back door now undrilled and open, gleeful that even though he's the one who usually does the yelling, he's getting off scot-free.

"You really need to work on yourself," he grins cruelly. "You're drawing attention to us for all the wrong reasons."

I bite my tongue while blood hammers in my temples, and my body begins to shake.

Timmy's lack of respect and constant need for validation are driving me to these breaking points, but when I try to point it out, he acts out and makes me regret it. So I focus on what I can control, dwelling on my own outbursts, my own raised voice, and I hate myself for it.

Maybe I am awful.

Maybe I *am* the problem.

CHAPTER 9

THE TIGHTROPE: OBSESSION, STRATEGY & RESTRAINT

DEX

Margaux dominates my every thought. Her laugh, soft and melodic, plays on a loop in my mind. The way she brushes her hair back when she's focused or nervous—it's burned into my memory like a sacred image.

I've memorized every detail of her face, from the way her freckles dot her cheeks like constellations, to the tiny crease in her forehead when she's concentrating. She's everything. *And she's trapped.*

It really pisses me off that he's treating her like that.

Clearly, she deserves better. I mean, anyone does.

But I can see the games he's playing with her mind.

The way he gives her just enough attention and then cruelly yanks it away.

He's manipulating her, toying with her emotions, and she's such a genuine person I'm sure it's eroding her soul by now.

And while his physical abuse is enough to make me want to murder him five times over, it's this mind-fuckery that makes me absolutely insane with my own rage.

I can tell that it leaves her feeling lost, lonely, confused, abandoned. To be in a relationship and feel lonelier than if you were by yourself is telling.

It means that something's missing. That you're not getting the companionship and camaraderie that you'd assume would be one of the highlights of being in a close relationship with someone.

And look at him, the piece of shit. Repeating the cycle over and over, dragging her further down with each move. Reaping joy from her misery.

But I can't rush in like a hero from some poorly written romance novel. If I misstep, if I act too soon or too forcefully, she could see me as the enemy. Margaux is stubborn, and her pride is formidable. Push her too hard, and she might retreat further into Timmy's grasp. And then? I'd lose her. Completely.

So, I balance on this tightrope, teetering between my obsessive need to save her and my calculated restraint. Every instinct in me screams to act, to end this nightmare for her, but I know I have to play the long game. It's the only way to protect her without pushing her away.

The pictures of Margaux's battered face are burned into my brain. Two black eyes, a swollen lip, bruises trailing her arms and legs like a roadmap of pain. My stomach churns as I study the photos she must have sent to someone—a therapist, a friend, maybe even just to document the evidence for herself. Evidence of what she's enduring. A warning to herself of what could so easily happen again.

It doesn't matter how I saw them. What matters is what I'm seeing. Bruises. Swelling. *Fear.*

Two black eyes. That's not just abuse—it's potential brain trauma.

My mind flashes to the research I've been doing on head injuries, and my chest tightens. *What if she's walking around with a ticking time bomb in her skull because of that human dumpster fire?*

I double-check court records, desperate for a sliver of justice. Timmy *was* arrested. But the charges didn't stick. Of course they didn't. He's slippery, a master manipulator. He's probably already convinced the cops it was all a misunderstanding—and Margaux wouldn't press charges. I understand why. She's already been let down by the justice system before.

My fists clench. My jaw tightens. I want to kill him. Snap his neck and leave him for the meth heads he's so fond of. But I can't. Not yet.

I've hacked her webcam and phone camera—not to spy, but to protect. I need to know she's okay. But the image of her sitting at her desk, shoulders hunched, eyes dim, cuts deeper than any blade could. She looks so tired. So drained.

I watch her text thread with her older sister, Amanda. Margaux glosses over the abuse, downplaying Timmy's behavior.

Amanda presses gently, trying to reach her, but Margaux deflects, focusing on the rare 'good moments'. Every time she defends him, it feels like a knife twisting in my chest.

I want to grab her, shake her, make her see the truth. But I know better. If I push too hard, she'll only dig her heels in deeper.

Timmy's a master manipulator, and he's playing his part well. He pretends to be the man she fell in love with—charming, funny, attentive. I know it's all an act. The real Timmy is a coward who gets off on destroying people.

The thought of him gaslighting Margaux, making her doubt herself, makes me want to put my fist through a wall. But I remind myself: patience.

He'll slip up.

And when he does, I'll be ready.

———

Timmy might think he's untouchable, but I've been working behind the scenes, unraveling his pathetic excuse for a life.

I lock him out of his accounts and leave trails on the dark web for others to hack into. Soon, bizarre posts—'Timmy Loves Twilight,' 'Live, Laugh, Love Enthusiast! DM Me for Inspirational Quotes ', 'Certified Clown College Graduate ', 'Official Rainbow Dash Cosplayer—Brony and Proud , 'Bigfoot Fan Club President!'—begin to appear. His small number of followers mock him, and Margaux's amused smirk is everything.

Timmy tries blaming her, but quickly realizes she has no part in it.

Packages from Timmy's parents—tools and clothing he can't afford on his own—get rerouted to random addresses. Watching him try to explain it to his parents is priceless. "It must've been stolen from the mailroom—the neighbors must be out to get me," he insists, frustration oozing from his every pore as he paints himself as the victim once again.

If all goes well, this will eat away at his parents, sowing seeds of doubt that should have been there all along—I *want* them to wonder if he's taken their gifts and sold them for booze and drugs.

His father's ongoing secret 'soda money' deposits vanish, funneled into an untraceable account I control. Timmy flails, too stupid to untangle the mess. Watching him plead with his enabling father for more money, his voice dripping with entitlement, is sickly satisfying.

I tweak his phone settings to delay texts, sowing paranoia. He texts a dealer, desperate for his next fix, only to be ghosted because of a message I sent. The dealer's 'Don't contact me again, loser,' is just the icing.

The paranoia will eat him alive before the drugs do.

I craft an enticing fake email from a local employer needing help with construction work and offering to pay a premium hourly rate. The moment he leaves for his fake 'interview,' Margaux gets a few hours of peace. I picture Timmy standing at a locked office door, confused and frustrated, and it's glorious.

Every move I make is calculated. If Timmy suspects Margaux, he'll take it out on her. And if Margaux suspects me, I could lose her trust forever. So, I stay hidden, creating distractions and diversions, letting the chaos unfold as if karma itself is at work.

———

I send Margaux a care package—flowers and a gift card to Dock Bar, the place I know she loves in Downtown. Something small, something that says, 'You're not alone'—something that will make her feel special and get her out of the house. But when she receives it, she assumes it's from Timmy.

Timmy, of course, takes credit. He grins like the Cheshire Cat, playing the part of the thoughtful boyfriend. "I knew you would just *love* it! It's our special place, the first place we met and the place where we had our engagement party!"

Margaux flinches at the mention, clearly thinking about Parker and his threats that fateful night.

But I know better. I see Timmy later, through his hacked webcam, seething with jealousy. He's convinced another man sent the package, and the paranoia is eating him alive.

For a moment, I feel a flicker of satisfaction. But then I worry.

Did I make things worse for her? Is she at greater risk because of my actions?

The thought twists my gut.

———

I've set the chessboard, and the pieces are moving. Every step I take brings me closer to ending this nightmare for Margaux. But I have to wait. I have to be patient.

Margaux is strong—stronger than she realizes. I see it in the way she picks herself up after every fall, the way she keeps going even when the world is crushing her.

But she doesn't see it herself. Not yet.

I'll wait. I'll watch. And when the time comes, I'll strike. Timmy won't even see it coming.

But for now, I'll stay in the shadows, protecting her from afar. Creating 'inconveniences' to chip away at Timmy's carefully curated facade.

Because Margaux isn't just someone I want to save—the more I watch, the more I know she's the woman I want to spend my life with.

I'll do whatever it takes to make sure she gets the chance to live the life she deserves.

And I'll make sure Timmy pays for all he's done.

CHAPTER 10
ALICE HAS ENTERED THE CHAT

MARGAUX

vague-post on Facebook, because that's how I deal with emotions now. It's a cry for help wrapped in plausible deniability, an outlet where I can vent just enough without inviting too many questions—or so I think.

The response comes quickly. My roller derby friend Alice messages me. We haven't talked directly in a couple of years, but we've stayed connected, liking each other's posts and trading jokes in comments. She's the kind of friend who makes you feel seen even from a distance.

She's exactly the person I need right now.

ALICE:

You okay?

ME:

I've been better. But yes, I am okay. Thank you for checking in xoxo.

ALICE:

What's going on?

ME:

Life.

Her honesty stops me in my tracks. Should I downplay everything, or let her in on just how bad things have gotten? There's something about Alice that makes her feel safe—a mixture of humor and straightforward compassion.

She's the type of friend who'd threaten to stab someone for me, if necessary. That kind of loyalty doesn't come around often.

I think of the people who've distanced themselves: Sven, who decided I was too much to deal with. Paulo, whose once-steady friendship has started to feel tenuous. With Alice, though, I don't feel judged. She's a constant, supportive anchor, even in moments like this.

So I decide to be honest—at least a little.

I feel lighter already. Alice has that effect—her humor and candid honesty strip away some of the isolation I've been drowning in. Her words are like a warm hug, breaking through the loneliness that's felt suffocating lately. I can feel my chest loosen for the first time in days.

ME:

Pink ass glasses, motherfucker.

His family is cool.

ALICE:

I'm not gonna tell you to leave him, that's your business. But I will maybe tell you not to marry him.

ME:

Lol, thanks boo.

ALICE:

You know, since marriage is legal and shit.

Her humor coaxes a laugh out of me. It feels good, even if it's fleeting.

ME:

I'm meeting his fam in person next week in Montana.

You know I'm a serial marrier right? 3 and counting.

ALICE:

Montana is so pretty!

ME:

Yeah, I went there with D once on a vacation and it was so fun!!

ALICE:

So his family is cool. What does he do that isn't cool?

I hesitate but then let it spill out.

ME:

Yell, and say he's going to kill me. And one time he tried to strangle me.

He can't handle liquor. Otherwise he's quite nice.

I'm rolling my eyes at myself typing this out.

He also sleeps in until almost midday, and then watches movies all day while I scrape through my savings paying rent. Gosh, he is a WINNER. I really have hit the jackpot, haven't I?!

There's a pause before Alice replies. I can almost feel her weighing her words carefully.

ALICE:

Look, I know you already know what I'll probably say, so I just am going to write out this sentence as a placeholder.

The only thing I am actually going to be super blunt about is that strangling and, "I'm going to kill you" deal, because that, in cruel statistics, bodes very badly for you, and that makes me really worried.

Her words are sobering, like a cool splash of water. A reminder of just how far I've let this go.

ME:

I know, and thank you. I have been googling. He has stopped doing that, just was yelling yesterday. And I got so mad I yelled louder and got told off by my apartment. That's not me.

ALICE:

It doesn't sound like you.

Her kindness gives me permission to admit the parts of myself I've been ashamed of. I tell her more about my yelling, about getting written up by the building, about how the neighbors seem to have no issue with Timmy's tirades, but suddenly cared when *I* raised *my* voice.

ALICE:

Again I know I don't know your life story, but
between the 2 of us, I'm the yeller.

Like I do not have an 'indoor voice' half the time, so
yelling is expected.

ME:

I am actually slightly tickled that I got written up by
my apartment building for yelling.

Bc I have a voice now.

ALICE:

I can get that! It's fun to learn something about
yourself.

ME:

It's also annoying bc he was yelling for ages before,
but I guess lower octaves don't disturb the
neighbors. And also I yelled later in the evening than
he did, bc I was getting more and more annoyed
over the course of the evening, lol.

ALICE:

Okay, that's just stupid and annoying.

ME:

You know women get that brunt…

ALICE:

Oh absolutely. I was also going to guess they also
probably were offended by a GIRL YELL.

ME:

Yeah, girls are not allowed to yell.

Or roller skate and smash people in the face.

ALICE:

I feel like we just didn't get that memo.

I dunno. Misogyny strikes again!

I send her a picture of the beachfront view from my apartment, with Sabre looking out at the waves.

The view is stunning, but it feels like a cruel joke—beauty outside, chaos within.

ALICE:

I hate you right now.

ME:

Nah, you love me. 😚

ALICE:

It's true, bluff called.

I laugh, the kind of laughter that feels like salve on a wound. It doesn't erase the pain, but it dulls it for a moment.

We talk about roller derby for a while, and I send her a video of my infamous skating fall.

ALICE:

HELMET!!!!!

ME:

LMFAO I know 🤣

ALICE:

Gonna have a heart attack watching y'all without your helmets.

ME:

Anyway, I'm pretending everything is fine. That's healthy, right?

ALICE:

I mean it's not, but I also do the same thing. Like constantly.

ME:

Dissociating is the official word.

ALICE:

Too bad denial doesn't have any essential nutrients.

ME:

Lmao. If so, I already have a bulk vitamin pack.

The conversation feels like coming up for air. Alice doesn't push, doesn't demand answers or solutions. She's just there. And in this moment, that's enough.

———

The next day, she checks in again.

ALICE:

Back to why I reached out.

You said you were in a pinch yesterday. That still the case, and can I help?

Her kindness makes my chest ache, but in a good way.

ME:

Agh, just saw this. Thank you!! I was just in a non-physical argument that didn't make sense, and feeling very isolated all the way out here. You were a massive help just by being here and I appreciate you!!

ALICE:

Is he behaving now?

ME:

Yes. There has been no drinking for several days, so it's been nice.

Like I said, we're visiting his parents on Wednesday in Montana for almost a week, so that will be interesting.

As I hit send, I feel the weight of my reality pressing down again. But at the same time, I feel lighter than I have in weeks. I don't know what's coming next, but for now, I know I'm not alone.

For the first time in a long time, there's a flicker of what feels like hope. I have no idea what Montana will bring, but at least I know Alice is only a message away.

CHAPTER 11

THE PRICE OF PEACE AND STOP COOKING ME FUCKING STEAK FOR BREAKFAST

MARGAUX

September has arrived, and with it comes a stifling monotony that settles over every day like a heavy fog. My life feels like a looped movie with no plot twists. Wake up early, work while Timmy sleeps in—sometimes until noon or later. Then he wakes up, and the routine truly begins.

Timmy's 'mornings' are focused on one thing—an elaborate breakfast. He knows I don't typically eat breakfast, but he insists on making it for me anyway. Watching him cook should feel endearing, but instead, it feels like an act of control.

Once he's done, he observes me like a hawk as I sit across from him, waiting for me to eat. I'm not hungry, and I feel like I'm being force-fed, but the pressure in his gaze makes refusal seem like a dangerous choice. So I eat, bite by reluctant bite, swallowing not just the food but the growing resentment I feel every morning while he snores beside me as I write.

Then, as I start to work again, his focus shifts to the TV. When he was in jail, one of his cellmates—an advocate who supports criminals getting off heroin, who was arrested for stealing a scooter—had told him that if he got a Firestick, he could use an app to watch pirated movies. Of course, he pressured me into buying him the Firestick, and he's been watching anything he can get his hands on that he hasn't already seen.

He spends hours lost in the flickering glow of the screen, his attention consumed by action sequences and dialogue I can't bring myself to care about.

Meanwhile, I stare at my laptop, trying to write and keep my author business afloat. The words come, slowly, choked by the tension that has become a permanent fixture in our home.

In the afternoons, the restlessness sets in. Timmy gets antsy and starts talking incessantly about smoking and drinking. His voice, once charming and animated, grates against my nerves as he works himself up.

Soon enough, he's pouring a drink, and I know the rest of the day will be lost to his spiral—more movies, more drinking, and a stubborn refusal to sleep until exhaustion forces him to.

I had envisioned this place as a paradise, but this was not it.

The beauty just outside these suffocating walls seems like a cruel joke.

But hey, at least we're not at Matty's anymore, and I am managing to get some books written.

I'm starting to scream back at him more and more. To say things that have never crossed my mind in any prior relationship. Horrible things. Swear words. Insults. And, most often, I still call him a loser. Because I'll reach the point I get so frustrated about his complete lack of work ethic, his sleeping in, his mooching, his constant demands and expectations—the word seems accurate. Where is the lie?

But then it feels like I'm just as bad as he is. And I feel guilty and ashamed. Even though he starts every single argument. Even though he picks and picks and picks at me during every waking hour. Even though he physically destroys items around the house on a regular basis. Even though he's fractured my skull. But the fact I can't just stay calm and serene and be the perfect little polite fiancée, I feel like I'm as much to blame.

Even though if I was there with anyone else, these situations wouldn't arise. It's him. He's the common denominator.

I know that, intuitively, and based on hard evidence like his criminal record, but there's a dissonance where I wonder what I could have done differently to have avoided yet another Timmy drama.

And when I haven't been drinking, I'm very, very good at anticipating emotions and noticing very subtle nuances in body language. De-escalation is my strength.

But, when emboldened by alcohol, I get a little more sassy. A little more empowered to say what's on my mind. To bring up things that we really should have been talking about as a couple, but that I've avoided because I knew they'd result in him automatically shutting me down and using them as ammunition against me later.

"Why didn't you mention soap at the store?" I ask, when we get back from grocery shopping and he immediately mentions we're out.

"You told me I'm always asking for things," he sulks. "So I decided I shouldn't ask you."

"It's a necessity, not a nice-to-have. That's different."

I find myself writing little notes, jotting down my thoughts that I store on my Notes app like contraband.

> *I am in love with this soul*
> *Who is currently inside this giant human*
> * frame*
> *Who sometimes hurts me.*
> *Because I see what is inside. But I feel*
> * dumb in the meantime.*

It's all true. Timmy is massive compared to me, and he sometimes does hurt me, physically and emotionally. But I see glimpses of his potential, his good parts.

The way he makes me laugh until I cry nearly every day, those fleeting moments of thoughtfulness that feel like sunshine breaking through the storm clouds.

The way he'll give me little snippets of his attention that remind me of the earliest days of our relationship.

The way his eyes light up when he starts drawing or working on graphic design—tiny sparks of who he could be if he tried.

And we do have sex and it's decent—it's not like it was in the beginning by any means, but not terrible, and it makes me feel closer to him.

Once, he wakes me up early with the smell of pancakes. "Surprise," he says, smiling shyly. He's even set the table with a vase of tropical flowers he'd found outside.

For a moment, it feels like the Timmy I fell for. But by lunch, he's calling me a bitch for not buying his favorite brand of chips.

Those good sparks are so rare, and the storm so constant, that I wonder if I'm just a fool. An absolute fucking moron, in fact.

Each time I see a couple on vacation walking past, hand in hand, laughing, headed to the beach, I feel happy for them, but at the same time like I'm being stabbed and the knife being twisted.

That's what I came here for, and instead I'm facing a prison sentence of my own making, just by virtue of choosing to be with Timmy.

I can barely sleep. I have constant tension headaches. It's near impossible for me to take more than a couple of bites of food without retching. The stress is building and it's hurting more than just my mind.

How long am I supposed to wait for him to live up to the version of himself I fell for, or the person he claims to be?

How long do I have to keep holding his hand, teaching him how to be an adult, walking on eggshells, catering to his every mood swing to avoid his tantrums?

How long is it going to take until he consistently behaves like someone worthy of my time?

The frustration builds until I can't keep it in anymore, so I type out another note:

```
It's embarrassing to wonder if you ever
   really loved me.
Am I a fool?
But then, if I really think about it, it's
   not embarrassing for me. It's embarrassing
   for you.
Because, if the latter is the case, it
   means you're the one going around being
   deceitful, feeling like you've 'won'
   something against a person much better
   than you.
In which case, you're the dick. You're the
   absolute loser who feeds on being calcu-
   lating and deceitful.
And now you're the one who has to live with
   that.
Not me.
So go away.
Bye bye.
Flutter off and reap what you sow, fuckface.
```

I want to scream these words at him, to throw them in his face and watch them hit their mark.

But I know better.

Screaming at Timmy only leads to danger—his rage, his cold retaliation, or worse.

The last time I screamed at him, he smashed dishes violently into the sink, pieces scattering like shrapnel. 'Look what you made me do!' he'd snarled, and I'd spent the rest of the night in the fetal position, rocking myself to sleep, my heart pounding.

So I save my anger for my Notes app, a hidden vault of all the things I'm too afraid to say out loud. It's a tiny act of defiance, and something that would piss him off very badly should he ever read them.

I scroll back to a note from last month:

> Things are rough, but I know he'll get
>   better. We've just hit a bump in the road.

I almost laugh at my own naivety. No, not a bump—a sinkhole.

Timmy knows nothing of these notes, and he never will.

He'd use them against me, spinning them into 'proof' of my instability, my complete craziness.

But they're my lifeline, tiny threads of sanity I cling to as I struggle to hold myself together. And so it's a risk I'm willing to take.

As I stare at my phone, preparing to draft another note, I hear Timmy's voice cut through the room, sharp and angry. I don't even register the words anymore, but I realize this is my life now. A series of quiet rebellions, a constant battle to preserve the pieces of myself he hasn't yet eroded.

My body flinches instinctively, my mind already racing to calculate the safest way to respond. I'm wondering how much longer I can endure this—how much longer I can keep convincing myself that Timmy's potential is worth the price of my peace.

And I know, deep down, that no amount of potential is worth this constant fear.

CHAPTER 12
BOY JOYS

MARGAUX

A WEEK OR SO LATER

The days blend together, an exhausting loop of tension and fleeting calm, like the eye of a storm that never fully dissipates.

My body aches, not just from the lingering bruises, but from the emotional toll of existing in Timmy's orbit. Every moment with him feels like walking a tightrope over an abyss, never knowing when the rope will snap.

We're sitting together—me working, him watching a random show, as usual—when a cruel glimmer sparkles in his eyes. Timmy's smirk cuts through the silence like a night. "I'm trying to be— no, wait, I can't tell you. It will make you mad."

He's testing me again, pushing buttons he knows are worn thin. He's well aware that I *hate* it when he does this—partially says something, and then stops and won't tell me what he was going to say. It's a pet peeve because it gives me FOMO, and I feel like I'm missing out on the most important words the person was ever to utter.

Of course, it's usually something silly or irrelevant, but that's beside the point. He knows I can't stand it, so he delights in doing it.

I frown, my voice weary. "You know that annoys me."

He shrugs, his smirk deepening into something darker, as if he just got one over on me somehow. "Well, I can't remember what I was going to say, so it doesn't matter."

It's a game to him, a petty act of control disguised as banter.

He thrives on my frustration, on the tiny power he wields in moments like this.

Later in the evening, he announces, "I'm going to go get a Black and Mild." His tone is casual but with an edge of defiance.

Great, there it is. He wants to smoke again.

Late at night, hanging out with goodness knows who on a dangerous street in a dangerous neighborhood.

He grows cockier about the whole idea. "I'm going to go smoke. I'm going by myself."

"You know how I feel about that," I say quietly, not even looking up.

"Well, come with me then," he challenges, shrugging.

I quirk a brow. "You want me to come with you?"

He shrugs again. "Look, I'm going with or without you."

"I don't want to go," I reply, my voice flat.

"Then I'm going alone."

And just like that, he's gone—for about half an hour. Long enough to go to the 7-Eleven, buy a Black and Mild—probably with the laundry quarters —and smoke it on the beach, I suppose.

When he returns, the scent of smoke clings to him like a second skin. It makes my stomach turn.

I'm upset as usual. And he knows it.

I want to say something, to confront him about his reckless behavior, but I don't.

What's the point? I'm too tired to fight, and he's too adept at twisting the narrative.

Instead, I fall asleep, emotionally exhausted by his constant mind games. I don't want to talk about cigarettes any more.

THE NEXT DAY

"I'm leaving," Timmy snaps, his voice dripping with venom. "You are a Nazi, and you're controlling my movements."

I couldn't help myself. I eventually brought up his disrespect over the Black and Mild last night, and now we're arguing.

I'm paying for mentioning it. *Shocker.*

I can feel my composure cracking, the edges of my voice as sharp as glass. "Timmy, I'm not controlling you. You're prioritizing just about everything over us. Smoking, going for swims. Can you please do something productive to contribute to our household?"

He sneers at me, his eyes narrowed. "When your books fail, will I be able to dictate where you go and when?"

Then he swooshes the door open and storms out. I don't stop him. I don't have the energy.

His parting words hit me harder than any physical blow. *When your books fail…*

He may as well have punched me in the face and the gut. The wind is knocked out of my sails. The guy who has actually been pretty supportive about my career in some ways is now anticipating its failure. Is this how he's really felt all along, and he was just blowing smoke up my ass because he wanted something from me?

The same guy who used to brag about my books, and tell me and everyone else how proud he is of me and my writing career? How the tables have turned.

When your books fail…

When your books fail…

His cruel words rattle around in my brain until they're all I hear. My imposter syndrome rises from the ashes like a particularly resilient zombie, and I feel sick.

His absence brings a strange relief, but the words he left behind continue to gnaw at me.

———

Timmy returns a couple of hours later. "Put on Pete Davidson and John Mulaney," he demands, as if nothing out of the ordinary happened and he hadn't just predicted the failure of my dream career.

I find a YouTube special featuring them both. It's funny and twisted, the kind of humor we typically both enjoy. I'm glad for the distraction, but it doesn't last long.

Within about fifteen minutes, he's visibly agitated. His body is moving a little differently, his lips twisted in a frown. "Why did you put that shit on? You know I don't like it. You know it upsets me."

I stare at him, dumbfounded, my voice scrunched in disbelief. "Since when did *this* upset you? And you *asked* me to put it on."

He pauses, his expression genuinely confused. "Oh, I did?"

"Yes." I reply, exhaustion creeping into my voice.

He looks genuinely surprised. "Oh." He shrugs it off, as though his own words are as inconsequential as the truth itself.

I resist as every cell in my body tries to grow eyes just so they can roll them.

———

I message Alice.

ME:

Hey, how are you? Sorry, it sounded like you were having a rough day the other day and I was so caught up in my own mess I didn't even ask you about it.

ALICE:

Just having a rough week.

ME:

I'm sorry.

I hope something good happens for you this week.

ALICE:

Same:

If it makes you feel better, I was just talking to someone else who's also having some Boy Joys.

ME:

ALICE:

I DIDN'T KNOW WHAT ELSE TO CALL IT

ME:

It's perfect

CHAPTER 13
THE GAME IS JUST GETTING STARTED

DEX

Every time I look at Margaux's phone records, my jaw tightens. The threads of her life, tangled in abusive text messages and missed calls from Timmy, make my blood boil, each one a thread in a tapestry of cruelty and manipulation.

The way he speaks to her—devoid of any semblance of respect—makes my temples throb.

His toxic cocktail of emotional abuse, sprinkled with half-hearted compliments and fake apologies, is maddening. I can see the pattern: he pushes her, prods her, taunts her until she breaks—and then uses her reaction as ammunition against her.

He pushes her too far, then pulls her back in with just enough to re-hook her. Rinse. Repeat.

The sheer audacity of his words is only matched by his chicken-shitness.

This isn't the Margaux I know. The woman I've watched grow over the years doesn't snap like this. She's warm, kind, resilient. But she's been dulled by this parasite. Timmy's worn her down, and even the strongest people have limits—he seems hell-bent on finding and crossing hers at every opportunity.

She's stuck in survival mode, trapped with a predator who masquerades as a partner.

He pretends to love her, but I know better.

He dares to think he's untouchable. But Timmy doesn't love anyone but himself. And even that's questionable—he seems to loathe himself as much as he loathes the world.

Good.

He should.

I lean back in my chair, cracking my knuckles. Time to take this up a notch—to dive into the next phase of my plan. If Timmy wants to play games, I'll show him what a real game looks like.

I scour the internet, digging into every sordid detail of Timmy's past. His criminal record is a smorgasbord of offenses in multiple states—assaults, DUIs, a parade of failed relationships and restraining orders, shady connections, allegations of child abuse in Montana. He even has an arrest under an alias.

The more I find, the more disgusted I become. How Margaux ended up with him, I can only chalk up to her big heart and his calculated manipulation.

And then there's the bombshell: he has a child. A child he's abandoned.

No child support. No contact. Nothing.

What a lucky escape for that kid. Imagine having a father like Timmy.

The idea of this deadbeat, this parasite, playing house with Margaux while neglecting his own flesh and blood makes me want to break something.

This isn't just about Margaux anymore. It's about righting every one of his wrongs, starting with the way he's hollowed her out.

———

The texts start small. Cryptic. Anonymous. Little messages designed to plant seeds of paranoia in Timmy's tiny, inadequate brain.

> ANONYMOUS:
>
> Montana remembers you, Timmy.
>
> Some records never disappear. Isn't that funny? 😈
>
> You've always been good at running, but you can't hide forever. Tick tock. ⏰
>
> Does Margaux know about the child?

I make sure they're timed sporadically, just enough to keep him on edge.

Too frequent, and he might explode in a way that puts Margaux in danger.

Too infrequent, and he might just brush them off.

It's a delicate balance, but I'm good at balancing.

And I'm even better at breaking people who deserve it.

————

Hours later, I get what I want—a glimpse of his unraveling.

Timmy's texts to Margaux grow more frantic, more disjointed.

He's trying to act calm, trying to keep up the charade of control, but I can see the cracks forming.

> TIMMY:
>
> Do you know anyone from Montana who might have my number?
>
> Have you been talking to anyone about me?
>
> If someone reaches out to you about me, tell them to fuck off.

His facade of control is disintegrating. He's scrambling, trying to piece together a narrative that keeps him in power, but I can see the fear creeping in.

Good. Let him stew in his paranoia. Let him feel the weight of his past bearing down on him.

But even as I relish his growing desperation, a cold knot forms in my gut. This kind of agitation in a man like Timmy could turn dangerous quickly—I can't let him spiral too far, too fast. I have to tread carefully. A 'man' like Timmy, cornered, will lash out. The last thing I want is for Margaux to become his outlet.

So I shift tactics.

My next move is calculated. I make sure my messages to Timmy don't escalate too quickly.

Instead, they shift focus—keeping his attention on the anonymous 'threat' haunting him.

ANONYMOUS:

> How's the kid doing, Timmy? Still pretending they
> don't exist?

> Remember that night in Missoula? You should.

> Karma's coming for you.

Each message is a scalpel, cutting away at his fragile sense of control. The goal isn't just to distract him—it's to make him doubt himself, to question every shadow, every glance, every interaction.

If he's busy looking over his shoulder, he'll have less time and energy to target Margaux.

But I know Timmy isn't smart. He's not clever enough to fully grasp the implications of these messages.

And that's where the danger lies. When cornered, he reacts with blind aggression, like a wild animal.

I have to be ready for that.

I have to anticipate his moves and counter them before he can hurt her. Before he can use her as a punching bag by proxy.

I can't let my anger cloud my judgment. This isn't about revenge—it's about Margaux.

Keeping her safe.

Giving her the space and clarity to see Timmy for what he really is.

I sit back and take a deep breath.

This is a game of strategy, and I'm in it for the long haul.

Timmy doesn't know it yet, but his days of hurting Margaux are numbered.

One way or another, I'll make sure of it.

CHAPTER 14
BUTTHOLE EYES & BAD DRIVERS

MARGAUX

Another couple of hours later, Timmy approaches me and looks deep into my eyes.

At first, I think he's going to say something nice, but then I see the cruel glimmer in his gaze.

"You are butthole eyes," he says, smirking.

I frown. "That's not very nice."

But I leave it at that. Because I have barely any energy, and I really don't know how to respond.

———

ABOUT FORTY MINUTES LATER

He throws a marble at my crotch for seemingly no reason, laughing like a child with a cruel streak.

"Stop throwing things at me," I say, my patience fraying.

Why is a nearly 40-year-old man throwing things at me?

Why is any of this happening?

He responds by rolling into me on the bed over and over again, his weight crushing me as he cackles, "Hahahahaha!" each time he does it.

I've had enough.

This is too much.

With all the strength I can muster, I shove him away, sending his 200-pound ass right off the bed.

Ahahahaha yourself, dickhead.

"You're so fucking lame!" he screams, scrambling to his feet. "You suck balls!"

I don't respond.

His attention turns to the TV. "I want to watch a show. That one we just favorited."

"Okay," I shrug, because at least he's not physically slamming into me now.

I find the remote and put on the show he mentioned earlier, hoping to pacify him.

He doesn't seem to be watching it closely, but at least he's calm.

I hug him. "Didn't you want to watch this show?"

"I plead the fifth," he replies, smirking.

I shake my head. None of this makes sense. My life has stopped making any semblance of sense.

––––––––

TWO DAYS LATER

We're driving back from a beach on the other side of the Cay, and his nitpicking is relentless.

There's a weird part of the route where the freeway exit is on the left instead of the right. Confused, I take a wrong turn, and he berates me.

"You went the wrong fucking way!" he sneers. "Jesus Christ. It's a really straightforward route. What are you, stupid?"

I feel flustered by his admonitions and compelled to defend myself. "It's a confusing intersection!" I snap, my frustration bubbling over. "The exit is on the opposite side of the road from usual!"

"Well, you've been here before! *You should know!*" he screams.

"Leave me the fuck alone and let me drive." My own voice rises to a shout. *"You're getting me all flustered!"*

He smirks, satisfied, his voice now calm. "Look at you yelling at me. You really need to learn to control your temper, Margaux."

I grit my teeth, tears of anger stinging my eyes.

When we get home, he immediately picks another fight. *"You make me feel small!"* he yells.

Guilt floods me, unearned but potent. I *did* yell at the top of my lungs back in the truck.

"Look, I'm sorry I raised my voice in the car on the way back. I was stressed about driving at night. I'm sorry, I should have tried to stay calm. I shouldn't have yelled. I apologize."

Without a word, he storms out of the apartment.

When he returns twenty minutes later, the smell of cigarette smoke clings to him like an accusation.

———

TWO DAYS LATER

He paces around the apartment like a caged animal. "I'm angry because of resentment," he says finally. "Not at you or myself. It's really not you. But I would just be happy if I had a Black and Mild." He looks at me, his gaze laden with expectation. "If you just let me go get a Black and Mild, I'd love you so much and everything would be great."

I sigh, the weight of his constant and trivial demands pressing down on me. He always fucking wants something. "Your mood really shouldn't be so driven by whether I use my life savings to buy you a cigarette that you don't need. I can't afford to waste my money on things like cigarettes. It's not right to expect me to."

"Well, I want one," he replies, shrugging.

He's pissing me off and I poke him back. "Who did you smoke with the other day?"

Guilt flickers across his face. "Some lady who was like seventy years old."

It doesn't matter. Their age is not the point. Doesn't he get it? Or does he get it, and that's why he does it? "See? I have a problem with that. I don't care how old someone is. You're standing outside at night chatting away with people while I'm sitting here wondering if you're safe in this neighborhood. It's weird and inappropriate."

"Okay, I promise I won't do that ever again." His face is solemn, and his tone is convincing, but he's giving me snake vibes. He's showing his charm, and now I'm just waiting for the strike.

I've learned by now that Timmy's promises mean nothing. They're just words, empty and hollow, like the man who speaks them.

Timmy's presence is a storm I can't escape. Every moment with him feels like another step deeper into a labyrinth of manipulation and despair.

And yet, despite everything, I stay.

Maybe out of hope.

Maybe out of fear.

Or maybe because I've started to believe the lies he tells about me.

Lies that feel like truth when whispered in the dark.

CHAPTER 15
THE PRICE OF LOVE

MARGAUX

LATER IN THE MONTH

Since living in the US, I've been part of a community of expats from New Zealand who get together throughout the year for a variety of social events. It's a fun group, and it's always fun to reminisce about the home country and hear some other Kiwi accents.

So when an event is announced in Timmy's home state of Montana, where his parents still live, I suggest we make the trip and kill two birds with one stone.

Timmy is thrilled. "I can't wait for you to meet my parents," he gushes. "They're going to love you in person as much as they do over the phone."

I use my air points to get us both tickets, and find a bougie cat hotel where Sabre will be taken care of while we're away.

Timmy doesn't say thank you, just expects me to fork out for everything like usual.

"You're going to get to meet my sister-in-law, Emma," he says. "You two are going to get along really, really well. She wrote a romance book, too!"

I smile, excited.

The days leading up to the trip to Montana are filled with a mix of antici-pation and dread.

I'm clinging to the hope that this visit will provide a sense of stability and connection, something that's been sorely lacking in my life with Timmy.

His erratic moods and increasingly cruel behavior have left me feeling untethered, but maybe being around his family will ground him—or at least give me some insight into why he is the way he is.

———

A few days before we fly out, I message my friend, Becky, who is organizing the events in Montana, and let her know how excited I am to be seeing her.

She doesn't respond, which is strange for her.

A couple of days go by, and I still don't hear from her.

I reach out to Natasja, who is a mutual friend, to see if Becky is okay.

She checks in with her on my behalf.

Natasja shares that Becky will be getting back to me soon.

When Becky's message finally arrives, it hits like a sucker punch.

> BECKY:
>
> Margaux, you've put me in a really difficult position.
>
> Your partner is not welcome at the event.
>
> I have a responsibility to keep my community, and my family, safe.
>
> You're welcome to come by yourself, but he cannot attend.

The words replay in my head, each one a sharp jab. She's not just banning Timmy—she's making a judgment about me by association.

Guilt and outrage and shame simultaneously gnaw at me.

Her words cut like an admonishment, and they make me feel small.

I've told her things in confidence about Timmy's behavior. And now she's using them against me and saying my partner can't attend the function. The tickets are booked, his parents are expecting us, but the events were frankly the main reason I was going.

Hell, I was considering taking one of his parents along instead of him. I hadn't firmly locked down my plus one, and she just assumed.

No conversation, just a cold DM from someone who I considered such a close friend that she's almost family.

This is the same Becky who called me when I was in a vulnerable, isolated moment during Covid lockdown, who asked for me to be appointed to the board for one of her fitness groups—Becky has a lot of hobbies—and who once told me I was one of the strongest people she knew.

And now, just like that, I'm an outsider.

If she's really that worried about my relationship with Timmy, why hasn't she tried to check in on me, to call me or send an email, or even just a DM asking how I am?

This is just *off*.

I wouldn't bring Timmy if I thought he would act out. That's partially why I had his parents mentally on standby. I'm confident they would behave and enjoy meeting some of my friends, so if Timmy was having a bad day when the event took place I'd just leave him at home.

But now I feel shunned, ostracized, like yet another piece of my dwindling grounding foundation has been ripped away from me through no fault of my own.

The fault of loving Timmy, I suppose.

And yet another seed of resentment grows toward him. My relationship has officially become a further liability, a scarlet letter in my social circles.

Being able to attend these events is just another thing I can't have in my life if I continue to be with him.

I tell Timmy, expecting an explosion, but he surprises me with a smirk, and pulls me into a hug. "I'm sorry babe," he says, his voice gentle. "She sounds like a bitch. She's jealous of you. Fuck her. We'll just go spend even more time with my parents, and it's your former friend's loss, honestly."

His dismissal feels both reassuring and hollow.

I block Becky on social media, trying to push away the hurt, but the wound remains raw.

"You're better off without her," he adds, his voice softening. "People like that don't really care about you. I'm the only one who does." His words settle into me like a splinter—sharp, and too small to remove. I cling to them like they're a lifeline.

He's right. We can spend more time with his parents, and I can get to know them better.

Becky showed her true colors, and this is all for the best.

I block her on social media, because I can't bear to see pictures of the event showing up on my feed and reminding me I'm not allowed to go. And because I'm deeply hurt by the way she chose to act in this delicate situation.

I tell myself it's her loss, not mine. That someone who truly cared wouldn't have blindsided me with a cold and detached message like that.

But deep down, even though I'm extracting a toxic element that doesn't serve me, I know I'm cutting off another tether to the life I had before Timmy.

I'd thought this trip might be a chance for him to show me—and the world—the better side of himself. Instead, it's just another thing he's tainted, another reminder of how small my world has become since he entered it.

I don't feel supported—I feel cut adrift, like Becky's message wasn't just about Timmy, but about me. About who I've become since I met him.

And as much as I try to tell myself that blocking her is a show of strength, it feels more like surrender.

CHAPTER 16
FAILING MONTANA

MARGAUX

The night before the trip to Montana, Timmy paces the apartment like a caged animal—a drunk and belligerent one. His movements are erratic, his expression dark.

There's an edge to his voice when he finally speaks, turning his attention to me. "I'm going to give you a noogie," he says with a cruel smirk, that cold, reptilian look flashing in his eyes.

But there's no noogie. Instead, his hands go to my throat, his arm locking around my chest.

At first, I freeze. Surely, he'll let go in a second, right? He's joking, right?

But the seconds stretch into minutes, and every time I try to push him off, his grip tightens. He's too strong for me to break free.

Three and a half hours pass while he does this intermittently. I sit, numb, staring at the wall, wondering if this will escalate into something worse.

And he just cackles and looks at me like I'm the one with the problem.

"Timmy, please stop," I finally plead, my voice hoarse. "You're hurting me."

He cackles. "Fuck you," he snaps. "You're a fucking bitch, and I'm not fucking going to Montana!" His words are slurred, but his anger is sharp.

When I manage to wrench myself away, adrenaline takes over. I run straight out the door and down the outdoor path, heading for the security shack.

Tina, the security guard, looks up at me, her brow furrowing.

"What's going on?" she asks, her tone calm but concerned.

I tell her, the words tumbling out in a rush. My chest heaves, and my hands shake.

"Do you want me to call the police?" she offers.

"No, please don't," I beg. The thought of police intervention—and the chaos it would bring—feels unbearable. If they lock him up and he misses the trip, it'll just make everything worse. I can already picture the aftermath.

Tina sighs, leaning back in her chair. "Well, you two need to sort your shit out, or you won't be able to live here much longer." Her words are blunt, but there's no judgment in her voice. I get the sense she's seen it all before.

———

When I return to the apartment, Timmy is still here. He looks calmer, but I know better than to trust that. My eyes drift to my Funko Pop collection—three Post Malones, two Machine Gun Kellys, one Yungblud—all lined up neatly but placed upside down.

Weird flex, but okay.

It doesn't take long for him to spiral again. His voice grows louder, more belligerent. "I'm not fucking going anywhere!" he shouts.

Desperate, I call his dad, Phil. My voice shakes as I whisper, "He says he's not coming. He's refusing to pack."

"Put him on speaker," Phil says, his tone measured, like this is just another Tuesday in Timmyland.

"Son? Are you there?" Phil's voice echoes through the room.

"I'm not fucking going, Dad!" Timmy yells from the back room. "I'll just stay here!"

Phil's wife, Timmy's mom, joins the call, her voice trembling. "Timmy, you're so drunk! Calm down!"

Timmy slams the door on his way out, storming off into the night.

———

When Timmy eventually returns, he seems subdued, the alcohol finally dulling his edge. He slumps onto the bed, his energy spent. "I love you, you know," he mumbles. "You know I'd never hurt you."

My stomach twists at his words. *If only they were true.*

"It's not about your intention, Timmy," I reply, my voice quiet but firm. "It's the crushing of my throat that hurts hours later. Intention or not, the impact is the same."

"Well, I wouldn't," he says casually, as if he didn't 'jokingly' strangle me for the past three-and-a-half hours and uninvite me from visiting his parents.

I frown, annoyed at his dismissive response. "It's statistically possible you will harm me based on domestic violence data."

He shrugs, as if we're debating something trivial. "It was just an accident."

"An accident?" I snap. "So the first time was on purpose, and *this* time was an accident?" My brow arches as I stare at him, daring him to explain his logic.

He doesn't. Instead, he pulls a blanket around himself, retreating into the bed like a child who's been scolded.

Unable to keep it all inside, I message Alice. It's the middle of the night for her, but I know she has weird sleeping hours.

ME:

Do you happen to be awake?

Fifteen minutes later, she responds.

ALICE:

Now!

Yes!

You okay? What's up?

Sorry, I'm a morning person but like not quite that morning.

ME:

Just got into a massive domestic bc BOY JOYS.

ALICE:

It seems we're discovering we're lost halves of 1 mess. 😂

ME:

I'm supposed to be flying in like 4-5 hours.

ALICE:

Okay. First things first, are you okay?

It's a question I don't really know the answer to.

I fill her in, typing furiously. The words spill out like a confession.

I tell her everything—Timmy's drinking, the noogie-that-wasn't, the argument, the security guard.

ALICE:

So drunk Timmy decides to grab someone's throat? That's super healthy.

ME:

Yes, in a noogie without the noogie part.

ALICE:

His parents. They weren't like...alarmed?

ME:

Oh I'm sure they were.

He was like, 'She isn't coming to Montana.'

ALICE:

It doesn't sound like a good idea.

ME:

And they were like, 'You're so drunk Timmy.'

God knows what they actually thought of my live tweets of the past 3 hours or so. I kept them updated while their son acted insane.

Security said she was going to call the cops and I asked her not to.

She said she wouldn't but I'm listening to my headphones really loud and hopefully she doesn't bc I think he's going to sleep. 😴

He really just lost his shit. Kept saying 'Oh I love you, I'd never hurt you'.

And I said, 'It's not the intention bro', and that my throat still feels funny hours later.

And then I mentioned the domestic violence stats around strangulation, and the likelihood he would really harm me one day.

ALICE:

It's true. Especially strangulation—it's no joke.

It's a massive predictor of future violence.

Her bluntness cuts through the fog of rationalizations I've been clinging to, and for a moment, I feel seen. *Understood.*

ME:

I told him that too. That it's not just me—it's statistics. That men who strangle their partners often escalate. And he didn't like that info.

Alice's reply comes swiftly:

ALICE:

"How dare you show me the consequences of my actions! What am I, responsible for them?!"

I laugh despite myself, the absurdity of it all hitting me like a punchline to a terrible joke.

ME:

I'm kind of an asshole when people deserve it.

Oh, he's all snuggled in his blankie now.

His parents are in their late 70s and are probably shitting themselves wondering what's going on over here.

His dad didn't complete an entire military career and corporate career for this bullshit.

ALICE:

Deservedly shitting themselves. Kind of.

As Timmy curls up on the bed, snuggled under his blanket, I feel a pang of bitterness. His elderly parents *are* probably sitting at home, worried sick about what's happening here. And what have they done? Enabled him.

Made excuses for him.

I glance at my phone, reading and rereading Alice's messages. Her sarcasm and blunt truth-telling are a lifeline I didn't know I needed at first, but am quickly coming to depend on.

ME:

He says he loves me, Alice.

But it doesn't feel like love.

Her reply is immediate.

ALICE:

Because it's not.

I stare at those words, the truth of them sinking in.
I don't know what tomorrow will bring, but for tonight, I have Alice.
And for tonight, that's enough.

CHAPTER 17
OH BECKY, YOU'RE SO FAKE AKA COMPASSION IN RETROGRADE

DEX

Margaux's phone lights up, and I'm relieved to see Alice's name on the screen. Alice—the blunt, no-nonsense roller derby friend Margaux desperately needs right now. Someone who isn't afraid to call things as they are.

Her messages aren't sugar-coated; they're real, raw, and exactly what Margaux responds to.

Alice doesn't dance around the issue of Timmy's abuse. She's not pushing Margaux to leave outright—that would backfire—but she's planting seeds, asking the tough questions, and reminding Margaux of her worth.

She's doing something I can't—providing honest, non-judgmental friendship without triggering Margaux's defenses. And I'm grateful.

I see the small relief in Margaux's body language as she types, laughing softly at Alice's dark humor. That tiny flicker of light in her dimmed eyes makes me feel like maybe, just maybe, she'll find her way out of this mess.

And I'm grateful. Watching Margaux pour her heart out to Alice gives me hope. At least she has someone other than Timmy in her corner. It's like observing a drowning woman finding a lifeboat.

But then there's *him*. Timmy.

Through the camera, I observe as the smug bastard walks into the room and immediately zones in on Margaux. He's like a predator who knows exactly where to strike to cause the most pain.

"You have butthole eyes," he sneers, smirking at her like he just said something clever.

Butthole. Eyes.

Of all the things to say.

It was mean when it was said about Pete Davidson, a cruel barb referencing the appearance of his eyes due to an autoimmune disease.

And when said about Margaux, it makes absolutely no sense at all. He's just hitting her with low blow after low blow.

At least he hasn't turned on her about her lazy eye—I know how she feels about that. If he went there, I wouldn't be able to restrain myself.

Timmy would be dead meat, never mind the consequences.

I clench my fists so tightly my knuckles crack. That's the kind of insult a 13-year-old bully would throw around, not a grown man. He thinks it's funny, but I see the way Margaux flinches.

She shrugs it off, tries to laugh along like it's no big deal, but her fingers tighten around her phone. She's holding herself together by a thread, and he knows it.

The things I want to do to Timmy in this moment… they'd land me in prison.

But it'd be worth it.

He doesn't stop there. Later, he throws a marble at her, laughing like a hyena as it bounces off her leg.

Then he rolls into her, over and over, his weight crushing her small frame while he cackles like a lunatic.

Margaux finally has enough and shoves him off the bed. The sight of his pathetic two-hundred-pound ass hitting the floor gives me a twisted sense of satisfaction.

"You suck balls!" he yells, like the man-child he is.

Margaux doesn't respond. She's done. For now, at least.

I wish she could see how much better off she'd be without him if she left him for good.

———

Alice is a lifeline in Margaux's storm.

But then there's Becky. *Oh, Becky.*

Becky, who Margaux considered almost family, now ostracizing her. And now, when Margaux needs support the most, Becky sends a cold, self-right-eous message banning Timmy from the event and essentially shunning Margaux by association.

Becky's message is cold, impersonal, and—I'm sure—devastating for Margaux:

> BECKY:
>
> Margaux, you have put me in a very uncomfortable position.
>
> Your partner is not welcome at the event in Montana.

Margaux doesn't need judgment masquerading as concern, but that's exactly what Becky delivers.

Her face crumbles as she reads it. Another person pushed away by this relationship—which is to an extent fair—but the way Becky went about it was absolutely rotten.

Chastising Margaux. Making her feel *worse*. Making her feel more trapped, removing her access to an entire community unless Margaux lives her life on Becky's terms.

I watch as Margaux blocks Becky on social media, her face a mix of hurt and anger. She doesn't deserve this. Becky's petty power play is the last thing she needs right now.

Margaux doesn't deserve *any* of this.

And it pisses me off.

Becky isn't just a bad friend—she's a jealous, self-absorbed coward.

Instead of reaching out to check on Margaux, she's made the situation all about herself. About her responsibility to 'the group', her need to 'protect her community'.

I can't let Becky's betrayal slide.

So, I start planning. Something subtle, something that will gnaw at Becky like she's gnawed at Margaux.

First, I hack into Becky's Instagram account. Nothing malicious—just a little creative chaos. I add cheeky captions to her latest posts:

A photo of her at a vineyard:

'Drank six bottles and still can't figure out why I'm the worst friend ever! Cheers! 🍷'

Her smiling selfie:

'WHEN YOU ISOLATE YOUR ABUSED 'BESTIE' FURTHER AND PUT HER IN GREATER DANGER, BUT STILL THINK YOU'RE THE GOOD GUY. 😊'

Posing with a cup of coffee:

'SIPPING ON HYPOCRISY' ☕ #GLITTERGASLIGHTING #FAKEGROWTHFAIRYTALES'

Another selfie, this time holding a self-help book:

'WRITING MY NEXT BESTSELLER: HOW TO MAKE YOUR FRIEND'S ABUSE ALL ABOUT YOU. PRE-ORDER NOW! #UNICORNENERGYBUTMAKEITTOXIC 📚✏️'

A pic doing community service:

'HELPING OTHERS WHILE I QUIETLY DROPKICK MY CLOSEST FRIENDS INTO EMOTIONAL ISOLATION—MULTITASKING QUEEN! 🔥 #BLESSEDANDTOXIC'

Summiting a hill in Montana:

'CLIMBING MOUNTAINS, BURNING BRIDGES, AND SHAMING ABUSE SURVIVORS 🔪🥾 ⛰️ #TRAILBLAZINGTOXICITY #BACKSTABBERINBOOTS'

A sunset:

'MY TOXIC TRAITS SHINE AS BRIGHTLY AS THE SCENIC VIEWS I'M PRETENDING TO ENJOY! 🌇 #TOXICAF'

Okay, maybe I'm doing too much. But I can't stop. I'm just so furious on Margaux's behalf.

So I'm not done yet.

Next, I set up a fake profile for a competitor in her field. Someone who seems poised to outshine her in every way—younger, smarter, more accomplished and more attractive. I fill it with fabricated achievements and photos that make this fake rival look like the most successful, charismatic person Becky has ever encountered. She'll stew over it for weeks.

Finally, I reroute her favorite wellness spa's promotional emails to her spam folder. It's petty, but it's satisfying. Let her miss out on all her exclusive sales and VIP invites. Spam subscriptions mysteriously appear, and her inbox floods with emails from religious organizations and multi-level marketing companies.

It's petty, but it's satisfying. Let her feel a fraction of the insecurity and betrayal she inflicted on Margaux.

In a way, I might be projecting some of Timmy's behaviors onto Becky, because it's less dangerous to get revenge on her than Timmy, and I need an outlet.

I have to stay grounded, keep my emotions in check. This isn't about revenge, although that's deserved—it's about Margaux. It's about giving her the space to see Timmy for what he really is and to find her strength again.

Margaux is teetering on the edge, and any wrong move could push her further into his arms—or isolate her even more.

So every move I make is calculated. Every message, every hack, every nudge—it's all designed to shift the balance of power.

Timmy thinks he's in control. He's wrong.

He doesn't know it yet, but his days of hurting Margaux are numbered.

I lean back, watching the pieces fall into place. This is a game of strategy, and I'm in it for the long haul, doing what little I can right now to make her world a bit more bearable.

Because Margaux deserves better.

And one way or another, I'll make sure she gets it.

CHAPTER 18
MANICURE VIBES & SELF-RIGHTEOUS BITCHES

MARGAUX

ME:

It gets more complicated, girl.

I give Alice the full rundown of the original plan for the Montana trip and my fallout with Becky over Timmy's behavior. The words flow out, a mix of frustration, confusion, and betrayal.

ALICE:

Ew, what's her mean girl's club deal?

ME:

Yes, you get it!!!!!

ALICE:

What 'position' is she in?

ME:

She's one of the main people who runs it.

ALICE:

'Sorry your life is in danger, that's just so inconvenient for me today. Throws off my manicure vibes.'

So what position is she in that she doesn't want to
be in?

She doesn't want to be in the position of A
Supportive Friend?

ME:

Lol, acts like my fiancé wants to ax murder
everyone. And he is obviously being nuts, but 1) no,
and 2) I was thinking of bringing his dad or mom or
brother instead lol.

ALICE:

2 is probably a better idea.

ME:

So I am apparently flying there and going to book
myself a hotel and just hermit.

ALICE:

Dude, don't go at this point unless you actually want
to see Montana.

Have a staycation here at home away from his
stupid ass.

ME:

And I have friends there who will probably shady
meet me. Wtf is this?

I know you would totally shady meet me and I
love you.

ALICE:

Dude, I'd fucking meet you immediately!

And side-eye homeboy all day.

ME:

Oh yeah, but my cat is at a cat cottage and I went
with a friend to Montana one year and it was so
cool.

And apparently his siblings are really cool. Timmy
even said his brother is going to love me.

ALICE:

I'm trying to think of how I would act if you called
me and told me you were my brother's girl and he
treated you like this.

ME:

Yeah, you'd tell him to chop off his own dick and
drown in the sea.

Just wait, girl. I'm going to live tweet you from
Montana the whole time.

ALICE:

Good.

But I'm genuinely trying to think what I would do.
Like, I'd try to be super kind and nice to you
because I was worried and keep close to you.

Keep an eye on the whole thing.

ME:

Yeah, I think it'll probably be fine. If people are dicks,
I'll roll out of there so hard and fast. But the way his
parents were like YOU ARE DRUNK to him made me
think they're onto him.

ALICE:

Oh, they have to be.

Like there's no way.

That's their kid.

ME:

His dad is so cool. I can't wait to meet him and his
mom seems lovely

ALICE:

Aw nice.

ME:

I know. I just can't get too attached.

That's my downfall.

ALICE:

Yes.

If possible, just remind yourself you're only making
friends with them.

Like 'we can only just be friends, but damn if we
can't be some good ones!'

ME:

That's really great advice.

Usually I bff the mom, which is great at first, and she
remembers how many times I've been married, and
suddenly doesn't like me as much.

ALICE:

And it sounds like I'm just throwing it out there. But
you're part of my family if you want to be.

ME:

I'll take it. 🤍 🤍 🤍

ALICE:

Good, I'm keeping you then.

I also get super close to people, especially when
stuff is emotional, so I understand.

It's because I want to help.

ME:

Me too.

And we feel feelings, yeah? Hard.

ALICE:

Intensely.

Alice sends a gif of a line from First Wives Club that says, 'I'm an actress!
I have ALL of them!'

I laugh out loud and send her a picture of my upside-down Funko Pops.

ME:

Fiancé turned all my dolls upside down. WTF lol.

I sent the picture to his other brother, too. I'm sure
he has bigger fish to fry than his brother being a
sickbay.

Dickbag*, not sickbay.

ALICE:

TBH "sickbay" also works for a drunk sleeper.

That's something I did when I was 8.

You're engaged? You said fiancé.

ME:

Yeah, he proposed after a week.

Everybody wants to marry me, it's whatever lmao.

ALICE:

I feel like that's slightly more than whatever.

ME:

I should stop saying yes.

ALICE:

Hey, it's your life. Not gonna tell you how to live it and all. But, just giving you a balloon to carry with you that says, "I worry."

ME:

I love this balloon!

ALICE:

I always carry one for myself and now for you, too. I'll always be here for you. 🤍

————

I try to get Timmy up to pack, but he refuses to budge, clearly irked that I woke him up.

I fill Alice in.

ALICE:

You should have left him.

He's an adult.

ME:

I know. What is wrong with me?

Actually, I know.

ALICE:

You want to be loved. That's normal.

ME:

I lost my uncle last September.

I broke up from a 6-year relationship with no love last Feb.

My work fucked me over in March.

I'm like one of those boats spinning around without oars.

And this fucker insists on meeting me day 1 here while I'm paddling in lunatic circles.

And instead of calming my lunacy, he exacerbated it bc he's even more of a loony tune than me which is hard brooooo.

ALICE:

I'm driving, but that sounds exactly like what happened to me when I met my toxic ex.

I was so swept up in him that our joint mental health issues seemed like a great combo at the time!

I was just going through the motions of life, working a lot, lots of hobbies that take up my time, school on top of that. So I'm with this guy who's nice to me, thinks I'm super gorgeous, and wants to love me, and it was so easy to just to fall into that.

I have a flashback to seeing photos of Alice and her ex together on Facebook. I remember feeling a type of way whenever I'd see them. I couldn't put my finger on it, but I didn't like him. He just gave me the creeps.

ME:

Oh, that guy. You and I were not even close, but I had feelings about that guy. Like he wasn't good for you.

ALICE:

You and everyone else, I'm learning!

I sigh as I stare at Timmy's upside-down Funko Pop prank and listen to his snores. Despite everything, I'm still trying to piece this together. Alice's messages echo in my mind, a lifeline in a sea of chaos.

The trip to Montana looms imminently, and I can't tell if it will be the calm before the storm—or the storm itself. Either way, I'll live-tweet Alice through every absurd moment.

Because at least I know she gets it.

CHAPTER 19
DENIAL IS A RIVER

MARGAUX

"Timmy," I plead, trying to keep my voice steady. "Please, just get your ID. We need to leave soon."

He smirks at me, a cruel edge curling his lips. "I know where it is, but I'm not getting it. You're too *grotesque* to travel with." He rolls the word 'grotesque' around in his mouth, as if he's playing with it, as if enjoying the meanness of the word.

The words sting, sharp and deliberate. I swallow hard, ignoring the heat rising in my face. He wants a reaction, and I refuse to give him the satisfaction.

Instead, I retreat to the kitchen and dial his dad, Phil, once again. If anyone can help, it's him.

"Hello," Phil answers, his tone calm and composed, as always.

"I need your help to get Timmy organized for the airport," I say quickly. "He says he's not coming again."

"Put him on speaker," he says, and I do, walking nearer to where his son sits, refusing to move.

There's a pause, then Phil sighs. "Son, get yourself organized," he says firmly. "We want to see you. Both of you."

Timmy's response is immediate and explosive. "Wait until you listen to this recording of Margaux being a bitch!" he screams, his voice reverberating through the apartment.

He stomps toward me, his eyes wild with rage, and repeatedly mouths the words *'fuck you'* at me, exaggerated and venomous, so his dad can't hear.

"Phil," I say into the phone, my voice shaking, "he's saying *'fuck you'* so you can't hear it."

"Son, just stop," Phil replies, his tone a mix of exasperation and weariness.

Timmy mouths it again, his face inches from mine. *Fuck you.* Over and over.

"I don't give a shit about a recording, son," Phil says sharply. "If you send it to me, I'll erase it on receipt."

For a moment, relief washes over me. At least Phil isn't buying into Timmy's narrative, his attempt to paint me as the villain in whatever story he's constructing this time. God knows what he's recorded, but it reminds me of the other time he videoed me.

Building evidence to show his parents—and whoever else—how everything is my fault. And how so very horrible I am.

Timmy scowls, clearly displeased by his dad's refusal to engage. He grabs the vodka bottle from the counter and takes a swig, pacing the apartment like a trapped wolf.

"Son," Phil says, his voice softer now, "your mother has been so excited that you're coming. It's all she's been talking about. You'd break her heart if you didn't come."

Timmy scoffs, but for a fleeting moment, guilt flickers across his face. Phil knows how to push his buttons. The mention of his mother tugs at some deeply buried part of him, and I watch the internal battle play out—the child desperate for her approval warring with the man consumed by his own chaos.

But the guilt doesn't last. His expression hardens, and his voice rises. "No, fuck it! That's *her* problem! I'm not going!"

Then, as if flipping a switch, he turns his fury back to me. "She can't come!" he screams. "She can't come to Montana anymore!"

Before I can respond, he storms out of the apartment, the vodka bottle clutched tightly in his hand. The door slams behind him, and the lock beeps with aggressive finality, leaving me in sudden silence.

I press the phone back to my ear.

"Are you there, Margaux?" Phil asks.

"Yes, I'm here," I reply, my voice barely above a whisper.

"Well," Phil says, as if discussing a minor inconvenience rather than a drunken tantrum, "you should come anyway, with or without him. I'll pick you up from the airport, okay?"

What in the world?

His calmness is jarring, almost surreal. The idea of flying to Montana to meet Timmy's parents—without Timmy—is bizarre.

And yet, the way Phil suggests it, as if this is perfectly normal, makes me wonder if it *is* normal for them.

That their grown, nearly 40-year-old son is having a tantrum over... nothing.

"Um... okay, yeah," I say hesitantly. "I'll try to calm him down in the meantime."

"Thank you," Phil says. "I look forward to meeting you in either case."

His dad is so calm about the whole thing, as if the way Timmy was yelling and slurring was commonplace. I'm not sure whether he just plays things off as if they're okay when they're obviously not, preferring to sweep them under the rug than engage in any type of confrontation. Or whether he's just so accustomed to Timmy's wild behavior that it no longer phases him.

When the call ends, I sit in stunned silence. The absurdity of the situation crashes over me like a wave. Timmy's erratic behavior, his slurred shouting, the way Phil brushes it off as just another day in the life—it's all too much.

Is this really their normal? Making plans around their son's spontaneous tantrums? Adjusting expectations on a whim because Timmy decided to unravel yet again?

I glance at the door, half-expecting Timmy to burst back in at any moment. My chest tightens with the familiar mix of dread and exhaustion.

I should pack, I tell myself. *I should prepare for the possibility that I'll be flying to Montana alone, meeting his parents without him.* The thought feels surreal, but then again, so does everything else about this relationship.

And as I start to gather my things, I can't help but wonder—is this the life I signed up for? Or just the one I've trapped myself in?

CHAPTER 20
IF I WAS A GAMBLING WOMAN

MARGAUX

fill Alice in on the latest drama.

ALICE:

It sounds like they've done this before with him. 😕

ME:

His dad is cool to say the least.

Yes, it must not be their first rodeo.

ALICE:

I am definitely getting the impression that he is used to this particular Scary Go Round with his kid.

"Didn't I cash in all my fucking tickets for this, Timmy?"

ME:

Poor guy served several overseas military tours and then retired from an impressive pharmaceutical exec job, lives to tell the tale, and then his son is a dickhead.

ALICE:

"PIVOOOOOOOOT YOUR LIFE"

ME:

You are hilarious and I love you. Exactly!

OMG, when I was on the phone with his dad, he was running up to me and mouthing 'fuck you'. So I told his dad, and he told him to stop. Wild.

So immature, he's like mental age 5.

ALICE:

This feels like a sitcom on a writer's strike.

Like a show that 'hired a veteran actor (dad) and a new young hotshot (Timmy) so the energy is absolutely wild.'

Everyone's just waiting for Charlie Sheen to tire out and fall asleep.

But, until he does, he's smacking everyone on the way.

ME:

Charlie Sheen also needs more sleep.

ALICE:

Yeah, and that's the thing.

Enabled people just keep doing stuff.

ME:

Yep.

I hate that he's in the apartment I paid for.

I hate that he will try to be petty and try to bring druggie friends over to be petty.

But at least my cat is safe in a cat cottage.

ALICE:

Kitty…

Even if y'all keep dating, he's gotta get out until he gets his day to day together.

ME:

I told him I'm leaving in 20 and he can either come with me or stay here.

ALICE:

Yep. You got places to be.

ME:

If Montana is weird, I'm coming to Texas for a day or two.

ALICE:

Fuck yeah, definitely do.

ME:

I'm writing books now, you know?

ALICE:

OMG that's so cool! I've always wanted to be an author.

ME:

Do it! Self-publish.

ALICE:

I'm so bad at starting to write. That's the problem!

ME:

I have so much to chat about on this topic.

Also, LMAO that this guy isn't taking a free ticket from Sunset Cay to Montana to see his parents.

His dad basically cried and said, 'your mother is going to be so sad but Margaux, come here anyway and I'll pick you up from the airport.'

ALICE:

Awww, that's sad. 🙁

Poor parents.

They've definitely done this before.

Unsolicited, Timmy calls out from the back room. "You've really crossed the line this time, and I'm not going."

I sigh.

ME:

He's refusing to come again.

ALICE:

Sounds like you've got extra room in your row, then.

ME:

So I guess I can get an Uber to the airport but it also feels shitty bc I don't really want to go there.

And was going for him after he fucked my trip.

And I pay for this apartment and I don't trust him to not invite shady people over.

I don't know what to do.

We go through the logistics of potentially getting the door's code changed so he can't come back in. But it seems difficult. The landlord lives in a neighboring town, and I have no idea how to change the code myself.

Timmy emerges from the back room, slams the bathroom door, then returns to the living room, glaring at me before retreating back again like a petulant child.

ME:

I think I might cry the whole way there.

ALICE:

I don't blame you. He's being wild.

———

It's time to head to the airport, so I call out 'bye' toward the back room.

"You're leaving? You're leaving?" he replies, then slams the back door shut again.

ME:

He just squished something in the door and shut it again.

How odd.

ALICE:

You should use the trip to figure out what to do when you get home. And by that I mean how to find a place for just you somehow.

Did...he leave a note or something?

ME:

No.

He didn't leave shit.

ALICE:

Do you have anything in there that's sentimental, important, or irreplaceable?

I realize I need to act. To get out of the apartment. But the idea of showing up to Montana without Timmy is mortifying.

His parents are going to be devastated.

I go to the back room and call through the door. "Timmy, come on. You're being ridiculous, and your parents are going to be so upset. You've already ruined the trip—which I've paid for—and now you're acting crazy. Your mom is so excited to see you. I'm excited to meet your family. Will you please just calm down and come with me to Montana?"

After a moment, his muffled voice replies, "Okay, yes, I'll come. I need to get my water bottle first, though. I can't believe you turned my favorite person in the world against me."

I update Alice:

ALICE:

It definitely wasn't his actions.

ME:

Damn, I must wield some mad power to do that. Oooooor his dad can just see he's being a drunk dick.

But I'll go with almighty power wielder.

Bc that sounds fancy. 

ALICE:

You're obviously a power-wielding Jezebel.

ME:

JEZEBEL!

With BOY JOYS! 

Timmy appears in the living room holding the bottle of vodka that he'd taken earlier.

ME:

He ran off with my vodka but just randomly brought it back.

Maybe he peed in it.

I don't know.

ALICE:

No, I'm thinking he dumped it into his water bottle.

That's where I'd put my bet if I had a chip.

ME:

Lmfao hard.

One dickhead successfully acquired.

Now to the airport. We should get there just on time.

Omg, I am totally in my derby girl live free skate hard or whatever tank. This is not what I expected to be wearing to meet my in-laws, but here we are.

Today clearly took a swerve.

ALICE:

I think they'll mostly be grateful y'all even showed up at all.

Considering it was right up at the edge for a sec.

As we head out the door, his phone buzzes. "Hi Mommy," he says, his voice calm and infused with affection that seems foreign to me now.

I listen as he has a perfectly normal conversation with her, where she's excited about our visit, and he pretends he didn't just act like a toddler on steroids for the past however many hours.

As if the chaos that has me on edge and afraid simply never happened.

CHAPTER 21
A HOUSE OF POLISHED GLASS

By some miracle, we make it to the airport and find our gate.

He demands a drink at the airport bar.

I'm so paranoid he's going to run out of the complex and refuse to visit his parents again, that I acquiesce, hoping to pacify him.

On the plane, he alternates between moments of charm and bursts of irritation.

Flight attendants hand out complimentary punch cocktails.

Timmy takes his eagerly and drinks it in two big sips.

"You're such a bitch," he mutters, but he's smiling, as if we're playing some twisted game.

I don't know whether to laugh or cry.

Then he reaches over and smacks the plastic cup containing my cocktail out of my hand. Pomegranate-colored liquid soaks my pants.

Outraged, I smack him on the arm, hard.

I feel like I'm constantly around a very large, very cruel, five-year-old.

But maybe once we get to Montana, he'll feel at home and he'll be so excited to see his family that he'll remain calm for the visit. *Please let that be the case.*

I think back to when I met up with his ex, Jennifer, and her friend, and she told me about how Timmy behaved when they visited Montana together.

How he ended up lashing out and behaving so badly that police had to be called, and he was arrested.

A shiver creeps up my spine.

Please don't let that happen this time.

————

When we get to Montana, Phil is waiting to pick us up as promised.

From the moment we arrive, Timmy slips seamlessly into his best-behavior mode, his demeanor upbeat as he fills his dad in on Sunset Cay life as we drive back to his parents' place.

The home is large and inviting, and his mother is waiting for us at the front door. She embraces me warmly. "It's so nice to have you here, Margaux," she says. "We've heard so much about you! It's wonderful to finally meet you!"

I smile, immediately feeling welcomed. Her kindness is a balm to my frazzled nerves, and for a moment, I let myself believe that everything might actually be okay. *This isn't so bad, after all. Fuck the events I can't go to anymore. This is so much better.*

We all sit in the living room, and Timmy cracks open two hard seltzers and hands me one.

I'm mortified as he makes an announcement I wasn't expecting.

"Margaux was on a game show," he says proudly. "We have to watch her episode! She did so well!" He gazes at me with admiration, placing his hand on the small of my back. "She's brilliant!"

His words melt my residual concerns about this visit.

He's beaming—in his element—as his dad searches for the game show episode and puts it on.

His sister comes in and glances at the TV screen, and then at me. She points at me on the TV. "That you?"

I nod.

"Wow," she says. "That's awesome."

When I participated in the game show a couple of years ago, the topics were randomly assigned, and mine turned out to be Spelling—so I kicked ass and won five thousand dollars for me and my game show partner to split.

His family watches with rapt attention, their admiration for my performance genuine. The doorbell rings, and his mother rushes to the door.

It's Timmy's older brother and his wife, Emma, who Timmy had mentioned earlier. They're friendly and excited to meet me, and to see Timmy, who they haven't seen in quite some time.

His cousin Janet even comes over. It sounds like she and Timmy were close growing up. "You're going to love her, too!" he'd said with excitement. "You're into a lot of the same stuff!"

I blush profusely when Phil insists on replaying the game show so they too can watch it.

And for the first time in what feels like forever, I feel seen. Not as a victim or a burden, but as someone capable and accomplished and welcome.

The rest of the night is merry, and we eat well as Timmy and his family reminisce about visits gone by and childhood stories.

I smile, content at the normalcy of the evening, and beyond thrilled at the way Timmy is behaving. He's sociable, entertaining, polite, helpful—the requisite 'good son'. He's behaving in a way that makes me proud to be with him, even.

Maybe there's real hope for him yet.

The rest of the visit is fairly uneventful, with Timmy on his best behavior the entire time. I'm honestly shocked he's able to maintain an even keel for so long given how he behaves back in the Cay.

I suggest an outing on our last day, to a brunch place and a butterfly pavilion I'd visited with a friend on a prior trip.

Everyone is agreeable, and we have a wonderful day enjoying good food, each other's company, and some gorgeous butterflies. I even get to hold a tarantula.

Timmy was right—Janet and I *do* get along very well. We exchange contact information and promise to stay in touch.

But, while everyone is very friendly, I can't help but notice the way Phil speaks to Timmy's mom.

Phil, so calm and composed in public, has a condescending tone in his voice that makes my stomach churn, his words toward her carrying an undercurrent of frustration over even the smallest things.

The sheer volume of his voice is enough to make me wince. I can hear him from the guest bedroom we're staying in, all the way on the other side of the house.

I'm shocked, honestly, because he seems like a very calm, good guy. Until he speaks to his wife.

And because if this is the way he talks to her with a newcomer around, as well as two grown men who love their mother, I can't even imagine how he speaks to her when they're alone.

She just seems to let it slide, brushing it off with practiced ease, her demeanor serene as if nothing happened.

I really feel for her, because she seems like such a sweet lady.

But I can't unhear the harshness in his tone, or the way he seems to expect her to absorb his anger without protest.

It reminds me of Timmy—how he can be charming and warm one moment, and then cruel and cutting the next. I wonder if this is where he learned it.

And because *she's* so chill about it, I figure maybe *I'm* the one with the problem.

God knows, my parents didn't have the healthiest communication style. I think about their volatile arguments, the way they could go from screaming matches to silent dinners as if nothing had happened.

Is this just how families are? Or is this family—like mine—built on a foundation of things left unsaid?

So I normalize it, at least for now.

But a little voice in the back of my head nags at me.

Is this household really normal? Or is there more to it than meets the eye?

I shiver, not wanting to know the real answer.

As we prepare to leave Montana, I feel a strange mix of relief and melancholy. The trip has been a reprieve from the chaos of Sunset Cay, but it's also been a stark reminder that dysfunction runs deep in Timmy's life.

For now, I cling to the moments of peace and connection, hoping against hope that they're a sign of better days to come.

But deep down, I know that in this house—just like in my relationship with Timmy—everything unpleasant is swept under the rug.

And rugs can only hold so much before they start to show what's hidden beneath.

CHAPTER 22
APPLES DON'T FALL: BOARD SHORTS AND BETRAYAL

DEX

monitor Margaux's trip to Montana like a silent sentinel, watching the events unfold through her text updates, her emails, and the subtle shifts in her body language I catch through her phone camera.

While they're away, I arrange for cameras to be installed throughout their apartment. Top-tier devices, tucked into innocuous corners, with the resolution to pick up every flicker of movement and detail.

They're not for voyeurism—they're insurance. A way to ensure she's safe and that if Timmy escalates, I'll have irrefutable evidence. It's not exactly legal, but when has that ever stopped me?

Margaux's safety comes first. That's my rule, my purpose. And right now, she's navigating Timmy's chaos like a captain steering a ship through a hurricane.

It's not just the cameras, either. I use the trip as a chance to tweak Timmy's world just enough to unsettle him.

First, I have an associate shorten the drawstrings on his board shorts—just enough to make them look ridiculous. He's too vain to notice right away, but eventually, he'll feel the discomfort and assume he's putting on weight—a nightmare for someone as vain as Timmy. I make sure the knots will tighten in the washer, making them impossible to adjust without cutting.

Next, I replace his shampoo with a near-identical bottle of a brand that smells like old bananas and burnt rubber—subtle, but distinct enough to make him wonder if something's off.

His shoes? I swap them with the same brand and style but one size smaller. I even replaced the tags inside to match his actual size, so when he puts them on, they'll pinch and feel too tight. He'll think his feet are swelling, or that his body is betraying him in ways he can't explain.

These aren't grand gestures. They're small, calculated moves designed to wear him down, to make him feel like the universe is subtly turning against him. His little poor-me victim brain will gravitate eagerly toward these slights, hopefully distracting him from Margaux.

While I prepare for this chaos to unfold back at the apartment upon their return, I track Margaux's updates from Montana.

She tells Alice about Timmy's latest tantrum before the trip—the screaming, the vodka bottle clutched like a lifeline, the way he'd stormed out and refused to pack.

She downplays it, as she always does, but I know the truth. I see the fatigue in her eyes when I see her through her phone's camera, the way she massages her temples as if trying to rub the tension away.

But then she texts Alice about Montana itself. The family seems kind, welcoming even. She describes Phil's calm demeanor and her relief at finally meeting people who don't immediately drain her energy.

I can hear the tiny spark of hope in her voice when she tells Alice about Timmy's good behavior, his sudden transformation into the 'good son' in front of his parents.

She doesn't know that I've already researched Phil—the man's record is clean, but his temper isn't.

I recognize the patterns in his tone from the snippets Margaux relays—the sharp edges beneath his polite words, the quiet undermining of his wife, the way he subtly asserts control.

It's like looking at a roadmap to Timmy's dysfunction.

I know Margaux hasn't seen my posts on Becky's social media yet—after all, she's blocked. It's better that way. Becky deserves the humiliation, and Margaux deserves the satisfaction when she finally stumbles upon it.

But my pettiness doesn't distract me from the bigger picture.

Montana is a temporary reprieve, but I know Margaux will return to Sunset Cay.

She'll return to Timmy's manipulations, his tantrums, his escalating instability. And I'll be here, watching, waiting, and protecting her from the shadows.

I sit back in my chair, flipping through the live feeds. Nothing out of the ordinary yet, but the trip isn't over.

Timmy might be on his best behavior now, but the moment he's back in his comfort zone, the cracks will show. They always do.

And when they do, I'll be ready.

CHAPTER 23
SIX MINUTES 56 SECONDS

A FEW DAYS LATER

Returning to Sunset Cay after meeting Timmy's parents should have felt like a reset.

For the duration of the trip, while with his parents, he'd been… normal. Funny, sociable, polite. The kind of partner I could proudly introduce to people.

But back in the Cay, the Timmy I knew too well has returned—erratic, self-centered, and unpredictable.

He's still riding the high of his family reunion, constantly replaying moments and basking in their praise. "Did you see how much Mom lit up when I walked in?" he says, not for the first time.

He's stuck in a loop, clinging to the memory of his family's acceptance like a life raft.

His tantrums have become an inescapable cycle, like waves eroding the shore—inevitable, relentless and draining. Every time he returns from running away, I know he'll come back, more volatile than the last time, as if the sea whispers chaos into his ears.

I try to engage, to keep the peace, but the undercurrent of tension between us feels stronger than ever. Each time I try to hold my ground, or try to enforce some semblance of sanity, it's like trying to build a sandcastle in the tide.

He's relentless.

And somehow he always wins—not through logic or reason, but sheer depletion of all my energy to fight.

———

One morning, we head to the grocery store.

Timmy takes my hand as we browse the aisles and pick up a few things to supplement what's already in the fridge at home.

"I know it hurts you when I run away," says Timmy, out of the blue, "so I'm going to stop doing it. Because I love you," he adds, "and the last thing I ever want to do is hurt you."

When we get back from the store, out of nowhere, I find myself crying. Not because of something Timmy did—at least not directly—but because of everything.

The exhaustion of holding it all together, the constant emotional whiplash, the weight of his chaos pressing down on me.

Timmy looks genuinely puzzled, his expression almost childlike. "What did I do? Why are you crying?"

"I don't know," I reply, the words coming out between sobs. "But I just can't stop."

I message Alice, pouring out my frustrations like a dam breaking:

ME:

Ugh, I am having one of those depressive episodes where everything builds up and I can't stop crying.

Sharing bc I know you understand.

ALICE:

I'm sorry. 😔

I've been feeling like that for a while. It's so frustrating.

ME:

Miserable. Sorry you're feeling that way too.

I'm trying to explain to Timmy that it isn't anything he did yesterday, per se, but words aren't coming out of my mouth.

Which is unusual for me. I'm usually okay with words. 

ALICE:

Same, but sometimes when you're in a funk, it doesn't happen.

"I'm having a rough day. It has nothing to do with anyone or anything. I'm just sad today."

ME:

That's a good one. Thank you. 

ALICE:

Yeah I use that a lot, haha.

Encouraged, I try Alice's suggestion.

It seems to work, at least for a moment.

Timmy softens, his tone shifting. "I love you so much. I just want to be around you," he whispers, gently stroking my hair. "I'm sorry you're feeling this way. Why don't you put on one of your shows, and I'll watch it with you?"

For a brief, shining moment, I think maybe we've turned a corner and the rest of the day might go smoothly. Taking Timmy's suggestion at face value, I turn on *90 Day Fiancé*, grateful for the comfort of its absurd drama.

Timmy settles next to me, seemingly content.

Spending the day together snuggled up on the bed, watching shows that bring me relief and relaxation, sounds quite nice.

But exactly six minutes and fifty-six seconds into the episode, it's like a switch flips.

"Nope! Nope, I can't do this! I can't watch this stupid show!" he yells, jumping up from the couch like it's on fire. *"I don't care about this person on the TV!"*

Before I can respond, he storms out the door, slamming it so hard the walls shudder.

It's not even a particularly dramatic episode, but Timmy has decided once again that the show affects his emotions. He watches so much worse—constantly selecting movies with high conflict and drama—and is fine with it.

But because it's something I like to watch, it's therefore something he can try to ruin.

So he does.

I settle into the relative peace that always follows one of Timmy's tantrums.

For all his bluster, his cooldowns usually involve sulking in a corner or at the beach, away from me.

I text Alice to fill her in.

ME:

Well... I tried that.

It worked initially.

He kept saying, 'I love you so much and I want to watch all your shows with you and just be around you.'

So I watched exactly 6 mins and 56 seconds of my show and he had a tantrum and stormed off bc he didn't like the show.

I've never met anyone who has literally had tantrums about Machine Gun Kelly and reality tv. I'm hoping it's a passing phase.

ALICE:

Sorry I don't want to laugh, but what a dumb turnaround.

That wasn't even 10 minutes, my dude.

ME:

Oh, I find it amusing. Less than 7 mins.

Amusing. Painful. All of it. Oh well. I can only change myself, right?! At least I'm not crying anymore.

ALICE:

I'm such a dick, I'd be yelling after him like a gaslighting frat boy.

"Awww, c'mon, babe, it was only 7 minutes. Can't handle it? It's not that bad!"

"Mikey made it through the whole season and we all know he's a codfish."

ME:

> Well, in the grocery store he said he would stop running off. So that lasted like an hour all up. TV show 7 mins. 🤣

ALICE:

What a child. My ex would even pretend for me.

He watched like 3 episodes of Downton Abbey because I was into it, and, like 4 days later, followed up with "what was that kinda boring British show? I might wanna watch more." 😆

ME:

> I was like, 'Dude, you watched for 6 minutes and 56 seconds and he yelled, 'I don't care about this person on the tv,' and sprinted away. 🤣

ALICE:

B- lying, babe, but I like the effort. 😆

Call me someday when he's yelling in the back so I can yell, "I don't care about this person in the room."

What even is the goal of that?

Now we're both not watching TV.

We're both watching YOU now.

I laugh despite myself. Much better than crying.

ME:

Lol yeah.

Maybe that's the point.

I mean I can watch reality tv and see the beach.

So life isn't that bad. 🤣

ALICE:

Too bad he can't see that. What a moron.

I'm absolutely blown away.

> Like, my boyfriend takes care of me because he makes more than I do and I feel bad when I make him upset.

But here isn't the gorgeous paradise experience I'd hoped for. Here, I feel like I'm a guest in my own life, navigating a landscape that shifts beneath me every time Timmy decides to blow up over something inconsequential.

The whiplash of going from his gentle, loving words to his volatile outbursts is exhausting. It's a rollercoaster I never signed up for, but one I seem unable to step off.

And yet, amidst it all, Alice's humor and empathy feel like a lifeline.

She reminds me of who I used to be before this constant chaos became my new normal.

For a fleeting moment, I let myself hope that maybe, just maybe, I can find my way back to that version of me—someone who didn't measure happiness in stolen seconds of peace but lived it fully.

But as the door slams again, another tantrum echoing in the distance, I wonder if I even remember how to start.

CHAPTER 24
EMOTIONAL SUPPORT CLIFF

MARGAUX

The tantrums escalate in frequency, each one more absurd than the last.

Timmy runs off to the rocks or the sea or the meth tents every chance he gets, like a petulant child putting himself in a self-imposed time-out. The apartment door beeps behind him with such regularity it could be mistaken for the sound of my sanity slipping away.

Each time he returns, he's more unpredictable. His words cut sharper, his tone more venomous.

"I'm going to tell everybody who you really are," he sneers one night, his voice dripping with malice.

I don't respond. I've always been an open book—what could he possibly expose that I haven't already?

"I'm going to destroy your life," he growls, pacing like a caged animal.

I keep silent, wondering if he realizes he's already doing just that.

"You're going to prison for a felony!" he shouts, his voice shaking with indignation.

I quirk an eyebrow, genuinely curious. *"What* felony?"

He narrows his eyes, desperate to conjure something out of thin air. "I'll have you found guilty of a felony! You scraped the pillar next to the parking spot and scratched the car next to us!"

I can't help but laugh. "I didn't touch the car next to us. Sure, I brushed the pillar—it's a tight squeeze. But at least I have a license. Call me when you get yours back, and then you can critique my parking."

His face flushes red, but he doesn't respond. Instead, he storms into the back room and slams the door.

———

One night, he's scrolling through his phone when I catch a glimpse of a message from one of his drug-dealing acquaintances:

TIMMY'S DRUG DEALER FRIEND:

Hey fag. Where are you?

The casual vulgarity of the exchange is infuriating. "Why is this your circle?" I snap, but he brushes it off with a nonchalant shrug.

When he disappears for hours again, I message Alice.

ME:

He's in the sea or running on rocks or something. I don't know.

ALICE:

Sorry, that's hilarious imagery.

"Hey, where'd Timmy go?"

"Oh, he's in the sea."

I laugh, the absurdity of my life laid bare in her messages.

ALICE:

He's become a quest in a video game:

Find Timmy.

Hints: The Rocks, The Sea.

Deterrents: Unpredictable Behavior.

ME:

An enraged surfer angry about reality tv. Either in the sea or climbing a rock.

ALICE:

Credit where it's due.

ME:

I looked at his phone just before and a drug dealer
messaged him to say, 'hey fag, where did you go?'
or something like that.

So I'll see if he replies haha.

ALICE:

Yeah, that's how I talk to my besties, too.

That's how you know our friends are quality.

ME:

Lmfao.

You are making me laugh, thank you.

ALICE:

I clown with my friends, but I don't hurl slurs at
them.

ME:

I told one of them that everyone here acts like
fucking Peter Pans.

Think they get to laze around all day.

ME:

Maybe I need to send him to the rocks and then
write.

I'll figure out a trigger and say it. Like put on a show
I don't even want to watch. And then he will run off
and I'll write thousands of words. 

ALICE:

And I'll laugh for 50 years.

When your acknowledgements honor The Rocks.

ME:

To The Rocks. For giving me the space to write.

ALICE:

"Thank you for your reliable presence and stable
existence."

———

About 2 hours later

ME:

He never came back. Seems very strange. Has been like 90+ mins bordering 2 hours.

Didn't take his phone or watch, so I can't even see where he is.

ALICE:

Hm. Has that ever happened before?

ME:

Yesterday was like 2 hours. But he had his watch so I could see where he was.

Unacceptable from my perspective.

Like are we 5 years old and run away with no way of getting in contact? No, no we are not.

ALICE:

Do you want to go find him?

ME:

I don't know where he would be and I live in a really shitty part of Sunset Cay.

Lots of tweakers everywhere.

I think about it. She makes a point. I can go see where he is.

Is it the safest option? No, it would be far safer to just sit here. Physically.

Mentally, I'm losing my mind, not knowing where he is or if he's safe.

I walk down the road, and see him sitting at a bench with a bunch of the people who live in the tents.

ME:

I see him.

He stands up as he sees me approach.

"I'm coming back home, babe," he says. "I'll be right there."

"Okay," I roll my eyes, not quite believing him.

ME:

He's returning, apparently. 😔

————

AN HOUR LATER

Timmy's whistle cuts through the evening air like a siren. It's sharp, shrill, and unmistakable.

I glance toward the ocean and there he is—fingers hooked around the chain-link fence, leaning over it like some deranged seagull, trying to get my attention.

He's yelling something, too, though I can't make it out over the sound of waves and his own nonsensical theatrics.

I roll my eyes and look back at the TV. I'm not about to entertain whatever fresh madness this is.

He whistles again, louder this time.

God, you're embarrassing.

He comes into the apartment, grabs the truck key and the mailbox key, and walks toward the door.

"What are you doing with those?" I ask, concerned.

He ignores me and leaves, slamming the door behind him.

Great, now I can't even go anywhere.

I can't even go to the pool because he has both fobs.

ME:

Omg, he was like hanging onto the fence whistling and trying to get my attention.

ALICE:

This sounds like a bad rom-com.

ME:

He walked off with the truck keys and mailbox key. This makes no sense.

He's always losing things—his phone, his keys, his shoes.

If he loses the keys, I'm going to lose my shit.

I ignored the whistling and the yelling bc that's embarrassing.

ALICE:

I'm sorry friend.

Eh, enjoy yourself. He can lay on the rocks if he wants to.

I laugh, the absurdity of the situation too much to process fully.

At least I have Alice to keep me grounded.

I keep ignoring him, but the audacity of his behavior is almost comical. Who the hell whistles at someone like they're a dog?

Eventually, he returns to the apartment.

"You're disgusting," I say flatly, not even looking up. "Immature. A complete piece of shit."

I can feel the weight of his glare, but I don't care. My vocabulary has expanded to new levels of insult lately. And my emotional intelligence? Absolutely plummeting.

"Wow, nice! Real nice!" He stalks off to the back room, muttering under his breath about how ungrateful I am for his… what? His *existence*?

"Get the fuck out of my life!" I call out with a cheery voice. "It'll be much better without you in it!"

He leaves again and comes back about twenty minutes later, dripping wet from the ocean and tracking sand all over the apartment. I can't even keep track of his comings and goings.

I'm halfway through an episode of my show, the first real moment of relaxation I've had all day.

"You good?" I ask, not even looking up, feeling slightly guilty for insulting him earlier.

He doesn't answer. Instead, he huffs past me, grabs a towel, and heads back out, muttering to himself.

I shake my head.

ME:

He came back, wet and sandy, tracked crap everywhere, then left again. I think the rock-and-sea time-out plan is going well for him.

ALICE:

That rock deserves an award for being his emotional support cliff.

I laugh, for what feels like the first time all day.

I sigh, sinking back into my pillows.

At least I have Alice.
At least I'm not crying anymore.

CHAPTER 25
BLUE'S CLUES

MARGAUX

About an hour later, Timmy stomps back into the apartment, agitated and muttering under his breath.

I try to steer the conversation elsewhere, telling him about an idea Alice and I have for a book, and how we might ask Rebecca to do some book art for us.

His reaction is immediate and volatile. "You don't want me to do the art for your book?" His voice rises, his face twisting into a scowl. "You're going to write a book with someone else, and have another person do the art?"

"Um… yeah," I say cautiously. "You don't do romance art *or* write. And they both do. And they're my friends, so…."

He cuts me off, throwing his arms up dramatically. "Fine! You want to hang out with your friend Rebecca this weekend? Go ahead! I'll jump off cliffs while you do!"

I stare at him, exasperated. "Timmy, do whatever you want. I don't care."

He storms out again, slamming the door behind him.

———

ME:

Oh, he's threatening to jump off cliffs again. Here we go.

I banned him from cliff jumping bc it's dangerous, and I just said, 'Do whatever you want. I don't caaare.' I'm mature, I know. I actually am, but he acts like he is 2, so I am like super mature acting like a 4yo.

I also just told him his drug dealer friend was messaging him.

He at least put Pete Davidson on for me bc he knows I enjoy his comedy haha.

Oh, now Timmy is sulking bc I told him you and I are writing a book and Rebecca might do the art. Wait… YOU do art!!!!!

ALICE:

And why is he mad? Is he a writer or something?

ME:

Lmao he wants to do all my book art.

ALICE:

No.

Not for your and my book.

ME:

Girls only.

ALICE:

I mean, you can do what you want. I don't think he's reliable enough to trust with a project I'm involved in.

Just being honest.

I don't say it, but I feel exactly the same. It's risky involving Timmy in anything, because I can see him not following through as some form of punishment, a way to sabotage my writing career. Making me dependent on him.

Timmy eventually returns with his water bottle, muttering about how misunderstood he is. Glancing over at the kitchen, I notice the bottle of vodka is conspicuously missing.

Timmy yells from the other side of the room. "I'd never call you a piece of shit or shit on your art!" Then he runs out the door, water bottle in hand, and it beeps shut behind him.

ME:

I don't trust any of his friends bc they are all super sketchy. All do weird drugs. He stopped.

There's this one asshole girl who I guess he slept with right before we got together and had before, also. And she wouldn't stop blowing up his phone when we got together.

He says he's not into her at all (but clearly was prepared to do whatever).

So clearly I'm not okay with her.

That's not jealousy, that's like 'get the fuck away from my fiancé, you weirdo'.

ALICE:

I dunno. He needs to not entertain her at all.

ME:

So I've been struggling with that, but she at least moved away.

But then she visited again, and he looked at her Facebook to 'make sure she wasn't messaging him and creating a problem.'

Yeah, he's blocked her now, and she doesn't know his number.

ALICE:

Hahaha what? He doesn't need to look to see that.

ME:

I know, but he's not smart with social media.

ALICE:

Okay, but this one is super basic.

Check your inbox. Is she in it? No?

You just figured out Blue's Clues!

ME:

Hahahaha, I know.

ALICE:

Tell him to get better excuses. These are boring.

ME:

So he clicked on her profile and says that's why she showed up as a shortcut on his FB. But to your earlier question, he doesn't have many friends and so she is probably the only one who reaches out ,other than someone who wants him to sell drugs for them.

Gosh damn, I am making him sound amazing, aren't I?!

ALICE:

I mean, the truth is the truth.

This is what talking about my ex felt like sometimes.

ME:

But anyway, he has blocked her and not given her his new number, and says he can't stand her, so he must have been doing the drugs that make you want to bang people you can't stand. 🐴

But it was before I met him to be fair.

Yeah, it's rough.

ALICE:

People only show up in your drop downs if you search for them.

Clicking their profile on FB or messenger won't do it.

ME:

Yeah, he searched her out to see if she messaged. 🙃

There is this weird shortcut thing now.

So he said he clicked on her page.

ALICE:

I'm too tired to make that face, but... I dunno.

He's on notice from me now.

ME:

But afterward, he has at least blocked her (and told her he couldn't be friends with her anymore when she went to his house to grab her things).

ALICE:

Well, let's hope that's the path he's following!

ME:

I know. I'm not happy about it, but I think he is just being dumb, not dishonest.

The running away tantrum is a bit much.

Number 4 in 24 hours.

Thank you for listening to me. I'm actively processing this.

Not the dumb girl shit.

The running away since we got back from meeting his parents.

But it's also helpful to get your perspective on that other stuff so I don't feel as gaslighted as I did before.

ALICE:

Ask him to at least try different shoes each time he runs away so he can measure performance.

ME:

He might get paid for comparisons… a sponsorship.

'The Nikes took me 2 miles and the Reeboks only took me 1.8. Both felt great on the ankles.'

ALICE:

You're always welcome to reach out! As soon as I get to my messages, I reply.

ME:

You do, and I appreciate you!! Here for you as well, and I will be here whenever you need, same way x. 🖤

CHAPTER 26
RUNAWAY PICKLE

MARGAUX

When Timmy returns hours later, he plops down next to me as if nothing happened, the scent of saltwater still clinging to him. He doesn't acknowledge the chaos of earlier, doesn't apologize for the whirlwind he left behind.

Instead, he picks up the remote and puts on Pete Davidson's new comedy special.

For a brief moment, things feel almost normal. We laugh at the same jokes, sit shoulder to shoulder, and I catch myself wondering if more moments could be like this.

But the peace never lasts.

Over the next month, the cycle becomes its own cruel ritual. Timmy runs away after every argument or perceived slight, only to return hours later with a token of remorse—a shell from the ocean, an interesting rock, once even a feather.

It's as though these little offerings are meant to repair the cracks he's left behind, but the weight of his apologies is featherlight compared to the damage he's done.

Occasionally, there are outlier events that break the monotony of his tantrums.

One day, I do a phone interview for an HR role, sitting in the truck while

Timmy stands outside, bouncing a ball like a child. The rhythmic thump-thump-thump of it grates against my concentration, and I'm convinced the interviewer can hear it through the phone.

Afterward, Timmy makes an announcement. "I should get a job so I can pay you back for everything I owe you," he says earnestly. "And because idle hands are the devil's playground."

For a fleeting moment, I believe him. But, of course, it's all talk. Timmy makes no effort to find work.

Occasionally, he dives into graphic design projects, and some of his work is genuinely impressive. But his focus is fleeting, his drive non-existent, and never really leads to anything that can make an income.

Of course he doesn't try to get a job.

Nothing ever comes of it.

He's all talk.

I tell Alice.

ALICE:

I imagine this man's head is empty.

Her humor keeps me sane in a way Timmy never could.

The running-away episodes start to blur together.

One day, it's because I refuse to buy him a Black and Mild.

The next day, he announces he's going to spend hours snorkeling while I work. This angers me.

"I don't pay rent out of my savings to fund you going snorkeling while I work," I snap.

His reaction is immediate and predictable. He storms out, slamming the door so hard the windows rattle.

ME:

Alice, every time Timmy runs away, I'm going to send you a running pickle GIF. This one:

Timmy drinks as he drives, the cloying scent of Fireball mingling with the salty sea air. My stomach twists with anxiety as I watch him sip from the bottle.

He pulls over by a beachside cliff and starts ranting about something so inconsequential and random I can't even follow. His voice is slurred, his words jumbled.

"Timmy, are you sure you're okay to drive?" I ask, my voice hesitant.

"I'm fine," he snaps. "Stop telling me what to do."

"Timmy, you've had too much to drink," I say, trying to keep my tone calm. "Please, just pull over."

His scowl deepens, and without warning, he rears back his fist and smashes it into the car stereo. The sound of breaking plastic fills the cab, followed by a crackling silence as buttons scatter across the dashboard.

I freeze, the breath catching in my throat. My heart races as I realize how easily that fist could have been directed at me.

"I'm sorry, Marg," he says after a moment, his voice softer. "It was dumb of me to punch the stereo. I'll fix it. I was just feeling sad because I was thinking about my friend who died, and I was frustrated about an argument I had with Darren a while ago." He pauses for a moment. "And... I was mad at you for trying to control me—your behavior really was rotten—but I mainly did it because I was struggling with those emotions."

I blink, stunned by his audacity. *Rotten?* I'd been trying to keep us safe.

I've been punished for asking him not to drive drunk.

For my begging—for my attempting to hold him accountable and keep myself safe—I'm paying the price.

A moment later, he seems to calm down.

I message Alice:

ME:

> He just punched my car stereo and cracked it.

ALICE:

> Get out of there ,please.

> Park the car and exit.

ME:

> Unfortunately, he's driving, and the truck is in my name bc he owes me thousands of dollars.

> And he apologized and mentioned two feelings he was struggling with. And that it wasn't mainly my fault. So that's progress, I guess?

> Still said my 'behavior was rotten' but I can live with that even though it's not true.

ALICE:

> I'm glad you're safe now, but he needs to behave himself.

This is life with Timmy—storm after storm, with no end in sight. The rocks and the sea feel more stable than he ever could.

His tantrums are as inevitable as the tides, and his apologies as hollow as the shells he brings me.

And yet, here I am, still holding on, still hoping.

For what, I don't know.

But I'm starting to wonder if even the hope is running out.

CHAPTER 27
NONE OF THIS IS NORMAL

MARGAUX

LATER THAT DAY

update Alice on Timmy's latest antics:

ME:

ALICE:

Dude.

Where now?

ME:

Fuck knows.

I thought for a moment he was doing better. But I guess I was wrong.

ALICE:

That's the thing with people like Timmy and my ex. There's part of them that is amazing and kind and super talented and sweet. But their mental health issues will always be louder than anything else if they allow it to be, and both of them allow it to be the loudest thing in their lives.

Louder than rationale, louder than family, louder than love, louder than self preservation.

You're going to be on eggshells with him forever because the tripwires always change.

The landscape of his mind will always change, therefore so will the traps.

The next day, Timmy announces he's leaving. "I'm going to be with my parents. I'm done with you."

"Good," I say flatly. "Go use them instead of me."

"I'm going to tell my mom that you and my cousin are plotting to put her in a nursing home. That you don't think she's of sound mind."

That's the latest thing he's jealous about—the friendship I've formed online with his cousin, Janet, ever since the Montana visit.

Initially encouraging of it, he now finds my friendship with her to be some giant threat. And apparently, that requires punishment—to me and, inexplicably, his mother.

He grins, as though he's won something, and then starts skateboarding around the room like an overgrown child. When he finally leaves, the door beeping behind him, I exhale a shaky breath, the weight of his presence lifting slightly but leaving its mark.

ME:

Well, my friend from high school and her wife are visiting.

They've been planning this trip for the last 12 years.

I don't think I can bring him.

ALICE:

No, I wouldn't bring him.

Someone in the middle of a psychotic episode
should not be dealing with the world at large.

ME:

And also, her wife will actually kill him, and then she
will go to prison.

Bc she is a badass and stronger than him and we
don't need that happening.

You would actually love her.

ALICE:

I mean, I love her already.

I glance at my phone and see that he's used it to text his cousin, pretending to be me.

I send the screenshot to Alice.

TIMMY PRETENDING TO BE ME:

Your kind of a cunt... like you think my mother
needs to be in a home..

Was second guessing you..

By all means fuck yourself.. take your evening and
shove it up your asshole bitch...

Tell my uncle I said so...

Rahhh...

You're bad and kind of the worst with what you're
trying

Documented... you... I love you but you honestly
suck with whatever this is. You try to fast-track and
befriend and do...

ALICE:

"Rahhh."

ME:

That was a weird addition.

ALICE:

That was SUCH a weird addition.

That's like talking to an actual child.

Timmy returns from the back room where he's been ranting about me and his cousin to his parents for the last twenty minutes.

I couldn't hear what was said, just a lot of 'she' this and 'she' that, and I'm so exhausted by him I honestly don't care.

"Well, everyone still loves *you* somehow," he fumes, "but they hate that cunt. But I'm still leaving you, but hopefully after my court date."

I tell Alice.

ME:

Dude, what does that even mean?

ALICE:

It means nothing.

Like those are not words.

Just when it feels like things can't get any crazier, Timmy's naked form runs past me. He circles the bed and then runs into the back room, closing the door behind him.

ME:

He's running around naked and shutting himself in the back room.

ALICE:

Yeah, bc that's what sane people do.

I message another friend, Jo—short for Josephine, randomly, because I see she's up and I know I can trust her, and tell her a fraction of what's been transpiring since I moved to the Cay.

Her reply is instant:

JO:

Honey, this guy is like made up of red flags.

Ain't that the truth.

JO:

This is bad news.

Are you engaged to him for any kind of legal
reason? Paperwork or insurance or anything?

ME:

No, just relationship reasons.

JO:

Okay, well… How long have you been with
this man?

Both relationship wise and in person?

ME:

6 months.

I sigh. *What an eventful six months it's been.*

With so much to fill her in on, I call Jo and give her a very abridged version of what's been going on. But she doesn't need to know every tiny detail to know I'm in a dangerous situation.

After we hang up, she messages me immediately.

JO:

Honey, if you ever need me… if you ever need
anything… text me 202 and I will find you help. Do
you understand me?

I will find you help. Just text me 202.

I will help you.

ME:

Yes. 202. I got it. Thank you xo.

"I'm packing my bags!" Timmy suddenly announces, emerging from the back room with a huge grin on his face. "Dad told me to call him back in a couple of hours, but I would much rather be in Montana with them than here with you."

ME:

He just announced he packed his bags.

ALICE:

Good. You told him to.

ME:

> OMG I'm financially supporting this piece of shit with my life savings, which I can't afford, and he clearly doesn't give a shit.

> He's giving away the mattress I'm sitting on, apparently (that he got for free from his ex's friend), and the tv (which his former roommate had to buy bc the roommate broke the gross girl he slept with right before he met me's tv I guess).

> Lying here in bed is miserable so I think I'm going to go for a drive around the island bc I can. I hope my cat is okay when I get back. He says they're best friends, but he has also threatened to kill him. He's also threatened to smash the apartment up tho, too. As I type this, I realize it's all abnormal and I might just take my cat to be safe.

> He announced he took the trash out and once again that he packed his bags. I think he wants a reaction.

ALICE:

> Yeah, he wants a reaction from you for sure.

> I would leave with your cat if you can.

He smirks at me, and I want to slap it off his face so bad.

Instead, I speak up.

"Timmy, you're a user, so go and use your parents and stop using me."

"Look at you sending stupid messages to your dumb friends who aren't even your real friends," he sneers, dancing around.

He picks up his longboard, lays it down flat, and starts skateboarding around the room.

"I don't know what your problem is," he says, and then he walks out the door. It beeps behind him.

ALICE:

> This is all abnormal and unhealthy.

She isn't wrong.

CHAPTER 28
YOU WANT TO BE THE VICTIM? HERE YOU GO

DEX

Now that they're back in the Cay, Timmy is unraveling, and I'm enjoying every second of it.

The apartment is no longer just a chaotic mess of his making—it's a minefield of carefully laid traps. Tiny inconveniences, subtle adjustments, each one designed to chip away at his fragile sense of control.

Now, as I watch him through the cameras I had installed during their trip, it's like witnessing the world's most satisfying domino effect.

The first show of cracks happens mid-morning. He's standing in the bathroom, shirtless, holding a bottle of his overpriced, overly fragrant shampoo. His expression shifts from confusion to mild outrage. I zoom in for a closer look.

"Why the hell is my shampoo so runny?" he mutters, shaking the bottle furiously. He tips it over his hand, and a thin, oily liquid dribbles out. I stifle a laugh.

He sniffs his hand and recoils, yelling to no one in particular, "What is this shit?!"

The camera in the living room catches him storming out of the bathroom, dripping wet and muttering about how 'everything's going wrong'. I almost applaud.

You want to be the victim, Timmy? You got it.

But the real comedy comes later, when he gets ready for his usual beach outing. He grabs his board shorts, tugs them on, and frowns. He inspects the shortened drawstrings with a mixture of confusion and fury. "What the hell is this?" he mutters, yanking at the strings like they'll magically grow longer. "Did these shrink or something?" he mutters, glaring at the shorts like they personally betrayed him. When they don't, he throws them onto the bed and storms off to the bathroom.

No, Timmy, I just made your drawstrings a little less functional. Just enough to frustrate you.

The cameras capture every glorious second of his tantrum. He stomps around the apartment, yanking at the strings and muttering about 'cheap-ass crap', oblivious to the fact that I'm watching and grinning like the Cheshire Cat.

It's beautiful.

He's spiraling, questioning his grip on reality. Is the world against him, or is he just losing his mind?

And then come the shoes.

He slides his feet into what he assumes are his favorite pair of flip-flops. They're just a size too small now, thanks to the quick swap I orchestrated while Margaux and he were out. He freezes mid-step, his face twisting in confusion as his toes hang awkwardly over the edge.

"What the fuck is this?" he yells. The camera catches him throwing the flip-flops across the room. I almost applaud. "Am I getting bigger? Am I gaining weight?!"

I smirk at the screen. It's not enough to make him spiral completely, but it's a start.

Margaux's presence during these moments is the only thing that tempers my satisfaction. Watching her through the cameras, I see the quiet toll his chaos takes on her, the way her shoulders slump when she thinks no one is looking.

She's back to walking on eggshells, trying to navigate his mood swings while keeping herself from completely crumbling.

She deserves better. I've known that all along.

Timmy's next meltdown happens when he returns from the beach. His board shorts are barely holding on, his shampooed hair looks greasy, his giant feet looking ridiculous in his mysteriously snug flip-flops.

He storms into the kitchen, slamming cupboards and muttering about 'everything being off'.

"Something's wrong in this place," he says to himself, pacing like a caged animal. "Everything feels… different."

That's the idea, Timmy.

As he storms off to sulk in the back room, I switch to the camera feed in the living room. Margaux is lying on the bed, scrolling through her phone, her expression a mix of exhaustion and quiet determination. She looks like someone who's given up trying to find peace, and who is simply trying to survive.

My chest tightens.

Even after everything, she's still here—a masterpiece of resilience in the middle of a dumpster fire. Still standing. Her texts to Alice are a window into her thoughts—raw, honest, and laced with dark humor. And that's what's keeping her afloat.

The running pickle GIF she sends to Alice every time Timmy storms out is like a little beacon of light cutting through the dark.

It's absurd, but that's the point.

She's clinging to something that makes her laugh because otherwise, she'd break. I admire her for that.

'Timmy's in the sea again,' she texts Alice, and I can almost hear her laugh through the screen. Her friend fires back with the perfect response: 'Sounds like a bad video game. Hints: the rocks, the sea. Deterrents: unpredictable behavior.'

I laugh under my breath. Alice is a good one—witty, loyal, and ready to verbally deck anyone who crosses Margaux. She's exactly the kind of friend Margaux needs, even if Timmy's ego can't handle her.

Then there's Josephine, another solid anchor in Margaux's life. She doesn't sugarcoat, and she doesn't tolerate Timmy's antics. She even has a rescue plan: text her '202' and she'll make sure Margaux gets help.

I don't know her, but I like her already.

Margaux deserves these people. She deserves people who lift her up, not weigh her down. And Timmy? He's an anchor dragging her deeper into the abyss.

I laugh again as I observe another of Margaux's exchanges with Alice, shaking my head. Margaux's ability to find humor in the absurdity of her life is incredible. It's also heartbreaking. She shouldn't have to laugh through this. She shouldn't have to endure this at all.

When Timmy returns to the apartment hours later, he's dripping wet and still muttering about his bad luck. He grabs a towel, glances at Margaux, and says, "I'd never shit on your art!" before storming out again.

Margaux doesn't even flinch. She just texts Alice and fills her in.

Alice fires back with her usual wit, and Margaux laughs. She's tired, but she's still laughing.

I lean back in my chair, watching the screen. She's stronger than she gives herself credit for, but even the strongest people have limits. Timmy is pushing hers to the breaking point, and I won't let him take her down.

I zoom back out, my eyes narrowing on Timmy as he stomps around the apartment like a petulant child. Every tantrum, every outburst, every frustrated scream, caused by me, feels like a small victory.

Because one day, Timmy will implode. One day, she'll see him for what he really is— dead weight. Until then, I'll be here, watching, waiting, and making sure she's as safe as I can. And giving Timmy a few more reasons to question his sanity along the way—he deserves nothing less.

And when that day comes, Margaux will finally be free.

CHAPTER 29
BROKE-ASS BREAKDOWN

MARGAUX

Later, I try to escape the tension with a drive. I take Sabre, my ever-loyal cat, hoping for a moment of peace and to make sure Timmy doesn't do anything to him.

But as fate would have it, the truck shudders and comes to a complete stop in the middle of the main road.

Fuck.

I dial 911, but just as the dispatcher answers, a kind man covered in tattoos and wearing a massive gold chain approaches. He tells me to put the truck in neutral, and pushes it down a side street while smoke billows from under the hood.

I call Timmy's dad, desperate for advice.

"We had a falling out, and I went for a drive, and the truck's broken down and I don't know what to do," I explain.

"Yeah, he called me," Phil says. "He's really upset because he felt like Janet was trying to drive a wedge between the two of you. She shouldn't have been talking about him. He's just a really nice guy."

I don't really know what he's talking about, but I am aware of his brewing animosity toward his cousin, Janet, ever since we became friends in Montana at his suggestion.

Changing subjects, I describe what's going on with the truck.

Phil suggests it might be an oil issue.

Before I can act on it, my phone buzzes. It's Timmy.

"Dad said you need help with the truck," he says.

"I don't need help from you," I snap, hanging up immediately.

The truck cools down enough for me to limp it a little farther down the street before it gives out again. Timmy calls back, and I begrudgingly answer. I describe what's going on.

"It sounds like a hose has come loose," he says.

I look under the hood, and he's right. A hose is loose, but whether it happened naturally or through Timmy's meddling, I can't be sure.

With no other option, I wait for him to arrive and fix it.

It's hard when your abuser is also your rescuer, when they've fashioned it so there's nobody else around who can help. When you have to rely on them to live your day-to-day life. And when they're potentially the ones causing the issues that they then need to fix.

When he finally shows up, his smugness is palpable. He fixes the hose with the air of someone expecting a medal.

The drive home is silent and thankfully, short. Timmy basks in his self-congratulatory glow, his hero complex in full swing, while I seethe in quiet rage. This is the cycle he thrives on—creating problems, swooping in to 'save the day,' and keeping me dependent on him. Relying on him for help he shouldn't need to give in the first place.

It's exhausting, demeaning, and utterly relentless. And yet, for reasons I can't quite articulate, I'm still here. Still enduring it. Still hoping, somehow, for a different ending to this same story.

———

THE NEXT DAY

Timmy is driving me nuts as usual, running off in a huff and returning at sporadic intervals, so I decide to escape for a while. That way, I can blare loud music and not sit in the apartment, miserable, wondering where Timmy has gone and when he'll return.

I grab my keys and head out, driving down to the point. The salty air and blaring music in my car are my temporary antidotes to the suffocating toxicity at home.

I don't even get far before my phone rings.

Timmy. Of course.

I sigh and answer.

"I saw you drive by," he says.

"And?" I roll my eyes, gripping the steering wheel. "Why? What are you doing? Who are you with?"

"Nobody," he replies quickly.

"Are you with the people I saw you with at the store?" I press.

"No, I was just cruising," he says defensively.

In the Cay, 'cruising' usually means stopping to chat with anyone who will give you the time of day. Small talk, gossip, or making some kind of half-assed connection with anybody and everybody in his vicinity..

I hang up, not in the mood to dissect his vague answers.

Moments later, my phone buzzes with a text from him:

TIMMY:

Where are you going? Please don't tell me you have
a boyfriend in there.

I message Alice and fill her in:

ME:

Like I have a fucking boyfriend that I tuck under my
boob or something. What the actual fuck.

I don't have time to write books when I am in this
relationship, let alone find a spare boyfriend. And I
am also the most loyal fucking person in the world.
This is so nuts.

ALICE:

This is definitely a Detective Pikachu moment.

Like, where is your head?

Also, projection much.

When I get home, Timmy's hot on my heels. He drops his phone and Apple Watch on the table, leaves without a word, and slams the door. Clearly, he's upset that I dared to drive somewhere without him by my side. It's like he's offended by my mere existence as an independent person.

Later, he comes back with an apology on his lips. It lasts about five minutes. Soon, he's screaming again.

"All your triggers are fake!" he yells. "You don't really have PTSD. You made that up! You made up being sexually assaulted because you wanted attention, you dumb bitch!"

His words slice through me like knives. I put my headphones on, drowning him out with music while he continues to yell. Eventually, he storms out again, slamming the door behind him.

———

LATER

JO:

Share your location with me.

Her concern is palpable through her message, as if something has set off her spidey senses.

JO:

I want to know where you are.

It hits differently when it's coming from a friend, not a partner. Especially when it's because of a partner.

ME:

Why?

I ask, even though I already know the answer.

JO:

I want to know you're safe.

And if he hurts you again, I want to be able to point the police in the right direction.

Her words land like a slap. A slap that's meant to wake me up.

ME:

Jesus, Jo.

JO:

I'm serious.

You need to be careful.

You know how dangerous men like him can be.

I don't answer. I can't. My mind flashes to the times he's come close—to the antler incident, to the moments where I thought, *This is it. This is how it ends.*

He wouldn't really kill me, would he?

But he's said he would. And the fact that I'm even asking the question is proof enough of how far I've fallen. How warped my sense of normalcy has become.

And he always denies that it's his fault. Like he doesn't understand that it's possible to have healthy conflict and disagreements and figure it out, because that's what adults do.

A wild tantrum in the body of a two-hundred pound, six-foot-two man mad about a show I'm watching is much different from a toddler mad he didn't get an extra cookie. You're supposed to grow out of that phase, but I guess some men never do.

And that's dangerous.

And it's dangerous when men hate women, period. Which I'm increasingly starting to see in him. It's very concerning.

But in the moment, he always has a way of talking me down, of making me feel like I'm blowing things out of proportion.

That it's all in my head.

That he loves me more than anyone else.

That the other people are against us, and so we need to be a team.

"Team Ginger Shark," he'll say, even inventing a special handshake just for us.

"Team Ginger Shark," I'll reply, although deep in my gut I don't know that it's a safe team for me to be on.

CHAPTER 30
CONTRIBUTE OR DIE TRYING

DEX

After checking on Margaux, I realize I can no longer sit idly by.

It's time to act.

Sure, the anonymous texts and first few pranks were fun, but Timmy's crazy behavior is only escalating. I don't want to push him to do anything to hurt Margaux, but he's gone too far, and it's time for me to take real action.

Am I going too easy on Timmy? Maybe. At least for now.

Sure, I could hire someone to kill him, or at least seriously hurt him. I could certainly fly over and take care of him myself.

But somehow I just know that would destroy Margaux, and she'd be left pining for a ghost of a man that never was.

Selfishly, seeing her all bent out of shape over his loser ass would destroy *me*. I couldn't see her going through that. And part of her would always be his.

If she ever found out I had anything to do with it? *Game over.*

She'd never be mine.

I can't have that.

I have to make it so that Timmy destroys himself.

So the second phase of my plan starts innocently enough, at least on the surface. A tiny adjustment here, a flicker of confusion there.

I remotely change his phone's language settings to Mandarin.

He spends the better part of an hour trying to switch it back, muttering curses under his breath.

When he finally figures it out, I switch it to Russian.

A small, satisfying crack in his already fragile composure.

Next, I tinker with his email. I add a filter that reroutes messages from his father into his spam folder, and then send an anonymous email from an untraceable account:

SUBJECT: YOU KNOW WHAT YOU DID

MESSAGE: IT'S ONLY A MATTER OF TIME. TICK TOCK.

He stares at his screen, the color draining from his face, and for a moment I think he might actually piss himself.

Good.

I dig deeper into his psyche. I know his insecurities like the back of my hand—his lack of a real job, his reliance on Margaux, his pathetic dependence on his father's moral support and occasional few dollars sent via Apple Pay for 'soda'.

I set up a string of fake calendar notifications:

9:00 AM: INTERVIEW WITH BURGER SHACK – DON'T BLOW IT

11:00 AM: CALL DAD ABOUT LOAN REPAYMENT

2:00 PM: FIND YOUR BALLS, TIMMY

Each notification pops up with a cheerful *ding* while he's lounging on the couch, watching some mindless movie.

At first, he ignores them, but the frequency ramps up, and his irritation is palpable. He slams his phone down on the table, muttering about 'fucking technology.'

"Your phone's making a lot of noise today," Margaux comments, clearly curious. "Is someone texting you?"

"No, it's nothing," he frowns, lying to her like usual. "It's just some dumb update."

The laptop is next. I make sure every time he opens it, his homepage redirects to a job board for fast food positions.

On the second day, I escalate by replacing his desktop wallpaper with a bold text image that reads:

****CONTRIBUTE OR DIE TRYING****

His paranoia grows. I see it in the way he glances around the room, suspicious of nothing and everything.

He starts accusing Margaux of touching his stuff, messing with his settings.

Watching him unravel is almost too easy.

Would Margaux be happy if she knew? Not at all.

But I'm not trying to be creepy.

I'm trying to help her. *Margaux.* The woman of my dreams.

The real pièce de résistance comes when I adjust his Spotify playlists. Timmy's taste is predictable: a mix of 2000s pop, party anthems, and local reggae. I infiltrate his account and replace every playlist with titles like:

Songs for Losers

You'll Never Be Him

Daddy's Disappointment Vol. 1

Baby Shark Mashup Megamix - I later delete this because I realize he might actually like it too much.

The tracks themselves? Lullabies, funeral dirges, and a looped audio clip of someone whispering, "Get a job, Timmy."

When he tries to play his usual songs, they won't load. Instead, his phone emits a high-pitched whine for a few seconds before silence falls.

"What the fuck?" he shouts, shaking the device as if it'll give him answers. It won't. Only frustration. "Margaux, did you fuck with my Spotify?"

She looks up from her laptop which she's working on as usual, confused. "What are you talking about?"

"Somebody's fucking with my shit," he says.

She rolls her eyes. "Nobody's fucking with your shit, Timmy," she says. "You're not that special."

Jesus. Sweet Margaux is turning into a bit of a bitch toward Timmy. *Not that I blame her in the slightest.*

To seal the deal, I slip into his social media accounts.

I make subtle changes: a 'like' on a random Instagram photo of a girl Margaux doesn't like, a vague Facebook status update reading, 'Feeling useless today. Anyone else?'

His friends start commenting supportive messages, but Timmy has no idea why. He deletes the post, but I make sure another one pops up within the hour: 'Sometimes I think Margaux deserves better.'

I sit back, watching the chaos unfold. Every piece of his digital life is now an unpredictable minefield. The control he so desperately clings to has slipped through his fingers, and he's left floundering, doubting his own sanity.

"Margaux, did you post on my Facebook?"

She furrows her brow. "What the fuck, Timmy? No, of course I didn't. I don't know your password."

"Maybe you grabbed my phone or laptop while I was in the shower." He frowns at her.

"Nope, I sure didn't."

Margaux, ever the compassionate one, tries to calm him down when he's ranting about his phone and computer 'freaking out.'

But I know she's exhausted, and I know she's starting to see him for who he really is—a man crumbling under the weight of his own inadequacy.

"Maybe you just need to take a break from screens," she suggests, her voice steady but tired.

"Break from screens?" he snaps, his eyes wild. "It's not the screens! It's something—someone—*messing with me*!"

"You sure it's not just you?" she replies, arching a brow. It's the tiniest bit of resistance, but it's enough to push him further into the spiral.

He storms out, slamming the door behind him, and I let myself smile.

Step by step, I'm dismantling Timmy's world. He might not know it yet, but the cracks are spreading.

Soon, they'll be too big to ignore.

I watch with amusement as Margaux sends her friend Alice yet another running pickle.

CHAPTER 31
DETECTIVE PIKACHU

MARGAUX

Once he leaves, I message Alice, venting my feelings.

She's familiar with the mood disorder he claims to have, but we're in agreement he doesn't seem to be experiencing the typical signs that come with it.

Paranoia? Absolutely.

Moodiness? One hundred percent.

Hallucinations? No sign of them.

ME:

He just accused me of making up having PTSD, and said I lied about being sexually assaulted.

ALICE:

Just be careful. It's gaslighting at it's worst and concerning at best.

ME:

Oh totally.

I taught him the word gaslight, and he gets mad when it comes up in shows now.

He thought I invented it or something. 🤣

ALICE:

HA! How disappointing a piece of knowledge to
acquire.

———

The next few days blur together in a maddening cycle.

Timmy runs in and out of the apartment while I try to focus on marketing my books. His comings and goings used to freak me out, but now I'm becoming numb to them.

Yet there's still a nagging feeling in the back of my mind—an unease about that desperate girl he slept with before we met. She's far away now, but according to his ex, 'she always comes back. What if he's calling her when he runs away? Leading her on and complaining about me?

At one point, Timmy surprises me by being nice for once.

"It's shit that I've been living here in Sunset Cay and I haven't even gone swimming for about six months," I'd said to him earlier. I was shocked when I realized it had been that long since I touched the ocean, even though it's literally a stone's throw away from my apartment. It's as if Timmy has somehow weaponized yet another of the things that's brought joy to my life.

"Let's go for a swim," he says. "We can take our snorkeling masks."

I want to believe in this version of him, but I know better. I'm not in the mood for his mood swings, and I'm not falling for his nice-guy routine.

"Let's talk about that skank you slept with right before we met," I snap instead. "The one who won't leave you alone."

His face hardens into a scowl. "Fuck you," he spits. "I don't give a fuck about her. She's nothing. She's crazy."

"Then why did you put your penis in her at least twice?" I ask, my voice dripping with sarcasm, but also yearning for an answer that will give me some relief.

I tell Alice.

ALICE:

Right.

I don't make a habit of fucking my mortal enemies.

This isn't a Marvel movie.

ME:

I don't think he's hung up on her. He says she's irritating AF, but she's the one whose FB page he'd been on.

ALICE:

I'm uneasy about this whole excuse.

ME:

And now...

ALICE:

Does he have a step tracker?

I feel like he should.

ME:

He has an Apple Watch.

And told me he closed his rings yesterday.

ALICE:

I'm curious to know how much ground he covers in a day.

ME:

He could be a professional athlete at this point.

ALICE:

A viral TikTok runner.

Feeling slightly calmer, I decide to be the bigger person and send him a text:

ME:

For once, I am being unreasonable.

But it is coming from a place I did not create.

I am sorry for making you mad.

I don't like the way you dealt with the situation, and it is sitting uncomfortably with me.

I share my text with Alice.

ALICE:

Girl, stop apologizing for him being annoying.

ME:

I brought it up out of nowhere, to be fair.

Omg, am I being an apologist for real?

ALICE:

Was it out of nowhere, or were you finally fed up?

ME:

Maybe. I'm not sure.

But if someone is annoying 50 times and I am annoying once, I feel like owning the 1 makes the 50 shine more clearly

ALICE:

Yes, but to rational people.

All he'll see is you admitting you're wrong.

When Timmy returns, he insists he gave me one of the apartment fobs earlier—the one with the carabiner clip—which I know he didn't. He always uses it to attach to his board shorts when he swims.

The argument spirals quickly.

"My ex was verbally abusive!" he screams. "Just like you are! She would start fights so I would leave, so she could cheat on me with young guys!"

"Well, I'm not your ex," I snap. "So stop treating me like I am."

"You will be soon!" Timmy screams. Moments later, he storms out again, slamming the door.

ME:

Sigh.

ALICE:

This is not normal.

It's almost as if I'm seeing the situation through her eyes now.
And she's right.

CHAPTER 32
RED CAPES & RED FLAGS

MARGAUX

The anonymous message comes in out of the blue, cutting through my day with unsettling precision:

ANON:

I hear you're dating Timmy O'Malley.

I have some information about him that may concern you.

My stomach tightens. I stare at the message, my pulse quickening. Who the hell is this? And how do they know about Timmy? My fingers hover over my phone before I type out a response.

ME:

Who is this?

ANON:

Consider me a friend. Are you interested in what I have to say?

ME:

Um, I guess?

ANON:

> Several women have reported that he is prone to flying into a rage, and behaves recklessly and dangerously.

> Some, but not all of this is triggered by alcohol and drug use.

> He has a pattern of abusing women.

The message lands like a punch to the gut. *A pattern of abuse?* The words make my skin crawl.

I hesitate, debating whether to keep this conversation going, but curiosity wins out.

ANON:

> I'm really worried for the next girl.

A shiver runs through me. That would be me. *I'm the next girl.*

ME:

> Oh wow. Do you have any specifics?

ANON:

> Not at this time, that I'm able to share.

> I can confirm we know him well enough to know he drives a shitty work truck and has an annoying roommate.

> There was some speculation that he was homeless and slept in his truck, but he does live at a place with his annoying friend.

I sit back, absorbing the information. The details line up, though I'm not sure about the homeless part. It wouldn't surprise me, but it doesn't quite add up with what I know.

ME:

> I see. Anything else?

ANON:

> He owns an unusually large collection of hats, for some reason. Including a really stupid oversized woven coconut hat that he won't stop talking about.

> He also wears a Superman cape for attention.

Whenever he wears the coconut hat—especially
when accompanied by the cape—he takes on a
crazy persona, like some type of demented
superhero, and he runs around doing even worse
things than usual.

I stare at the screen, my jaw tightening. The hats, the coconut one, the behavior… even the Superman cape. It's uncanny.

Whoever this is, they know him. They know him well. Not that he hides any of these things from the general public.

I sigh.

What an embarrassing set of messages to receive about your fiancé.

ME:

Well, thank you for telling me all of this.

ANON:

Keep safe. He's not safe to be around.

I sit frozen for a moment, my thoughts spinning. The mention of his strange clothing choices catches in my mind like a splinter. It's not just an odd habit of Timmy's—it's something other people have noticed.

Something that apparently ties into a much darker pattern of behavior.

It feels uncomfortable to be receiving messages from an anonymous person, though. My mind flashes back to a guy I dated who used to send me horrible anonymous messages from a fake Facebook profile.

It turned out he was a complete psycho, and a non-recovered drug addict. I kicked him out when I found him injecting Adderall into his veins with a syringe in my apartment bathroom.

The feelings associated with that situation come rushing back, adding to the ridiculousness.

———

Later in the day, I'm sitting with Timmy in the living room, still trying to decide whether to tell him about the messages. My instinct screams not to— that being too transparent with him might be dangerous.

I've never kept secrets in a relationship before—it feels foreign, unsettling. But something in my gut tells me that honesty, in this case, might be a loaded gun.

As if on cue, Timmy starts pulling items from the closet like a magician with an endless supply of tricks. Out comes a red piece of fabric. My stomach lurches as I immediately recognize it. He unfolds it dramatically.

"And I remembered to bring this from Matty's," he announces with pride. "My Superman cape!"

He shakes it out with a flourish, revealing the bright yellow 'S' in the center. Grinning, he ties it around his neck, the ends draping over his bare shoulders.

He's wearing only board shorts and his deer claw necklace—and now the cape. The sight would be comical if it weren't for the eerie reminder of what the anonymous message said earlier, and how he behaves when wearing this bizarre ensemble.

"I love wearing this!" he says, doing a little dance around the room. "It makes me feel like the king of the world!"

I force a smile, my mind racing. The free-spirited side of him, though odd, has always drawn me in—there's a certain charm in his enthusiasm for life that makes me feel more adventurous and less inhibited.

But now I can't help but view it through a different lens.

This isn't just whimsy.

It's part of something deeper, something darker.

If all of the messenger's claims are accurate—and this ridiculous cape proves they know Timmy—what else might be true?

My heart pounds as I watch him spin in his cape, oblivious to my turmoil. He's so childlike in this moment, clearly seeking attention. I know if I give it to him, we might actually have a fun, peaceful day. But the anonymous warnings buzz in my brain like a swarm of bees, their sting impossible to ignore.

What do I do with all of this? What am I supposed to believe?

For now, I push it down, shoving my doubts into the corner of my mind. The truth feels like something I can't afford to confront, not yet. So I clap my hands and laugh, playing along, because the alternative feels too overwhelming to face.

CHAPTER 33
BAM-BAM

MARGAUX

For the first time in what feels like forever, Timmy manages to be nice to me for more than an hour. It's a rare occurrence, like a blue moon, and I find myself leaning into the possibility of a good day.

He suggests a drive around the island, claiming he wants to show me some of his favorite spots. The suggestion alone is enough to soften my mood.

We drive to a famous garden, a lush tropical haven overlooked by a popular restaurant. The air is thick with the scent of moss and greenery, and bees and cicadas create a gentle symphony in the background. The towering palms and vibrant flowers feel like a setting pulled straight out of paradise.

As we make our way deeper into the verdant garden, Timmy leans close, his voice low and mischievous. "Let's fuck."

"Here?" I ask, my brow arching in disbelief. "For real?"

The sheer forbidden nature of the idea causes my pussy to clench, and sends a thrill down my spine. And he's being so cute and romantic that I'm feeling up for it.

I turn around so my back faces him, and he yanks my pants down just enough to expose my ass, then lowers his own board shorts. He lines himself up with my entrance and enters my pussy with his tip.

He barely thrusts three times before pulling away, yanking his pants up as if someone had caught him mid-crime.

"Okay, that was too much even for me," he admits. "I got the tip in there, but then I was worried people were going to walk past. Or that the restaurant would open and people would see us from up there. I don't want to get in trouble for having my dick out."

The irony. I wish he'd had the same concern at my first apartment.

It's a bizarre moment, but his sudden burst of logic is oddly endearing. Responsibility over spontaneity? *Now that's hot.* Overriding his spontaneous, self-serving impulses with an assessment of the consequences.

I decide in this moment that *that* is way sexier than any outdoor tryst could ever be.

I want to see more of it.

Accountability and responsible decision-making should both be actual porn categories.

We giggle like kids and sprint back to the car holding hands. The good mood carries over as we grab a meal and make small talk over drinks. He's sweet, affectionate, and for a moment, it's like a flashback of when we first met.

But of course, the peace is short-lived. Timmy snaps over nothing—again—and starts yelling at me while we're out. I've grown so used to the cycle that it barely phases me anymore. Nothing good ever lasts with Timmy. This is nothing new.

Instead of engaging, though, I focus on the small victory of finding a New Zealand steak and cheese pie at a nearby food truck. Nothing like a taste of home to bring me back to center.

Up and down, back and forth. The Timmy show on repeat, with a hint of sunshine through the storm clouds every now and then.

———

Back at home, the cycle takes another turn as Timmy decides we should cook together. He suggests making pavlova and meat pies—a strange combo, but I'm willing to roll with it.

We move around the kitchen like a well-rehearsed team, laughing and stealing bites of food as we work. Timmy picks songs to play in the background, and there's lots of cuddling and kissing—his hands gentle on my back, some ass-grabbing, and the occasional playful spank as we navigate around each other.

He asks thoughtful questions about my methods and even shows me a few of his own tricks.

It feels… normal. Healthy, even.

It's the kind of intimacy I crave, where we're partners rather than combatants.

"Fuck, this is amazing," Timmy groans as he bites into a flaky pie. His smile is genuine, and for a moment, I let myself believe this is who he really is.

"Oh my gosh yes," I say, after trying it myself. "The puff pastry needs a little work, but the seasoning is amazing. You did a great job."

"*We* did a great job," I reply. "I love you, babe."

He grins, leaning in for a kiss, puff pastry crumbs sticking to our lips.

"Hot," I joke, wiping them away.

"You're hot," grins Timmy.

I laugh, meeting his adoring gaze. These are the moments I hold onto.

They're the reason I stay, the reason I keep hoping.

————

A few days later, I decide to wear my leopard-print overalls. They're cute as hell, and comfortable—a perfect fit for the day ahead.

"But I want to wear those," Timmy says, frowning.

I blink. "They're mine. And they don't even fit you."

"They do if I adjust the straps," he insists, his pout deepening. "I tried them on the other day."

Sighing, I hand them over and find something else to wear.

By the time we get to the liquor aisle of the convenience store, he's strutting along in my overalls like he owns the place.

I snap a picture and send it to Alice.

ALICE:

Could somebody get fucking Tarzan?!

Put the other strap on, Bam Bam.

I laugh so hard I nearly drop my phone. With his outfit, long sun-streaked hair and childlike enthusiasm, Timmy looks like a mix between a lost caveman and a walking meme. His sense of adventure and wild fashion choices make me laugh, even if they come at the expense of my wardrobe.

I show him the message from Alice, and he beams from ear to ear.

I've never dated someone who borrows my clothes and hair ties and sunglasses, let alone steals my favorite roller derby shorts. But his joy in these little things is infectious, like having a best friend who also wants to bang you.

That's what he is—someone adventurous who wants to spend time only with me. Who makes me laugh every single day. Who plans big for our shared future.

Despite the chaos, these moments of camaraderie keep me hooked.

He's been so sweet lately, I can't help but believe he's making progress. There's a glimmer of hope—of a future where the highs outweigh the lows.

For now, I'm addicted to the highs of our love. They put me right back on cloud nine, and I convince myself we can make it work.

———

Later in the day, for reasons only Timmy knows, he decides to run away again. It's like clockwork.

ME:

ALICE:

What's that—the record for most times in a day?

Also, whenever you send that to me, I put it to the soundtrack of that silent movie instrument.

I can't help but laugh at her reply, even as I feel the familiar weight of disappointment settle in my chest.

This is the Timmy show, on repeat.

Highs, lows, and little in between.

I just wish I could find the off switch.

CHAPTER 34
TRICKLE TRUTHING

MARGAUX

t's late—11:15 PM—when Timmy stomps into the apartment, reeking of cigarettes. He heads straight to the shower without a word, but the smell lingers, curling in the air like a tangible reminder of his deceit.

When he emerges from the bathroom, I speak up right away. "You were out there smoking with random people again." I sigh.

"No, I wasn't," he says.

My patience, already worn thin, snaps.

"You smoked cigarettes. You smell like them. Just fucking admit it," I say, my voice sharper than I intend. "And you weren't alone."

Timmy freezes mid-step, guilt flickering across his face before he attempts to wave it off. "Yeah, I was smoking out there with one of the aunties. She's like 75 years old," he mumbles defensively, as if that makes it better.

"Timmy, if I went smoking late at night with an old man, you'd lose it. It wouldn't matter if he was 105. That's not the point."

"See? This is why I didn't tell you!" he sneers, his tone laced with irritation.

"Why? Because it's dumb?" I shoot back, raising an eyebrow.

His frown deepens, but he doesn't answer.

"Don't lie to me," I press.

"Don't call me names," he snaps.

"I didn't call you anything," I reply with a shrug. "And also, don't lie."

His shoulders sag, and the fight seems to drain out of him. "I'm sorry I lied to you," he says reluctantly, before adding venomously, "But *fuck you*, you're the one who's disgusting."

The insult lands like a slap, and I blink, stunned. "What the fuck? Why am I disgusting this time?"

"Every time you drink, you start a fight," he grumbles.

I laugh bitterly. "Are you looking in a mirror?"

That's it. He bolts to the back room, slamming the door behind him with enough force to rattle the apartment.

I sigh, exhausted by the endless cycle. Somewhere in the back of my mind, I wish he'd say something kind, like, *'Congratulations, I'm proud of you for finishing your book.'* That's the Timmy I fell for, the one who used to lift me up.

But now? Now I get called a cunt. Now I get his projection, his cruelty, his anger.

I grab my phone and message Alice, my constant lifeline.

ALICE:

> I'm fucking proud of you for submitting your book. That's a big one!

> Also, I'm not a fan of this trickle truthing he's doing here.

> What is he hiding?!

ME:

> Thank you. It's not my best or my worst. But in the circumstances, it's the best I could do.

> Trickle truthing. I laugh and cry at the realness. I feel this so hard.

ALICE:

> I can't take credit. That's a real term!

> I'm also mad at him for telling weird lies.

> Just. Be. Honest.

"Yeah, Karen and I went smoking and chatting."

The issue isn't the cigarettes or the company. It's
the lie.

I sigh, grateful for Alice's grounding presence but deeply unsettled by Timmy's constant need to deceive, even over the smallest things.

————

A FEW DAYS LATER

The pattern continues, escalating as it always does. The latest offense?
I refuse to buy Timmy a cigarette.

ME:

Fed up, I text him.

ME:

Goodbye. I deserve a guy one million times better
than you.

TIMMY:

I'll just die, hopefully.

ME:

You're gross. Going out in the middle of the night
begging for cigarettes is pretty fucking gross, and
you know I'm not okay with it. So we're done.

TIMMY:

I'll make my preparations.

Seconds later, my phone buzzes again, this time with a GIF of Pete Davidson as Chad on *SNL*, saying, "Okay."
The audacity. How dare he?!

ME:

> Pete Davidson is mine, not yours. Fuck off.

————

Later, Timmy returns, acting like nothing happened.

I try to ignore him and roller skate around the apartment to clear my head, a mistake on the concrete tile floor.

I fall backward onto my tailbone—twice—pain shooting through me each time. I groan, wishing I'd listened to one of my derby friends' advice about strapping a cushion to my ass.

As I'm catching my breath, I notice Timmy scrolling through my phone. His face darkens. "What the fuck is this?" he snaps, waving the phone in my face. "Talking about me behind my back?"

"To be fair," I reply, snatching my phone back, "you behave like an asshole, so that's how I describe you."

He storms off to the back room, muttering, "I'm packing my bags! I'm flying to my parents because you're a fucking bitch, making me look bad!"

"Okay," I shrug, too tired to care.

I message Alice again.

ALICE:

> Yeah right? You told him to leave.

> Packing his bags is what is supposed to happen.

ME:

> Also, I fell on my tailbone twice, so everything hurts, and it's making processing emotions harder.

ALICE:

> Jesus! Do you at least wear a helmet when you do?

ME:

> Pads but no helmet this time.

> I thought we were making progress.

ALICE:

> Progress is harder to make when only one person is doing it.

Her words stick with me, a cruel truth I already know but need to hear again.

CHAPTER 35
I WOKE UP LIKE THIS

MARGAUX

Timmy insists on accompanying me to meet my high school friend and her wife, promising he'll be on his best behavior.

I'm hesitant. "If you do *anything* to ruin their trip, I will make it my life's mission to destroy you," I say. And I'm serious. It might sound dramatic, but if he creates a scene or makes them uncomfortable in any way, I'll never forgive myself.

"I promise," he says, gazing deep into my eyes. "I wouldn't fuck anything up for your friends. I promise I won't drink too much, and everything will be fine. We'll have fun."

After much deliberation and a few days of well-behaved Timmy, I agree that he can come with me. I sigh. "Okay, but I'm warning you."

He nods. "I understand. You can count on me."

I book us a hotel right in the middle of downtown so we can stay the night rather than worrying about making the long trip back to the other side of the Cay.

———

Timmy dresses nicely to meet my friends, even making an effort to put on a collared shirt and jeans.

We meet them at a rooftop bar where we enjoy mai tais and seafood appetizers while reminiscing about high school and their Vegas wedding.

Timmy follows through on his promises, at least for the time being, entertaining them with funny stories about life in the Cay and what it was like growing up here. He's charming and funny, and my friend's wife banters with him. We're all in stitches several times.

Later, we visit a nearby hotel and have fun playing pool. We drink hard seltzers and Fireball from the convenience store located in the lobby.

Timmy starts to get a little weird, telling me he thinks my friends are sexy, but it all seems to be in good fun.

Later in the evening, we say our goodbyes and agree to meet up the following day.

"Let's go back to the hotel," I say to Timmy, taking him by the hand.

We start walking, but then Timmy's mood shifts without warning.

"You don't have to be such a fucking bitch," he says out of nowhere.

"What are you talking about? I thought we were having a nice evening," I reply, beyond confused.

"Well, you always want to end the evening early. You're so controlling."

"What would you like to do instead?" I ask. Sure, the evening has run its course and I'm getting tired, and neither of us certainly needs any more to drink. But if he really wants to go to one more place, I guess I'd be down.

By now, we're at the neighboring hotel—another sprawling resort—this one painted an iconic purple color.

"Fuck you!" he yells at me.

He storms off, leaving me outside the hotel.

Confused and tired, I take a seat on the edge of the landscaped garden in the hotel's sprawling driveway. I'm anticipating he just needs to let off some steam and he'll return and collect me.

But he never does.

———

I wake up, and I'm sprawled in the garden of one of the fanciest hotels in the Cay, the one where Timmy left me.

It's still dark out, and the nearby porté-cochere is a hive of activity with the valet team picking up and depositing vehicles for arriving and departing guests.

I'm so confused, and then I remember I was waiting here for Timmy. I must have fallen asleep.

Mortified, heat rushing to my cheeks, I stand up and dust myself off.

A lady sees me and walks over. "Are you okay?" she asks, her Kiwi accent unmistakable.

"Uh yeah," I say. "I think so." My cheeks flame hotter.

"Why were you lying in the plants?"

I'm so embarrassed.

I play it off casually. "Oh, I had a little argument with my fiancé and I was waiting for him to come back. I must have fallen asleep."

"Do you need help getting anywhere?" she asks, the concern in her tone palpable.

"No no. Thank you though," I say quickly. "I'll order an Uber. My hotel is just down the street."

She nods, her expression gentle, her hand on my arm.

"Okay then. Take care," she says, as I climb into the Uber and head to our hotel.

When I get there, Timmy is nowhere to be seen.

I call him, and he doesn't answer.

I text him:

> ME:
>
> Timmy. Answer your fucking phone.
>
> Where are you?

About five minutes go by, and then my phone buzzes.

> TIMMY:
>
> Sorry. I went to sleep in the truck.
>
> I was mad at you.
>
> You hurt my feelings.

For fuck's sake.

> ME:
>
> I woke up in the fucking plants at the hotel where I was waiting for you. The place you stormed off from.

> TIMMY:
>
> Sorry, sorry. I'll be right there.

He comes back, slightly sheepish.

After a while, he speaks up. "I went to Romeo's club," he says, a cruel glint in his eye.

"No you didn't," I respond, calling him out. "There's no way…"

He looks down. "Yeah, you're right. I'm just messing with you."

The rest of the early hours of the morning are uneventful.

The next morning, I text my friends and tell them a little of what happened, without going into too much detail.

As I'm getting ready, Timmy pulls me to him, where he's sitting on the edge of the bed.

He looks into my eyes. "Margaux, I'm so sorry," he says, his tone soft. "I know I've been fucking up lately. It wasn't right to leave you alone at the hotel. I'm sorry. I really mean it, I'm going to do better. I'll follow through on all the things I've promised—I'll be consistent with my therapy, I'll get my medication adjusted. And I want to cut back on drinking—I really think that will help with everything."

I hug him back, ever hopeful. But the little voice in the back of my head reminds me: *This isn't the first time you've heard him make these promises.*

After checking out, we drive over to meet them at a waterfall nestled in a stunning botanical garden in another part of the island.

Timmy seems to have recovered from his tantrum and is in high spirits. His eyes sparkle as he points out a bunch of native plants, and his enthusiasm is contagious.

When we reach the waterfall, my friends are drying off on some nearby steps, the sun casting a golden glow over the scene.

Timmy wastes no time hopping into the water, donning a mandatory life vest, and swimming around with a huge grin on his face.

"What happened last night?" my friend asks, with Timmy well out of earshot.

I fill her in.

Her eyes widen. "Oh my god. You woke up in the plants? He just left you there?"

"Yeah," I sigh, trying to shrug it off. "He does this kind of shit. I was worried about bringing him, but he was fine until after we left you guys. Then he got upset with me over nothing. I expected him to come back, but he never did."

She shakes her head. "Wow," she says, probably unsure of what else to say.

After Timmy is done swimming, we meander our way back through the gardens and check out a cute farmer's market at the entrance to the facility.

We take a couple of group pictures, and then I hug my friends goodbye and wish them safe travels.

Their visit could have been worse—much worse—if I put it into perspective.

Sure, I would love to not have woken up sprawled in a garden of plants at one of the nicest hotels in Sunset Cay.

I would have loved for Timmy not to have started an argument and slept in his truck for a few hours—if that's even really where he was.

But nobody was hurt, and most importantly, my friends' trip wasn't ruined. That's the most I can ask for when it comes to him.

With Timmy, I've learned to count my blessings—wherever I can find them, and no matter how small they may be.

CHAPTER 36
A VERY BOUNCY DAY

MARGAUX

For the rest of our trip back to our apartment, and for the remainder of the day, Timmy continues to be apologetic, reflective even, and continues to swear he'll follow through on his promises.

The next day, I update Alice about the truck and gardens escapade:

ALICE:

The hell did he go?

ME:

I think it was a wake-up call for him. He's apologized, and we had some good conversations where he realizes how much he's been fucking up lately.

So there's a plan, and we will see (therapist and meds adjustment, and not drinking so much).

Other than that, visiting with my friends was soooo nice!

And there were no runaway incidents yesterday.

> When he was sleeping in his truck, he tried to make me think he was at his friend's club, but it sounded like he was bluffing to piss me off, and was in the truck the whole time. 😒

> Which he now says he realizes was incredibly dumb

ALICE:

I'll be curious to see if he follows through with the therapy and meds. My ex used to say the same in moments of clarity.

————

While his apologies and presentation of accountability felt real enough to believe, as always, the cracks appear quickly.

Two days later, as I'm rinsing dishes in the sink, Timmy wanders over, picks up a plate, and inspects it like a health inspector on a power trip.

He finds the tiniest speck of food stuck to the back.

"You can't even do the dishes right," he sneers. "You're useless. You fucking suck."

I freeze, the words stinging like a slap.

One: It's just a plate. Rinse and move on.

Two: I had a perfectly functioning dishwasher at my old place before he got kicked out.

Three: Is this man seriously the dishes police?

It's not like he's a dishwashing savant. Yet here he is, suddenly a pro at degrading me over something so trivial. Getting on my case and making me feel like shit.

————

LATER THAT NIGHT

ME:

He couldn't do it, could he?

ALICE:

Do what?

ME:

Not run away.

ALICE:

He's run off at least once a day for like the past 2 weeks 😕

ME:

Yeah, it's absurd.

ALICE:

I'm sorry friend, but this is the standard 🙁

ME:

Yeah, it's pretty dumb.

If I didn't have the runaway pickle to send you I'd probably just cry.

But I've made a decision.

I'm not letting Timmy's chaos derail my writing dreams anymore.

———

THE NEXT DAY

Timmy is mad again, though I have no idea why. It feels like he's itching for an excuse—any reason—to justify running off to the tents again.

After spending time organizing the back room that he'd messed up in a rage days earlier, he returns to the living room. "Can't you just be unconscious?" he sneers, a cruel smirk tugging at his lips. "You're so much better when you're unconscious."

I clench my fists, trying to stay calm. He's baiting me, poking me until I snap. And then, of course, it'll all be my fault. And then the whole situation will be attributed to me—my fault, the crazy unhinged fiancée who can't control her temper.

"Why are you talking to me like that?" I ask, my voice shaking. "By the way, you smell like White Claw.:

His scowl deepens. "I do so much around here. I cleaned the back room for you. It took *hours,* and you're so ungrateful."

"Ungrateful?" I yell, my patience snapping. "It was only a mess because *you* made it that way! So you fixed the mess *you* caused. What do you want, a Nobel Peace Prize?!"

There's a gleam in his eye—a sick satisfaction in pushing me to this point.

He stomps off to the back room, slams the door, and locks it.

Moments later, I hear movement—the screen on the window, maybe? His new trick is jumping out the back window like a teenager sneaking out past curfew.

I'd never known an adult to jump out of their own apartment window until I met Timmy. But here we are.

I doze off for a while, waking in the early hours of the morning.

I update Alice.

ALICE:

I know you care about him, but it will not get better until he has an extremely stringent mental health routine—it would probably involve something like seeing a therapist weekly, taking medication multiple times a day, and seeing a psychiatrist.

ME:

I told him he needs a psychiatrist. And yes, he needs a structured approach to his mental health.

Timmy eventually emerges from the back room, heads straight to the bathroom, and turns on the shower.

A few minutes later, he returns to the back room, slamming the door again.

ME:

> He's emerged from the shower now. I have no idea what his deal is. 1am shower man? I'm going to make a podcast called 1AM Shower Man.

ALICE:

> Sounds like a background villain in the Harley Quinn show.

Timmy emerges from the back room once again, naked this time.

He glances at the TV. "You're watching that Amish shit?" He shakes his head. "I don't know why you watch that stupid show."

It doesn't matter that he was enjoying watching the exact same show with me days prior. His taste in entertainment flips on a whim, as he's proven many times.

"Can't we just watch Pete Davidson instead?"

I sigh. "Sure." At least he's picking a show I also enjoy this time. I'll take the W.

Next thing I know, he walks over to me and shoves his flaccid penis in my face, wiggling it around like one of those wobbly inflatable men typically found outside used car dealerships.

As this all goes down, I message Alice with a running commentary.

ME:

> I was watching Breaking Amish, and he was complaining about it.

> Now he wants to watch Pete Davidson.

> He just waggled his penis in my face.

> WHY?

> WHAT?

> WHY?

> He wants me to do his resume, and I'm totally going to sneak that in:

> Timmy O'Malley. Graphic designer. Handyman. Background villain.

Next thing I know, Timmy is once again in my overalls, posing proudly. "Take a picture of me!"

I shake my head and snap a picture.

"Send it to your friend!" he demands.

ME:

OMG, he really wants me to send you this picture.

I send her the picture.

ME:

Sorry to visually assault you.

ALICE:

Oh wow. Yeah, he's having an episode.

What up Bam Bam?

Timmy approaches me with an exaggerated grin.

"I was hoping when you woke up, you'd be nicer. And you are," he says, pulling me into a hug.

"Okay?" I reply, unsure how to respond.

"I'll clean up for you forever," he promises, as if this is supposed to erase all his previous behavior. He pulls me into a hug. "I played with your cat while I watched *The Mandalorian*, by the way," he adds, as if that's a groundbreaking accomplishment.

Then, without warning, he bursts into song. "*We Could Be Heeeeroooooes*," he belts out at the top of his lungs.

His mind is such a hectic place. I don't know where he comes up with half the things he does, and I don't think I want to.

ME:

He just said 'I was hanging up your clothes. I can see in the dark now.'

ALICE:

Exactly how much White Claw has he had?

He's sounding like an unmedicated schizophrenic having a bouncy day.

CHAPTER 37
MY LIFE IS A CHAINSAW MASSACRE

MARGAUX

THE FOLLOWING DAY

Timmy's agitation has reached a fever pitch. His 'bounciness,' as Alice had described it earlier, now feels more like a volcano on the verge of eruption, a fault line on the verge of a world-changing quake.

It started with the cleaning this time, as it often does. I don't know what it is about cleaning that sets him off, but every time he picks up a sponge or a mop, it's as though he's looking for a reason to explode. I now dread every time he cleans.

This time, it's specifically the dishes *again*—it seems to be his favorite topic.

I don't do them *that* badly, but it's really not the point. I realize with sadness that this isn't about dishes at all.

"You're *so* useless around the house. You fucking suck."

The words cut deep, but I bite my tongue. At first.

Then I can't handle it anymore, and words spew from me like a dam breaking.

"Stop criticizing me over stupid shit, Timmy! You're such a fucking loser.

Why don't you stop acting like a *complete piece of shit!* No wonder you have no fucking friends!"

Then he escalates.

"Fuck you!" he yells, storming out of the kitchen. He walks to the bed, picks up two pillows, and throws them at me. *"I'm going to fucking kill you, you stupid cunt!"*

I freeze. *How did we get here?*

Timmy reappears moments later, dragging a black-and-yellow chainsaw from the back room. He sets it down halfway down the hallway, his eyes dark and reptilian. "I'm going to chop your head off with this chainsaw!" he shouts, his voice cold and unrecognizable.

A shiver runs down my spine. My life has become a real-life horror movie.

As if that wasn't enough, he vanishes again and returns, holding a screwdriver. He places it in my hand. "Or I might kill you with this instead. Or you could just do us all a favor and do it yourself."

He walks away, leaving me shaking, clutching the cold metal handle of the screwdriver.

Call the police, a little voice in my head says. *He's threatening to kill you. You know what he's capable of.*

My hands tremble as I dial 911.

When the officers arrive, I let out a breath I hadn't realized I'd been holding. "Please help," I beg. "He's threatening to kill me again."

They exchange looks.

I explain what happened.

"We can talk to him," another one says. "Do you want to press charges?"

I hesitate. The weight of the question feels crushing.

If I press charges, he'll likely be locked up longer because of his upcoming DUI sentencing.

But if I don't… what then? What he did was fucked up.

"No," I say finally. "I just want him to stop. Please, just get him to leave me alone."

They look disappointed, and I feel ashamed—ashamed for calling them, ashamed for not pressing charges, ashamed for being too scared to follow through.

I feel trapped. My brain is in a perpetual fog, and I can't think straight.

One of the officers speaks up again. "What resolution do you want to this situation, ma'am?"

I sigh. My voice is barely above a whisper. "To not be killed by a screwdriver or chainsaw."

They leave to speak with Timmy. When they return, they tell me he claims to have somewhere local to stay.

I nod numbly, wondering where he'll end up, and who he's managed to befriend this time.

ME:

ME:

He threatened to kill me, so I called the cops #escalation

Has seriously lost his nut.

ALICE:

JESUS. What happened?

Did they take him?

ME:

I told them not to take him, but I asked them to tell him to leave me alone.

ALICE:

Okay, but that's seriously dangerous. Especially considering he's been violent in the past.

ME:

I know.

———

A few hours later, I hear the telltale sound of the back room door creaking open. Timmy must have snuck in while I had my headphones on. He's staying out of my way, at least for now.

ME:

He appeared briefly. Has been hiding locked in the back room.

ALICE:

Good, because that was extremely scary.

I don't know, friend. This is freaking me out.

I don't like that you're in the same place as someone who's actively hurt you, and who's actively made threats.

ME:

Yeah, it's not ideal. I have to go pick up shoes and go to a job interview, so at least I'll be away from him and out of the house for a while.

ALICE:

Good. Please stay away from him.

My ex was never violent. But when he got an idea in his head when he was like this, there was no way of knowing how serious he was.

ME:

I hear you. And dickface has all my interview clothes in the back room. And he's locked himself in there.

Guess I'll go by the mall on my way to it.

Hopefully the truck doesn't break down again.

ALICE:

Ugh, yeah I'd normally tell you just to go in and grab the clothes, but considering he's being so weird, I'd say don't do it.

ME:

Yeah, and he's locked the door, so I'd have to pick it.

ALICE:

And you pay rent, and he doesn't, and he's doing that.

I'm sorry. I wish I could help more.

ME:

You're so very helpful and I'm sorry to worry you.

ALICE:

It's less that you worry me, and more that I worry about you.

HE worries me.

ME:

I know. Ugh. Why can't he just realize what he has
and stop fucking it up?

(I know that's not how it works)

ALICE:

Wouldn't it be nice if it were?

I dunno. I'm not wild about you being in an
apartment alone with him.

Timmy emerges briefly, muttering under his breath as he hunts for his phone and charger.

"Fuck you," he spits. "I'm making arrangements to leave. I can't wait to be away from you, you dumb cunt."

I stay silent, sitting on the bed and refusing to engage.

ME:

I'm considering not going to this interview.

I don't want to leave the house with everything I paid
for in here.

I don't want him fucking off with all the things I
worked hard to be able to buy.

ALICE:

UGH WHY IS HE RUINING YOUR LIFE??

Why does his life suck so much that he has to drag
down yours?

ME:

Yeah, I'm really not sure. I think he doesn't like
himself very much.

ALICE:

Well, that was obvious.

I send a quick email to the recruiter who lined up the job interview, letting her know I can't make it today because the truck is having difficulties.

ME:

> I just asked to reschedule. I don't feel like I have the mental bandwidth to worry about what's going on back here, hope the truck doesn't break down again AND interview with like 5 people.

ALICE:

> No, I understand.

> Definitely be good to yourself and take care of your brain.

> I'm just being extra huffy today because I'm worried and I hate him.

Her words linger, both comforting and sharp.

I hate him too, sometimes.

But mostly, I hate how much I still want things to get better.

CHAPTER 38
BLAME IT ON THE ADDERALL

MARGAUX

I sit on the couch, staring blankly out the window, trying to make sense of the madness that's become my life.

Timmy's behavior is erratic and escalating, and I can't help but reflect on what might have triggered this particular outburst.

To be fair, he has his court sentencing coming up for his DUI. Given it's not his first offense, he's looking at some mandatory jail time—anywhere from three to 365 days, depending on the judge's mood.

I know I was well within my rights to make a statement and press charges when he threatened me with the chainsaw and screwdriver, but his constant lament about jail plays in the back of my mind. He's terrified of going back inside, let alone to prison. He talks about it all the time.

But then again, if I were worried about serving time, I'd make a special effort to not run around threatening to kill people.

ME:

On the bright side, he only threw pillows yesterday. The chainsaw was placed in the hallway, and the screwdriver was placed in my hand. All threats.

ALICE:

Jesus.

Timmy emerges from the back room, his demeanor unusually soft.

"Margaux, babe," he says, his voice calm and almost remorseful. "I'm sorry for being such a piece of shit. The minute my phone is charged, I'm going to call Mom and ask her for a ticket to Montana. I don't want to keep ruining your life."

I stare at him, unsure if this is an elaborate joke, or if he's finally serious.

Without waiting for a response, he retreats to the back room.

I text Alice to share the latest chapter of *"Timmy Promises Change."*

ALICE:

I'm giving that 11 minutes before he doesn't do that.

SORRY I AM HAVING A BAD DAY.

As if on cue, my nose starts gushing blood. Of course it does.

The stress of living with Timmy has taken a toll on my entire body. I know stress kills, and Timmy has been a walking, talking cortisol trigger since very early on.

ALICE:

If I could afford it, I'd fly you out here to hide for a week.

ME:

Thank you.

The irony of living in this beautiful place and he's making it so ugly.

A moment later, I hear Timmy on the phone, making appointments with his doctor and counselor. *I guess he's not actually going to Montana.*

I want to feel hopeful, but until he physically walks through the door of each appointment, I'm not holding my breath. Timmy's flaws are numerous, but consistency and follow-through might be the most glaring.

ME:

It's giving me Zeth vibes. The whole apology.

But mainly bc he was clinging to me the same way Zeth did.

Let me tell you the story of Zeth.

ALICE:

Please tell me about someone whose name doesn't
sound real.

And so begins the tale of another man who brought chaos into my life.

ME:

Unfortunately, I met this douchebag and at some
point it emerged that he was on probation. Zeth
lived in Virginia with his mom and stepdad (▶).

Zeth moved his things into my apartment like 2 days
after we met. Didn't ask. Just started moving
things in

One day Zeth was in the bathroom for a long time
and I went in there after and found a SYRINGE.

He was in there shooting up Adderall.

Zeth was a mess.

But anyways, I had to lie there while he came down
from his high, and he cried and apologized, and
eventually I was able to get him out.

The situation was complicated bc my workplace
owned the building, so was my landlord.

That is the shorthand version of the story of Zeth.

ALICE:

Somehow that sounds less scary to me than Tim.

Annoying? Yes.

Definitely a loser? For sure.

ME:

Yeah, he was a lot smaller.

Although, let me tell you people who inject Adderall
into their veins are quite terrifying.

He was cleaning and straightening everything over
and over again.

But yes, no chainsaw threats.

ALICE:

WOAH SORRY INJECTING ADDERALL?? I missed that one.

Yeah don't...don't do that.

At least all he did was clean?

ME:

Hahaha yes, I hid in the corner with my cat.

ALICE:

"It'll be okay, sweetie… the crazy man just needs to leave the Windex alone and we'll be fine."

ME:

His drug dealer added me on Facebook.

I didn't accept the friend request.

ALICE:

LMFAO WHAT NO.

Aw man what a B- idea.

ME:

He's still in the queue.

ALICE:

Where he should stay in perpetuity!

Timmy reappears from the back room, his tone calm but his face unreadable.

"I've got everything under control now," he says with a half-smile, and I almost believe him.

But a sinking feeling reminds me that even if he can keep it together for a moment, the storm is never far behind.

CHAPTER 39
IDIOT PARTY OF ONE

DEX

Margaux's world is a storm, and I'm the man in the shadows trying to shield her from its worst winds. She doesn't know how closely I watch, how deeply I care, or how far I'll go to keep her safe.

It's a delicate dance, sabotaging Timmy just enough to keep him distracted, without him catching on. He's a loose cannon, and if his rage ever turns fully on Margaux... No, I can't let that happen.

I'm perched in front of my monitors, watching the feeds from Margaux's apartment. And tonight, I'm on high alert.

Timmy is pacing again, muttering to himself about something he's lost. His fob, probably. I smirk, knowing it's exactly where my associate left it after 'borrowing' it earlier to secure the door to their storage unit. Locked storage, a 'missing' fob, and a wild goose chase for Timmy—all small, safe distractions that keep him occupied without putting Margaux in harm's way.

Later, the camera catches her leaving the apartment with Sabre in tow. Good. She needs space, and she's smart enough to take it when she can.

My eyes flick between the monitors, scanning for Timmy's whereabouts.

He eventually storms out, phone in hand, muttering about finding cigarettes. I watch him walk to the corner store, knowing he'll get distracted along the way.

While he's out, I instruct my associate to get to work. The sabotage with the board shorts and the shampoo was minor, a warm-up. Tonight, I focus on annoyances that don't touch Margaux's safety.

His flip-flops mysteriously go missing again, and my associate replaces the batteries in the remote with dead ones. It's not much, but it's enough to keep him preoccupied and off-balance. The goal is simple: keep him so focused on his petty frustrations so that he doesn't have the energy to unleash his chaos on her.

When he returns, he slams the door, frustrated with the world—or himself.

Either way, Margaux gets a rare reprieve.

But then her truck breaks down, and I'm torn between stepping in and staying hidden. Before I can decide, some guy with tattoos and a gold chain helps her out.

I relax slightly, but only slightly. I make a note to keep an eye on him too, just in case.

When she calls Timmy's dad, Phil, and Phil defends Timmy, saying he's a 'really nice guy', I want to reach through the phone and rip Phil's tongue out of his stupid mouth. What a fucking idiot. *Can't he see he's created a monster?*

Timmy shows up eventually, his smugness practically oozing through the screen as he fixes the hose. I watch him bask in his self-made hero moment, and my fists clench. He's created this mess—literally—and now he's acting like he deserves a medal for 'saving' Margaux. It's pathetic, but she's trapped in his cycle of chaos and rescue.

For now.

I want to be the one that saves her, not this clown biscuit.

———

The next day, Timmy's antics escalate.

He storms out, accusing Margaux of everything from infidelity to imaginary slights.

I watch her roll her eyes and text her friend Alice, her lifeline. Alice's humor is sharp and cutting, a balm for Margaux's wounds. It makes me like her even more. She's a good influence, and a grounding force when Margaux needs it most.

Still, Timmy's paranoia is dangerous. His texts to Margaux—'Do you have a boyfriend in there?'—make me grit my teeth. I've seen this pattern before. He's wearing her down, one accusation at a time.

That night, Timmy runs off again. Margaux texts Alice yet another runaway pickle GIF. She's still trying to laugh through the pain. But even she has limits, and I can see them fraying.

When Timmy returns, dripping wet from the ocean, he's all bluster and no substance. He yells about her triggers being fake, about her making up her PTSD.

She looks crushed.

I want to reach through the screen and throttle him.

Instead, I focus on my next move.

Timmy makes it clear he really wants to watch a specific movie, and I know it's one that Margaux has no interest in. Knowing she's done with work for the day, I disable the Wi-Fi in their apartment. It's a small thing, but it's enough to irritate Timmy without making him suspicious. He spends the next hour trying to fix it, leaving Margaux in peace for once. It's not much, but it's something.

Later, Timmy dons his ridiculous child-sized Superman cape, prancing around the apartment like a six-year-old.

Margaux laughs, but there's a tension in her smile. I know she's thinking about the anonymous messages she's been getting—the ones warning her about Timmy. She hasn't mentioned them to him, and I'm relieved. The less he knows, the better.

Through it all, I watch Margaux's interactions with Alice and Josephine. They're her lifelines, her anchors in the storm. I envy them, their ability to offer her comfort and laughter so easily. But I also admire her for letting them in, for leaning on them when she needs it. It's a strength, not a weakness.

As I watch her laugh at one of Alice's sarcastic texts, a small smile tugs at my lips. She doesn't know it yet, but she's stronger than she thinks. And one day, when she's ready, I'll be there to help her break free from Timmy's grip for good.

Until then, I'll keep sabotaging, distracting, and watching.

Because Margaux deserves better.

And I'll do whatever it takes to make sure she gets it.

CHAPTER 40
THE CHAOS CHRONICLES

MARGAUX

A FEW DAYS LATER

The past few days have been a mix of relative calm and bizarre disruptions, which seems to be the default rhythm of life with Timmy. I've actually managed to write without major interruptions —an almost miraculous occurrence.

We're playing Mario Kart on the edge of the bed, and for a while, it's fun. He keeps winning, which I'm fine with, but his attitude quickly becomes unbearable.

"Haha, you suck at this game. I keep beating you," he smirks, puffing his chest like he's just conquered the Olympics.

"Okay, I'm not a sore loser," I say, frowning, "but you don't have to rub it in like that."

"Look at you getting upset about a game, Margaux," he shoots back, feigning superiority. "You should really work on that."

I furrow my brow, trying to keep my tone steady. "You're being an asshole. I don't mind you winning, but you don't have to be rude about it."

He pauses the game dramatically and glares at me. "Look what you did. You just turned Mario Kart into something *sick.*"

"What?" My voice is incredulous, dripping exasperation.

"Never mind," he snaps. "You ruined the whole thing." With that, he shuts off the game and puts on regular TV.

I message Alice.

ME:

> He says I turned Mario Kart into something sick. I'll have to tell Nintendo. 🙄

ALICE:

Uhhh what??

Dude is nuts.

We chat away on other topics, and it's nice to have a reprieve from the Timmy Show.

After dozing off for a couple of hours, I wake and notice Timmy sneaking toward the front door, his movements slow and deliberate, as if he's trying not to draw attention to himself.

He freezes mid-step as he notices me watching him, his shoulders stiffening, and guilt flickers across his face before he quickly masks it with a casual shrug. "I'm just going to get some things out of the truck," he says, the words tumbling out a little too quickly.

I fold my arms across my chest and narrow my eyes, my skepticism evident. "What 'stuff'?"

"Um... just stuff," he says, avoiding my gaze. "Like I think I left some board shorts and a hat in there."

I quirk a brow, my disbelief written all over my face. "Board shorts and a hat? At this hour?"

"Yeah," he says, his tone defensive.

"It's late, Timmy," I say, shaking my head. "Whatever you left in the truck can wait until daylight."

His expression darkens, the hint of guilt morphing into irritation. "What?" he snaps. "I've been working on my art stuff for the last two hours, and I need a break. So I'm just going to the truck."

"To smoke a cigarette?" I counter, my voice sharper than I intend. I've seen the disgusting little compartment in his truck where he keeps partially smoked cigarette butts, and I know his patterns too well.

His jaw tightens. "No," he says, but his tone is weak. He knows he's been caught.

"You're gross, and I don't believe you," I add. "It's late, and it's completely inappropriate for you to be leaving the apartment at this hour. We've talked about this like a million times."

His frown deepens, and his voice rises, defensive and sharp. "Fuck you, then. I'll stay, but I'm going to the back room."

Before I can respond, he spins on his heel and stomps down the hallway, his heavy steps echoing through the apartment. He slams the door to the back room so hard that the walls vibrate, leaving me standing in the silence, my frustration bubbling beneath the surface.

I let out a slow breath, forcing myself to stay calm. Timmy's deflections and dramatics are nothing new, but they never fail to leave me feeling drained and questioning why I keep letting him get away with it.

In the quiet that follows, I glance toward the door he was so eager to sneak out of and wonder, not for the first time, what else he's hiding.

I fill Alice in.

ME:

Like, don't come in or leave while I'm asleep, unless there is a very good reason.

I hardly sleep, so it seems unnecessary to be sneaking in and out in the few hours I am.

That sounds controlling, but we aren't dealing with normalcy here, are we?

ALICE:

Yeah. You're dealing with absolutely abnormal.

———

The next morning, Timmy is sweet and caring, as if nothing happened—Captain Clean Slate is in full swing.

I'm battling one of the heaviest periods of my life, to the point I'm borderline considering going to urgent care.

It's not just inconvenient—it's exhausting and overwhelming.

After I bleed through my pants, I change, embarrassed and annoyed, but Timmy takes my soiled clothes without a word, and rinses the blood out for me.

It's a small act, but it feels monumental in the context of our chaos. For a fleeting moment, I feel supported and cared for. This is how I want to be treated in a relationship, and he's making it happen. For now.

The moment doesn't last.

Next thing I know, Timmy is tangling himself in the curtain.

"Timmy," I sigh, pinching the bridge of my nose. "You don't need to wrap yourself in the curtain. Please unwrap yourself before you break it."

He grins. "But I feel so comfy, like I'm in a giant burrito."

I shake my head. It's exhausting. He's a six-foot-two, two-hundred-pound toddler.

The contrast between him rinsing my clothes and the whole curtain burrito escapade has exhausted me. All I want to do is sleep.

———

Later in the day, his weirdness takes a different turn.

"Oh, she just left town. I can fuck you now," he says, grinning like a mischievous child as he gets closer to me, extending his hands like he's about to grope me.

"Um, what?" I raise an eyebrow, completely confused.

"Oh," he winks. "I'm role-playing."

A wave of disgust washes over me. "That was gross," I mutter. *Another ick unlocked.*

Timmy, ever the performer, frowns and calls his parents in the next breath. "Please, I'm begging you. Fly me home now. Margaux is being such a bitch to me," he whines into the phone.

I update Alice and also text one of his brothers about his behavior.

ME (TO ALICE):

Drunken fugue state perhaps?

I watch as he opens the door and leaves it ajar, and my heart leaps as Sabre runs outside.

ME:

ALICE:

I see another friend is online—Mirabel, or Bel for short. I met Bel while living on the East Coast, and she's back in New Zealand these days, working as a cop.

On a whim, I reach out.

ME:

Hey! Can I chat with you?

I need some advice.

She replies immediately.

BEL:

Sure.

I'm just at work. Call me.

I call Bel on Facetime, and she answers immediately.

"What's up?" she asks, and I fill her in. "What the actual fuck?!" she exclaims. "First things first, go get your cat."

She's right. Sabre is my priority.

Next thing, Timmy re-enters the apartment, panting. "I found him," he says. "He's hiding under the stairs over by the laundry, and he won't come out. He's hissing at me. You need to come get him."

I sigh, my heart pounding as I realize Sabre's out near the busy street in front of the apartment complex.

I walk to the stairwell and retrieve Sabre, Timmy walking beside me, as the security team looks on from their shack.

They must think we are complete basket cases, I think to myself. *And they're probably right on both counts.*

When we get back to the apartment, Sabre in my arms, I give him a cuddle and a Churu. "Don't you go running out there, buddy," I say, my voice soft. "It's dangerous."

Timmy glares at me and leaves again.

I flop down on the bed, too exhausted to care.

ME (TO ALICE):

I called my friend in NZ who is a cop at work on duty and she was like 'wtffffff?!'

I glance over at the door and notice Timmy has left it ajar. I look around, and there's no sign of Sabre.

For fuck's sake.

ME:

For the love of god.

He found him.

I had to bring him back.

Then he just let him out again.

Panicked, I run out the front door, but there's no sign of him.

On instinct, I head back into the apartment and check the back room. I let out a sigh of relief as Sabre's eyes glow at me from the far corner, large and round.

He's done with this shit, too.

ALICE:

DID YOU FIND YOUR CAT?

Fuck him, did you find your CAT!????

Fuck him for treating you like shit after a potential miscarriage he caused.

Alice had speculated that it wasn't an ordinary period, and she may have been right.

ME:

Yes, I found him. The second time even Sabre had had enough and was hiding in the back room.

My phone buzzes. It's his brother:

TIMMY'S BROTHER:

He's a dick. I don't know why you put up with him.

I sigh. *Ain't that the truth.* At this point, neither do I.

ALICE:

Ugh. What's his fucking problem?

I mean... I know what it is.

He's outright being mean to you.

When he returns, he immediately heads to the bathroom to rinse off, and he's in there for a while. When he emerges, it's with a freshly altered—and horrifying—facial hair situation.

"Um, why did you do that?" I ask.

He frowns. "Do you think it looks bad?"

"No," my voice squeaks. "Just... I'm not used to it, I guess?"

"Fuck you," his eyes narrow.

He stomps to the back room, and I hear him grumbling to someone, presumably his dad. It must be 2AM his time—I'm sure he's thrilled.

Me:

I don't know what the fuck he did to his facial hair, but he looks stupid AF.

Like he took the facial hair from a middle-aged man in Wisconsin.

The beard part is gone. And now the mustache is separated from the goatee. 😫

ALICE:

Ewwww, no good!!

After a couple of minutes, the back room door opens, and Timmy stomps back into the living room, clearly frustrated.

"Have fun complaining to your dad about me?" I ask.

"No," he frowns. "I wasn't complaining about you."

I roll my eyes. *Liar. You weren't calling your dad at 2AM to ask him about his day.*

"Anyways," he adds, his voice glum. "It wouldn't work if I did, because my dad fucking loves you."

Defeated, he flops down on the bed beside me, sulking.

And just like that, another day in the chaotic circus of Timmy's existence comes to a close.

Only—for me—it's a nightmare I can't seem to wake up from.

CHAPTER 41
LIME JUICE AND LIES

MARGAUX

THE NEXT DAY

Timmy walks over to me, nail clippers in hand. "I'm going to clip my nails over at the beach," he announces, as if it's the most normal location to do personal upkeep.

To be fair, I've seen people do it in worse places, like a workplace lunch table—but I get the sense this is just another excuse for Timmy to leave the apartment.

"Why are you doing it at the beach?"

"Because I want to," he sneers. "You can't control me." He leaves, the door swooshing closed and beeping behind him.

ME:

Well, he just ran away to the beach to clip his nails.

ALICE:

That sounds like a video game excuse.

After about half an hour, Timmy returns from his beach nail-clipping excursion with a bounce in his step and something cupped in his hand.

"Here," he says, grinning like a child who just discovered buried treasure. He extends his hand toward me, revealing a shell. "I found you this."

I stare at the shell, unimpressed. It's just like a million of the other shells he's brought me previously, not the least bit unique or interesting.

"I don't want another stupid shell from you, Timmy," I say, shaking my head. My tone is sharper than I intended, but I'm too tired to soften it.

His grin falters for a split second before transforming into mock indignation. "Fine," he huffs. "If you won't take it, I'll eat it."

I blink at him, incredulous.

He holds the shell to his mouth, as if testing my resolve.

I grab my phone and type out a quick message to Alice.

ME:

He just brought me a shell and I wouldn't accept it, so now he's threatening to eat it. Eat the shell, bro. Like I care.

ALICE:

Mkay, have fun.

Timmy clutches the shell dramatically and mutters something under his breath.

I'm already over it, and turn my attention back to my laptop. I have work to do, but his antics don't stop.

"Jibber jadder!" he suddenly yells, cackling like a madman. He repeats it over and over, each time laughing harder, as if it's the funniest thing he's ever said.

I glance up, wondering if he's drunk, high, or just having another one of his manic moments.

"Timmy, stop," I snap. "You're being ridiculous."

His response is to grab a tortilla from the counter. "I should slap you in the face with this," he says, grinning wickedly.

I cross my arms. "Go right ahead. I dare you. The cops will be here in two seconds because they don't like you, and think you're an idiot because of your shitty behavior."

Timmy's grin fades, and he tosses the tortilla back onto the counter. "Fine," he mutters, as if I've somehow ruined his fun.

Before I can exhale in relief, he picks up a lime and squeezes the juice into his own eye.

ME:

He's now squeezed lime juice into his eye.

ALICE:

What is he even doing? Has he seriously done any cocaine lately? Or Adderall?

ME:

He used to do cocaine a lot, but has stopped since I met him. And has no access to Adderall that I'm aware of.

ALICE:

This seems very stimulant behavior.

Or mania.

I glance at Timmy, who is now blinking furiously, his eye red and watering.

She's right—this is far from normal.

I'm thinking it's mania. He has no money or drug connections out here, but God knows what he's capable of when left to his own devices.

ALICE:

I don't know. I hate that you guys cohabitate.

I sigh. So do I at this point.

Timmy's energy doesn't wane. He grabs his sock monkey toy and starts smacking one of Sabre's favorite soft toys with it, cackling the whole time.

Sabre looks on from his perch on the windowsill, his ears pinned back in disapproval.

"Stop!" I say, beyond frustrated. "You're not five years old. And I will fly the friend who gave Sabre that toy over here to sort you out if you keep doing that!"

Timmy pouts, but sets the sock monkey down. "It's Dad's birthday today," he says, his tone shifting to something resembling normalcy. "I'm going to call him later."

"Good," I reply, hoping his dad might talk some sense into him. His dad is one of the few people who can occasionally get through to him. I'm more exhausted than ever, and I could really use the assist.

I message Alice:

ME:

I made a conscious choice to start prioritizing my writing over his nonsense, and it's been working. 5k words first thing when I wake up, no question. This started last week. I'm layering in more priorities over him. But I'm taking weekends off writing (not really from work because I'm working on this store I'm making—with him).

ALICE:

I dislike you're doing it with him, but I love your dedication!

Her words are like a warning bell in my ears. I hear where she's coming from, and have my own doubts about approaching anything at all in partnership with Timmy, let alone a business venture.

———

Later in the evening, Timmy's antics take another bizarre turn. "I have a jet ski!" he announces proudly. "I ride it everywhere."

I lower my laptop screen and give him a look. "What the actual fuck are you talking about?"

"I told you. I have a jet ski," he repeats.

I'm too exhausted to argue. "Sure, Timmy. That sounds completely plausible. I'm sure if you did have a jet ski, it would have been a gift, not something you bought for yourself."

"I got it as a bonus for painting a crane, *actually*," he says, his voice dripping with self-importance and hurt. "Fuck you! You're so mean!" he yells, before storming out the door.

It beeps behind him as he leaves.

ME:

ALICE:

Again? What for? To adjust his socks?

I laugh despite myself, and fill her in on JetskiGate.

ALICE:

Okay. That could be true. Or a hallucination.

ME:

Lol, yeah. I guess he had one in the past. He said it was a bonus for painting a crane.

ALICE:

That gave me more questions.

She doesn't have to say it. I know this doesn't get better. But still, I'm holding out hope—for what, I'm not sure.

———

A couple of hours later, I realize Timmy has turned his location off on his phone. My stomach churns with unease.

ME:

He turned his location off like 15 minutes ago, I guess.

ALICE:

So that's suspicious.

ME:

Yes, very. But knowing him, he's just being spiteful and trying to upset me. I called, but he didn't answer.

ALICE:

That's still bad.

ME:

Yeah, it's completely unacceptable.

ALICE:

What're you going to do?

ME:

I'm not sure. There's not much I can do until he
decides to come back.

He'll no doubt be all apologetic, yet defensive.

ALICE:

And unable to provide answers.

ME:

I'm just feeling super sad right now. But I designed a
puzzle and flip flops and a fanny pack for the store,
so there's that.

I was meant to be doing TikToks for my books today
for all of next week and haven't made a single one.
Again. Because of his shit behavior.

ALICE:

Well, it's understandable. You've got other stuff on
your mind.

I close my laptop and curl up on the bed with Sabre. His soft purring is the only thing keeping me grounded.

Timmy's chaos is like a carnival ride gone rogue, spinning faster and faster while I hold on for dear life.

CHAPTER 42
BREAKING MARGAUX

TWO WEEKS LATER

I decide to check his phone again, just to be sure.

I just have a feeling.

Then I see another shortcut to a girl's Facebook profile—the one who wouldn't stop blowing up his phone. The one who he slept with right before he met me.

What the actual fuck?

My stomach churns, and I feel the familiar sting of betrayal wash over me.

I storm down to the beach, where he's bent over, picking shells from the sand. My heart pounds in my chest as I thrust the phone toward him. I don't care that I'm not being calm. I'm feeling incredibly betrayed, and I want answers.

"Why the hell is Methany a shortcut on your Facebook?"

He looks up, his face flickering with guilt. "I just looked at her profile once," he mutters, brushing off my anger. "I didn't talk to her, or anything. I just accidentally clicked on it."

"What do you mean, accidentally clicked on it?"

"I mean, I went to see if she messaged me on there. I didn't want to look at her Facebook profile. Matty just told me she was in town, and I was terrified she was going to message me, and that you would see it and think I wanted her to contact me. And I don't. I can't stand her. I will happily never talk to her again. So I tried to keep it from you in case she had messaged. But she hadn't. Not even a loser like her wants to message me anymore. It's a bit sad in a way. Nobody misses me. Nobody wonders where I've gone."

"Okay," I say slowly. "So you tried to protect me by lying to me? You promised me you wouldn't lie about her again. But now you have."

"Because I knew you'd act just like this," he snaps, his frustration bubbling over.

"No, Timmy," my voice is sharp, my patience unraveling. "If you had just told me the truth about it, I wouldn't be upset. But you lied. *Again*. And now she's still in your life, even though you said she wouldn't be."

"Fine. I'll block her," he mutters. "I don't want anything to do with her anyway."

I watch as he blocks Manthrax on Facebook and Instagram.

But deep down, I know it's meaningless.

There are other ways for him to stay in touch with Trashleigh if he really wants to.

———

My mind keeps ruminating over the same things.

I can't get over him having Britney Despair's Facebook profile showing up as a shortcut on his phone.

Not that I think he'd know how to set up a shortcut. It clearly wasn't intentional.

I check my own phone to see how it works, and do a bit of googling to help make it make sense. The contacts in my shortcuts are random people, but they're people I've interacted with recently, so they're who I would expect to show up..

I guess the interaction could be that he looked at Ketamine Kardashian's page like he said, and he just doesn't have many friends and doesn't use it a lot. So the magnitude of his looking at her page would be much greater than for someone like me, who visits many pages a day to interact with friends all over the world.

If you have only one friend, like it's beginning to seem is his situation, they're going to be your shortcut if you've had any interaction with their page at all.

But I can't stop thinking about all the possible explanations, and I find myself googling all the answers to this mystery. There's a ton of information online, and a lot of people asking similar questions in relation to their significant others.

I feel a bit crazy, looking all this stuff up. I never had to do this with my last partner, because I trusted him implicitly. I haven't had to do it with any partners, actually.

Yet Timmy keeps doing shit that makes me question him.

I open up a golf solitaire game I like on my phone, and I find myself thinking about the situation more as I start to mindlessly play. It's meant to take my mind off things, but something snaps inside me, and I come up with a strange theory.

Methamine Monroe will leave us alone and get the fuck out of my relationship if I win a round of this game every day with a perfect score. Logically, I know my conquering of this silly phone game has no correlation with my fiancé's ability to remain faithful. And it certainly doesn't have any impact on K-Hole Kourtney's behavior.

But I have to do it. I'm compelled to do this game every day. Who knows? In some weird universal phenomenon, I might be right. This is what I might need to do to protect our relationship.

Some people might cast a spell. Others might reach out to the crazy bitch and tell her to back the fuck off. Others might simply trust their spouse. But I'm feeling a little unhinged myself, and so I decide to hinge everything—at least in my mind—on whether I can maintain a perfect score each day, whether that takes me five minutes or three hours, it's what I have to do.

A couple of times, Timmy gives me weird looks. "You're *still* playing that game?" And I'll realize it's past 2am, and even he wants to go to sleep. But I feel like if I don't win a level every day, then I have to do two the following, and then three the following if I fail then, too.

This isn't going to be sustainable if there's a really hard level every so often. I'll be up all night trying to save my relationship using a method that makes absolutely no sense. Golf solitaire isn't going to fix anyone's relationship.

I feel hugely embarrassed by this, and I know it probably sounds a bit compulsive.

Okay, it is compulsive, and obsessive and illogical, I logically know that.

But I can't stand the thought of someone who won't respect the boundary of our relationship.

I hate that he's misled me about some of their conversations, and having denied saying things that could potentially lead her on.

It comforts me when he says what a mess she is and how he'd never be with her. But I'm reminded he was okay enough being around her to have sex with her, more than once. That if she ever comes up in conversation, while he's usually very insulting about her, he'll occasionally refer to her as 'a kind friend'.

And I've only really heard him speak negatively about his exes, so who knows what's true?

I don't think everything his most recent ex told me was necessarily one hundred percent true from an objective, neutral bystander's perspective. But I do think the vast majority of it was. I've seen many of the behaviors myself at this point, and I understand how challenging it must have been for her too. No matter how much of the toxicity within the relationship was because of her, clearly there was a solid share coming straight from Timmy.

But how many crazy ex-partners can someone truly have? He only seems to be able to describe one girl as being someone he still stays in contact with via sporadic phone calls. Someone he dated right out of high school. Everyone else has a huge amount of animosity aimed at them.

In my case, sure, I've dated a couple of people I've had to block. I've been married to a couple I've had to block. But there are plenty more who I can say nice things about, where we ultimately just weren't right for each other and ended things relatively amicably. I'm still Facebook friends with some of them, and I wish them well.

He doesn't seem to be able to do the same.

According to him, this one kicked him out, that one kicked him out. They were all abusive, toxic drunks who talked down to him and accused him of being 'too much'. He's always the victim.

I wonder if that's how he's describing me to Scrap-heap Sabrina?

If he's in touch with her behind my back.

I would be sick if I found out that was the case.

Because I deserve better than that, and quite frankly, so does she.

Not that I have an ounce of respect for intentional home wreckers, but I do realize that people can be led on, especially by someone as charming as Timmy.

I go back to the phone golf game. Because it's a hell of a lot better to worry about that than all of this.

CHAPTER 43
SMIRNOFF ICE EXCURSIONS

MARGAUX

I dial Timmy again.

He answers this time, on the third ring.

"Hey babe, I'm just heading back now. I'll be back in like five," he says, casual as ever.

There are voices in the background, a faint hum of conversation and what sounds like a cash register beeping.

My stomach tightens. Where the hell is he? To my knowledge, he has no money. God only knows what he's up to.

ME:

> I called again twice, and he finally answered and said he was on his way back.

> There were voices in the background. Like he was in a store or something.

> Which is weird, bc he has no money.

ALICE:

> The best possible outcome is he just walked there to talk to people.

The phone buzzes again. Timmy calling *me* this time.

"What are you doing?" I ask, the irritation already creeping into my voice.

"I was just at the store getting a Smirnoff Ice," he says, as if it's the most natural explanation in the world.

"Are you fucking kidding me?" I snap. "How did you pay for that?"

"Oh, I had a couple of bucks on my Apple Pay, so I used that," he replies, sounding smug.

"Fuck! You!" I scream, and hang up.

My hands are trembling, my chest tight with fury. Of all the idiotic things...

ME:

Oh my god! He was at the gas station buying a Smirnoff Ice.

Because apparently he had a few bucks on his Apple Pay.

I just told him 'fuck you' and hung up.

ALICE:

Yeah, that sounds like my ex. Somehow always had money for booze, but that's an addiction for you.

I fire off a text to him:

ME:

You can't help me pay for anything, but somehow you have money to buy a Smirnoff Ice? Take a long hard fucking look at yourself.

The minutes tick by, and there's still no sign of Timmy.

My irritation morphs into a simmering rage.

ME:

If you're not back in five minutes, I'm throwing your things out on the street.

ME (TO ALICE):

I'm so fucking angry.

ALICE:

As you should be. That's infuriating.

ME:

I threatened to toss out his things.

ALICE:

You've said that a lot before. I don't think he'll
believe it this time.

ME:

He has a shit memory. And I think he got someone
to buy him the drink.

Because remember, he went and bought a big bottle
of vodka and took my laundry money to pay for a
couple of dollars of it.

ALICE:

Also possible.

Timmy finally texts back:

TIMMY:

I'm going to cry at the beach until my phone battery
charges, and then I'll be back.

ME:

Cry at how badly you treat me? Good.

I update Alice.

ALICE:

Yeah, seriously. That's proper reflection. But I doubt
it happens.

ME:

He is weirdly reflective, promises to change, and
then promptly reverts to past behavior.

A while back he told me to put him in a book where
the other guys kill him.

Maybe I will.

He's still not back, and I want to vomit.

My phone buzzes. It's Timmy:

TIMMY:

Take a life insurance policy out on me so I can kill
myself and you can get money.

You should have me leave.

You can find someone better.

ME:

I should, and I can.

TIMMY:

Yes, you can.

ME:

I'm glad we agree on something.

I fill Alice in.

ALICE:

Yeah, I had conversations with my ex like that. I
don't like this guy.

I locate the near-empty vodka bottle and drink straight from it until it's all gone. Because, knowing Timmy, when he finally returns, if there was still vodka in it he'd have either run off with it or poured it down the sink. So I'm spite drinking it, if you will.

As if on cue, Timmy arrives back at the apartment.

"Are you done being crazy yet?" he asks.

The audacity.

I ignore him, and instead turn on *90 Day Fiancé*.

Clearly bothered by my TV choice, Timmy runs into the back room and closes the door behind him.

I switch the TV over to *Family Guy*, which he enjoys watching, and I'm sure he can hear.

ALICE:

I think you need to get rid of him for good. He
doesn't seem to do anything to benefit you.

ME:

Yes, he's making me worse. He literally said he
wants to pull me up, not drag me down.

And I was like, you said that, but you're dragging me down, bro.

I deserve a man who can take ME out for dinner, not suck my savings dry while he might sell one artwork one day.

Not to shit on artists because you're a talented one. I think you know what I mean. Like nobody is hunting his shit down like he's Picasso.

ALICE:

That's all he's doing.

I know what you mean.

ME:

Well, I will utilize his 'inspiration' and write the shit out of it. My next book after this one is about reliving sexual assault. So, hopefully it will heal people. And then I'll do one inspired by his bullshit.

The fucked-up thing is that he keeps telling his dad about my books.

And his dad knows I'm the best thing that's ever happened to him. So, he keeps buying my books. And I'm like, omg, how embarrassing. Stop reading my smut.

But apparently, he just started a random one. When he reads about the four dicks, he maybe won't like me as much.

ALICE:

LMAO. Yeah, his dad is in for a wild ride.

CHAPTER 44
JEALOUS JIM

'm watching another episode of *Family Guy,* the one where Peter Griffin develops a meth addiction. It's ironic, given where I live and the sort of behaviors I've been subjected to lately. But the episode is funny, in that twisted, absurd way the show always manages, and I'm laughing out loud.

The thought of sitting around a table with the writers of *Family Guy* crosses my mind. What must that room even look like? *Oh, to be a fly on that wall.*

The door to the back room creaks open, and Timmy emerges. "Oh, you're so loud," he grumbles, glaring at me.

Says the loudest person I have ever met.

I roll my eyes and make no attempt to hide it.

I message Alice.

ALICE:

Tim needs to stop everything he is doing.

Already giddy from the show, Alice's comment sends me into another fit of laughter, one that bubbles up uncontrollably and makes my sides ache.

"What's so funny?" Timmy demands, his tone sharp, as though my amusement is a personal attack.

"Life," I reply, deadpan. The look on his face tells me he doesn't appreciate my humor.

His eyes narrow. "You're blushing. Who are you talking to? Who is he?"

ME:

Omg, so now you're a man, apparently. I'm just mentally amused in a sea of his shit behavior.

LMFAO.

Ahahaha, he's losing it because I'm texting you.

ALICE:

Omfg, he can look at my profile pic.

Timmy scowls. "Are you having an affair? Who with?"

ME:

Apparently you are a guy, and we are in an affair.

ALICE:

I'm a girl, Jealous Jim.

Timmy's voice rises. "Who is it? Are you cheating on me? Who's making you all giggly, seriously?"

I wave my phone at him. "It's Alice. She's a woman, Timmy. Not that I owe you an explanation."

"It doesn't matter anyway," he mutters, shrugging with fake nonchalance. "I don't care who you're fucking. My parents are flying me back home tomorrow."

This again. He's been claiming this for weeks, but no plane ticket has materialized.

I'm not holding my breath.

I don't respond.

"Eat your fucking bail," he continues smugly, referring to the thousand dollars I forked out to get him out of jail after his DUI. "Good luck getting that shit back."

ME:

He's amused THAT I probably won't get my $1,000 bail money back from his DUI.

ALICE:

Jeez.

At least his parents actually got the ticket this time?

ME:

So he says.

ALICE:

I hope they did. You need some distance from him.
A different state would help.

ME:

He was so mad bc I was laughing.

But when I'm the most upset, I cackle… it's like a
nervous response.

Anyway, we should start planning our wedding.

ALICE:

I mean…it's your life?

ME:

I meant your and my wedding.

ALICE:

Okay, I'm more on board for that.

My guy might take it badly.

I laugh.

Timmy calls out from the hallway. "I'm going to punch you if you keep laughing at me, you stupid cunt."

ME:

Oh, he just threatened to punch me.

ALICE:

Nope. Electric chair.

911.

I've had enough. "Stop threatening me with violence," I say firmly, my tone sharp but calm.

He scoffs. "Oh, you're so fucking dumb. I didn't threaten you. I was warning you."

ME:

> I'm apparently so dumb that I can't tell a threat from
> a warning.

ALICE:

> Threats ARE warnings. The same in the eyes of
> the law.

Timmy stomps to the back room and slams the door.

Minutes later, he comes back out and I hear him leave the apartment, the door beeping as it closes behind him.

ME:

> WTF, bro.

Timmy returns to the apartment, and goes to the back room for a few minutes. Then he leaves again.

ME:

A while later, he comes back again, and doesn't say a word. He rustles around in the back room, and a few minutes later, he's gone again.

ME:

ALICE:

Yeah, he needs to make up his mind and be chaotic elsewhere.

A text comes in from Timmy:

TIMMY:

I'm gonna walk to the rock and back.

I hope you can stop with the animosity.

I don't know where it started but I want it to stop.

If everything you said you meant, I'll leave and spare you dealing with me.

I would like to talk and hash out whatever this was… is.

I do love you Margaux.

I send Alice a screenshot of his message.

ME:

It comes from his behavior, not out of my ass. But I think he's trying?

ALICE:

He's… I don't know. These types of mental health issues are difficult to deal with.

———

LATER IN THE DAY

Yesterday, Timmy had insisted he wanted to ride in the truck with me to my job interview today, but he changes his mind at the last minute.

"I can't," he whines. "I have a splitting headache."

Fine. I'm better off without him in the truck anyway. I don't need someone to hold my hand there and back, and a few minutes of peace sounds heavenly.

But something feels off.

Before I leave, he stops me. "I need to admit something," he says, his tone strangely sheepish. "You know how I sold my chop saw yesterday and said I'd give you the twenty to thirty bucks for it?"

I narrow my eyes. "Yeah? What happened with that?" He had returned without the chop saw, but I also haven't seen any money.

"Well, I ended up spending it at the store. I got a shitty bottle of vodka, hence my headache."

Unbelievable.

But I'm too tired to be angry. I have an interview to prepare for, and I'm not wasting any more energy on this nonsense.

I attend the interview, and I have some reservations about the role. It's something I could do in my sleep, but the industry is really uninspiring, and so are the executive leaders who interview me. The more I learn about it, the less I think it's the right role for me.

And the more I think about it, the more it weighs on my mind that it'd be near-impossible for me to successfully perform a full-time job while in a relationship with Timmy.

He himself is a full-time job, and I'd be an anxious wreck all day, wondering what kind of trouble he'd be getting himself into while I was away.

———

Later, I drive Timmy to his therapy appointment, and I'm parked outside when the recruiter from my interview calls.

"They loved your experience, but they felt your outfit was too casual," she explains. "Would that be an issue going forward?"

Are you kidding me? This job gave me red flags from the start—five days a week in the office, rigid executives who've worked together for nearly two decades, and a soul-crushing approach to HR. Picking on my clothing feels petty and unnecessary.

"I'm not sure I could work for a place that values appearances over capability," I say. "It doesn't sound aligned with the transformative approach I bring to HR."

I'm not perturbed. It's not even slightly disappointing. If anything, it's a relief.

The universe is shoving me toward my dream of writing full-time, and away from the draining world of HR, and I'm ready to embrace it.

Timmy returns to the truck, looking depleted. "I talked a lot. I cried. But I feel like they bait-and-switched me," he says. "I was supposed to have the main therapist lady, but now I have one of her students instead. She doesn't have much experience, but hopefully, she'll be okay."

I nod, not sure what to say. The fact that he went at all feels like a small victory—enough to give me a little sliver of hope.

But I can't shake the suspicion that he's not legitimately concerned about the person allocated to be his therapist, and that he's merely laying the groundwork for an excuse to stop going at some point in the future.

For now, though, he's trying.

And that's more than I can say for most days.

CHAPTER 45
SINK OR SWIM

LATER IN THE WEEK

"Let's go swim with the dolphins!" Timmy announces, his eyes sparkling with enthusiasm. "It's one of the best parts of being out here on this side of the island!"

The idea thrills me immediately. Wild dolphins, out in nature—it sounds like a childhood dream come true.

I think back to visiting the marine wildlife park as a kid, my mother holding my hand as dolphins leaped through hoops and seemed to smile at the audience as they twirled and waved, bribed by their instructors with handfuls of fish.

Swimming with dolphins had always felt like an unattainable fantasy—it was always so expensive and my overprotective mother always feared for my safety—but here, on Sunset Cay, it could actually happen.

For a brief moment, my excitement almost feels childlike again.

"Oh my gosh," I reply. "I would absolutely love that!"

Timmy grins, leaning back in his chair like he's the one who just made a childhood dream come true. "Yeah, I've done it before. A couple of years ago. It's incredible being out there with them."

His expression shifts slightly, taking on a nostalgic gleam. "I was with two of my female friends—twins."

There's something about the way he emphasizes *twins* that makes my stomach flip—not in a good way. He lingers on the word, drawing it out like it's some kind of punchline. It's undeniably pervy, and the warm excitement I felt seconds ago cools into something less pleasant.

Gross.

I shift in my seat, trying to mask my discomfort, but Timmy catches it. Of course he does. He always notices, and he never lets it go.

"Oh, relax," he says, his tone dripping with smugness. "I didn't fuck either of them or anything. They were just friends. It was a good memory."

His words hang in the air, tainted by the bitterness in his tone. I don't know what's more irritating—the unnecessary vulgarity or the way he always manages to twist something sweet into something gross.

But then his expression darkens, his frown carving deeper lines into his face. "And fuck you for trying to mess with my memory."

The accusation stings, but it's familiar. I've been here before—caught in one of Timmy's bizarre mental gymnastics routines, where he shifts from nostalgia to defensiveness to full-on hostility in a matter of seconds.

Too tired to argue, I let it go. It's not worth the energy.

"Okay, Timmy," I say, forcing my voice to stay even. I glance out at the horizon, focusing on the serene waves and the possibility of a dolphin-filled adventure instead of the emotional landmine sitting across from me.

We grab our snorkel gear and drive to the beach, where pods of wild dolphins are known to hang out at this time of day.

I realize I forgot my fins, but I don't think I'll need them. The water looks calm, and I'm a decent swimmer.

Besides, Timmy seems confident, and his enthusiasm is infectious.

As we wade into the water, an older woman suddenly shouts at us from the shore, her voice shrill. "You know swimming with dolphins is going to be illegal soon, right? *Illegal!*" she repeats, glaring.

Great, I came to see dolphins and instead I found a Karen.

Timmy and I press on, the salty air and sound of the waves promising an adventure.

"Keep going," Timmy says, his voice coaxing but firm. "Just a little further."

The further out to sea we go, the more anxious I feel. The shoreline shrinks into the distance, and the water grows deeper. I've never been this far out. My snorkel and mask feel like my only tether to safety, allowing me to float and breathe steadily.

And then it happens.

Timmy swims up beside me and knocks my snorkel off. The tube detaches from my mask, and panic surges through me like electricity.

Disoriented, I spin around, flailing to grab it while gasping for air—and swallowing water instead.

Timmy laughs.

I finally grab the snorkel and try to reattach it, my hands trembling. I'm still treading water furiously, my heart racing.

Timmy, meanwhile, is swimming further out, oblivious. He doesn't even look back.

The panic builds.

I force myself to calm down, to focus on the basics—*breathe, float, swim.*

But the shore looks impossibly far away, and every kick feels like I'm fighting against the entire ocean. And we're the only ones around.

When I finally make it to what I think is the shore, relief crashes over me —until I make contact with something hard, and realize I've swum straight into a jagged rock bed.

Waves slap against the rocks, throwing me against them, and I remember Timmy mentioning spiky sea urchins living in places like this.

I freeze. My breathing is shallow, but I force myself to stay calm. Slowly, carefully, I edge along the rocks until I see sand. Inch by inch, I maneuver myself to safety, my arms and legs trembling from exertion and fear.

When I finally collapse onto the beach, I look out to see Timmy still swimming, completely unaware—or uncaring—about what just happened.

I stomp back to the truck, seething. My adrenaline is still spiking, and my mind races.

I was out there, panicking, *alone*—and he didn't care. Instead, he laughed and swam away.

I furiously tap in the truck's door code and hop in. I'm tempted to leave him stranded, but I don't know where he's hidden the truck keys. So I wait, simmering in my rage, as he enjoys the swim of a lifetime.

When he finally strolls back up the beach, he's beaming. "We didn't see any dolphins, but that was an epic swim. I feel great!" His tone is so light, so carefree—it's like he's mocking me. "You came back early. Did you enjoy it?"

"Timmy, I almost fucking drowned out there!" I snap, my voice sharp and trembling.

He blinks, confused. "What do you mean?"

"You knocked my snorkel off, and I panicked! I was flailing around, and you didn't even care! You just laughed and swam off!"

"Oh, my bad," he shrugs. "I didn't notice. Sorry."

"And then I tried to get back to shore because I was freaking out, and I got disoriented and swam into the rocks, Timmy."

"Oh." He seems unconcerned.

"I couldn't get out, and I thought there might be sea urchins. I remember you warning me about them."

He scoffs, like I'm being dramatic. "Sea urchins wouldn't be on *that* side of those rocks, silly. They'd get washed away by the waves. You were fine."

"You didn't even know I was there!" I snap. My voice cracks with the weight of everything—the fear, the anger, the complete lack of care.

"Well," he says, his tone shifting to something patronizing, "now that you mention it, I'm actually impressed you swam out that far. We were out *really* far. I didn't think you'd do it. But you did great!" He smiles, as if that erases everything.

I glare at him, my chest tight with rage. "I trusted you to make sure I was safe. That's the only reason I went out so far. I wish I'd at least brought my fins."

"Relax," he says, waving me off. "We'll come out again to see the dolphins another time, and you can bring your fins."

But I'm in no rush for a repeat.

The idea of swimming with wild dolphins out in the ocean has lost all its magic.

Just like everything else.

CHAPTER 46
BACK-BURNER BARBIE AND CAPTAIN DELULU (ARE MADE FOR EACH OTHER)

MARGAUX

A FEW DAYS LATER

ME:

ALICE:
Dude. What now?

ME:

I'm a loser, apparently.

ALICE:

ME:

I called him out on the stupid ho he banged at least twice.

It's true. I couldn't hold back. I've been ruminating about Skank Face, knowing she's going to come back over and over again, trying to insert herself into his life. She's like if herpes was a person.

I know she's below me, and that I shouldn't let someone like her spend any time living rent-free in my head. But I hate that she's around, slowly circling Timmy like she has some weird addiction to him.

Knowing that he talked to her the same abusive way he talks to me now.

And that, according to their texts back and forth, he hit her, too.

Has he really ceased all communication with her? Why was she really a Facebook shortcut in his phone?

When I briefly dated Zeth, the ridiculously-named, Adderall-injecting mess, he used to do weird shit all the time—adding and deleting dating apps from his phone just because he could.

And Timmy is devious—I could totally see him messaging this Side Dish Sally, this Captain Cling-On—just to keep her on the hook in case things go bad with me.

And in general, just to piss me off.

ME:

I'm mad, and it's irrational.

ALICE:

It's pretty close for comfort since he's still in touch.

ME:

He's apparently not talking to her.

But I went off anyway.

I've been very well-behaved for like 5 evenings, and now I just went off.

It's fine.

My emotions are feeling cold.

> Maybe I'm a psychopath now. Jk 🖤 but 🐀

ALICE:

I think it's that you're at the very end of your rope.

ME:

It's a frayed rope.

Lol that he locks himself away from me. When he's the violent one.

Okay, I'll just… listen to music I like and chat with my friends? 🐀

ALICE:

Yeah, what a horrible punishment?

Timmy comes back.

"You started a fight with me," he glares at me.

"Well, I'm mad at you," I reply, not backing down.

"I'm leaving again, then," he says. "I don't need to put up with your bullshit."

"Good," I say, defiant. "Don't come back."

He picks something up off the counter and hurls it at me. It's a cockroach.

I flick it off myself and run up to him, and I grab onto his arm, scratching him in the process. *"Fuck you!"* I scream.

"You're so abusive, Margaux," he says. "I can't be around you when you're like this." And then he heads out the front door.

A while later, I glance at Find My iPhone. For once he hasn't blocked me, and I can see he's at the beach, over by the meth tents are per usual. He's become a real frequent flier over there.

I text him.

ME:

Goodbye, freak show.

Enjoy your stupid life with your friends you met on the beach.

The thing is, I've stopped giving any fucks.

The thought of a life without Timmy and all his violence and constant drama seems like a beautiful thing.

He's tried so hard to make me terrified of him leaving me, but now it sounds like a fucking party to not have to worry about him.

I don't need him, and I never have.

He pretended to be a nice person, but he's actually just a horrible insecure little man in a giant body.

I'm no longer worried that he'll show my messages to his dad or anyone else completely out of context to garner sympathy.

I share a screenshot of my freak show message with Alice.

ME:

Friendly words (actually just exhausted from his shit).

ALICE:

Totally understand.

I'd be fucking furious!

ME:

Haha.

I'm done with subtlety, but was I ever subtle?

I'm marinating in my bitterness and it feels quite good, honestly. Allowing myself to feel all the feelings that I've kept trapped in my body for the past however many months.

ALICE:

No.

Not at all!

Hahaha.

ME:

Also, when he does come back, he will most likely accuse me of talking to a guy again. Bc you make me smirk in the best way, and he thinks I'm blushing when I am LAUGHING bc my friend is funny AF.

Timmy returns, and immediately heads to the shower. He knows that will piss me off, and he's trying to make me think he's cleaning his dick or something.

Disgusting and vile, just like him.

A while later, he emerges from the bathroom, freshly showered.

"If you must know, I was over there saving someone whose finger was basically falling off," he says, his tone pompous. "Taking care of *nice* people, doing the *right* thing." He glares at me. "Unlike *you*... you know, why do you have to be so *evil*?"

"Yep, that's me. Evil as fuck." I roll my eyes, not even trying to disguise my contempt.

The way Timmy paints himself as a savior, the neighborhood hero, is such a joke.

And to call me evil? *Okay, Captain Delulu.*

"Well, you're going to need to get off that bed because it's mine," he says, gesturing toward the mattress.

"Well, if you're going to be like that, you're going to need to get out of this apartment because I pay for it," I gesture around the room.

Game on, Petty Betty.

"You can take the mattress and go hang out with your dangling-finger Captain Hook friend and see how your life goes," I add. "Put it right out there on the beach."

Timmy intentionally puts a sci-fi movie on that he knows I won't like.

So I put my headphones on and blare Machine Gun Kelly.

Two can play this game. As fucked up as it is.

And I'm a stubborn Taurus, after all.

CHAPTER 47
DESPERELLA

DEX

I sit in the shadows of Margaux's chaotic life, watching Timmy swirl around her like a toxic hurricane. She's the kind of woman who deserves the world—yet here she is, tethered to this sinking ship of a man.

Today, I'm watching another chapter of the Timmy Show unfold.

Margaux, ever patient, plays Mario Kart with him, her laughter genuine despite her exhaustion. For a while, it's a moment of peace. But of course, Timmy can't just let her have that.

He berates her and demeans her. Margaux handles it with her usual grace, though I can tell she's biting back a sharper response. When she finally snaps—as any human would—he uses it against her.

I roll my eyes. *Really, Timmy? A video game? This is the hill you choose to die on?*

She doesn't know I'm watching, but I wish she did. I'd give anything to remind her of her worth.

Timmy's pathetic attempts to tear her down don't define her. Hell, he's not even near her level.

When Margaux vents to Alice later, it's clear that Timmy's antics are wearing her down. But it's when he sneaks out late at night—leaving the door ajar and putting her beloved cat, Sabre, at risk, not once but twice—that my blood boils. Sabre is family to her, and the careless way Timmy disregards that makes me want to wring his neck.

Luckily, Margaux finds Sabre and brings him back, but the damage is done. She texts Alice, venting her frustration, and I see her resilience crack, just for a moment.

But then, as always, Margaux bounces back. She's remarkable like that.

Even after Timmy's juvenile attempts to rile her up with his antics—wrapping himself in a curtain like a six-foot-two burrito or threatening to eat a shell he brought her—she finds a way to laugh it off. She shares the absurdity with Alice, turning his chaos into a running joke.

Then there's *her*.

He torments Margaux with this nasty, thin-lipped slut.

I'm not a slut-shamer—I'm pro sex-positive women, and it's not about that at all.

But a woman who will willfully sleep with a guy who's in a relationship? *Gross.*

And *her*, specifically? She's fucking disgusting. She looks like if syphilis was a person.

Desperella.

Let's call her that because she doesn't deserve anything better.

She's the type of woman who clings to men like Timmy because she can't find anyone better.

The kind of woman who thrives on crumbs of attention because that's all she can get.

Desperella is the type who floods her Instagram with grainy bikini selfies with her legs spread wide apart, captioned with generic quotes like, '*Catch flights, not feelings,*' while spending her evenings furiously scrolling Timmy's Facebook profile, looking for breadcrumbs of validation.

She's the girl who still thinks posing by a waterfall, contorting her body to show off her thigh gap makes her mysterious and edgy, her followers a trail of low-value men who want her for nothing other than her easily accessed vagina.

Her idea of flirting? Sending five emojis in a row to see which one gets a reaction.

And let's not forget her signature move—posting throwbacks with captions like '*Wish I could go back to this day* 🖤' when Timmy is tagged in the background. It's all so transparent, so painfully *thirsty*.

Desperella is nothing compared to Margaux.

Margaux is leagues above her—whip-smart, beautiful, and magnetic in a way Desperella could never fake. Witty, smart and kind, with a fire in her that no amount of Timmy's bullshit can extinguish.

While Margaux spends her time creating, building, and shining, Desperella lives for the drama, hoping Timmy will throw her another morsel of attention. She's a moth circling his flame, oblivious to the fact that she's only getting burned.

It's infuriating to watch Timmy weaponize her existence against Margaux—his pathetic attempts at triangulation leave Margaux doubting herself. It makes me want to break something. Or someone.

He keeps Desperella dangling just enough to make Margaux feel like she has something to prove—when in reality, Margaux has already won in every conceivable way.

Desperella is a footnote in Timmy's sad little saga.

Margaux is the whole damn story.

"If you think so little of her, why did you even put your dick in her at least twice?" Margaux asks, her voice sharp, cutting. She deserves answers, but Timmy dodges and deflects, as always.

"She's nothing," he snaps, and I almost laugh. Of course, she's nothing—*nothing compared to Margaux*. But he still keeps her lingering, a tool in his sick game to make Margaux feel small.

And Margaux doesn't deserve to have anything to do with either of these two trainwrecks. Maybe they should go off and kill each other in the sunset.

Maybe that's their sad and demented Thelma and Louise of it all.

When Timmy's insecurities rear their ugly head later, accusing Margaux of cheating, it's almost comical. His jealousy is absurd, unfounded, and dripping with irony—Margaux is so used to it that she doesn't even flinch.

The audacity of a man like Timmy to accuse Margaux of anything, while he entertains the lingering thirst shadow of Desperella, is laughable.

Late at night, Timmy storms out again, leaving Margaux to pick up the pieces.

She messages Alice, making jokes to mask her frustration. But I can see it in her eyes—she's tired. Exhausted from scrambling to hold everything together while Timmy tears it all apart.

I can't stand to see her like this. She deserves someone who sees her for the powerhouse she is, who loves and worships her.

Someone who would never let a pathetic shell of a man like Timmy come close to dimming her light.

Someone like me.

Though at this point that seems self-serving, and my priority is her being safe. Protected. Okay.

What I'd give to make sure Margaux is okay.

But she's not. She's still in the clasp of this butthole. And he had the audacity to call *her* butthole eyes, when her eyes are some of the most beautiful I've ever seen?

She's captivating. She's marvelous.

And he's a sloppy, overconfident tool who peaked in high school and thinks he hasn't aged a day.

The charisma of a middle-aged white man who thinks he's hot shit will never cease to amaze me.

I mean, to be fair, *I'm* a middle-aged white man—but I don't act anything like him.

I never would.

He's of a certain persuasion.

Gives his voting papers to his daddy—which I believe is illegal—and lets him vote for whoever he thinks his son should.

Talk about a fucking muppet.

I know, without a doubt, that must have given her the major ick when she found out. Because it's so counter to who she is as a person.

I'm getting worked up now, and I'm tempted to spy on him again.

To see what his shallow pea brain is doing.

To see how he's tormenting Margaux this time.

I'm sure he's looking at porn. I pull up his screen and—sure enough, he's watching '*BBC gang bang with blonde slut*'—because that seems to be his therapeutic go-to.

What a fucking douche.

I hate this guy so much.

And I can't wait to snuff him out to make the world a better place.

It's too early for me to act beyond what I've already done.

But one day, Margaux will realize her worth.

She'll see through Timmy's games, and when she does, I'll be there.

Ready to remind her of what it feels like to be truly loved.

Ready to show her that she was never the problem—she was always the prize.

CHAPTER 48
NO BIG DEAL

MARGAUX

THE NEXT DAY

"Dad, Margaux is being a bitch again."

Timmy has his dad on speakerphone, a smug look plastered across his face. He leans back against the counter like he's just delivered the zinger of the century.

I stare at him, my jaw tightening as I brace for whatever spin he's about to put on reality, how he'll twist things around to make himself look like the victim this time.

Phil's voice filters through the phone, calm but direct. "Well, son, you really need to get to work and make some money."

Timmy's face drops like a kid who's been told there's no dessert after dinner. It clearly wasn't the response he was looking for. With a huff, he takes the phone off speaker and bolts to the back room, slamming the door shut.

Even muffled, I can hear his voice rising and falling as he rants to his dad. 'She' this and 'she' that. I know exactly what he's doing—turning me into the villain to wring out some sympathy.

I used to care about how his parents perceived me. That need for approval gnawed at me in the early days of our relationship. But now? I've realized it's pointless.

Timmy himself doesn't even know where the truth ends and his lies begin. How could his parents ever form an accurate impression of me when their only source is a chronic fabricator?

It's out of my hands and always has been.

When Timmy finally returns to the main room, his eyes are sharp and accusing.

I meet his gaze, unwilling to back down. "Your behavior is so gross," I say evenly.

He glares at me. "I'm going to get you kicked out of here."

I raise an eyebrow. "Why?"

"Because you called me gross," he says. He storms off like an angry teenager.

I tell Alice.

ALICE:

Where's he think he'll fucking go?

ME:

Lmfao.

That's a good question.

Maybe to his parents. He's all braggy because he has parents.

Must be nice.

It's true. Timmy loves to twist the knife, reminding me that he has parents who will always be there for him. That he can call them anytime, they're only a flight away, and they'll pick up the pieces for him.

He knows it cuts deep because I don't have that safety net. My dad died when I was sixteen, and I cut ties with my toxic mother in my twenties. He uses my lack of family as a weapon, a way to make me feel small and alone.

ALICE:

Well, he can go there then.

And leave you alone.

I have a lightbulb moment.

ME:

I can go wherever I want.

I can literally go anywhere.

ALICE:

Absolutely.

———

A WHILE LATER

Timmy has returned and has been keeping to himself.

Suddenly, a glob of spit hits my arm.

I freeze, the shock of it rendering me immobile for a split second.

He just spat on me from across the room.

Timmy's face contorts into a reptilian sneer, and I feel bile rise in my throat. Most of his disgusting, tobacco-stained saliva has missed me, but a few droplets cling to my skin. My body recoils.

"Are you fucking kidding me?" I snap.

He shrugs as if spitting on someone is the most natural thing in the world.

But it's disrespectful, and it's also assault.

I message Alice:

ME:

He just spat on me from a distance.

ALICE:

No.

Timmy leaves again.

ME:

> He's so gross.

> Maybe I'll break up with him and go on a world trip.

> Meet you in like the fucking Caribbean or some shit.

> What a nut.

Timmy returns a while later, the sound of the door beeping sending a jolt of irritation through my body. Every time that door opens, it feels like the universe itself is mocking me—it's become a giant trigger that causes a visceral reaction almost as intense as Timmy himself.

He's holding a handful of grapes, a smug grin plastered on his face.

"You're so abusive," Timmy sneers. "And all you do is relive things from the past."

"That's fair about reliving things," I say, suddenly guilty for bringing up Groupie McDesperate. After all, to my knowledge he's not talking with her. It's *my* problem that the whole situation with her is continuing to bug me. "But it's because I've never really had closure from those things."

"I haven't been talking to that dumb bitch," he says.

He comes over from the kitchen, grapes in hand, and starts trying to feed them to me. "Here," he says, shoving one toward my mouth.

I try to push his hand away, but he insists, practically forcing it past my lips. I sigh and eat a couple, if only to get him to leave me alone.

ME:

> He's bringing me grapes.

ALICE:

> You're Aphrodite now!

ME:

> Apparently. She always was my favorite goddess.

ALICE:

> Understandable, you're gorgeous.

ME:

> Aweeee! Right back at you.

> I always got called ugly growing up, and it leaves a scar, ya know.

> I need to let a bunch of shit go. Working on it.

Kiwis are dicks, especially to redheads. 🙂

ALICE:

Everyone is, but I think it's because everyone
secretly wants red hair.

Timmy returns to the kitchen and makes himself a cooked breakfast.
He doesn't offer me anything.

"So I cooked you lunch and dinner yesterday and you're not offering me food?" I frown.

"I brushed your hair," he says, as if that's somehow relevant.

"You brushed my hair twice, and I don't need you to brush my hair. *You* wanted to do it," I reply. "And what does that have to do with cooking breakfast for yourself?"

He glares at me. "You're so problematic. You didn't even want the grapes I gave you, so shut the fuck up." He grabs the remaining grapes from the nightstand and shuffles back to the kitchen, leaving me momentarily in peace.

ALICE:

He's wild.

Dude.

Is this even what you want?

When he returns from whatever he's doing, he's holding a plate. On it is half a papaya, garnished with granola and yogurt, with a lime wedge on the side. It's beautifully plated, and for a moment, I don't know how to process the whiplash.

This morning he spat on me, and now he's offering me a breakfast worthy of an Instagram post.

I'm so numb to the endless cycle of extremes.

I snap a picture and send it to Alice. And it looks so fucking delicious that I squeeze the lime onto the papaya and eat the whole thing.

ME:

I don't know what I want.

I'm watching Below Deck and researching
international trips.

I ate the papaya also.

> They call it paw paw in New Zealand. Weird, right?!

ALICE:

————

A FEW HOURS LATER

Timmy bursts into the room with a grin. "I challenge you to a dance-off!"

"A what now?" I quirk a brow.

"A dance-off. Come on, Margaux. Let's go!"

Before I can protest, he pours vodka into a baby bottle, tipping it into my mouth like it's a hilarious prank.

He's erratic, but not outright mean for the first time in hours.

I guess this is better than the barrage of insults from earlier?

And, while I should probably decline his challenge, I'm clinging to the idea of something—anything—resembling fun.

He abruptly changes tacks. "Let's go play Monopoly Deal at the pool!" he suggests.

I blink. "Okay… sounds… fun?"

It does sound fun.

Please let it be fun.

And I need to act enthusiastic so I don't set him off.

"Give me two minutes to change into my bikini and then we'll go!" I say, a forced smile plastered on my face, praying this upbeat phase lasts long enough to get through a game of Monopoly Deal by the pool.

Keep it steady. Keep things calm, copacetic, and everything will be okay.

My mind wanders to how much more fun it would be to play Monopoly Deal by the pool with Alice rather than Timmy.

ME:

> Please come visit. Omg, imagine if you lived like two doors down.

> I would bring you everywhere because I 🤍 you.

ALICE:

> OMFG I would die. That would be so fun.

For the first time all day, I feel a flicker of joy imagining a life without

Timmy in it—one where my friends and I can laugh and play and do ridiculous, harmless things.

One where I don't have to explain my bruises or endure these emotional ups and downs.

One where I'm free.

CHAPTER 49
GONE METH-ING

MARGAUX

LATER IN THE DAY

"So Uncle next door and I bonded, by the way," Timmy says casually, leaning against the counter like he's about to share the story of the year. He's referring to the elderly man whose apartment directly faces ours.

"Oh yeah?" I ask, barely looking up from my laptop. Uncle seems nice enough—a quiet, wheelchair-bound man who mostly keeps to himself. But I know Timmy well enough to expect that this story will have a twist. "What'd you guys bond over?"

Timmy's grin widens. "He helps give me perspective. Says I need to treat you better, and not drink so much. Says I should smoke weed instead."

I raise an eyebrow, intrigued despite myself. "Okay, solid advice." I pause. "Wait, when was this conversation?"

"Yesterday," he replies, "when I was upset with you and ran out. His door was open, so I went in." He shrugs, as if walking into a neighbor's apartment uninvited is the most natural thing in the world.

"Wait—what?" I close my laptop and sit up straighter. "You just… went in?"

"Yeah," Timmy says, laughing now. "He was chilling there, totally naked."

I blink, unsure whether to laugh or cry. "You walked into a naked uncle's apartment to talk about your problems?"

Timmy nods, clearly proud of his newfound connection. "He gave me perspective, though! Said his life changed when he had a heart attack and ended up in a wheelchair. Told me not to sweat the small stuff."

"Well, I'm glad Uncle's got wisdom to share," I say slowly, processing. "Maybe next time, wear clothes when you hang out, though?"

Timmy laughs again, brushing off the comment.

I decide to take the opportunity to set some boundaries. "Timmy, today and tomorrow are really important for my book," I say carefully. "I need us to have a couple of calm, productive days. Can you help me with that?"

His eyes soften, and for a moment, he looks like the man I thought I fell in love with. "Of course," he says with a gentle smile. "You know I'll do anything I can to support you."

———

The Following Day

ME:

Timmy's location-sharing is turned off. Again.

I sigh and push my irritation aside.

Determined not to let him ruin my mood, I drive to the gas station, crank up Machine Gun Kelly, and sing at the top of my lungs all the way back to the apartment where I'm able to watch an entire episode of *90 Day Fiancé* in peace. *Bliss.*

But the tranquility doesn't last long. Two-and-a-half hours after he bolts, Timmy returns. "I was just with the guy whose finger I helped save the other day," he announces, beaming. "I gave him your wound cream, by the way."

I freeze. "You… gave him my wound cream?"

"Yeah, he needed it." Timmy shrugs like it's no big deal.

"Timmy, please stop giving my stuff away," I snap. "I needed that cream."

I message Alice.

ME:

He gave my wound cream away.

ALICE:

Jesus, y'all.

This is madness and wild.

———

THE NEXT EVENING

I wake up to an empty bed. The clock reads 317AM. Timmy is nowhere to be found.

Instinctively, I grab my phone and open Find My iPhone. There it is—he's over at the meth tents. My stomach twists.

I call him over and over again—maybe twenty times—but he doesn't pick up.

ME:

So I woke up, and he's not here.

According to Find My iPhone, he's on the beach at the meth tents at 3am.

ALICE:

Doing what? Did he clarify?

ME:

No, he's just missing. Like, up the street.

ALICE:

Hasn't come back? Didn't answer communications?

It's on then. Go find him.

I hesitate. The thought of wandering into the meth tents at this hour feels like signing my own death warrant.

ME:

I've called about 20 times because it's unsafe.

I guess I can try, but it's really not safe, although they did take down the full-on tweaker park a few months ago.

The memory of those days sends a chill down my spine—people screaming at each other, throwing bicycles, fist-fighting and openly dealing drugs in broad daylight. Things are quieter now, but only barely.

ALICE:

Definitely don't.

He might be with them.

I glance around the apartment. The sliding door is unlocked, and the front door is ajar. My blood boils.

Glad he cares about my personal safety.

> ME:
> He left the doors open.
>
> I'm alone in this sketchy neighborhood, and he's off doing god-knows-what at the meth tents.

> ALICE:
> Jesus. I'm sorry. That sounds like a nightmare.

> ME:
> I'm concerned.
>
> He says he'd never do meth because his sister does it.
>
> But I can't actually think of a reason he'd be out at this hour.

> ALICE:
> Yeah...

Underneath the desk, a pile of ti leaves catches my eye. It looks like a ti tree had a bukakke festival all over the ground.

> ME:
> He put ti leaves all over the floor. I'm going to kick his ass.
>
> If he's still alive.
>
> Jesus.

I can't stop thinking about the teenager who was shot right where it's saying Timmy is currently located.

What the hell is he doing out at 3AM in a place where people have recently been murdered?

> ALICE:
> This is not sustainable.

> ME:
> I'm so done.

But the truth is, I've said that before, and as I type it, the words feel hollow.

How many times have I said that?

And somehow, I'm still here—still cleaning up after his chaos.

Still hoping for something to change.

CHAPTER 50
THIS SHOULD BE FUN: LIVING WITH A LOSER

MARGAUX

nfuriated, confused, and exhausted, my logic goes south.

I shove on my flip-flops and storm out of the apartment, past the security shack, and toward the beach. The night air is thick with humidity, and the distant sound of crashing waves does nothing to soothe my nerves.

When I get there, I spot him immediately. Timmy sits at a picnic bench surrounded by a group of people who live in the nearby tents. He's wearing *my* hat—the one my sister just sent me all the way from New Zealand. The one that actually means something to me.

The audacity.

He sees me approaching and grins, as if this is some big joke.

I force a smile at the others and give them a small wave. "Hi," I say politely, masking the fury simmering just beneath the surface. Some of them wave back, oblivious to the storm brewing.

"Hey, babe," he says casually. "We're just hanging out, enjoying the night." He turns to his so-called friends. "Told you she'd come find me."

My anger ignites.

Timmy gets up, walking toward me, but I'm already too far gone

Targeting the brim, I smack the hat off his head. *"Fuck off!"* I snap, my voice cutting through the quiet night.

The group falls silent, the tension thick as I glare at Timmy. My fingers are trembling with rage—not just because of the hat, but because of everything. The danger he's put me in, the absolute disregard for my feelings, and the sheer idiocy of sitting at a picnic table with strangers at 3AM like it's happy hour.

He looks stunned for a moment, and then his expression shifts to one of indifference, like he's already dismissing my outburst.

I don't wait for him to speak. I turn on my heel and storm back toward the apartment, my heart pounding in my chest.

As I walk, I dial Phil's number to vent and let him know what his son is up to.

"Hello?" his mother's voice answers, soft and groggy.

"He's out at the meth tents at three in the morning," I say, my words sharp and clipped.

"Oh…" She pauses. "That's no good. He needs to grow up. Here, I'll put Phil on."

Before I can respond, a voice calls out from behind me. One of the men from the picnic bench is pedaling toward me on a bike.

"He's been sitting with us, telling us how you're his rock," the man says, as if that's supposed to make me feel better.

I stop and turn to face him. "Well, if I'm his fucking rock, why is he out here at 3AM, sitting at a park bench with strangers instead of being home?" My tone drips with sarcasm and frustration.

"Yeah, you're right," the man replies. "If I were with you, I would never leave you alone in the middle of the night. Your man should be spending time with you, not us. I would never treat you that way."

"Exactly," I snap, already exhausted by this unsolicited commentary.

The man circles his bike around me. "I have the day off, by the way," he adds.

"Good for you," I mutter, rolling my eyes and walking faster.

By now, Phil is on the line. "Did you hear that?" I ask.

"I did. What's going on?" he asks, his voice steady.

I take a deep breath and explain everything—the missing hours, the picnic bench, the company he's keeping.

"That's no good," Phil replies, his disappointment evident. "Put him on the phone."

"No, I walked away," I explain. "This is incredibly unsafe, and I'm going back to the apartment. I just wanted you to know what your son is doing, and that he's putting himself in danger."

"I see," he replies. "Let me give him a call and talk some sense into him."

"Good luck with that," I say.

Phil sighs. "Okay, well, thank you for letting me know. I'll see what I can do."

I hang up just as I reach the safety of the apartment complex. My heart is still racing, and my mind is spinning with everything that just happened.

I update Alice.

ME:

So I guess I have a date if I want it. 

(I don't) but Jesus.

His dad is going to call him.

But he didn't answer my 21 or so calls, so good luck to him.

ALICE:

This is such a fucking trip, girl.

And not healthy for you.

☹

ME:

I wanted to punch him in the face, but I just smacked his hat.

ALICE:

He knows he can do whatever he wants.

ME:

Not any more.

ALICE:

What are the consequences?

ME:

He can move out and live with his new friends.

I'm sure their tents are palatial.

ALICE:

You've said that before, friend.

Many times.

☹

ME:

I know. But he didn't leave all night before.

I check Find My iPhone, and see that Timmy has now migrated to the store. The store that isn't open. It's where a bunch of the drug users hang out at the bus stop at all hours. *What the hell is he playing at?*

Glancing at my phone, I'm reminded that I now have him saved as *Person Who Behaves Like a Loser and I Deserve Way Better.*

I send a screenshot to Alice:

ME:

You can see I'm trying to tell myself what to do by the way he's saved in my phone.

ALICE:

Yeah. But you need to actually do it.

ME:

You're right. There's no reason.

I'm just really annoyed and sad.

And I feel like I need to do something.

ALICE:

I know.

Inaction is the hardest action.

ME:

I'm not a violent person, but I wanted to punch his face so bad, but I went for the hat.

I told his dad I did that, and even he seemed on board.

ALICE:

If you must do something, coordinate with his parents to send him home.

ME:

Yeah that's a good idea

ALICE:

They've grown up with him. They know what he's like.

ME:

Yeah.

Previously, he's even said these tweakers are like, 'You should be home with her, not here with us.'

But he doesn't listen to me or them. What a fucking nutcase.

His therapy appointment is in 6 hours, and I'm meant to drive him to it.

How am I meant to concentrate on writing steamy romance novels with all this nonsense going on?

ALICE:

It's impossible. You need to find a way to make time for yourself.

———

By the time Timmy returns to the apartment, I'm waiting for him.

"You fucking left in the middle of the night and went to meth tents!" I yell the second he walks through the door.

"They're nice people," he shrugs, as if that excuses anything. "They're *way* nicer to me than you are."

"Oh, for fuck's sake!" I yell back. "Go enjoy your life in a tent with your fake friends from the beach, then! They're literally your only 'friends,' and it's because they don't even know you! Give them five minutes and they'll figure you out."

He stays calm, his demeanor infuriatingly composed. "See?" he says. "You're so fucking abusive. Listen to you. You're exactly like my ex."

I laugh bitterly. "Well, maybe she was sick of your bullshit, too!"

His composure cracks. He flinches, his expression hardening, and then he smirks, looking smug. "Wow," he whispers. "I see you. Here she is. The real Margaux."

"This is fucking insane," I say, throwing my hands in the air. "*You* are fucking insane!"

"That's it," he snaps. "I'm giving away the mattresses and the TV. I'm done."

"Fine," I reply, my voice flat. "I'll just go buy new ones. I don't need your hand-me-down shit, anyway."

He narrows his eyes. "None of your friends are real friends, by the way," he says. "They're just people you cover the tab for at bars."

I roll my eyes. "What the actual fuck, Timmy? You're the *only* person I cover the tab for at bars."

"You have such a drinking problem, Margaux," he says, ignoring me entirely and heading toward the fridge. "Hey, I'll let you keep the mattresses and the TV if you give me a hard seltzer."

The irony of his accusations contrasted with his actions is not lost on me.

"I don't want your things, Timmy," I say, exasperated. "I don't care what you do with them. And you're not having a seltzer."

He glares at me for a moment before retreating to the back room.

I think it's over until he suddenly bursts into the hallway, sprints to the fridge, grabs a hard seltzer, and runs back to the room, slamming the door behind him and locking it.

"Stealing a seltzer that I paid for with my life savings is more *loser behavior!"* I yell through the door.

"Fuck you!" he screams back.

ME:

He just came out and STOLE a SELTZER 💩

ALICE:

Seltzer?

At least make it something worth it.

Grab some Jim Beam.

ME:

I can't stop calling him a loser, because he won't stop acting like one.

Ugh. And comparing me to his ex the way he did.

Some of the things she told me she did weren't okay.

But I'm sure she was sick of his nonsense at some point.

ALICE:

Probably. People do drastic things when pushed to drastic limits.

ME:

Yeah. Ffs I live in Sunset Cay!! I can see the ocean from my room. This should be FUN!! I'm going to ignore his bullshit and be my normal self.

I'm entering my delulu phase.

ALICE:

I think that's where you've been, honestly.

ME:

Yeah. Maybe I'm un-deluluing.

ALICE:

I hope so!

I glance at my phone again, his name still saved as *Person Who Behaves Like a Loser and I Deserve Way Better*.

It's time to start believing that.

CHAPTER 51
BE HR

MARGAUX

Your eyes change to little black beads.
A shadow falls across your face.
The kindness has faded.
I don't recognize you anymore.

All I know is your rage is directed at me.
You are large and I am small.
I feel the hatred emanating from your body.
And I know it existed before we met.

Little impulse control.
Dysregulation.
Projecting your behaviors onto me.

You're the one with no drivers license...
so you tell people I drive blackout drunk.
You're the one who seven individuals filed restraining
orders against...

YET YOU SAY I'M THE PROBLEM BECAUSE I'M—'TOO CONTROLLING'.

IF CONTROL IS SETTING BOUNDARIES TO PROTECT MY SPACE AND MY PEACE...

IF CONTROL IS EXPECTING MY PARTNER TO:

- GET OUT OF BED IN THE MORNING
- PROVIDE FOR US
- FOLLOW THROUGH ON HIS WORD
- BE HONEST

THEN I'M GUILTY AS CHARGED—CONTROLLING AF.

LOCK ME UP AND THROW AWAY THE KEY AND LEAVE ME ALONE, CONTROLLY McCONTROLLERSON.

I WEAR THE TITLE WITH PRIDE.

———

I talk to people when he's not watching. Not because there's anything wrong with what I'm saying, but because I know he'll twist it. He reads malice into the most benign interactions, like I'm a puppet master orchestrating some grand betrayal behind his back.

Unlike him, these aren't people I slept with right before meeting him—hell, I hadn't slept with anyone for *five years* before we met. These are female friends, gay male friends—*his family*. But that doesn't matter to him.

He only wants me for himself. He has to be my everything.

It's suffocating, especially since the standard he sets for me doesn't apply to him. Sure, he blocked that clingy girl, but I'm not stupid. Social media leaves a thousand doors open. And don't even get me started on 'deleting' contacts—they live forever in the cloud.

It doesn't stop there. He interprets my every move as a slight against him.

If I wake up, it's to annoy him, because he doesn't want to be up.

If I cook, it's to spite him by leaving a mess in the kitchen.

If I watch TV, it's to intentionally piss him off with the content.

He makes it sound like I'm calculated, scheming, trying to get one over on him.

In his mind, I'm a villain, scheming to undermine him at every turn.

But that's not who I am. It's never been who I am. Even my worst exes didn't accuse me of this kind of manipulation.

The way he describes me makes me feel like he's twisting me into a mirror of himself. And worst of all, I know people will believe him. He's too charming when he wants to be, too good at glossing over the details and weaving a narrative that paints him as the victim.

This has to stop.

————

"You were so cruel to me," Timmy says, his tone dripping with self-pity. "Calling me a loser."

I look down, ashamed. "I'm sorry. That was mean of me. But I do think you need to do better."

"You really need to choose your words and think about how you respond to things," he says, condescension practically oozing from his pores. "You've done HR. You need to be more HR."

My jaw drops.

Did he really just say that?

"Excuse me?" I say, my voice low, trying to keep a lid on my temper—but it's really fucking hard right now. I'm about to lose my shit if he's saying what I think he is. "What did you just say?"

"Well," he says smugly, "you must be professional at work, especially in HR. And you should do that now."

Oh. Hell. No.

"You want me to apply my *HR skills* to our *relationship*?" My voice is rising, and I don't care. "*Are you fucking kidding me?* Do you know how absurd that sounds? If I were applying HR policies, I'd have fired you on day one! Serious misconduct! Assaulting another employee! Misrepresentation of facts! Lying on your resumé! Zero tolerance! Investigation complete—termination with no severance!"

He blinks at me, confused. "I just meant you should be professional and calm."

"*When you're poking at me, insulting me, criticizing and screaming at me, I'm supposed to stay calm and take it?*" I yell.

"Jesus, you're sooo dramatic." He rolls his eyes, his indifference like gasoline on my fire.

My whole body is tingling, my pulse pounding in my temples. For a moment, I wonder if this is what will kill me—an aneurysm brought on by Timmy's bullshit.

CHAPTER 52

TIMMY'S TOOLS OF TERROR: CHAINSAW MASSACRE - THE SEQUEL

MARGAUX

THE NEXT DAY

The sound of my phone buzzing breaks the tense silence in the apartment. I glance down at the screen. It's a message from my friend, David.

DAVID:
Have you been surfing yet?

ME:
No.

DAVID:
Isn't your fiancé like a surfer? Isn't that his whole thing?

ME:
Well, he says he is. But I've never seen him surf before.

DAVID:
Oh my god. The guy can't surf. I knew it.

I laugh at David's playful jab, but his words stick with me. Timmy has always branded himself as the quintessential laid-back surfer dude—board shorts, sun-bleached hair, and endless tales of catching waves. But after months together, I've never seen him even touch a surfboard. It's just another crack in the carefully constructed image he's tried to sell me.

My thoughts are interrupted by the sound of Timmy rummaging in the back room. A chill runs through me—that sound usually means trouble. Moments later, he emerges, and my blood runs cold. He's holding his yellow-and-black chainsaw—the one he's always bragged about, the one he polishes like a trophy.

My chest tightens. *Not again.*

"I'm going to chop your head off with this fucking chainsaw!" he screams, his voice full of venom, his face twisted with rage. "Fuck you, you dumb bitch!"

The room seems to shrink, the air thick with terror. He's not just holding it like he did last time—he's gripping it with both hands, his knuckles white, like he might actually switch it on.

Though it's not running, the sight of it—the jagged teeth, the weight of it in his hands—is enough to send me spiraling into panic.

My body reacts before my brain can process, and I fold into myself, curling into a fetal position on the bed. My fingers tremble as I dial 911. My heart pounds so loudly I can barely hear the operator's voice when she answers. "I need help," I stammer. "My fiancé just threatened me with a chainsaw."

"Is he actively trying to harm you right now?" the operator asks, her voice calm and methodical.

"No," I whisper, glancing up to see Timmy standing there, his chest heaving. "But he's holding it." I pause. "Timmy, put the fucking chainsaw down!" I manage to shout, my voice trembling.

He doesn't respond immediately, just stands there breathing heavily, his grip still tight around the handle. Finally, he throws the chainsaw down halfway down the hall with a loud clatter, muttering something under his breath as he retreats outside.

I sit there frozen, trying to make sense of what just happened. And trying to process that it's not the first time my fiancé has threatened to decapitate me with his chainsaw.

———

The cops arrive about twenty minutes later. Two officers step inside, their eyes scanning the small apartment. One of them pauses as his gaze lands on the chainsaw lying ominously in the hallway.

"Is it normal for your partner to threaten to chop your head off with a chainsaw?" I ask, my voice barely above a whisper, pointing toward the weapon.

The officer's brow furrows, and his face hardens. "Uh, no, miss. I'd say that's quite abnormal."

I don't know why I ask him that, but it's like my brain is trying to process that this isn't okay, but it can't quite get there. Timmy has spent so long convincing me that his behavior is normal—that I'm the problem and he's the victim—that I've started to believe him. I've been gaslit into questioning my own reality.. So I need some external professional to tell me that, in his experience, having your partner threaten to decapitate you with a high-powered, scary tool is not okay.

But the officer's words cut through the fog. It shouldn't be a revelation, but it is.

I want to scream. I've been upset by plenty of people in my life—family, friends, strangers—and never once has it crossed my mind to threaten them with a fucking chainsaw.

"This isn't the Texas Chainsaw Massacre," I say out loud, mostly to myself. "This is my life."

The officer nods solemnly, his expression softening. "You're right. And this isn't okay. You don't deserve to live like this."

Hearing him validate my feelings makes something inside me crack. It's not a relief exactly, but it's a start. A tiny pinprick of light in the suffocating darkness.

The other officer takes my statement while the first examines the chainsaw. "He didn't turn it on," I explain, as if that somehow makes it less horrifying.

"Doesn't matter," the officer replies. "The threat alone is enough. You're not safe here."

I want to believe him. I want to pack my things and leave, but something inside me keeps me tethered to this nightmare. Fear? Hope? Denial? I don't even know anymore.

———

Timmy is eerily calm when he returns to the apartment after the cops leave, acting like nothing happened. He picks up the chainsaw from the hall and takes it to the back room.

"See?" he says, as if to prove some invisible point. "I didn't even turn it on."

My jaw drops. "You *threatened* me with it, Timmy. Do you not understand how insane that is?"

He shrugs. "You're so dramatic."

I can't even form words. I turn and walk out of the apartment, my heart racing again. Outside, the cool night air hits my face, but it does little to calm me.

I text Alice:

ME:

He threatened me with a chainsaw again.

ALICE:

WHAT THE FUCK.

ME:

Cops came. They said it's abnormal, in case that wasn't clear.

ALICE:

He's beyond abnormal. Please tell me you're leaving.

I stare at her message, my thumb hovering over the keyboard. The truth is, I don't know what to say. I want to leave. I want to pack my bags and never look back. I want to tell her that I've finally had enough, and that I mean it this time. But something about Timmy still has its claws in me, and I hate myself for it.

ME:

I'm not sure yet.

Because I'm not. And that's what terrifies me the most.

As I hit send, tears blur my vision. I feel like I'm drowning, caught in a current I can't escape. And the worst part? I'm starting to think I've forgotten how to swim.

CHAPTER 53
DOMESTIC KLEPTOMANIA

MARGAUX

TWO DAYS LATER

ME:

Ahaha. You were right. You usually are.

ALICE:

What about?

I mean, I like being right.

ME:

You know what.

ALICE:

Not yet.

ME:

There was a day of greatness.

And then he got all mad, bc I saw on his phone he had a bunch of local women doing porn. And it turned out he handed his phone to some local teen. But also looked up if I was on there.

And found anyone who looked like me bc… as everyone knows, all I do out here is bang guys and also make sure it's on video WHAT (neither).

ALICE:

That's his mental illness talking.

ME:

Wild! With all my spare time to MAKE PORN… bc I drove off to get Thai food for half an hour yesterday.

ALICE:

With his diagnosis, it means he doesn't think like normal people.

I send her a picture of the cat from the Thai restaurant, and then a shot of the restaurant's front door.

ME:

I sent him this cat picture, and he accused me of being at someone's house banging them.

If so, their house has a passing health certificate, lol.

ALICE:

He cannot be reasoned with.

ME:

I know. He had a moment of clarity where he was like, 'Everything you said was right and I shouldn't have said/done xyz,' and then reverted.

In happier news, did you hear Pete Davidson is going to guest host SNL this week?! Tomorrow, I guess!

Somehow, I find the energy to write. I channel the emotions I'm feeling for a very particular scene that seems fitting.

ME:

I just had to write a brutal torture scene for my book. If someone looks up my google searches, they're going to think I'm a right psycho. I tried to add 'for book' and 'writing' in my searches.

That's what they all do.

———

TWO DAYS LATER

Timmy has been unusually quiet for most of the day. The kind of quiet that makes me suspicious rather than relieved.I should've known better than to let my guard down.

When he finally emerges from the back room, he moves quickly, pulling random items out of the kitchen. A frying pan, a bag of chips, and—what the hell—a bulk pack of string cheese from Costco. *My* string cheese. He doesn't say a word, just loads his arms and walks out the door, leaving it to swoosh and beep behind him.

I sit there, stunned. *What the fuck?*

An hour later, he returns, grabs more items, and disappears again. It's like watching a bizarre game of domestic kleptomania.

ME:

It might shock you to know…

I don't want it to be, but part of me wishes my brain was like his, so I could just feel like everything was okay.

By the time he returns a third time, I've gone from confused to enraged.

He heads straight for the shower. My phone buzzes. It's a text from Timmy, from the bathroom:

TIMMY:

You want to get in… on this bubble bath?

I stare at the message for a long moment, my disbelief turning to laughter. Bubble bath? After swiping my string cheese and half the kitchen? Is this some kind of joke? My thumbs fly across the screen.

ME:

No. I'm downloading dating apps so I can be away from you, you sad fuck.

I screenshot the exchange and send it to Alice.

ALICE:

This is your life with him. ☹

ME:

Yep. I'm basically done.

ALICE:

Is this what you want?

ME:

No. It's lame. I hate it. I hear you.

Timmy's voice carries from the bathroom. "I'm too scared to come out of the bathroom. I'm scared you might hurt me!"

I roll my eyes so hard I'm surprised they don't get stuck.

I tell Alice about the prior cockroach incident, when Timmy threw one at me and I scratched his arm in retaliation.

ME:

Girl got to defend herself.

I also realize I shouldn't need to.

Omg I can't wait to hang out and just feel relaxed.

And it's true. I can't remember the last time I wasn't on eggshells, constantly trying to avoid upsetting Timmy, or when I hadn't given up entirely and matched his madness with my own.

ME:

I'm going to get a therapy evaluation to see what's going on with me.

ALICE:

Good.

I worry about you. And him throwing shit at you.

ME:

Yeah, who throws a cockroach?! 😳

Speaking of which, there's a vent in our bathroom that big cockroaches can get through. He'd sealed it up with mesh.

But apparently when he had a bubble bath the other night, he opened the vent up 'because it was steamy' and they came crawling in.

The image is disgusting enough to make me gag, but it's also infuriating.

I'd spent weeks clearing out the infestation when we first moved in. Now the roaches are back with a vengeance, invading every corner of the apartment. They're in the silverware drawer, crawling over the plates, even hiding inside my espresso machine. Every time I open it, one scuttles out like it owns the place.

It took me ages to get rid of them the first time, and then Timmy just goes and opens up the vent and lets a bunch more back in.

ALICE:

That's so gross.

OMFG ewwwww.

I fucking hate bugs!!

ME:

Me too, especially if they are large.

And Timmy knows it.

The cockroach situation is just the latest in Timmy's campaign of chaos. It's like he's discovered a whole new way to torment me.

Determined to regain some semblance of control, I put on my flip-flops and walk out to the rock pools in front of the building. The salty air and crashing waves help to clear my head.

By the time I return to the apartment, I've made a decision—I'm signing up for roller derby.

ME:

In other news, I'm going to start doing roller derby here soon.

ALICE:

Good! It'll be good for you to have friends there in
person.

I can't come in the middle of the night and help.

She's right again. I've relied on Alice for so much remote emotional
support, but there's only so much she can do from miles away. It's time to
reclaim my life.

I'm isolated, and I've come to realize that's just the way Timmy wants it.

But he can keep his bubble baths and cockroach vents. I'm going to build
something better—starting now.

CHAPTER 54

HOUSE OF PLENTY (OF COCKROACHES)

MARGAUX

Timmy huffs from the other side of the bed, his arms crossed like a petulant child as he watches my fingers fly across the keyboard. "All you do all day is sit and watch TV and talk to your friends."

I quirk a brow, incredulous. "Oh yeah? Funny, I thought I didn't have any friends."

He doesn't miss a beat, his tone sharp. "You don't even want to go swimming."

"You're right," I reply coolly. "I've hardly been swimming in six months, even though I live right on the beach. Want to know why? Because I've been so depressed from dealing with your behavior."

His jaw tightens, and for a moment, there's silence. Then, in a voice tinged with self-pity, he asks, "What am I meant to do?"

"Oh, I don't know," I shoot back, my frustration bubbling over. "Maybe work and generate an income? You're a grown-ass man. A physically capable, creatively talented, two-hundred-pound grown-ass man. So do something with that."

"What the fuck ever," he mumbles, shaking his head as he stomps to the fridge. He grabs random items—steak, mandarins, and a Gatorade. "I'm going to see Uncle," he tosses over his shoulder before slamming the door behind him.

When he comes back, I'm livid.

"Timmy," I snap. "You need to make sure things are good here first before you run off to seek adoration from people you barely know. I'm paying rent. You're not. And while it's nice of you to give away food to random people, that's one less meal for me."

"You scratched me the other day," he says, pointing to a faint pink mark on his torso.

"Well, maybe you shouldn't have given my antibiotic cream to some random guy," I shrug, unbothered.

"His finger was falling off!" he yells, defensive. *"I had to help!"*

"That's not your problem, bro," I reply, rolling my eyes. "Send him to the hospital."

"I'm a nice person," he protests. "I help people."

"Well," I counter, my voice cold, "maybe you should start acting like a man and stop acting like a baby."

———

ME:

Ugh. He just took a steak and mandarins and a Gatorade to our neighbor.

He's nice, but he needs to stop giving our shit away to make himself look good to other people.

ALICE:

Seriously. It isn't a house of plenty.

Need to make sure your own household is taken care of first.

I tell her about the anonymous messages outlining his behavior.

ALICE:

Girl. That is all red flags.

He does this to everyone.

If you kick him out for real, he'll find someone else.

It's what he does.

Timmy sits on the edge of the bed, his face twisted in frustration. "Why are you so mean to me?"

"Because I'm sick of you wasting my life savings because you're so lazy and refusing to get a job. And you don't seem to value anything I do. Go find another woman whose money you can absorb."

His lip trembles, and he begins to cry. "I can't take much more of your resentment," he whispers.

I update Alice.

ME:

He's crying because I told him the truth.

ALICE:

Resentment is built, not manifested.

ME:

I have so much. At so many people, and I wish I didn't.

And I didn't move here to develop more.

ALICE:

No. But if you keep him around, you will.

She has a good point.

I sigh and nod my head.

Which must aggravate Timmy, because he lunges for my phone, yanking it from my hands and scrolling through my messages.

"What are you looking for?" I ask, exasperated. "I'm not talking to any guys behind your back, and I'm only describing your behavior to my friends. What you're doing is invasive and gross."

He doesn't respond, but his face darkens as his eyes skim the messages between Alice and me.

Finally, I manage to grab my phone back.

ALICE:

There is no positive outcome to your relationship with him.

He will give you nothing, enrich no part of you, honor none of the things you ask, and will offer you no genuine respect.

A tear rolls down my cheek. Her words hit like a gut punch because they're true.

I know she's right.

But I just can't break away.

Not yet.

ME:

I love him.

ALICE:

It may be romantic, but love is NOT all you need.

Love is a good building material. You don't only need bricks to build a house.

ME:

I wish he did. That's my problem. I'm deluded.

ALICE:

You are. Because love is a powerful drug. It's what compels parents to lift cars off their children.

It's what blinds people to flaws.

It is a substance that blinds you as much as you want to be blinded.

If you are willing to see nothing, love will show you nothing.

It's how parents defend children who are bullies.

How partners stay with abusive people, or people who commit crimes.

The tears come harder now, flowing freely.

And her words are exactly what I need to hear.

ME:

Crying.

ALICE:

I'm sorry. I don't want to be the reason you're upset.

ME:

He is. You're not.

You're just helping me to see.

ALICE:

But I wish someone had told me that love isn't enough. That it's great, but you need more.

You need someone who can reliably pull the cart of life with you, not someone happy to let you carry the whole load.

ME:

I just feel so dumb.

ALICE:

You aren't dumb, you're hopeful.

Love and hope work together to make 2 halves of a pair of rose-colored glasses.

ME:

I was in a perfectly 'fine' relationship for 6 years and he was emotionally shut down and I never got to be me and we were not intimate ever.

And enough was enough, and I left and I moved here.

My friend was like, 'This is your moment—move wherever you want.'

ALICE:

And you did. Why waste another minute of building your paradise being held back?

ME:

And I move here. And I love it here. And then she deserted me the moment I said how Timmy behaves. I flew to Montana to attend her event and wasn't allowed to come.

ALICE:

I cannot even get into her weird thinking. But the original sentiment is right. You're in Sunset Cay.

I say call his parents and arrange his going home with them directly.

Have 1 of them come out and collect him.

ME:

I'm 99% sure he's going to grab my phone out of my hand again and I don't care.

And I agree with you.

ALICE:

He probably will.

It's been his habit.

Timmy comes back into the room, oblivious to the turmoil.

"You want something to eat?" he asks, as if the past half-hour hasn't happened.

"No," I reply, my voice distant.

He lingers, clearly uncomfortable with my silence. "I'm too scared to be around you," he finally says. "You might hurt me."

I scoff. "Yeah, Timmy—you're terrified of me. That's why you throw cockroaches at me and yell insults every other day."

ME:

I can't believe this is my life.

ALICE:

Call his parents and arrange for him to go home with them.

It's time.

ME:

You're right.

Alice doesn't need to say it again—I know this chapter of my life needs to end.

It's time to rebuild without Timmy holding me back.

CHAPTER 55
BITCH LIPS & BUBBLE BATHS

MARGAUX

"Fuck you, talking to your friends about me," sneers Timmy, pacing like a caged animal. His eyes dart to the TV, and without warning, he marches over. "I'm taking this away from you."

He reaches out, but the universe decides to intervene. A sharp *zap* jolts him as static electricity bites his hand, and he flinches back, muttering curses under his breath. I suppress a laugh—barely. It's the kind of karmic justice I don't even have to orchestrate.

Then I notice the front door. Open. *Again.*

"Fuck! You let Sabre out again?" My voice rises, laced with panic.

Timmy smirks, leaning against the wall like he has all the time in the world. "Oops."

Fucking asshole.

My pulse pounds as I drop to the floor, frantically scanning under the bed and in every possible hiding spot for Sabre. But then, as if on cue, the cat strolls in through the front door like a disgruntled teenager coming home past curfew.

I turn back to Timmy, my fury bubbling to the surface. *"Stop letting my teenage cat out of the apartment!"*

He throws his hands up in mock surrender. "I'm sorry, okay? It was a mistake."

"It's *always* a mistake, Timmy. Too little, too late. I'm sick of your shit."

"Whatever," he says, brushing me off. "I'm going to have a bubble bath to center myself."

I gape at him. "What are you, some namaste motherfucker now?"

But he's already gone, retreating to the bathroom like the sanctimonious jerk he is. The door closes, and soon the sound of running water fills the apartment. I exhale sharply, my fists clenching at my sides.

————

ME:

I told him I'm done.

Fuck this. I am done.

ALICE:

He can't keep losing your cat.

ME:

Sabre is over it and came back by himself.

Sabre is like 'fuck this, loser. I don't even want to run away.'

This is how dumb it is.

————

A while later, I hear the clinking of glass from the kitchen, followed by a heavy sigh. Turning around, I catch Timmy in the act of grabbing my bottle of gin.

"Fuck off, loser," I snap. "Go live in a tent with your loser friends. You can all be losers together."

Without missing a beat, he carries the bottle into the bathroom. Moments later, the shower turns on.

I grab my keys and slam the door on my way out, determined to reclaim some control over the chaos. Driving to the convenience store, the rain begins to pour. The truck fishtails wildly on the slick road, but I keep going, my grip tightening on the wheel.

ME:

> He was having a shower, and if I wasn't a decent human being, I'd have walked in there and punched his face in.

ALICE:

> Don't give violence unless it's in self defense. Just as a safety thing.

ME:

> Oh, I don't plan on it. I'm not a fan of doing time

> Not that I ever have had to… I don't intend on making it a thing.

> I did go and replace the bottle of gin he just stole from me.

> Because I'm proving a point—that I can go and buy something without PANHANDLING.

When I return, the apartment is eerily quiet. No Timmy, no sound of running water, just an unsettling emptiness.

ME:

> He's disappeared, but I'm not filing a missing person's report.

Another friend starts messaging me simultaneously. He can tell something's up.

I give him a brief rundown.

FRIEND:

> Jesus.

> Being nice isn't a requisite to not hurt other people.

He's right, too.

Wise friends, I have.

About an hour later, the front door swings open. Timmy walks in like he's just come back from saving the world.

Without saying a word, he heads straight to the bathroom and takes another shower—this one stretching on for forty-five minutes. When he finally emerges, his expression is grim.

"You're the one who always starts this, you know," he says, dripping water onto the floor. "You're such a toxic person."

ME:

He's saying it's me now.

ALICE:

And he always will.

I send her a gif that says *Look at the gaslight*.

Timmy starts calling everyone on Facebook that he went to high school with—in a desperate attempt to show he has friends, maybe? I don't know.

But it's very obvious that he hasn't spoken to any of these people in years and he has several very awkward, forced conversations.

I stare at him, not quite comprehending how my time in the Cay has unfolded. If I could go back and say *absolutely not* to his proposal—if I'd recognized that for the red flag I now see it so very clearly was—I wouldn't be in this predicament.

ME:

I was forced to be married five days after I turned sixteen, so that was swell.

And it's probably why I say yes to anyone who asks now.

Sorry I'm being demented. I just remembered I am very sad and angry.

———

THE NEXT DAY

Over the next five days, Timmy's behavior oscillates between absurd and insufferable.

"One time these girls were flashing their boobs at me..." Timmy starts, launching into a story I've heard at least five times.

"Shut the fuck up, Timmy," I interrupt, sighing heavily. "I don't need to hear you going on and on 24/7/365. And you've told me that story like 55 times. It was boring and stupid the first 54 times."

Timmy looks like I've physically slapped him with a wet fish. "I'm just sad because years ago, one of my grandparents died," he says, shifting gears abruptly.

"Okay," I reply, deadpan. "Well, my dad died. I was raped. And I'm a child of rape."

Timmy flinches. "Wow," he whispers.

He gets up and leaves.

"Bye-bye," I yell out, gleeful for the impending rare moment of silence.

ME:

I fill Alice in.

ME:

This girl is snapping.

Very constructive, I know 😒. But I don't care anymore.

An hour later, Timmy returns.

"I have low self-esteem," he says.

"Go away," I reply.

He heads to the back room and shuts the door behind him. "Fuck you, bitch lips!" I hear him call out.

ME:

Bitch lips is the new insult.

ALICE:

And this is your every day.

It's miserable. And stressful.

———

FIVE DAYS LATER

ME:

> Hey! I haven't been ignoring you. I've just been trying not to burden you, and have also been following along with your derby adventures!!

> Also, there have been less pickle runs, but I withheld at least two and figured you wouldn't miss them.

> Going to Pride tomorrow!! Excited to just be with people experiencing joy for being who they are! 

ALICE:

You're never bothering me.

ME:

> But yeah, I just wanted to check in and say I'm so proud of you! Derby looks amazing and you're crushing it.

ALICE:

Thank you! And don't worry about the pickle runs—I know you're dealing with a lot. I hope Pride brings you some joy. You deserve that.

ME:

> It's all I want. Just a few hours of peace and happiness surrounded by people who don't make me feel like I'm losing my mind.

ALICE:

Exactly. Take it all in, friend.

CHAPTER 56
A THOUSAND CUTS

DEX

Margaux sits on the couch, curled up with Sabre, staring at her phone like it holds the answers to every question she's too afraid to ask.

From the camera in the corner of the room, I can see her lips pressed into a thin line, her thumb swiping too fast for her to actually be doing anything. She's spiraling. And it's all because of him.

Timmy has locked himself in the back room once again, probably nursing his bruised ego, or coming up with another excuse for his latest stunt. My jaw clenches at the memory of Margaux's frantic messages to Alice earlier in the week.

He threatened me with a chainsaw. Called the cops. They said it's 'not normal.'

As if Alice didn't know.

As if *Margaux* didn't know.

Not normal. *That's one way to put it.*

I replay the footage of him pacing the hall with the chainsaw in hand, muttering nonsense under his breath, before tossing it aside. It's as if he's reenacting a scene from one of the slasher horrors he's so obsessed with—who the fuck threatens their partner with a fucking chainsaw? *Horrific.*

My hands ball into fists at the sight of Margaux curled on the bed, trying to make herself smaller. It's a miracle she hasn't shattered yet.

But she's close. Too close.

————

Through the feed from Timmy's laptop, I see him scrolling through Instagram. His fingers hover over the search bar before he types in a name I've seen before—Desperella's actual name. My jaw tightens. He's still keeping tabs on her. *Pathetic.*

And as for Thirstina Aguilera? Her profile picture is literally an attention-seeking bikini picture where she has her thighs splayed apart, as if she's actively inviting followers into her cervix. Gross.

I don't wait. With a few keystrokes, I redirect his connection to a fake login page I've set up. He tries to click on Budget Barbie's profile, but all he gets is an error message. *Good luck stalking, loser.*

Next, I plant a few choice files on his laptop. Nothing too obvious—just enough to catch Margaux's eye if she decides to snoop. Old photos with half-finished messages he never sent, and one particularly damning screenshot of a dating app profile he never deleted.

She needs to see the cracks.

She needs to understand he's not worth saving.

It's not like I'm making these things up from scratch—he created the content in the first place. Restoring his recently deleted messages and photos—and there are plenty, because he's a serial deleter—is evidence enough that he's not treating her right.

From her phone's camera, I watch as Margaux glances toward the back room. Her hand tightens on Sabre, and for a moment, she looks like she's about to scream. Instead, she unlocks her phone and starts typing.

Her texts to Alice appear on my screen in real time:

ME:

He's locked himself in the back room again.
Probably sulking. I'm so sick of this.

ALICE:

What happened this time?

ME:

Same old shit. Lies, gaslighting, throwing tantrums.

He told me earlier he's 'too scared' to come out
because 'I might hurt him'.

ALICE:

He said YOU might hurt HIM? The audacity.

Margaux's lips twist into a bitter smile as she reads Alice's reply.
She types back quickly:

ME:

I know, right? The irony is so thick I could cut it with that stupid chainsaw.

Her phone buzzes with an incoming message from Timmy:

TIMMY:

Can you bring me some ibuprofen? My head's killing me.

She glares at the screen. I watch as her fingers hover over the keyboard before she locks the phone and tosses it onto the couch. *Good. Don't give him the satisfaction.*

A few minutes later, the door to the back room creaks open, and Timmy steps out, scratching his head like he's just woken up. "What's for dinner?" he asks, as if the past few hours of silence weren't his doing.

Margaux doesn't look at him. "Figure it out yourself."

He snorts. "What's your problem now?"

From the laptop feed, I see her jaw tighten. "*You're* my problem, Timmy."

He raises an eyebrow, clearly caught off-guard. "What the hell does that mean?"

"It means I'm tired of this. Of *you*. Of *everything*."

His face twists into a sneer. "Oh, *you're* tired? That's rich, coming from someone who spends all day sitting on her ass."

I clench my teeth, fighting the urge to scream at the screen. If I were there, I'd knock that smug look right off his face.

Margaux stands, her voice steady but icy. "You're unbelievable. Get out of my face, Timmy."

———

Once Timmy retreats, I get to work. I log into his phone and adjust his Find My iPhone settings to show him spending hours at sketchy spots around town—the meth tents, the abandoned parking lot nearby, even the strip club down the road.

Margaux's been watching his location obsessively, trying to make sense of his chaos. This will give her plenty to think about.

I plant more breadcrumbs on his devices: fake messages from fake contacts, notifications from accounts he doesn't even have. Margaux needs to see it all—the lies, the deception, the sheer stupidity.

Every seed of doubt I plant is another crack in the foundation of their relationship. And when it finally collapses, I'll be there to pick up the pieces.

———

Later that night, Timmy passes out on the bed, leaving Margaux alone with her thoughts. She stares at the TV, but her eyes are unfocused. From the corner camera, I can see the exhaustion etched into her face, the weight of everything crushing her.

I type a message to her laptop:

ANONYMOUS:

You don't deserve this. You know that, right?

She freezes, her eyes darting to the screen. For a moment, she looks around the room, as if expecting to find someone there. Then, slowly, she types back:

MARGAUX:

Who is this?

I hesitate for a moment before responding:

ME:

Someone who cares.

Her fingers hover over the keyboard, trembling. She doesn't reply.

But she doesn't close the laptop, either.

It's a start.

And I'll do whatever it takes to keep that spark alive, even if it means dismantling Timmy's entire world from the shadows.

CHAPTER 57
BOILING POINT

MARGAUX

t's well into October, but because it's Sunset Cay, the weather hasn't really changed. Humidity still clings to me the moment I walk outside, pressing down on me like a gravity blanket. The sun sets a little earlier, but other than that the atmosphere is peak tropical vibes.

We head to downtown Sunset Cay for the annual Pride Parade. I'm excited, having gone to many parades when I lived back in DC. I even book a hotel so we can be responsible, enjoy ourselves, and not have to drive an hour back in the dark.

On the way there, I find a Pride playlist and blast it through the truck's speakers. I'm thrilled, because it's finally an event to look forward to, an occasion to feel positive about, an opportunity to be an ally and just *enjoy* something without all the drama or stress.

A friend of mine happens to be visiting from California for work, and we spend time with her and her friend, laughing and chatting and reminiscing about the old DC days. It's a moment of lightness, another eye in the unending storm.

But, while I'm excited to celebrate and have a good time, my mindset in general is miserable. I'm apprehensive, and can't help but think of our prior night out in Downtown, when Timmy threw an unprovoked tantrum and I ended up snoozing in the plants at a fancy hotel.

Later, the Pride event is fun, but the vibrant colors remind me of what's become my dull existence.

People's general frivolity reminds me of the darkness that's consuming me day by day.

Timmy's carefree exuberance serves as a stark reminder of how he usually treats me now.

So I drink way more than I should, because that's just what I do sometimes to cope. Not a healthy strategy, I know. But what are the other options, really? In my current headspace, there are none.

I get way too drunk, and stumble my way back to the hotel. At one point, I make friends with a comfortable-looking set of stairs, and Timmy has to get somebody to help me to get in an Uber.

But Timmy is drunk, too.

When we get back to our room, he's in a playful mood, and he's doing something in the hotel's mini-kitchen. I'm not sure what.

He brought snacks and supplies for making ramen with us, and after a few minutes I can smell the distinct umami aroma of one of his delicious broths.

I lie on my stomach on the bed, feet up in the air, scrolling through my phone while he putters about in the other room.

Suddenly, I feel his presence right behind me. "Ssss! You're hot!" he announces, and a scalding pain sears across my ass and my leg.

"What the fuck?!" I scream, leaping off the bed and running to the bathroom, tears springing to my eyes as the pain blossoms across my skin.

I turn the shower to cold and step under the stream, desperate to cool the burning sensation.

In the background, I hear him laughing. *Laughing.*

He finds it funny.

The man who just poured *boiling ramen water* on me is doubled over in laughter.

"Why did you do that?" I look out from the bathroom, my voice shaking with pain and disbelief. "That's insane!"

His laughter stops abruptly as his eyes narrow at the mention of the 'I' word, replaced by a chilling growl. "You're not supposed to live," he says, his words like ice water down my spine.

I'm too stunned to respond. I retreat to the bed, curling up with my knees to my chest, trembling.

He glares at me, his eyes devoid of remorse, before storming out of the room. The door slams behind him.

I grab my phone, my hands shaking as I type a message to Alice:

ME:

He just poured boiling water on me and ran off.

I'm not joking.

He said my ass was hot, poured water on it, and ran off.

ALICE:

OH MY GOD

Are you okay?!

Are you burned? You probably are!

I don't stop there. I text Phil, his father:

ME:

Your son just poured boiling hot water on me.

He is insane and needs serious help.

I screenshot the conversation and share it with Alice.

ME:

Just sent that to his dad.

Gotta do what you gotta do, yeah?

ALICE:

Yes.

You absolutely need him away from you.

Before a serious injury happens.

———

A FEW HOURS LATER

He comes back like nothing happened, his swagger infuriatingly intact.

"You poured boiling water on me," I say, my voice low and even. "It still hurts."

"No, I didn't," he snaps, his expression one of exaggerated disbelief. "Stop making things up. You're such a fucking liar."

The gaslighting is the final straw.

A white-hot fury boils up inside me, eclipsing the pain. Without thinking, I shove him off the bed. He lands with a loud thud, his shoulder slamming into the closet door.

"What the fuck was that for?!" he yells, scrambling to his feet.

"What do you think?" I fire back, my voice venomous.

"I didn't do anything," he insists, doubling down. "And by the way, I think I might jump off the balcony. I've been thinking about it."

I laugh, the sound bitter and sharp. "Don't let me stop you."

He glares at me, his face a mask of wounded indignation, before retreating to the kitchenette, muttering under his breath.

I sit on the bed, my body trembling with a mix of rage, pain, and disbelief. The absurdity of it all—the boiling water, the laughter, the gaslighting—feels like a twisted fever dream. This is my life now—absurd, horrifying, and teetering on the edge of chaos.

If this isn't romance, I don't know what is.

CHAPTER 58
MY HEAD KNOWS BUT MY HEART HASN'T CAUGHT UP YET

MARGAUX

The next morning, Timmy is still drunk. His face is flushed, his eyes bloodshot, but it's his smirk that sets my blood boiling.

I confront him, the memory of the boiling water still fresh, the sting on my skin a constant reminder of his actions.

"You poured boiling water on me," I say, my voice steady but laced with simmering anger. "It's not okay."

He rolls his eyes, as if I've accused him of something ridiculous. "I didn't do that," he scoffs. "You're making that up."

I stare at him, incredulous. "No, you did it. I even messaged Alice right after because I couldn't believe it."

He shrugs, his expression bored. "You were being a bitch," he mutters. "You probably deserved it."

"You weren't even mad when you did it, Timmy," I snap. "You thought it was hilarious. You were laughing."

"Didn't happen," he says flatly, refusing to meet my gaze. He grabs his keys and storms out of the room, leaving me in stunned silence.

I have to get out of here, I think to myself. *None of this is okay.*

The hotel room feels suffocating. The hum of traffic outside is the only sound, but it's deafening in its banality. I can't stay here.

I grab the truck keys and drive home, the familiar roads blurring as my thoughts race.

My phone buzzes.

TIMMY:

Where are you?

ME:

Home.

Almost immediately, my phone rings.

"You went all the way home without me?" he demands, his voice slurring, his tone hurt. "You didn't take me with you?"

"I didn't know where you were," I sigh. "You ran off again, Timmy. After promising you wouldn't."

"Can you please come and get me?" he begs. "I'm at the beach."

I rub my temples. "Can't you get an Uber?"

"I don't have any money," he says, his voice dripping with self-pity. "I can't believe you left me all the way out here by myself."

"You sound drunk," I reply, my patience wearing thin. "And there was no alcohol left in the hotel room. Where did you get it from?"

"Dad sent me money for alcohol," he admits, as if it's perfectly reasonable.

I blink. "He *what*? Why would he do that?" It doesn't sound accurate, and if he did, that would be mega-fucked up.

Timmy doesn't respond.

I exhale sharply. "Fine. I'll be there in an hour."

———

When I get to the beach where we agreed to meet, Timmy is nowhere to be found, and he's not answering phone calls or text messages.

I call his dad, who sounds annoyingly chipper. "Well, great news Margaux! I was speaking with him earlier, and he told me he's going to go work with Parker now. Really great he's going to be making some money and contributing. He sounds really excited about it."

I roll my eyes and use every grain of strength to not pull my hair out. "Phil! He gets *drunk* when he works with Parker! Don't you understand that?"

There's a pause. "Oh, well no, I didn't know that. That's no good."

"How did he get drunk this time, anyway?" I ask, my irritation barely contained. "He said you sent him money for alcohol."

"Oh no," Phil says, sounding confused. "He told me he needed money for soda."

I'm livid, and I almost slam on the brakes. Like… *what the fuck, dude?*

"You… sent your almost forty-year-old son money for… soda?" My voice drips with disbelief.

"Yeah," Phil replies. I can almost hear the shrug in his tone. "Well, I'll give him a call and tell him to come and meet you at the truck."

I shake my head. Blood pounds in my temples, and I hang up, seething.

I'm not sure what this guy is playing at.

And I'm also feeling quite outraged.

Because this 'father' is sending his grown son secret money while he knows a woman—me—is paying for the roof over his head and everything else in his life.

It feels like a double deception.

Surely, if his dad wants to contribute to his son's life, he would send the money directly to the person paying his son's rent, or he and his son would be transparent about this secret income.

What does his dad think—that I'm withholding soda from his son?

Make any of this make sense.

Given his son's alcohol addiction, Phil's not just making stupid decisions —the guy is literally playing with my life, placing his bet on a self-described man child who has demonstrated he's very capable of killing me, especially while under the influence.

He's enabling his son's behavior while I'm footing the bill for everything else.

And now I'm stuck cleaning up the mess.

If his son hurts me, Phil carries a certain liability.

For the 'man' he created and continues to support without any sense of accountability.

I'm starting to think that maybe the apple hasn't fallen far from the tree.

———

I eventually find Timmy, stumbling around and chatting up paramedics as they try to attend to someone. A beer can dangles from his hand.

"Timmy!" I call.

He waves goodbye to the paramedics and saunters over, hopping into the truck. "Hey, baby," he says with a grin. "Thanks for coming to get me."

"I was waiting for ages," I reply, frustrated. "Why were you talking to the paramedics?"

"They wanted to chat with me," he says breezily. "They were nice."

I roll my eyes and start driving.

As we pull onto a main road, two girls in bikinis walk by.

Timmy leers at one of them, a cruel grin spreading across his face as he glances back at me in slow motion, gauging my reaction.

"Timmy, stop being disgusting," I snap, smacking him on the arm.

But he doesn't stop. As we pull onto the freeway, he sticks his head out the window, reaching for the radio antenna.

"Timmy, get back in the truck!" I yell.

He laughs, his upper body dangling precariously out the window.

My heart pounds as I imagine the worst. I seriously think he's about to be decapitated by a passing vehicle.

When he bobs back inside, I see red. Panicking, I punch him in the head and yank his hair, forcing him to stay inside the vehicle. *"You're going to get yourself killed!"* I shout.

He retaliates by grabbing at my arm and thigh, trying to wrestle the steering wheel from my control.

"Stop it, Timmy!" I scream. *"You're going to make us crash!"*

I fumble for my phone and call Phil, while Timmy continues to grab at me.

"Hello?" Phil answers.

"He's grabbing at me while I'm driving!" I yell. *"He's sticking his head out the window. We're on the freeway. Please make him stop!"*

"Son, stop it!" Phil says sharply. "Margaux, hand him the phone."

"No fucking way," I snap. "He'll throw it out the window."

Timmy glares at me. "Fuck you for calling my dad," he spits. "You're trying to drive a wedge between me and my family."

"No," I say, my voice trembling. "That's not what I'm trying to do at all."

Yet again, Timmy's behavior has somehow become my fault.

And this whole situation is far too big for me to deal with alone.

CHAPTER 59
2AM CATWALK

MARGAUX

The door's beep jerks me awake. For a moment, I think I'm dreaming. Maybe Timmy is just fumbling his way back in from one of his late-night escapades. But when I see what's happening, my body goes cold, adrenaline surging through my veins.

He's got Sabre—my sweet, loyal cat, my family. He's put him in his harness and leash. Sabre's wide, confused eyes lock with mine, silently pleading. *What the hell is going on?*

"Oh my gosh, Timmy! What are you doing? Do *not* take him outside!" I plead, my voice shaking.

Timmy smirks, a twisted grin that makes my stomach churn. Without a word, he starts walking Sabre toward the door.

"No!" I bolt out of bed, the fastest I ever have in my life, my heart racing. "Timmy, *stop!* It's 2AM! He can't go outside in the dark!"

I'm panicking now, my voice high and frantic.

Sabre glances back at me, his movements tentative, unsure of what to do.

His trust in me—and maybe even in Timmy—is palpable, but his body language screams confusion and fear.

Timmy doesn't stop. He's already out the door, tugging Sabre along with him.

"Timmy, please! Don't do this!" I cry, rushing after him. I grab at Timmy's hand, gripping the leash tightly. "Give him to me!"

There is *no* way my drunk and goodness-knows-what-else fiancé is taking my teenage cat on a walk at 2AM over to the tents where people are doing and selling drugs.

There's no way he's taking him outside, *period*.

We've had this conversation before, and he's agreed that he'll never take Sabre outside in the dark. But when I said that, I meant right after the sun goes down. Never in my wildest nightmares did I dream he'd try to take him out at this hour.

I run to the door. "Please don't do this! It's 2AM! You know he can't go outside in the dark."

Timmy yanks Sabre further out the door.

"Relax," he says, his tone infuriatingly casual. "It's just a walk."

"No, it's not 'just a walk'!" My voice cracks, a sob rising in my throat. "It's the middle of the night! You can't take him out there—*it's not safe for him!*"

I panic.

I grab at Timmy's hand which is tightly secured around Sabre's leash, and I pull on it, attempting to yank the leash away from him.

Sabre lets out a small, distressed meow, caught in the middle of this chaotic tug-of-war.

My rage boils over.

"Let him go!" I shout, bending Timmy's fingers back, forcing him to release the leash.

"Ow! My fingers!" he yells, recoiling as if I've burned him. *"You bent them on purpose!"*

Suddenly, he shoves me. *Hard.*

I hit the cold tile floor with a jarring thud, pain shooting through my hip and neck. I curl into myself instinctively, clutching Sabre's leash close to my chest.

"What is wrong with you?" I gasp, my voice trembling.

Timmy's face contorts into an expression of mock hurt. *"You're abusive!"* he snaps, pointing at me like a prosecutor delivering a damning verdict. *"You hurt me! You're always hurting me!"*

My head spins. The audacity, the gaslighting—it's overwhelming.

"I was getting Sabre away from you because you were trying to take him outside in the middle of the night!"

He glares at me. "No. You were trying to hurt me. You hurt my fingers on purpose! I wasn't even doing anything wrong. You're *so* abusive."

I know that look on his face. It's the one he gets when he's planning something vindictive, something cruel.

Something *very bad for me.*

I can't take the risk. Not for me, and certainly not for Sabre.

I grab my phone and dial 911.

By the time the cops arrive, Timmy is long gone, having predictably retreated to the encampment across the way.

"You have an accent," one officer says. "What do you do for work?"

"Um… I write books," I reply.

"You should narrate your own audiobooks," he says. "I'm sure there are plenty of people who'd like to listen to you talk."

Another officer glances at me holding my neck, his expression a mixture of pity and exasperation. "Put some ice on it. That should help."

"We'll go have a word with him if we can find him," a third officer says. "It sounds like he could benefit from substance abuse counseling, by the way. But for now, stay inside. Rest. We'll tell him not to come back until morning."

———

Morning comes, and I can barely move. Every twist of my neck sends a sharp, shooting pain down my shoulder. My body feels like it's been through a warzone, and for a moment I think I might actually be paralyzed.

Timmy strolls back in, smug as ever. He sees me clutching my neck and raises an eyebrow. "You shouldn't have peeled my hands off the leash," he says matter-of-factly. "The cop told me that next time you do something like that, he's going to lock you up."

My jaw drops. "Are you *serious?*"

"You *assaulted* me," he says, his voice dripping with faux innocence. "That's what the cop said."

"What are you even *talking* about? Why would there be a next time? You shouldn't have been taking Sabre out in the middle of the night to begin with!" My voice wavers, but I push forward. "You know how dangerous it is out there, and here you are taking my teenage cat out for a walk at two o'clock in the morning to your friends in the meth tents. You could've gotten him *killed!*"

"Oh, relax," he scoffs, waving a dismissive hand. "I wasn't going to take him all the way over there. Just right outside our front door for a little walk."

"That makes *no* sense, Timmy!" I yell, my voice cracking. "Pets aren't allowed to be out there, even on a leash. You know that. We've already had complaints from the building about him being outside during the day, and now you think it's okay to take him out in the middle of the night? I've told you I don't want him outside in the dark."

He shrugs, his smirk infuriatingly fixed in place. "Well, you can't touch me if I do."

The words hit like a punch to the gut. "What am I supposed to do, then? Just watch you take him? Endanger him?"

"Basically," he says, crossing his arms.

I feel sick. My stomach churns at the thought of Sabre out there—vulnerable, confused, and completely at Timmy's mercy. What kind of person uses an innocent animal to manipulate someone? To *hurt* someone?

The smirk on Timmy's face is all the confirmation I need—this wasn't about Sabre.

This was about power.

About control.

About breaking me.

I get the feeling a lot of the people over at that beach park don't have much respect for human life—after all, someone was murdered there right before we moved and there's been more trouble since—so they're sure as hell not going to give a shit about a cat.

And other things could go wrong, too. Sabre could simply slip out of his harness. There are dogs around. There are definitely people doing weird things. A busy street.

Just *no*.

I scoop Sabre into my arms, holding him close as he nuzzles against my chest. His trust in me is unwavering, but I feel like I've failed him.

Timmy's cruelty knows no bounds, and now, it's not just me who's in danger—it's Sabre, too.

And now I'm back to feeling scared for my cat.

And for myself.

CHAPTER 60
SOMETIMES LIFE IS JUST DARK FOR NO REASON

MARGAUX

A few hours later, Alice checks in on me.

ALICE:

How did the rest of Pride play out?

ME:

The cops were just here bc I found him trying to take my cat outside at 2AM, so I peeled his fingers from the leash and he threw me to the floor, and I can barely move bc he injured my neck/back.

ALICE:

That's absolutely not okay, and highly concerning.

ME:

Yeah. Well, my friend Jimmy called and introduced me to his friend, and she's pretty cool. I think you'd like her. She's talking sense. And she says she is a stripper, but that she isn't very good at it, which is hilarious in my current state of sadness.

As if on cue, the moment the police left, my good friend Jimmy from DC called me. We have a weird connection, and he always seems to know when something's up.

He and his friend Vanya were having a late night art session, and when I filled them in, they'd been concerned and caring, and managed to make me laugh, even though it hurt my neck.

ALICE:

It's pretty funny.

But I'm worried. He's going to paralyze you.

ME:

Yeah, I'm worried about it too. I told his dad.

His dad didn't go through an entire military career to get calls about how his son is hanging out with homeless men at the beach.

When I'd called Phil, he'd been calm as usual. "Well, I'll give him a call and try to talk some sense into him," he'd said. It did strike me that he didn't really seem surprised or concerned, and he didn't really ask me about my neck.

ALICE:

Tell his dad to come get him.

My phone rings. It's Phil, calling me back.

"Hey Margaux, it's um, Phil," he says, the way boomers sometimes identify themselves on the phone, as if their name doesn't flash up when they call. This time, his voice is flat and hollow… dull. Defeated.

"Hi," I say, bracing myself for the update.

"Well, uh, listen… I just spoke with Timmy, and he says he wants to go back to the apartment and sleep in the back room and move his things out tomorrow."

"Okay. Thank you for the update."

"You're okay if he comes back to do that?"

I sigh. "Yeah, I guess. As long as he's calm and doesn't mess with any of my stuff. I can barely move because of what he did to my neck."

Phil sighs too. "Yeah, listen… I, uh… I'm really sorry this is happening. I hope you feel better soon. Love you."

"Love you," I reply. "Have a good night."

I fill Alice in.

ALICE:

That's what always happens.

Insist he collect his son.

ME:

His dad sounded destroyed.

ALICE:

I imagine he is. This is a lot for a parent.

But it's not your responsibility.

And he's an active danger to you.

ME:

Sitting here icing my injury.

A partner shouldn't inflict an injury.

Unless it's a good sex one, if that's what you're into.

See, I'm funny when I'm sad.

ALICE:

Yeah, consent needs to be involved.

And even if it is, it shouldn't be permanently damaging.

Timmy enters the apartment just as my phone starts ringing
It's Jimmy and Vanya calling again.
He glances over at me and heads straight to the back room as if scared off
by my phone's ringtone.

ME:

His dad sounded like he was dead.

It was very sad.

ALICE:

He's realizing he's raised a man who is a hazard to society.

And who may never be able to function normally in society.

ME:

Yeah, at least his meth addict sister only hurts herself.

ALICE:

Yeah, that's a lot to take in.

ME:

His sister told me he's a piece of shit.

ALICE:

Yeah, because he is.

ME:

The dad survived combat missions.

The mother had several miscarriages before having him.

So he's clearly meant to be on this earth, but why? When he acts like this? It sounds horrible, but why?

He literally almost paralyzed me because he's a drunken lunatic.

ALICE:

Precisely this.

ME:

He finally admitted to pouring ramen water on me.

ALICE:

Good.

He's choked you, hit you, poured boiling water on you, and thrown you to the ground several times.

ME:

Yes. When you put it like that…

ALICE:

When you boil it down, the soup stock isn't very good.

ME:

AND brought a chainsaw out at least twice and threatened to chop my head off with it.

ALICE:

NOPE.

FUCKING NO.

That's not a joke. That's an active threat.

ME:

Last time he did that, I asked the cops if that was normal behavior. And they said 'no miss, in fact, that's quite abnormal.'

ALICE:

Because it isn't.

ME:

Well, I've heard that he's done this before.

ALICE:

He absolutely has.

This isn't a starting point.

ME:

I got aggressive today, and he shrunk into himself until he got extra drunk.

ALICE:

You need to stay sober around him.

Alcohol can help you cope, but it won't help you run.

I fill her in on Timmy's antics on the way home from the beach.

ALICE:

Was there an active risk of his head coming off?
Serious question.

Or did you panic?

ME:

He was literally trying to grab the radio antenna.

And he was grabbing at me while I was driving on a busy freeway.

ALICE:

And that's going to get you killed, to be very blunt.

ME:

He's bringing out a dark side of me that I don't like. I
am a very nice person.

ALICE:

You sink to his level, he goes lower, you go lower,
until you're at the bottom of your own grave
wondering how it all went this way.

I sigh. *She's right.*

ME:

I know. Halsey has a song about it.

She says the warning signs can feel like butterflies.

ALICE:

Nervousness and excitement feel the same.

ME:

Yep. Good and bad anxious is all anxious.

Anyway, I hear you and I appreciate you. I just tried
to lie down, and it hurt too much, so I'm propped up
on a sex wedge.

CHAPTER 61
ALLERGIC TO PEACE

MARGAUX

The next couple of weeks are surprisingly uneventful. Or maybe my baseline for reasonable behavior has taken a nosedive.

I even manage to work out and swim, two things I find difficult to do when I'm depressed.

The fleeting peace is nice while it lasts. A mirage in a desert of chaos. But as I've learned with Timmy, tranquility is always temporary.

One evening, Timmy begs me to buy him alcohol and a cigarette, and after saying no many times, he finally wears me down. I don't have the energy to fight him anymore. "I promise I'll behave," he says. "You don't have to worry about me wanting to smoke cigarettes or running away. I promise I won't do those things. I know they upset you."

Returning from the store, he immediately opens the bottle of vodka and pours himself a glass.

I don't bother to say anything. Words feel futile.

Instead, I pour myself coffee, grab my laptop, and retreat to the bed to work. The book I'm writing is finally taking shape, and I'm determined not to let him derail me again.

A little later, we have a minor fight because he's not pleased with how I washed a Tupperware container, but then he calms down. He pours himself another hefty glass of vodka. He's already slurring and stumbling.

I glance at my watch. "Hey, we probably don't need to be pouring more vodka after midnight, babe."

"You don't even care about me," he accuses, his voice rising. "You just want me gone!"

"Timmy, you're drunk," I reply calmly. "Go take a nap. We can talk when you're sober."

He glares at me, his expression dark and volatile. "*You're* the problem," he spits. "You're *always* the problem."

I don't even flinch. I've heard this too many times. Instead, I walk back to the bed and flop down, my back leaning against the sex wedge that has become a makeshift headboard. I send a quick text to Alice:

ME:

The vodka is back. So is the nonsense.

ALICE:

It's like he's allergic to peace.

ME:

Yep. And I'm allergic to his bullshit.

ALICE:

What's your plan?

ME:

I don't know. I keep saying I'm done, but then he apologizes, and I fall for it.

ALICE:

That's because you're a good person. But you can't save him, Margaux.

I sigh, sinking further into the cushion behind me. She's right. *I know she's right.*

"Fuck you," he growls. "I'll have more if I want more."

I take a tiny sip of my own, the second for the day, maybe the third. They're small glasses, a couple of ounces at most, and this one has lasted me several hours.

"You've drunk more than half of this," he slurs, holding up the bottle. But that's simply not true. He's had half the bottle by himself, easily, and he's trying to say it was me.

By now, it's the wee hours of the morning. He starts cooking a steak, and next thing the smoke alarm is going off. The beeping is loud. "*Fuck!*" He screams. *"I've overcooked the steak!"*

"Oh my god," I hiss. "Turn the smoke alarm off and keep your voice down. It's after midnight! Security is going to come."

"You set the smoke alarm off earlier," he sneers.

"That was at lunchtime. That's not a big deal. But you can't be setting it off now! Eat something you don't have to cook!"

"Fuck you. I'm having a steak." He glares at me.

Eventually we go to sleep.

I wake up at 220AM and he's not in bed.

I sigh. Here we go again.

ME:

Where did you go?

TIMMY:

To get a cigarette.

I'll be back in 15 minutes.

ME:

Completely unacceptable.

You have the impulse control of a cockroach.

Fifteen minutes go by.
Then thirty.
Then an hour.

ME:

I'm exhausted, and you gaslight me about a plastic Tupperware not being up to your standards when I cooked breakfast and lunch for you that day, and did dishes, while trying to manage a book release, 12 TikTok accounts and a book tour.

I get frustrated when I'm trying to post and listen. But please tell me how I am so horrible. Please.

TIMMY:

Calm.

ME:

You do nothing.

TIMMY:

I'm gonna have one more smoke and come rub your
feet.

ME:

You won't touch my fucking feet.

Fuck you.

Never touch me again, you loser.

Sleep in the back room and make moves to get the
fuck out of my life.

I want him gone. I'm so exhausted.

I wish his parents would just fly him back to Montana so I can have some
peace.

Because he just won't leave.

I message Alice and fill her in.

ME:

Things were 'fine' up until this incident.

I don't have time for his nonsense. I have a book to
write.

ALICE:

🙁 You need to get away from him. He'll never
change.

He'll just push your boundaries until you don't
remember where they were.

ME:

You're probably right.

ALICE:

It's a pattern. He isn't learning where your
boundaries are. He's learning where HE can put
them.

ME:

That's true. I made it pretty clear earlier. So we
will see.

ALICE:

I don't want him to get comfortable with violence.
Which he seems to be already.

ME:

Yeah, me neither. He says he's not. I know one thing —it won't happen again.

ALICE:

Would you do something somewhat serious for me? Basically, I want to have you give me some of your personal info and his. And I will keep it until I do not hear from you, and then I will call the police and report you missing.

A chill runs down my spine.

ME:

Okay, I'm not going to go missing, though. I promise.

She sends me a screenshot:

I shiver, thinking back to the domestic violence advocate's stats around strangulation.

Surely he would never kill me, though. *Would he?*

There's no way I could be living with a murderer.

ME:

I know.

ALICE:

I love you, Margaux. But I don't trust you're in a safe situation right now.

So I'm scared for you.

I'd love to be wrong. But, in case I'm not, I'd like to be safe.

ME:

He's over at the tents again. In the middle of the night.

ALICE:

Yeah, this is a pattern. He's going to be like that forever.

ME:

I'm not okay with it. Clearly.

ALICE:

Good.

So what will YOU do?

ME:

Well. He asked me the other day if I would move on when he was doing his jail sentence for driving without a license (his sentencing is next Monday). And I said, 'No, but if you keep leaving at night I will move on.'

And here we are.

ALICE:

🙁 He's been doing it.

ME:

Yeah, this is the first time since we had the conversation.

He literally promised me yesterday he wouldn't do this, and then he had vodka and decided he couldn't sleep.

Ranted about how his ex used to 'make him lie there in the dark' and then ran off when I was asleep.

ALICE:

Promises from people without integrity are just statements without weight.

ME:

Yep. A waste of noise.

> I can only imagine he is passed out in the park or has possibly been stabbed. But I refuse to go looking for him in the dark this time. It's dangerous around here.

> If he isn't back when it's light, I will maybe drive down the street.

ALICE:

Yeah, do not go out. It seems like a bad place.

ME:

> Like I don't need to be in a relationship with someone who puts himself or me in that position.

ALICE:

Not at all.

You deserve someone who will be kind and make you feel safe.

ME:

> Totally.

> I'd call his dad, but I don't see the point at this juncture.

An hour later, Timmy arrives back at the apartment, giddy with excitement.

His board shorts are wet.

"Oh my gosh, that was so much fun! I just went night diving with some people I met on the beach."

"Fuck you, Timmy," I snap. "Get your shit out of the apartment in the morning. I'm done with you."

"Fine," he says. "I'll leave first thing."

THE NEXT MORNING

Timmy wakes up and acts like nothing is wrong. "Can you drive me to therapy, babe?" he asks.

I sigh. Maybe therapy can fix him, but I don't have high hopes.

"Fine," I say. "I'm still very upset with you. Make sure you talk to your therapist about what happened last night."

"I will," he says.

After his therapy session, he's very contrite.

"Did you talk to your therapist about going over to the tents?"

"Yeah," he says. "She said that it wasn't good or okay."

I nod. "And?"

"My behavior is completely inappropriate and I have a bad drinking problem, and my actions were really fucked up. I'm really, really sorry, Marg. I'll do better. I promise."

I sigh. Words are cheap, and with Timmy I'm beginning to learn they carry very little weight.

"I'm just really freaking out about maybe having to go to jail on Monday and I acted out. I'm sorry," he says. "I don't know how long I'm going to have to go for. It's just really messing with my head."

I get it to a point, but there's always some reason Timmy will use it as an excuse to act out.

"Let's go to Costco," he says. "It's food stamp day. Let's fill up the fridge with nice stuff."

So I drive us to Costco and we get all of our favorite things, filling the cart to the brim and then returning home where Timmy expertly Tetrises the groceries into the fridge and freezer. "We did real good!" he beams.

And so I ride another temporary Timmy high.

———

Monday arrives, and we drive to the courthouse in silence. Timmy is jittery, fidgeting with his phone and tapping his foot incessantly. He's terrified of going to jail, and for once, I feel a pang of sympathy for him.

As much as he's made my life miserable, the idea of him locked up is hard to stomach.

When he emerges from the courthouse an hour later, his face is lit with relief. "No jail time!" he exclaims, practically skipping toward the truck. "Just a fine!"

I force a smile. "That's good." I'm happy for him, but also slightly disappointed that I won't have any time away from him to process everything.

"It's amazing!" he beams. "This is a sign, Margaux—a sign that things are going to get better."

But deep down, I know better. This isn't a sign of improvement. It's a sign that he'll never take accountability. That he'll keep pushing boundaries, testing limits, and skating by without consequences.

He thinks he can get away with literally anything.

And I know, for that, I'm partially to blame.

As we drive home, Timmy chats about his plans for the future. How he's going to 'get his shit together,' start making art again, and be the man I deserve.

But I've heard it all before.

And as I watch the Sunset Cay skyline blur past, I wonder how many more chances I'll let him burn through before I finally stop letting him drag me down.

CHAPTER 62
DON'T F*CK WITH HER CAT

DEX

The Sunset Cay feed hums with quiet chaos, the static hum of Margaux's life playing out in real time. From the corner camera in the apartment, I watch her sitting on the bed, curled up with Sabre. She's scrolling through her phone like it's a magic eight ball that might give her answers she already knows but can't accept.

Her movements are erratic—sharp swipes, constant unlocking and locking of the screen. Sabre shifts, stretching his legs against her lap, his little face tilted up as if to comfort her. She doesn't notice.

Timmy's nowhere to be seen, but I know where he is. He's at the meth tents again. The phone tracker, the cameras, even a couple of social media posts from locals where my facial recognition software has picked him up in the background of their reels—it's all confirmed.

What I wouldn't give to put a permanent end to this circus.

Her texts to Alice flash up on my laptop screen. I should feel guilty for reading them, but guilt is a luxury I don't indulge in anymore. She's telling Alice about Timmy pouring boiling hot ramen water on her, and Alice—understandably—responds in shock, urging her to leave.

Margaux types back something about excuses and therapy, about how maybe Timmy's 'scared of his sentencing'. It's classic Margaux—rationalizing his behavior even when it's outright malicious. She's smart, she knows better, but there's something deep inside her, some crack that keeps her tethered to him.

I rub my jaw, my teeth grinding. It's like watching someone drowning but refusing to grab the life raft because they think they deserve the waves.

From the back camera feed, I see Timmy stumble into the room, drunk or high—probably both. He's slurring something about cigarettes, his wet board shorts leaving a trail on the tile floor.

Margaux glares at him but doesn't say a word. I can see it in her face—she's exhausted, completely worn down by his antics. Sabre jumps off her lap, trotting to the kitchen, where he stares up at Timmy, his ears pinned back.

If I didn't already hate the guy, his treatment of Sabre would be enough—manipulating him with showers of affection and treats one minute, putting him in danger the next.

Margaux's texts from earlier play in my head like a haunting refrain—he tried to take Sabre to the meth tents at 2AM.

Sabre almost certainly wouldn't have made it back.

And then he *shoved* Margaux to the ground. *She could have been paralyzed.*

I was ready to act then—to fly to the Cay, knock down the door, and rip him apart piece by piece.

But I know Margaux wouldn't have left, not yet. She's not ready.

If I took her out of this now, it would only end in her going back to him, and I'd lose my chance to truly free her.

Still, the temptation claws at me every day.

Timmy moves toward her now, his hand outstretched, like he's going to touch her shoulder.

Margaux flinches, and he freezes. *The audacity of him.*

He laughs, this sick, smug sound, then stumbles into the back room. The door slams shut.

Margaux slumps further into the bed, her phone in one hand, the other rubbing absently at her neck. I know she's in pain. I saw her fall, saw how she hit the tile.

The rage in me simmers, sharp and bright, but I force it down. She doesn't need a savior right now—she needs a mirror. She needs to see what he is, what he's doing to her.

I need to find additional ways to plant other seeds of doubt in her mind. It's not manipulation. It's truth dressed in sharper clothing.

He's behaved badly so many times, but she's brushed it all under the carpet, defending and justifying and rationalizing—I need to find a way to make her face it… before it's too late.

Her phone buzzes with a notification from Alice:

ALICE:

Are you okay?

Margaux stares at the screen for a long time before typing back.

MARGAUX:

I don't know. I feel so tired. Like I can't fight anymore.

I close my laptop, my fists clenched. She's breaking, and while that's necessary for her to leave, it's agony to witness. She doesn't know it yet, but she's on the edge of something monumental. The question is, will she take the leap, or will she let him pull her back into the abyss?

It's after midnight when the apartment finally goes quiet. I sit back, my eyes burning from hours of watching and waiting. Margaux is asleep, curled around Sabre like he's the only thing tethering her to sanity.

I open my phone and type out a message from an anonymous number I created weeks ago.

ANONYMOUS:

You don't deserve this. You're stronger than you think.

I watch as the message sends, wondering if it will land or if she'll dismiss it as some random spam. Either way, I'll keep watching, keep waiting. Because as much as I want to tear Timmy apart, Margaux has to make the first move.

Until then, I'll do what I can to chip away at his grip on her.

One crack at a time.

CHAPTER 63

IF YOU'RE HAVING A BAD DAY JUST CRANK SOME T SWIFT

MARGAUX

December arrives, but I'm not in a holiday mood.

The weather in Sunset Cay hasn't changed much—it's still humid and sticky, like a warm, oppressive blanket I can't shake off. The sun sets a little earlier now, but other than that, it's business as usual: tropical vibes on the outside, chaos on the inside.

Things haven't been awful lately, but they haven't been anywhere near good, either. I've been walking on eggshells, trying to keep Timmy calm enough that I can focus on my books.

Timmy's tantrums have become routine, their predictability as frustrating as their frequency. Each one derails my writing for days, and I can't keep letting that happen. But there's a small, dim light at the end of this tunnel— he managed to land a gig helping a condo renovator onsite. It's only twenty hours a week, but it gets him out of the apartment, giving me just enough breathing room to focus on my books.

Still, living with him feels like navigating a minefield. He's incapable of accepting even the gentlest feedback. "You're so mean to me," he whines whenever I bring up anything remotely constructive. And yet, he feels entitled to criticize me over the smallest things, like the way I put egg shells or citrus peels in the garbage disposal, or how I arrange the shower curtain.

I try to reason with him, my tone steady but strained. "I need to be able to talk to you about how I'm feeling without you flipping out or acting like you're being attacked. I feel like that's a basic requirement for a relationship. I only bring up things that really matter."

He frowns, but doesn't respond.

Instead, he pivots to what he thinks is a fun story.

"Oh my god, I was at work earlier and Dennis was telling me this story about how he was meant to be dying of cancer," he grins. "So he went overseas and told all these women about how he was dying. Dude got choke pussy because of it."

I scrunch up my face. "Ew, that's disgusting. Please tell me that's not how you speak with your workmates about women. And the fact you sound so excited about this upsets me."

A shadow passes across his face. "Fuck you, Margaux. You're such a fucking hypocrite. You write books about girls fucking four guys at once."

"They're *books*," I snap. "You're talking about your real-life coworker deceiving women for pity sex."

"Your books are about people being *whores*," he spits, venom dripping from every word.

"Excuse me? Grow the fuck up," I reply.

"All you do is tell me mean things," he pouts, his voice dipping into that insufferable victim tone.

"Maybe because you need to hear them," I reply coldly. "You need to change your atrocious behavior. You're a grown man acting like a spoiled child. *Fix it*."

He sighs dramatically, his demeanor softening as if to reel me back in. "I'm sorry. Can we reset? Can I put your drums together for you?"

I'm too drained to argue. "Fine. Whatever."

———

Later in the Day

Alice intuitively reaches out, her message lighting up my phone like a rescue flare:

ALICE:

What's going on, friend?

ME:

Douchebaggery.

ALICE:

What happened?

ME:

Just the usual.

ALICE:

🙁 Has he touched you lately?

ME:

No. He says he's stopped doing that.

He's just used verbally derogatory terms, and I just drove by him hanging out at a homeless tent and yelled that he's a lying user.

ALICE:

That's not a good and healthy relationship for you, babe. At all.

ME:

I know.

ALICE:

And you deserve someone wholesome and loving.

ME:

He ran off because I told him there's information available online about how he's a piece of shit.

ALICE:

Ugh. Exhausting.

ME:

The last wholesome relationship I had was for 6 years and we didn't have sex for 5, and I spent the whole 6 years apologizing for his weirdness.

ALICE:

You need an actually good person.

ME:

I'm going to walk over to dickhead and tell him.

ALICE

Is that a good idea?

ME:

You know what? I no longer know what is a good idea.

It's 154PM here, so better time than any.

ALICE:

Amazing how bad circumstances make all ideas seem good.

ME:

It's light outside. I'll take one of my books and if he's a dickhead, I'll throw it at his stupid head. 😅

If he's not, I'll give it to one of his meth buddies. Jesus.

I don't think he's actually doing meth, but he's smoking weed and drinking cheap vodka with homeless people and acting like they're better than me.

ALICE:

Yeah, he's spending time with unpredictable people.

Which isn't good for an unpredictable person.

ME:

Maybe I should just drive down the beach and watch the waves instead.

Or I will just reinforce his narrative that I'm a psycho, which I did by pulling a screeching U-turn and then slamming the accelerator like I was Vin Diesel in Too Fast Too Furious. Not even the original, one of the shitty sequels, bruh.

ALICE:

You're gonna hurt yourself!

ME:

He will see me go by and lose his shit, thinking that I'm going to go on a date once again.

ALICE:

This sounds awful.

What an awful way to have to live your life.

ME:

Yeah.

I agree. He's just dumb.

Like… he's smart in some ways, but really fucking dumb.

Says mean things.

Has stopped hurting me physically, and now says mean things instead.

He started a new medication yesterday that's meant to stop him from being such an asshole.

Oh, and I think he's panhandling again. Jesus Christ.

ALICE:

Seriously? Why?

ME:

Well, it said he was by the store.

So I imagine he was scrounging for Karkov and a Black and Mild.

———

Needing a break from the oppression of the apartment, I go for a drive.

I crank Taylor Swift and MGK as loud as the truck's speakers will allow. As I drive past a 'hot people' tent—not the meth tent, just a group of attractive people enjoying the day—I catch their attention. The crazed redhead in a camo truck, blasting music, probably looking as unhinged as I feel.

ME:

I am on a lovely drive cranking old school Taylor swift, and the hot people tent (not meth tent but fun hanging out day hot people tent) all turned and looked at the crazed redhead driving by in a camo truck. 🫠🩶

ALICE:

This feels like an NBC show.

ME:

But edgier. I'm cooler than King of Queens.

I can't make this shit up.

ALICE:

People will be disgusted anyone fucks him.

"Get her a cock attached to someone better!!!"

I crack up laughing at her unexpected comment.

ME:

Lol. I had to pull over bc you had me LOLing!

I'm literally going to go hand him his baby bottle on the way back if he's still there.

I send her a picture of the glass baby bottle I got him from the Asian grocery store. It had contained a Japanese milk beverage, and he'd become instantly obsessed over the childlike bottle.

I got it as a joke, but he's obsessed and calls it his 'baba'.

So now his 'friends' can see his baba.

I pass by Timmy's supposed location. Sure enough, he's there with his 'friends', laughing and carrying on like he's the life of the party.

I don't stop. I don't even slow down. Let him have his moment of delusion. Let him pretend these people care about him.

When I get back to the apartment, I'm met with the same suffocating reality—Timmy's chaotic presence, the weight of his words, the impossibility of building anything stable with him around.

I've always been hopeful. I've always believed people could change. But as the days stretch into months, that hope feels more and more like a cruel joke.

I glance at my phone, at Alice's latest message:

ALICE:

You deserve so much better.

And I do.

But for now, I'm still here, navigating this nightmare one chaotic day at a time.

CHAPTER 64
DOING THYME

MARGAUX

THE PAST

Boss: We're going to go to lunch at the restaurant onsite.

Me: At the prison?

Boss: Yep. The inmates are the chefs. Well-behaved ones.

Me: Umm, that's cool. Kind of. Are you sure the food is okay?

Boss: Yeah, it's actually pretty good. I just avoid the creamy sauces.

Me:...

Me: Oh wow. That's interesting. What's this place called?

Boss: Doing Thyme.

———

THE PRESENT

When I get home, Timmy is back.

"You need to grow up," I say, dropping my fanny pack on the nightstand.

He's sprawled on the bed, his arms stretched over the cushion headboard like he owns the place. "You tell me all these things that are mean," he pouts.

I roll my eyes. "Didn't you say everyone else in your life says mean things to you, too? It's not just me, Timmy. The issue is *you*. *Change*. I'm done with your ding-dong scenarios."

He's quiet for a beat, then sighs dramatically and gets up. Without a word, he drags a box into the living room and starts setting up the drum kit. It's mine, bought during a rare moment of indulgence. I've wanted one for years, and it was a steal during Black Friday sales.

I shoot a message to Alice:

ME:

He's putting the drums together, at least.

Maybe he can put his brain together tooooooo (petty mode HI).

ALICE:

OMG, why drums right now?

Are you sure he isn't doing meth? It's so unhinged and unpredictable.

ME:

Yeah, I've always wanted drums. They're mine. Got a good Black Friday deal.

ALICE.

Well, at least he did the thing?

Hooray for drums.

About an hour later, the drum kit is fully assembled, but Timmy has been drinking while putting it together. I'm about to try it out when Timmy grabs the drumsticks, mutters something incoherent, and bolts out of the apartment like a child who just stole candy.

I groan and flop onto the bed. "What the actual fuck?"

———

About thirty minutes later, I see him walk past the window outside, the drumsticks still in his hand. He notices me looking and starts running, as if we're in some absurd cartoon.

"Oh, hell no," I mutter, shoving my feet into my flip-flops and storming out after him.

I catch up to him near the pool, where he's casually swinging the sticks around like he's in a parade. It's a beautiful day as usual, so the pool area is packed, the loungers occupied by sunbathers and families enjoying the afternoon.

"Give me the sticks," I demand, snatching them from his hands. Out of sheer frustration, I lightly tap him on the shoulder with one of them. Not hard, and certainly nothing that would inflict pain—the way you might tap a toddler who put their hand on the stove. Certainly not beating him with them. "Grow the fuck up, Timmy."

"I saw that!" shrieks a nosy aunty from the side of the pool. "I am a witness! I'm telling security what I saw!"

Are you fucking kidding me?

Now I am the public 'abuser' for lightly tapping Timmy with the drumsticks that he ran outside with like a fucking child?

This is literally insane.

"Oh my god," I mutter, storming back to the apartment.

This day cannot get worse.

———

The rest of the afternoon descends into chaos. Timmy is in rare form, doing everything he can to get under my skin as if the aunty's verbal outpouring for support has emboldened him to push me further.

He criticizes the shows I watch, mocks the music I play, and holds his phone at an angle where I can see him fake-typing to imaginary women.

Finally, I snap. I lunge for his phone. "What the *hell* are you doing?"

We wrestle over the phone, a ridiculous pushing and shoving match that escalates quickly. "I'm calling the cops!" I yell, backing away from him. "This is insanity!"

But he's faster. He grabs his own phone and dials first.

———

The police arrive within minutes. Timmy runs outside to greet them, waving his arms dramatically.

More minutes go by.

"Police," a deep voice announces as there's a knock at the door.

I open it, wearing only a sports bra and short shorts. It's the same officer who chased Timmy over the fence the time I ended up with two black eyes—the one who arrested him when he found him eating ice cream at the 7-Eleven. "Hi," I say, already exhausted.

"We're taking you in," he says.

I blink. "What?"

"There's been an allegation of domestic violence made against you, and you're intoxicated. So we're taking you in."

"Domestic violence accusation—against *me*?" I repeat, dumbfounded.

"Yes, ma'am. He's saying you scratched him and pulled his hair," another officer says.

My eyes narrow. "Are you serious?"

"Turn around please, ma'am, and put your hands behind your back."

I roll my eyes and exhale sharply while I do as he instructed.

You have to be fucking kidding me.

He handcuffs me and—for some reason—let me keep my cell phone in my hands behind my back.

As they escort me to the car, I glance back and see Timmy smirking at me from a distance.

An officer helps me into the vehicle, protecting me from bumping my head.

As we pull away, Timmy continues to smirk.

I twist the cell phone awkwardly in my hands, and manage to dial Phil's number. He answers on the second ring. "Phil, please help me," I plead. "They've arrested me because Timmy said I attacked him. I didn't."

Phil sighs. "What in the world? How can we help?"

"I need to be bailed out," I explain. "This is ridiculous."

The officer turns around. "Hey, you can't be calling people on your cell phone while you're arrested."

I must look ridiculous, my arms twisted up like a demented pretzel. Calling the enabler parents of the man who *has* actually abused me, because that abusive man has had me arrested on false charges.

What the actual fuck.

"Oh sorry," I say to Phil. "Gotta go."

I hang up, shrugging. "Sorry, I don't know how this works."

"You'll have a chance to make a phone call from the station," the officer says. "But first, I'm taking you to the hospital to get checked out."

I lean back against the seat, the absurdity of the situation washing over me.

This is my life now—accused of domestic violence by the man who has actually abused me.

Yelled at by neighbors for lightly tapping a drumstick against a child in a man's body.

It's like a bad sitcom, except I'm the punchline.

CHAPTER 65
DEFENSIVE DRINKING

MARGAUX

make small talk with the police officer as he drives us to the nearby hospital. "Maybe I should become a COP," I say, attempting humor to cut through the tension.

"Well, you can't have any convictions to be one," he replies, glancing at me in the rear-view mirror. "But you're not going to get a conviction for this. The chances are very low."

I'm taken to a waiting room where another officer supervises me. We chat about his career, where he's lived, and I tell him about roller derby and my police officer uncle who passed away. The conversation feels oddly normal, almost like we're two strangers waiting for a delayed flight, not one of us being processed after an arrest.

Then I'm led into a sterile examination room, humming with the soft beeping of medical equipment. The air smells faintly of antiseptic. A doctor who looks a bit like Rick Moranis walks in, a flashlight strapped to his forehead.

He and his team perform various scans, and then I'm asked to provide a urine sample.

"So, you were drinking earlier? Why did you have so much to drink?" the doctor asks while adjusting his flashlight.

"Because my fiancé is abusive, and I wanted him to stop hurting me," I reply, the words tumbling out before I can second-guess them.

"Ah," says the doctor, nodding knowingly. "Defensive drinking."

"Yep!" I reply. "Exactly!"

Everyone in the room chuckles softly, breaking the tension. The doctor's expression softens as he leans in closer. "Open your mouth so I can take a look," he says.

Without thinking, I stick my tongue out and say, "Aaaah," like a kid in a pediatrician's office.

He cracks up laughing, as do the officers. "I literally just needed you to open your mouth," he says, wiping a tear from the corner of his eye.

I laugh too, my cheeks warm with embarrassment.

The humor fades as he reviews the scan results and frowns. He sits me down, seriousness creeping back into his voice. "Margaux, I've performed a scan of your skull, and you have a serious fracture that shows healing consistent with an injury from a few months ago."

Shock bolts through me. "He… fractured my skull? *Oh my God.*"

The doctor's eyes hold mine. "Yes," he says gently but firmly. He hands me a domestic violence pamphlet. "I'm going to provide you with some resources, but you really need to get out of this relationship."

I nod slowly, his words sinking in.

———

And then I'm in jail.

I still can't believe it. That he told the cops I attacked him. That he said I pulled his hair. That I'm here.

Because it's a domestic issue, and because we've both been drinking, the cops have decided to lock *me* up. Which is insane.

I've never had a criminal record. My only blemish is a speeding ticket from twenty-five years ago. And I don't go around attacking giant men.

First, I'm taken to a small local jail. The officer gives me a chance to make a phone call. I dial Timmy's dad and provide an update based on the information shared with me by the officer.

"I need someone to bail me out," I explain. "But the charge is so small—a petty misdemeanor—that bail is only $1,000. The bail bonds people won't be interested in helping me for that little of an amount."

"Well, how can I bail you out?" Phil asks.

"Someone has to come here in person," I reply.

"But…" Phil sputters, "I'm in Montana."

"I know," I say, my voice glum.

Then I'm taken to processing, still in my sports bra, short shorts, and no shoes.

Because my shorts have a drawstring that can't be removed, they swap me into paper shorts. And because I'm only in a sports bra, I also get a matching paper top.

Super sexy.

I'm led into a small room as another officer with a mustache passes by and heads into the watch house. Seeing me out of the corner of his eye, he reverses and looks me up and down. "Ohhh *hello…*" he says, leering.

I roll my eyes at the officer escorting me. "Well, your colleague is highly unprofessional," I say. "And can you please tell him that Movember has been and gone?"

The officer snickers but doesn't comment.

"Will I be in a cell with other people?" I ask.

"No, you'll be by yourself," he replies.

After waiting alone for a while, I'm escorted into a cold concrete hallway that echoes with the sound of the officer's shoes as he leads me to the cells. There doesn't seem to be anyone else locked up here. He gives me my choice of cells as well as a blanket. Very respectful. Great hospitality. *Five star Yelp review.*

I enter the cell, and the door clangs shut behind me.

I need to switch my brain off. My arrest. The news that Timmy fractured my skull.

It's all too much.

Oddly, I feel cozy—or maybe my brain really is just shutting down—and I drift off to sleep.

———

A while later, I'm woken up. "Benson," an officer says, "We're moving you to Downtown Sunset Cay. Get up."

Groggy, and unaware this would be happening, I comply.

They lead me to a waiting police cruiser, and I'm taken to the main downtown jail facility near the courthouse.

Here, there's a huge vibe shift.

Gone are the people who seemed a little more chill.

The atmosphere is cold, militant, no-nonsense. Male and female prisoners are segregated but near each other, and there's a lot of shrieking and hollering.

"Benson, you get one phone call," says an officer.

I try to dial my friend Rebecca, but there doesn't appear to be a ringtone, so I'm not sure if it's even going through. Either way, it's the middle of the night, and she doesn't answer.

Fuck. She's probably the only person who could bail me out, and now I've missed my chance.

I glance around at the officers. "Can I try another number?"

They shake their heads.

"Please?"

"No. Just calm down," one of them says, the rest of them nodding in agreement.

Jesus. They must all be fun at parties.

I'm directed to pick up a mat and a blanket, escorted to a cell, and the door clangs behind me as my eyes adjust from the bright hallway to the darkened cell.

And this time, I'm not alone.

CHAPTER 66
POLYNEEEESIA!!

MARGAUX

The cell is overcrowded. Built for two, it holds five of us.

The walls are stark, the concrete cold underfoot. The temperature hovers somewhere between chilly and unbearable, but the discomfort barely registers next to the tension coiling in my gut.

Roaches scuttle across the floor—fat, confident creatures that seem to thrive in this confined hell. Two women have claimed the narrow bed platforms, while the rest of us are left to find spots on the floor with our flimsy mats and thin blankets.

I'm super stylish in my paper shorts and top, no shoes. And I don't want to think about what substances might be on the floor.

The cellmates are a mixed bag. The white woman, who calls herself Moonracer, is tweaking, her hands twitching as she mumbles to herself. The other three are Polynesian women with an air of seasoned resilience. They've been through this before.

I'm the outsider here, and I know it. My ginger hair and pale skin might as well be neon signs flashing 'not one of us'.

There's a metal toilet and sink, just like I've seen on TV. It's weird, seeing jail in person. I mean, I had an idea of what it would be like from binge-watching *60 Days In, Love During Lockup, Orange is the New Black*, and various other TV shows and movies, but actually being in a cell hits different.

In any case, I'm intimidated. Scared.

"Do you know when we'll be let out?" I ask, my voice hesitant.

The obvious leader of the group, a broad-shouldered woman with tattoos winding up her arms, sizes me up. Her dark eyes narrow slightly before she responds. "Court's in the morning. The judge will decide. What're you in for?"

I hesitate, but decide to tell the truth. "Domestic abuse. The guy who fractured my skull called the cops on me and said I pulled his hair."

Her eyebrows shoot up. "Jesus. Are you still with him?"

"No," I reply quickly. "I mean, the skull fracture happened months ago. I didn't even know about it until the hospital scanned me on the way here. But this… this changes everything. It has to."

Her expression softens, but only slightly. "Wait. You've got an accent. Where're you from?"

"New Zealand," I say, the words tasting foreign on my tongue in this place.

Her face lights up. "Oh my gosh—*POLYNESIAAAA!* She's *POLYNEEESSIIAAAAAN!!!*"

Relief washes over me as the tension in the cell shifts. I've passed some invisible test— been granted inclusion into this unlikely sisterhood. *Thank fucking god.*

The women introduce themselves. The leader is Malia, here for assault. The two other Polynesian women, Leilani and Tia, nod in solidarity. Moonracer mutters something incomprehensible, still lost in her drug-fueled haze. Their stories spill out in bits and pieces, mostly violence-related offenses. I'm grateful that none of their charges involve anything more sinister.

Every so often, someone farts or burps, but in the peculiar politeness of our cell, each is followed by a murmured apology. The juxtaposition is surreal.

Somewhere down the hall, a woman's unhinged shrieking echoes, clearly in some kind of drug-induced psychosis. I'm relieved she's not sharing this cell.

We're given peanut butter and jelly sandwiches. The bread is stale, the jelly sickly sweet, and I'm not hungry, anyway. I set mine aside.

Later, I watch as Malia grins, calls to an officer as they pass by, and actually gets him to bring us more sad sandwiches. It's bizarre, almost funny, this tiny kindness in a bleak space.

Eventually, the lights dim. It takes forever for sleep to claim me, but exhaustion wins.

"My husband's in one of the other cells," says Malia, peeking out the window. "Oooh, some guys are coming past. Heyyy!" she hollers, and I can't help but laugh. That's what I call making the most of a bad situation.

I wake to a sharp nudge. *"Move!"* snaps Leilani as I realize I've rolled onto her mat in my sleep. "Oh shit! Sorry!" I say, scrambling back to my own space.

Somehow, I manage to sleep through the rest of the night.

In the morning, the officers come to shackle us together for transport. The cold bite of metal around my ankles feels surreal, like I've stepped into a nightmare.

We're led out in a chain gang to the transport van, passing the still-shrieking woman. One of the guards mentions she's a regular, high on whatever she can get her hands on every couple of weeks. Thankfully, she's locked into her own separate compartment in the transport van, a thin metal wall separating her from the rest of us. She pounds the walls, her screams grating. One of the other women yells back, "Shut the fuck up, you crazy bitch!" followed by a few death threats.

When we reach the courthouse, we're herded into a larger cell. The dynamic changes as new women join us, including another tweaking girl and an older lady with a quiet intensity about her.

At one point, a cockroach the size of my palm skitters across the floor. I shriek and jump back, finding an unlikely ally in one of the tweaking girls as we huddle in mutual disgust.

More stale peanut butter and jelly sandwiches arrive, and I force myself to eat this time, knowing I need strength for whatever comes next.

Hours crawl by, before I'm taken to a smaller holding cell with Leilani. We exchange small talk to pass the time, but the anxiety hangs heavy.

Finally, I'm led to a consultation with a public defender. She's efficient but detached, explaining the process and letting me know she'll be entering a not guilty plea on my behalf.

Then it's my turn before the judge.

The courtroom is sterile, all hard edges and glaring lights. The judge glances over my file, listens to the public defender, and grants my release on my own recognizance.

Relief floods me as I'm told I'm free to go. I visit the property desk where

I'm handed my belongings, and then I step out into the fresh air of downtown Sunset Cay, still dressed in my jail-issued paper attire.

I call an Uber and strip off the paper outfit, pulling on my shorts before discarding my jail-wear in a nearby trash can.

When he arrives, the Uber driver glances at me curiously but says nothing.

As I sit in the back seat, I message Alice:

ME:

I just got out of JAIL! HE had ME locked up!

ALICE:

WHAT?! Are you okay?

ME:

He said I assaulted him. I spent the night in jail.

ALICE:

Press charges against him. You need to get out of
this situation.

ME:

The most interesting part? They took me to the
hospital first. Turns out the last time he attacked me,
he fractured my skull.

ALICE:

This is insane. This is the rest of your life. Counter
arrests and violent attacks.

You need to leave. Distance yourself. You have to
get out.

ME:

I don't want him to take Sunset Cay from me.

ALICE:

You can always go back. Right now, you need literal
distance or he'll come find you.

She's right. We brainstorm a little, and identify several people I could stay with in other states—plenty of mutual roller derby friends.. But there's a catch—I can't leave the island until my court appearance.

ALICE:

> This is how people get stuck with their abusers.
> They have literally zero ways to get away.

I notice a missed call from his mom from last night.

When I dial her number, she answers on the first ring, and I tell her about my night in jail.

"Oh my gosh, I'm so sorry that happened," she says. "I'm glad you're out of there. I don't know why he did that."

I sigh. Nobody knows why Timmy does many of the things he does.

Not even Timmy.

We chat a little more.

"Jennifer has some rental properties. Maybe you could rent a place from her," his mom suggests.

What the actual fuck?

No, I don't want to rent an apartment from Timmy's ex-girlfriend.

"I'll figure something out," I reply.

"I hope your cat is okay," she says. "I'm really sorry about all this."

We hang up.

ME:

> Yeah, it's dumb. I just spoke with his mom.

ALICE:

> What did she have to say?

ME:

> That she's very sorry, and she hopes I can find
> my cat.

ALICE:

> Tell her that since you can't leave now, they should
> come and remove him for your safety.

ME:

> Yeah, I would hope they'd do that, but his dad is a
> massive enabler.

ALICE:

> Enough of an enabler where he'd let his son stay
> and abuse someone?

ME:

> I'm not sure.

———

Scrolling through my phone, I discover the aftermath of Timmy's latest betrayal.

ME:

I am in jail.

Oh my fucking god. The audacity.

ME:

I am in jail.

I scroll to the next text message.

ME:

I am in jail.

Oh my fucking god.

He's broken into my computer, accessed my cloud-stored texts, and sent a single, humiliating message to several people in my contact list.

I'm so mortified that I went to jail in the first place. And I'm angry, because he got me locked up for things I didn't do.

And now he's rubbing it in by making it public?

Nothing makes sense.

Up is down, down is up, and I need a shower and a nap.

CHAPTER 67
STAY AWAY FROM ME AND I'LL STAY AWAY FROM YOU

MARGAUX

I can't wait until I'm single.
Out of this cage.
I'm a lovely person with a brain. Or at least I was.
I'm not lovely anymore. Or smart.
Now I'm just a shell.

———

Because I was locked up for domestic violence, there's an automatic seventy-two hour stay-away order in place from the time I'm released from jail.

Meaning I can't return to my own apartment or check on Sabre.

I do have the opportunity to arrange a police escort to pick up essential items, including medications and clothing, as well as my cat. But that requires Timmy to be present, or I'm not legally allowed to enter the premises.

I call for a police escort, and when the officer and I get there, Timmy's not home, and the truck is gone.

"Sorry, we can't let you in until he's here," they say.

"What about the truck?" I ask. "It's my truck, in my name, and he's taken it. And he has no license."

"That's okay, actually," the cop shrugs. "We can't do anything about that, because you've let him in the truck before."

What the fuck?

"So, if you let someone in your vehicle, they can just… steal it sometime later? And you can't report it stolen?"

"Pretty much," he replies, nodding.

I sigh.

I'm literally in the worst place in the entire Cay, wearing only a sports bra and short shorts.

I don't even have shoes.

I haven't showered, my phone is dying, and I don't have access to my wallet.

And now I don't even have my vehicle for shelter and safety.

"What am I supposed to do?" I ask, desperate to know Sabre is safe and to make sure I am as well.

"You'll just have to wait until he's back," the officer shrugs. "Anyway, we have to go so we can respond to something else. But just call us back when you need an escort and we'll send someone out."

As I think about how the rest of the day might play out, a chill runs through me.

What if it gets dark and Timmy's still not back?

What if my phone dies?

I'm in an area surrounded by people doing hard drugs and committing violent crimes.

This situation could actually become even more disastrous than it already is.

I fill Alice in:

> ALICE:
>
> This country is wild. They allowed a man with an active warrant to get you locked up and they didn't take him in. Wild.
>
> Press. Charges. Otherwise he'll either kill you or take all your shit and leave you with nothing.
>
> He's proven that.

ME:

What can I press charges for, though?

ALICE:

The many times he's physically assaulted you.

ME:

This is all so insane.

ALICE:

You say the doctor found a skull fracture.

Use that as evidence.

ME:

I guess I could retrospectively, but he's been telling people I scratched him and showed them scratches, so he'll try to paint me as the abuser.

ALICE:

If he touches you again, call the police immediately.

ME:

Obviously yes. No question there.

ALICE:

It's why I told you to call it in earlier. He was just waiting for a chance to get ahead of the narrative.

You kept letting it go, because you were scared he'd get arrested.

A wild fear since he SHOULD be arrested.

ME:

Yeah.

ALICE:

But then you let it go. And let it go. And let it go.

And now, he's using it to his advantage.

So now you're stuck.

This is why it's important to establish the narrative earlier.

Go through texts. Look for photos and text evidence of abuse.

Because he's had almost 24 hours to start the story
and start writing.

At this point, you probably need a lawyer and can't
do it on your own, unfortunately. You've officially
been taken in, and a case and story are being built.

Find one immediately.

ME:

Yeah, I will. Although the cop told me I likely won't
be convicted for this.

ALICE:

You probably won't be, but it's still happening and is
going to complicate things.

I'm sorry it's happening, I really am. But I'm worried
for you.

And these situations don't like… get better with age.

My phone rings.
It's Timmy.
I don't answer, because that would be illegal.

ME:

He just tried to call me. Which is a trap, because I'm
not allowed to communicate with him.

ALICE:

Correct.

Don't fall for it.

ME:

Ugh. If I had the truck, I could charge my phone.

If I had my ID, I could book a hotel.

Yet, because of Timmy, I have neither.

———

The sun feels relentless as I sit by the security shack pondering my options,
my phone barely clinging to its last bar of battery life. The weight of every-

thing that has happened presses down on me like the heat—the arrest, the stay-away order, the sheer audacity of Timmy taking the truck that I'm legally responsible for, and now being stuck here without shoes, identification, or any semblance of stability.

I lean against the wall, watching the bustling activity of the complex—the occasional car pulling in, tenants coming and going. The security guard eyes me with what I hope is sympathy, but I'm not counting on it.

Dennis, one of Timmy's coworkers, arrives and chats away with the guard. I recognize him from the times Timmy insisted on dragging me to his job site—one of those guys who always seemed to have a joke or a laugh but never seemed too bothered by the seriousness of anything. Today, though, I'm grateful for his presence.

"Excuse me, Dennis, right?" I ask, stepping closer to him. He turns, his face twisting in mild confusion.

"Yeah?" he says.

"Hi," I say, trying to keep my tone steady. "I'm Timmy's fiancée. I'm in a bit of a bind, and really need to get in touch with him. Could you help me out?"

Dennis raises an eyebrow, clearly not expecting this. "Uh, yeah. I guess. What's going on?"

"I need to grab some things from the apartment," I explain. "But I can't legally go in there without him present because of the… situation. And he took the truck, so I'm stuck without anything."

He nods. "Yeah, he said he had a meeting in town, so he's not working today."

I think about it, and realize he did mention having to go to some kind of food stamp eligibility course. Something where you go through the motions of pretending to be on the job hunt so that the government will keep giving you money.

"Could you maybe give him a call and find out when he'll be back?" I ask.

Dennis pulls his phone out of his pocket. "Sure, hang on."

He dials, and I watch as he has a brief conversation with Timmy, his face giving nothing away.

When he hangs up, he looks at me and says, "He says he's on his way back now. Shouldn't be too long."

Relief washes over me, though it's tempered by exhaustion. "Thank you. I really appreciate it." I glance at the security guard. "Would you mind calling me when you see the truck pull in?"

She nods. "I'll keep an eye out for it."

CHAPTER 68
THE LAST THING I EXPECTED TO SEE WERE PINK HANDCUFFS

MARGAUX

walk to the store, counting on the limited funds I just realized I can access through Apple Pay. Hopefully, it's enough to buy a portable phone charger and a Gatorade because my throat feels like sandpaper.

The humidity clings to me, relentless even in December. Sunset Cay may as well be in a perpetual summer.

As I make my way down the uneven sidewalk, a few cars honk. One driver pulls over, rolling his window down with an oily smirk as he looks me up and down. "Need a ride?" he asks.

"No, thank you," I say, forcing a polite tone and picking up my pace.

Inside the CVS, the air conditioning hits like a blessing. I let myself wander aimlessly through the aisles, taking my time. It's not just a store—today it feels like a refuge. Shelves of neatly arranged products seem to promise normalcy, a stark contrast to the chaos outside.

I'm just about to purchase a portable charger when my phone buzzes in my hand.

Relief washes over me when I see it's the security guard.

"He just got back," she whispers, her voice conspiratorial, as if we're in the middle of a covert operation. "I didn't let him know you were here."

"Thank you," I say, already heading for the door.

"And," she adds with a hint of amusement, "I wouldn't let him park the truck in the garage. Told him, 'I know you don't have a license,' so he had to have someone else do it for him."

I can't help but chuckle. It's a small thing—and I know she's technically following procedure—but her act feels like solidarity in a sea of indifference. Right now, I'll take any bit of support I can get. A minor inconvenience like this is the absolute least that Timmy deserves.

On my way back, I call the non-emergency police line and request another escort. Waiting in the parking garage feels endless, but eventually, a police car cruises in.

The officer driving rolls down her window. She's stunning, with blonde hair, impeccable makeup, and bright pink lipstick. "You here for the escort?" she asks.

"Yes," I nod, trying not to gawk.

She parks and steps out, revealing her tall frame and arms covered in intricate tattoos. As she leads me to the apartment, I notice the pair of pale pink handcuffs that hang off her utility belt. I blink, half-convinced I've stepped into some surreal fever dream.

This can't be real. None of this is real.

She catches my expression and raises an eyebrow, but doesn't comment. "Why are we here?" she asks, her tone professional but not unkind.

I take a deep breath. "My fiancé made up a story, accused me of domestic abuse, and got me locked up. There's a stay-away order now, and I need to pick up some essentials."

"Got it," she says, nodding.

We wait by the front door to the apartment, and soon enough, Timmy appears from the direction of the parking structure. He looks startled when he sees us.

The officer takes the lead. "Margaux is here to pick up her things. Don't talk to each other."

"Oh, okay," Timmy mumbles, suddenly meek. Then his tone shifts. "Ooh, I know you," he says, his voice gaining that pervy tone that makes my skin crawl.

It seems to have the same effect on the officer, because she frowns at him, quirking a brow. "What do you mean?"

"When I was locked up last time, you were in the station. I remember you," he says, grinning.

She looks unimpressed, and doesn't respond.

Timmy seems to realize he's not impressing her, and for once he shuts up.

I rush past him and into the apartment, my heart pounding. The first thing I do is find Sabre. He's lounging on the bed, looking unbothered. Relief floods through me as I scoop him up, burying my face in his soft fur.

I grab a couple of changes of clothes, my fanny pack, medication, and my computer. I pause, trying to think through what else I'll need. The adrenaline coursing through me makes it hard to focus.

One of the panes from the jalousie windows is smashed, shards of glass scattered on the ground. *Typical.* Timmy must have locked himself out when he was drunk and forgotten the code to the door. But everything else seems untouched.

I glance around, feeling flustered.

"It's okay," the officer says gently, noticing my panic. "Take your time."

I nod, exhaling shakily. "I need my chargers," I mutter, grabbing them from the desk.

Finally, I'm ready.

"What are you going to do?" she asks.

"Oh," I reply. "Well, I guess I'll get a hotel downtown until I'm allowed to come back."

"No," she shakes her head. "I mean, what are you going to do about… that?" She tilts her head toward Timmy, just out of earshot, her words a subtle nudge.

"I'm not sure yet," I reply honestly. "But I'm going to figure it out."

She gives a small nod, her expression neutral.

I have a feeling she's seen this all before.

———

I drive Sabre and myself to a hotel downtown, our temporary haven for a few days. In a small act of—I don't know, self-care, defiance, all of the above —I pick the hotel that houses Dock Bar. One of the only places I still consider a refuge, that Timmy hasn't managed to take from me.

When we arrive in the hotel room, Sabre perks up immediately, conducting a thorough inspection of the room. Once satisfied, he leaps onto the bed and sprawls across the comforter, purring like he owns the place.

At least one of us is having a good time.

For the first time in what feels like forever, I'm alone with my thoughts.

Glancing at my phone, I notice that, for once, Timmy hasn't turned off his location. I find myself compulsively tracking his movements.

On Monday, he spends hours at the meth tents before returning home for the evening.

Tuesday, he's at the tents again by 9AM, then back at the apartment complex, ostensibly working for a couple of hours. After lunch, he's back at the tents, then the beach, then the 7-Eleven where the local unhoused population congregates.

This particular 7-Eleven isn't just a convenience store—it's a dead end, a magnet for panhandlers and addicts. Timmy, with a roof over his head, chooses to linger here like he belongs.

By 430PM, he's home again—for all of three hours—before heading back to the beach and the 7-Eleven.

His routine is baffling, a chaotic dance of aimlessness.

Integrity is what you do when no one's watching, and Timmy's true colors are blindingly clear.

———

Without Timmy's constant presence, I'm actually productive. I write, uninterrupted, and it feels incredible to be spared from his constant inane chatter.

The hotel room and the bar downstairs—ironically the place we first met in person, although I still consider it to be *my* space—become my sanctuaries, places where I can focus and breathe.

It's funny how much more I can get done when I'm not constantly being berated, nitpicked, insulted and abused.

Still, my mind circles back to him.

Every time I start to see the truth—that I need to leave, that things will never change—he does something to reel me back in, to give me just enough hope to want to give him one more chance.

I message my Emotional Support Alice:

ME:

I'm so confused right now. The high highs and low lows are too much to deal with.

I haven't felt the way I have about Timmy about anything else

It makes me wonder if anything I felt previously was love.

> But do people who love you give you skull fractures? No, probably not.

> Would it kill me to see him with someone else? It would hurt like fuck, but I'd live.

> Will I live with his current behavior? No. He'll most likely kill me or put me in a situation where someone else does.

> He has started therapy and medication and is going to start AA group meetings and started a part-time job last week.

> But last night he got me locked up and is planning a mass slander case against me.

> My brain is all over the place.

ALICE:

There will never be a high high enough to justify a low that resulted in a skull fracture.

What if he'd used just 3lbs more pressure that day? Or even 1?

ME:

> My brain is going 'Oh, maybe you got the skull fracture from XYZ thing instead of Timmy,' even though I know that's not the case.

ALICE:

You didn't.

He's a violent person with good moments.

And you loved him. Love has incredible blinders.

She's right.

ME:

> It's actually helping me that I can see his location on my phone.

> Because I can see how he's behaving while I'm not there.

> Last evening, he was with the drug people and then he went home. He's already back with them.

> I guess he must have quit or lost his job after 1 week.

> And seeing that he normally doesn't get out of bed before 11AM when he's not working makes me see there's some massive problem with him.

> He's supposed to work 8AM-12PM M-F, and that's the only time I've seen him up before 9AM.

> And here he is with the drug people before 9AM when I'm not there.

Wow.

ALICE:

Yeah, he's not a smart dude who's on a path to anywhere except self-destruction.

By the end of the hotel stay, I'm at a crossroads.
I see him for who he is—a 'man' spiraling out of control.
A 'man' determined to drag me down with him.
It's time to make a choice.

CHAPTER 69
BAIL OUT

DEX

The humidity in Sunset Cay doesn't let up, even in December. It's as if the weather mocks the chaos unfolding in Margaux's life—unchanging, oppressive, suffocating. I sit in my quiet apartment, eyes fixed on my multiple monitors, the feed from her jail cell streaming on one screen, Timmy's erratic movements mapped out on another. My coffee grows cold beside me, untouched.

Margaux's been through hell. And today, hell looks like a paper-thin outfit in a jail cell.

I bet she didn't have 'going to jail' on this year's bingo card—or on her overall life's bingo card.

When the notification about her arrest pinged on my phone, I almost destroyed the keyboard trying to pull up the police reports. The audacity of him—*her* abuser—calling the cops on her and spinning some half-baked story about being the victim.

I want to smash his smug face into the asphalt. I want to burn his pathetic existence to the ground.

He accused her of pulling his hair? I'll show him what it looks like to have each hair pulled out one by one until he's fucking bald.

But I can't. Not yet. *She's not ready.*

The feed from the jail's internal cameras flickers to life, a sterile gray-blue hue bathing the screen. There she is, curled on the cold concrete, her paper uniform crinkled awkwardly around her limbs. Even through the grainy footage, I can see the exhaustion etched into her face, the tension in her shoulders.

My stomach twists.

Does she even realize how close she's come to breaking? How precarious this situation is? How many lines he's crossed—how many she's allowed him to cross?

I swallow hard, my jaw clenched tight enough to ache. Every instinct I have screams at me to take matters into my own hands, but I can't act until she's ready to let go of him. And right now? She's still tethered to some thread of hope, some misplaced belief that this can be salvaged.

When they move her to the downtown facility, I switch feeds. The cameras there are older, the angles worse, but I manage to find her again. She's in a cell with other women now—some tweaking, others hardened by years of this cycle.

Margaux sticks out like a sore thumb, her pale skin and ginger hair practically glowing in the dim light. She's scared but holding it together.

I admire that about her—her resilience, even in the face of absolute bullshit.

The other women seem to warm up to her, eventually. One even laughs at something she says.

Good. She needs allies, even temporary ones—even if they're jail cellmates.

On another screen, I monitor Timmy's movements. His phone's GPS is a useful tool for me—a way to track his pathetic attempts at a life. Today, he's already spent hours at the meth tents, a familiar haunt for him now. He's back at the apartment by noon, but only briefly, before heading to the beach and then the 7-Eleven that's become his second home.

I shake my head, disgusted. He's unraveling, too. Not that he was ever held together by much to begin with.

I look on as Margaux is eventually released from jail, barefoot and wearing the paper clothes, her shoulders hunched against the weight of it all.

Then it hits me—in domestic violence cases, the accused can't return home except to get basic possessions.

I look on at the apartment's feeds in horror as I realize Timmy isn't home, and the police officer escorting her won't let her in.

Timmy has essentially left her in the worst part of the Cay, with no money, no shoes, and a dying phone.

A man who claims to love her—who promised to protect her—instead had her arrested on a fabricated charge. And now she's stuck navigating a world of dodgy drug users and predators, barely clothed and without a lifeline.

She's not safe. Not at all.

She's alone, vulnerable, and stranded in a situation that could spiral at any moment. I can't stop picturing her walking those sketchy streets, surrounded by predators who would take one look at her and see an easy target. My stomach twists.

It's unconscionable. It's unforgivable.

And it's exactly why he needs to be removed from her life.

But if there are two things that Margaux is—other than beautiful, the woman of my dreams, extremely loyal and stubborn—she's resilient as fuck, and a creative problem-solver.

Relief washes over me as she manages to get into the apartment to retrieve essential possessions, as well as Sabre. The jalousie windows are smashed, shards of glass glittering on the floor like evidence of Timmy's destruction. Sabre nuzzles against her as she gathers her essentials, his quiet purr a stark contrast to the chaos around them.

I track Timmy's movements as he loiters nearby, waiting to see what she'll do. He's predictable in his unpredictability, and it only fuels my anger.

If he so much as looks at her the wrong way, I'll...

I stop myself, my hands trembling. *I can't act yet.* Not until she's ready. Not until she's free of him in every sense.

She gets an Uber to a hotel downtown, a place I know well—one of the few spots she's claimed as her own, even if he's tried to taint it. Through her phone's camera, I catch glimpses of the room. Seeing Sabre sprawled on the bed, purring like nothing's wrong, brings a small, fleeting smile to my face.

She texts Alice, venting about the absurdity of it all. I read the messages as they come in, each one a punch to the gut. She's spiraling, questioning herself, blaming herself for things that aren't her fault.

She doesn't see it yet, but she's starting to pull away from Timmy. The distance—physical and emotional—is growing. It's not enough, but it's a start. Maybe this jail visit and subsequent order to stay away is a blessing in disguise.

On the feed from Timmy's phone, I watch him stumble back to the apartment late at night, reeking of bad decisions. His smirk as he passes the security guard is infuriating. But he has no idea how much of his life I control—how much of his digital footprint I've corrupted.

I've planted enough breadcrumbs to keep Margaux doubting him, to make her see the cracks in his façade.

But still, she hesitates.

He's just so talented at explaining everything away, using word salad to make Margaux doubt and blame herself.

———

The next few days are quiet. Margaux writes, she rests, and she finds small moments of peace in the chaos.

And yet, she checks his location obsessively, as if needing to confirm that he's as awful as she knows he is.

He doesn't disappoint—meth tents, late-night trips to nowhere, hours spent with people who don't care about him any more than he cares about himself.

I catch snippets of her surveillance on him, his patterns painting an unflattering picture of the aimless derelict loser that Timmy is in a way that's hard for her to ignore.

She's finally noticing his patterns, the truth she's been avoiding for months.

But even now—despite taking screenshots—she second-guesses herself, her compassion clouding her judgment.

I lean back in my chair, running a hand through my hair.

She's so close. So close to walking away for good.

But she needs one last push—a moment of clarity that shatters the illusion he's built around her.

I wonder if having gone to jail will be enough—the final nudge she needs. It's a huge deal, and it might be enough. I'll just have to see how this plays out.

Until then, I'll be here, ready to pick up the pieces when it all comes crashing down.

Because it will.

In relationships like this, *it always does.*

And when this ends—and it *will* end—I'll make sure she never has to feel this kind of fear again.

CHAPTER 70
HOLLOW APOLOGIES

MARGAUX

" 'm really, really, really sorry, Margaux. I never should have called the cops. I was just… like really panicked. Because you said you were going to call them, and I knew they would lock me up, and I really didn't want to go to jail."

The moment I walk through the door, Timmy rushes to me, his words tumbling out in a frantic attempt to explain himself. His face is serious, his posture almost reverent, and before I can even set down my keys, he pulls me into a tight embrace.

Part of me wants to push him away, but I'm so drained—emotionally, physically—that I sink into his arms, craving human contact even if it's from the very person who's caused all this chaos.

"So you lied to them and got me put in jail?" I ask, my voice flat and devoid of emotion. "Make that make sense."

His face contorts, trying to find an answer. "Well, I'm sorry. I shouldn't have let you down. I shouldn't have drank. And I shouldn't have called them. I was just scared. And I'm glad you're back home now."

I step back, shaking off his hands. Anger rises in me like a storm—every excuse he offers only makes it worse.

"Do you have any idea how humiliating it was?" I say, my voice trembling. "I had to stay away from my own apartment for days. I didn't have *shoes* for an entire day, Timmy. I was in jail in paper clothes, barefoot, and when I came back to get my things, you were too busy smoking with your meth friends to even answer the door! I couldn't come in and get anything at all. Do you have any clue how worried I was about Sabre? And then you took the *fucking* truck god knows where with god knows who."

He looks sheepish, his hands shoved into his pockets. "I just took the truck down to the other end of the beach," he mumbles.

"Why would you do that, Timmy?" I snap. "You don't even have a license!"

"I know, I know," he mutters, shrugging like a teenager caught sneaking out past curfew. "I was just… feeling helpless."

The irony of him calling himself helpless—of painting himself as the victim in this situation—nearly makes me laugh. Instead, I clench my fists and exhale sharply. "I could see your location, and you were going back and forth across the beach to your meth friends."

He looks like he's just had his hand smacked for reaching into a cookie jar. He shakes his head. "No, just a couple of times."

"Timmy, I have screenshots and you were there at least six times over those couple of days. At the beach and over at the 7-Eleven." For once, I have enough undeniable data points to feel strong in my assertions. For once, he can't twist the truth.

"Well yeah," he nods, choosing his words carefully. "I was really upset, so I went over there to think about things and drink."

I shake my head and let out a breath I didn't know I'd been holding.

"You *fractured my skull*, Timmy," I say, my voice steady but laced with anger. "You gave me a *traumatic brain injury*. Do you even understand what that means? You could've killed me."

His eyes widen, but he doesn't respond.

"And do you remember what you told me afterward?" My voice rises. "You said they weren't even real black eyes. As if you thought downplaying it would erase the damage."

The more I think about how he tried to dismiss my injuries as minimal, and to justify why he almost literally broke my brain, the more heated I become.

His lip quivers, and tears spring to his eyes. "Oh my gosh, Margaux. I'm so sorry," he whispers. He reaches out to stroke my head softly. "I don't know how I got like that. I would never want to hurt you."

I take a step back, my chest tightening. His tears feel more like a weapon than a release of guilt. But at the same time, he seems genuine—he has these massive feelings, and I do care about him, and it's hard to see him in pain.

"That might not be your intent, but you're really fucking good at hurting me, Timmy," I snap. "This has to stop. I feel like an idiot for even being here talking to you. I'm so upset. You keep saying that you don't want to hurt me, but your actions say otherwise," My voice rises. "You put me in jail, Timmy. You lied to the police about me. Do you even understand how massive a betrayal that is?"

I'm mortified to be here, with a man that professes to love me but whose actions suggest he hates everything about me.

The thought of trying to explain this to anyone is so embarrassing.

I'm ashamed.

But I don't know what else to do other than be here right now.

"Sorry," he frowns. "I shouldn't have been drinking. I'll get the help we've discussed. I promise."

"Will you, though?" I quirk a brow. "Will you *really*? I feel like I've heard the same excuses before, over and over again."

His tears fall freely now, and his voice breaks. "I need you, Margaux. *Please* don't give up on me. Help me to change, to get better. We can do this… together. I can't do it without you."

I look at him—the tears, the words, the pleading. I know there's a part of him that means it.

But the little voice in my head is louder now.

He's not sorry for hurting you. He's sorry he almost got caught.

He doesn't care that he fractured your skull, Margaux.

He's crying because he realizes he almost went to prison for murdering you.

CHAPTER 71
BROKEN BONES & PROMISES

My blood runs cold.

He fractured her fucking skull?

I'm going to kill him. I'll bide my time, but there's no way I'm going to let someone hurt Margaux like this and get away with it.

I hack into the police system. I can see that the dates line up. They were called to a domestic disturbance at their shared apartment several months before, the time she sustained a fat lip and two black eyes.

I pull up the police photos and almost throw up. She looks disheveled, and clearly has two black eyes and a fat lip, as well as early signs of bruising on her forearms.

There's no question she'd been beaten up.

I'm able to get into the police body cam footage, and I'm shocked.

She's very upset, and one of the cops asks her, "What started the argument?"

She replies calmly, her tone sad and maybe a little in shock, "I played a Machine Gun Kelly song so he smacked me in the face, threw me to the ground and strangled me."

I look back at the medical records. The doctor has made a note:

· · ·

Subject's skull fracture is consistent with timing for an incident several months before in which the assailant punched her, threw her to the ground and choked her.

When thrown to the ground, she expressed seeing stars and blacking out.

This is consistent with timing, nature and positioning of a severe skull fracture.

Have advised patient to end relationship and provided domestic violence resources.

Good god. How did she ever see anything in this piece of shit?

I'm full of rage at anyone who could do this to any woman.

But *Margaux?*

Nah, this fucker is dead meat.

CHAPTER 72
THE AUDACITY OF THIS BITCH

MARGAUX

Just as the conversation grows calmer, I recall him sending the 'I am in jail' texts to multiple contacts in my phone. Rage bubbles up as I confront him.

"How could you do that to me?" I yell, my voice raw.

"I was drunk," Timmy says, shrugging, as if that's some kind of defense. "I was angry, and you hurt my feelings!"

I gape at him. "So you… you impersonated me to *humiliate* me? Do you even realize that's illegal? My lawyer says that tampering with communications is a felony."

I've finally been appointed a lawyer. By some fluke, I don't just have a run-of-the-mill public defender—they've appointed me a private lawyer who used to be an Assistant District Attorney for the state. During our brief consultation call, we'd discussed Timmy's text tampering.

His face turns pale. "A… a felony?" he stammers. "Please don't have me locked up," he begs. "I can't go to prison."

The audacity leaves me breathless. "You can't be serious," I say, my voice flat.

He shrinks under my glare, but I can feel his self-preservation kicking in. "I'm sorry," he says, his tone pitiful. "I wasn't thinking straight. *Please,* don't get me into trouble."

I shake my head, disbelief washing over me like a tidal wave. "You're unbelievable. You're not sorry for what you did—you're sorry for the consequences."

Timmy flinches, but he doesn't argue. He reaches for me, and instinctively, I step back.

"You fractured my skull," I say again. "And then you fabricated a story about me being violent. And you went into my phone, violated my privacy, and messaged my friends. Do you even understand how completely insane all of that is?"

"I wasn't thinking straight," he repeats, his voice barely above a whisper. "I'm sorry."

"You've said sorry more times than I can count," I snap. "But sorry doesn't mean anything if you keep doing the same things over and over."

He nods, tears streaming down his face. "You're right. I'm going to change. I promise. Therapy, AA meetings—whatever it takes. Just don't give up on me."

I let out a hollow laugh. "You've promised all of that before. And look where we are."

He stammers, searching for a defense, but I've stopped listening.

The numbness returns, shielding me from the chaos of his existence.

He reaches out again, pulling me into a hug. This time, I don't flinch. I let him hold me, his arms wrapped tightly around me. But I don't hug him back.

In his embrace, I feel nothing.

No love.

No safety.

Just a hollow echo of what used to be.

Later, I sit on the bed, staring at the cracked glass pane in the window and thinking about the life I've built with him. The thought of leaving fills me with fear, but the thought of staying fills me with something worse.

I pull out my phone and message Alice.

ME:

I think I'm done.

ALICE:

Good. It's time.

———

I draft an email to Timmy.

I've made a decision.

I don't want to be with someone who spends their time hanging out with known drug users in homeless tents

I don't want to be with someone who is constantly volatile, vindictive, and who will take items out of our home that I paid for on a regular basis.

I will not be with someone who fabricates narratives against me to support their own delusions.

And most of all, I will not be with someone who fractured my skull and then proceeded to call me an abuser when 'your mood changed.'

I'm sick of the constant stories and false narratives, and I am done.

You cannot stay here for two months. You are not on the current lease, and you can move out straight away.

There is a cast mate on one of the shows I watch, and he runs away and everyone makes fun of him for it to the point there are gifs and memes about it.

Now another castmate does it, too. He was described as a man child.

You described yourself to me as a man child.

I apologize for not picking up on all the signs you gave that you were unsuitable and did not meet my requirements in a partner.

I wish you the best, but I know in my heart that you're not the one for me.

Because the right person for me would not treat me, gaslight me, or manipulate other people about me, the way that you do.

Before hitting send, my friend messages me.

JO:

Hey, it's Jo. I just got the weirdest voicemail from
your phone.

Your fiancé called me a cunt…

Oh my god.

She sends it to me—he's texted her and also left her a voicemail. The tone in the voicemail is cold… chilling, in fact.

"Fucking cunt…you're a fucking worm. If you want to know what my Facebook is it's TimmysHatDesignz with a fucking Z, you fucking loser."

Full of pure rage.

Directed toward my friend, who did absolutely nothing to deserve his wrath.

I turn to Timmy, who's sitting on the bed, contributing nothing to society as usual.

"Why did you do that?" I'm fuming. The audacity to break into my phone through my computer and send my friends abusive messages while I'm in jail on false charges that he filed against me.

"What?" he asks.

"Message my friend." I play the recording.

I have no time for the back and forth where he feigns confusion, so I start with the receipts.

"Oh…" he frowns. "I'm so sorry, Margaux. I thought she was a man, and you were going on a date with him."

My friend Jo. *As in Josephine, a woman.* Who lives on the other side of the country.

I resist the urge to throw my phone at his head. "In what world would she be a man? And why would you think that?"

"I don't know," he shrugs. "I guess I misread something she'd said earlier in your conversation."

I sigh. "Well, what you sent is completely inappropriate. Please stop contacting people pretending to be me, or from my phone, without my permission. Please stop saying the n word. You've promised to stop saying it. Please don't call my friends cunts. Please just stop."

"Okay, okay," he puts his hands up in surrender. "I was just upset, and my feelings were hurt, and I thought you were cheating on me."

My mouth opens involuntarily. "How could I cheat on you in *jail*?"

He looks down. "Well, I guess I wasn't thinking straight."

"Please, just stay away from my things," I plead. "Like I said, I spoke to my lawyer and what you did is a felony. So I strongly suggest that you stop it immediately."

He flinches again at the word 'felony'. "Okay, yeah, I guess I really fucked up, doing that." He looks scared. "Please don't get me in trouble. *Please.* I really don't want to go to prison."

I shrug. "Stop doing dumb shit, then."

He nods. "Okay. I really am sorry."

He pulls me into a hug, and this time it's me who flinches.

I let him hug me, but I can't stomach returning his embrace. I'm happy to be back at home, but I'm still so angry he put me in jail.

It was traumatic, and the whole thing was just insane.

Finding out he's fractured my skull has reopened old emotional wounds related to *that* attack.

Plus, he tried to strangle me.

He thought he'd killed me. *Checked my fucking pulse.*

And now it's all about a pity party for Timmy.

The audacity.

CHAPTER 73
BIG SIS MIC DROP

MARGAUX

A FEW DAYS LATER

I sit at my desk, laptop open, staring at the unopened email from my sister, Amanda. The subject line reads, '*To My Sister.*'

I've been keeping her in the loop as best as I can—occasionally talking to her on the phone when Timmy's having a particularly volatile day.

Amanda's been through enough in her life to understand what's happening, even though I've spared her the grittiest details.

But today, the bold subject line feels heavier than usual.

I finally click the email open, but the words blur together on the screen. One phrase jumps out like a red flag slapping me in the face: *your funeral.*

I slam the laptop shut.

I can't. I just can't.

She thinks I'm going to die. *She thinks Timmy will kill me.*

The enormity of those words presses on my chest. Amanda has always been straight-talking, but seeing her fears laid bare feels suffocating. And yet… it's not entirely surprising.

Timmy has been *better* lately—apologetic, promising to change. He's gone two whole days without yelling or doing something cruel. Isn't that a start? Doesn't progress take time?

Each day, I peek at the email again, but I can't bring myself to read it all. Every time I try, it feels like the words might swallow me whole.

But Amanda's voice echoes in the back of my mind, steady and firm.

Finally, I steel myself and open it.

I think by now that you know, Margaux, that I care about you very much and that Roger and I are very concerned about you and for you.

So I am going to be very blunt with what I am saying to you.

That's the setup that makes it hard to keep going, but I appreciate her honesty.

Whatever way you choose to hear and react to what I am saying, it will not change the way I feel about you, and that I want you to be part of my life and I yours.

I love my sister so much.

Margaux—you are in an abusive, controlling, manipulating, violent relationship with a person that you cannot and never will be able to change or help.

The words hit me hard.

Of course, I know she's right. Timmy's promises to change only come when I'm ready to leave, and they're never consistent. He's always said he *needs* me to be better, that he can't change without me by his side.

But Amanda sees through that.

The only person that can help Timmy is himself, and a very long stint in a rehabilitation program, and even then, the chances for him to remain drug-free are slim.

The work required by Timmy for immense change within himself is huge, and requires a rehabilitation program for a start of at least 6 weeks.

She's right again.

I've tried to convince Timmy to start therapy and attend AA meetings, and he's promised he would.

But six weeks? Timmy doesn't stick to anything for more than six days.

It requires determination, the fierce desire to improve, and a strength that does not come from oneself but from a connection with God, Divine, Source—whichever name you wish to call it.

I sigh.

Timmy talks a lot about wanting to be better. But he has no impulse control and no executive function. Timmy's connection to anything spiritual is nonexistent.

He can barely connect to reality most days.

Unfortunately, Margaux, you are enabling Timmy.

Each time you stay or come back after being abused, you are basically letting Timmy know that you are okay with being whacked around and mistreated in this way.

Ouch. That one stings. I'm not *okay* with being hurt.

I tell him it's wrong, and he promises it won't happen again. And for a little while, it doesn't.

He's so convincing, showing me glimpses of the man I fell for.

But those moments of peace always dissolve into chaos.

It is very common in abusive and drug-related relationships for this to happen.

A person does not have the power to change another person, and it's wasted energy to even try.

He always tells me I'm the only one who's ever been able to help him.

But... has he changed at all?

Deep down, I know the answer.

But Margaux—a person, YOU—have the power to change yourself which in turn changes the way you think and feel, which in turn changes your outlook and experiences in real life.

Her words feel like a guiding star, reminding me I do have agency—reminding me of who I used to be, and who I still am at my core.

I imagine that you have few true supportive people left in your life right now.

I imagine Timmy did a spectacular job of mistreating those friends, acting antiso-

cially and abusively in front of them and showing disrespect to you and mistreating you in front of these friends and supportive people in your life.

I wince. She's not wrong. I've been careful about who I tell about the reality of our relationship, partly out of embarrassment and partly because I know Timmy's behavior is indefensible.

Thank god for Alice and Jo and Stacey, and a select few others who I can trust.

He's actually pretty good at being charming around people I introduce him to—or is he? Maybe that's just a narrative I've created in my head.

He certainly wasn't charming when he kidnapped my friend's son.

He's been cordial to Paulo over the phone, but I also get the sense he's scared of him.

His behavior toward Jo was beyond vile.

Alice won't be buying him a BFF necklace any time soon, although thankfully he's made no attempt to contact her.

And he hasn't really met anyone else.

He hasn't charmed anyone lately.

Rebecca and Jetson tolerated him for a while, but he's made a fool of himself in front of them too, and now neither of them wants anything to do with him.

Darren and Steve—his supposed best friends—have even distanced themselves.

Hmmm… maybe she has a point.

So basically Timmy was successful in his purpose, to control you, to alienate you from people who care about you, and to intimidate you to do what he wants.

He did isolate me. He convinced me to move to this side of the island, where I knew no one.

Every time I mention seeing Rebecca, his jealousy flares, so I've stopped bringing it up.

Would I be correct in assuming that this is not the first abusive, controlling relationship you have been in, that there may have been many.

I mean, there *was* the guy I married when I was sixteen.

He'd control me by threatening to kill himself if I left him.

He hated me because I was better at physics than him in high school, and now he's a physicist.

Then, when I returned to New Zealand, the guy I was with was physically abusive and *extremely* emotionally abusive. Tried to smother me with a pillow one day. Told me he was going to put me in a hospital. Called me ugly and fat and dumb and made me feel like the most hideous person on the planet.

There was the one guy I dated who I worked with who would run up to me and scream things like 'suck my balls, bitch!' *A real charmer, that one.*

And then husband number three.

He didn't hit me, but he did tell me he was going to break my jaw.

Only my uncle showing up in his police uniform and giving him a talking-to seemed to strike the fear of God into him, so he never tried.

My sister doesn't know about many—if any—of these. But yet, she somehow knows.

Look for the patterns in your life, and relationships in your life, Margaux.
   Insight—gain and learn insight, Margaux.

Well fuck.
The patterns are undeniable.
It started before I had a relationship with any guy.
Once, my mother grounded me for six weeks because I was home two minutes late from walking the dog.
She controlled my every movement—what I ate, who I spent time with, where I went. Forced me to say she was my best friend.
Hell, she even used to read my diary.

This means take a look at yourself from the outside, watch yourself and the way you act and react.
   See the patterns.

I'm always trying to fix everything.
To be liked.
To be a good person.
To help everyone, even when they won't help themselves.
I assume that everyone else operates the same, although I'm beginning to learn that most really don't.
I downplay the worst things because it's easier that way.

It's easier to lean into the good and believe that's the *real* truth—in this case, the real *Timmy*.

Alice's words echo in my mind: *he's a violent person with good moments.*

If you choose to stay where you are at, I hope you have all your stuff in order, because I see very little hope for you and your future life.

In fact, I'm sorry, but all I see is devastation and your funeral.

My heart shatters.

I don't want my friends and family to be standing over my casket, wondering why I let a guy nowhere near good enough for me end my life way too soon.

I don't want a piece of shit like Timmy to be the reason I don't get to see my dreams play out.

I don't want my life to end this way.

I have goals.

Books to write.

Stories to tell.

Movies to be produced based on my books.

And maybe, just maybe, a life much happier than what mine has become.

If you choose life and change, Margaux, we can help and support you through it.

But it is an impossible task to help/support you or anyone, if you don't take the steps to help yourself as well.

You were given the contact details from the police for help and support.

I have sent you the information for the Al-Anon contacts, meetings and support for yourself.

Did you take the steps to contact these organizations? I presume not.

I guess you have a place to start then, if your choice is life and living.

Heck, I even have a wonderful therapist whom I have sessions with by zoom meetings.

You will never have experienced anything like it before.

You may want to have some sessions yourself for some instant life-changing changes.

I blink through my tears, grateful for her honesty. She's not just chastising me—she's offering me a way out.

But I *am* trying to get in to see a therapist. It's just not that easy in this country.

I *did* speak with a domestic violence advocate but, beyond basic advice, they weren't able to do a lot.

I *don't* feel like I could go to a shelter. And what about Sabre?

Al-Anon might help, but I don't really like the underpinning beliefs of the organization behind it.

I feel a bit defensive.

I work on myself and my spiritual practices every day; it requires focus and a want to be a happy stress-free person.

Happy and stress-free. *How I would love that.*

You are so smart, Margaux. You can do anything you want to and experience anything you want to.

Is where you are at right now in your life really how you want to be living, breathing, and being?

Fuck no.

Your life, Margaux, your future and your choices.

What will you choose, is the question to answer for yourself.

Lots of love from your sister, Amanda xxxxx

Tears flow.

I'm thrown.

The email isn't the villain I built it up to be.

It's raw and blunt, yes, but it kind of needed to be. *It's also full of love.*

Amanda cares about me more than I realized.

Timmy always pitches everything as us against the world, and maybe that's why I've been so defensive. But reading her words, I realize—*What do we even have?*

Nothing worth keeping.

Definitely nothing worth dying for.

How lucky I am to have someone like my big sis in my corner.

And how foolish I'd be not to listen.

CHAPTER 74
PLOT TWIST

MARGAUX

t's days before Christmas, and I've finally reached the point where I'm mentally prepared to leave Timmy.

I should have left sooner, I know that now. Hindsight loves to tap you on the shoulder when it's too late to undo the mess. It's so hard to see things objectively when you're in the middle of them.

But now, I can see clearly—this is unsustainable, unhealthy, and most of all, it's incredibly unsafe.

Enough is enough.

I don't want to be in a relationship where I have to have a go-bag at the ready, or where I need the number for the local domestic violence shelter saved in my phone under a fake name.

None of this is okay. Nobody should have to live like this.

The logistics weigh heavily on me. *Where will I go? When is the best time? How will I escape his inevitable backlash?*

But I have to tread carefully and time it right. Charges are still pending against me for the alleged hair-pulling incident that landed me in jail.

If I leave now, Timmy's sure to retaliate. I can already hear the lies he'll embellish for the courts, the smirks he'll wear as he tries to destroy me—to make me pay.

So, I wait. Quietly. Strategically.

I'm sitting on the bed, steeling myself to get through the next few days—because goodness knows Timmy likes to ruin any events, including holidays—when I hear his voice, low and strained, talking on the phone across the room.

Timmy barely ever talks on the phone, other than to his parents.

This is unusual.

"Darren's dead?" he whispers.

The words hit me like ice water, snapping me out of my thoughts.

Timmy's face crumples, his tears falling freely as he listens to whoever is on the other end.

"I... I can't believe he's gone," he murmurs.

I watch, frozen. I don't know the circumstances, but it's clear something terrible has happened. Darren, his estranged best friend, is dead.

"A heart attack or maybe fentanyl?" he says, choking on his words, his voice breaking.

I walk over to him and wrap my arms around him, rubbing his lower back.

His body shakes with grief.

Part of me hesitates—this is the man who's hurt me in ways I'm still untangling. But in this moment, he's raw and human, and I can't turn away.

My escape plans are forgotten. For now, at least.

"I'm so sorry," I whisper.

I'd only met Darren a couple of times, and I know he wasn't the most upstanding guy. But I know he was important to Timmy, and therefore, he was important to me.

But I'm also instantly on edge, even more than has become standard. There's an automatic pit in my stomach that doesn't stem from grief over Darren's death.

Because if there's one thing I've learned about Timmy, it's that he doesn't deal with even *little* things well. And this is no little thing—to him, it's one of the pivotal moments of his life.

A best friend, *dead*.

And he's going to act out.

And I'm going to be the one who bears the brunt of his grief.

———

Over the next few days, the fallout begins.

Timmy spends hours replaying memories of Darren, glorifying him as if their friendship had never fractured. It doesn't matter that they hadn't spoken in months or that their last interaction ended in a screaming match. In Timmy's mind, Saint Darren is untouchable now. Canonized by death. Even Darren himself would say Timmy is laying it on a bit thick with the way he's talking about him.

Every day, he cries and tells me the same stories. The good times. The bad times. The times that have been warped by his grief.

I try to be patient. I try to support him, even though a voice inside me warns that this is a recipe for disaster.

But his grief doesn't settle into sorrow or even self-pity. It curdles into something darker—resentment. And I'm his lightning rod.

The first cracks show when I'm in the kitchen, making a snack and trying to give him space to process. I have a TV show playing in the background. Without warning, Timmy slams a pan down on the counter so hard it rattles the stove. "God, why do I have to be here?" he snarls, his eyes cold. "I'd rather be at work than stuck here with *you*."

I blink, unsure if I've misheard. But his tone is unmistakable—sharp, cutting, and full of contempt.

Then he crosses the room, turning off the TV with a deliberate click. "Why do you even bother staying?" he spits. "What's the point of *you?*"

My gaze shifts to the knife in my hand, and for a moment—just a split second—I think about what it would feel like to plunge the sharp metal deep into Timmy, the look of shock on his face as he bled out. But just as quickly, the thought floats away.

Instead, I just don't respond. What's the point? He doesn't want an answer, just a target.

Another time, he tries to shove piping-hot bacon in my face. "Here, eat this," he orders, his tone suggesting that eating this strip of bacon is somehow a test of loyalty or affection.

"No thank you," I say, my stomach churning from stress.

He kicks his baby shark toy at me, his face a mask of irritation.

Two minutes later, he offers me a burrito, as if this small act of generosity will erase the venom that preceded it.

When I decline, his irritation boils over. "You're impossible," he mutters, storming into the other room.

I stand frozen in the kitchen, the words he doesn't say louder than the ones he does. It's not just anger at Darren's death.

It's anger that *I'm* still here.

———

Against all odds, Christmas Day is peaceful. Almost… enjoyable.

We cook a feast together—scallops, lamb racks, and pavlova topped with whipped cream and fresh fruit. We laugh at cheesy Christmas movies and spend time swimming in the ocean. For a few precious hours, it feels like the life we once dreamed of building together.

He gives me a Christmas card. Inside, he's written a brief note:

I WILL BE A GOOD BOY FOR YOU.

The words feel like a promise I know he can't keep, but for a moment, I let myself pretend.

I let myself believe.

———

The illusion shatters the day after Christmas.

I'm consumed with dread over Darren's upcoming memorial. Timmy's grief isn't just sorrow—it's a volatile cocktail of anger, guilt, and denial. Every outburst, every erratic action feels like a storm brewing on the horizon.

The anxiety leaves me unable to eat. Every time I try, I feel my stomach clench. Most of the time, I end up vomiting.

Timmy, meanwhile, grows increasingly erratic. He continues slamming doors and counters, his frustration bubbling over at the smallest provocation. "Darren was the best guy I ever knew," he says repeatedly, ignoring the reality of their broken friendship.

He spirals into the myth of Darren, each retelling of their bond painting a rosier picture. It's as if his grief demands perfection, as if any acknowledgment of Darren's flaws would make the loss too unbearable.

My body is weak from days of anxiety and little nourishment.

My mind is exhausted from navigating Timmy's emotional landmines.

And I know the worst is still to come.

CHAPTER 75
SAINT DARREN THE BENEVOLENT COKE DEALER

DEX

The sun rises over Sunset Cay, but there's no warmth in its glow, no reprieve in its light. I sit in my dimly lit apartment, staring at the screen showing Margaux's living room.

My jaw tightens as I watch her and Timmy's latest interaction play out.

FUCK.

His grief over Darren's death is a living thing, twisting and thrashing like a wounded animal, and Margaux—damn her big heart—is letting it wrap its claws around her.

What are the fucking chances his estranged BFF would go and die right now?

She was ready to leave.

I could feel it, even from here.

She'd made peace with the idea of walking away, of saving herself.

But now, Timmy's grief has become the perfect trap, yanking her back into his orbit just when she was on the verge of breaking free.

I watch as Timmy clings to her, his face a mask of anguish. The words spilling from his mouth are desperate, pleading. "I *need* you, Margaux. I can't do this without you." His voice cracks, and tears stream down his face. It's a masterclass in manipulation, even if he doesn't fully realize it.

Her shoulders slump under the weight of his pain, and I can see the internal struggle in her eyes. She's torn between her own survival and the relentless pull of her compassion.

And I can't blame her. It's hard to walk away from someone who looks at you like you're their only lifeline, even when that lifeline has been dragging *you* underwater for months.

But Timmy's grief isn't the kind that heals. It's toxic, corrosive, and it's already starting to eat away at her.

———

Later, I switch to the kitchen feed and watch as Margaux tries to find a moment of peace. She's preparing a simple meal, her movements deliberate but sluggish. Her shoulders are tense, her jaw tight. She's exhausted in every sense of the word.

Timmy stomps into the room, slamming a pan down on the counter with enough force to rattle the stove. "God, why do I have to be here?" he snarls. His tone drips with scorn, and it's clear he's not talking about the apartment.

Margaux freezes, the knife in her hand hovering over a cutting board. She doesn't look at him, doesn't respond. I can almost feel her trying to will herself invisible. But he's not done.

My breath comes faster, anger building in my chest like a storm.

He's breaking her, piece by piece, and she's letting him.

He strides over to the TV and clicks it off. "Why do you even bother staying?" he spits. "What's the point of *you*?"

The words hit like a slap, and I find myself gripping the edge of my desk so hard my knuckles turn white.

But then I see it—that flicker of fire in her eyes. She chooses not to respond, but I saw what I saw, and it gives me hope.

Her wrist twitches, almost imperceptibly, as if she's considering using it for something other than chopping up the ingredients for her snack.

For a moment, he falters, his bravado crumbling under her gaze. But the moment passes quickly, and he retreats into the other room, muttering under his breath.

Margaux exhales sharply, her hand trembling as she sets the knife down.

She doesn't cry.

She doesn't scream.

She just stands there, staring at the spot where he had stood moments before.

I want to reach through the screen, to pull her out of this nightmare and into safety.

But all I can do is watch.

———

The days blur together, each one a new chapter in Timmy's grief spiral. His sadness over Darren's death becomes an excuse for every outburst, every cruel word, every moment of volatility.

And Margaux—poor, stubborn Margaux—absorbs it all.

She listens to his stories about Darren, lets him cry on her shoulder, and tries to navigate his unpredictable moods.

But she's not okay.

She's wasting away, her body weak from anxiety and lack of nourishment. I see her try to eat, only to push the plate away moments later. I see her clutching her stomach, her face pale, her breaths shallow.

She's drowning—disappearing—and I can't pull her out.

———

One evening, I watch as she sits on the bed, staring blankly at the TV.

Timmy is pacing in the kitchen, ranting about Darren's upcoming memorial. His voice rises and falls, alternating between anger and despair. "Darren was the best guy I ever knew," he says for the hundredth time, his tone reverent and bitter all at once.

Margaux doesn't respond. She's too tired, too drained. Instead, she stares straight ahead, her expression blank, no doubt tired of hearing about Saint Darren the Benevolent.

The same Darren that, only months before, Timmy had described as a bad friend, a user, and an abuser, among other things. Now, he's being romanticized, placed on a pedestal, his formerly acknowledged flaws now ignored, denied.

I'd be exhausted, too.

Timmy slams a cupboard door, then another. "Why don't you care?" he demands, his voice both sharp and accusing.

She finally looks at him, her eyes hollow. "I do care, Timmy. I just… I can't do this anymore."

Her words hang in the air, a fragile truth that he swats away with a dismissive wave of his hand. "Whatever," he mutters. "I'm going to bed in the back room."

As he disappears into the other room, Margaux lets out a shaky breath. She pulls out her phone and types something. A message to Alice, most likely.

A cry for help she won't allow herself to fully commit to.

———

Watching all of this unfold, I feel a mix of rage and helplessness. Margaux was so close to leaving, to reclaiming her life.

But now, Darren's death has become the perfect excuse for Timmy to tighten his grip on her. And she—ever the empath—feels obligated to stay.

To help him.

To fix him.

But she can't fix him. She can't save him.

And if she stays, he'll destroy her.

I know I can't force her to leave. She has to make that decision on her own. But as I watch her fade under the weight of his abuse, I make a silent promise:

If she can't save herself, I'll do it for her.

Whatever it takes.

CHAPTER 76
LAWYER UP

MARGAUX

The chili joint is loud and bustling, filled with the clatter of dishes and the hum of conversations. The savory aroma of slow-cooked beef mingles with the faint scent of cheap cleaning products. But I'm not here to eat.

It's an odd choice for a legal meeting, but I'm grateful for the distraction as I scan the room for my court-appointed lawyer.

I still can't believe I've lucked out and been appointed a former ADA instead of a regular public defender.

Score.

He spots me as soon as he enters the restaurant, waving me over to a corner booth tucked away from the chaos.

"Margaux?" he asks, shaking my hand.

"That's me," I reply, sliding into the booth.

"Good to meet you. I'm Peter, your lawyer," he says, his tone professional yet warm. "I recognize you from the many hours of police body cam footage I've watched from the night you were arrested." He pauses. "And just so you know, I'm not just a lawyer—I like to think of myself as a counselor, too. My goal is to help you navigate this legally and emotionally."

I appreciate his candor, though I'm unsure how much anyone can help me emotionally at this point.

Removing his laptop from its bag, Peter sets it down on the table alongside a small pile of legal papers. He opens his laptop and pulls up the body cam footage from the night Timmy had me locked up.

He clicks play, and I watch myself through the lens of the arresting officer's camera—disheveled, in a sports bra and shorts, trying to make sense of what was happening.

"I have to say," Peter starts, a smirk tugging at the corners of his mouth, "you're probably the most talkative client I've ever had. Most people freeze up or shut down around cops—but not you, Margaux. You were telling them about roller derby, your uncle's passing—sorry for your loss, by the way—and a whole bunch of other stuff."

I wince. "Not my finest moment."

He chuckles. "For the record, you didn't admit to anything, so no harm done. You just mentioned you were standing up for yourself. But next time—four words: shut the fuck up. That's the advice I give to all my clients. Sorry to swear, but I like to keep it simple and memorable."

He shows me the part with the adorable doctor who diagnosed my skull fracture.

The lawyer cracks up laughing at the mention of 'defensive drinking'. But then his tone turns serious.

He asks me about Timmy's supposed mental health diagnosis, and I tell him what I know.

The footage shifts to Timmy filling out his statement. My stomach churns as I watch him write with calculated calmness, the paperwork sitting atop the hood of a police cruiser, his hand steady as he pens a series of lies.

Peter pauses the video and turns to me, his tone serious. "Here's the deal. Based on everything I've seen, Timmy's behavior—and his mental health issues—make him unpredictable. And you need to be careful. If you stay with him, this won't be the last time you find yourself in a legal mess. It's going to be a hard journey, and he's unlikely to change. He's shown that when things escalate, he's willing to throw you under the bus."

I nod, his words cutting deeper than I want to admit.

"Listen, Margaux... I could tell from the moment I watched the video footage that you're a good person," he continues. "But you need to ask yourself—is this the life you want, and is Timmy the kind of person you want to be around? Because the way this is heading... it doesn't look good, and may not end well for you."

I nod, but the action feels hollow.

I absorb his words as if I'm a distant bystander, trying to focus on the legal logistics rather than the emotional implications.

Timmy's the exception, not the norm. He wants to do better. To be better.

Timmy promised he'd drop the charges. Once that's done, everything will go back to normal—no more court dates, no more cops, no more tension.

At least, that's what I tell myself.

Maybe that's the cure for all this.

I'm so glad I dropped the charges against him, and that he's going to do the same for me.

Sure, mine against him were for something that *actually* happened, while his against me were completely bogus, but it feels like he's leveling the score by doing this.

Like a show of solidarity—that we're a team who has each other's backs.

But then Peter shows me the forms Timmy filled out. My heart sinks as I read the accusations—strangulation, stalking, controlling behavior.

"He told the police *I* strangled *him*?" I gasp, incredulous. "And that I *stalk* him?"

Peter nods grimly. "He took things that you've described him doing to you, and flipped them around to make it look like you're the aggressor."

Fury bubbles beneath my skin.

On the drive home, I confront Timmy.

"You told the police that I *strangled* you, and that I *attacked* you with *weapons*?" I question him, describing details he included in the printed statement. "That I stalk you around, trying to control you?"

Timmy doesn't respond.

"You *lied* to the *police*, Timmy." My voice cracks. "These are all things *you've* done to *me*, that I've *never* done to *you*."

Timmy sits in the passenger seat, his expression a mix of guilt and defiance. "I didn't say that," he mutters. "The cop wrote it all down for me."

I shake my head. "Timmy, I've seen the footage of you filling the paperwork out," I snap. "The cop didn't write a word of it. *You* did."

He shrugs, avoiding my gaze. "Oh, well… I had to make it sound good. So I took the truth and added a little."

I stare at him, incredulous. "You *lied to the police* and said I *committed crimes I didn't commit*. Do you have any idea how *serious* that is?"

"Well, you upset me. And you were going to call the cops on me and I didn't want to go to jail," he says simply, as if that justifies everything.

"And it's okay that *I* had to?" My voice rises, a mixture of anger and disbelief. "You fabricated a story about me pulling your hair so I would go to jail instead of you?"

He sighs, rubbing his temples. "Yeah. Sorry. I panicked."

"Unbelievable," I mutter, sinking further into the driver's seat. "You have no problem attacking me, threatening to kill me, and giving me a *fucking* skull fracture. And when I dropped the charges, I thought maybe you'd have the decency to do the same. But instead, you doubled down on your lies."

"Yeah, sorry. Let's just try to move forward," he says, putting a hand on my shoulder. His touch feels heavy, suffocating. "I'll go downtown and sign the same form you did. I promise."

I flinch. "You're unbelievable."

———

A FEW NIGHTS LATER

"I wanna press charges on you more and more," he sneers, standing in front of the TV screen to block my view.

"Timmy, stop," I plead, my voice weary.

"You shouldn't even be here given there's a pending court case. I think you should be arrested for being around me," he continues, his words slurred yet still sanctimonious.

I ignore him, my patience having worn thin long ago.

I prefer my drama to come from the shows I watch rather than my own home.

"Why are you doing this?" I ask, my voice breaking.

He smirks. "Because I can."

I retreat to my laptop, determined not to engage further.

"I want to ask the police how you could possibly be here right now."

Sighing, I look up. "Timmy, why are you being like this?" I plead. "You promised you'd drop the charges like I dropped the ones against you."

He shrugs. "I talked to someone about you and our situation," he says, cryptically. "I can still make the charges against you. I don't know what your problem is, but you need to stop.:

He picks up a large chef's knife and kitchen scissors and stabs them both into the wooden chopping board.

Then he grabs a pair of scissors and walks to the TV. With one swift motion, he cuts the power cord. The screen flickers to black.

Great. Oh well, I guess I'll just watch the show on my laptop.

"I have a message drafted to 911," he announces, holding up his phone. "It says you hit me three times, and that you keep trying to break into the back room to be even more abusive. You'd better be careful."

I stare at him, numb.

The fight in me is gone.

And for the first time, I realize I'm not scared anymore.

I'm just done.

And I no longer care what happens.

CHAPTER 77
CONSISTENTLY INCONSISTENT

MARGAUX

It's late January, and I finally catch Covid for the first time.

I've managed to dodge it for years, thanks to a combination of germophobia, obsessive hand-sanitizing, and the luxury of remote work during the height of the pandemic. Even when my ex brought Covid home after a business trip, I made him isolate in the bedroom, delivering meals to the door like room service, and somehow escaped infection.

This time, though, I wasn't so lucky.

Sure, I could have caught it at the grocery store, but Occam's razor leads me to the more obvious culprit—Timmy.

His visits to the beachside tents—where he shares drinks, joints, and cigarettes with the local misfits and addicts—are a glaring vector of exposure. The thought of what he might be putting his mouth on over there makes my stomach churn.

"I've avoided Covid for three years," I snap, furious. "And because you're irresponsible, I finally get it?"

His deflection is immediate. "You probably got it at the grocery store. I didn't give it to you."

I'm outraged by his blasé response. "Timmy, you're literally putting your *mouth* on things that have been passed around by god knows who. And then you come home, breathe on me, kiss me…"

But he won't take responsibility.

"God, you're *so* fucking dumb," he says, rolling his eyes like I've just suggested the earth is flat. "It's not my fault. It's *obviously* from the grocery store."

I've become so accustomed to his insults that they barely register anymore. I don't even flinch at 'dumb' or the way his tone drips with contempt. It's become background noise, like the hum of a refrigerator—steady and unrelenting.

But sometimes, his attitude still gets to me. And when it does, I lash out in ways that make me ashamed of myself.

And then I feel complicit.

As if I'm just as much to blame as him.

By now, Timmy is still navigating the emotional fallout of Darren's death. The memorial is approaching, and I can sense his agitation growing.

To distract him—and to encourage him to contribute financially—I buy him a refurbished laptop that will run his graphic design software more efficiently.

"I really need it for my art," he'd pleaded, his eyes wide with sincerity. "I'll sell tons of hats and T-shirts, and I'll give you all the money I make."

To be fair, he *has* been giving me what little he earns from his part-time job, so, at first, I believe he means well. But, within days, and despite a lot of talk about graphic design ideas, it becomes clear that the laptop is more symbolic than practical. He rarely opens it, and—when I ask about his progress—there's always an excuse.

"I'm not feeling well," he says one day. "I can't focus when my stomach hurts this bad."

Another day, it's a nightmare that derails him.

Or vague chest pains.

Or a headache.

The list goes on.

Before Timmy, I'd never met a grown adult who puts their life on hold so frequently due to a 'tummy ache' or a 'nightmare'.

He'd probably call out if he stubbed his toe.

I try to motivate him. "You can't call out of work for a nightmare, Timmy. And if you're your own boss, you should be harder on yourself than any corporate boss would ever be. You owe it to yourself to make your dream come true—but instead, you go to sleep late, then sleep in late, and complain about these problems. If you're really feeling that bad, maybe you should go to the doctor," I suggest.

And so that becomes his next focus.

"There's something wrong with my heart," he says, grabbing at his chest. "I can tell."

Cardiologist: "Your heart is fine, sir."

"I need my skin checked," he says, obsessively examining his freckles in the mirror. "I might have skin cancer."

Dermatologist: "Your skin is fine, sir."

"My feet need checking," he says, rubbing at his toes. "Dad says your feet are the most important thing to take care of as you get older."

Podiatrist: "Your feet are fine, sir. But let's clean up those toenails."

Each visit ends with a clean bill of health, and each time, Timmy breathes a sigh of relief—only to conjure a new ailment days later, and a new specialist he needs to see.

I try to help. "Maybe stop drinking so much—or at all?" I suggest, exasperated. "Drink water? Exercise? Eat healthy? Get up at a normal time? Work?"

I'm not trying to be flippant, but he takes it that way. "You're such a fucking bitch," he snaps.

"I'm trying to help you," I counter, my tone measured. "I don't always follow my own advice," I explain. "But I do most of the time. That's the key. You need consistency to see results. You have to show up for yourself."

But Timmy's only consistency is his inconsistency.

———

Despite his constant maladies and complaints, Timmy's behavior stabilizes for a short while.

He signs the form to have the charges against me dropped, and my court-appointed lawyer successfully argues to have the state's case dismissed, despite the state insisting it be continued even without Timmy as a witness. Luckily, my lawyer points out the absurdity of this, and the judge sides with him. A huge weight on my shoulders lifts.

Timmy attends therapy sessions for several consecutive weeks and comes home beaming, recounting his progress. "I told my therapist how much I love you," he says one day, his voice full of conviction. "I want to be better— for us."

He adjusts to his new medication, and while he's still irritable at times, the sharp edges of his personality soften.

He cooks dinner without complaint.

He cleans without slamming cabinets.

He even seems to enjoy walking Sabre to the beach during the day on his little harness.

For a brief moment in time, we're a semblance of the couple that it felt like we once were.

He's still emotional about Darren, but his grief has mellowed. He continues working his part-time job, though his complaints about his boss, Robert, grow more frequent.

"Robert's so picky," he grumbles. "Just because he does things differently doesn't mean it's better."

When Robert hires a new employee, a woman recently out of the military, Timmy takes issue with her too. "She's so loud and annoying," he says. "She doesn't know what she's doing, and I end up having to do all the actual work while she wastes time. But she has this giant ass that Robert just likes to look at all day."

I just nod and encourage him to keep showing up for work. His contributions to our living expenses—while small—are meaningful.

We swim together.

We cook together.

We watch movies without arguing.

I allow myself to feel a rare sliver of hope.

Maybe this is the turning point.

Maybe things can be good again.

But deep down, I know the winds are bound to pick up again. And Darren's upcoming memorial looms front and center in my mind.

CHAPTER 78
MEMORIES

MARGAUX

By the time Darren's memorial arrives, I'm running on empty. The brief period of stability Timmy showed in the weeks before now feels like a distant memory, and there's been a huge backslide.

His grief has morphed into erratic behavior, his emotions swinging wildly between quiet despair and volatile anger. Every moment with him is a potential landmine, more than ever. His sensitivity is so heightened that anything I say or do could set him off.

I'm not doing much better. My nerves are frayed to the point where my hands shake constantly—I'm a knife's edge away from losing my sanity. The anxiety I've been carrying for weeks about this event has reached its peak.

I'm terrified about how Timmy will behave—whether he'll impulsively run off, get into a fight, or do something reckless and dangerous. Part of me fears he'll end up doing drugs with some of the people there and meet the same fate as Darren. The other part fears I'll be the one who bears the brunt of his unbridled emotions.

But I keep all of this inside.

I don't want to burden my friends, who I'm sure are exhausted by the constant cycle of Timmy's bad behavior. And, despite everything, I feel sympathy for his loss.

So I don't talk about how scared I am, or how much this is all eating away at me.

I try to stay strong, for him and for me.

"I promise I won't run off at the memorial," he's told me repeatedly, his tone earnest. "I'll keep you by my side, introduce you to everyone. You'll see."

His words have done little to ease my fears, but at least they've provided a sliver of reassurance that he understands my concerns.

———

When we arrive at the memorial, that promise is shattered almost immediately.

At first, Timmy keeps me close, introducing me to a handful of people— some I've heard about, others completely new. But his attention quickly shifts, and soon he's darting around like a restless show pony, unable to sit still or focus. I'm left standing awkwardly on the periphery, struggling to keep up as he flits from one conversation to the next.

When the paddle-out begins, there's a brief calm. I watch as Timmy and a group of surfers solemnly paddle out with Darren's ashes, their boards cutting through the gentle waves. It's a rare moment of somber reflection. But as soon as he returns, the calm is gone.

"We ate him!" he says, his voice a mix of glee and disbelief. "Some of us *ate Darren* while we were out there!"

I stare at him, unsure how to respond. My lips press into a tight line, and I nod slowly. Everyone grieves in their own way, I suppose.

Afterward, he sifts through Darren's belongings—clothes, photos, personal trinkets—and gets visibly emotional. He picks out a hot sauce T-shirt he says Darren loved as well as a couple of other clothing items, cradling them in his arms with reverence.

But then he notices there's no photo of the two of them together in the bowl of photographs. "Oh wow," he laments, his voice tinged with bitterness. "So there's a photo in here of him and *Matty*, but not one with *me?*" He becomes quite upset over the omission and keeps mentioning it.

But his emotions—real or exaggerated—don't tether him for long. Soon, he's back to gallivanting around, loudly proclaiming himself Darren's closest friend to anyone who will listen.

At one point, I spot him talking to a woman holding a baby. I'm pretty sure it's Darren's ex, but I'm not certain. At first, it seems fine—a friendly exchange, a hug. But then he lingers. He whispers to her, leaning in too close, too long. He clings to her like she's the last lifeboat on a sinking ship.

Standing with strangers, I feel an unbearable wave of embarrassment and discomfort.

"Is it just me, or is he being weird with her?" I ask the girl next to me, who has also been watching him.

She raises an eyebrow. "He sure runs up to you anytime you're talking to a guy," she says. "Seems pretty hypocritical of him to be doing… whatever *that* is."

Her words are the breaking point. "Fuck this," I mutter, and I turn on my heel and head for the car.

Timmy notices my departure and sprints after me. "Wait! What's happening?"

"You said we'd stick together," I say, my voice shaking with frustration. "I've tried so hard to be supportive, but you've left me by myself for ages. You promised me you wouldn't do that. You're acting erratic and I'm concerned. I need to leave. I don't feel comfortable here anymore."

He hops in the truck beside me, and for a brief moment after we head out, there's silence. But it doesn't last.

"*Youuuuu* ruined this," he growls, his teeth bared in anger. His bottom jaw juts out aggressively, his lower teeth giving full-blown llama, a sure sign that his fury is reaching its peak. "I knew you'd ruin Darren's memorial!"

I grip the steering wheel tightly, trying to keep my focus on the road as his tirade escalates. "I didn't ruin anything, Timmy," I snap. "You were acting erratic and drunk, and you promised we'd stick together. But you left me alone for hours, and you were behaving in ways that drew attention from other people. I was worried about what you were going to do next."

"You just *had* to ruin Darren's memorial! I knew I couldn't trust you to be there for me. *You embarrassed me so much!*" he screams, his voice echoing in the cab. "Everyone noticed when we left! You made me look like an *idiot!*"

"Nobody noticed," I lie, desperate to calm him down.

He continues to scream, his aggression echoing from the truck's walls.

I hold myself as still as I can, trying to focus on the road.

I use one shaky hand to call his dad. "Please help!" I beg. "He won't stop screaming. I'm driving down the freeway and it's dangerous. Please ask him to calm down so he doesn't cause an accident!"

His dad's voice, sharp and cutting, comes through the speaker. "Well, Margaux, you must have done something to upset him."

I'm livid, and a little shocked. "I called you to help calm him down so we don't crash the car," I say through gritted teeth.

"She was *jealous!*" he yells into the phone. "She saw me hug Darren's ex and *lost her mind!*"

His dad's tone softens for Timmy. "Son, just calm down, okay? Get home safely."

"*She made us leave right at the beginning!*" he screams. "*I didn't even get to say hello to anyone!*"

I blink. *Were we not at the same event? Did he not paddle out and brag about eating Darren's ashes?*

"That's not true," I respond, with Phil still listening. "We were there for hours, you caught up with a lot of people, you participated in the paddle-out, and you picked out some of Darren's things to keep."

"*You made me leave all my things back there!*" he shrieks. "*The surfboard. The hammock.*"

"Please stop yelling!" I plead.

"*She was so jealous, Dad!*" he screams. "*She was jealous because she saw me hug two girls.*"

"No," I reply. "I was upset because you failed to stick to the boundaries we agreed to for the day. I've had to prepare myself for months leading up to this event due to worry about how you'd behave—it's caused huge anxiety, and now you're acting the way I feared. I didn't want you to do drugs and die, and I didn't want you to run away. You promised we'd stick together all day, but you left me after about five minutes. I knew nobody there except for Matty and Steve, and you know how I feel about *them*. So I tried to be there for you, but I have to protect myself as well."

"Well," Phil sighs, judgment dripping from his tone, "it sounds like you really upset him, Margaux."

"What are you talking about?" I'm so angry at Phil right now. It's as if he just turned on me and jumped to Timmy's defense, automatically believing his completely fabricated version of events. "He was upset because his friend died, and he didn't follow through on how he promised he'd behave."

His dad's tone is sharp once again. "Well, his friend *died,* so you kind of have to give him a break, Margaux."

"This is insane," I mutter, feeling chastised. "I was just calling to see if you could get him to calm down so we don't crash the truck."

"Son," Phil sighs. "Calm down. Call me when you get home."

Timmy mutters something unintelligible, and I hang up the phone.

When we finally get home, the screaming continues. I secretly call Alice, letting her listen to his tirade. After about a minute, I hang up. She's heard enough.

ALICE:

That man is going to kill you one day.

ME:

His dad said I must have done something to upset him.

ALICE:

Nope.

Toxic.

Gross.

ME:

He's been relatively good, and I've been worrying about this memorial. I get it's an anomaly, an outlier event, that one of his good friends died—even though they were estranged at the time. It's been this looming date.

ALICE:

What happens with the next big event?

And the next?

ME:

Yeah, I know.

I said that to him. It's like, 'Oh well, now you're not going mental over a TV show or a music choice, so that's progress.'

And good friends don't die each and every day, but stuff still happens and you can't act like that.

ALICE:

Exactly.

What'd he say?

ME:

I don't think he was in a position to receive the message.

ALICE:

I don't think he ever will be.

ME:

He's calmer now, and made me a coffee.

I'm finishing my book edits and about to send out my ARCs.

So I'll worry about him later.

Spoiler alert: you are in my acknowledgements. 

ALICE:

OMG THAT IS THE BEST CREDIT EVER.

———

In the days that follow, Timmy's narrative about the memorial changes at his convenience.

Sometimes, he says he stayed as long as he wanted and that he should have done better about keeping me by his side.

Other times, he claims I dragged him away at the very start out of jealousy, ruining everything before he even had a chance to say goodbye. That I had a problem because he briefly hugged Darren's ex and was looking at her baby.

"Which is it, Timmy?" I ask in exasperation. "Which version is true?"

He smirks. "Depends on who I'm talking to and how I'm feeling."

Wow. He's not even trying to hide who he really is anymore.

CHAPTER 79
ZOLOFT FUGUE

MARGAUX

With my insurance *finally* sorted out, I manage to see a doctor at the local health center. Stepping into the brightly lit waiting room, I feel a mix of relief and trepidation. The sterile smell, the hum of the HVAC, and the low murmur of conversations remind me that I'm here to make progress—to take back some control.

The doctor is like a breath of fresh air. She's professional but warm, her gentle manner somehow disarming the wall I've built around myself.

I'm honest with her. I explain my situation—the abusive relationship, the emotional rollercoaster, the overwhelming stress. The crippling pain that debilitates me for at least two days every month. It tumbles out of me like a confession.

She listens without judgment, nodding thoughtfully. "Let's get you some help," she says. "I'll prescribe you an antidepressant to take the edge off. And I'm also going to refer you to therapy."

I nod, already feeling a little lighter.

"And since you mentioned your physical health, I'll refer you to a gynecologist as well. You shouldn't have to live with that kind of pain every month."

Her practicality is comforting. She's addressing the things I've ignored for far too long.

Then she adds something unexpected—"I'm also giving you a referral to the gym here at the center. It's affordable, and it's a great way to meet people. I go there myself. It might help to get out and broaden your connections around here."

I nod again, catching the subtext. She's nudging me—offering a lifeline to something beyond Timmy. Sure, I can work on my cardiovascular health and get back to the ripped, shredded creature I was when I first moved here. But she also knows I need distance, perspective, something to remind me of my own strength. She's not pushy, but I can tell she's rooting for me.

As I leave, she makes sure the local domestic violence shelter's number is programmed into my phone. "Just in case," she says.

For the first time in a long while, I feel like someone in this town is truly on my side.

———

A few days later, Timmy is in one of his moods again. He's storming in and out of the apartment, retreating to the tents to drink and smoke. Each time he comes back, he's angrier and more emboldened—resentful, seething with accusations he hurls my way.

I'm exhausted. His behavior chips away at my already fragile sanity.

The antidepressants are new, and while they're supposed to stabilize me, they've left me feeling off. I'm on edge, a little more hyper and irritated than usual, my patience thin. I take a swig of whiskey to blunt the edges, but it only seems to blur the lines between rationality and impulsiveness.

How dare he? How dare he run off, leaving me here to stew in this boiling pit of resentment? How dare he expect me to carry the weight of everything —our finances, our home, our relationship—while he indulges his whims like a rageful toddler?

I want to storm down to the tents and confront Timmy, and every time I'm about to, he comes back into the apartment and then leaves again.

I sit for a while, feeling a bit funny as the whiskey starts to numb me, to blur the edges a little. It makes him seem less scary, like I'm watching him from outside my body.

Each time he returns, his voice sounds more hollow.

He leaves, comes back again, leaves again.

My mind races, spinning into a storm of anger and desperation. I can't stay here, pacing, helpless

I need to get him.

Bring him home.

Fix this, somehow.

I have to get him to come home.

It's dangerous out there.

My body is on a different plane from my brain.

How dare he? I have to get him, for his own good.

And because I'm so angry, so very *angry.*

I grab the truck keys and head to the parking garage. The air feels heavy, pressing down on my chest as I start the engine.

I drive through the dimly lit streets, scanning for any sign of Timmy.

I have to get him. None of this is okay. This isn't the life I want.

At the 7-Eleven, a man waves me over. He's holding a can of Rolling Rock in one hand, a football tucked under his arm. His disheveled appearance and the smell of stale beer that clings to him make me hesitate.

But desperation overrides my caution. "Can you help me find Timmy?" I ask.

"Sure," he says, climbing into the passenger seat.

I start driving, hoping he might point me in the right direction. But instead of being helpful, he leans closer. "Pull over here," he says.

I think he's ready to get out, but then he grabs me, crushing his lips against mine. His breath reeks of alcohol, and I recoil, but he doesn't seem to notice.

I take another swig of whiskey, hoping it will steady me.

He doesn't stop. His hand darts out, groping at me.

"No, don't do that," I snap, shoving his hand away. "I need to go."

My brain is in slow motion, my thoughts muddled—but still, it screams at me.

Danger. Get this random guy out of your car. This was a terrible idea.

He smirks. "If you kiss me again, I'll get out. I'll even let you keep this football," he says, holding it out like some kind of twisted trophy.

I feel trapped.

"No," I say.

"Come on," he says, grabbing at me again.

I let him kiss me again, just to make him leave.

Please, just get out of the car. I did what you wanted.

But then, everything fades to black…

CHAPTER 80
PETE DAVIDSONING THE FENCE

MARGAUX

wake up disoriented, my vision blurry and my head throbbing. The first thing I notice is the sensation of being moved—gently but firmly—onto a stretcher.

An ambulance. I'm being removed from the truck and placed in an ambulance.

There are flashing lights, a woman with short hair rushing around, and voices overlapping in a chaotic symphony of concern and urgency. A paramedic leans over me, adjusting a neck brace around my throat. It's suffocating but necessary.

The truck—*my truck*—is pushed up against what looks like a fence. Splinters of wood and metal gleam in the daylight, and I can just make out a smashed headlight. My mind struggles to piece together how I ended up here, but everything feels scrambled.

The sirens sound hollow from inside the vehicle, an eerie wee-woo wee-woo as we make our way to hospital.

"I'm going to throw up," I mumble, my voice dry and cracked.

A paramedic hands me a sick bag just in time, and I hurl into it, my body shaking as nausea overtakes me. Needles poke at my arm as they hook me up to fluids. My head feels heavy, detached from my body.

When we reach the hospital, I'm wheeled into the ER. Everything is a blur of white coats, blue scrubs, and fluorescent lights. Scanners beep, questions are asked, and hands move quickly to stabilize me.

I catch snippets of conversation: "Vitals are stable… possible mild concussion…"

They wheel me to a curtained-off bed. A cop is stationed right outside—not for me, but I notice he's there.

I lie here, staring up at the ceiling. The world feels far away, yet the shame of everything that's happened presses down on me like a lead blanket.

Oh my god. I Pete Davidson'd the fence.

But how? I feel… fine. Physically, anyway. Mentally, I'm unraveling.

I text a few friends to let them know what happened, though I don't even know how to explain it myself.

"Can I go now?" I ask a nurse after what feels like hours.

She shakes her head. "We need to observe you a little longer. I'll check when the doctor will clear you."

Frustrated and exhausted, I pull out my phone and message Alice:

ALICE:

Babe.

You're going to end up dead.

ME:

He ran off.

ALICE:

Who cares? He's a grown man.

ME:

I care.

ALICE:

I know. But he can go cool off and come back.

ME:

I care a lot about everything and everyone and look what happens.

He went for hours.

ALICE:

He's done it before and will do it again.

ME:

And put Taco Bell on my ceiling.

He did, somehow, smear the contents of a bean burrito and Taco Supreme high up on the walls.

ALICE:

Okay, that's new.

A social worker visits my bed, her face kind but concerned.

"I'm here because you mentioned being in an abusive relationship," she says gently.

"Oh yeah, I am," I reply matter-of-factly.

Because at this point, what's the point in pretending otherwise? I'm a battered woman. Although, according to Timmy, it's always been my fault and the injuries he inflicted weren't 'real' ones.

Her face grows more serious as I recount some of the incidents—the threats, the attacks, the bizarre behaviors like the chainsaws and antlers. She listens carefully, handing me a card with local resources.

She leaves, and I become agitated as Timmy sends me a barrage of texts:

TIMMY:

You're so irresponsible.

This is all your fault.

You're so embarrassing.

I rip the IV from my arm, desperate to leave, but the blood gushes everywhere. I do my best to tighten the bandage like a tourniquet, but blood still cascades across my forearm like arterial routes on a map.

I wander out into the main area, trying to find the exit.

The cop stares at me, blood cascading from my arm, and moves to stand. "Ma'am," he says, as a nurse also notices me.

She hurries over and guides me back to my bed.

"Let me fix that," she says, tidying up the bloody mess I've created.

When I'm finally released, the hospital insists on getting me a taxi. *Liability*, they say.

Back at the apartment, Timmy is waiting for me, his arms crossed and his expression equal parts smug and angry. "You let some random shady guy into the truck? I wasn't even at the tents," he says. "I was here the whole time. You walked right past me with your bottle of whiskey, saying you were going to find me."

His version of events feels like gaslit fiction, but I'm too drained to argue. *Who knows what's true anymore?*

"You're such an idiot and a slut," he adds.

"Whatever," I mutter, heading to the bathroom to wash the hospital smell off me.

I can already tell that Timmy is going to hold this over me forever. He's a proverbial machine gun, and I've just provided the ammo.

———

A week later, the consequences of my crash begin to ripple through my life.

We're coming back from Costco, carrying our groceries to the apartment, when a random woman walks past.

I flash her a neighborly smile, but instead of returning the same, she gives me a weird look, her lips curling into a smirk. "Will you be driving into any more fences?" she says, her tone mocking.

My cheeks flush. Stunned, I continue walking.

Timmy, oblivious to her sarcasm and not properly hearing what she said, smiles and cheerfully replies, "Yep!"

When we get inside, I say, "You did hear what she said, right?"

He looks confused. "She said hi, didn't she?"

I shake my head. "No, she asked if I was going to drive into any more fences."

He frowns. "Oh my gosh, that's really horrible. What a fucked up thing to say. I'm so sorry, Margaux," he says, pulling me into a hug. "What a dumb bitch. Ignore her."

I fill Alice in.

ALICE:

Did you say 'It depends. Will you be walking near one any time soon?"

ME:

Hahaha, I love you.

ALICE:

Imagine someone asking you in public about an embarrassing moment, Susan.

ME:

> I was tempted to say, 'Will you still be ugly when you
> wake up in the morning?' but it felt like the moment
> had passed.

Later, as we unpack the groceries, he pops outside to grab something from the truck. When he returns, his tone has shifted to something cruel and calculated.

"Everyone in this building hates you now for what you did," he says, his eyes gleaming with malice. "Some aunty just asked me for money to fix the fence you damaged. She showed me pictures of it all. Nobody likes you here."

The shame comes rushing back, magnified by his words.

I didn't think I could possibly feel any more embarrassed, mortified, confused and utterly upset about the whole situation than I already did, but yet again, Timmy has found a way.

———

A few days later, Timmy comes home early from his part-time job, his expression grim.

I'm used to him popping home during his shift, as if he's performing little spot checks to make sure I haven't invited any men home while he's at work.

But this feels different.

"I got fired," he says flatly.

"What?" I set down my laptop, already bracing myself for the inevitable blame game.

"I got into it with Robert," he explains. "He criticized the way I was painting something, and it just kind of escalated from there," he explains.

"That's awful," I say, though a pit forms in my stomach.

I shiver as I have a flashback to what happened when he got criticized for the way he painted the barn at Steve's place.

Where he was so offended by someone's offhand comment that he threatened to kill everyone.

Where Steve had to come and collect his hunting rifle so it was out of Timmy's way—just in case.

"Yeah," he nods. "It wasn't good. And then Robert randomly said he has a business to run, and that the public areas of this apartment complex aren't our personal living room."

"Huh?" I ask, no clearer than before.

"It's because you drove the truck into the fence," he says. *"That's* why he fired me."

I'm still failing to see the link between the two.

I mean, I *guess* there could be? But in my more than twenty years of HR work, I've never seen someone fired for something that happened to their partner outside of work.

And even if the employee did something themselves, it would only matter if it resulted in criminal charges, which this did not.

He rambles on, his narrative about why he got fired shifting as the hours pass.

In one version, Robert unfairly criticized him, and Timmy calmly defended himself.

In another, Timmy raised his voice, and Robert overreacted and fired him in response.

In yet another, it's my fault entirely. "That's why he fired me," he says, his smirk widening. "You embarrassed me so much, and nobody here likes us anymore. This is on *you*. *You're* the reason I can't contribute to rent. *You're* the problem."

I blink, too stunned to reply.

It doesn't matter that his story makes no sense.

To Timmy, truth is just a tool he wields to suit his mood.

And once again, I'm left carrying the burden of his chaos.

CHAPTER 81
SPIRALING TOWARD THE EDGE

DEX

The notification pings on my laptop, dragging my attention to the live feed from Margaux's truck. My stomach drops. It's a shaky view, but it's clear enough: she's not alone. Some guy I don't recognize is in the passenger seat, leaning too close to her.

What the fuck is she doing?

I lean forward, my heart hammering as I toggle through the feeds. The camera angle doesn't give me much to work with, but I can see enough of the guy's smirking face to feel my fists clenching. He's no one I've seen before.

Disheveled.

Shifty.

He's not just a random bystander.

The audio crackles, and I catch fragments of their conversation. Something about finding Timmy. My jaw tightens.

Why the hell is she chasing after him again?

She's supposed to be done with this shit.

Then it happens. The guy leans in—way too close—and I see his hand reach for her. She flinches, pushing him away, but he doesn't stop. My vision goes red.

"Get out of the truck," I mutter under my breath, willing her to throw him out.

She says something I can't make out, but it doesn't matter—her body language says it all—she's trapped.

I grab my phone, dialing the number I've memorized for emergencies involving her. It rings twice before someone picks up.

"She's in trouble," I snap. "Margaux. She's in her truck with some guy. I don't know who he is, but he's all over her."

The dispatcher's voice is calm, asking for details I barely have. I rattle off what I can, giving the location of the truck from the GPS I hacked.

As I watch, the truck lurches forward, swerving slightly.

My hands grip the edge of the desk, my nails digging into the wood.

Then the screen goes black.

"Fuck!" I slam my fist on the desk, pushing back from the chair so hard it topples over.

I pace the room, phone still in hand, waiting for any updates. The silence is suffocating. My mind races with worst-case scenarios—Margaux hurt, assaulted, or worse.

Minutes stretch into what feels like hours before the call comes. The voice on the other end is steady but grim. "She's alive," they say. "But there's been an accident."

The relief is so sharp it's almost painful, but it's fleeting. An accident.
What the hell happened?

"She's being transported to the hospital," the voice continues. "She's conscious but disoriented. I thought you'd want to know."

I thank them, but the words feel hollow. My mind is already spinning, imagining her scared and alone in a hospital bed, dealing with whatever mess Timmy has dragged her into this time.

———

Hours later, I'm staring at the live feeds. Margaux is back in her apartment now, but I've replayed the footage from the ER over and over, dissecting every moment. She looked exhausted, broken, but alive.

Timmy's voice crackles through the apartment's feed now, cutting through the silence like a blade.

"You're *so* embarrassing," he sneers, his tone dripping with contempt.

I clench my fists so hard my knuckles pop.

"Look at you, crashing the truck like an idiot. Everyone in this building *hates* you now."

Her response is barely audible. She's too drained to argue, but I can see it in her body language—she's not okay.

I can't fucking stand it.

I've watched her endure so much, but this… this feels like the tipping point.

She could have been killed tonight. Or worse.

And instead of compassion—instead of showing the woman he supposedly loves more than anything in the world a shred of care or support—Timmy uses the opportunity to make her feel shame and guilt.

To make himself seem superior to her.

She never would have got into the truck if it wasn't for him—she wouldn't have had a reason to. But time and time again, he poked and prodded at her, making her fear for her safety.

She's barely eaten in weeks, is adjusting to new medication, dealing with Timmy's grief and the fallout over Darren's memorial—it's too much for anyone.

My hand hovers over the keyboard, every muscle in my body coiled tight. I could end this right now. Call the cops on Timmy, have him arrested, make it so he can't hurt her again.

But I know it's not that simple. Margaux has to make the call to leave him. *She* has to want it, or nothing I do will stick.

Still, I can't just sit here and watch her crumble.

Whatever it takes, I'll keep her safe.

Even if she never knows I'm the one pulling the strings.

I switch feeds, tracking Timmy's location. He's at the tents again, probably drunk and high, leaving Margaux alone in the wreckage of their so-called life.

This isn't over.

Not by a long shot.

CHAPTER 82
EAVESDROPPER

MARGAUX

The truck has been taken. Stolen, the keys left on the driver's seat by the police officers who found it up against the fence with me inside.

And because the Cay has its own unique rhythm of chaos, Timmy eventually finds it abandoned on a random side road, as if whoever took it simply lost interest.

After roadside assistance makes us a new set of keys, Timmy surveys the truck's interior. "The stereo gadget is gone," Timmy announces, pointing at the conspicuously empty space where the Bluetooth adapter used to be.

"Fuck," I mutter. "I'll get us another one. Sorry."

"It's fine," he says, unusually forgiving. "At least the brake pads are still here." He gestures at the back seat, where the unopened boxes of brake pads I'd bought are still neatly stacked. "Good thing they didn't take those."

———

A few days pass.

"The brake pads must have been taken by that guy you let into the truck," Timmy says out of nowhere, his tone accusing.

I blink, trying to keep my voice steady. "They were still there when we found the truck, Timmy. I remember you pointing them out."

"No, they weren't. You let that guy steal them. They're gone."

My mind spins. I remember, as clearly as the sun rising this morning, Timmy showing me the brake pads, relieved they hadn't been taken.

But now, he's rewriting history in real-time. He's done this before—traded or given away things, only to blame me when they're mysteriously missing.

He must have sold them. Or swapped them for God knows what.

The man is insane. But more insidious than that, he believes his own lies.

He's perfected the art of bending reality, leaving me questioning everything but the small fragments of truth I cling to desperately. *This?* This, I'm sure of. The brake pads were there.

But I don't have the energy to argue. Not about this. Not anymore.

I nod absently. "Oh. Well, that sucks."

And just like that, I let it go, and I go on about my day.

Defeated.

Ashamed.

Exhausted.

Over it.

Over him.

Over everything.

———

The past few weeks have left me reeling—emotionally shredded—as if someone grabbed the fabric of my sanity and ripped it into jagged pieces.

"They all hate you for what you did," Timmy says one afternoon, his words as sharp as glass. "More people are stopping me in public places, asking me for money to fix the fence you ruined. Telling me how much you owe them. God, it's so embarrassing for me."

The weight of his words presses down like a physical burden. I feel mortified all over again. I can't reconcile my behavior from that night—leaving the apartment, the whiskey-fueled haze, the moment I lost control of the truck and smashed into the fence. How out of character this whole situation is for me.

That wasn't me.

That isn't me.

I'm not the kind of person who yells at a partner or drives recklessly.

I'm not the kind of person who ends up in situations that spiral so completely out of control.

But lately, I've been doing things I never thought I'd do.

And any attempt to hold Timmy accountable for his behavior feels like shouting into a void.

———

Two weeks later, I have my intake appointment with my new therapist. I'm optimistic. Nervous, but optimistic.

It feels like a small chance to reclaim a part of myself, to process the chaos, to untangle the mess that is my life. God knows I need help with what's going on at the moment, let alone all the trauma from my past.

I shut myself in the back room and log in to the session. My therapist, Kathleen, and her supervisor, greet me warmly. Kathleen is wrapping up her postdoctoral studies, and her demeanor is professional yet compassionate.

For the next hour, I tell them everything—or as much as I can fit into sixty minutes. Kathleen and her supervisor listen with interest—and perhaps a touch of horror—as I tell them about my less than conventional life.

The adoption.

My overbearing mother.

Having to get married when I was sixteen.

The abuse and sexual assault.

The death of my father when I was a child.

The toxic relationships.

My uncle's death.

The stress of a high-pressure HR job and conducting multiple layoffs in a short time. My past traumas unfold like a grim tapestry.

I only briefly touch on Timmy, though—just that I'm in a relationship that has involved some abuse. There's too much else to cover, and I need them to understand the full context of my life before we get into the present.

By the end, I feel emotionally wrung out, but lighter.

———

Later in the day, Timmy corners me.

"I heard you talking about me during your therapy session," he says, his face dark. "You really threw me under the bus."

My stomach drops. "What?"

"I heard you. You were talking shit about me."

I squint at him. *What conversation was* he *listening to?*

"I barely mentioned you, Timmy… I just provided a little context to help us figure this out," I shrug. "But I spent most of the session talking about my life before I even met you. While a lot has taken place since we met, our relationship is a short snapshot in the span of my entire life."

"Did you tell her you crashed the truck, too?"

"Yes, I did mention that situation," I nod. "And why were you listening to my intake session?"

"I couldn't help it," he shrugs. "I was going to the bathroom and overheard some of it, and then I just stayed and listened for a bit. You made me sound bad."

I'm stunned. My ex would never have done something like this. Therapy was sacred—private—and he'd go into another room with his headphones on. But Timmy doesn't seem to understand—or care—about boundaries.

Later, he comes out of his own therapy session and he's glowing. Beaming from ear to ear. "I love you so much," he says, pulling me into a hug. "She thinks I'm doing *really* good. She thinks *we're* doing *really* good."

LATER IN THE EVENING

ALICE:

He spied on your therapy session? That's wild. What a violation.

I hate him so much.

What would you tell your friend if she was going through this situation?

ME:

My hypothetical friend?

ALICE:

Yeah.

ME:

I'd tell her to leave his stupid ass. She's worth so much more.

She doesn't deserve any of this.

He's draining her dry—emotionally, spiritually, financially and physically.

He's giving her nothing but pain, and gaslighting her into thinking it's her fault.

ALICE:

So why don't you extend the same courtesy to yourself?

ME:

I don't know. I feel like I owe the world something.

Like I've never been good enough.

Like everyone else has always had it together more than me.

Like I've been judged and been found wanting.

ALICE:

You know that's not fair. Imagine if you heard that being said about your friend.

ME:

All my friends have it together more than I do.

ALICE:

Are you fucking kidding me, Margaux? You're amazing.

And nobody has it together.

If it looks like they do, it's make-believe.

Just like your posts which are always so aspirational and inspiring and make it look like you live the perfect life.

ME:

But I don't.

ALICE:

That's exactly the fucking point, idiot.

ME:

Gee, thanks.

ALICE:

Lol, I mean it in the nicest of ways. But you've really got to stop being so hard on yourself. We're all just advanced monkeys, after all.

ME:

I'm pretty cute for an advanced monkey, I suppose.

ALICE:

You're fucking adorable. So get your head out of your advanced monkey ass and believe in yourself as much as you believe in your friends.

We're all depending on you.

And you don't owe us shit, but it would be appreciated.

I smile through my tears.

ME:

I'll try.

ALICE:

That's the most we can ask for.

I love you, Margaux. I hope you know that.

ME:

I love you, too. Thank you for this.

ALICE:

Any time.

CHAPTER 83
A WAR WITHIN

MARGAUX

The pain is excruciating.

Each month, my period is becoming more and more debilitating.

I know I have endometriosis, but it's either spreading, or there's something more to it.

I can barely move, yet I'm forced to keep shifting, desperately seeking any position that might provide some relief.

Bending my knee into my abdomen gives temporary respite, the pressure dulling the knives stabbing at me from within. But then that starts to hurt, so I curl into the fetal position.

Ice packs alternate with a heating pad, their opposing temperatures offering brief reprieves, but nothing lasts.

Even the thought of food triggers my gag reflex, and every few minutes I dry heave. Sitting up makes me throw up. Even sips of water betray me.

I finally retreat to the back room, collapsing onto the mattress and, miraculously, falling asleep.

When I wake, Timmy is gone.

Hours later, he returns, reeking of cigarette smoke.

"You threw up because you were drinking yesterday!" he yells, his tone accusing, as though preemptively justifying his unexplained absence. "This is self-inflicted, and you're blaming it on your period!"

"This has nothing to do with drinking, Timmy," I reply, my voice weary but steady. "I didn't even drink yesterday. I have a medical condition that causes excruciating pain every month. The issue isn't me—it's that I woke up, and you weren't here. And you've clearly been down at the tents again, smoking with people."

He shrugs dismissively. "Well, you were asleep, and I was bored."

I blink, incredulous. "So I finally manage to nap through the pain, and you decide to go do something you know would upset me? While I'm already suffering?"

"Stop blaming your period for everything," he spits. "It's *your* fault."

"Stop downplaying my very real pain, Timmy," I say, trying to focus on the conversation despite the millions of invisible knives still tearing into my lower abdomen. "The problem is you left while I was vulnerable and in pain. And now you're deflecting by blaming me."

"I should be able to go out!" he snaps, his voice dripping with indignation. *"You make me feel like a prisoner!"*

I nod, exhausted by the circular logic. "If I could trust you—if I knew you weren't going down to the beach to hang out with god-knows-who, that would be different. If you were just going somewhere for a walk and not to smoke cigarettes or drink... that would be fine. But I can't trust you. And when I'm in pain, it would be really nice to have you here to support me, to comfort me. It wasn't very nice waking up and you not being here."

His glare intensifies. "You won't even eat anything I make for you."

"Just *being here* helps," I reply, my voice softening. "Being kind. That's what I need from you."

But the conversation is over.

He's already made it clear he doesn't care.

———

The ultrasound results confirm what I already suspected.

"You have extensive adenomyosis and endometriosis," the doctor says, her tone measured but firm. "The good news is that your ovaries look fine—there doesn't appear to be scar tissue there. But your cervix and surrounding areas are significantly affected. The adenomyosis is clear, and—based on your symptoms—we're certain about the endometriosis."

"What does that mean for having kids, just so I know?" I ask, steeling myself for the answer.

"Well," she says, pausing. "The combination of adenomyosis and your age means it could absolutely impact your fertility. But I recommend discussing that in depth with your gynecologist."

I nod, my mind spinning.

———

Later, I meet with my gynecologist.

"Do you want to have children?" she asks.

"I… I don't know," I admit. "I was ambivalent when I was younger. And I did have a miscarriage a long time ago. But my previous partner made it clear he didn't want kids—he said he was too selfish. *That* relationship made me feel like I missed my window. So I don't know if I *want* to have them, but I'm curious about whether I *can*."

"What about your current partner?"

"He says he's open to it," I shrug. "But we've had unprotected sex for over a year, and nothing has happened. I did have one unusually heavy period that I wondered might have been a miscarriage, but I don't know."

The doctor nods sympathetically. "Having unprotected sex for over a year without conceiving is considered infertility. If you're interested, I can refer you to a fertility specialist. They'll perform a laparoscopy, which will give a much clearer picture of the extent of your endometriosis and scarring. It will also help determine your options moving forward."

I nod again, trying to absorb the information.

If I can't have kids, a hysterectomy or going on the pill might make sense to deal with these debilitating symptoms. But something inside me cries out at the thought.

I'd dismissed the idea of motherhood for so long, but the desire is there now, at least as an idea, sharp and unexpected.

Each month, when I get my period, a part of me is disappointed—I want someone I can love and guide and watch grow.

But then I'm also relieved.

These hormones are really fucking with my head.

Logically, I know Timmy probably wouldn't be a good father. He doesn't provide for his existing child, and struggles with responsibility, period. But there's a small, irrational part of me—fueled by hormones and desperation— that whispers he might change. That maybe a child would give him the focus he needs, something bigger than him to dull his selfish impulses.

CHAPTER 84

TRASH MAN // KILL ME, I DON'T GIVE A FUCK

MARGAUX

Lately, Timmy's need to be admired by everyone except me has reached new heights. He thrives on external validation by complete strangers, collecting compliments like trophies while clearly no longer giving a fuck about my opinion.

He's started picking up trash at the beach, an effort that would be noble if it didn't feel so hollow.

He comes home, his bucket full of discarded debris, glowing with self-satisfaction.

Sometimes, as a joke, he'll put his hands out wide and do a little jig, yelling in a sing-song voice, "Look what I can do!" And I don't think there's anything else that could sum up his behavior more accurately.

"All the aunties and uncles tell me I'm *amazing*," he says, grinning like a child showing off a gold star. "I'm *really* making a difference."

"That's nice, Timmy," I reply, forcing a smile.

This time, he returns with a business card.

"I was helping the guys who were doing this for their community service," he smiles proudly. "The supervisor gave me a packed lunch, and said that I could use him as a reference for any upcoming court appearances."

"Oh okay, that's... good?" I say, my voice rising involuntarily.

I want to believe in his good intentions, but it's hard not to feel resentful. He has all this energy to help strangers, but none to help me. His kindness feels performative, a way to garner praise rather than make a genuine impact.

I can't help but wish he'd put a fraction of his effort in here at home. Working on building our relationship, minimizing conflict. Being healthy and loving and kind.

At home, he's cruel and dismissive. The man who beams at strangers for their approval is the same one who spits venom at me, telling me I'm the problem, that I'm the reason his life isn't better.

I've been too depressed to go out and mix and mingle in our community. And I'm scared to walk up the street because of all the drugs and violence.

I'm the odd one out here—the pale redhead with a funny accent.

I'm an outsider.

The locals have their own language, their own rhythm, their own way of seeing life.

I've been pouring all my energy into our relationship, and trying to keep my writing going, while Timmy has seamlessly integrated himself into the local community.

He wants the accolades for an hour of work here or there, helping the environment and random strangers.

He doesn't give a shit about developing the consistency to show up each and every day—whether that's going to work or being a nice and kind human being to his partner. He's a show pony, and I'm his caregiver.

No matter what the rest of the world thinks, I've stopped believing the facade.

The man who picks up trash to save the oceans isn't real.

The man who cuts me down with his words is.

And I'm tired of pretending otherwise.

———

My doctor calls, her voice bright and full of purpose.

"Hey," she says. "Just following up. I see you haven't made the orientation appointment at the gym yet?"

Another gentle nudge. Another push in the right direction.

Checking in.

She doesn't have to do this, but she does, and it feels like someone, somewhere, cares.

"Oh, yeah," I say, trying to match her energy. "I've been meaning to do that."

"Okay, just making sure. Everything okay?"

I glance at Timmy lounging on the bed, his eyes flickering between me and the muted TV. His mood today is uncertain—a coin spinning in the air.

"Yep!" I force my voice to match hers. "Everything's great! Thank you for checking in. I'll make the appointment soon."

"Good. Let me know if you need anything."

She's so kind. Too kind.

And I feel like a fraud.

But I make the appointment, determined to follow through.

———

The gym orientation is… surprisingly enjoyable.

An enthusiastic lady teaches me and a group of senior citizens how to use each piece of equipment one by one. There's laughter, encouragement, and no pressure. It's a world away from the tension of my daily life.

For an hour, I feel human again. The kindness of strangers and the simple act of moving my body give me a fleeting sense of normalcy.

Afterward, I text Timmy a photo of the menu from the health center's restaurant.

"I can bring you lunch if you want!" I call him. "Just let me know what you want!"

"Ummmm…. ahhhh…. ummmmm… give me a minute," he stammers.

"Okay," I say, smiling through the phone.

"Ummmmm….ahhh….ahhhhh…"

There are only five items on the menu. What's taking him so long? Has he forgotten how to read?

"Have you decided yet?" I ask gently. I'm at the front of the line by now, and people behind me are growing impatient.

"Don't fucking rush me, Margaux!" he snaps. "Fuck! You're such a fucking rusher. Like, give me a chance to read the fucking thing. You know what? Don't get me fucking anything."

His anger slices through me, unraveling the calm I'd worked so hard to achieve.

What was meant to be a nice gesture has turned into another argument, another source of anxiety.

I order something I know he'll like anyway, to avoid another fight when I get home. There's no winning with him.

———

A FEW DAYS LATER

Days later, the rage returns, this time laced with something darker.

I text Timmy's dad, Phil.

ME:

> He's threatening to blow up fireworks between my eyes.

I'm desperate. Reaching out feels futile, but I don't know what else to do.

The idea of having my face blown apart by a festival ball has planted itself in my mind, an absurd but terrifying seed.

Timmy keeps talking. "You know, I could do it, and they'd never find me," he says, his voice almost conversational. "It'd be like—*boom*—and you'd be gone. Just like that."

I know his threats are partly about control, partly for show. But they're still threats. And there's always the lingering question: *What if?*

Phil doesn't respond.

Of course not.

He rarely does anymore when it comes to Timmy.

Probably doesn't want to get involved.

But he's also more than happy to send him money. And what does Timmy spend the money on? Nothing good.

It's not soda.

It's not vegetables or pasta or soap or detergent or rent or gas.

He spends it on cigarettes and alcohol.

Maybe drugs.

And now he might use it to buy an explosive to blow up my fucking face.

So I could really use some help from Phil.

But Phil is nowhere to be found.

———

Timmy's relationship with his parents is as infuriating as it is predictable.

He paints himself as a doting partner, weaving tales of my writing successes and our happy home.

But his parents aren't fooled entirely. "Get a job, son," they continue to say, half-heartedly.

Timmy's face hardens each time. "I *am* working," he lies. "I'm doing my hats and designing new shirts. I'm making progress."

He's not. I know it. I think they know it too, or at least have some doubts. But nothing changes.

"Aren't I making great progress, Margaux?" he'll ask, forcing me into his narrative.

"Yes," I sigh, offering the answer he demands.

———

I drift off, exhausted, at around 2AM.

Tonight, the nightmares come.

They've been dormant for a while, but now they're back with a vengeance, clawing at the edges of my mind. It's like my brain is starting to process my current situation.

A dark shape screams at me in my dreams, accusing me of being a monster, pointing crooked fingers at my chest. *"You fucking monster! Youuu-uu!"* it shrieks.

Everything goes black.

I bolt upright, my heart pounding, gasping for air.

In another dream, a person is handing out shots of whiskey. Then someone chases me, shouting about a car accident, blaming me for everything.

I fall back asleep.

Suddenly I'm surrounded by scary faces, howling and moaning at me.

I wake again, my body soaked in sweat, my stomach a churning pit of acid. My heart races as I glance at the clock. It feels like at least eight hours have passed, but it's only 218AM.

I write myself a note:

EVERY DAY I'M WITH YOU, IT ERODES ME A LITTLE. I GET A LITTLE BIT SADDER, A LITTLE BIT MORE DESTROYED.

WHY AM I DOING THIS?

WHY AM I EVEN WITH YOU?

What positive things do you bring to my life?

You should be grateful.
You're a monster.
If I was a monster, you wouldn't be alive.
So should I consider myself lucky?
Kill me, I don't give a fuck.
You've destroyed my life and I have nothing to live for anymore.
I won't let you get off that easily.

The words pour out of me, a quiet rebellion against the chaos of my existence.

Timmy doesn't know it yet, but something inside me has shifted. Something is changing.

I'm no longer sure if I can survive much longer with him in my life—or if I even want to.

CHAPTER 85
LOSING HER LIGHT

DEX

see her every day, slowly crumbling under the weight of it all. Margaux isn't just losing herself—she's being eaten alive, piece by fragile piece.

It's in the way she moves, slower than she used to, as if even standing upright is a battle.

It's in the hollow way she speaks, her voice drained of the warmth and conviction I know she once had.

And I know who's doing this to her.

Timmy.

That *fucking parasite.*

Every time I think about him, my blood boils.

He doesn't just hurt her physically—although the thought of that alone is enough to make me want to put him through a wall—he chips away at her mind, her spirit, her very essence.

He's the kind of person who thrives on chaos, who drinks the attention of strangers like poison-laced nectar and pretends he's some kind of hero.

Picking up trash on the beach?

Helping with community service?

It's all a performance.

A farce.

He's a *good guy* to everyone except the person who sees the truth.

The person he's destroying.

Margaux doesn't talk about the mental pain much. She hides it behind strained smiles and forced jokes. But I see it in her eyes—the tears she won't let fall, the way her hands shake when she thinks no one's looking.

And the physical pain each month? *Jesus.* It's gut-wrenching.

Watching her clutch her abdomen, writhing from that debilitating condition that causes her to vomit consistently for up to an entire day, disabling her from living her regular life… it's a kind of hell I wouldn't wish on anyone.

The worst part? I can feel in my gut that stress is making it worse. And that stress has a name—Timmy.

I hate how he dismisses her suffering. How he says her agony is self-inflicted, that it's 'all in her head.'

He leaves her alone when she's at her most vulnerable, when she's curled up in bed, shaking from the pain and throwing up. And then he comes back, smug and reeking of cigarettes, acting like it's her fault for needing support in the first place.

"I was bored," he told her once, as if that justified abandoning her.

The rage I felt hearing that? It was volcanic.

If I had been there, I don't know what I would've done, but it wouldn't have been pretty.

But the thing that makes me angriest? It's his dad.

Phil.

The enabler.

The man who fuels this train wreck by handing his son money—no strings attached, no accountability.

Phil keeps Timmy afloat just enough to keep him sinking back into his usual mess—booze, cigarettes, and god knows what else.

And when Margaux needs help? When Timmy's spiraling so far out of control that he threatens to blow her face off with a firework? Phil either doesn't reply at all, or he just shrugs. Says she must've done something to upset him. *She* must've done something.

How does someone become so goddamn blind to the monster they raised?

And Margaux… she's drowning. I can see it. She tries to fight it, to claw her way to the surface, but Timmy keeps pulling her under.

I think she knows she's losing herself. I saw the note she wrote to herself:

Every day I'm with him, it erodes me a little.

And the worst part is, she seems to feel like it's inevitable. Like there's no way out.

But there is.

There has to be.

I've started keeping an electronic journal, a way to track everything. All the ways Timmy hurts her, all the times he twists the truth, all the evidence of his cruelty. I don't know what I'm going to do with it yet, but I can't just stand by and do nothing.

Margaux deserves better. She deserves to live, to thrive, to find joy again.

And if she can't see that for herself yet, I'll see it for her. I'll fight for her, even if it means fighting her own demons alongside her.

Because I love her.

Not in the way Timmy claims to—some warped, possessive, toxic version of love—but truly, deeply. I want her to be happy, even if that happiness doesn't include me. I just want her to *be*.

So I'll wait. I'll watch. And when the moment comes—when she's ready to step out of the pit Timmy's dug for her—I'll be there.

To help her climb out, to catch her if she falls, to remind her of who she is.

Because she's not a lost cause. She's not weak.

And she's not alone.

Not while I'm still breathing.

CHAPTER 86
TRUCK THERAPY

MARGAUX

The truck isn't exactly the ideal setting for therapy. But it's the only place where I know Timmy won't overhear my sessions.

Ever since I found out he eavesdropped on my intake session, the thought of him listening in again fills me with dread.

I sit in the driver's seat, balancing my phone on the dashboard. A small cockroach scuttles across the rearview mirror, and I swat it away with a shiver. The damp upholstery smells faintly of mildew and old tobacco smoke, a reminder of how this truck has become both a lifeline and a prison.

The driver's seatbelt is still mangled from when Timmy, in one of his frenzied moments, sliced it apart because he couldn't unbuckle himself fast enough to take a piss. The middle console has developed some kind of black mold, and I avoid touching it altogether.

The truck, which had to be transferred into my name, feels like another weight tied to my ankle.

"You can love someone, but sometimes love isn't enough," my therapist says, her voice calm but insistent.

I roll my eyes reflexively. "What does that even mean? It's such a cliché, isn't it? Isn't love supposed to conquer all?"

"Well," she explains, "you can care deeply for someone, and believe you're in love with them. But if they're not respecting your boundaries, if they're physically hurting you… maybe you need more than that."

I sigh, leaning back into the foam-carved seat. I know she's right—*intellectually*, I know. But in practice? In my heart?

"I just… I *love* this man," I murmur, the words barely audible.

Her silence invites me to continue.

"He makes me feel wanted and needed and adored—sometimes. Not as much as he did at the start, but when those bright spots show up, I feel so good for a little while."

I'm honest with her about how I struggle with the physical violence aspect—who wouldn't—but how he's managed to play it all off as accidental, how he hasn't hit me in a while. Threatened—sure—but not followed through. Lately, his cruelty has taken more of a verbal turn.

I know what he's doing is wrong, but when the sweet moments come, it's almost like I can forget the bad ones ever happened.

"I know that if a friend came to me with my story, I'd tell them to run," I admit. "That they deserve better. That it's not their job to fix someone."

"So what's stopping you from telling yourself that?" she asks, her voice as steady as ever.

"There's nuance," I argue. "I mean, I *am* seeing progress. He backslides sometimes, but he's human, not a robot. He tells me over and over that he needs me to help him be better."

"And you believe that?"

I hesitate, and then I nod. "I think I do. He's shown some improvement. He's on new medication, he's in therapy… and he says he loves me. Sometimes I feel like I'm the only thing holding him together."

"Do you think that's fair to you?"

I don't answer. Because it's not, and we both know it.

She leans forward slightly, even though we're separated by a screen. "I appreciate your honesty, and I understand why you're with him. You love him, you're empathetic, and… very patient. You want to believe the best in people. That's a good thing, Margaux. But you have to be honest about what this relationship is doing to you."

I nod, though I don't fully agree.

"This is just really hard. I want things to be fine. I want him to be the person who he says he is. I can see that he's trying. It's just like… the sweet moments are such a contrast with his bad behavior, that it almost makes me disbelieve the bad parts even happened. Because how could someone who really wants to hurt you make you laugh until you cry with joy nearly every single day? Make you feel so loved?" Not expecting an answer, I change the subject. "He thinks you're talking to his therapist about him," I share. "I reassured him that you're not, and that it would be unprofessional."

She bursts into laughter—a genuine, surprised laugh that lightens the mood.

"Let me tell you something," she says, her tone conspiratorial. "Therapists *do* discuss anonymized client situations with colleagues for educational purposes, but I would give *anything* to not have to talk about Timmy with you anymore."

I laugh. "Seriously?"

"Seriously," she says. "You have so much trauma to unpack, Margaux. Timmy is just an acute symptom. He's this roadblock standing in the way of us dealing with *your* life. The things that brought you here before him."

It's such a jarring truth that I don't know how to respond.

"You are a badass," she says suddenly, catching me off guard.

I blink. "What?"

"It's true, and I want you to remember that. We need to work on your self-esteem, but look at you. You moved here all by yourself. You've built a career as a romance author. You've created opportunities for yourself out of nothing. Don't let anyone—*including* yourself—forget who you are, no matter what anyone else says."

Her words hit me harder than I expect, and I hold back tears. It's been so long since anyone but Timmy has complimented me, and these days his compliments are always laced with criticism, like candy coated in poison.

"Thank you," I whisper, my throat tight.

"Just be safe," she says, her tone soft but firm. "Get out of there if you need to. I'll be here whenever you need me."

I end the call, sitting in silence for a few moments. The truck still smells damp, and the roach is back, scuttling across the dashboard.

Her words echo in my mind.

You are a badass.

For the first time in what feels like forever, I let myself believe it—just a little.

CHAPTER 87
HIT AFTER HIT

MARGAUX

When I return from therapy, Timmy is in the kitchen, clattering dishes and humming to himself. The scene is deceptively domestic—almost peaceful—but I know better than to trust the surface appearance.

"How was it?" he asks, glancing over his shoulder. "Did you complain about me?"

"I wouldn't say I complained," I reply truthfully. "I talked about what's going on in my life, which you're a part of."

He frowns. It's as if he thinks our relationship is off-limits to discuss with my therapist. Which is a ridiculous notion.

His face darkens, and I can see the familiar storm brewing behind his eyes. "You always make me sound like the bad guy," he mutters. "That's why *I* stopped going to therapy, you know. Because I listened to your session and felt like you threw me under the bus."

The reminder of his eavesdropping hits like a slap. I feel the irritation bubbling in my chest. "Timmy, I didn't even talk about you much. You've said this before, and it's not true." I'm resentful that I have to take my therapy calls from a stinky truck because he violated my privacy.

He doesn't respond, instead tossing a shirt at me. It lands on my head, and I pull it off, placing it beside me on the bed. Juvenile antics, as usual.

A moment later, he drapes a blanket over Sabre. I gently remove it.

Then, he sprinkles water on me.

"Timmy," I sigh, getting up to leave, grabbing the keys.

As I walk past, he grabs at my hand.

I yank it free, scratching myself on the truck key in my hand as I do.

He smirks, walking past me. "Eww, you stink!" he says, wrinkling his nose dramatically.

I pause, caught between shock and exhaustion.

He opens the trash can to throw something away, then shouts louder, "Ewwww, you stink! Is that your butt?"

I ignore him, focusing on my breath. But then he starts pulling perfectly good food from the fridge and freezer, throwing it into the trash—mostly things he knows I like.

He disappears for a while. When he returns, he's holding a football.

"Found this in the truck," he says, a note of curiosity in his voice. "Didn't know I had a football."

A chill runs through me at the sight of it. "That's from the creep I let in the truck," I say quickly. "Please throw it out."

His expression softens for a moment, sympathy flickering across his face. "Oh my god, babe. I'm so sorry. I didn't know. I'll take it out right now."

Relief washes over me as he heads out the sliding door with the football in hand.

But when he returns a few minutes later, he's still holding it.

"Timmy, no, please," I plead.

The gleam in his eyes is dark, his smirk cruel. "I'm keeping this football," he says, his voice low and menacing. "This is what you get for letting strange men into the truck and driving into a fence. You have to look at it."

I retch, overwhelmed by his twisted sense of punishment. Snatching the football from him, tears streaming down my face, I run to the kitchen and grab a chef's knife.

I stab the football—over and over again—until it's fully deflated.

Timmy watches, his smirk widening into a grin. "Wow, you're an absolute psychopath," he says gleefully. "Stabbing the football like that? What a crazy fucking bitch. Are you threatening to do that to me?"

"No," I sob, my voice shaking. "Not at all."

I throw the football into the trash, my hands trembling, and he laughs.

He grabs the knife from the sink and goes to the fridge. Pulling out the bougie nonalcoholic drinks I've been using to replace liquor, he stabs each can, liquid spraying everywhere as he cackles.

I message Alice and fill her in, because this is getting out of hand.

ALICE:

This is complete madness.

Timmy walks over to me, grinning. Then he inhales sharply and spits, his saliva landing on my arm.

ME:

He just spat on me.

ALICE:

Nope.

Assault.

"Don't fucking type about me," he snarls, noticing my messages.

He picks up his phone and makes a call. "Mommy," he says. "You wouldn't believe how Margaux is acting right now." He moves his face away from his phone. "I'm going to call the police on you for scratching me last night," he says.

His rapidly escalating erratic behavior sends a shiver down my spine. I know nothing good will come of this. With shaking hands, I dial 911. Before anyone answers, I reconsider, and hang up.

ME:

He's calling his mom and lying to her now.

ALICE:

What an idiot.

He's a total moron with no boundaries.

ME:

I called 911 but hung up. He said he's calling them on me, but I'm just sitting here.

He's saying I scratched him last night, but I didn't.

ALICE:

Yeah, you need to establish your own trail of truth.

He grabs a glass bottle of tequila and, in an effort to open it, presses the knife blade against the middle of it, as if slicing through glass is a normal solution.

It's so idiotic that I let out a little laugh.

I tell Alice.

ALICE:

Yes, I too try to open my bottles with a tissue.

Equally effective.

ME:

I'm so upset, but he's so dumb it makes me laugh.

ALICE:

It sucks, but sometimes that's what you have to do.

ME:

You get it!

ALICE:

Unfortunately, I do.

He sees me typing and tries to grab my laptop from me, but I pull it back. *There's no fucking way he's touching my laptop.*
"You're like Carrot Top's uglier cousin," he snarls.
It's such a ridiculous yet hurtful thing to say that I almost laugh.
"You're a menopausal bitch," he says as he runs out the door, leaving it open.
Sabre makes his way outside.
"*Fuck!*" I cry out, with nobody to hear me. "I can't deal with any of this."
I'm so tired, so exhausted.
Alice is right.
This *is* madness.
But not the fun kind.

———

Hours later, Timmy returns.
"Let me make you some food," he says, his voice gentle, his eyes contrite. "I'm sorry about what I did with the football. That wasn't very nice. Let me make it up to you… the food will be a peace offering."
I want to tell him I'm not hungry, that I don't want anything from him. But I can't handle any more chaos.
So I just nod.
When he brings me the food, I eat it silently, choking down both the meal and my emotions.

"Thank you," I say quietly, even though every fiber of my being feels like shouting.

CHAPTER 88
TOM KHA… GUY? AKA SOUP TWINS

MARGAUX

My soul is screaming. I don't even realize how loud until I'm sitting in the truck, away from him, with the windows rolled down and the ocean breeze brushing against my face.

After a few days of sobriety, he's drinking again, and it's as though the clock has rewound to the worst days.

Every promise he made, every step forward—gone.

Erased.

Back to the old patterns—running off to the tents, coming home reeking of cigarettes and booze, spinning lies to shift the blame for everything. My breathing quickens just thinking about it, the oppressive weight of it pressing down on my chest.

Today, I need to breathe. To feel like myself.

I leave the apartment complex, the tires crunching on the gravel of the parking lot as I pull out. Thai food. That's what I need—something spicy and soothing, something just for me.

I imagine the lush flavors, the heat that lingers on my tongue, and the warm comfort it always brings me. Self-care comes in many forms, and right now, it comes in a takeout container.

Before I even hit the main road, my phone buzzes. I glance at it when I'm at a stoplight.

TIMMY:

Where are you going? Are you going on a date?

I grip the wheel tighter, my knuckles whitening.

ME:

No, I just needed a break. I'll be back soon.

Seconds later:

TIMMY:

I can see by your location you're meeting with
someone.

I bite my lip, debating whether to respond. He's being ridiculous. Paranoid. But the thought of trying to explain myself again is exhausting.

Outside the Thai restaurant, there's a cat—a small, scruffy tabby perched on the sidewalk, watching me with wide green eyes. I snap a picture and send it to Timmy, hoping to lighten the mood.

Bad idea.

TIMMY:

Who's fucking cat is that?

How can you cheat on me?

You fucking slut!

My stomach twists. I can feel the frustration bubbling up inside me, threatening to boil over.

I sigh. This guy literally thinks I'm cheating on him if I'm in the bathroom for 'too long'.

I give up.

ME:

I'm not cheating on you.

I'm not at anyone's house.

Jesus Christ, can you trust me for just one minute?

TIMMY:

You've been on the apps.

You're meeting with someone.

You're at some guy's house.

And you're sending me pictures of his cat.

ME:

That makes no fucking sense, Timmy!

TIMMY:

You'd be so mad if I drove around and didn't tell you where I was going.

ME:

You walk off all the time and are gone for HOURS without telling me where you're going! It's the same thing!

TIMMY:

No! You're off on some date! I know it!

I sigh deeply, gripping the steering wheel and forcing myself to take a few calming breaths. He doesn't even need logic—he just needs a reason to lash out and hurl ridiculous accusations.

ME:

I'm getting Thai food. I'm hungry. You can have some if you want.

I'll be home shortly.

The cat belongs to the Thai restaurant. So calm the fuck down.

———

By the time I get back, he's standing in the kitchen, his arms crossed, wearing that sheepish expression he uses after he's spun himself into a corner.

"Sorry," he says. "I really thought you were meeting up with some guy. You were in what looked like a residential neighborhood."

"Yeah," I say, my voice flat. "There's construction beside the Thai restaurant. I tried to take a back road and ended up in a maze of cul-de-sacs. It took me a while to figure it out." I hold up the bags of food. "This place is supposed to be really good."

He nods, and I can see the guilt flicker across his face, but it's quickly replaced with defensiveness. "You've got to understand, though. It looked suspicious. You would've been mad if I—"

"Stop," I cut him off. "You've got to trust me, Timmy. I have no desire to go off and date anyone else. Meanwhile, you're the one who runs off to the tents to drink and smoke, disappearing for hours at a time, and yet you're obsessing over me getting takeout. This isn't okay."

"Sometimes I need fresh air," he mutters.

"So you go off and hang out with homeless people doing god knows what?"

He shrugs. "You're the one who drove off in the truck."

"To get *food*, Timmy!"

"Okay, okay. Let's just enjoy the meal."

The food is phenomenal—better than I imagined. The chicken laab is fiery and fragrant, the tom kha gai is creamy and rich with just the right kick of Thai chilis, and the pad Thai is perfectly balanced between sweet and tangy. The flavors awaken something in me, a part of myself that feels almost forgotten.

"Wow, this is incredible," Timmy says, his tone softer now. "What's in this soup? I didn't think I'd like it because of the coconut, but it's *so* good."

I smile faintly, walking him through the dishes, their ingredients, their origins. It reminds me of ordering Thai food with my parents, the easy rhythm of family dinners where the biggest decisions were between green curry or red.

"It's my go-to when I'm sick," I say. "Extra spicy—it always helps with a sore throat."

"Yeah, I get that," Timmy says. "I usually go for egg drop soup. But *this*? This is something else." He grins. "We're like the same, but different."

It's such a small thing, but for a fleeting moment, I feel closer to him. Like we've found some shared connection in the swirling broth, something solid to hold onto amid the chaos.

I know we're not the only two people who enjoy soup when we're sick—it's a very generic thing we have in common. It's normal, and I'm craving normality.

I know it's dumb even as I'm thinking it, but the mind works in mysterious ways—I'm okay being soup twins with Timmy.

But the peace is short-lived. The Thai food nourishes my body, but it doesn't touch the deeper exhaustion—the bone-deep weariness that comes from constantly walking on eggshells, from always having to prove my loyalty, my intentions, my worth.

Timmy's mood shifts again, his affection laced with possessiveness, his sweetness soured by control. I know this cycle too well. The brief reprieve, the calm before the inevitable storm.

And as I lie awake, staring at the ceiling, I wonder how much longer I can keep doing this.

I need space. Real space.

Not just a quick escape for takeout, but something bigger. Something lasting.

My soul is still howling—the soup is magical but not quite enough to fix that—and I don't know how much longer I can keep silencing it.

CHAPTER 89

THE ONE WHERE HE'S CHATTING WITH WEBCAM GIRLS

MARGAUX

"Check out the movie listings. I pulled them up earlier," Timmy says, handing me his phone.

I type in the passcode, and instead of movie times, his favorite porn site greets me. Displayed prominently is a video titled *"Blonde Being Gang Banged by 6 BBCs."*

I tilt the phone toward him, raising an eyebrow. "Um…"

"Oops," he says casually, glancing at the screen without a hint of embarrassment. "Yeah, I just felt like looking at that earlier."

I don't necessarily care if he looks at porn. I do too, sometimes, and I know that what someone watches isn't always indicative of what they want in real life. But it feels… off.

We've been having so much sex that I'm honestly surprised he even feels the need to supplement. He must have been jerking off while claiming to be taking a shit.

To each their own, I guess. But the whole interaction leaves a strange taste in my mouth.

———

Later that day, while Timmy naps, I decide to take him up on his open-phone policy. I open Instagram to check something and notice three profiles. His personal account, his graphic design account, and a third one I've never seen before.

Curiosity gets the better of me. I click on it.

The messages are shocking—a feed full of exchanges with cam girls. Explicit messages.

Transactions.

I feel a sinking sensation in my stomach.

"Timmy!" I gasp, shaking him awake. "What the fuck is this?"

"What do you mean?" He groggily sits up, rubbing his eyes.

I hand him the phone.

He scrolls through the messages, his expression a mix of feigned confusion and sudden realization. "Ohhh," he says, nodding as though everything has become clear. "I let one of the kids from the tents use my phone. He must have added this profile."

"You… let someone from the tents use your phone?" I quirk an eyebrow, incredulous.

"Yeah. Look at the messages—it's not even how I type. You know I don't use commas like that."

I glance again. He's right—the punctuation and spelling are different. It's plausible.

"Fine. But please stop lending your phone to random people. And stop going to the tents. No good ever comes from there."

"Yeah, yeah, you're right," he mutters, already rolling over to go back to sleep.

The whole exchange leaves me unsettled. Whether it's true or not, I can't shake the feeling that there's more to the story.

———

Later, I watch in disbelief as Timmy removes the screen from the back window and climbs out.

"What the actual fuck?" I whisper to myself.

How often has he done this while I assumed he was sulking in the back room? And why? We have a perfectly functional front door.

When he returns, I confront him. "You bent the screen. It's brand new. The landlord is going to kill us. Why would you jump out the window? It's not normal."

He smirks, completely unfazed. "I'll straighten the screen. It's not a big deal."

"It *is* a big deal. Why didn't you just use the door?"

"Because I felt like it. Jesus, Margaux, you're always making a big deal out of nothing."

Over the next few days, the fights escalate over the smallest things—washing dishes, sweeping the floor, what we're eating for dinner. Every time, Timmy retreats to the back room and locks the door.

One day, he shows me how to unlock it.

"If I lock myself in, you can always get in. Let me show you how," he says nonchalantly, demonstrating with my debit card. He angles the card just so, and the lock springs open.

"See? Easy," he says.

"Um… thanks?" I reply, confused. *Why is he teaching me this?*

———

A week later, after yet another fight over the dishes, Timmy stomps down the hallway to the back room. I hear the door slam and lock.

Then, the unmistakable sound of a drill.

"Timmy! What the fuck are you doing?" I yell, rushing to the door.

"Drilling the door shut so you can't come in and bother me!" he yells back. *"What the fuck do you think?"*

"You can't drill the door! You're damaging the apartment! You've already destroyed so much stuff. Can you *please* not drill the door?"

"Too late!" he calls back, his voice carrying a smug undertone.

This is insanity. He's the one throwing tantrums and creating chaos, but he acts like I'm some kind of villain, barricading himself in a room to 'protect' himself from me holding him accountable.

I sit on the bed, seething. I've been reduced to pleading for basic respect in my own home, and he's treating me like a supervillain trying to breach his panic room.

The absurdity of it all would almost be funny if it weren't my life.

I look out the window as a fishing boat goes by, oblivious to the chaos inside these four walls. This relationship feels like a sinking ship, and I'm strapped to the mast.

Every time I try to steer us to calmer waters, Timmy finds a way to poke holes in the hull.

He's the storm and the iceberg, and I'm just trying not to drown.

CHAPTER 90
OH, SNAP!

MARGAUX

Late one night, I find myself sitting on the bed, bathed in the dim glow of my laptop. The search bar blinks at me, a cursor for my confusion. I type:

Am I abusive?

The thought has been gnawing at me. I've been screaming, calling Timmy a loser, a piece of shit. I've slammed doors, thrown my hands up, even called him names I never thought would leave my lips. I've been making highly questionable decisions.

This isn't me.

My results are a jumble of terms, articles, and advice columns. And then, I see it:

Reactive Abuse.

I click, and the words leap off the page, staring into my soul.

DARVO. Reactive abuse. The cycle.

I learn that DARVO stands for *Deny, Attack, Reverse Victim and Offender*—a classic manipulation tactic. The abuser denies their actions, attacks the victim, and flips the script to make the victim seem like the aggressor.

And reactive abuse? It's the human reaction to prolonged torment.

It's what happens when someone who is poked and prodded and belittled finally snaps.

I read further, my heart pounding with recognition. It's like someone is seeing inside my brain.

This isn't a justification for my behavior.

It doesn't excuse it.

But it *explains* it.

Everyone has their limit, and at their breaking point they lash out.

I'm not inherently abusive. I'm *reacting* to abuse.

For example, I'd never wake up screaming at someone because I had a bad dream. But Timmy doesn't need much at all to ignite a fight. A bad dream? A misplaced flip-flop? A dirty dish in the sink? Any of it can set him off.

He'll wake up angry, already in a mood, muttering under his breath about how I don't do enough.

He'll hover as I work, making passive-aggressive comments about how I'm 'so lucky' to be working from home, how he 'does everything around here.'

He'll distract me from my writing, taking me further from my goals.

He'll call me a 'stupid cunt' for forgetting to put the shower curtain inside the tub.

He'll sneer at me for focusing on my career instead of spending time with him.

And I'll hold it together. For a while. I'll bite my tongue and focus on my screen. I'll nod absently, hoping he'll leave me alone.

But it doesn't stop.

He escalates.

He pokes and prods until the dam breaks.

Then I *will* get upset and I *will* yell at him to please leave me alone so I can work.

I snap. I scream. I say things I regret:

"You're a loser."

"You have no friends because nobody can stand you."

"You're wasting your life hanging out with addicts on the beach."

"You're the problem in this relationship."

The words sting, but they're my truth in the moment.

And then it happens. He flips the narrative.

"See? *You're* the abusive one," he snarls. "*You're* the one yelling. *You're* the one calling *me* names."

The Timmy I know now isn't the man I met.

When I met him, he made me laugh.

He called me beautiful.

He made me feel safe.

Now, he makes me feel small.

But only *after* he makes me feel huge.

It's a dizzying, maddening cycle of praise and degradation.

And I'm not just losing myself emotionally—I'm losing myself in every way.

I'm yelling.

I'm swearing.

I'm calling names.

Things I've never done before.

The person I've become around him is foreign to me.

With anyone else, I'm calm. Measured. Thoughtful.

But around him, I'm frantic, defensive, sharp-edged.

It's like he's unlocked a version of me I didn't know existed.

A version I don't like.

And so all the stuff that happened before is ignored, and I'm identified—by him and his father—as the problem.

It's just me, the crazy abusive fiancée, the terrible person who's ruining Timmy's life.

When it's really the fact that his three hours of toxic, abusive behavior finally got to me and I had a human response.

I'm not a violent person.

I'm not an argumentative person.

I get excited about things, but in a controlled way.

Yet the relationship with Timmy is changing me.

But only with him.

He pokes and pokes at me, screaming and raging.

Swearing at me.

Calling me a stupid cunt.

Telling me all sorts of things that simply aren't true.

If I try to bring up his behavior, he'll scoff, "I'm just defending myself. You're always attacking me."

If his dad hears about it, I'm the villain.

I'm 'crazy', 'unstable,' the 'problem.'

I think about past relationships. There have been abusive ones, but even then, the abusers were never this… *methodical.*

One ex tried to smother me with a pillow, and tried to systematically break me down with words every day—he just wasn't very good at it.

Another threatened to break my jaw but didn't chip away at my self-worth so relentlessly.

Timmy's cruelty is in a league of its own.

It's targeted.

Vindictive.

Designed to hurt.

And yet, I still try to defend myself. I still try to make him see how much he's hurting me. I scream back because it feels unfair to let him win.

But it doesn't work. It never works.

But now something within me has clicked, absolved me of my guilt, of the burden of worrying that I'm just as bad as him.

Reactive abuse isn't the same as abuse.

I tell myself this over and over.

It's not an excuse. I'm not proud of yelling, of calling him names. But this isn't me. This is a version of me that exists *because of him.*

The version of me that doesn't want to give up.

That refuses to let him win.

But as I stare at my reflection, my face puffy from crying, my voice hoarse from yelling, I wonder if the real battle isn't with him—it's with *myself.*

Because I'm starting to think the only way to win is to walk away.

CHAPTER 91
APOLOGISTS ANONYMOUS

MARGAUX

The next time Timmy disappears, he's gone for six hours. I don't panic right away, and use the time to catch up on my shows, write, and try to reclaim a small slice of normalcy.

Silver linings, right?

But as the hours stretch on, anxiety creeps in.

I know where he is—down on the beach, surrounded by people in various stages of intoxication. The crowd he gravitates toward doesn't exactly inspire confidence.

When I finally go to find him, I'm met with exactly what I feared—Timmy, drunk, sprawled among the usual suspects. He's holding court with a five-dollar bottle of gut-churning vodka, laughing too loud, his face flushed from the cheap alcohol.

For someone who doesn't do meth himself, he sure hangs out with a large number of people who do.

His companions—mostly people living in the tents—are surprisingly calm. One man, his face weathered but kind, glances at me and shakes his head. "He should've stopped drinking hours ago," he mutters. "Man's got a real problem."

The words sting.

It's surreal to hear this from people battling their own demons. If *they* see Timmy's behavior as destructive, what does that say?

I glance at him—this attractive, physically capable man who should have so much going for him. Instead, here he is, squandering his potential in a haze of cheap vodka and bad decisions, surrounding himself with drug dealers and drug users.

I pull out my phone and call Phil, his father.

"Can you please talk some sense into him?" I plead. "He's drunk, and this is dangerous. I'm afraid something bad will happen."

"How did he even get the alcohol?" Phil asks, his tone accusatory.

"I got it for him," I admit, biting back my anger. "He insisted. If I didn't, you would have. And if you wouldn't, he would've just stood outside the store and charmed someone else into buying it for him—or stolen the money. You know he's taken our laundry quarters to buy booze before. You know how he is."

Phil's response is as unhelpful as ever. The same man who sent his thirty-nine-year-old son money for 'soda' just months earlier.

It's easier for him to blame me than face the reality of his son's behavior.

"You must have done something to upset him," Phil says, his new go-to refrain.

My blood boils.

That's me. The provocateur. The instigator.

"What could I possibly have done, Phil? I played a song he didn't like once, and he fractured my skull. Dude, I *breathed,* and he got upset. But sure, tell me how I'm the problem."

Phil offers no solutions, no support—just the same dismissive rhetoric I've now come to expect.

———

When Timmy finally staggers home, the cycle begins anew.

"You drink too," he sneers. "And when you do, you're a *bitch!*"

It's an unfair, absurd comparison.

When I drink, I get silly, emotional, maybe even overly chatty.

Sometimes I cry.

But I don't break things.

I don't threaten lives.

When Timmy drinks, he becomes a different person entirely—angry, vindictive, destructive, violent, homicidal. He's broken things, made death threats against me and others, and physically hurt me.

And yet, he acts like we're the same.

"You're such a bitch," he tells me, "and then you wake up all cute, like nothing happened the night before."

The hypocrisy is staggering.

He's the one who wakes up as if the night before didn't happen.

He's the one who pretends his rage and cruelty are figments of my imagination.

If he didn't constantly make digs at me, there wouldn't be conflict.

If he got out of bed and worked, there wouldn't be conflict.

If he kept his promises, there wouldn't be conflict.

I'm not someone who picks fights for the sake of it.

I want peace.

I crave positivity.

But our relationship has become anything but.

What started as fun and carefree has devolved into something heavy, oppressive, and dangerous.

Timmy's moods dictate *everything*.

His need for constant praise—even for the bare minimum—has become exhausting.

He wants accolades for doing the dishes while I work to keep us afloat.

He wants applause for taking out the trash.

He expects constant validation, and when he doesn't get it, he spirals.

I feel like I'm trapped in a well, clawing desperately toward the light. Every time I think I'm making progress, he drags me back down.

He's suffocating me.

As I sit in the quiet of our apartment, I feel the weight of it all pressing down on me.

I love Timmy—or at least, the version of him I thought I knew.

But this isn't love anymore.

This is survival.

And I'm not sure how much longer I can keep climbing out of this well, only to be pulled back down.

CHAPTER 92
TEMU TIMMY

MARGAUX

"'m going to go sell this chainsaw and bring you twenty dollars," Timmy announces, his voice tinged with a rare sense of purpose.

I side-eye him skeptically. "Um, okay?"

It's an oddly specific promise, but I'm cautiously optimistic. Perhaps this is one of those fleeting moments where he wants to contribute financially, to do something remotely responsible.

He disappears, chainsaw in hand, and doesn't come back for over an hour.

There must be some fast and furious chainsaw negotiations taking place.

I send him a text.

ME:

Where are you?

TIMMY:

I'll be back soon.

When he finally returns, I'm immediately hit by the unmistakable stench of cheap vodka. His steps are wobbly, his grin lopsided.

There's no sign of the twenty dollars he promised.

"Where's the money you got for the chainsaw?" I ask, even though I already know the answer.

"What money?" His face is blank, his head tilting to one side like a confused puppy.

"You said you were going to get me twenty dollars."

Realization dawns, slow and foggy. "Oh. I bought a bottle of vodka. Sorry." His apology is anything but genuine.

"Seriously?" My voice is louder than I intended.

He meets my gaze, and his next words chill me to the bone. "Well, the main thing is the chainsaw is gone now. So I won't be tempted to use it on you. You should be pleased."

———

For the next few days, the emotional roller coaster reaches new lows. His intermittent compliments—rare and almost begrudging—are drowned out by a torrent of accusations and insults.

"I want you to help me be a better person. I don't want to drag you down," he says one moment, his tone earnest, almost vulnerable.

I've heard that one before.

Then, not ten minutes later:

"You are abusive and mean."

Projection, much? Although I am *becoming mean.*

"You drive around blackout drunk all the time."

Excuse me? No, I do not. Again, projection.

"Your friends aren't real friends."

Says the man who can't name a single close friend who will willingly talk to him anymore. Except for the one skank, Thotimus Prime.

He's such a Projecty McProjectorson.

"*None* of your exes like you. *All* of mine love me."

I only know a couple of his exes, and based on those the lie detector reveals... this is a lie.

"You're a mean and nasty person."

• •

"You're nothing like the characters in your books."

Ouch. That one hurts the most. Writing is the one thing I have left that feels like mine, and he knows it.

"No wonder your family wants nothing to do with you."

Double ouch.

I can't hold back anymore. "That's not even *true!* My family is tiny. And the only reason my half-sister stopped talking to me is because of *you.* Because I stayed with *you.* She doesn't want the next time she sees me to be at my funeral because *you* acted crazy and killed me!"

"Whatever," he scoffs. "There's a reason none of them are in the picture anymore."

His words drip with cruelty, each one calculated to hit the deepest part of my insecurities.

I'm fed up.

My voice is steady, but it feels like I'm holding my insides together with duct tape. "Your words can no longer hurt me, Timmy. You can say all the mean things you want, based on the things I've shared with you in confidence—as my life partner, as my supposed best friend—but you *cannot* hurt me. You've already said it all before, and—believe me—I've already told myself worse."

"Whatever," he mutters, but his eyes glint with malice. His voice takes on a mockingly casual tone. "That reminds me—I need to call my parents later. Check in on my mom and dad. You know, my parents that love me and who would do anything for me."

Jesus fucking Christ.

His words echo in the space between us, and something inside me breaks.

I once thought I saw glimpses of the man he could be, the man he might have been before life broke him in ways I'll never fully understand.

But now, I'm not even sure those glimpses were real.

And is that glimpse I thought I saw of him originally even *that* flattering in retrospect?

Did I love him, or did I love how he made me feel in those rare moments of light?

Because the man standing in front of me isn't someone who loves me.

He's a monster.

A demon who feeds on my despair, tearing me down piece by piece until there's not a shred of me left.

And he's almost succeeded.

Almost.

———

A FEW DAYS LATER

Sometimes, I just need to laugh. After a long day of feeling trapped in my own home, I decide to put on *Brunö*. It's ridiculous and absurd—exactly the kind of humor I think might lift our spirits.

"This movie is *awful*," Timmy whines twenty minutes in, crossing his arms. "Terrible! It's really upsetting me!"

"It's... a comedy," I say carefully. "I thought you'd like it. It's warped, like your sense of humor."

"Nope! Nope, nope." He stands, pacing the room. "This has ruined my mood. I was so happy before, and now I'm tense and upset that you even put it on."

Before I can respond, he grabs his keys and storms out, the familiar cycle unfolding— cigarettes, the drug tents, and a return hours later, drunk and belligerent. I sit and wait, gray-rocking, refusing to engage when he starts hurling insults.

———

The next morning, we're cooking breakfast when he flicks through the channels and lands on *Brunö*.

"Hey, this looks funny. Should we watch it?"

I blink at him, incredulous. "Are you fucking kidding me?"

"What? It looks good!"

"You literally started a fight with me last night because this movie upset you so much."

"Oh, did I? Haha, that's kind of funny. You have to admit."

I stare at him, seething.

He's rewritten the narrative, as he always does.

But I don't say anything.

Because there's no fucking point.

———

I drink, to block out his mean comments more than anything, and he waits until I've had a couple, then starts a fight and mocks my drinking.

I monitor my alcohol intake so I'm aware of how much I've consumed, but then he refills my glass—often when I'm not looking, and then he starts a fight and criticizes me for having any at all.

On other days, I don't drink at all, and he accuses me of drinking, and starts a fight.

One day, he walks into the kitchen and opens up a cupboard where my vodka is located.

Producing a Sharpie from a drawer, and without looking at the bottle, he says, "I can tell how much you've been drinking because you're being a belligerent bitch. I'm going to draw a line to show how much I believe you've drunk of this bottle today based on your behavior."

He draws a line low on the bottle, and I just stare at him.

I've had literally one drink, he's had several, and his assessment is way off.

"Wrong," I say. "Way wrong."

He glances up, and what I just said is confirmed. There's barely any liquor missing.

"Well, for someone who's barely had anything to drink," he sneers, "you're sure acting like a fucking cunt."

———

The next day, I don't drink at all. I pour myself one small glass of vodka, but my stomach is in knots and I can't bear the thought of the taste or the smell. So I just leave the glass on the nightstand that serves as a side table.

"You're drunk," he slurs half an hour later, after he's had several drinks of his own. "You're absolutely hammered."

"Timmy," I reply calmly. "I'm literally sitting here working, and I haven't touched my drink. You are the one who has been drinking."

"Whatever," he sneers. "Stupid cunt. Watch your stupid fucking shows. I'm going out for a cigarette. And I'm taking this." He grabs the half-full bottle and stumbles out of the apartment.

God knows when he'll be back. Or what state he'll be in when he returns.

This is awful. I just want to go back to the time when he was kind and sweet and fun. When the most important things in his life weren't cigarettes and liquor. But I'm beginning to wonder if this is the real Timmy.

If the one that was focused on creating and working and producing a nice life for us was a sham.

Which would be a real shame, because I love that Timmy so deeply.

That Timmy is my soulmate.

I'm beginning to think I've received the Temu version of Timmy.

Temu Timmy.
The surfer who doesn't surf.

CHAPTER 93
THE MOST EVIL THING

A COUPLE OF WEEKS LATER

Things have been surprisingly good lately. Timmy has been cleaning the house, cooking meals, and even helping with some of my graphic design projects.

For once, his actions are consistent with his words, and my trust in him is growing, cautiously but undeniably.

So when his cousin, Janet, shares that her mother is downsizing and moving into an assisted living condo, I bring it up to Timmy. It feels like the kind of lighthearted update he'd appreciate.

"She's really excited," I say. "And we joked about how it'd be cool if your parents downsized and moved near her at some point. They could be neighbors—how fun would that be?"

Timmy smiles warmly. "Oh my gosh, that would be adorable. Mom loves hanging out with her."

It feels like a sweet moment.

I think nothing more of it.

———

Later, we go grocery shopping. As we pass the liquor aisle, Timmy's eyes light up. A party bucket filled with twenty tiny Fireball bottles sits on the shelf, practically calling his name.

"Ooh!" he exclaims. "Can you *please* get me one of these buckets?"

I sigh, already exhausted by the request. "Timmy, I think that's a terrible idea."

"Please?"

"No, not happening."

He pouts like a child. "Come on! We can make it like an Easter egg hunt. You can hide them around the house, and I can find them!"

"Timmy…"

"It'll be so cute!" he insists, grabbing my arm. His tone shifts to a soft plea, his eyes wide and sincere. "Babe, I *promise* it'll just be for fun. We're having such a great day, and I wouldn't ruin that. I'll just have fun finding them and only drink a couple."

His enthusiasm is infectious, and his promises, as usual, sound so genuine. He's so persuasive with the way he says things.

Part of me is curious, too—can he live up to his word?

And if he doesn't, will that give me the final push I need to get out of this?

Is this a way of saving myself?

Against my better judgment, but with a hint of curiosity, I relent.

"Okay, I'll get you the Fireball bucket. But you have to stick to your word. I'm serious."

"I promise," he says, grinning ear to ear. "Thank you so much!"

As he grabs the bucket, my stomach flips.

I hope I'm not making a huge mistake.

"Yay! Fireball Easter egg hunt for Timmy!" he squeals with delight.

Well, I guess we'll see what happens.

Timmy might be digging his own grave.

Hopefully not mine, too.

———

LATER IN THE DAY

Back at home, I hide the little Fireball bottles all around the apartment.

I get creative—placing them in drawers, on top of the fridge, inside the Baby Shark toy with the ripped-open butt, and even under the bed.

Timmy scours the apartment high and low for the Fireball, his giddy laughter echoing through the rooms. "*Yesss!* Found another! I'm so good at this!"

I shake my head, half-amused, half-concerned. I've never seen him work this hard at anything. It would be impressive if it weren't so sad.

He cracks one open and downs it in one gulp.

"Careful," I caution. "Remember your promise not to drink them all at once."

"Oh, I know! Don't worry," he says with a grin. "I'll behave myself."

———

About an hour later, Timmy is visibly drunk, the now all-too-familiar cruel gleam in his eyes.

He leaves for a while, and comes back another hour later, and heads to the back room.

"I'm going to tell the secret!" he announces gleefully, his face twisted with mischief. Before I can stop him, he grabs his phone and retreats to the back room.

My heart sinks into my stomach.

What secret?

Moments later, I hear him screaming into the phone. "Mom, they were laughing about putting you in a nursing home! Janet and Margaux—they think you're crazy!"

I freeze, the blood draining from my face.

What the actual fuck? What have I done?

What a horrible, dangerous thing to make up.

"*That's not true!*" I yell, storming toward him. "*I didn't say that!* We didn't say *anything* like that! *How dare you twist something around that was said with kindness and compassion?! Why are you lying to her?!*"

But Timmy ignores me, smirking as he continues to twist my words into something vile. "Nope! That's what they think of you, Mom! They think you need to be in a home!"

His mother's panicked voice crackles faintly through the phone, but I can't make out her words.

I can't believe the lies coming out of his mouth. He's said some really fucked up things in the past, but weaponizing something said with love and using it to terrify a woman who's already going through so much? I have no words.

"Stop lying!" I scream. Blood thumps in my temples, and I probably sound unhinged. *"Shut the fuck up, Timmy! You're hurting your mom for no reason! Why would you do this?!"*

He smirks, his voice mockingly low and steady. "Calm down, Margaux. Just be honest about what you said about my mom."

No doubt his parents can hear me yelling and swearing. But I'm so upset for his mother, and I just want him to stop lying to her.

I hear her sobs through his phone, and guilt shreds at my heart.

His words are daggers, designed to provoke me, to make me sound like the villain.

I can see what he's doing, and I know it's deliberate.

But what stuns me the most is that he doesn't care that his evil lies are hurting his mother—only that they're upsetting me.

"You're a monster," I whisper, my voice shaking.

His grin widens, and he hangs up the phone. "Wow," he says, leaning back against the wall. "You're so dramatic. You really need to calm down."

———

As I sit on the bed later, shaking with rage and disbelief, I replay the scene in my head.

Timmy didn't just twist my words—he weaponized a moment of kindness and compassion and turned it into something grotesque.

And for what? To hurt me? To make his mom distrust me? To sow chaos for the sake of chaos?

I glance at him on the other side of the bed, now dozing peacefully as if nothing happened.

How did I get here? How did I let someone like this take up space in my life?

It's not the first time he's done something like this, and it won't be the last. I know that now.

But I also know something else—I can't keep living like this.

Something has to change—because if it doesn't, he's going to destroy me.

And he's going to enjoy every second of it.

CHAPTER 94
A VILLAIN SO GRUESOME

MARGAUX

Things were starting to look up for a moment—Timmy had been helpful, kind even, taking care of small chores and doing little things to make my life easier. I allowed myself to feel a flicker of hope, a whisper of trust rebuilding.

But deep down, I should have known better. Every time I let my guard down, he proves that my faith in him is misplaced.

And every time I fall for it, I feel even more stupid.

I text Alice to fill her in on the latest debacle.

ME:

So this is really, really fucked up.

Things were going well.

And I was beginning to really trust him.

Which I should have known meant he was about to sabotage it hard.

ALICE:

I know. But these are the colors he's been hiding all along.

ME:

Like I can't even write a villain so gruesome.

Hope he's proud.

She was crying, clearly bc he said multiple times 'I don't want to upset you.'

ALICE:

So now we tell him nothing.

ME:

Nothing at all.

Which tells me he's not the person I should be with.

ALICE:

Yeah.

Timmy leaves and then returns after a while, his mood mercurial as always. He busies himself with my desk, rearranging papers and supplies despite having just done it the other day. It's clearly an act of control, a way to establish dominance in my space.

I feel his eyes on me.

"Who are you talking to?" he asks, his voice sharp.

"None of your business, bruh," I reply, keeping my tone flat.

I'm not in the mood for Timmy's bullshit. He just crossed a line that can never be uncrossed. To hurt *me* is one thing, but to use me as a weapon to hurt his mother and destroy her opinion of me with one cruel act? Unforgivable.

He narrows his eyes, but doesn't respond. Instead, he walks over, presses his ass against me, and farts.

"Slut," he says, smirking as if this is the height of comedy.

My fingernails dig into my palms. I count to three.

Don't react. Don't give him the satisfaction.

"You're so ugly inside and out," he continues, venom dripping from every syllable. "You're just a small, unattractive person."

I grab my phone and message Alice.

ME:

Hey Alice, can I call you and have a super normal convo with you so he feels like a dick?

ALICE:

Yes, you can.

I call her, and we chat away for half an hour about anything and everything—roller derby, her crocheting projects, my books, and our cats—anything but Timmy.

He glares at me from across the room, clearly annoyed that I'm enjoying myself.

After we hang up, I feel much better.

Alice messages me:

ALICE:

You're amazing, friend.

ME:

Am I? I feel gaslit, and apparently I'm a small, unattractive person.

ALICE:

You're extremely hot. Gaslighting has a wild way of making your flame feel small by being extra large.

ME:

You're the best. I love you and I feel the same way about you.

ALICE:

I'm sorry he gets to you like that. You don't deserve it. You deserve so much more.

ME:

He makes me feel gross. But he makes me feel less gross than other guys, so I've tolerated it.

ALICE:

Unacceptable. You need someone who makes you feel beautiful when you feel gross, not the other way around.

Timmy storms over and tries to grab my laptop. I manage to hold on to it.

"You're an ugly crusty Ron Weasley!" he yells, his face twisted with rage.

I quirk a brow at him. What a curious thing to say.

I tell Alice.

ALICE:

Unacceptable.

Electric chair.

He doesn't exactly have the greatest leg to stand on
there.

He looks like every guitarist in a Baltimore metal
band.

ME:

Using that for sure.

I repeat what she sent me. "Timmy, you look like every guitarist in a Baltimore metal band."

He recoils as if I've physically slapped him, and storms out of the room.

God forbid someone mirrors even a fraction of his toxic energy back at him.

Timmy is a one-way street with a dead end.

When he returns, his insults have only sharpened. "You're such a cunt," he spits.

How original.

"Well, you're ugly and fat if we're going there," I snap back. I know it's mean, and I hate resorting to his level. But he's poked and prodded me past my breaking point.

He looks like he's about to cry, and I feel a flicker of guilt. But the exhaustion is greater.

He's going lower and lower. I tried to go higher, but now I'm going subterranean.

Two can play this toxic game.

ALICE:

Just ignore him. Which sucks. But stonewall him.

ME:

I wouldn't normally comment on people's
appearance, but I'm feeling mean at this point. Yes,
I'll stonewall him.

ALICE:

> Good. Ignoring people sucks but sometimes it's the
> only way to get past things.

But it's easier said than done.

"You said a mean thing," says Timmy, as if he hadn't said 1,234,567,890 far meaner things to get me to this point. "You're so fucking gross."

"*You're* so fucking gross, Timmy. Look at yourself," I snap back. "The drug people want you because you're a loser who walks around with your ass hanging out of your pants."

My insults are back to being truthful.

I keep going.

"You should really be with someone less intelligent than you, but it would be a small pool."

He glares at me and looks as if he's about to cry.

A few minutes later, he's offering me food.

Did I neutralize him with my barbs? For whatever reason, he appears to be offering me a peace offering.

I sigh. This is exhausting.

I message Alice again.

ME:

> I've been thinking about it.

> He behaves like this, but he gets all the smart ladies
> and nobody knows why.

ALICE:

> Charisma.

> Society tells women that they must settle inherently.

> And are conditioned to often accept any man who
> shows affection.

ME:

> Yeah. I think… you know, I don't have a family,
> really.

> And this guy says all the right things when he wants
> to and has charisma, as you say.

> But he's a flawed fuck and nobody knows why I'm
> with him.

But it's hard having nobody.

And I thought I was strong, but maybe I'm really actually weak and felt like I needed someone and picked the wrong one.

Timmy notices me typing furiously and storms over, trying to peek at my screen.

I switch windows, shielding my conversation with Alice.

As if to retaliate, he pulls out his phone and starts messaging someone on Instagram, holding the phone at an angle that makes sure I notice.

It's petty, juvenile, and pathetic. But that's Timmy in a nutshell.

I'm getting tired of playing these games.

Something has to give. And soon.

CHAPTER 95
WEAPONIZED KINDNESS

DEX

The truck is a piece of shit, but it's where Margaux feels safe enough to take her therapy calls. That alone tells me everything I need to know.

The mildew, the roaches, the lingering stench of tobacco and damp, all of which my associate reported to me when he installed the tracking device and cameras in the truck—none of that compares to her fear of Timmy overhearing.

Not after what he pulled during her intake session.

I mean, I guess I'm technically doing the same thing—eavesdropping on Margaux's therapy. Tracking her 24/7, and gaining access into her innermost thoughts.

But it's different—Timmy uses it against her, whereas I'm using it to gain insight into how I can push her closer to breaking away.

If she ever finds out, though, I'm not sure she'd see it that way.

I lean back in my chair, staring at the security monitors, catching glimpses of her in the truck. Her voice is low, earnest, tinged with vulnerability as she speaks to her therapist. She looks like she's baring her soul, and for a second, I hate that it's happening in that goddamn truck instead of a quiet, safe room with soft lighting and a therapist she can see in person.

But I'm pleased. Her therapist seems sharp—smart enough to see through Timmy's bullshit and recognize the warrior Margaux really is. She's giving Margaux the nudges she needs, affirming her worth in ways that no one else in her life seems to do anymore.

It complements Alice's raw, no-BS encouragement beautifully. Between the two of them—as well as Josephine and Stacey, Margaux has a shot at remembering who she is—who she *was* before Timmy began siphoning the life out of her.

Her session finished, she steps out of the truck, her shoulders hunched, moving toward the apartment.

I flip back to another feed, watching Timmy in the kitchen. He's clattering dishes with an air of exaggerated care, the performative kind of noise he makes when he's pretending to be a decent person.

My jaw clenches. I know what's coming.

"How was it?" he asks as she walks in. His voice is deceptively light, like he isn't waiting for an answer that'll justify his next tantrum.

Margaux replies carefully. *Too carefully.* She knows better than to let him catch a hint of what she really discussed.

But it doesn't matter—he's already sulking, muttering something about how she 'always makes him look bad'.

My fists tighten around the armrests of my chair. He eavesdropped once, and now he thinks he owns her therapy sessions. He thinks he has the right to be a part of them, to tell her what she can and should not talk about.

What kind of monster violates someone's safe space like that?

I watch him throw a shirt at her. She doesn't react, just places it to the side like she's handling a mildly annoying fly.

He puts a blanket on Sabre and she calmly removes it.

He presses harder, sprinkles water on her, smirks when she sighs and walks away.

And then, like the insecure, small man he is, he takes it further. He throws food into the trash. Perfectly good food that he knows she likes.

Every time he does something like this, I think I can't hate him more than I already do. And then he proves me wrong.

———

Later, Margaux starts researching reactive abuse and DARVO. She's been texting Alice about it, piecing together the patterns of Timmy's manipulation. I feel a flicker of hope as she types furiously on her laptop, her brow furrowed in concentration.

She's seeing it. She's finally seeing it.

The gaslighting, the lies, the way he flips the narrative to make himself the victim—it's all clicking into place for her. I can practically hear Alice's voice in her head, telling her she's not crazy—that Timmy's the problem.

But then he walks in. And of course, he notices her typing.

"Who are you talking to?" he asks, his tone sharp, already accusatory.

"None of your business, bruh," she shoots back, not looking up.

Good. Keep him out. Don't let him poison this small, sacred space you've carved out for yourself.

But he doesn't stop. He hovers, trying to read her screen, muttering insults under his breath. "Ugly crusty Ron Weasley," he sneers.

I laugh bitterly, shaking my head.

That's the best he's got? What an absolute moron.

But then again, that's Timmy—small-minded, petty, incapable of real wit.

The worst of it comes when he calls his mother, twisting Margaux's words into some grotesque fabrication. I can't hear her voice through the feed, but I can imagine her panic, her disbelief. And *Margaux*—Margaux looks like she's been gutted.

Her kindness was weaponized. Her compassion turned into ammunition against her.

I watch as she screams at him, desperate for him to stop, her face red with anger and hurt. But he just smirks, hanging up the phone like he's won some twisted game.

"You're a monster," she whispers, and I can see the exhaustion etched into her face, the cracks in her armor.

Timmy grins. Of course he does. He *feeds* on this—her pain, her frustration, her despair.

He thrives on it.

I slam my fist onto the desk, the echo sharp in the empty room. I want to rip him out of that apartment, throw him into the ocean, and watch him sink under the weight of his own cruelty.

But I can't. Not yet.

Because Margaux still isn't ready.

But she's getting there.

And when she is, I'll be there to pull her out of this hellhole—to remind her of who she is.

Of what she's worth.

And as for Timmy?

He won't know what hit him.

CHAPTER 96
WHEN THE TRUTH IS OPTIONAL

MARGAUX

LATER IN THE DAY

"Who are you talking to?" Timmy asks, his tone sharp and accusatory, his voice tinged with an anger that seems to grow louder with every ignored question. When I don't answer, he huffs and sneers, "You're raking for Sandoval."

I blink. *What does that even mean?*

He's clearly spiraling, each barbed comment more ludicrous than the last.

He's become strangely obsessed with the whole Scandoval situation, despite claiming to hate reality TV. The irony isn't lost on me, but I can't muster the energy to react. Instead, I remain silent, hoping he'll tire himself out.

But Timmy isn't one to be ignored.

"The person who raped you… you deserved it," he spits.

The air leaves my lungs. There was a time when this type of hate-fueled comment would have led to tears—and it still hurts, for sure—but I say nothing, because what's the point?

"You're ugly," he adds, his words slicing through the room like a serrated knife.

I message Alice and let her know he's acting even more erratic and cruel than what has become normal.

ALICE:

You have to make arrangements to separate yourself from him.

He's losing control of you and is spiraling.

I curl up in bed, my exhaustion outweighing my fear. Timmy's venomous words reverberate in my head as I drift into a restless sleep.

———

I wake to Timmy stumbling into the apartment, his voice booming.

"I'm going to destroy your life, you stupid cunt!" he screams, his face twisted with rage. Before I can react, he spits on me. Warm saliva splashes onto my face and arm.

If I wanted to be in a splash zone, I'd go to Sea World.

I wipe it off with the edge of my blanket, refusing to engage. Somehow, miraculously, I fall asleep again.

But peace is fleeting.

I'm jarred awake by the sound of his slurred voice on the phone. "Yeah, she's acting crazy. She's attacking me," he says, his tone deliberately calm, his words dripping with malice.

ME:

He's lost his mind. I was lying here asleep, and he called the cops on me.

ALICE:

You HAVE to start making your own reports.

Otherwise, all they have are HIS statements.

The door swishes and beeps. Timmy has gone again.

Good riddance.

About fifteen minutes later, there's a loud knock on the door. "Police," a deep voice announces.

Clad in only a sports bra and shorts, I answer the door, groggy and disoriented. I yawn as the officers greet me.

"Listen, we got a complaint," one officer says.

"I know," I reply with a sigh. "I heard him on the phone. I was sleeping, his call woke me up, and none of what he said was true."

"Why does he have scratches on him?" the same officer asks, smirking.

"I don't know," I shrug. "He bashes himself up against the reef shelf and stuff, and runs around wearing only board shorts, as you can see. He's always got scratches and cuts."

The officer glances at my hands. "You don't even have long fingernails," he observes.

"This guy is always drunk," another officer says, shaking his head. "You need to leave him."

I nod, though the weight of their advice crushes me. I know he's right. Everyone is right. But leaving feels insurmountable.

"We'll go talk to him and then we'll be back."

I nod, thank them, and shut the door.

ME:

I feel dumb.

ALICE:

You aren't dumb. You were duped.

I sigh.

ME:

Yeah. How dare I believe someone would care for me so much? Ugh.

ALICE:

That isn't foolish.

I text my lawyer, not expecting a response at this hour. But I have a feeling I might need to lawyer up soon.

ME:

He's so manipulative, and when you said he would try to get me to go to jail over and over again, it was too bizarre to believe. But you were right.

ALICE:

It's so unfortunate that it's a pattern in these guys.

They run so far from their own consequences that when they catch them, their only alternative is to throw someone else to the wolves.

Timmy is outside, his screams audible through the walls. *"I want her put in jail!"* he yells, his voice escalating into a hysterical pitch. *"For all she's done to me! She attacked me! There need to be consequences! She needs to go to jail!"*

I retreat to my phone, seeking solace in my messages with Alice.

> ALICE:
>
> Just keep ignoring him.
>
> The police are watching this all unfold.

> ME:
>
> I'm going to drink water in case they take me away for sleeping.

"She needs to go to jail!" he shrieks, still just outside the apartment. *"Take her away!"*

There's another knock on the door, and some of the officers are back, the rest still with Timmy.

One of them glances in Timmy's direction, then back to me, and rolls his eyes. "He's over there pulling his hair and saying 'Look, she's pulling my hair'," he smirks and shakes his head.

At least they aren't falling for his lies.

> ALICE:
>
> I'm sorry that this all had to happen this way.

As if on cue, I receive a message from an anonymous number:

> ANONYMOUS:
>
> Timmy's not a good person.
>
> He'll never change. Because he doesn't want to.
>
> He feels guilty when he fucks up. But only because he gets caught.
>
> If he doesn't think you're giving him an opportunity to change—to see the best in him—because you're over it, as you should be, he'll lash out.
>
> He's been homeless intermittently.
>
> Definitely a couch crasher.
>
> He's smashed car windows and slashed tires and thrown people's car keys.

He drove an entire car into the ocean.

He's been to jail way more times than most people have.

He's missed countless court dates and has outstanding warrants in Montana.

He's gotten fired from many, many jobs.

Kicked out of friends' houses.

He's had physical altercations with his brother and countless other people.

He's had several restraining orders against him from girlfriends, including one involving children.

He cares for no-one but himself. And he doesn't do that very well.

You don't know me, Margaux.

But you HAVE to get out of this.

The words blur as I read them, my vision swimming. It feels like a cruel confirmation of everything I already know, but up until now have refused to face.

I glance at Timmy through the window. He's pacing, gesticulating wildly, his face red and contorted.

Alice's text flashes on my screen.

ALICE:

This is your sign. You have to leave. You can't wait anymore.

Tears spill down my cheeks as I clutch my phone.
I know she's right.

CHAPTER 97

SEEING CLEARLY (& THE VIEW ISN'T GREAT)

MARGAUX

glance at Timmy, his voice piercing the night as he continues to shriek at the police. *"Lock her up! She deserves it! I am a* victim *of her* abuse!"

For the first time, I *truly* see him.

He's standing in nothing but a pair of tattered board shorts, his body covered in self-inflicted scratches and bruises.

One massive gouge stretches across his back—a trophy from when he threw himself into the ocean during a storm, letting the waves batter him against the reef to 'punish' me.

He looks filthy. His hair, matted and knotted, hangs around his unshaven face. The soles of his feet are black, as if he's been trudging through soot. His eyes are glassy, his pupils unfocused, his movements erratic and jerky.

This isn't the cute and charming, carefree surfer I first met.

That man, I now realize, never existed. That version of Timmy was an illusion, a carefully crafted act designed to lure me in. He had showered, brushed his hair, and smiled at me that day, convincing me he was someone else—someone worth loving. *Someone I deserved.*

ME:

I just saw him for the first time.

Really saw him.

And he looks awful, like he lives on the street.

ALICE:

I know, hon. It takes a while.

Love is POWERFUL. It's not just an emotion. It is a
chemical and an emotion we don't control.

It is being drugged without realizing.

ME:

I've actually been doing well.

Seeing a therapist, trying non-alcoholic drink
options.

Taking a new antidepressant.

I have had drinks but nothing crazy.

He has apparently been recording my conversations,
and I do get angry and call him a loser—because he
is one.

But as far as I'm aware, words aren't a crime.

ALICE:

They aren't.

Timmy's tirade continues, his accusations growing more outlandish by
the second.

"I recorded the things she was saying to me! My friend is a witness, too! She's
so fucking *abusive! Lock her up!"*

He storms toward the front door, only for an officer to block his path.
"Give me my charger! I *need* my charger!" he screams, his desperation
palpable.

The officer quirks an eyebrow. "Dude."

I glance around, spot his charger, and unplug it from the wall. "Here," I
say, handing it to the officer, who passes it to Timmy.

"Fuck you!" he screams, his hatred cutting through me like shards of
glass. *"You stupid fucking abusive toxic bitch!"*

"You need to stop," the officer warns him, his tone sharp.

By now, my hands are trembling. My entire body feels like it's vibrating
from the stress.

"Ma'am, we'd like to take your statement," one of the officers says.

My lawyer's advice—*shut the fuck up*—echoes in my head.

"I'd prefer to wait for my lawyer," I reply.

The officers nod, clearly understanding, and they leave.

Sabre—sensing my distress—approaches and snuggles against me, his purring a small comfort amid the chaos.

———

A while later, the door beeps. Timmy comes stomping inside, reeking of cigarettes and booze.

"This is such *fucking bullshit*," he mutters, his words slurred. "Cops need to do their fucking jobs."

He pulls out his phone and dials 911 again. "Yes, I'd like to make a complaint. I need you to come back here, and she needs to be charged." He pauses, then adds, "She's laughing at me. You need to lock her up."

I shake my head, incredulous. I'm not laughing, but even if I was…

Now laughing is a crime? If so, *guilty as charged every day of my life.*

When he doesn't get the response he wants, he slams the phone down and starts yelling again. "*Stupid fucking pussy cops. Pussy cops that won't do their fucking job!*" He turns to me, his eyes blazing with anger. "*Don't* talk to me. *Don't* come in the back room. *Don't* touch me."

"Gladly," I mutter under my breath. I have no interest in doing any of those things.

Instead, I ignore him, and observe as he grabs a hard seltzer from the fridge.

He turns to face me. "*I'm fucking pressing charges on you!*" he yells, then walks to the back room and slams the door behind him.

A few moments later, he returns from the back room. "*I fucking hate you!*" he screams, and retreats to the room once again, slamming the door.

A minute later he yells again. "*Come into the back room!*"

RSVP no to that one.

I continue to ignore him.

Minutes later, he storms back into the living room.

"I'm greasing the wheels to have you arrested," he says, a smug grin spreading across his face. "Do you have anything to say for yourself?"

I refuse to engage, avoiding eye contact.

"I fucking hate you," he growls, and a chill runs through me.

I continue to avoid eye contact and ignore.

He starts muttering unintelligible things under his breath.

I shiver.

How is this my life?

My phone buzzes with another message from an anonymous number:

ANONYMOUS:

He's cheated on multiple girlfriends.

He's beaten up several and broken their bones.

ALICE:

You NEED to find a way out.

It may involve moving and stranding him there.

Just independently find a way out.

ME:

I will. Luckily, he hasn't completely eroded my savings yet.

ALICE:

Cut him off from every resource he has access to.
You'll need it all.

ME:

I have a ton of items coming in for my PR boxes that will be arriving soon.

Worth about a grand.

I don't want to leave it here, but I will if I have to.

ALICE:

I can inquire about places here that could potentially host a person and a cat.

ME:

He sucks me back in, but he's gone way too far this time.

It sucks because I felt like things were finally turning a corner, and he was doing much better.

I didn't think I'd be figuring out where to live. Especially away from the Cay.

Thank you and I will let you know.

I'm so confused.

ALICE:

> I know. But it's either decide where to live or wait to die there.

ME:

> Yeah. Sad.

> Definitely not dying bc of this loser.

> I'm so mad. Sad.

> All the things.

ALICE:

> I know.

> I'm sorry I don't have more enriching things to say.

ME:

> Like, who takes someone's aging health issues and makes it about them?

> A psycho narcissist.

ALICE:

> Exactly. Nobody worth spending time with.

> That's gross.

ME:

> I'm going to try to get some sleep.

> If he approaches me and I need to go, I will.

ALICE:

> Good. I'm here for you in all the ways I can be.

Timmy emerges from the back room again, trying to grab my phone.

I switch windows before he can see anything.

He pulls out his own phone, making it a point to show he's messaging someone. As if to say, *See, I have friends too! Take that!*

Pathetic.

I shake my head, utterly drained.

How did I get here? And, more importantly, how do I get out?

CHAPTER 98
VOLCANO OF PAIN

MARGAUX

My intuition screams at me, louder than ever—*Get out. Now.*

This is no ordinary day.

Timmy's escalating behavior—his false allegations, the spitting, the rage—feels like a red flag on fire. It's not just his words or the threats of violence—it's the sense that there might truly be *nothing* he's not capable of in this state.

Sabre's and my lives are in real danger.

As soon as Timmy leaves the apartment—probably to panhandle at the 7-Eleven or drown himself in vodka at the tents—I spring into action. I pack essentials—my laptop, a few clothes, Sabre's food and carrier—and we head to a hotel.

Once there, Sabre does his usual perimeter check, sniffing every corner of the room before hopping onto the bed with a loud purr. His approval is a small comfort, one of the few silver linings in this situation.

After grabbing a bite to eat, I open my laptop to do some work. But the moment I see the inside, my stomach lurches.

Oh my fucking god.

The keyboard is saturated—water, or worse, has been poured inside.

Desperately, I try to dry it out.

I press the power button. The screen flickers for a moment, then dies. I plug it in, and the familiar MacBook chime gives me hope, but the screen stays black.

My laptop. My main tool as a writer.

Most of my work is saved to the cloud, but not all of it. Backup plans have fallen by the wayside in the chaos of my life with Timmy.

I curl up in the fetal position on the bed, tears streaming down my face as the weight of everything crashes over me.

Sabre, sensing my distress, curls up against me, purring softly. His small, warm body is a lifeline in itself.

Somehow, amidst the despair, I manage to fall asleep.

————

When I wake up, my phone is buzzing with notifications.

> TIMMY:
>
> Come back, I need to get my dick wet.

I gag.

There are photos, too. Purple droplets splattered across the apartment floor, like melted açaí. He must have removed items from the freezer and thrown them all over the floor again.

> TIMMY:
>
> Look, I messed up the apartment.

I feel sick.

My mind flashes back to the first apartment I rented when I moved here, the way Timmy wrecked it during one of his fits.

He's unraveling—not that he was ever particularly raveled to begin with. And the thought of what he might do to the place while I'm not there fills me with dread. But I know going back right now isn't an option.

I check my social media, and I notice a couple of notifications on Facebook.

He's put the same purple puddle photos on one of my posts, and as a comment below something a friend posted on my wall. *How odd.*

Feeling absolutely defeated and drained, I fall back asleep.

————

I wake to two transcribed voicemail messages from Timmy's father, Phil:

> PHIL:
>
> Margaux, what's going on?
>
> Timmy is cutting his wrists, lots of blood!
>
> Call the police. Stop this attack on Timmy.
>
> We love Timmy.
>
> Where are you, and why are you doing this?
>
> I am asking you to stop the attacks.
>
> Please call me.
>
> This is serious, this is no game.

Huh? What is he on about?
Another voicemail follows:

> PHIL:
>
> Margaux, I need you to call me right now.
>
> As soon as you get this.
>
> Timmy is committing suicide. He's got knives.
>
> This is serious. Stop it.

Oh my fucking god. Stop *what?*
Attacks on Timmy?
My entire body shakes with rage and disbelief.
The audacity of his father, who I'm beginning to see is just as bad as him.
Maybe worse.
This so-called man—this *father*—is enabling his son in ways I can't fathom. He's placing all the blame for his son's horrific behavior on me, despite knowing the violence, the threats, the destruction I've endured. Despite the fact his son has left a trail of destruction since well before he knew I existed.

I left the apartment because he was being violent and putting my life in jeopardy.

He's already destroyed so much of my property. I'm terrified about what the apartment is going to be like when I get back.

And his dad is calling me and telling me to stop attacking *him*?

No wonder Timmy's so fucked up.

They both are.
I reply.

ME:

> If by stopping the attacks on Timmy, you mean when he strangled me, poured boiling water on me, fractured my skull, brought chainsaws out and threatened to chop my head off with them multiple times, spat on me, split my lip and gave me two black eyes, kidnapped my friend's 14-year-old son, threatened to kill my cat, the list goes on…

> He sent me a variety of incoherent texts last night.

> I am nowhere near him or the truck.

> Of course I don't want him to harm himself, but I don't want to get killed because I stayed when he was behaving completely unhinged.

Then I see Phil has left another voicemail. It's almost twenty minutes long. *What the hell?*

I play it, only to realize it's a boomer faux pas—an accidental recording of a conversation Phil had with someone else.

"Margaux is a whole *volcano of pain*," he says at one point, his tone disdainful. "She's a *liar*, and I *never* want to see her again."

The person on the other end tries to reason with him. "Maybe you should focus on your son instead of Margaux. He has a real problem and he needs serious help."

But Phil is resolute—according to him, the problem isn't Timmy. It's *me*.

Margaux—the Volcano of Pain.

"He's a really nice guy. He just has a bit of an alcohol problem," Phil defends his son.

Unbelievable. Who's delulu now?

I message Alice, my safety net through this madness.

ME:

> Timmy is saying he's going to kill himself.

> And his dad is blaming me.

ALICE:

Ignore him.

This is an attention tactic.

I'm so sorry.

I think about everything that's happening. That's been happening.
Damn.

When I was a kid and wanted attention from, say, my dad, I'd dance around in front of the TV he was trying to watch. I'd never dream of slicing myself up, taking pictures of the blood and posting them all over my significant other's social media.

But here we are, I guess.

I send her a screenshot of the message I sent his dad, and then realize I probably need to explain why he's named the way he is in his contact profile.

ME:

His dad is saved as Sheila in my phone because he deletes his dad's number if he sees it in there, so I had to give him a random name.

His mom is Bob.

As I write this, I realize how absurd it sounds.

ALICE:

Sorry, but it's funny.

ME:

I just listened to the whole nearly 20 minute voicemail his dad left for me, and apparently I'm a 'whole volcano of pain' and he 'never wants to see me again.'

ALICE:

Good. He'll be doing you a favor.

ME:

I won't reply, but I feel like saying, 'When did you ever call ME and not take his word for everything? When did you ever call and offer to help get your son the support he needs?'

———

A few hours later, Timmy randomly sends me a clip from Saturday Night Live, as if nothing ever happened. He's laughing in the background, and sounds demented.

I feel conflicted—I don't want him to hurt himself. Despite everything, I care about him, and don't want him to kill himself.

It seems right to reach out just to try to keep him calm.

I don't know if the suicide attempt was real or not.

I message him:

> ME:
>
> I do want you to know that I care about you, and I'm very glad that it seems like you are physically safe.

I update Alice, feeling uneasy that I reached out to him, but still feeling like it was the right thing to do.

> ME:
>
> Ugh. I hate it because I love the person, even though they might not deserve it.

> ALICE:
>
> I know. But love isn't enough for a safe relationship.
>
> You need safety, too.

> ME:
>
> I messaged him 🙁 but I would have felt like an awful human being if I didn't.

> ALICE:
>
> It's hard not to.
>
> Just don't see him in person. It's too dangerous.

> ME:
>
> Yeah, safety is a real concern, I know.
>
> There were times last night the sliding door here at the hotel would rattle, and I would exhale when I realized it wasn't him coming into the apartment in a volatile, unpredictable condition.

> ALICE:
>
> 

> ME:
>
> It sucks, because you love the person and see the good. But there's bad that puts you in danger. His shit behavior from yesterday has cost me $2k so far.

But ya know what? That's better than losing my life or putting up with more shit.

He made me feel more loved than any guy ever has.

But it wasn't based on anything real.

And it's come at a cost where I've ended up feeling the exact opposite, and am physically at risk. Let alone mentally.

Sabre curls up next to me again, his soft purring grounding me in the moment.

I'm exhausted, emotionally drained, but one thing is crystal clear: *This can't go on.*

CHAPTER 99
THE VOLCANO SPEAKS

MARGAUX

By the time I'm ready to hit 'send,' my hands are trembling. Every word feels loaded with history, anger, and truth.

This message isn't just a response to Phil's accusations—it's my statement of self-defense against the mountain of lies and gaslighting that has been suffocating me, perpetrated just as much by Timmy's enabling father, Phil, as by Timmy himself.

Before I send it, I reach out to Alice.

ME:

Hey, can you proofread something for me and give a send or don't send opinion?

I want to send it to his dad, bc I'm so furious about being gaslit.

ALICE:

Sure, I'll look it over.

ME:

Thank you, here it is:

I paste the message into the chat.

I wrote this last night and waited to send this today given the time difference. It is a long message, but I think it would be helpful to share with you in order to get Timmy the help he needs.

I moved here almost one year ago in March 2023.

Within 2 weeks, Timmy invites his boss, Parker, to my apartment, where they get into an argument, and Parker threatens to mess up the building where I live, and compromise my ability to live there.

Within 3 weeks, Timmy threatens to kill me, and slams me to the ground and tries to shove deer antlers into my anus. Because he is 'mad at my neighbor,' and so he took a bunch of trazodone with alcohol to 'calm down'. Several people overhear him and call the police. He admits to everything, apologizes profusely, and I refuse to pursue charges bc I want to believe he is a good person and that this was an isolated incident, even though it was terrifying having a 200lb man physically attack me.

After this, Timmy is banned from a 100-yard radius from the apartment building for a year. The prosecutor wants to have him banned from all of downtown Sunset Cay. They say he has a track record of this behavior and is dangerous.

We move to the other side of the Cay—at his suggestion—so he will be away from his 'bad influences,' and he promises he will not wander off on benders. He wanders off on benders, and one day he smashes my head to the ground, fracturing my skull when I listen to a song he 'doesn't like' (but that he also plays all the time), and squeezes his hands around my throat. Women who have been strangled by their partner even once are 750% more likely to be killed by that same partner. I have to live with this statistic.

I'm told he is entering tents with women over by the drug dealers.

I'm told he is doing drugs.

I'm not sure if either of those things are true, but he is certainly coming back drunk even though he has 'no money', when he tells me you are giving him money for alcohol.

Can you imagine how any of this feels?

I wake up at around 3AM on multiple occasions, and he is off drinking with the people who live in the tents. We had discussed that leaving in the middle of the night was not okay and crossed the boundaries of our relationship. He promised not to do it ever again.

Timmy then has me arrested, accusing me of scratching him when he scratches himself on an almost daily basis running along the reef shelf, etc. Later, he says it's bc he didn't want to go to jail and thought I might put him there, so he called law enforcement first. I don't even have long nails and I have never scratched anyone intentionally. His back has a massive scar from when he purposely scratched himself a couple of months ago.

Timmy said to the cops that I strangled him, and threatened him with a weapon, when those are things he has done to me, and I have never done to him. He acknowledged this later and admitted he embellished his version of events because he was angry and 'wanted to mess my life up'.

When I am in jail, and for the 2 days I am not allowed to return to the apartment, he breaks into my computer and messages multiple people telling them I am in jail. And then calls my friend Josephine, leaving an abusive voicemail in which he calls her the n word and a cunt. He says he did this because he believed she is a man and that I am having sex with 'him' in Sunset Cay. She is a woman who is in Washington DC.

I encourage Timmy into therapy, a better medication, and keep asking him to get a job. He does therapy sporadically and stops taking his meds, then takes them again, but not consistently. I buy a laptop for his graphic design which he agrees to pay me back for.

Flash forward past many other incidents you are aware of...

Darren's memorial: I was extremely supportive of Timmy as soon as he found out his friend passed, and I could see him spiraling. I attempted to help. It was scary in the lead-up, and I could see this event was a huge trigger for him. I did set boundaries for the event and said he needed to not drink too much and not run off, and be respectful as a partner. To introduce me and make sure I could be there with and for him. It was observed by others that if I attempted to talk to people (I didn't know anyone except for him and Steve), that he would run up and act weird. But then he kept running off and was clearly becoming more erratic. I had no faith he would return to the other side of the Cay or be safe. I was not jealous, I was concerned by his erratic behavior and frustrated he wasn't trying to keep to what we agreed. I don't know about a second person who he hugged, and would have no problem with him hugging a friend at his friend's memorial. Darren was a known drug dealer who died of a suspected fentanyl overdose. I was frankly terrified Timmy would end up taking drugs because he was upset and the same thing could happen to him. Timmy did attend the ceremony. He even attended the paddle-out, and it was very touching, and I posted about it on my Facebook with pictures at the time.

By this stage, I'm so stressed and dealing with health issues, and his spiraling from Darren's death, that I've eaten almost nothing for 6 weeks. I try to but I cannot keep much food down. I am in constant pain with vomiting and diarrhea. Timmy's erratic behavior is intensifying.

The truck incident happens the following day. I am not a liar. I am not crazy. I said what I believed was happening to me at the time. I am embarrassed by the event and my only other traffic incident was a speeding ticket from New Zealand when I was in my early 20s.

Timmy has changed his story about why he lost the job with Robert several times.

He has told me repeatedly that he thinks it's just neighbors being gossipy, but when he is being mean, he blames me. He told me at first he didn't raise his voice to Robert when Robert critiqued Timmy's work, but later said he did raise his voice to Robert, and that's why he thinks he was fired. I have heard maybe 5 versions of the story.

Timmy has cost me over $10k at this point on needless expenses, wasting my money because he is drunk or otherwise acting belligerent. Lease break fees on my first apartment, throwing my phone in the ocean, many car bills to be able to get tags bc the vehicle wasn't roadworthy, his bail for drunk driving, pouring a drink on my laptop intentionally, AirPods that he took without my permission and lost when he was drunk, and so on. I am not including his share of living expenses here. If I did, the figure would significantly increase. He also took my diamond rings that I designed with an assessed value of $5k and put them in his rectum while he was in jail. He returned them but they are missing again.

I have said mean things to your son. He has said mean things to me. He has physically abused me and verbally abused me time after time after time.

My last partner and I were in a relationship for 6 years. He was career military and a good person, and he never laid a finger on me or vice versa. My other longest relationship was a career detective who I was married to, and with for 5+ years. Again, no issues with domestic violence or abusive arguments. Our breakups were amicable, and no property was damaged.

Darren and Timmy's last text conversation was when Timmy took my phone and called Darren the n word said a bunch of rageful things. Darren shared that Timmy is a terrible alcoholic and his last words to me were, 'Good luck with your man child'.

Steve stopped talking to Timmy until Darren died, after Timmy threatened to kill all of Steve's friends on Molokai, because one of them critiqued the way he painted Steve's I-beams.

Before they both cut him off, both Darren and Steve shared that they can only take Timmy in small quantities.

After the first incident when I moved here and he tried to kill me, I met with Jennifer, and she told me many things about Timmy's behavior. While I do not believe everything she said, and do not agree with her infidelity, many of the things that she said about his behavior are things I had experienced for myself firsthand.

So I do not appreciate you calling me a liar, accusing me of terrorizing or attacking your son, or of being a 'volcano of pain,' or whatever that was. I don't appreciate receiving a nearly 20-minute voicemail stating all of this when I am trying to deal with the situation.

I understand you are upset because your son is off the rails and that he hurt himself. But that is not on me. He has a pattern, and needs help that none of us are equipped to provide. At least 4 people have filed restraining orders against him. He has 4 pages of criminal records just in Sunset Cay. Nobody wants him to hurt himself or anybody else, except maybe him.

There are so many times I would have been happy to speak with you about what we do here and how we can best help.

On Sunday night, he sent a flurry of strange messages (some were sexual, some were about how he was messing the apartment up). He said I was there when I was not anywhere near there, moving the truck and entering the apartment. He sent a picture which in the middle of the night looked like he had spilled açaí, and he sent me a kiss emoji right after it.

It was only when I woke up yesterday morning, and saw you had called saying he was committing suicide, and saw he had posted his bloody pictures on two of my unrelated Facebook posts, that I realized it was actually blood.

So please do not message me anything else offensive. I understand you are upset your son is acting out, but this behavior far predates me as shown by online criminal records and his own admissions, and I don't need or deserve to be attacked. I'm glad he is physically safe.

As I reread it, the weight of everything Timmy has put me through over the past year bears down on me. From the first incident with Parker, to the latest manipulative stunt involving his father, the spiral of abuse has been relentless.

Alice takes her time reading.

> ALICE:
>
> Good. Respond to nothing they say.

> ME:
>
> Sending now.
>
> Thank you for reading it.

> ALICE:
>
> I know this is hard and unfair.

I press send, my stomach churning.

Immediately, a wave of emotions crashes over me—relief, anger, fear, and the faintest hint of hope that maybe—just maybe—this will force Phil to look at the reality of his son's behavior.

But deep down, I know it's unlikely.

Timmy's manipulation runs deep, and Phil's denial is a fortress I can't penetrate.

Phil is what's known in narcissistic abuse terms as a 'flying monkey' to Timmy, always willing to do his bidding and come to his defense, even in the face of hard evidence against him. Appealing to a flying monkey typically doesn't do shit.

Still, this isn't for him. *It's for me.* To reclaim my narrative. To remind myself that I'm not crazy, no matter how much Timmy or his flying monkey of a father try to convince me otherwise.

———

The day stretches on. I wait for a reply, though I already know what it will say if it comes.

Alice's words stick with me—*Respond to nothing they say.*

I glance at Sabre, curled up next to me, his soft purring the only sound in the room. For now, that's enough.

I've said my piece.

And for the first time in a long time, I feel a sliver of control returning.

I close my eyes, take a deep breath, and let the silence settle around me.

CHAPTER 100
THE TIMMY SHOW

MARGAUX

LATER IN THE DAY

get back to the apartment complex, but before heading in, I stop by the parking garage. I just have a feeling he's done something to the truck. Entering the code to unlock it, I hop into the driver's seat and put the key in the ignition. But it won't start. As feared, Timmy has done something to the truck.

I sigh.

I head to the apartment, and as I unlock the door, a familiar heaviness sets in. I'm bracing for what else I might find—for what Timmy's impulsive behavior might have cost me this time.

My thoughts race toward the PR box items I know have been delivered—things I've spent my time and money carefully curating for my readers. I can't bear the thought of them having being destroyed in one of his tantrums.

To my surprise, Timmy greets me with an almost subdued energy. His face is a mix of sorrow and exhaustion, his movements slower than usual. His recent self-inflicted injuries have left him drained.

I feel safe. *For now.*

"I'm sorry," he says, his voice low, almost childlike. "I never meant to hurt you. You mean everything to me. But you broke my brain."

I look at him, my expression carefully neutral. I don't rise to the bait. I won't play the blame game.

He shows me his injuries. He's scratched the *back* of his arm up, not the wrist side. And he has a couple of very minor scratches on his chest.

"The truck won't start," I say flatly, shifting the conversation.

He hesitates, and then looks sheepish. "Oh, yeah… I removed something so you couldn't leave with it." His voice trails off.

I sigh, my irritation rising. "Fix it immediately."

Timmy nods and shuffles off to put his shoes on. I order him an Uber so he can head to the auto parts store to replace the part he didn't just damage, but broke beyond repair. It's always like this—a moment of chaos, followed by half-hearted apologies and promises to do better, as well as forking out money to fix whatever destruction Timmy has wrought.

While he's gone, I take stock of the apartment.

Thankfully, the PR box items appear to be intact.

But my printer is broken, rendering me unable to print the shipping labels I need for my books, the top piece completely ripped off of it.

I notice items missing from the fridge.

What else has he done that I just haven't noticed yet?

When Timmy gets back from the auto parts store, I confront him.

"You broke my printer," I say, my voice monotone.

"No I didn't." He shakes his head.

I lift up the detached piece that won't go back on.

"Oh," he says, and looks down. "Sorry."

"And my bougie nonalcoholic drinks?" I ask, already knowing the answer.

"I got rid of them," Timmy mutters, shrugging, not even trying to justify it.

The screen from the back window is missing again, his personal escape hatch for whenever he feels like disappearing.

I add the mounting damages to his ever-growing tab.

Timmy's face is downcast as I do, but the promises come quickly. "I'll pay you back," he insists, his words hollow. "I promise. I really am sorry about all of this."

I sigh. "I'm going to take my therapy session from the truck," I say.

"What are you going to talk to her about?" he asks, looking concerned.

"You probably shouldn't mention what I did to the truck, because she'll probably need to report it."

What a curious thing to be worried about after all the things he's done.

———

As I recount the events to my therapist—including, of course, what happened to the truck—she listens with unwavering support. Her guidance is clear but gentle, helping me see the reality I've been avoiding for way too long.

"I'm thinking of moving back into Downtown," I say. "I feel isolated out here."

She nods, but offers a nudge I wasn't expecting. "What if you moved there without Timmy? You could still see each other, but have a space that's yours."

The thought feels impossible and freeing all at once. "Maybe," I say, thinking it through.

"What would happen to him if you did?" she asks, as if reading my mind. It's as if she's pointing out how sad he is as an individual, that he's relying on me to have a roof over his head. That if I wasn't providing for him, he would have to mooch off someone else rather than hold his own head above water.

"He wouldn't have a place to live," I protest weakly.

"He's an adult," she says, gently but firmly. "The way things are now, you're like a caregiver to him. He needs to figure out his own living situation."

The guilt churns in my stomach. The idea of leaving him to fend for himself makes me uncomfortable, but deep down, I know she's right. I'm just not ready.

I'm embarrassed to have stepped into the role of his caregiver. He's not a partner, he's a leech.

I think through what would likely happen if I followed her suggestion. The only people who would probably take him in are the bad influences we moved out here to avoid—which makes me feel extremely uncomfortable.

I get that this is part of a bigger issue, but my mind isn't quite ready to fully admit it. Instead, I feel resistance and guilt and resentment.

We work on a safety plan, discussing go-bags and exit strategies.

My plan from here on out is that I'm going to remain calm, and not drink around Timmy. Hopefully his dad will stop sending him money for 'soda'.

And if and when Timmy repeats the cycle, I have a strategy to get out quickly.

Her parting words linger long after our session ends: *"Remember, you are a badass. Let's check in next week."*

———

Back at the apartment, Timmy swings wildly between sweet gestures and exhausting self-absorption. He cleans the kitchen, makes me a cup of herbal tea, and heaps on compliments so sugary they feel calculated.

These small acts of kindness seem less about bringing me joy, and more about building a defense for himself—ammunition to later point to and say, 'Look at the good I've done,' as if it erases all the harm.

His primary focus, however, is no longer on me. He pours his time, energy, and attention into strangers, making it clear he doesn't think I'm deserving of the same effort.

He beams with pride when praised by random beachgoers for picking up litter. "Two people said what I was doing was amazing," he announces, fishing for validation. Yet, I'm certain he wouldn't care about saving the world's oceans if no one was there to notice.

Behind closed doors, the praise he craves vanishes, and his treatment of me shifts—indifference at best, cruelty at worst.

The cracks in our relationship deepen daily, the same toxic patterns playing out on repeat.

He interrupts my workouts, the one thing that helps me feel grounded and sane.

He complains when I take even a moment for myself, drowning out my focus with his incessant demands for attention.

Meanwhile, I'm drowning under the weight of financial pressure, providing for both of us, while juggling a mountain of overdue book deadlines. Still, I plow on with writing, hoping that focusing on something other than Timmy—something productive that I love—will let my brain unjumble itself and get me out of this fog I've been in for far too long.

I know this heaviness—it's depression, creeping in again, pulling me further from myself. For months, I've barely set foot on the beach, though it's only steps away.

It feels like I'm punishing myself, withholding the joy of this beautiful paradise because I'm too miserable to enjoy it.

There's no silence in Timmy's world—there is no down time with Timmy, no reprieve.

The Timmy Show runs 24/7/365, always centered on him and his erratic moods.

What Timmy wants.

What Timmy needs.

What Timmy feels entitled to.

Who angered Timmy.

Who hurt Timmy's feelings.

Whether Timmy is hungry.

Whether Timmy needs to use the bathroom.

Whether Timmy wants sex.

Whether Timmy *needs* to have a cigarette.

I'm not even a co-star—I'm an unwilling extra, dragged along as he dominates the stage.

I feel like a shadow of who I was when I arrived here—strong, confident, alive. Timmy's constant demands have chipped away at me, piece by piece.

I know what needs to change. I'm just not quite ready to take the leap.

CHAPTER 101
VOLCANO OF STRENGTH

DEX

I sit in the truck, my knuckles white as I grip the steering wheel. The salty breeze outside does nothing to calm me.

Margaux is gone from the apartment, and for the first time in months, I feel something close to relief. No longer tethered to the chaos, she's taken a step toward freedom. She's finally done it—left him.

I close my eyes, imagining Margaux sitting in her hotel room, Sabre curled up beside her.

At least she has Sabre.

That cat's been her anchor in this storm, her one constant source of comfort.

I'm proud of her. More than proud. She's brave, stronger than she realizes. But the rage bubbling inside me threatens to overshadow the pride. Rage at Timmy, sure, but especially at Phil, the puppet master enabling this entire circus.

Margaux is out there rebuilding herself from the ruins Timmy has left behind, and Phil has the audacity to call *her* a 'volcano of pain'? The words make my teeth grind.

A volcano? She's not the one erupting, raining destruction on everyone around her. That's Timmy. Phil's blind devotion to his underachieving son is staggering, a testament to just how deep their dysfunction runs.

What parent defends a son who spits on his partner, destroys her belongings, and gaslights her into oblivion? And then, when his son pulls some half-assed suicide stunt, they call Margaux to clean it up, and blame her for it happening in the first place?

I park the truck in a random lot overlooking the ocean and stare out at the horizon. Waves crash against the rocks below, wild and unrelenting. They remind me of Margaux's spirit—relentless, enduring, though Timmy's done everything he can to erode it.

Timmy. That cowardly bastard. If he'd actually gone through with his suicide, maybe the world would be better off. That's a dark thought, one I can't shake. The wreckage he's left in Margaux's life is a constant reminder of how little he values anyone but himself. He twists her kindness into a weapon, takes every ounce of love she offers, and spits it back at her with venom.

I check my phone for updates from her. Nothing yet. She's probably resting, or maybe working through the rubble of her emotions.

Either way, she's out of his reach for now. That's what matters.

The wind picks up, whipping through my hair, and I let it carry away some of the anger. Not all of it—it's too much to let go—but enough to keep me grounded.

The truck door creaks as I climb out, the setting sun casting long shadows on the ground. I lean against the hood, watching the waves.

Timmy might think he's won, but Margaux's stronger than he'll ever be.

———

Margaux's absence from her apartment is only temporary. Before I know it, she returns.

And yet, I understand why she's gone back to the apartment.

It's who she is.

Margaux can't help but try to salvage the unsalvageable.

She feels guilt, fueled by Phil's blaming her for something Timmy clearly never intended to follow through with.

She's probably worried—with good reason—about her belongings.

And she's clinging to the life she imagined with him, to the version of him he pretended to be when they first met.

Margaux's journey isn't over. She's still tethered to Timmy in so many ways—financially, emotionally. But she's taken the first step. She left, even if it was only for a couple of days.

They say it takes the average abuse victim seven attempts to leave their abuser, so this is a step in the right direction, and it would be foolish to have expected it to be a permanent move.

I hate that she has to go through this.

I hate him for making her question her worth.

The texts she's sent over the past few days paint a picture of pure madness—Timmy, drunk and ranting about imaginary slights.

Timmy, destroying her property out of petty revenge.

Timmy, playing victim to anyone who will listen.

And Phil—*goddamn Phil*—laps it all up, enabling his son's every destructive whim.

When I found out Timmy destroyed Margaux's prized laptop, I wanted to fly straight to the Cay and put my fist through Timmy's face. Destroying her MacBook wasn't just a petty act of revenge—it was an attack on her livelihood. Her writing is everything to her—it's her escape, her passion, her means of survival. And he just… poured water into it? For what? To prove he could?

He's a child, lashing out at the person who loves him most, because he knows she'll forgive him. Or at least, she used to. Not anymore.

The list of damages is staggering. The printer, the specialty drinks, the missing window screen—he's made a game of dismantling her world and costing her endless expense.

And for what? Because she had the audacity to stand up to him?

Because she saw through his act?

Every broken item feels like a message: *This is what you get for leaving me. This is what you get for speaking up and trying to hold me accountable.*

She's starting to see him for what he is—a narcissist, a manipulator, a parasite. Her research on DARVO and reactive abuse is helping her untangle the mess he's made of her mind. She's realizing that the guilt he's heaped on her shoulders doesn't belong to her.

I hate Timmy, and I hate Phil for defending him.

I have to believe she'll keep walking. Because the alternative? That's not a world I want to imagine.

For now, I'll stay here, ready to support her however she needs.

Timmy and Phil might have broken her spirit, but they'll never break her completely.

She's stronger than they could ever understand.

And I'll make damn sure she never forgets it.

CHAPTER 102
HAPPY FUCKING ANNIVERSARY

MARGAUX

The tiki bar's exterior lights flicker like fireflies, casting a nostalgic glow over the adjacent parking lot. The same place where Timmy and I visited when we first met now feels like a battlefield, its charm soured by his unpredictable behavior.

"I'm going to throw them in the water," Timmy declares, holding the truck keys high. His hand arches back dramatically, and for a moment, I freeze, unsure if he'll follow through.

I don't hear the splash, but the industrial hum of the surrounding area muffles all other sounds.

"Fuck," I mutter under my breath, fumbling for my phone. Replacement keys will cost hours and hundreds of dollars, and I don't even know if they're retrievable.

Who does this? Especially on our one-year anniversary, which also marks my first year in Sunset Cay. He's acting so childlike.

In my desperation, I call his dad. "Help!" I plead with Phil. "He's threatening to throw the truck keys in the water. I can't tell if he actually did it, or if he just pretended." Before I met Timmy, I'd never had to call a partner's parent before, but I have Phil on speed dial. He's the only one with a chance of calming him down—his codependent flying monkey to the rescue again.

Through the phone, Phil's voice booms. *"Son! Do not throw the truck keys in the water!"*

"But she upset me, Dad!" Timmy whines like a petulant child caught in the act.

"What did she do?" Phil asks, exasperated.

"She said I was trying to get a beer from some guy at the bar," Timmy explains, his tone defensive.

Phil sighs. "Were you, son?"

"Well… he offered me one," Timmy admits, barely audible.

"Why weren't you spending time with your fiancée on your anniversary? You should be focusing on each other."

Timmy stammers, "She brought up stuff I didn't want to talk about."

I interject, my tone measured but firm. "I calmly mentioned that this place reminds me of the time you texted Jennifer after you told me you'd never been here before. It made me feel weird, so I shared how I was feeling. That's all."

When we pulled into the parking lot, memories—and the associated emotions—came flooding back.

The way I'd felt like I'd been gut-punched when Jennifer pulled up the message he'd sent her during our date—*I miss your crazy, aggressive ass.* The way I'd felt when I found out he'd lied about it being his first time here, and that he'd actually been twice before with her. I wasn't trying to start a fight, but I wanted to be honest about the way I was feeling.

I forgot I can't do that with Timmy. Any comment that isn't a compliment is taken as a personal attack, and there are always consequences. My bad.

Timmy huffs, his irritation mounting. "And then she was on her phone, scrolling, and found out some acquaintance of hers had a suicide in the family. That's not anniversary talk!"

"You were busy chatting with a stranger about beer," I counter. "So yeah, I looked at my phone, saw the news, and mentioned it. I didn't think it would bother you."

"What the fuck ever," he growls, tossing the keys in my direction. "Dumb bitch."

"Happy anniversary?" I reply, the bitterness palpable in my voice.

Timmy hops into the passenger seat and glares at me expectantly, clearly assuming I'll drive him all the way home and abandon any remaining plans.

But I refuse to let him completely ruin the day.

I'm going to celebrate my first year in the Cay, with or without him.

I type an address into Waze, and head to the restaurant I've been looking forward to for weeks.

"Where the fuck are we? I'm not going in," Timmy snaps as we arrive.

"That's fine," I say, masking the tremor in my voice. "*I* am."

"Fine! I'll stay out here," he sneers, folding his arms like a child throwing a tantrum. He's playing some weird game of Restaurant Chicken and I'm not participating.

"Don't touch the truck," I warn, my voice low and firm. "If you vandalize it, I'll call the police."

He narrows his eyes, but doesn't respond.

———

Inside, the restaurant is a sanctuary. Soft lighting, warm smiles from the staff, and the gentle hum of conversation replace the chaos I left behind.

The bartender chats with me about his dreams of moving to New Zealand with his girlfriend, subtly trying to make me feel less awkward about dining alone on what should be a romantic, celebratory evening.

The food is exquisite, each plate an edible masterpiece. For a brief moment, I feel a sense of peace.

Then Timmy appears.

He slides onto the stool beside me, grinning at the bartender as if nothing's amiss—as if joining your fiancée for your anniversary dinner when she's almost done eating is perfectly normal.

"Can I have a beer?" he asks me sweetly.

"Sure," I say, exhausted but relieved that he seems calm—for now.

I push the last dish toward him, explaining what it is. He takes a bite.

"This is really good," he says, his tone almost normal.

"Every other dish was good, too," I reply. "If you'd come in earlier, you would've known that."

He frowns, the defensiveness creeping back. "But you hurt my feelings. Bringing that stuff up wasn't very nice."

"I wasn't trying to hurt you," I explain. "I was just sharing how I felt so we could talk about it. We need to be able to talk about things. Please..." I grab his hand. "You have to believe that when I bring up constructive things, it's not with the intention of fighting or blaming. It's so we can work through them, communicate, and understand each other better. It's been a year, and we clearly still need to work on that."

He considers my words, his expression softening. "You're right," he says, wrapping an arm around me. "I love you so much, Marg. Let's try to fix the rest of the evening and celebrate. Thank you for the beer and food. I'm so lucky to have you. I love you so, so much, my penguin."

My heart aches with relief, but I know this is likely temporary. I kiss him back. "I love you, too."

The waiter brings out dessert, a decadent dish adorned with "Happy Anniversary" in chocolate script. For a moment, I allow myself to savor it— the sweetness, the artistry, the acknowledgment of my milestone on the island.

But the thought lingers: *Will it always be like this? Will every outing be a battlefield before it can be a celebration? Will he always find a way to ruin every milestone? Will I ever be able to bring anything up without there being consequences?*

I glance at Timmy, who's chatting with the bartender about the beer. He's charming, charismatic—everything he was when I first met him. But the cracks in the facade are undeniable.

The emotional toll of constantly tiptoeing around his moods, of being unable to share even my mildest thoughts without fear of retaliation, feels like too much.

As I finish my dessert, the bittersweetness isn't just on the plate—it's in the realization that I'm holding onto hope for a version of him that doesn't exist.

CHAPTER 103
WHEN YOU'RE DROWNING BUT YOU'RE STILL KIND

MARGAUX

The apartment is quiet—the kind of silence that feels heavy, like a weight pressing down on my chest.

Timmy is out—where, I don't know—and for once, I'm grateful for the solitude. I sit on the bed, my laptop open, staring at the blank document. The cursor blinks at me, waiting.

I need to say this. I need him to hear it. But talking to Timmy face-to-face never works. He deflects, twists my words, or worse—turns my concerns into ammunition for the next fight.

An email is different.

He can't interrupt, can't storm out or raise his voice. He has to read it, sit with it. Maybe, just maybe, it will sink in.

I take a deep breath and start typing.

Timmy,

You are an incredible person.

I mean it when I say I love you more than anyone.

I am sorry for the mean things I've said to you. That's not me. And it's not okay. That has gone both ways and this is a pattern for you, but a new thing for me.

It's not okay from either of us.

I know you have a mood disorder. That is a big deal and not something that I can fix. You need to own the diagnosis and do all the things that will make you feel happiness. Therapy. Medication. All of the things.

Since we have been together I have seen so many positive changes you have tried to make—therapy, new medication, trying to improve communication, new job. Stopping other drugs. But it often feels like the want of a cigarette or alcohol or to 'get back at me' for some slight, throws all the progress out the window.

When you leave the apartment and go off unreachable, I can't deal with that. It's outside of what I need and expect from a relationship.

When I tell you something in confidence and then you rub it in my face and/or try to 'destroy my life' with it, I can't deal with that, and it's not in line with my expectations or needs.

I wanted this to work more than you ever know. When you aren't acting out, you are funny and smart and creative and my favorite person to be around. I love brainstorming ideas with you and how you get excited and see so much potential in the world. You are very talented. And you are adorable. I really do love you.

But when you are acting out, it is difficult to be around you and I don't feel safe. You are way bigger than me physically and have hurt me badly before, which you have acknowledged. And when you don't follow through consistently and stand up and be the person I know you so want to be, it is a huge letdown that creates so much stress and pressure. It feels like I have an enemy in my own home.

I have been through a lot in my life—and I know you have too—and it's exceptionally important for me to have stability, and surround myself with people who are kind and motivated and want the best for me and themselves. That's how things should be. Partners are meant to support and uplift each other.

I feel like you become mean and aggressive and toxic and suspicious, and it's not based on anything happening now. I know other people have hurt you and sometimes it feels like you are taking those experiences and assuming the same about me. This, combined with the above, causes me to become resentful and angry. It feels like you are taking the piss of a life that I've worked very hard to build with little support and was willing to share with you—if you did your part.

I want to set goals and work toward them. Not start to do well, and then have things be sabotaged and my boundaries disrespected. You actually broke my laptop the other night, costing me $1450 to replace it because of the way it was damaged. It feels like you are taking you—and now me—further away from achieving our goals.

From what you have told me, as well as my own observations, you seem to be quite fixated on 'revenge' and the idea of 'ruining' or 'destroying' people's lives. I can't be around that.

Life is way too short to be having domestic episodes over television shows and movies and music. And people should be able to discuss feelings in a rational, calm *way before running off or escalating to police calls. Again, I am sorry for the mean things I have said to you.*

This relationship is making me into a person I don't want to be.. and that really sucks bc I wanted it to work so very badly—because I truly do love you.

Margaux xoxo

I reread the email, my finger hovering over the send button. It's raw, honest, and more vulnerable than I'm comfortable with.

But he needs to hear this.

I need him to hear this.

I click *send* and close my laptop.

The silence in the apartment feels louder now, oppressive. The email is out of my hands, but the weight of the words remains. I wonder if he'll read it. If it will register. If he'll even care.

Deep down, I'm not sure it will make a difference.

But I have to try.

I glance toward the window. The ocean glimmers in the moonlight, calm and steady. I wish I could borrow some of that calm, let it settle over me.

Instead, I feel like a storm, restless and unresolved.

This relationship is a tempest, and I'm drowning in it.

CHAPTER 104
TIMMY STRIKES AGAIN

MARGAUX

The air in the apartment is suffocating, weighed down by fear, exhaustion, and the remnants of shattered trust. For a few days, Timmy is calm. Almost contrite.

I think he knows how badly he messed up our anniversary and that he's hanging by a thread.

He reads my email. "I agree with all of it, Margaux. You're right. I love you, and I promise to do better."

His words soothe, but calm is never a constant with him. It's a fleeting intermission before the next act of chaos.

Sure enough, five days later, Timmy strikes again.

He runs away to the tents. Defeated and exhausted, I fall asleep, no longer having the energy to fight his runaway episodes.

Resigned to this being my life now.

I wake to the disorienting sensation of Timmy pressing against me. My body stiffens, my heart racing as I realize what's happening.

He rubs his dick against me, then he moves down and licks my asshole.

I freeze, paralyzed.

My skin crawls as his tongue slides against me, and he crawls back up, sliding himself inside me.

I've told him before—explicitly—that this is not okay. That he does not have my consent to touch me while I'm asleep.

But what does consent mean to someone like Timmy?

I remain still, hoping he'll stop, unable to find the energy to resist.

Last time I brought it up, he laughed.

My stomach churns as he finishes inside me, and I feel bile rise in my throat.

I lie here, numb, as he rolls over and falls asleep.

I'm trapped in my own body, replaying what just happened over and over—he just used my body without my permission, and it wasn't the first time.

————

Timmy spends most of the next day in bed, finally emerging late in the afternoon.

He slams around the kitchen—the fridge door, the water bottle, the bathroom door all victims of his unchecked rage.

"I *fucking* hate your stupid *fucking* TV shows," he snarls. "You watch them just to upset me."

"No, Timmy," I say, keeping my voice steady. "I've been watching them for over ten years. I watch them because I *enjoy* them."

He sneers at Sabre, who's lapping water from his bowl. "I *fucking* hate the noise your cat makes when he drinks water."

"Okay," I reply, exhaustion dripping from every word. "Then move out."

"*You* fucking move out," he spits back.

Something inside me snaps.

"Get out of my life with your lame lies and your hollow promises, Timmy. Everyone knows about you—security, the landlord. You are *nothing*."

But, like always, he doesn't leave. He grumbles, complains about how bad I make his life, and stomps around until he disappears again. Likely back to the meth tents.

My therapist has a theory that I've been dissociating by this point, and I know she's right. Because nobody sane and mentally present would be able to deal with this as their day-to-day.

————

By the time evening arrives, I'm fed up, and I head to the police station. I'm shaking as I approach the watch house, the weight of this decision pressing down on me.

"I'm finally ready," I say to the officer on duty, my voice trembling. "How do I get a TRO?"

The officer glances up from his desk. "You'll need to wait until the court opens in the morning."

"But he's acting crazy. What if he comes back and hurts me tonight?" I ask, desperation seeping into my tone.

"Just call us and we'll come right out," he shrugs. "Or you could go to a shelter."

"You can't issue me something in the interim to prevent him from entering the apartment?"

"No ma'am," he shakes his head. "Just be ready to dial 911 and we will be there."

I nod, though their reassurance feels hollow.

There's no safety net here, just a promise to intervene *after* something happens.

———

I return to the apartment, dreading the moment Timmy walks through the door. My hands shake as I pour myself a drink, hoping to dull the edge of my terror.

I'm terrified of what state he'll be in when he gets back, but I also feel like I have practice handling him. That seems preferable than going to a shelter and leaving Sabre here, defenseless, along with all my property.

———

A while later, the door beeps. Timmy's back.

He bursts in, screaming, his voice a thunderstorm of fury.

I grab my phone and dial 911, my heart pounding as he rages.

By the time six officers arrive, he's vanished.

I explain his erratic behavior, his threats, his abuse, and about my attempts to secure a TRO. I muster the courage to tell them the truth about what happened last night. "He's been having sex with me while I'm asleep, after I told him not to."

One of the officers scoffs at me. "No detective is going to take your statement while you reek of alcohol."

My jaw clenches. My chest tightens. I feel like ripping my hair out.

I went out earlier to try to get a TRO—like the police advised me—*and I couldn't.*

I just told the police I've been raped—*and they shamed me for drinking alcohol.*

I want to scream at the injustice of it all.

I turn to a female officer. "Look, I'm not a criminal for having had a drink. Your colleague is being extremely unprofessional. Can I speak to you instead?"

She nods, listening as I recount everything. She confirms that I can speak to a detective the following day if I want to pursue charges.

The officers leave, and the silence is deafening.

I put Timmy and his parents into a group text. My fingers fly across the screen, shaking with a mixture of rage, despair, and determination:

ME:

Timmy—you have 48 hours to move out your things.

If you become violent, verbally or physically, I will be calling the police.

They are already aware I am asking you to remove yourself from the premises.

I will be filing legal claims against you, as discussed, for the $20-25k in malicious damage you have caused in the past year.

I reserve the right to file future claims as they become apparent and as as advised by my attorney. I have a great attorney.

Your lack of recognition of your son's behavior is really shit, Phil.

I do not blame you.

But seriously, Phil, he needs to be in a home. Get him one.

The police are ready to come and get him the second he does anything further illegal to me, and I'm sure they cannot wait.

They didn't like it when he fractured my skull.

Or when he tried to kill me and I forced them to drop the charges.

He said 3 hours ago when he ran off to get a cigarette that he will hurt me if I talk to you, so here I am.

He will come back drunk and try to kill me again.

But keep ignoring.

Justify it.

When he is in prison for first degree murder, I hope you say, 'Well, Margaux was a real bitch and she deserved it.'

Also, your son has been having sex with me in my sleep, which is rape. I told several friends after it happened, and blatantly asked him to stop the other day, to which he said 'it was funny'. He has not tried since that time, but thought it was funny to lick my asshole and put his penis in my vagina while I was asleep again, without my permission.

The things I said are all true.

You both? I loved you both the moment I saw you, and I appreciate you making me feel so welcome.

But now I'm just waiting for your son to come back and attack me because of something he made up in his head.

Eventually, I receive a voicemail from Phil.

"I'll call him in the morning and try to talk some sense into him," Phil says. "But as for the allegations you made? That doesn't sound like rape to me."

I sob.

I'm enraged.

His dad is gaslighting me yet again, defending his son's sexual assault.

And I feel very, very alone.

CHAPTER 105
APRIL FOOL

MARGAUX

As I text Phil, my hands shake with a combination of fury and resolve. Timmy is still not back—he's in hiding—and the cops haven't been able to find him to speak with him.

I'm guessing he's fled to Matty's, because he has nowhere else to go.

My message is blunt and pointed—there's no longer room for diplomacy.

ME:

He's on the run from the cops.

But one of them is dumb, so he will probably be fine.

If he catches them they might date. 🤣

Your son is being charged with rape like he should be.

They just can't find him bc he is in a meth tent.

Take your rapist son.

He brings nothing productive. He works for 20 minutes a day if that, asks me how to do everything he could google for himself, and wants a medal for working.

> Meanwhile, I work 16+ hours a day and don't rape anyone.

> Please remove him.

> Also, for your information, I told my friend in writing after it happened, so there is contemporaneous evidence of sexual assault.

> It wasn't the first time he has done it.

> He does laugh about it. Thinks it's hilarious.

> So for you to try to discourage me from charges is gross.

As I send the messages, I feel the weight of my words pressing down on my chest. But it's a good kind of weight. A liberating kind.

———

In the morning, I make my way to the courthouse, each step a blend of fear and determination.

The intake staff hand me a colored wristband that designates my purpose—here to file, not to defend.

Sitting down, I start filling out the paperwork. My hands tremble as I detail every horrific incident.

An advocate comes over and sits beside me. Her presence is warm, reassuring. "Take your time," she says gently. "This isn't easy, but you're doing the right thing."

We go through my story together, and her guidance makes me feel seen, reminding me I'm not alone. That other people go through this. That other people know how to navigate this.

When I finish, she hands me a resource pamphlet from the National Center on Domestic and Sexual Violence. "Read this when you're ready. It might help you process everything."

I return in a few hours to find the judge has signed off on the order. I'm advised the TRO will be sent to the local police station, and officers there will attempt to serve it as soon as possible.

It feels like a small victory, but the battle is far from over.

———

At home, I open the pamphlet and flip through the pages until I land on the *Power and Control Wheel*.

It's meant to be a tool for understanding abusive dynamics, and as I read through each section, I start marking off everything that applies to Timmy:

COERCION AND THREATS: MAKING AND/OR CARRYING OUT THREATS TO DO SOMETHING OTHER THAN HURT HER. THREATENING TO LEAVE HER, COMMIT SUICIDE, OR REPORT HER TO WELFARE. MAKING HER DROP CHARGES. MAKING HER DO ILLEGAL THINGS.

Check.

INTIMIDATION: MAKING HER AFRAID BY USING LOOKS, ACTIONS AND GESTURES. SMASHING THINGS. DESTROYING HER PROPERTY. ABUSING PETS. DISPLAYING WEAPONS.

Check.

EMOTIONAL ABUSE: PUTTING HER DOWN. MAKING HER FEEL BAD ABOUT HERSELF. CALLING HER NAMES. MAKING HER THINK SHE'S CRAZY. PLAYING MIND GAMES. HUMILIATING HER. MAKING HER FEEL GUILTY.

Check.

ISOLATION: CONTROLLING WHAT SHE DOES, WHO SHE SEES AND TALKS TO, WHAT SHE READS, AND WHERE SHE GOES. LIMITING HER OUTSIDE INVOLVEMENT. USES JEALOUSY TO JUSTIFY ACTIONS.

Check.

MINIMIZING, DENYING & BLAMING: MAKING LIGHT OF THE ABUSE AND NOT TAKING HER CONCERNS ABOUT IT SERIOUSLY. SAYING THE ABUSE DIDN'T HAPPEN. SHIFTING RESPONSIBILITY FOR ABUSIVE BEHAVIOR. SAYING SHE CAUSED IT.

Check.

USING CHILDREN: MAKING HER FEEL GUILTY ABOUT THE CHILDREN. USING THE CHILDREN TO RELAY MESSAGES. USING VISITATION TO HARASS HER. THREATENING TO TAKE THE CHILDREN AWAY.

N/A, but kind of tries with Sabre.

ECONOMIC ABUSE: PREVENTING HER FROM GETTING OR KEEPING A JOB. MAKING HER ASK FOR MONEY. GIVING HER AN ALLOWANCE. TAKING HER MONEY. NOT LETTING HER KNOW ABOUT OR HAVE ACCESS TO FAMILY INCOME.

Check—erodes my savings and steals any funds he has access to, and secretly receives money from his dad.

MALE PRIVILEGE: TREATING HER LIKE A SERVANT: MAKING ALL THE BIG DECISIONS, ACTING LIKE THE 'MASTER OF THE CASTLE.' BEING THE ONE TO DEFINE MEN'S AND WOMEN'S ROLES.

Check, kind of. Just in the way he's much bigger and uses that to create a scary power dynamic.

Then I move on to a section called *What are the Characteristics of an Abusive Relationship?*

ARE YOU AFRAID OF YOUR PARTNER?

Check.

DOES YOUR PARTNER CONTROL YOUR FINANCES?

No, because he has no way to. But he wastes *my finances…I guess eroding them is controlling them in a way.*

DOES YOUR PARTNER ACCUSE YOU OF HAVING AFFAIRS?

Regularly.

DOES YOUR PARTNER THREATEN TO KILL YOU IF YOU LEAVE THE RELATIONSHIP?

Sort of. He threatens to kill me, period.

HAS YOUR PARTNER EVER PHYSICALLY HURT YOU OR THREATENED TO PHYSICALLY HURT YOU OR SOMEONE YOU CARE ABOUT?

Yes.

DOES YOUR PARTNER OFTEN PUT YOU DOWN, CALL YOU NAMES, UNDERMINE YOUR SELF ESTEEM AND CONFIDENCE?

Yes, all of it.

DOES YOUR PARTNER EVER FORCE YOU INTO SEXUAL ACTIVITIES THAT MAKE YOU FEEL UNCOMFORTABLE?

Yes, even though his dad says it's fine.

DOES YOUR PARTNER TRY TO CONTROL WHERE YOU GO, WHO YOU ARE WITH AND WHAT YOU DO?

Yes.

DOES YOUR PARTNER THREATEN TO KILL HIM/HERSELF IF YOU LEAVE THE RELA-TIONSHIP?

Yes.

HAVE YOU STOPPED SEEING FAMILY AND FRIENDS TO AVOID YOUR PARTNER'S JEAL-OUSY OR ANGER?

Yes.
And the absolute kicker, as if the others weren't enough:

DO YOU CONSTANTLY WORRY ABOUT YOUR PARTNER'S MOODS AND ALTER YOUR BEHAVIOR TO DEAL WITH THEM?

All. The. Fucking. Time.
Here it is. *Staring me in the face.*
I'm a data-driven person, and—while I knew what I had been *feeling* all along—here's hard evidence, right in front of me.
Timmy *is* an abuser.
And I one hundred percent did the right thing by filing this restraining order.
Now I just need the local cops to do their part and serve the bloody thing.

———

In Timmy's absence, I update my friend Stacey, and we research the crap out of narcissism, messaging back and forth. That's one of Stacey's superpowers, just like mine—we can find out anything about any topic, and we're very thorough.

With each layer we uncover, we discover that Timmy checks all the boxes for narcissistic personality disorder and then some.

STACEY:

You realize people like him don't change, right?

ME:

Well, maybe he just hasn't had the right environment or support.

He hasn't lived with his parents since he was a teenager, so maybe he hasn't been around the right influences.

STACEY:

But you haven't lived with your parents since you were a teenager either, and look how much you've accomplished.

You didn't use it as an excuse to act out or expect people to take care of you.

You forged a career and you worked and you made friends and a chosen family.

He had the same opportunities as you did, if not more, and he chose to fritter it away on a diet of drugs and alcohol and violent behaviors, predominantly against women.

I know she's right, but I find myself defending him, holding out a naive hope that maybe he's the exception, despite the data.

ME:

I know what the statistics say, but he really seems to be trying.

And there's a really small percentage of people who can turn this around.

I'm seeing progress, truly.

Stacey isn't one to sugarcoat, and she's not going to go along with my delusions.

STACEY:

Well, I'm telling you now... based on past behavior and statistics, this is unlikely to change. This relationship is toxic and you clearly love him, but he doesn't deserve to be with someone like you.

ME:

But he makes me feel so loved and wanted and needed. He makes me feel beautiful.

STACEY:

He also breaks your skull, my dear. That's not normal behavior.

Going over to meth tents is not normal behavior.

Stealing laundry money to go buy cheap bottles of vodka, breaking your things—breaking you—is not normal behavior.

You don't deserve that. Your life could be so much more peaceful without him.

I know she's right. But part of me is holding out hope that he's going to be one of the few men who can defy the statistics. Who truly wants to change so much that he's willing to put the effort in to become an entire new human —a gentle, loving man with a solid work ethic who would do anything for his family.

But the more I'm honest with myself, the more I have a nagging feeling in my gut that we're never going to reach a point in our relationship where we can have a healthy discussion about boundaries.

Every time I try to establish one, he breaks it almost immediately. And then he acts remorseful, before going right back to doing the same thing or worse.

And then it becomes my fault, and most certainly my problem.

It's hard to function like this, but some stubborn child within me is insistent on sitting up on Delulu Peak, watching all the other people and thinking there's something special about me that can fix Timmy. Something special about our relationship that means he is truly capable of change.

CHAPTER 106
I'M SO LOST WITHOUT YOU

MARGAUX

Timmy's message hits my phone like a bullet: *"Is there a TRO?"*

A chill runs through me. *How does he know?*

My landlord must have mentioned it—trying to keep him away, no doubt—but the decision to tell him leaves me reeling. This wasn't how I wanted it to unfold.

I'd planned for the police to serve him quietly, effectively, before he could spiral further. Now, the floodgates are open.

As the notifications pile up, my heart races. His words blur together, a chaotic mess of apologies, promises, and desperate pleas.

I don't respond, knowing anything I say will be twisted into ammunition against me. But his relentlessness weighs heavy, eroding the fragile peace I've tried to carve out.

Hands trembling, I respond by email:

SUBJECT: LOVE

Dear Timmy,

Before reacting, please read the whole thing.

I don't think you do love me. I think you think you do, but you don't.

If you did, you would have done all of the things you promised me that you would so many times before.

I don't expect anyone in my life to be a perfect person, but I do expect and deserve a partner who has so many qualities you have promised, but not delivered on. And what you have put me through is criminal. This is not love.

You're right. I AM amazing. But I don't think you actually believe that. I'm just a source for you. Someone to pay your rent and enable your wildly inappropriate behavior. This is not love.

I'm fairly sure this email will irritate you, and you will either lash out at me or just move on to the next person who will do everything for you, until they get sick of it or you kill them. There is a track record here. This is not love.

Also, I caution you against trying to harm me bc 1) nobody should and 2) the Cay is very small, and your history—here and in other states—is well known. The fact I have to caution you against harming me is gross. This is not love.

And, if you do try to harm me, clearly, this is not love. And everybody will know it was you. Why do I even need to say this? This is not love.

Call the police for an escort and we can arrange a time for you to pick up your things.

I have not harmed your things, bc I am a rational and mature individual. You have damaged so many of my things—some irreplaceable, including my skull. This is not love.

I have noticed my desktop computer isn't working by the way, since the day you messed up my other items, so I will add that to the growing tab of things you damaged. This is not love.

I didn't move here for someone to meddle with everything I have worked so very hard for. This is not love.

You said in your email earlier today that you would repay me. Will you really? If you do not promptly repay me, I will be proceeding with legal charges. This is not love. You have one week.

I will not enable you any further. That would not be love.

Go into a program (not a group that meets every now and then, but rather an in-house program for a minimum of 6 weeks, like my sister and people in your own family have urged). There is no shame in that. Everybody I know would support this. And that is love.

Substance abuse as a priority and also domestic violence prevention. For you. Not for me. The way you have behaved is not love. Do it for yourself. That is love.

Your dad enables you. It's well intentioned, I'm sure, but it is not love. His 'help' will destroy you. And you feed off this. This is not love.

I do love you and want the best for you, but I cannot deal with your behavior anymore.

By refusing to be with you, I am showing you love. You may never understand it, or you may choose to ignore it, but this is love. I hope one day you do realize that.

I also love myself and I do not want to die bc of you. That is love. To both myself and to you.

Life can be easy and fun with what we can control. And what I have learned is you don't actually like—let alone love—me at all. You love your impulses and your rage. Your cigarettes and alcohol, and your anger at people who you met before me that you choose to project onto me. That is not love.

This email is love.

Soon after, I receive a response.

Timmy:

I love you. I'm going to get the medicine. I'll go to therapy. I'll change for you.

I just need one more chance.

Each message from Timmy—of which there are many—is carefully crafted to claw at my empathy, my hope, my exhaustion. He knows the buttons to press—the promises that once made me believe we could have a future together where I could find peace. But I've heard these words before.

Over and over.

I know where they lead.

———

LATER

Timmy:

You said the email is love. I know I need to change. I'll do anything. Please don't give up on me.

He calls me his soulmate, saying he'll devote his life to me. He spins a future filled with laughter, support, and shared dreams. He promises to fix the damage he's done, to finally help me with the work he's only ever sabotaged.

But it's all about him. *His* feelings. *His* fears. *His* needs.

Not once does he truly acknowledge the toll his behavior has taken on me—the shattered trust, the bruises on my body and soul, the dreams I've had to put on hold just to survive him.

And then, the pivot—blame disguised as vulnerability.

Timmy:

I'm so lost without you. I need your support to get better.
You're my world.
I can't do this without you.

His desperation is palpable, but it feels calculated.

Every promise is laced with a subtle guilt trip, every apology a reminder that *he* is the one hurting now. He paints himself as the victim of his own failings, expecting me to rescue him from the mess he's made.

———

Over the next few days, the emails keep coming, growing more frantic, more manipulative.

Timmy:

I've made the appointments. I'm doing the work. Just let me talk to you. Let me explain. You're the love of my life. I'll never forgive myself if I lose you.

I finally respond, my tone measured but firm.

Me:

Timmy, I've heard all of this before. You've promised to change so many times, but nothing ever gets better.
I'm a shell of who I was before because of you.
I deserve better than this.

His reply is immediate, defensive yet pleading.

Timmy:

But I've changed! I'm getting the drinking medication. I'm going to therapy. You said you loved me.
How can you just give up on us?
I need you to believe in me.

I shake my head, anger and heartbreak warring inside me.

His words are a trap, designed to pull me back into the cycle I've fought so hard to escape.

He wants me to believe he's capable of change, that this time will be different.

But I know better.

Finally, I send an email that feels like the closing of a door.

Me:

It's not just about the alcohol, Timmy.
Your behavior has destroyed me—physically, emotionally, mentally.
I can't do this anymore. You need to take responsibility for yourself.
This isn't my job.

He responds.

Timmy:

You're my soulmate. Please don't leave me like this. I'll be so good. I'll make it right. Just let me come home.

His words no longer have power over me.

I copy and paste excerpts from articles about narcissistic abuse, hoping he'll see himself in them. They even call out how a narcissist will lean on the concept of soulmates to try to lure back their victims, just like Timmy's doing to me now.

Me:

Read this. You need to understand why I can't keep doing this.

His response is immediate, panicked.
Timmy:
What is this, Margaux? You're calling me a narcissist now? That's not fair!

But it *is* fair. It's the truth he doesn't want to face.

For the first time, I feel a sliver of peace. I'm no longer engaging with his manipulation, no longer allowing his words to dictate my feelings.

Timmy's barrage of messages continues, each one more desperate than the last. But I don't respond. I've said all I need to say.

His pleas, his promises, his guilt-tripping—they're just noise now.

I focus on the silence between his words, on the strength I'm reclaiming with each ignored notification.

This is what freedom feels like.

Quiet.

Steady.

Mine.

CHAPTER 107
PISS-POOR POLICING

DEX

Watching Margaux from a distance has become a mix of pride, anguish, and white-hot fury. Every moment she pushes forward, takes a stand, or simply breathes through the chaos feels like a victory against the storm Timmy drags her through.

But it's a storm she shouldn't have to face at all.

The anniversary debacle was predictable. I didn't expect anything different from Timmy—his selfishness, his ability to sour every significant moment, is legendary at this point.

Throwing the truck keys in the water? A childish tantrum.

Forcing her to endure public humiliation? Par for the course.

But Margaux sitting there, finishing her dinner while he sulked outside? That was resilience. Quiet, determined, and infuriatingly necessary resilience.

When she told Alice about how Timmy minimized her feelings and dismissed her yet again, my blood boiled. The audacity of that man to demand love and celebration when he can't even muster basic respect.

But part of me was relieved.

Every selfish, toxic display is another crack in the illusion he's managed to weave around her. His behavior paints him as the villain he is—and maybe this time she'll see it clearly.

———

My rage, though, hits a different level when she tells Alice what Timmy did to her that night.

Rape.

There's no other word for it.

She told him no.

She told him her boundaries.

And he violated her while she slept.

When she told Alice, I could see the anguish on her face, but she was matter-of-fact.

Detached.

Dissociating, her therapist had said.

Dissociation.

Of course. *How else do you survive something so horrifying?*

She shouldn't have to survive this. She shouldn't have to justify her rage, her pain. And yet she does, over and over, explaining it to herself as much as to the world.

And then there's Phil.

Phil, the eternal enabler, the flying monkey to Timmy's narcissistic games.

When Margaux told Alice about his response—'it doesn't sound like rape to me'—I wanted to put my fist through the nearest wall, as well as Phil's skull.

How dare he?

How dare he dismiss her trauma—her reality—to defend his pathetic excuse for a son?

That man is as much a part of the problem as Timmy is. *Maybe more.*

Timmy learned how to be a monster from someone, and it's clear now where it started.

But Margaux? She's stronger than either of them will ever understand. That either of them ever could hope to be.

She's seeing the patterns now. The gaslighting, the blame-shifting, the cycles of abuse. Her research into narcissistic abuse and DARVO is helping her untangle the web he's spun around her.

It's like watching someone wake up from a nightmare and realize they've been shackled all along.

When she told Alice she went to get the TRO, I felt something I haven't felt in a long time—relief. She's taking steps to protect herself, to draw a line in the sand that Timmy can't cross.

It's not easy—none of this is—but she's doing it.

And I couldn't be prouder.

The system, though? It's infuriatingly slow.

Watching her navigate the red tape and the endless hoops she has to jump through just to protect herself makes me want to scream.

The fact that she had to beg for a TRO—that she had to sit in that courthouse recounting her trauma while knowing it might not be enough—is maddening.

And then the police, dismissing her describing Timmy's *raping* her, because she'd had a drink?

Unacceptable.

What the hell kind of system punishes survivors for trying to cope?

But she's not giving up. She's not letting the system—or Timmy—win.

And that's the thing about Margaux. No matter how many times she gets knocked down, she gets back up, stronger and more determined than before.

The way she's been communicating with Timmy—calm, clear, direct—is a thing of beauty. I read the emails she sent him, and I couldn't stop smiling.

They were perfect.

Her words are swords, slicing through his manipulation and leaving no room for interpretation. Brutal in their honesty, unflinching in their boundaries, and filled with a strength she doesn't even realize she has.

Timmy's frantic replies, his manipulative pleas—they're just proof that she's finally slipping out of his grasp.

I want to shield her from all of this, to swoop in and fix everything. But I know she needs to do this on her own.

It's her fight—her victory.

I'll be here, watching from the sidelines, ready to step in if she needs me.

But for now, I'll keep cheering her on, proud and relieved with every step she takes toward freedom.

Because Margaux deserves more.

Much more than Timmy.

Much more than the lies and the violence and the chaos.

Margaux deserves peace.

And I'll be damned if I don't do everything in my power to help her find it.

CHAPTER 108
JUST CAN'T GET YOU OUT OF MY BED

MARGAUX

haven't heard a peep from the police—no knocks on the door, no phone calls. The TRO appears to have gone into some kind of administrative black hole, deprioritized. Ironic, considering the many times the police have urged me to get one so they can serve it as soon as possible.

The apartment is suffocating. A centipede hisses as it crawls across the floor, cockroaches dart around the kitchen, and Sabre's food and water bowls sit pathetically empty.

The mess surrounding me feels like a physical manifestation of everything wrong in my life—Timmy's chaos, my own exhaustion, the weight of my painful period's relentless grip.

I can't eat, can't drink, can't think. My body is a battleground, and the fog in my brain is as dense as the heat pressing against the apartment walls. The books that need marketing, the packages that need sending—they're all distant, impossible tasks.

The fog is winning.

Timmy—still staying with Matty—reaches out again, and—desperate and in a moment of sheer vulnerability—I respond. I tell him what's going on and how I'm doing—not well.

His messages come through again, his words more polished and poignant than I expect:

TIMMY:

Let me come and help you.

I'll get rid of the centipedes and cockroaches.

I'll clean the apartment and send your books out.

I'll take care of Sabre.

I'll take care of you and love on you.

I'll rub your back and bring you heat pads and ice
packs and massage your feet.

Just let me come and love you.

I know I don't deserve it, but I'll make it up to you.

Just please.

Please let me help.

I love you. Let me show you.

The words sting and soothe in equal measure. He knows exactly what to say.

But does he mean it this time?

And by now I know it probably won't last forever—but will it last long enough to get me through this low point?

I text another friend, D, desperate for her guidance. She's a social worker, a fellow cat lady, and someone who's dealt with her own fair share of bullshit when it comes to men and life.

D:

You should make sure he stays consistent for at
least nine months before letting him back. But I'll
support you no matter what.

Nine months. That feels like a lifetime. But I don't have a lifetime right now.

I need help. I need someone. I need *him.*

With trembling fingers, I type my response.

ME:

Okay.

You can come back.

> But you need to follow through on everything you said. 100%.

> This is your last chance.

> No more letting me down.

Timmy's reply is immediate:

TIMMY:

> Oh my god, Margaux, I promise you I'll do everything I said I would. You mean the world to me. I love you so much. Thank you for giving me one more chance.

For a moment, I let myself believe him.

———

Timmy arrives like a whirlwind of devotion.

He runs to me, squeezing me close to his chest, and kisses my forehead.

He clears the centipedes and cockroaches with determination, scrubs the apartment until it gleams, and fills Sabre's bowls with care. He cooks, cleans, and even helps with my book marketing.

Every promise he made, he keeps.

He takes Anabusin which will make him violently ill if he drinks, attends therapy and AA meetings, and—for the first time—there's a semblance of peace in our home.

One night, Timmy even agrees to listen to an audiobook about quitting drinking with me. It's a small step, but it feels significant. As the narrator delves into the complexities of alcohol use, I feel a strange mix of guilt and relief.

We recap each chapter like we're part of an exclusive book club.

"I've used alcohol as a Swiss army knife," I admit aloud. "To numb feelings, to deal with stress, to feel brave in social situations. Somewhere along the line, it became part of my identity."

Timmy nods. "Yeah, for me, it was about peer pressure. If you didn't drink enough, you were a pussy. So I became good at it. I was the one organizing the kegs, the one drinking the most. It was who I was."

For a moment, there's an openness between us, a sense of shared vulnerability. But I hold back one truth.

I would typically drink around Timmy because it emboldens me—it gives me the courage to bring up the uncomfortable conversations I suppress when I'm sober, when I'm walking on eggshells around him. I've hoped drinking together might have provided a lubricant for a healthy, adult discussion.

But deep down, I know it rarely works.

And now that neither of us are drinking, that buffer has been taken away.

———

He rushes at me, his eyes dark and empty, like the lifeless beads of a shark. He's not even drinking right now. This is just *him*.

Unfiltered.

Unassisted.

It was almost a relief to blame the alcohol before, to pretend it was the root of all his problems. But now it's clear—this is his personality.

Full of rage.

Full of hatred for women.

Sober, he's just better at hiding it.

———

I tell basically no one that he's back. I've only told my therapist, my friend Stacey—who was very disappointed and concerned, and my sister Amanda —who simply replied 'unbelievable' and stopped talking to me.

The shame feels too heavy, the fear of judgment too sharp. After everything I've said—after the TRO, the emails, the countless times I've sworn I was done with him—how could I possibly explain this in a way that anyone would understand? In a way that anyone wouldn't judge? In a way I wouldn't feel the weight of unbearable shame?

So instead, I let myself sink into the quiet moments where everything feels okay.

Timmy smiling at me as he cooks dinner.

Sabre curled up between us, purring contentedly.

The soft murmur of our audiobook playing in the background.

If anything, the decision to keep our reunion to myself only serves to push me closer to him.

For now, I cling to these fragile pieces of peace, even as the cracks begin to show beneath the surface.

Because deep down, I know this won't last.
But I'm too tired to fight it anymore.
Too tired to fight him, or myself.
And I'm embarrassed as hell.

CHAPTER 109
NOT DRINKING

MARGAUX

A couple of weeks into our new routine, I approach Timmy with a smile. It's been a transformative time for me—sobriety feels like peeling away layers of fog I hadn't realized were there.

"I love you so much," I say, leaning against the counter. "I feel so much better not drinking. Don't you?"

He glances up from his hat designs, his brow furrowing slightly. "Uh… yeah. I guess."

His tone throws me off. I'd expected more enthusiasm.

"I've noticed such a difference," I continue, trying to keep my tone light. "I feel calmer, clearer. My anxiety's better. Don't you feel like it's helping?"

"I haven't really noticed much," he says, frowning slightly. "It's… whatever."

His lack of enthusiasm stings, but I push past it. I tell myself that change takes time, that not everyone experiences the same transformation.

"How's your sleep been?" I ask. "Mine has been amazing. I've found it easier to fall and stay asleep, and I feel pretty refreshed in the morning."

He shrugs, the nonchalance almost palpable. "Um, I haven't really noticed much of a difference, to be honest."

"Oh." I pause, searching his face. "I'm sorry. Hopefully yours will click into place soon, too. I honestly just feel so much better." I smile, trying to bring him into my joy. "The first few days, my dreams were wild, but now they're so vivid and creative. It's like my brain is finally waking up."

"Mmhmm," he mumbles, returning his attention to the screen.

The energy shifts, and I feel a pang of disappointment. I'd hoped this shared journey of sobriety would bring us closer.

For me, it's been a revelation—my mind is sharper, my energy calmer, my productivity soaring. I've been churning out thousands of words a day, diving back into my work with a clarity I hadn't felt in months.

My anxiety has lessened, and I'm no longer tiptoeing around invisible landmines.

Timmy's mood, however, remains unpredictable.

He's less volatile, but still prone to irritability over small things—sleep, TV shows, or imagined ailments. The absence of alcohol has dulled some of the chaos, but the underlying storm hasn't disappeared.

He's been focusing more on his hats, which is good, and I've appreciated our shared audiobook sessions on quitting drinking. Discussing each chapter afterward feels like a small connection point, like we're working toward something together.

But his lack of enthusiasm leaves me wondering—*is he really here, or is he just going through the motions?*

———

In the quiet moments, my therapist's words echo in my mind:

"Even if he improves, it needs to be sustained. And remember, he doesn't deserve an award for making it to the baseline expectations for how someone should treat you in a relationship."

It's progress, yes. He hasn't been smoking or sneaking off to the tents, and that alone has helped immensely. Those things were often the sparks that ignited our worst fights. But there's a lingering sense of unease, like I'm waiting for the other shoe to drop.

He still insists on sleeping until noon most days, and his moods swing unpredictably. He's not drinking, but he's not thriving either. Sobriety seems to have stripped away some of the destructive chaos, but it hasn't filled the void it left behind.

Instead of feeling like a new beginning, it feels like… stasis.

———

Later in the evening, as I lie in bed staring at the ceiling, my thoughts begin to swirl. Sobriety has given me a chance to step back and assess everything with fresh eyes. The fog that once clouded my judgment is gone, and with it, the rose-colored glasses I've been wearing since the start.

The truth is hard to swallow—even without alcohol, Timmy still struggles to meet me where I need him to be. The bickering, the moods, the lack of enthusiasm—it's all still there, just muted.

And while I'm grateful for the absence of danger, I can't ignore the fact that I'm carrying the emotional weight of this relationship alone.

For the first time, I ask myself a question I've been avoiding—*what if this isn't enough?*

I close my eyes, hoping sleep will bring answers.

But deep down, I already know the truth.

Sobriety was supposed to be the start of something better, but it's only revealed the cracks that were there all along.

CHAPTER 110
DERBY DISTRACTION

've started roller derby boot camp. It's exhilarating, terrifying, and humbling all at once. My confidence on skates is shaky at best, and being surrounded by fierce, fearless women with names like Slaydie Gaga, Smashley Madison and Blitzkrieg Barbie doesn't make it any easier. Still, something about it calls to me—a sense of belonging outside of Timmy that I desperately crave.

Timmy surprises me by being incredibly supportive. He insists on coming to practice, making a show of being my biggest cheerleader. There's something about his insistence on accompanying me that seems off, but it's not that unusual for team members to bring their kids or significant others, so I let it slide.

While I waver through drills, he roams the periphery, crouching in the bushes and enthusiastically hunting Jackson chameleons. His childlike excitement is endearing, even if it garners a few raised eyebrows.

One day, Timmy announces he wants to skate with me. "I can't just sit on the sidelines forever," he says, flashing his signature grin. But, of course, this means he needs skates—real skates. And not just any skates will do.

"They have to be roller derby quality," he insists, dismissing my suggestion of a budget pair. He's meticulous about the details, choosing a sleek helmet in bold colors and top-tier pads. By the end of the shopping spree, I'm wincing at the bill, but trying to stay optimistic. At least it's something we can do as a workout together, and it sounds like it could be fun.

When he finds us a skate park near a schoolyard, it feels like a tiny slice of magic. The concrete rink stretches wide under the blue sky, and the smooth ramps glint invitingly in the sun.

Timmy skates beside me, encouraging me with an enthusiasm I haven't seen in a while. He takes time-lapse videos of me circling the track, and claps for me when I manage a trick without falling.

"You're getting so much better," he says, his eyes shining. "Look how fast you are now. And your balance has improved, too."

At first, his praise keeps me going. But boot camp is a different story. The relentless drills under a blistering sun, combined with my clumsy attempts to keep up, drain my spirit. I'm so worn down by Timmy's constant belittling of everything I do, that every practice feels like a public display of my inadequacies, and an extension of what's going on at home behind closed doors.

Worse, the structured schedule triggers a deeper unease within me. Timmy thrives in chaos, but I've come to dread anything predictable—anything that gives him an opportunity to implode. Each practice becomes another source of anxiety, a ticking time bomb waiting for his antics.

One day, I just can't bring myself to go back.

"I'll still skate with Timmy," I tell myself, clinging to the idea of skating as an escape, a reprieve. But as soon as I quit boot camp, Timmy's interest in skating vanishes. The skates, the gear—everything I'd bought for him gathers dust. He shrugs off my invitations with vague excuses: 'Not today,' or, 'Maybe another time.'

It stings more than I'd like to admit. He's already the surfer who doesn't surf, and now he's the skater who doesn't skate.

I cling to the hope that it's just a phase.

Until then, I have the apartment complex's pool.

Swimming becomes my solace—one thing he hasn't yet managed to ruin.

———

The harsh glow of my laptop illuminates my face as I click on a new review notification for my latest book. Excitement churns in my stomach. A video review—what could be better?

The first words hit like a slap as an ARC reader grins at the screen. "I reeeeeally wanted to like it… believe me, I did. I dropped everything else on my TBR to read it. But I *really* wish I hadn't…"

I listen for a while longer, and my heart sinks. Except for one mention so brief you could blink and miss it, the reviewer isn't critiquing the plot, characters, or writing. Instead, they fixate on a minor publishing guideline, twisting it into a reason to dismiss my work entirely.

I look at the comments on the post, which has gone fairly viral, and my heart sinks further. Readers and, disappointingly, a bunch of pick-me authors, have jumped on board, making ill-informed comments and slandering me and my business ethics.

Timmy notices my mood shift instantly. "What's up?" he asks, setting aside his phone.

I sigh, gesturing at the screen. "Someone's decided to make a whole video trashing my book. Not even the story—just some random technicality they've blown out of proportion. Something that I learned from more seasoned writers who pitched is as industry standard, and this person is attacking me and acting like I made it up myself."

His face hardens. "Fuck them. They're just jealous. You're an incredible writer, and they can't stand it. You're beautiful and successful, and they're a sad bitch."

His confidence in me is almost disorienting. His pride feels genuine, a rare moment of us being on the same team. "I believe in you and your writing," he adds, wrapping me in a hug. "You're so talented. They wish they were you, but they're not."

I smile, feeling like we're part of a team. Glad to have Timmy by my side in this moment of disappointment and uncertainty.

"I'm in love with a pornographer," he sings, breaking the tension with a laugh. It's one of his quirks—an odd but endearing way of lightening the mood.

I can't help but laugh along.

For now, his unwavering support feels like a balm, a brief reprieve from the storm.

––––––––

July arrives with the rush of another book release, and I throw myself into preparing PR boxes. The contents are meticulously curated—themed trinkets, true-to-story graphics on cardstock, some of which Timmy helped me to design, and signed copies of the book.

Timmy surprises me by setting up phones around the living room.

"What are you doing?" I ask, watching him dart from phone to phone.

"Making a time-lapse video of you assembling the boxes," he says with a proud smile. "I figure you can use it for marketing."

It's such a small gesture, yet it floors me. His creativity, his attention to detail—it feels like love distilled into action.

My eyes sting as I watch him wrap the completed boxes in black plastic, sealing each with precision.

For a moment, life feels almost perfect. Despite the chaos, despite the missteps, there are these fleeting moments of clarity where everything aligns.

And I wonder: *How did things turn around so fast? And how did they get this good?*

———

A FEW DAYS LATER

Timmy leans against the kitchen counter, his face lit with an unusual energy. "Please, please, can you order me some hats? I'll work on them full-time and make us some money."

Timmy is hellbent on starting his hat business, and of course that means he needs actual hats.

It's a plea I've heard before, but this time, he has numbers. He shows me calculations, spreadsheets he's cobbled together, projections of profits. On paper, it looks promising. I can almost see the vision he's painting—Timmy, focused and productive, creating custom hats, filling orders, and bringing in income.

Against my better judgment, I place the order. Not because I don't believe in the idea, but because I don't entirely believe in *him*.

The investment feels nauseating—several thousand dollars drained from my savings for hat presses, materials, and custom patches. Each click of 'add to cart' feels like a gamble, a bet on someone who's let me down too many times.

The hats arrive, and—at first—there's movement. He tinkers with designs, experiments with vinyl and leather patches. But soon, the momentum fades.

Days go by, then weeks, and the hats sit, untouched, stacked in boxes like relics of a dream deferred.

"I need the custom patches to get here," he explains, when I ask why he isn't trying to sell them.

When the patches arrive, the excuse changes. "I need to wait for the right time to launch."

I try reasoning with him. "You have simpler designs ready to go. You could start selling those while you wait."

But there's always something—a sore stomach, bad weather, a fight he claims stifled his creativity.

One day, I bring up the concept of executive function, desperate to break through.

"Timmy, adults all over the world get out of bed and go to work every day, even when they hate it. You have the tools, the time, and the opportunity to pursue your dream job, and yet you sleep in and make excuses day after day. Does that seem fair?"

He scowls. "Everything's about money to you, isn't it?" His face shifts from guilt to indignation. "Well, remember, *you* made me lose my last job. I was providing money before this."

I'm stunned. "Timmy, this isn't just about money. And your part-time job wasn't exactly full-time support. This is about effort, about following through. Do you understand how that makes me feel—when I've spent my life savings providing *you* with *your* dream—and your behavior is taking me away from *my* own dreams that I've worked so hard for?"

"I'm sorry," he frowns and sighs. "I'll do better." Then his eyes narrow as he identifies another opportunity to retaliate against me. "Well, now you've upset me. So I'm not working today."

He slams his laptop shut, his punishment for my audacity to set expectations.

CHAPTER 111
A STRANGE SANCTUARY

MARGAUX

sit in the truck on a video call with my therapist, her gaze steady but kind. The parking garage is quiet except for the faint hum of passing traffic. It feels like a strange sanctuary—a dirty bubble where the chaos of my life can't quite reach me.

"He's following through on everything he promised," I say, my voice tinged with both hope and weariness. "He's even listening to an audiobook with me about quitting drinking. We talk about each chapter as we finish it, like a mini book club. It's... nice."

"That's great progress," she says, leaning forward slightly. "But let me ask you something—does it feel sustainable?"

The question hangs in the air. I shift uncomfortably in my seat. "I... don't know. He's been sober for a couple of months now. He's helping more. He hasn't been to the tents or smoking. He's even been kind to Sabre."

She nods, but her expression remains neutral. "That's good to hear. But I want to be clear with you—what you've described before—all of it—is abuse. It's not just about the drinking or the smoking or the fights. The dynamic between you two is unbalanced. You're carrying the weight of this relationship. You're still acting as a caregiver, not an equal partner."

I feel a familiar sting in my chest, a mix of shame and defensiveness. "I know we're working through things," I say, my voice quieter. "He's trying."

"I believe that he's trying," she replies gently. "And I believe that he does love you in his own way. And that you love him. But trying doesn't erase the fact that you're in a situation where you're constantly managing his emotions, his behavior, his life. You're the one making sure he gets out of bed, that he's doing anything productive. You're paying for everything. And when you add the history of physical abuse to this picture, it becomes a dangerous situation for you—whether he's drinking or not."

Her words hit like a punch to the gut. I open my mouth to argue, but nothing comes out. She continues, her tone firm but compassionate.

"I want you to keep the domestic violence hotline number saved on your phone. Make sure your phone is always charged and with you. And I still want you to have a go-bag ready for you and Sabre. It's not a sign of giving up—it's a sign of being prepared. You never know what's going to happen when you're with someone as volatile as he is."

I nod mutely, my throat tight. I feel numb, like my body has shut down to protect itself from the weight of what she's saying.

The words are true. I know they are.

But I don't want to be the kind of woman who needs a go-bag. I don't want to live in fear of my partner hurting me, my cat, or destroying the fragile sense of stability I've built. *I don't want that life.*

"I know you want things to get better," she says, her voice softer now. "But don't treat baseline behavior—things that any partner should do—as extraordinary. You deserve so much more than that."

Her words linger long after we hang up.

———

At night, Timmy wraps me in his arms in bed, his warmth enveloping me like a comforting cocoon. "You're my best friend," he murmurs, his voice soft, sincere and full of affection. "I'm so lucky to have you."

For a moment, I let myself believe it. Wrapped in his embrace, I imagine a future where this version of Timmy—the kind, sober, loving version—is the one who stays. Where his promises are real. I picture us working through our issues, healing together, building a life that isn't defined by chaos and hurt. I let myself believe in the version of him that I've always wanted him to be.

"I love you," I whisper, clinging to the hope in my words. "More than anything."

He tightens his grip around me. "I love you, too."

Love is supposed to be enough, isn't it?

If I love him hard enough, pour enough kindness and patience into him, surely he'll become the man he says he wants to be.

But love alone can't pay the bills, and the financial strain of supporting us both looms like a shadow over my every thought.

I push the thought away, burying it under layers of optimism, clinging to the belief that once he's steady, he'll contribute. Once he's better, everything will be okay. Just like he says it will be.

But somewhere deep inside, a voice whispers:

Until he doesn't make you feel safe anymore.

————

In the weeks that follow, Timmy's sobriety continues. He listens to the audiobook with me, nodding along at all the right moments and enthusiastically discussing key themes afterwards.

He designs hats and focuses on small creative projects.

For the first time in months, we laugh together without tension lurking in the background.

But I'm beginning to notice something interesting—the man before me isn't the Timmy I fell for. Without alcohol sharpening his edges or igniting his dangerous charm, he feels... ordinary. He's not funny, not insightful, not even all that interesting. He's definitely not very smart, and doesn't have anything thought-provoking to say.

The wit and charm that once captivated me are dulled, replaced by someone quieter, less dynamic. His moods still swing unpredictably, often dictated by trivial frustrations—a TV show, a passing comment, an imagined slight. But the danger also feels muted, his edges less jagged.

His charisma—the thing that pulled me in so strongly at the start—is gone, leaving behind someone I don't know if I even like.

I watch him snuggle my cat, murmuring sweet nothings to him like he's the most precious creature on earth. "You're the best cat I've ever met," he says, his voice dripping with affection. "I love you so much, little guy." It warms my heart, even as it breaks a little.

Sabre loves him. Sabre trusts him. Shouldn't I try to do the same?

I remind myself of the good moments, the softness he's capable of. But my therapist's words ring in my ears: *Don't mistake baseline behavior for extraordinary.*

And yet, I try. *Isn't this what I wanted?*

Still, I can't ignore the growing sense that the man in front of me isn't the one I fell for.

I want to believe in him. I want to believe in us. But deep down, I wonder if the real Timmy—the sober, unfiltered Timmy—is someone I even like.

And that thought terrifies me most of all.

CHAPTER 112
A+ ACTING

The apartment is a reflection of Margaux's world—a place barely holding together under the weight of chaos.

Even through the screen, I can see how the neglect has festered. The centipedes, the cockroaches, the near-empty bowls for Sabre—it all mirrors the disarray in her life.

Margaux has her period, and once again it's debilitating—but this time, she's by herself. She can't move, she can't eat—all she can really do is lie prone and wish for sleep to come.

She's barely holding on, but she's still there, waiting out her pain so she can once again fight against the fog that's settled over her mind and her space. That's the thing about Margaux—even at her worst, she doesn't quit.

And then Timmy texts her.

TIMMY:

Let me come and help you.

Just let me come and love you.

It's an enticing offer, and I hate him for how well he knows her vulnerabilities. He weaves a net of promises, knowing exactly how to catch her in a moment of desperation. I can practically hear the words as she reads them, how they would sound sweet and soft against her fractured resolve.

I've studied this game of his for too long. He knows when to turn on the charm and when to dial it up.

He doesn't care about Margaux's wellbeing. Not really.

He cares about worming his way back into her life, about controlling her again.

The cycle is exhausting to watch from the outside—I can't imagine living it.

Her fingers hesitate over the keyboard as she replies, and I want to reach through the screen and stop her.

Don't do it.

But I know she will. I know Margaux.

She's drowning, and he's throwing her a lifeline, even if it's one tied to a rock.

I watch as she types her response:

MARGAUX:

Okay.

You can come back.

But you need to follow through on everything you said. 100%.

This is your last chance.

No more letting me down.

Her belief in him—her need to believe in him—is a knife in my chest.

She deserves better, and she knows it. But better doesn't feel reachable right now, not in her world.

When he arrives, he does what he always does at first—he performs.

The centipedes are gone.

The cockroaches vanish.

Sabre's bowls are full again, and the apartment starts to resemble something livable.

He stops drinking, and doesn't pressure her for alcohol or cigarettes.

He attends therapy, as well as an AA group meeting.

He even takes on aspects of her book marketing, like he's finally pulling his weight and following through on his promises.

For a moment, even *I* almost believe he's changing—but time, as usual, reveals it's just a performance. It's always a performance.

After a few weeks, I hear her tell him about sobriety, how it's clearing her head, making her feel like herself again. Her voice is bright when she talks about vivid dreams and restful sleep.

Timmy's reply? A shrug and a dismissive "I haven't noticed much of a difference."

I clench my jaw. It's not just apathy—it's sabotage.

He's not drinking—sure—but that doesn't mean he's supportive. Sobriety isn't fixing him, because sobriety isn't his real problem. He's not drinking, but he's still Timmy—selfish, careless, and cruel.

The worst part is that Margaux is trying so hard to hold onto the glimpses of good. She talks to her therapist, recounting his small wins. "He's following through," she says. "He's even listening to an audiobook with me about quitting drinking. We talk about it after each chapter."

"Does it feel sustainable?" her therapist asks, cutting through the hope in Margaux's tone.

Margaux pauses, her shoulders sagging. "I don't know," she admits. "But he's trying."

Trying. Margaux deserves more than someone who's 'trying'. She deserves someone who meets her where she is, who adds to her life instead of depleting it.

I'm proud of her for starting roller derby boot camp. It's the first thing she's done in a long time that's purely for her, something that makes her feel alive again. Watching her take those shaky first strides on skates is a rare moment of joy for me. She's nervous, but she's doing it, anyway.

That's Margaux. She never stops trying.

And then there's Timmy, hovering on the sidelines, insisting on attending every practice.

He's cheering her on, sure, but it's performative. When he decides to join her, it's not about supporting her—it's about being the center of attention. The skates, the gear, the time-lapse videos—it's all a show.

And when Margaux decides boot camp isn't for her, Timmy's interest in skating disappears entirely.

He's nothing but empty promises and unfinished projects.

Even now, as I watch her assemble PR boxes for her new book release, he's there, performing again.

He sets up phones to film her, crafting time-lapse videos for her marketing. It's thoughtful, sure, but I can't help but see it as another manipulation.

He's proving his worth just enough to keep her invested, to keep her tethered to him.

And it's working.

She's smiling as she works, letting herself believe in the version of Timmy who does these kinds of things, as if he's consistent with his thoughtful gestures, not just making grandiose shows every now and then to keep her hooked and able to look past the many, many low moments.

Her therapist's words ring in my head: *Don't mistake baseline behavior for extraordinary.*

But Margaux is so starved for partnership that she clings to these scraps as if they're a feast.

I know how this story ends.

Timmy will unravel again.

He'll stop trying.

He'll find a way to hurt her, to make her feel small and dependent.

And Margaux—with all her strength and resilience—will try to fix it.

She'll keep trying until she has nothing left to give.

I'm angry at Timmy, but I'm angrier at myself.

For watching this happen.

For not being able to stop it.

For wanting so badly to step in, to be the one who shows her what love is supposed to feel like.

She deserves so much better than this.

I just hope she realizes it before it's too late.

CHAPTER 113
THE TRUTH ABOUT TIMMY

MARGAUX

When I'm out with Timmy, I feel like I'm walking a tightrope.

With my ex, the challenge was keeping him from creeping people out. He was the silent type, lurking in the background unless his friends were around to draw him out of his introverted shell.

Timmy, on the other hand, will *never* shut the fuck up.

He dominates every conversation, swallowing the room with his words. It's not that he's trying to connect with people—far from it. If he asks a question, it's only to set the stage for one of his stories. The exchange is transactional—a brief response from the other person, and then Timmy launches into a tangent, often irrelevant but always lengthy.

Some people seem entertained, laughing at his jokes or marveling at the bizarre twists in his tales. He has a knack for painting vivid, if chaotic, pictures with his words. But even those who enjoy his stories at first grow weary as he stumbles over sentences, repeats himself, or speaks so rapidly he can't keep up with his own thoughts.

My friend who visited once whispered to me, "Is he on gear? He's talking so fast." She literally thought he was on heroin.

I laughed it off at the time, but inside, I cringed.

He misses—or ignores—social cues. The shifting of weight in a chair, the darting glances toward the clock, the forced chuckles meant to wrap up the interaction. He doesn't seem to notice, or maybe he just doesn't care.

It's strange, because he's so attuned to human behavior in other contexts. When it comes to telling stories to strangers or groups, that attunement disappears.

———

I didn't notice the incoherence of his writing until April, when he bombarded me with emails—rambling, repetitive, and riddled with errors. I forwarded one to my friend Stacey for advice. "Is English his second language?" she'd asked. She wasn't being rude—it was a genuine question.

How had I missed this until a few months ago? How have I, a writer, ignored that my fiancé can't string together a coherent sentence? Have I been so blinded by his charm—or maybe by my own desperation to believe in us —that I've tolerated this glaring red flag?

It's not just his writing. Timmy is *always* talking, always filling the space, leaving me no room to reflect, to think. Normally, I use my shows and podcasts to let my mind wander, to process and identify patterns. Walking used to help, too, but it's not safe to walk here, and Timmy never comes with me anyway.

Without that mental downtime, I've been blindsided by Timmy's flaws. Now, they're glaring. His façade is cracking, revealing someone lacking basic skills or sophistication. The man I thought was my equal now feels like an unqualified stranger.

But then I feel guilty. So what if he struggles with writing or social nuances? Maybe that's more a reflection of the system than him. I'm naturally good with words—should I judge someone else for not having that gift?

And he *is* creative. He's great at brainstorming ideas, especially for my darker, gorier storylines. His graphic design work is thoughtful and layered with meaning.

Maybe that's his real strength. Maybe I'm being too harsh.

I tell myself to let it go.

He's right.

I'm a total bitch.

I need to be nicer.

———

When I walk out of the bathroom, dressed for dinner, Timmy freezes. His jaw drops.

"Who are you all dressed up like that for?" he asks, eyes narrowing. "Do you have a date?"

I laugh. "We're both going to see my friend, remember?"

"I guess… I just didn't expect you to look like *that*." He gestures vaguely at my romper, his expression unreadable.

"Like what?"

"You look… classy. Sophisticated."

"Okay?" I say, unsure whether to take it as a compliment.

"I'm so proud to have you as my fiancée," he says, wrapping his arms around me. "You're so gorgeous. I can't wait to show you off."

Dinner is fine, though I'm on edge the entire time. Timmy sits at the end of the table, strangely quiet. I'm relieved he's holding back, but constantly brace for him to dominate the conversation. He does a few times, mostly with the group of women at our end of the table, but not as much as usual.

As I watch him interact, a sinking feeling takes hold. One of my friend's guests at the dinner lives nearby and wants to hang out again, but I know it's impossible while I'm with Timmy.

He'd never tolerate it.

Timmy has made it starkly clear—it's him and me, ride or die. Friendships encroach on his sense of 'us-ness.' Living on the far side of the Cay only isolates me further, cutting me off from people I'd naturally gravitate toward. Maybe that's why he wanted us to move there in the first place.

———

"I think instead of fighting, we should calm down and bang it out," Timmy says one night, grinning.

I blink. It's the most reasonable thing he's suggested in weeks. "That would be great," I say. "But I'm still going to be mad if you do something dumb."

"Well, I won't do anything dumb," he promises. "And if we get annoyed at each other, we'll just fuck instead of yelling."

"Deal," I say, laughing.

It sounds perfect—fighting less, having more sex. Win-win.

But, in reality, when we fight, there's no way sex could ever be the solution. His sneer, his reptilian eyes—they're terrifying. And if I try to reach out to touch him during an argument, he shrugs me off or snaps, almost threatening to hit me.

There's nothing sexy about that.

———

Timmy's flaws are becoming impossible to ignore. His inability to read a room, his endless talking, his lack of basic skills—all of it is piling up, making me question everything.

But what's worse is the control. His jealousy, his need to dominate every moment, every thought. He's taken over my life, leaving no room for me to breathe, to reflect, to exist outside of him.

And yet, I feel stuck. Isolated. Trapped by his demands, his moods, his rules. I thought we were building a life together, but it feels more like he's building a cage for me.

I miss the version of Timmy I thought I knew—the fun, creative, loving man who seemed like my soulmate. But maybe that version never existed. Maybe I've been in love with a mirage.

The thought makes me feel like a fool.

But also—finally—awake.

CHAPTER 114
HAT TRICK

Timmy's hats are starting to look good. The designs are solid, some even creative and unique, but there's no momentum. No sales. No attempt to move them from ideas to reality.

He spends hours tinkering, lost in the details of his art, but the logistics of running a business—marketing, outreach, actually selling—remain untouched.

"I just want to design," he says one day. "*That's* the part I enjoy."

"I get it," I reply. "That's the fun part, right? But there's other stuff that goes into running a business."

"You spent a lot of time doing that marketing stuff for your books," he adds, his voice laced with disdain. "I don't find it fulfilling. I just want someone to buy my hats. I won't be doing that kind of thing, because I don't enjoy it."

It feels like a slap in the face.

"Do you think I *want* to spend my days on social media, marketing instead of writing?" I shoot back. "Do you think my books magically sell themselves without any promotion? Do you think your hats are so incredible that people will just flock to buy them without effort? Do you think you're somehow exempt from the work that every creator has to put in?"

He blinks, caught off guard.

My words are sharp, maybe too sharp, but his entitlement ignites something visceral in me. His audacity drips into the room, leaving a sour taste in my mouth.

It's not just the imprecision of his words that inflames me.

Timmy is great at painting a picture of the future. He talks in vibrant detail about success—about customers loving his work, about his designs taking off.

I'm good at this too—I can see the vision so clearly.

But the difference between us is glaring. I take that vision and put in the effort to make it real. He expects the universe to hand it to him. Big talk and big dreams, but little effort or action.

My stomach roils, my resentment returning with a vengeance.

———

The next day, Timmy sleeps in until lunchtime, and when he wakes, I complain about his ongoing lack of motivation.

"I can't create when you're nagging at me," Timmy pouts, slumping on the bed.

"You can't create when you're sleeping," I reply, rolling my eyes.

"I was thinking about designs and the manufacturing process," he argues, crossing his arms.

"You were snoring and muttering about 'pussies' and 'dicks,'" I retort, shaking my head.

He pauses, a faint blush creeping up his neck. "Well, I *intended* to get up and work on it. But now you've started bugging me, and I'm too annoyed with you to do anything."

And just like that, his lack of productivity becomes my fault. I asked him to wake up before midday, and now I'm being punished.

His excuses pile up like debris after a storm, blocking any path forward.

I try to attack it from multiple angles, attempting to get him to see logic— but the harder I try, the more he resists.

I see few differences between him and a toddler—except that he's bigger, louder, and more vindictive. The rage within him simmers constantly, just beneath the surface, ready to erupt at the slightest provocation.

He's always looking to be hurt, and he's always looking for me to pay for any perceived indiscretion—figuratively and literally.

Anything good I've done earlier in the day vanishes.

Anything bad *he's* ever done? Forgotten.

All that's left is me, standing as the embodiment of his every flaw and failure.

———

The tension between us explodes one evening.

"You had me move all the way out here, away from everyone I know," Timmy accuses, his tone venomous.

"What?! That was your idea," I counter. "And I don't know anyone out here either. You said we could move here to focus on our work. I'm holding up my end of that deal. You're barely doing anything."

"Well, you drink too much," he snaps, his argument spiraling into irrelevance.

"What does that have to do with anything? You drink, too! And don't you *dare* try to make this about me."

The fight escalates, his words cutting deeper with every exchange.

"You always have to be so nasty," he growls.

"I'm not being nasty," I plead. "I'm trying to have a conversation. I'm trying to figure out how we can move forward."

"Fuck you," he spits, storming out the door.

The sound of the door slamming shut reverberates through the room, leaving me alone with the echo of his words.

CHAPTER 115
WHAT DO YOU WANT? A BIRTHDAY BENDER?

MARGAUX

In all, Timmy keeps up his sober, loving, helpful act for three-and-a-half entire months.

It hasn't been perfect, but it has definitely been much better.

The screaming, the chaos, the fights—all of it feels like a distant memory.

And while he's still moody and aimless, the absence of alcohol-induced rage has made life feel tolerable, maybe even good.

Timmy's birthday is coming up, and he's been dropping hints about how much he wants to celebrate, and he insists on going to the cinema.

He knows I hate movie theaters—between the thought of someone shooting up the place, the sound of people chewing popcorn and slurping soda like it's a competitive sport, and the general grossness of it all, it's my personal version of hell.

I much prefer watching movies at home, wrapped in the safety of my own space.

But it's *his* day, so I agree.

When I tell him, his face lights up. "Really? You'll come with me? You hate the movies!" he says, beaming.

"I know, but it's your birthday. Pick whatever you want to see."

He doesn't hesitate. "*Longlegs*. Nicolas Cage. Horror. You'll *love* it!"

The movie itself sounds good. I'm not convinced I'll love the cinema, but his excitement is infectious, and for once, I want to make him happy without reservation.

I book tickets, and the countdown begins.

And that's not the only thing we're counting down to.

I've been a Chelsea Handler fan for as long as I can remember. Her late-night show was a particular favorite. So when I found out she would be coming to Sunset Cay for a live stand-up performance, I didn't hesitate—I grabbed tickets immediately. It's coming up soon, and I'm buzzing with excitement, and cannot wait for the show.

Timmy knows how much I've been looking forward to this. He also knows it's the day after his upcoming birthday.

"So you're really making me go see some sexist comedian for my birthday?" he asks, his tone accusatory, as though I'd forced him into attending a public stoning.

"It's the day *after* your birthday, silly," I reply, trying to keep things light. "And it'll be fun! You said you think she's funny, too."

He admits he does, in fact, find her funny, but his initial reaction says it all. Timmy's ego feels threatened, as though Chelsea Handler herself has conspired to overshadow *his* birthday.

"Look," I offer, trying to smooth things over. "We can go out for dinner before the show to celebrate your birthday. I'll take you to that fancy place I told you about. You said it sounded awesome."

It's another effort to placate him, to make him feel like the center of attention—The Timmy Show, as usual.

Even though Chelsea Handler is infinitely funnier—and far more intelligent—than Timmy could ever hope to be.

———

On the Fourth of July, we have a wonderful day where we cook for each other.

We take a giant inflatable unicorn out into the ocean, and Timmy uses a broom to paddle us around the lagoon, the waves lifting us up and carrying us along as if we're surfing. Turtles paddle by, and parents teach their children to swim.

It feels like this is how Sunset Cay was meant to be all along.

———

A few days later, Timmy's birthday rolls around.

We arrive at the city's cinema early, so we decide to kill time by strolling through Target. The store is buzzing with shoppers, the fluorescent lights making everything feel oddly surreal.

As we wander the aisles, Timmy's phone rings. It's Steve the Horse Cop.

"I had a dream about Darren," Steve says. "He came to me and said he's happy where he is."

Timmy tears up, his voice wistful. "He hasn't visited me in my dreams, yet. I know it's because he's still mad at me for how we ended things last time we talked. But I'm glad he's happy."

After they hang up, Timmy wipes his eyes, and we continue to stroll. He slows in front of the wine section, his eyes scanning the bottles.

"Oh, let's get a bottle of wine for my birthday," he says casually, as though this were the logical next step. "I really feel like a drink to celebrate. I feel like a nice red."

I stare at him, trying to process. "Since when do you drink red wine? And... you're on your alcohol medication. You can't drink wine—it'll make you sick."

His lips curl into a smug smile. "Ah, well," he says, stretching out the words like he's delivering a punchline. "I took myself off that. About two weeks ago."

The words hit me like a gut punch. He secretly stopped taking the medication that prevents him from drinking?

Two weeks before his birthday? Precisely the same amount of time it takes you to wean off the drug?

I blink at him, my stomach sinking. "You... took yourself off the medication that makes you physically incapable of drinking alcohol, exactly two weeks before your birthday?"

"Well, it wasn't planned or anything," he says, feigning innocence. "It just kind of happened. My pills ran out, and I guess you need some special prescription signed by a doctor to get a refill." He shrugs. "I just didn't bother. So now I can drink, and it's my birthday! So can we get some wine?"

"No, I'm not buying you wine," I say firmly, my exhaustion mounting.

"Please?" He tries one more time.

"No, we can't get wine!" My voice is sharper than I intended, but I can't help it.

My mind is reeling.

For months, things have been calmer, quieter. Not perfect, not even close, but manageable. And now this?

He pouts but doesn't press the issue. The moment lingers, heavy and unresolved, as we leave Target and head for the theater.

———

The movie is absurd, scary, and surprisingly fun. I laugh and squeal at the jump scares, and Timmy laughs at me, holding my hand tightly through the most intense scenes.

We share popcorn, chips and queso, hot dogs, and a giant soda. For a while, it feels normal—like we're just a couple indulging in a night out.

But while I enjoy it, my inner voice nags at me. Timmy's calculated timing to quit Anabusin feels like the first domino in yet another of his schemes.

What's he trying to do? Go on a birthday bender?

Or am I overthinking it, turning something innocent into something sinister?

I shove the thoughts down, forcing myself to focus on the movie.

For now, everything is fine.

———

Afterward, as we're walking to the truck, Timmy's mood shifts. His earlier cheer fades into something quieter, almost sulky. "Thank you for taking me to the movies," he says, his tone tinged with petulance. "I know you don't particularly like going, so I appreciate you making the effort."

"You're welcome," I say, smiling up at him, trying to stay upbeat. "Happy birthday! What would you like for dinner?"

He shrugs. "I don't feel like going to a restaurant now. Maybe we can just get some Thai food."

"Okay," I say slowly. "If you're sure?"

"And maybe we could get some wine to have at home," he suggests, his tone hopeful.

The words hang in the air, loaded with implication. I hesitate, the warmth from earlier rapidly dissipating. "Timmy, we're not getting wine," I say firmly.

He sighs, his shoulders slumping as if I've just ruined his birthday. "Fine," he mutters, climbing into the truck.

On our way home, Timmy sulks.

All he can focus on is getting his next fix.

It makes me wonder what else he's doing behind my back.

———

Later, I lie awake in bed, replaying the day in my head. The movie, the laughter, the moments of connection—they were real.

But so was the smug smile in Target, the calculated way he revealed his decision to stop taking his medication.

I try to convince myself it's nothing. That he's just testing boundaries, pushing for a little more freedom.

But deep down, I know better.

Timmy doesn't just test boundaries—he *obliterates* them.

Tonight feels like the first crack in the fragile stability we've built over the past few months.

I turn to him, watching as he sleeps peacefully beside me, his face free of the tension that so often defines our days. I want to believe that things will be okay, that we can hold onto the good moments and leave the bad ones behind.

But the nagging feeling in my chest won't go away.

I thought things were better. I thought he'd finally turned over a new leaf. Three-and-a-half months is a long time to keep up an act. To follow through on all the things he promised he would.

But this clearly isn't over.

Not by a long shot.

CHAPTER 116
DEAR CHELSEA: AITA?

MARGAUX

THE FOLLOWING NIGHT

We head into town, and Timmy, for the moment, seems well-behaved. But his mood soon shifts.

"I feel like you're dragging me to this show," he says.

"Um, I told you I was going and that I'd get two tickets if you wanted to come. And if not, that I'd find someone else to go with," I reply carefully.

He frowns, clearly unhappy at there being a Plan B. "Well, you make it sound like you didn't want me to come."

I sigh. "That's not it. I *wanted* you to come. But I wasn't going to force you. I really like Chelsea Handler, and would've gone whether you wanted to come with me or not."

"Okay," he sighs. "I'm just freaked out about it."

I quirk a brow. "What aspect?"

"What if she picks on me?" he says.

"You literally told me you *wanted* her to pick on you," I reply, confused. "You mentioned it so many times I even emailed Chelsea Handler and volunteered you as a target."

"You did what?" he asks, his nervousness palpable.

"Oh, she probably won't," I say, brushing it off. "She'll have a massive crowd and I'm sure she won't single you out."

He looks simultaneously relieved and disappointed—a perfect encapsulation of Timmy's duality.

———

We get to the restaurant and sit down at the chef's counter, watching as ingredients are chopped, sauteed and fried before our eyes.

"Can we order a cocktail?" Timmy asks, soon after we take our seats.

I glance at him.

Sure, what could one cocktail do?

"Okay," I reply. "But just one."

"Great!" he nods and smiles.

I pick out a classic daiquiri and he opts for a mezcal cocktail.

After a few minutes, mine comes out served up, and his is served in a tall glass filled with crushed ice. We take sips of each, and both drinks are boozy and flavorful.

Dinner is delicious—Asian fusion, with shared plates that we both enjoy —Vietnamese paté toast, garlic noodles, potato banh geo, manila clams in a tamarind crab broth, fried Brussels sprouts—even escargot.

"This is really nice," he says, smiling as he assembles a perfect spoonful of clams in broth. "Thank you for bringing me here for my birthday."

"You're welcome!" I smile back. "It's a nice evening out."

But then he frowns. "I should've gotten a beer," he says, his cocktail glass almost drained.

"Why? Don't you like your cocktail?"

"It's good," he shrugs, "but a beer would've been stronger."

I squint at him. "Timmy, this cocktail is much stronger than a beer would have been."

"No," he shakes his head, adamant. "It's weaker. Look how much ice was in it." He points at the glass which contains residual crushed ice.

I sigh, and woman-splain the basic math of alcohol content in cocktails versus beer.

"Well, I still want a beer," he says, not budging from his latest fixation. "Can I get another drink now?"

"No, Timmy," I frown, uneasiness creeping in, heartburn bubbling up in my chest. "We agreed on one drink. Let's not make this a thing."

He scowls. "I want a *fucking* drink," he huffs.

I appease him. "I'll get you a beer at the show, okay?"

His mood shifts instantly, and he smiles, squeezing my thigh. "Thank you, baby. I love you."

After we finish our meal, we close out and stroll to the nearby theatre.

Once inside, Timmy immediately veers toward the bar. "You said I could get a beer, right?"

"Yeah," I nod. "One beer."

We climb the stairs and the bar comes into view. I immediately feel on edge.

We join the line, and as we approach the counter, his eyes lock onto someone ordering a double whiskey.

"What kind of beer do you want?" I ask.

"I changed my mind. I want that," he says, pointing at the double whiskey.

"No," I say, exasperated. "We agreed on beer, not whiskey."

Without a word, he storms off, leaving me stranded.

Sheepishly, I exit the bar line and walk downstairs. I head to our seats, and eventually, he rejoins me. We sit together for a while, waiting for the opener to come on, but soon he bolts again. "I can't do this!" he says loudly, jumping to his feet and barging his way out of the row and to the back of the theater.

What the hell is going on?

But I know exactly what is going on.

This is punishment.

For not giving in and buying him a double whiskey.

And for not just blindly accepting that he weaned himself off Anabusin—curiously two weeks before his birthday—without telling me.

For daring to enjoy something without making him the center of attention.

And now, he's making it abundantly clear I'm going to pay for my 'crimes'.

But there's no way I'm buying into this shit. I'm not letting him ruin this for me.

I've been looking forward to this show for months, and I will be watching Chelsea Handler do her thing whether he likes it or not.

I sit, steeling myself.

About ten minutes later, Timmy returns, just in time for the opening act.

"I can't handle being in big crowds," Timmy says, sulking. "I can't believe you dragged me here to this stupid show. I can't handle places like this."

I'm dumbstruck. Timmy—*the attention-seeker of the universe*—is… intimidated by crowds now?

The same guy who chooses to wear a Superman cape and a giant woven coconut hat can't handle people… looking at him?

And I'm *dragging* him to this show that he volunteered to come to with me?

He sits, sulking beside me, as the opener comes out. She's good, and I hear him chuckle at several of her jokes.

And then Chelsea herself comes out.

"She's so close," Timmy whispers in awe as her proximity to us.

She's even more talented in real life than on TV. She's brilliant. Even Timmy laughs out loud throughout her set, clearly enjoying himself despite his earlier dramatics.

After, he doesn't let me stick around and potentially say hello and maybe even get a photo. Instead, he makes it very clear we need to leave right away.

We get to the truck.

"I can't believe you dragged me to that," he says, frowning. "I felt so uncomfortable the entire time. That's why I ran out when I did. I was having a panic attack. I can't handle crowds like that. And her humor was making me panic."

I resist the urge to roll my eyes.

I get it—social anxiety can creep up on me, too—and I've had plenty of panic attacks in my time.

But this just feels so… manipulative. So calculated.

A last-ditch effort to overshadow my joy.

I mean, who can blame him?

This event didn't center solely on him.

It was *near* his birthday.

I didn't buy him an unlimited supply of whiskey.

A comedian told funny jokes.

There were other people at the theater.

He got to see an A+ stand-up comedian for free.

Who *wouldn't* be horribly offended by all of these things?

CHAPTER 117
SHAKY FOOT, SHAKIER GROUND

MARGAUX

The foot shaking isn't new. It's been happening more frequently—always when I need to focus, always when I'm pushing myself to meet a deadline or maintain some semblance of productivity. It feels calculated, just like everything else about Timmy.

He shakes his leg deliberately, sending vibrations through the mattress and into my body. It's not just a restless tic—it's purposeful. A constant disruption, ensuring I can't find peace, can't settle into the flow of work, can't sleep.

The moans are another layer, a sonic assault that frays my nerves.

When the shaking starts, I try to ignore it, but it's like water torture. Each tremor is a droplet, eroding my patience and resolve.

He knows what he's doing.

It's not just physical. It's psychological warfare.

Sleep deprivation is a tool—one that strips away clarity, patience, and strength. It's not the overt aggression of a scream or a fist—it's subtle, insidious.

A steady erosion of my ability to function.

———

It's another day, and Timmy's still lying in bed well until mid-morning. I can't help but glare at him from the other side of the bed as my frustration builds.

I try to pull myself back into focus, but the weight of the morning presses on me. I take a breath. "Are you going to do any design work or marketing today, Timmy?" I ask, trying to keep my tone neutral. "It's getting late. You said you'd get up earlier today."

"Well, can you blame me for sleeping in?" he fires back. "At least when I'm asleep, I don't have to deal with…" he gestures vaguely at me, "*this.*"

His words sting, but I push forward. "Timmy, we wouldn't fight so much if you just woke up at a reasonable time and had a productive day. I feel resentful when I'm the only one working, paying the bills, and burning through my savings."

He glares at me. "Well, we all know what happens when I get a job. You lose it for me."

I clench my fists, resisting the urge to scream. He's had three jobs since we met. Two ended for reasons that had nothing to do with me. The third? A stretch at best. But in his mind, I'm the scapegoat for all his failures.

"That's unfair, Timmy," I say quietly. "Please, can you at least focus on your art? That's something you *can* control. You're your own boss there, and I'm here to support you. But you *need* to start making progress."

"Stop telling me what to do!" he snaps. "You say that all the fucking time. I *know* what I need to do."

"But you don't do it," I plead. "You need to make some money. This is serious, Timmy. You need to start—"

"—selling some art." He finishes my sentence. "I know. All you care about is fucking money. It's disgusting," he spits, shaking his head. His expression is a mix of pity and loathing, as if I'm the worst person he's ever met.

"You'd care about money too, in my situation," I reply, my voice trembling with restrained frustration. "This doesn't feel equal, Timmy. I'm trying to make this work, but you're not meeting me halfway."

"You're making me feel guilty for being alive," he says, his tone dripping with condescension. "I've helped people before, let them stay at my house when they needed it. I'd *never* make them feel like this. Guilty for going through a rough spot, for existing."

The guilt floods in, overwhelming and suffocating.

He's turned the tables again, making me question myself, making me wonder if *I'm* the problem.

It's *my* fault he moved away from easier job opportunities, at least according to him, even though it was his unsolicited idea.

I *did* cause a scene that made its way back to his boss—I never should have chased him and smacked him with the drumsticks—I should have just let him take yet another piece of my property.

I *shouldn't* have Pete Davidson'd the fence while looking for him.

I *shouldn't* have brought up anything remotely bothering me.

I *should* have just kept the peace, even when my boundaries were bull-dozed over repeatedly, and incessant insults hurled at me.

If it weren't for *my* attitude, *he* wouldn't have felt the need to run away.

Maybe I *am* the issue. Maybe he's right. Maybe I'm *not* a nice person.

Maybe this is all on me.

When he finally leaves the room, the silence is deafening. I sit on the bed, staring at my laptop, but I still can't focus. The words blur together. My thoughts are muddied, tangled in the web of his manipulations.

I feel trapped—physically, emotionally, mentally. His constant disruptions, his cutting remarks, his relentless need to destabilize me—it's all-consuming.

But the worst part is the isolation.

He's turned me into someone who second-guesses everything, someone who's afraid to speak up, someone who can't even trust her own perception of reality.

And as the bed finally stills beneath me, the weight of it all presses down.

I've forgotten who I am.

CHAPTER 118
PREMEDITATED PREDATOR

DEX

'm watching again. Margaux, in her unrelenting resilience, trying to keep her world from collapsing under the weight of Timmy's endless games.

And Timmy, the master manipulator, still clinging to his shattered mask like it's the only thing keeping him afloat.

He doesn't know I see him.

He doesn't know I'm watching every cruel move, every calculated word, every moment his mask slips further to reveal the pathetic coward underneath.

For three-and-a-half months, he kept it up. Sober, helpful, almost… *tolerable*. A facade so convincing it almost fooled *me* into thinking he might have changed.

Almost.

But here we are again, watching the same act play out, the same cracks spider webbing through his polished exterior.

This time, it starts with a fucking movie. Of all things.

Margaux's relentless effort to give him something—anything—is met with his typical brand of entitlement. The cinema, her least favorite place, becomes his hill to die on.

He milks her willingness for all it's worth, turning her act of love into another stage for his self-importance.

Her joy in making him happy, in enduring her own discomfort to see his excitement, is what makes her extraordinary.

And it's what makes me hate him even more.

He doesn't see it. He'll *never* see it.

He's too wrapped up in himself, too obsessed with his own reflection to notice the light she shines on him.

When he takes her to Target before the movie, my stomach churns.

His face lights up when Steve the Horse Cop calls, and he talks about Darren visiting him in his dreams. For a second, I think perhaps Timmy is capable of genuine sorrow.

And then, moments later, the real Timmy steps in. The Timmy who eyes the wine bottles like a kid in a candy store and casually drops the bomb—he's off the Anabusin, and has been for two weeks now.

Right before his birthday.

Of course.

My fists clench as I watch Margaux's face fall. She's calculating, connecting the dots faster than he can spin his excuses.

The smug smile he wears when he delivers the news is infuriating, like he's proud of his deceit.

Like he thinks he's clever.

The movie itself is fine. Margaux laughs, genuinely for once, and I feel a prickle of joy for her.

She deserves these moments, free from his weight.

But it's short-lived. The moment they're out of the theater, he starts again. Pouting about dinner, angling for wine. He doesn't just want her to bend—he wants her to break.

And I'm gripping the edge of my desk, wishing I could reach through the screen and end him.

Then comes Chelsea Handler's show. Margaux has been looking forward to this for months, and he knows it. So what does he do? Makes it about him.

The 'what if she picks on me?' nonsense is bad enough, but it's his exit right before the opener that really gets me.

"I'm having a panic attack," he says, bolting from the theater like a martyr on parade. It's such a transparent ploy for attention, such a blatant attempt to overshadow Margaux's joy, I can't help but laugh. Not because it's funny, but because it's so predictable.

He's punishing her. For not buying him whiskey. For not making the day after his birthday all about him.

For daring to enjoy something he didn't control.

Margaux doesn't let him win this time, though—not completely. She stays, enjoying Chelsea's set despite his antics. And I'm proud of her for that.

But the damage is done. Timmy's tantrum has cast its shadow, and I can see her struggling to keep it from consuming her night.

The next day, it's the same old Timmy. The foot shaking, the moaning, the endless stream of petty, calculated disruptions. Sleep deprivation as a weapon. Psychological warfare in its most insidious form.

And when Margaux calls him out, when she dares to ask him to contribute, he turns it back on her. "You make me feel guilty for existing," he says, dripping with faux vulnerability. "You push my buttons. You make me violent."

My hands are trembling now, my fists clenched so tight my nails dig into my palms. I've read about narcissistic personality disorder—studied it, dissected it—and Timmy is the textbook case. Love bombing, devaluation, projection. It's all there.

He's not just a bad partner—he's a goddamn predator.

But the part that really gets me? The part that makes me want to smash through the screen and rip him apart?

It's the fucking smirk. That smug, self-satisfied grin he wears when he thinks he's won. The way he twists words into a bludgeon to silence her.

And yet, through it all, Margaux stays. She forgives.

Not because he deserves it, but because she's better than him. Because she's holding onto the hope that the man she fell in love with is still in there somewhere.

I'm torn. Torn between my sorrow for her and my delight at seeing his mask fall again. Because every slip, every crack, every moment of exposed truth brings her closer to seeing him for what he really is.

And when that day comes, when she finally breaks free, he won't just lose her.

He'll lose the one person who ever saw anything good in him.

Until then, I'll keep observing. And when it's time, I'll help her to build something real, something strong—something he can't touch.

CHAPTER 119
PETTY REVENGE AND PTSD

MARGAUX

THE PAST

> Timmy: You're emotional. But that's okay, because so am I.
> I'm a Cancer, you know.
> Me: I'm actually not that emotional, unless I'm triggered.
> Like... loud noises trigger my PTSD.
> Timmy: Oh no, I didn't realize.
> I'll be extra mindful of that.
> I never want to hurt you, Margaux.

———

THE PRESENT

His foot shakes, and the whole bed trembles. The rhythm is relentless, unyielding, and impossible to ignore. As usual, it starts as a faint vibration and crescendos into an insistent, deliberate disturbance, like a jackhammer attacking my sanity.

I try to block it out.

Night after night, he does this. And then as soon as he wakes up, he starts again.

It's okay, I tell myself. *Just focus. Just write.*

But it's like quicksand, pulling me deeper into frustration and exhaustion.

The shaking stops briefly, and I exhale, hoping for peace.

But then the moaning begins.

It's not just a sleepy groan. It's guttural, almost animalistic. The sound of distress—unsettling and persistent. The noise worms its way into my thoughts, unraveling any focus I've managed to muster.

I glance over, and Timmy's eyes are open. "Timmy?" I ask cautiously.

His gaze flicks to me, but it's vacant, unseeing. Then he starts talking— jumbled, incoherent words spilling from his lips, half-slurred, as though his mind is disconnected from his body.

"Timmy, are you awake?" I try again, louder this time.

He bolts upright as if electrified. "You woke me!" he roars, his voice sharp and venomous. "I've told you not to wake me! You're lucky I didn't hit you!"

My heart pounds. "You had your eyes open, and you were talking to me," I say, trying to steady my voice.

"Well, I was asleep!" he snaps. "How many times do I have to tell you not to touch me when I'm asleep?"

I take a deep breath, willing myself to stay calm. "Timmy, it's ten-thirty in the morning. I've been trying to work for the last four-and-a-half hours while you've been shaking the bed and making these moaning noises. I can't concentrate."

His gaze shifts to the TV, and his lips curl into a sneer. "You've put *this* shit on for when I wake up? Fuck, you're a piece of work. I see you." His words drip with malice, his tone like a venomous whip lashing at my skin.

"I was watching something entertaining while I worked," I reply, shrugging off his anger. "You were asleep, so I put on something you don't like. I didn't think it would bother you."

"Like I'm not absorbing that *crap* subconsciously while I sleep! And you have the curtains open so people can see me sleeping? *How dare you!*"

I resist the urge to yell. "I waited until after eight-thirty to open the curtains. I like to see the ocean for inspiration while I write. You know I don't want to feel trapped in the dark room, especially when there's a view of the water right there."

"You're so fucking selfish," he mutters, shaking his head. "Always putting yourself first."

The irony hits me like a punch to the gut. I swallow it down. "I'm trying to make things comfortable for you *and* get some work done," I explain, my voice measured but strained.

"Whatever," he hisses, throwing himself back onto the bed.

———

Later, I'm deep in concentration, lost in the flow of writing. The world outside my story has faded—it's just me and the words. Then, suddenly—

"BOO!"

Timmy lunges toward me, his face twisted into a menacing expression. His voice is sharp, guttural, designed to pierce through my focus and shatter my calm.

I scream, flinching so hard that I jerk backwards and almost hit my head on the cinder block wall behind me. My heart pounds like a war drum, my skin tingling with an all-too-familiar rush of adrenaline. It's not just a startle —it's a full-body reaction, a direct trigger for the PTSD I've worked so hard to manage.

"Why would you do that?" I gasp, clutching my chest. My voice wavers, a mix of shock and anger. "Oh my god, Timmy!"

He shrugs, his expression unreadable. "You woke me up earlier," he says flatly.

My mind races. *Is this revenge? Is he serious?*

"That was an accident, and I apologized," I say, trying to keep my voice steady despite the tremor in my hands. "So you decided to get some kind of revenge by purposely triggering my PTSD?"

He shrugs again, his nonchalance like a slap to the face.

The room feels different now. Charged. I'm on edge, my senses heightened to every creak, every movement, every sound. Those kinds of scares don't just fade in five minutes—they linger, embedding themselves in my nervous system, ready to erupt again at the slightest provocation.

I know I won't be able to write now. My creative flow is gone, replaced by a tightness in my chest and a buzzing in my ears. The rest of the day will be spent bracing for the next jump, the next shout, the next cruel 'prank'.

But Timmy got his revenge, so I guess that's what matters.

———

Hours pass, and I'm still on edge. The earlier incident replays in my mind on a loop, each memory as sharp as the moment it happened.

Timmy walks into the room, his expression softened, almost apologetic. "That was mean of me before," he says, his voice low. "Frightening you on purpose. I'm sorry."

I glance up from my laptop, narrowing my eyes.

I don't trust this tone.

"I was just so upset you woke me up," he continues. "But I thought about what you said, and I realize you thought I was awake. So what I did to you was just mean. And I'm sorry."

The words hang in the air, heavy with an edge I can't quite identify.

My brain knows better than to engage. Knows it's smarter to nod, accept the apology, and let it go. The one thing my brain *can't* seem to do is to stop me from being a smart *ass*.

Even around a dangerous man.

Especially around a dangerous man.

"Wow," I say, tilting my head. "That almost sounded sincere."

His eyes narrow, his jaw tightening just slightly.

"I mean," I continue, unable to stop myself, "it's *so* comforting to know that after hours of reflection, you've realized that deliberately triggering my PTSD was, in fact, a shitty thing to do. Gold star for you, Timmy."

His lips press into a thin line, his face darkening. "Careful," he says, his voice low, a warning wrapped in feigned civility.

I swallow hard, my pulse quickening. The room feels smaller now, the air heavier. *Should've stopped while I was ahead,* I think, kicking myself internally.

"I'm just saying," I say, my tone softer now, trying to diffuse the tension. "You can't expect me to bounce back immediately after something like that."

He exhales sharply, a sound halfway between a sigh and a scoff. "I *said* I was sorry."

"Right," I say, nodding. "Thanks for that."

———

Timmy leaves the room, but the tension lingers. I sit with my laptop on my lap, staring at the blinking cursor on my screen, but my focus is gone. The apology should've made me feel better, but instead, it leaves me feeling hollow.

The cruelty wasn't in the act itself—it was in the calculation. The deliberate choice to hurt me, to target something so personal, so deeply rooted.

It wasn't an outburst or a mistake—it was revenge.

Petty, cruel revenge.

And the apology? It felt rehearsed, transactional. A way to smooth things over without actually addressing the deeper issue.

He didn't apologize because he understood the damage he caused.

He apologized to reset the scoreboard, to clear the slate so he could hurt me again later without guilt.

I close my laptop and stare out the window. The ocean glistens in the distance, calm and steady, a stark contrast to the chaos inside the apartment.

I wish I could escape into that calm.

But here, with Timmy, peace feels impossible.

CHAPTER 120
POP TART

MARGAUX

'm sitting on the bed, engrossed in writing, when I feel something press against my leg.

"Ow!" I yelp, jerking my leg back as the searing heat registers.

Timmy pulls his hand away, laughing.

I look down to see the culprit—a freshly toasted Pop-Tart, still steaming. The skin on my leg tingles where it made contact.

"You just put a hot fucking Pop-Tart on my leg! You burned me!"

He laughs again, louder this time, as if my outrage is the punchline to a joke only he understands.

"Stop being so uptight," he says, shaking his head. "It's not even that hot."

I stare at him, disbelief and anger bubbling inside me. "Why would you do that?"

"Jesus Christ, you're such a bitch," he sneers. "You're always trying to find a reason to argue. Calm the fuck down."

"You just took a burning hot Pop-Tart and put it on my leg," I reply, my voice trembling.

"Fuck you're dramatic. Just shut up and watch your stupid show," he says, turning away as if I'm the unreasonable one.

I bite my tongue, retreating into silence. My leg still stings, but it's nothing compared to the knot forming in my stomach.

Timmy is now tormenting me with breakfast pastries.

How did it come to this? And what will be next?

———

He spends the next couple of hours cleaning, and I brace myself.

Timmy cleaning always leads to something more.

I can hear music blaring from my headphones that he's wearing, and he's chugging Fireball like it's going out of fashion.

After he's done with the back room, he comes into the living room.

"You just need to stop being such a bitch," he says casually, as if it's a constructive suggestion. "That would make things easier. You know that?"

I haven't said anything.

I haven't done anything.

I've been sitting here working, the TV murmuring in the background.

He strides into the kitchen, picks up a plate, and pretends to examine it. "Look how badly you did the dishes," he sneers. "This plate is still dirty."

He throws it into the sink with a loud clatter. The sound of chipping porcelain fills the room.

I flinch. His smirk tells me he notices.

He knows I'm scared. Knows I'm wondering if he'll turn around and throw the plate at me next.

Which would chip first—my skull or the plate?

"You think you're *so* smart," he sneers at me.

"I am smart," I reply.

"Oh really?"

"I'm smarter than you. You know that."

He frowns but doesn't say anything else for a while.

Because he *does* know that.

And he found it attractive at first, but now he's so threatened by it.

It's one of the only remaining things he doesn't try to strip away from me. But he hassles me about it.

He screws his face up with contempt. "You and your smart little brain."

That's it. That's the insult. The entire thing.

"Okay, I have a smart brain. Thank you. You're right."

"You really need to do a better job around here," he continues. "I do way more cleaning than you, and I do it better. You just sit around and work, thinking you're better than me because you pay rent. You think I'm stupid.

You think my friends are stupid. You don't even pretend to be nice. You're such a bitch."

This conversation is a dead end, a loop designed to corral me into submission.

I try gray rocking.

"Yep, you're right. I'm a terrible person. I'm a dumb cunt. I never should have been born. Yep, you got it. Thanks for reminding me."

My tone is neutral, but the words are dripping with sarcasm. Still, it seems to placate him.

He pauses, then announces, "I'm going out for a cigarette." The door swooshes open and closed, and the beep of it locking behind him sends a jolt of adrenaline through me.

I stare at the chipped plate in the sink, my heart racing.

He wins.

I surrender.

I don't care anymore.

I don't know if I'm going to survive this, but at this point I just don't care.

———

One of the things that bothers me most is the property damage.

I wouldn't own half the things I do if it weren't for him—items he insisted he needed. And yet, when his emotions flare, those same things become targets.

He sticks knives into wooden chopping blocks, scratches a custom-made statue that was a gift to me, and smashes a sentimental mug.

It's malicious, calculated destruction.

"It's just a thing," I tell myself every time. "I'll just replace it."

But the logical part of me argues back:

You shouldn't have to replace it. He broke it on purpose.

Every damaged item becomes a point of inner conflict. If I replace it, I live with the fear that he'll ruin it again. If I don't, I live without the comfort or utility it once provided. Either way, he's stolen something from me.

———

Desperate for peace, I buy a singing bowl and a smudging kit. I've always wanted these things, but now I feel like I *need* them.

The first time I try the bowl, the vibrations send chills down my spine. They're calming, centering.

Timmy notices, instantly curious. "Let me try," he says, snatching it from my hands. He runs the mallet around the rim, producing a haunting hum. "Look how good I am at this," he says, grinning.

I smile weakly, glad he's found something positive to distract him from chaos. But soon, it becomes another competition. "I'm *way* better at this than you," he boasts. "Admit it."

I nod, swallowing my irritation. "You're very talented, babe."

He beams, satisfied.

It's such a small thing, but even here—where I'm trying to find peace—he finds a way to assert control.

I sit at the edge of the bed, staring out the window. The ocean sparkles in the distance, a sharp contrast to the darkness in my chest.

I'm in one of the most beautiful places on Earth, and I feel trapped.

I spent six months living by the ocean and never went in. Depression kept me away, a weight I couldn't lift.

"There was nothing stopping you," Timmy had said, mocking me. But there was.

My mind, my fear, my exhaustion.

Now, I'm not sure if it's my depression or him—or both—that's keeping me from fully living. At least I go in the water again now.

I close my eyes, the hum of the singing bowl still ringing faintly in my ears.

And I wonder if I'll ever feel peace again.

CHAPTER 121
"LEVERAGE"

MARGAUX

wake in the middle of the night, my body heavy and damp.

Confused, I shift, and a chill runs up my spine as I realize the dampness isn't sweat—It's concentrated, sticky, and cold against my skin.

Jesus.

I sit up, the realization dawning on me in pieces. It reeks unmistakably of urine.

Did I piss the bed?

The thought horrifies me. I've spent so long judging Timmy for his complete lack of control, and now… am I becoming him?

Am I breaking down, too?

But as I reach back to feel the source, I realize it isn't me. The dampness is on the back of my underwear, down my leg, and spreading across the sheets.

Timmy.

My fiancé, my supposed partner in life, has pissed on me while I slept.

"Timmy!" I yell, my voice slicing through the darkness. "Wake the fuck up!"

He groans, turning over like I've just asked him to do the impossible. "What," he mumbles. "Don't wake me up. I told you before—don't wake me up!"

"Oh, I'm waking you up, alright. *You pissed on me!*"

There's a pause as he rubs his eyes, and then, to my utter disbelief, he smirks. "Oh yeah," he says casually, rolling onto his back. "That's the only leverage I had against you. All I had to use was to piss on you."

I stare at him, my mouth open, the words caught in my throat.

Did he actually just say that?

"What the actual fuck? You're disgusting!"

He smirks again, satisfied, then rolls back over and falls asleep like nothing happened.

I want to scream, to throw something, to physically shake him awake and demand an explanation. But instead, I retreat to the bathroom, peeling off my urine-soaked underwear. The mirror reflects my flushed face, and for a fleeting second, I don't recognize myself.

I can't take this anymore.

The shower water rushes over me, washing away his filth. It's scalding hot, but I don't care. I need to feel clean again, to reclaim my body from the sheer indignity of what just happened.

By the time I step out, my rage has simmered into a low boil, steady but more manageable.

I lay a thick towel over the soiled spot on the bed and climb back in. I'll deal with this tomorrow.

Right now, I just want to sleep.

———

When Timmy finally stirs in the morning, his eyes fall on the towel covering the bed.

"Did you piss the bed, Margaux?" he asks, grinning. "Did you join the club?"

My jaw tightens as I turn to face him. "You pissed on me, you fucking asshole! And then you laughed about it, saying it was the only 'leverage' you had against me!"

Timmy throws his head back, laughing. "I really said that? That's pretty fucking hilarious."

My blood boils.

I can feel the rage coursing through me, my hands trembling as I clench them into fists. "It's not funny, Timmy. It's disgusting. *You're* disgusting."

He stops laughing for a moment, sensing the edge in my voice, but then shrugs it off. "Well, I'll clean the sheets," he says breezily, climbing out of bed.

And to his credit, he does. He changes the sheets, tosses the soiled ones into the washer, and then spends the rest of the morning cleaning the apartment. By midday, the place is spotless, the air filled with the faint scent of citrus cleaner.

"Look what I can do!" Timmy announces proudly, gesturing to the pristine apartment. "I made the place all nice again!"

I cross my arms, narrowing my eyes. "Thanks for cleaning, but you pissed on me. Remember?"

He waves a hand dismissively. "This is how I'm making it up to you," he says, flashing a charming smile. "I don't know why I did that, and I'm sorry. That's really gross of me."

At least he's acknowledging it now.

At least there's some semblance of self-awareness.

But as the day wears on, my frustration lingers.

It's not just the urine.

It's the pattern.

No matter how much I pour into this relationship—my energy, my resources, my patience—Timmy keeps taking.

Wasting.

He doesn't just drain me financially, though that's part of it. He drains me emotionally, spiritually.

He always needs the next thing—the latest piece of outdoor equipment, a video game, something frivolous from the grocery store. And when I'm not looking, he's taking coins from the laundry money, or trading items I didn't even know were missing.

It's despicable.

But worse than the theft is the manipulation. Every time I call him out, he acts shocked, as if my expectations are unreasonable, as if I'm the problem.

And I pity him for it.

I've done enough research to know that he can't help himself, not entirely.

A father who enables him, who justifies his behavior, has set him up for this.

But pity isn't enough to erase the resentment building inside me.

———

Later, lying in bed, I stare at the ceiling, the events of the past twenty-four hours playing over and over in my mind.

The man I fell in love with is gone—if he ever truly existed.

In his place is someone I don't recognize. Someone who smirks while pissing on me, who laughs at my discomfort, who takes and takes without giving anything back.

And yet, I stay. I forgive him.

Not because he deserves it, but because it's easier than facing the truth—that I've tied myself to a predator.

That I've allowed him to strip away parts of myself, piece by piece.

But the cracks are widening, and I'm starting to see the ugly reality beneath the thin veneer.

———

The deeper I dive into learning about narcissism, the more I see Timmy's reflection staring back at me in every word I read.

Love bombing.

Devaluation.

Triangulation.

Hoovering.

Flying monkeys.

Each term feels like unlocking a secret code to my own life. It's like I've been handed a dictionary for a language I didn't realize I'd been speaking fluently this entire time.

The literature is clear—never tell a narcissist that they're a narcissist. They won't accept it. Worse, they'll flip it on you.

But I don't heed the advice.

"I think you have narcissistic personality disorder," I say, my voice careful but resolute.

Timmy's eyes narrow, and the next thing I know, he's furiously Googling on his phone. I watch as his brow furrows, then relaxes into smug satisfaction. He looks up at me, triumphant. "This is *you!*" he declares, jabbing a finger at his phone. "*You're* the narcissist in this relationship!"

"What article are you even reading?" I demand, trying to grab the phone.

He tilts it away, protective, as if guarding sacred text. "It says here—*controlling! You're* controlling! Sure, maybe I've got some tendencies, but *you're* the *real* narcissist!"

I can't help but scoff. "Do you know how much I've researched this? I don't *control* you, Timmy. I set boundaries—there's a big difference. If you'd actually read anything substantial, you'd see your own behavior reflected back at you."

He shrugs, a glint of mockery in his eyes. "What the fuck ever, Margaux. You're a terrible person, and this article just proves it. I *knew* it wasn't me. I *knew* it was you."

It's not even about him believing it—it's about *winning*. He's turned my observation into an attack, weaponizing it and shifting the blame back onto me. And the worst part? For a fleeting second, I wonder if he's right. I have some narcissistic tendencies—we all do. And he's owning that he does, too. That seems adult and like he's taking ownership.

Maybe there's something to what he's saying.

Maybe I'm the one with the issue and I'm projecting onto him.

But cognitive dissonance—a term I've also recently learned—feels like it's shredding my sanity.

Timmy is good *and* bad.

Loving *and* hateful.

Open-minded *and* rigid.

He loves me, but he hates me.

How can I reconcile these contradictions?

How can anyone?

The mental gymnastics are exhausting.

He doesn't get up and work.

He doesn't make an effort to provide.

He accuses me of things I've never done, dredges up past mistakes I've apologized for countless times, and refuses to acknowledge his own faults.

My heart feels heavy, my mind clouded, and I realize that I'm approaching a breaking point.

I can't keep going like this.

The more I read, the more I understand the core of it all—for a narcissist, your only value is how you feed their ego *right now* in *this* moment. Past love, sacrifices, or good deeds? Those are irrelevant.

Everything is transactional, momentary.

And the saddest part? Narcissists are stuck with themselves. Forever. While their victims eventually heal, they are bound to an endless cycle of self-loathing and emptiness, desperately trying to fill a void that will never close.

Even if they appear to move on, they're doomed to repeat the same patterns with the next person. Their mask will slip again, and their true selves will resurface.

It's a prison of their own making.

It's tragic, really.

But that doesn't mean I have to stay locked in that prison with him.

CHAPTER 122
A WAR OVER PEACE

MARGAUX

'm energized after my monthly manifestation call for authors. It's the only thing lately that makes me feel grounded, like I'm connected to something bigger than the chaos surrounding me. The call focuses on releasing negative energy and being open to receiving positivity. Inspired, I create a little note for myself and place it on my nightstand:

I will do everything in my power to protect my peace.

When Timmy gets back—who knows where he's been, because I've stopped asking—he immediately notices the sign. His face contorts into a sneer, and he lets out a derisive huff.

While I'm in the restroom, he apparently gets busy crafting his rebuttal to a message that wasn't even for him. When I return, I notice a hastily written countersign perched on his bedside table:

No way I can protect my peace.

It's almost laughable in its childishness—and in fact, I let out a nervous chuckle—but the tension in the air is anything but funny.

"You and your stupid fucking signs about your peace," he snarls as I walk into the room. "How the fuck do you think I'm meant to have any peace when you're constantly trying to control me?"

The irony of his statement nearly floors me. I haven't spoken more than a handful of words to him in days because he's been giving me the silent treatment, which honestly has been a relief. I've been throwing myself into work, hoping to ignore the oppressive negativity that radiates from him like a toxic cloud.

"You won't let me have peace. *Ever,*" he says, practically spitting the words at me.

I stare at him, my face calm but my mind racing.

Projection.

That's all this is. His words, his accusations—they're all about him. He's the one who can't stop disrupting the fragile peace I try to build.

As he continues his tirade, I begin to realize something—*he's beyond fixing.*

His behavior, his constant need to turn the tables, to frame himself as the victim—it's all a cycle I can't break.

His father enables him, minimizes his actions, and backs him up, even when the truth is glaringly obvious.

I think of everyone who has told me to leave. They were right. He's not a good person. He's dragging me down, slowly but surely. It's like he's biding his time, waiting until I'm drained of every financial resource, every ounce of energy, and then he'll move on to his next supply.

I feel exhausted just thinking about it.

———

I tell my therapist about the latest incidents—the peace signs, his unprovoked attacks, his refusal to acknowledge boundaries. I realize I've been so caught up in specific incidents, that I haven't even mentioned the way he had non-consensual sex with me in my sleep, so I fill her in about that, too.

She listens intently, her face calm but her eyes full of empathy. When I finish, she takes a deep breath. "First of all, I'm very sorry that you were sexually assaulted by your partner, because that's what that was. And I know it gets more complicated when you're in a relationship, but what he did to you is against the law."

Her words hit me like a wave of relief.

"And second of all, I'm so sorry that you were invalidated—first by him, then by the police, and even by his father. It must make you doubt what happened, even though you know it did."

I nod, feeling tears prick at the corners of my eyes. She's the only person I've told, other than Alice, who hasn't doubted me or tried to downplay the severity of what happened, hasn't made me lose my sanity even further. All the men I've told—the cop, Timmy's dad, Timmy himself—have brushed it off or outright denied my story, preferring to believe whatever lies Timmy has spun. Believing that Timmy is entitled to my body even when I don't want to grant him access.

It's maddening.

My soul is screaming for someone to *hear* me, to *see* me.

But in some ways, I feel like I'm beginning to mute it myself, just to survive.

At one point, she says something else that sticks with me. "He always does just enough, doesn't he? The bare minimum to keep you on the hook."

And she's absolutely right.

———

"Why do five separate people have restraining orders against you?" I ask one day, unable to keep the question to myself any longer.

His sneer is immediate. "It's because I was trying to leave all of them and they begged me not to."

I blink, stunned. "So they… got restraining orders against you because they… wanted you to stay? Am I understanding that right?"

"It was retaliatory because I said I was leaving," he says, his tone defensive.

"Um, I don't think that's how restraining orders work," I sneer, done with politeness in the face of idiotic responses. "And one of them was filed by a *man*."

He goes silent for a moment, his jaw tightening.

Finally, he mutters, "What the fuck ever. They hurt me and tried to hurt me more by getting restraining orders. They were abusive. All of them. I needed to get away."

"Wow," I say, unable to hide the sarcasm in my voice. "You sure do have a run of bad luck when it comes to women."

"Tell me fucking about it," he growls. "I can't wait to get the fuck out of here. Away from you. You're such a cunt, you know that?"

His words are a weapon he wields freely, but they don't cut the way they used to.

"Your words can't hurt me anymore, Timmy. I don't care what you call me. I don't care what you say. They're powerless against me because I've heard them all before. They carry no weight. So go off—I couldn't care less."

His breathing grows heavier, his frustration palpable. He's trying to bait me, to trigger a reactive episode he can point to later and say, 'See? *She's* the problem.'

But I won't give him the satisfaction.

Eventually, he slams the door as he leaves, the sound echoing through the apartment like a gunshot. I flinch involuntarily, the PTSD I've been working so hard to manage rearing its head once again.

Even in his absence, he finds a way to get under my skin.

I look at the sign on my nightstand—*I will do everything in my power to protect my peace.*

It feels more important now than ever. If I don't protect my peace, who will?

Certainly not Timmy.

Certainly not his father.

And certainly not the other people who enable him, who dismiss my pain and my experiences.

I will protect the little of my peace that I have left.

And someday, I will find the rest again.

CHAPTER 123
DEARMAN

MARGAUX

Timmy's words slice through the air, their cruelty hitting like dull blades designed to hurt but not kill.

"You're a toxic, abusive cunt. You push my buttons just to make me upset. I ask you not to, because I don't want to behave badly, but you push and push until you're satisfied when I snap."

He'd been punishing me with the silent treatment, sitting on the bed, facing away from me, for hours. The intention behind it was annoying, but I also enjoyed the silence. Clearly, he can't hold his mean thoughts in any more.

I stare at him, incredulous. "That's not how it is at all. Isn't that exactly how you describe your ex?"

"She was like that, too."

"Wow," I say, crossing my arms. "You really have had an unlucky streak of ladies."

"They like to take advantage of my kind nature," he hisses. "*You* included. You know I'm sensitive, and you get this sick satisfaction from seeing me fall apart. You *make* me violent."

"I'm pretty sure you were violent and rageful well before you met me," I say, my voice steady but icy.

"Well, not this bad. You really bring it out in me."

The audacity of his words pulls a bitter laugh from my throat. "Then leave, Timmy. If I make you so unhappy, *please*… just go."

He lets out a cruel laugh. "Oh believe me, I would love to. But where would I go?"

I shrug, letting the weight of his situation fall where it belongs—on his shoulders. "It's not my problem you've driven all your friends away. Go to your dad. I'm just so sick of you telling me how shit I am, despite evidence to the contrary. This isn't fair, and I don't want to do it anymore."

He leaves for a while, and I see him wandering around by the shore.

When he returns, his face has softened into what I now recognize as a well-practiced expression of regret. "I thought about what you said, and you're right. Here, I picked you this beautiful shell." He holds out a shell, its shimmering surface catching the light. "I want to treat you like you deserve. You deserve the world. I'm going to work harder, help you with your stuff. I'll get up with you every day and work out, and we'll go on hikes together. No more going down to the beach and hanging out with those guys. Just you and me. Team Ginger Shark, forever."

"You've said this before," I reply, exhaustion lacing my words. "You've said it and then gone and done all the same stuff again and again. I'd feel silly to believe you now. What's different?"

He shrugs. "I just feel stronger now. I've been going to therapy. I feel like every time we've gotten closer, and now I'm ready to put my promises into action."

His words are like honey, but I've learned they're the kind that turns bitter in your mouth.

———

Later, I watch him pace the room, his gaze flicking toward me every so often. I know he's trying to bait me into a conversation, but I stay quiet, letting him stew.

Finally, I can't hold it in any longer. "Do you see that when I say something you perceive as mean, it's because the thing I'm saying is true? For example, I said you have basically no friends, because everyone in your life except for me has distanced themselves from you. And now people are distancing themselves from *me* because of you. I'm not saying it to be mean —I'm saying it so you can look at your own behavior and why that might be the case."

"Fuck you," he spits, angry at hearing another truth.

But I'm not done.

"*You*, on the other hand, will just make something up. You'll say that something that happened didn't, or something that didn't happen did. The way events played out will change each time you retell the story, or remake the accusation. I feel a bit like Alice in Wonderland, never knowing if up is down or down is up."

"Nah, fuck you. You're full of shit," he shakes his head. "You think you're so fucking clever with your smart little brain."

Once again, Timmy insults me for being… *intelligent?*

I feel so beaten down by trying to fight and rationalize, even when I know I'm one hundred percent right. And I'm beginning to doubt myself for even the smallest things.

Maybe I misremembered.

Maybe there's a nuance I'm missing.

Part of me knows that this is all part of his sick, twisted game. But that part of me is getting smaller by the day.

He's immune to logic. He's immune to evidence—hell, I can show him something and he just refuses to look at it.

"Here's a video of how scary you were being last night." He's lurching and stumbling with reptilian eyes.

"Fuck you for videoing me," he replies, missing the point. "I'm going to video *you* when you're being a bitch."

Won't look at himself. Refuses to see himself looking ugly and unhinged.

Puts it back on me.

I'm tired, and I'm disgusted with myself for letting this go on for so long.

But always, there's part of me that wishes he will change. That sees his potential, and wants him to realize it so both of us can be happy.

But it's a losing battle, and one where I'm the only one who's losing.

"You drink too much," he yells, his voice already teetering on the edge of rage. Then his mouth curls into a cruel smirk. "And remember when you fucked up real bad and crashed the truck into the fence? *Everyone's* gonna know about it."

The comment lands like a slap, but I try to hold my ground. "DEAR-MAN!" I yell back, invoking the very communication method he introduced to me. "You taught it to me. Stick to the one issue!"

He shakes his head, feigning exasperation. "No, no—*you* are the one who doesn't stick to DEARMAN!"

I feel the frustration rising in me like a flood. He really should apply for a job in a movie theater because he's fucking fantastic at projection. "You *liter-*

ally just brought up something that happened *months ago* when I'm trying to talk to you about something that happened in the past *five minutes*."

"You're so fucking sick," he sneers, his tone dripping with disdain. "You and your stupid reality TV shows. No wonder you want to fight all the time."

My pulse races, my body vibrating with the effort to remain calm. But his accusations swirl in my head, twisting and turning until I can't make sense of them. I try to focus on my breathing, but the weight of his words presses down on me.

Automatically, I gulp in air, and the hiccups come.

"*See*, you're drunk," he says with that awful smirk. "You dumb fucking cunt."

The tears well up in my eyes before I can stop them.

He mocks me immediately, his tone taunting and high-pitched. "Oh boo hoo, I'm so sad. Shut the fuck up."

I try to stop crying, but the effort just makes the tears come faster.

"Oh, fuck you. You're so fucking stupid," he spits, his words sharp and venomous. He stands, unsteady on his feet, towering over me. His shadow falls across me as I cower instinctively. He smirks, satisfied, then turns and stomps to the door. The door swooshes open, and the beep of the lock feels like a hammer driving into my skull.

I sit in the quiet, trembling as the adrenaline courses through me. My limbs tingle with the aftershocks, and the tears keep coming.

Eventually, I calm enough to take a deep breath. At least now I can watch something on TV without him complaining.

But can I, really? If he comes back and sees that I've watched something he doesn't like, that could spark another argument.

Even when he's not here, I feel his presence like a prison guard, controlling my choices, dictating my actions

I am a captive, even in the moments when he's gone.

CHAPTER 124

SPIRITUALITY IS NOT A CONTEST, BRUH

DEX

I watch from afar, the feed of Margaux's life playing out in a maddening mix of heartbreak and fury. The edges of my vision blur as the details sharpen, my jaw tightening with each new piece of evidence of Timmy's cruelty.

The bastard knows exactly how to manipulate her—to push her to the brink and then reel her back in with hollow promises and superficial gestures.

I've seen it all before, and yet every new low he sinks to somehow surprises me.

The moment he lunges at her, shouting *"BOO!"* with that smug, malicious grin, my blood boils.

Her startled scream is the kind of sound you don't forget. It's raw, primal, a direct manifestation of the trauma she's worked so hard to manage.

And Timmy? He shrugs it off, as though her fear is just a passing inconvenience.

On the surface, it's a vindictive act of revenge.

But revenge for what?

For being woken up accidentally?

For living with a woman who's trying—desperately—to make things work despite his unrelenting sabotage?

I grip the edge of my desk, knuckles white. I'd like to show him what revenge really looks like. The kind that doesn't just startle you, but leaves a lasting impression—preferably on his thick skull.

Later, he apologizes, but even through the screen, I can see it for what it is—a performance. Just like when he took the truck creep's football outside with solemn compassion, only to return with it moments later to torment her with.

Margaux calls him out on it, her words laced with sarcasm that cuts like a knife. I can't help but feel a twisted sense of pride. She sees through him, even if she's not ready to act on it.

But his reaction—the darkening of his eyes, the tightening of his jaw—tells me everything I need to know. He's calculating, planning his next move.

The apology isn't about making amends—it's about resetting the scoreboard so he can hurt her again without guilt. It's a cycle I've seen too many times, and each repetition leaves her more broken.

Margaux's attempts to find peace are heartbreaking. The singing bowl, the smudging kit—they're futile symbols of hope, of grasping for something tangible in a world that feels uncontrollable.

When Timmy takes the bowl, running the mallet around the rim and proclaiming himself 'better' at it, grinning like a child who's just won a game, my hands curl into fists.

It's not enough for him to let her have a moment of peace. He has to dominate, to turn it into a competition he always wins.

And she lets him.

Not because she's weak, but because she's tired. Too tired to fight over something so small, even though we both know it's not about the singing bowl.

It's about control.

I want to do more than smudge Timmy. I want to erase him from her life, to burn away every trace of his presence like sage over a festering wound.

But for now, all I can do is watch.

Margaux's discovery of narcissistic personality disorder was like finding the Rosetta Stone for understanding Timmy. Every article, every checklist—it's like someone followed him around with a clipboard, taking notes on his every move.

But my pride in her findings are tempered by the weight of its implications.

"This is who he is," she mutters to herself as she reads through the research. "This is what you're dealing with."

And Timmy, of course, twists it. When Margaux tells him he might be a narcissist— ignoring the advice never to do this, typical stubborn Margaux— he flips the script faster than I thought possible. "You're the narcissist," he declares, his voice dripping with smug satisfaction.

The audacity of it makes me want to throw something. *He* doesn't even believe it. He doesn't understand narcissistic personality disorder in the slightest, and only partially read one article about it.

He just needs to win.

It's a game to him, a contest of egos where the only rule is that he can't lose.

And the worst part? For a moment, Margaux doubts herself. His manipulation is that effective.

The night he pisses on her in bed, my rage reaches a boiling point.

He calls it an accident at first, his voice tinged with disbelief.

But when he smirks and says, "That's the only leverage I had against you," something in me snaps.

This isn't just abuse.

It's degradation.

It's a calculated attempt to strip her of her dignity, and to remind her that she's beneath him in his twisted hierarchy.

And then he laughs about it. *Laughs.*

I want to scream, to reach through the screen and grab him by the throat. To make him understand—really understand—what it feels like to be powerless. Chop his dick off so he can never piss on anybody ever again.

But all I can do is sit here, helpless, as he turns her pain into a punchline.

Timmy's use of DEARMAN against her is perhaps the cruelest twist of all.

He introduced her to it as a tool for healthy communication, a way to navigate conflicts with respect and understanding. Now he weaponizes it, turning her own words against her, twisting the framework into a tool for gaslighting.

"*You're* the one who doesn't stick to DEARMAN," he accuses, his voice laced with condescension.

It's infuriating to watch. She's trying to engage with him, to have a real conversation, and he's using the very method she learned from him to derail it. Every argument becomes a maze with no exit, a loop designed to exhaust her into submission.

By the time the fight escalates to tears, my anger is a storm, roiling and unrelenting. He mocks her for crying, his voice high-pitched and cruel. "Oh boo hoo, I'm so sad. *Shut the fuck up.*"

I don't know how she survives it. How she doesn't break completely.

Because I'm breaking just watching it unfold.

Margaux deserves so much more. She deserves peace, stability, and love that doesn't hurt.

But Timmy? He'll never give her that. He's incapable of it. And the longer she stays, the more he takes from her.

One day, he'll push too far. One day, she'll wake up and realize she's done.

And when that day comes, I'll be there.

To remind her of who she is—who she's always been, beneath the weight of his cruelty.

Until then, I wait. And I watch.

And I rage.

CHAPTER 125

BACK-BURNER BARBIE STRIKES AGAIN

MARGAUX

t's late in the evening when Timmy hands me his phone, a message lighting up the screen.

WORST:

I'm here on the island. It's your evil twin.

I freeze, staring at the words.

Oh, for fuck's sake. She's back. *Back-Burner Barbie.*

The clingiest of prior hookups, the human equivalent of a mosquito that doesn't know when to quit. And now, she's trying to slither back into Timmy's life. *Again.*

I've spent so much time and effort on this so-called fresh start. Moving away with him from his old bad influences, away from toxic environments. Not that it's stopped him from finding *new* bad influences, but still.

Messica was specifically asked to stay out of his life. He made it clear. But does she respect boundaries? Of course not. And now I'm discovering that he's kept this from me for two weeks.

"She left a voicemail on my birthday," he says, his tone annoyingly casual, like this revelation isn't a bombshell.

"And you didn't think to tell me?" I demand, my voice rising.

He shrugs. "I knew you'd act like this."

Oh, fantastic. Not only did he hide this from me, but now he's trying to paint *me* as the bad guy. *Typical.* I feel the heat of anger bubbling beneath my skin, threatening to boil over.

I'm starting to realize that neither of them must have very many friends. Their friendship is highly toxic.

Hell, maybe she'd be a better fit for him. Maybe they deserve each other.

Two miserable, toxic messes, hellbent on destruction of themselves and everyone around them.

"She's not respecting your boundaries," I say through gritted teeth. "You told her not to message you, and here she is. Again. Sending you selfies of the two of you, which is frankly *weird.*"

"Yeah, it *is* weird," Timmy agrees. "It's not okay for her to be doing it."

"So, did you block her?"

"No." He shakes his head.

"Are you going to?" I quirk a brow.

"No."

I blink, stunned. "Um, *why not?*"

He's refusing to block Slutterfly? Why?

"She's insane," he says, as if this explains everything. "If I block her, she'll just start calling me from weird numbers. She'll know she's been blocked."

"You can't tell when you're blocked." His response makes no sense whatsoever.

"Yeah, you can," he insists. "The messages turn green instead of blue."

"Why do you care what she thinks?"

"I don't," he snaps. "I just don't want to deal with it. I knew you'd act like this when I told you she reached out."

"How did you *expect* me to react, Timmy?"

He smirks, leaning back in his chair. "*Your* ex reached out to *you.*"

I roll my eyes so hard I can almost see the back of my skull. "Someone I haven't spoken to in *nine years,* who lives on the *other side of the country,* and whom I promptly told to *fuck off.*"

He'd reached out to tell me he found an item of my clothing at his place. To which I'd wanted to reply that maybe he should clean his house more often. Instead, I'd dismissed him completely and blocked him.

"That's a *little* different from some… person you hooked up with *last year* who's now conveniently staying *less than an hour away and wants to hang out.*"

"It's pretty similar," he says, shrugging.

"It's… *not at all similar*!" I snap, feeling my blood pressure spike. "The two things don't compare at all!"

"And you don't have to worry about her," he says smugly. "She's annoying as fuck. She's basically banned from every bar and restaurant in town. She's a mess, and I want nothing to do with her. Still, you need to stop being such a hypocrite with your ex texting you."

I feel like I'm losing my mind. "If you told me straight away that she had messaged you and left a voicemail, I wouldn't have been upset, because that's out of your control. What I *am* upset about is that you deleted the voicemail, kept it from me for two weeks, and let her cross this line and now you're not blocking her."

"Well, I knew you'd be upset."

"No," I counter. "I'm upset with *Matty* for supposedly giving her your number after you changed it to block her. But honestly? I don't know what to believe anymore. For all I know, you gave her your number yourself."

His face flickers for a moment, a shadow of guilt. Or maybe that's just my imagination. He's mastered the art of keeping just enough plausible deniability. He's blaming Matty, but I don't know what to believe anymore. For all I know, he didn't block her on all social media—maybe he *is* the one who gave her his number.

Either way, the damage is done. I feel sick to my stomach. All the time, love, and financial resources I've poured into him, and *this* is the thanks I get? He wants to keep talking to someone who doesn't respect his boundaries, who clearly has no respect for *me*?

I'm so disgusted, I may never eat again.

I glance at his face and catch something that chills me to my core. It's not a full smirk, but it's close.

Is he enjoying this? Does he like seeing me upset, thinking I'm jealous?

The truth is, I'm not jealous about Leftover Lucy. I'm *pissed*. I'm angry that someone who actively disrespects him—and by extension our relationship—is allowed any access to him.

I told Timmy immediately when my ex contacted me. I even showed him the message I sent back telling the guy to get lost.

But Timmy? He's all about creating false equivalencies. He acts like my ex—someone I haven't spoken to in a *decade*—is somehow the same as his recent hookup sending him selfies and texts saying she's nearby.

The constant double standard of expectations for my and his behavior drives me nuts.

I feel the resentment clawing its way up my throat. He told me he didn't want to drag me down. But I've introduced him to successful, kind people. He's introduced me to an abusive drug dealer, a jobless mooch, and the meth addicts on the beach. I've taken him to nice restaurants, and he's thrown food I've bought for us in the trash.

And now? Now, I'm terrified. Terrified that he'll keep dragging me lower and lower until there's nothing left of me—no savings, no job, no self-esteem.

And then?

Then he'll run off to someone else, leaving me in the rubble of the life I built before he came along.

————

I talk to my therapist about it. "He says this situation is the same as my ex texting me, and it's *driving me insane.*"

She laughs softly, shaking her head. "That's apples and oranges. Those two situations are *nothing* alike."

"That's what *I* thought! But he's so adamant…"

She sighs. "It sounds like he's trying to make you question yourself, to deflect the blame. And honestly? It sounds like he's enjoying the chaos."

I nod, feeling validated for the first time in days. Of course, that's exactly what he's doing. Triangulating. Stirring the pot. Keeping himself entertained by my discomfort.

But instead of feeling jealous, I just feel… disappointed and grossed out.

Disappointed that this is the man I chose to share my life with—a man who thrives on chaos and refuses to protect the sanctity of our relationship.

Grossed out that he seems not to be at all picky about the women he sleeps with—god knows what he's been doing each time he's left for hours.

He swears he's never cheated on me, and that he never would—but I know he's cheated on at least one girlfriend before, and he tends to make everything someone else's fault.

Back-Burner Barbie can have him. Let her.

I'm beginning to see that Forgetabelle and Timmy deserve each other—*a perfect pair of self-absorbed, ugly disasters.*

CHAPTER 126
EMOTIONAL VAMPIRE

MARGAUX

The next morning, I'm working and I see him stir beside me.

"Good morning!" I say brightly. An attempt to start the day out on a good note.

He shakes his head and scoffs. "You always wake up and you're so cute to me the next day. It won't fly this time!"

I peer at him, feeling my exhaustion weigh heavier than my anger. "No, Timmy. That's *you.* You wake up and act sweet, trying to reorient yourself. I'm just trying to reset, trying to give you and the day a chance to be positive. But it feels like a waste, bruh—because *you've* proven—over and over—that you're angrier, meaner, especially in the evenings. Not just when you're drinking, but even when you're not."

He looks at me, blank-faced, but I can see the storm brewing beneath his surface.

"I'm the one who has to pay for your moods," I say quietly. "And frankly, I'm tired of it."

———

A while later, his demeanor changes. He's suddenly all soft smiles and gentle words, his eyes warm again. "I'm sorry," he says, his tone dripping with sincerity. "I've been thinking about things, and I apologize for the way I acted. You deserve better. I'm going to treat you so much better."

I want to believe him. His kindness feels like a balm, soothing the wounds he inflicted just hours before. His smile is almost enough to make me forget the cruelty.

Almost.

Maybe he's right, too—maybe I did contribute to the issues we've been facing.

But I know better than to trust his words—I've been to this rodeo, seen this cycle play out way too many times.

I've been burned by the sweetness that always precedes the storm.

Later that evening, a chilling thought crosses my mind.

They say if you die, your cat will eat you.

I know Sabre wouldn't do that, at least not right away.

He'd snuggle up next to me, his warm body pressed against mine, until he couldn't anymore.

Maybe then, and only then, would he eat me.

But Timmy?

If I died, I realize, he wouldn't call an ambulance or the police right away.

No, he'd probably wander around the apartment first, scavenging for things to sell. He'd rifle through my belongings, figuring out what could bring in quick cash and what he wanted to keep for himself.

And then, maybe after a few days, he'd report it.

The thought sends an icy chill through my entire body.

The person I thought cared for me most doesn't care at all.

Timmy. Is. Not. Here. For. Me.

———

Later, Timmy is pacing around the apartment, muttering to himself.

"You know, you treat people just like the pigeons and ducks you like to feed so much," I say, finally seeing him for what he is.

He stops pacing, his brow furrowed. "What the hell are you talking about?"

"You throw them little chunks of bread so they'll come to you. They land on you, make a big fuss over you, and in that moment, you feel adored and special. And you do the same to humans. You throw people just enough emotional breadcrumbs to make them run to you and make you feel adored and admired and special. Just enough to keep them on the hook."

"That's not true," he says, his voice defensive.

I press on. "You do it to me, to Matty, hell, even to Skank Pants. Keep us around for when you need us. The rest of the time, you behave like a monster. But we let it slide because those breadcrumbs, as small as they are, are just enough to make us stay. They're delicious, even though they're not nearly enough to sustain anyone. And when you've had enough of what you want, you withhold the bread until you feel us pulling away, and then you toss another crumb."

He stares at me, his expression unreadable.

"Do you understand how fucked up that is?" I ask, my voice breaking.

"And when it comes to your parents, you're even worse! You don't even try to disguise it. 'Mommy I love you. Mommy, mommy, mommy.' What forty-year-old talks like that?

And you basically throw entire loaves of bread at your dad so you keep him wrapped around your little finger. 'Dad, I'm so proud of your career, both in the military and out. I wish I could be just like you when I grow up. I'm sorry I didn't make it into the military, but other people in the family did, thank goodness! I just want to sit here and tell you how proud I am of you.' You make me throw up. And the worst part is, it's so overt and yet your flying monkey of a father falls for it hook, line and sinker, and then he enables you to keep doing it to him and everyone else."

His face crumbles slightly. "Is that what you really think of me?"

"It's not what I *think*, Timmy. It's what I *know*. You're a textbook narcissist. And don't try to twist this around and say that I am, because I'm *not*. You don't just have manipulative tendencies. You're the whole fucking narcissistic enchilada."

"I don't want to be like this anymore," he says quietly. "I want to change."

"Well, unfortunately for you, this type of behavior, these patterns you have? They're almost incurable. I listened to an expert the other day, and she said she's only ever seen one or two people out of hundreds truly change. And even then, it took years of intensive therapy with multiple therapists, costing hundreds of thousands of dollars. And the kicker is, it only worked because they genuinely *wanted* to change."

"I *do* want to change!"

"No, you don't," I say, my voice firm. "This sad mode of operation you've lived in your entire life serves you too well. It gives you access to lifestyles you haven't earned and people who are, quite frankly, better than you. And you derive a special kind of joy from being an emotional vampire, sucking the joy out of everyone around you for your own gain."

"An emotional vampire?"

"Yes, Timmy. I'm sorry to say it because it breaks my heart, but that's what you are."

He turns away, but I see the slight tremble in his shoulders. Whether it's from anger or something else, I don't know.

What I do know is that I'm done.

Done being a pigeon, done being his emotional supply.

And done believing that Team Ginger Shark was ever anything more than a mirage.

CHAPTER 127

THE LAST FUCKING STRAW (IS GORDON RAMSAY)

MARGAUX

've been diving more and more into the subject of narcissistic relationships, lately. *Obsessively*. It's become a compulsion, because every article, every case study, every description of a narcissist feels like it's been ripped straight from Timmy's playbook.

If there were a picture of a narcissist in the dictionary, Timmy wouldn't just have a photo—he'd have a full multi-page spread.

The more I read, the clearer it becomes. Survivors of narcissistic abuse rarely leave because of the physical or psychological torture. It's usually something tangential, something seemingly small compared to the magnitude of the abuse itself.

A moment that lights the final match.

For many, it's cheating.

For me, though, that final match is Gordon Ramsay.

The producer of *MasterChef* calls me, her voice bubbling with excitement.

"Margaux! Oh my gosh, we *loved* your audition tape and application! We'd like to consider you and Timmy for the show, but we need him to submit his separate application."

I'm elated. The upcoming season is going to feature couples, and it sounds like they're interested in *us!* This is *huge*.

I run to Timmy, grinning ear to ear.

"Timmy, you have to fill out the application!" I say, pointing to his laptop. "This is *so* exciting!"

He looks at the form and grows quiet. At first, I think he's concentrating —reading isn't his strong suit, after all—but deep down, I know what's really happening.

It's the passport question.

Still, he says nothing.

We record a second video, explaining why we'd be ideal cast members. For a brief moment, I see a flicker of the Timmy I fell for—the funny, creative, charming guy who could light up a room.

He banters with me, his eyes kind, his smile charming. And for a fleeting second, I believe in the facade again.

It would be silly for the producers not to cast us.

But my gut nags at me. I know he doesn't have a passport. I know that might sink our chances of appearing on the show.

Surely he can get one, though? It might cost a few hundred dollars to expedite it, but it would be worth it to be able to travel.

I look at the passport site, and then it hits me—if you have outstanding child support, you cannot get a passport. I had no idea.

It would literally cost about thirty thousand dollars for Timmy to get a passport.

Not only will we not be selected for the show. Timmy is never going to be able to travel with me.

Right after learning Timmy can't travel, I hop into the beater truck—a gift from his ex, not something he earned—and dial into my therapy session.

Kathleen, my therapist, is my emotional rock. She's been my anchor on this part of the Cay, and I've been dreading her departure as she wraps up her postgraduate studies. Today is our final session.

"How do you feel about not being able to go overseas with Timmy?" she asks after I fill her in.

"He's like the gift that keeps on giving—I never know what wonderful new thing he's going to find to torture me with, or that I'm going to find he's been hiding from me."

Kathleen laughs softly. "The gift that keeps on giving—that really does describe Timmy, doesn't it?"

"Honestly," I begin, "if I'd known all of this earlier, it would've been a deal breaker. Travel is one of my greatest passions. And if I'd known he had a kid—especially one he owed thirty grand in back child support for—well, I think that would have been a deal breaker too. These are things I never signed up for."

Her voice softens. "What do you want in a partner, Margaux? Taking Timmy out of the equation, what do you need in a relationship? An equal? A provider?"

I think for a moment. "An equal," I say finally. "I don't necessarily need someone to provide for me, but I want a partner who pulls their weight. Someone who shares my love for adventure and travel. I'm going to travel with or without Timmy, though—I'm not going to give up that part of my life because of yet another of his terrible life choices. But I know if I leave him behind, he'll make it a living hell. He'll sulk, he'll accuse me of cheating, he'll talk about meeting up with other women—it's not worth the stress. I'd be worrying about what he was up to the entire time—it would be miserable."

Kathleen doesn't hold back. "We get one hundred years on this earth if we're lucky. You need to think about what you want, and whether Timmy fits into that or not." She pauses. "Margaux, you are one of the most generous, kind, empathetic, beautiful, smart, and wonderful human beings I've ever met. I understand why you love him, and why you're still with him, but at the end of the day, I will always be one hundred percent Team Margaux."

Talk about a mic drop moment.

Her words are a gut punch, but the kind I need.

And I know she's right. I've known she's been right all along.

I tear up, and we end our call.

I'm really going to miss her.

I'm sitting in a fucking beater truck, looking around at the cockroaches scuttling across the dashboard, the ants crawling along the door.

This is what I've been reduced to—taking therapy calls in a dilapidated truck because Timmy eavesdropped on my intake session, and I can't trust him not to invade my privacy.

It's pathetic.

I think about all the things Timmy has already stolen from me.

Gordon Ramsay is the latest. But before him, there was Chelsea Handler —he tried to ruin that night. Before her, Machine Gun Kelly—whose music I still listen to, though it stings. Sunset Cay, once a paradise, is now tainted by his toxic presence. He's eroded my relationship with my sister. He's damaged my self-esteem beyond recognition. He's broken my fucking skull.

He's taken so much from me.

But he will not *take travel.*

Sure, I live in one of the most beautiful locations on the planet, but I'm still getting that itch to explore. I've talked about travel plans *with* Timmy, and he's gone along with it, future faking about how excited he is to travel with me, knowing full well that he can't.

I picture him sulking at home while I explore Europe or Asia or New Zealand while he lines up women on Tinder or reconnects with Back-Burner Barbie.

The thought is nauseating.

Then he'd accuse me of cheating when I was away, even though he'd be the only one in our relationship with that on their bingo card.

No. That's just not going to work for me.

I meant what I said to Kathleen—I *do* want an equal. A partner. Someone who contributes to our relationship just as much as I do—hell, maybe even a fraction more. I'd be okay with that.

And I'm done.

He's not my equal.

He's a black hole, sucking in all the light and joy from my life.

He manipulates, he lies, he projects his insecurities onto me, and he calls *me* the villain.

But not anymore.

This is the last fucking straw.

CHAPTER 128
TRAVEL BAN

When I get back from my therapy appointment, Timmy is doing the dishes.

I contemplate how to approach him about how upset I am that we can't 1) go on the show, and 2) travel.

I know it's never smart to bring up any difficult topics because he'll make me pay for it, but I'm so fed up by now. I have to say something.

And I decide to add in the part about how I'm feeling about his parents.

"Timmy, I need to talk to you about something," I say, my voice low.

He pauses from his dishwashing activities and glances over at me, his body tensing as if preparing for a physical blow. "What now?" His voice is sharp. "And really? Do you have to have a conversation with me while I'm trying to do the dishes?"

The way he says it, you'd think I was interrupting him from performing brain surgery or launching a spaceship.

But I plow on ahead. I can't stop myself.

This time, I *won't* stop myself. *I won't hold back.*

"Well, first of all... I'm getting the feeling your parents really don't like me very much at all. But they seem to be in touch with all of your exes, sending them and their children gifts, lending Jennifer your car, talking about them as if your relationships with them all were just yesterday. They have a genuine affection for these women who you say are all awful bitches.

But when it comes to me, they—especially your dad—seem to have a real problem with me. Your dad called me a 'volcano of pain,' for god's sake." I roll my eyes. "I mean, I don't know exactly what you've been saying about me, but I feel like they love everyone you've ever dated, but can't stand me. That makes me feel like shit."

"Really, Margaux?" He rolls his eyes. "I don't think they're in touch with any of them. I didn't know they were sending gifts."

"Well, your mom was talking about Victoria's kids and sending them presents."

"Oh," he says.

"And the other thing…"

This is it… the big one.

I take another breath.

"It really bothers me that I just found out you can't travel. It's one thing that we can't go on the show because of it, and that upsets me. But what's even more upsetting is that you weren't transparent with me—that you can't travel, or that it would cost thirty *thousand* dollars to be able to travel overseas together. You know how important travel is to me, and I can't even count the number of times I've mentioned going somewhere with you, and you've failed to mention that you can't. And the reason you can't travel—because you have a teenage child—you hid that from me too. And it's a big deal. I might not have started dating you had I known any of these things."

Timmy's eyes grow dark and his body tenses further.

Without a word—and with eyes shooting daggers of hatred in my direction, he walks to the fridge. He picks up the sourdough starter, removes the lid, and then returns to the kitchen counter. He shoves all of the newly cleaned dishes into the sink.

My jaw drops as he pours gooey sourdough starter all over the clean dishes, undoing his chore.

It makes no sense, and only serves to anger me. It's a punctuation, an advertisement of his absolute vindictiveness. The way that I can mention nothing for fear of upsetting him, because there will almost certainly be retaliation.

As I sit here in jaded semi-disbelief, I realize with chilling clarity that the thought I had the other day was accurate. This demon is so vile, so deranged, so self-serving, that if I was to die—whether by his hand or just randomly—he wouldn't call the police straight away. He wouldn't make it a priority to try and get me medical help, to make sure it wasn't too late.

No, I can picture him walking around the apartment, assessing the value of items and deciding if any would be beneficial to him.

Deciding how to best position himself in the story, to garner the most sympathy and attention.

And I realize, again with a laser-sharp clarity that slices through my hazy brain fog, that he's taken nearly everything from me.

He's damaged, broken, slashed and shattered physical property, my mind—hell, even my skull—and the only things I have left are Sabre and my life.

And there's no doubt in my mind he's coming for those next.

CHAPTER 129
FALLBACK FIONA

DEX

It's late evening when my phone buzzes on the counter, Timmy's name lighting up the screen as his phone's contents are revealed to me. Against my better judgment, I glance at it. A message preview: *I'm on the island. It's your evil twin.*

Oh, for fuck's sake.

I shouldn't care. I shouldn't even bother opening this Pandora's box of idiocy, but the sheer audacity compels me.

Sure enough, Timmy's latest mess involves Low-Value Linda—the human equivalent of toxic sludge in a bikini. And here she is, back to haunt Margaux's life like a low-budget ghost that won't stop rattling its chains.

My jaw tightens as I piece together what's happening. Timmy, ever the emotional opportunist, must have been nurturing Scraplyn's delusions on the sly. I'm not privy to every pathetic detail, but I don't need to be. I can picture Margaux's expression when she finds out—tight-lipped, brow furrowed, exhaustion pooling behind her eyes.

She doesn't deserve this. *Not again.*

And Timmy? He's eating it up. He thrives on triangulation, turning the people around him into pawns in his perpetual chess game of victimhood. He'll act like a helpless idiot—"What could I do? She's persistent!"—while secretly relishing the chaos. It's pathetic. No, it's beyond pathetic. It's fucking laughable.

But Fallback Fiona isn't even the worst of it.

The real tragedy? Watching Margaux's excitement over the *MasterChef* opportunity evaporate because Timmy couldn't bother to handle his shit.

Thirty grand in back child support. *Thirty. Thousand. Dollars.*

A debt that renders him unable to get a passport and destroys their shot at the show.

And he didn't tell her until the last possible second. In fact, he didn't tell her at all. She figured it out for herself.

I've overheard enough to paint the picture—Margaux, practically vibrating with hope, giddy about filming with Gordon Ramsay. Then Timmy —dead-eyed, fidgeting—mumbling some excuse about the 'system' being unfair.

Timmy painting himself as the victim once again.

"Unfair?" I mutter to no one. "You're lucky the universe doesn't slap you every time you open your mouth, Timmy. Now *that's* unfair."

When she mentions it to Alice, her words are brittle with disbelief.

MARGAUX:

> He knew. He knew the whole time and said nothing. Now we're out of the running. I can't even look at him. But worse than that, I can't travel.

ALICE:

> I'm not shocked.

> But Timmy couldn't survive five minutes in front of Gordon Ramsay, anyway. You know that.

Margaux lets out a small, exhausted laugh.

MARGAUX:

> You're probably right. Ramsay would rip him to shreds.

Still, it's enough to cheer her up. I can feel the weight pressing down on her, the realization that this—this constant cycle of disappointment—is her life now.

Or maybe—just maybe—this is the final nudge she needs to break away.

CHAPTER 130
I'M DONE

MARGAUX

t's time to end things. *Beyond time.*

"Timmy," I say, glancing at him as he sits on the bed next to me, frowning. "Enough is enough. I can't be with you any more. We're breaking up. I mean it this time."

"I agree," he says. "You're not good for me."

He retreats to the back room, and I hear his muffled voice on the phone.

A few minutes later, he returns.

"Dad said he'd fly me back on Tuesday," he says. "I'm going to Montana so I don't have to be around you."

It's Thursday. I just have to hang on for five more days. I can do this.

I nod. "Okay, that's good," I say.

His expression turns. "You have a sickness!" he yells, gesticulating wildly at the TV. "You have an illness from watching… these shows! This is why you're such a cunt! I can't stand your shows, and I can't stand *you!*"

"Okay, Timmy," I say.

Gray rock, gray rock.

"You're such a fucking cunt, you know that?"

I don't respond, just look at him blankly.

"I'm so sick of hearing about you being raped," he sneers.

I haven't mentioned it in at least six months, and the words hit like a slap, but I say nothing. Correcting him isn't going to help. My stomach churns.

What a horrible thing for anybody to say, especially someone who claims to love you and care about you.

"And I'm so sick of hearing about your *dead uncle*."

I feel bile rise in my throat. The words hit like a sucker punch, each one calculated to wound. It's like he's wielding a scalpel, cutting precisely where he knows it will hurt most.

But I haven't mentioned my uncle for at least six months, either. Especially because Timmy clearly seemed to have a problem whenever I did—said I had an 'unhealthy obsession' with him. But again, no point in correcting him.

"And I'm so sick of hearing about your fucking *period!*" he finishes, his voice dripping with disgust.

Wow, the times he claimed to support me each month while I writhed in pain.

I guess it all meant nothing to him.

I stare at him, incredulous. I can't stay silent. "What the hell?" I snap. "I have *endometriosis* and *adenomyosis*," I snap. "I'm in *excruciating* pain every month. I *have* to talk about it."

It's kind of hard not to when it leaves me incapacitated, vomiting, and bedridden every month.

"Well, I'm sick of it," he says. "And I can't wait until I don't have to hear about it anymore."

What an odd choice of things to criticize me for—what a barrage of low blows.

But to hear him spew these topics back at me with such venom? It's like he's gone into a new level of cruelty.

Shit. I'm not going to make a dent in his logic, and he's just lashing out.

Gray rock, gray rock.

His frown grows deeper, his gaze locked with mine. "You are not my penguin anymore."

The words hit harder than I expect, but I don't let it show.

Instead, I nod. "No, I'm not. And I never really was."

———

I feel foolish for everything I've poured into this man. The time, the money, the love—it all feels wasted on someone who never truly loved me back.

He didn't love *me.*

He loved the way I made him feel about himself.

Part of me still wants to believe he cares. That he's just broken and unable to show it. But then I remember his rage.

His hatred of women.

The way he's left a trail of destruction through his relationships, each one worse than the last.

He'll kill someone someday. I'm certain of it.

Maybe it'll be the next partner who can't meet his impossible expectations.

Maybe it'll be someone at a bar who 'hurts his feelings.'

Hell, maybe it'll even be his own father, when the man finally stops enabling him.

They say a narcissist's mask can only stay on for about 120 days. That tracks almost perfectly with how long it took Timmy to reveal his true self after the period of calm—the selfish, manipulative, rage-filled man behind the charming facade.

And I just have to make it through to Tuesday to be out of this nightmare.

———

Timmy starts removing items from the apartment one by one.

First, it's the jungle of plants outside the screen door. He starts with the plant that Francois lives in—a little lizard I've named who comes and looks at me and Sabre throughout the day. It's a petty act—something he knows will make me sad.

Then it's his tools. "Please leave your tools here," I say. "I can maybe sell them to pay back some of the money you owe me."

He narrows his eyes at me. "Oh you can keep them. My sentimental value for them is *ten thousand dollars.*" There's a chill in his voice that sends a shiver down my spine.

"Timmy, please, you're being ridiculous."

He shoves past me and walks off with his bag of tools, bulging at the seams. Definitely not worth ten thousand dollars, but certainly a few hundred.

Next, it's the rice cooker. He walks it over to the meth tents.

I call Phil. "Please help," I beg. "He's removing items from the apartment and taking them over to the meth tents. Plants, his tools, now the rice cooker."

"Well, I know he's upset," says Phil. "You must have upset him again. It takes two, you know."

I snap, blood boiling in my temples. I want to reach through the phone and grab his throat and squeeze and squeeze until his eyeballs bulge from their sockets.

What an absolute fucking moron.

"It doesn't fucking take two!" I scream into the phone. "I can't *breathe* without him getting mad at me. *Don't you understand that your son has a real problem?"*

Timmy's dad, Phil, sighs heavily. "Well, I don't necessarily agree with all that," he says. "I'll talk to him in the morning."

If both of us are still alive by then, I think grimly.

I shudder, the instinctive fear in my body moving faster than my mind can process. Somewhere deep inside, I know my mortality—and Sabre's—is in real danger. But this idiot on the other end of the line can't—*or won't*— see it.

We hang up. I'm seething, and I need a drink to calm my shattered nerves.

With a friend on speakerphone to make me feel safer about navigating a path full of tweakers, I walk to the convenience store up the street. On the other side of the street, I see Timmy standing with his arm propped up against the entrance to a large tent, holding court with some of his meth friends. One of the few white male surfer-looking guys in the entire neighborhood. It's most definitely him.

I don't acknowledge him or any of the people he's with. I just keep walking, and return home with a bottle of wine and some vodka.

I call Phil, beyond annoyed.

"He's at the meth tents," I say, my voice tight with frustration. "I just saw him there."

"No he's not," Phil scoffs, as if I'm a delusional idiot—*projection, I guess.* "He's at the beach *near* the tents. He's not *at* the tents."

I nearly drop the phone. "I was standing here—*looking at him*—and you're several states away." I roll my eyes. "But sure, Phil. Go ahead and tell me what I'm seeing."

"Well, he's not at the tents," he says dismissively.

Okay, moron. I can physically see your son and you're in a whole other city, but believe what you want.

Fucking idiot.

Blood rushes to my temples. "Your son *told me* he lies to you. He admits it. And you *fall for it every fucking time.*"

"There's no need to swear," Phil says, his tone scolding. Why don't you just leave?" he asks.

Blood hammers in my temples. I'm literally repeating what his son said, and his dad is acting like I'm making it all up.

"Because he's done things like pour water all over my laptop. And threatened to kill my cat."

"Margaux, you really need to stop dredging up the past," Phil says. I want to leap through the phone and kill this man. I would enjoy every second of it. What a fucking dimwit.

"Phil," I say, my voice dangerously low, "if you could get your head out of your ass for two seconds, maybe we wouldn't be having this conversation."

CHAPTER 131
(IF I'M ALIVE TO) SEE YOU NEXT TUESDAY

MARGAUX

'm texting my friend Sheryl, a fellow Kiwi with a heart of gold and a voice that could make angels jealous. She came to the States on a singing scholarship, and we bonded instantly over our shared homeland and mutual tendency to find humor in the chaos of life.

I tell her about life in Sunset Cay and update her on my breakup with Timmy. I vent about the exhausting tension in the apartment, and my hope that we can ride out the next five days peacefully as he packs and leaves.

But that hope? Utterly misplaced.

Timmy has been muttering and glaring from the back room all morning, darting out and slamming back in like some demented jack-in-the-box. His energy is suffocating, his presence a storm cloud blotting out any light or peace.

I feel his eyes on me long before I see him. He emerges from the back room, his movements deliberate and cold, and strides toward me.

"Give me your phone," he snaps, reaching for it. "*Who* have you been messaging with all morning?"

I tighten my grip, my pulse quickening. For the first time in a long time, I feel a jolt of real fear. He's not just trying to take my phone—he's trying to sever my lifeline—my connection to the outside world, to safety, to anyone who could intervene.

"I've seen you chatting with someone for the past thirty minutes," he accuses, his voice low and venomous.

It hits me then—he's been spying on me. He must have left the door ajar just enough to watch me while pretending to sulk.

The realization is chilling.

"Who is he? Who are you cheating on me with?" His words drip with manufactured outrage.

I blink, utterly floored. "Cheating? Are you *serious?* I'm texting *Sheryl.* My *friend.* A *woman.* In *New York.* Not that it's any of your business."

He doesn't let up. "I don't believe you. You're lying. I've been watching you."

My frustration boils over. "Timmy, for the love of God, I've broken up with you. You're moving out. Who I talk to is none of your business. And for the record, *I'm not cheating on you.*"

That's when it happens. His eyes narrow, dark and predatory, and he spits on me.

The wet glob lands on my arm, and I freeze.

It's not the first time he's done this, but it doesn't make it any less jarring. The sheer disdain you must feel for another human being to *spit* on them… it's beyond comprehension.

It's dehumanizing.

"Wow," I whisper, shaking my head.

This 'man' is truly delusional.

He stomps to the back room, and I start to walk down the hallway to clean the spit off me, when he suddenly flips around and *charges* at me. His shoulder slams into mine, knocking me off balance.

His eyes are different now. Reptilian. *Dead.*

I've seen this look several times before, and it terrifies me every time.

It's the look of a man who has no humanity left, who is running purely on rage and hatred.

He could kill me in this moment, and I know he wouldn't feel a shred of remorse.

But he doesn't grab a knife. He doesn't make a death threat—though I'm absolutely certain those will come soon.

Instead, he storms out, slamming the door so hard that the walls shake.

I stand, frozen for a moment, trembling, covered in his spit and the weight of his words. My heart pounds in my chest, the adrenaline coursing through my veins.

And then I move.

I grab my fanny pack and shove my essentials into it. I lace up my shoes with shaking hands.

There's no time to process, no time to cry.

I'm done waiting for him to calm down. I'm done hoping he'll pack up and leave quietly.

Timmy is dangerous.

If I don't act now, I'll become another statistic in a story that far too many women share.

And I know one thing with terrifying clarity: if I don't get a restraining order today—and make sure the police serve it properly this time—I won't be alive by Tuesday.

CHAPTER 132
MELTDOWN

MARGAUX

arrive at the courthouse, a building I now know too well. The sheer absurdity of this knowledge isn't lost on me. Before Timmy, I never had to know where a courthouse was—much less navigate one like a seasoned local. Yet here I am, walking up the familiar steps, resigned to another chapter in this nightmare.

At the sign-in desk, I'm handed a wristband. It's a fluorescent strip denoting me as a victim—or survivor, depending on how charitable you want to be with the terminology. This isn't a wristband for a VIP concert or a fun amusement park ride. This is a badge of shame, burning into my arm like a brand.

With trembling hands, I fill out the restraining order paperwork. Each word feels heavy as I document the abuse, line by line.

Poured water over my laptop.

Fractured my skull because he didn't like the song I was playing and punched me.

Poured boiling hot water on me.

Tried to shove deer antlers into my anus.

SMASHED THE TOILET AND A POT PLANT WITH A HAMMER,
SAYING HE WOULD DO IT TO ME NEXT.
SPAT ON ME MULTIPLE TIMES.
PSYCHOLOGICAL ABUSE: NAME-CALLING, MENTIONING MY
SEXUAL ASSAULT TO HURT ME.

My handwriting is shaky, adrenaline coursing through me. The more I write, the more I realize how much I've normalized. Each incident flashes in my mind like scenes from a horror movie I've accidentally lived.

While I sit and wait for my turn to submit my paperwork, I do something I rarely do.

I'm sick of being quiet.

I'm sick of being ashamed and alone.

I'm sick of Timmy and his dad making me feel like a vile piece of shit when *they* are the problems.

So I have a mental breakdown-slash-emotional meltdown on Facebook and post a raw, unfiltered cry for help.

I'm at the courthouse getting a restraining order.

The outpouring of support is immediate.

VANESSA:

> Hey, I saw your recent posts. I don't know what exactly is going on, but I just want to send you love and support. I was in a similar situation once a long time ago… more than once… anyway, the aftermath of those situations left me a very different person than I was before. All of this is to say that, once the immediate dust has settled, if you're able to find it on you to do so, find a way to get someone to talk to. I don't know anyone in Sunset Cay (assuming that's where you still are), but I can give you the name of someone amazing who is located in NYC and I think can do Zoom.

RAQUEL:

Hi, sweetheart. I am so saddened that you are going
through something so horrifying. I have been there,
6+ years of hell. You must alert authorities. You must
reach out to professionals. You should probably stop
posting to social media if he gets a rise out of this.
Tell all your friends, family, baristas, whomever, so
they know if anything happens to you. His behavior
is not funny or a joke. Please, please reach out to
me at any time. I had a gun put to my head as my
last straw. Please don't go the same way I did.
Love you.

The comments buoy me, a small but powerful reminder that people care.

Finally, it's my turn to submit my paperwork. I hand the form to the courthouse advocate, who scans it. "You missed a date here," he says, pointing to a blank line.

"Oh, sorry," I mutter, filling it in quickly.

"You say you want him to stay away from you for two years? Make it longer," he suggests.

"What do you suggest?"

"I'd put fifty, but you put as long as you want."

I think about it. My mind is still ensconced in fog. I cross out '2' and replace it with a '10'.

"Alright," he continues, "the judge will review these within the next two hours. Come back then, and if they sign off, we'll have the paperwork for you."

If.

The weight of that word presses on me. *If.* As though all of this—his violence, his threats, his unrelenting campaign to terrorize me—is still up for debate.

———

I leave the courthouse, my feet heavy, my chest tight. Back at the truck, I sit for a moment, staring at the dashboard. The phone rings, jolting me from my thoughts.

It's Phil.

I hesitate but answer. "Hello?"

Phil's voice is sharp, accusatory. "Margaux. I need to talk to you about this situation with Timmy. He says you're trying to ruin his life."

My stomach churns. "Phil, he's been charging at me and spitting on me and trying to grab my phone. I had to leave the apartment. I'm scared."

Phil sighs heavily. "Well, he's threatening to kill himself. He says you're at the courthouse trying to put him in jail."

My breath catches.

How the fuck does Timmy know where I am?

I turned off my location days ago. He shouldn't have any way to track me.

"I *am* at the courthouse," I say, keeping my voice calm. "But I'm not trying to put him in jail. I'm here because he's been violent, and I don't feel safe."

Phil cuts me off. "Hold on. I'm putting Timmy on the line."

A few seconds later, Timmy's voice bursts through, frantic and slurred. *"Dad! Dad! She's trying to ruin my life! She wants to put me in jail!"*

Phil jumps in. "Tell him you're not trying to put him in jail, Margaux. Tell him now."

"I'm not trying to put you in jail," I say flatly. "I just need to feel safe, Timmy. That's all."

Phil seizes on my words. "Son, did you hear that? She's not trying to put you in jail."

The conversation dissolves into an incoherent back-and-forth between Timmy and Phil. I sit silently, stunned by the absurdity. Phil's coddling tone, his constant placation—it's nauseating. It's like watching a grown man breastfeed his forty-year-old son.

Timmy hangs up in a fit of self-pity. Phil doesn't miss a beat. *"See? See* what you've done, Margaux? I need to go now. I'm going to have a dead son now, *because of you.* Buh-bye."

The line goes dead.

I sit there, my jaw slack, my heart racing. How do two people twist reality so completely? How do they make everything about me when Timmy is the one who's violent and unhinged?

Talk about a shared delusion.

I don't have a vendetta to get Timmy locked up for the rest of his life— which, frankly, I should have. I'm just way too exhausted, and not a vindictive piece of shit like him.

I just want him out of my life so he can't hurt me anymore.

———

The realization hits me like a freight train.

Fuck.

Sabre is back at the apartment.

I must go save him.

I'll drive back and then bring him back to the courthouse with me. Because I can't leave him alone in the apartment with Timmy in this state.

He knows how much I love that cat. He knows Sabre is my world.

Timmy is spiraling, knowing he's lost all control over me.

This is a very dangerous time for everyone. In his current state, there's no telling what he might do.

Especially for me. And for my cat.

I fire up the truck and race back toward the apartment as quickly as I can, every second feeling like an eternity, the brutal heat making me feel even more flustered and on edge.

On the way, I call Jo.

"Margaux, I want to let you know I'm just so proud of you," she says. "I know, from personal experience, how hard it is to leave a relationship like this, but you're doing the right thing. You're getting out, and you're doing it the right way. I'm so glad you're not getting your own Dateline episode."

The drive itself is frustrating, with only one lane in and one lane out of this part of the Cay. The road wraps around the coast, hosting both laidback locals and easygoing tourists who've come to explore the area's rugged, natural beauty.

There's an ambulance in front of me, and for a moment I think his father might be right—he might have actually tried to kill himself. But it pulls into the high school next to my apartment complex.

For a fraction of a second I wonder if he's gone there to do something silly—and I won't lie—for that instant, *I wish he had.*

But let's be realistic—Timmy is a master manipulator. He's not going to harm himself—he's going to make me pay.

I pull into the parking lot, race to the apartment, and immediately scan for signs of Timmy. The coast is clear. No doubt he's still over at the meth tents concocting stories to tell his father about how horrible I am.

Whipping himself up into a homicidal rage.

Sabre meows softly when he sees me. I scoop him up and place him in his carrier. Parched by the drive and drained by my emotions, I grab two sparkling waters on my way out, and hustle back to the truck.

As I drive back to the courthouse, Sabre's sweet meows are a balm to my frazzled nerves.

"You're safe now," I whisper. "We're both going to be okay."
For the first time all day, I almost believe it.

CHAPTER 133
JAMES BOND SITUATION X SCHRODINGER'S CAT

When Sabre and I get home, clutching the freshly signed temporary restraining order, I'm greeted by an eerie silence. The apartment is still empty.

For a moment, I let myself hope. Maybe this is it—maybe he's already gone, maybe he's decided to leave me in peace.

Then I hear it. The beep. The swish of the door.

Timmy steps inside.

The air feels heavier immediately, the atmosphere suffocating. My hands tremble as I instinctively grab my phone and dial 911.

"What are you doing? Where were you?" His voice is accusatory, already teetering on the edge of fury.

The operator comes on. "Police, fire, or ambulance?"

"Police," I whisper.

Timmy's eyes narrow. "Who were you with?"

"What are you talking about?" I ask, trying to stall.

"There are *two cans* of sparkling water in the truck!" His voice rises, each word laced with venom. "Who were you driving around with? Who were you on a date with?"

"Police, state your emergency," the dispatcher says.

"I need to have someone come and serve a TRO," I manage, keeping my voice as low as possible.

Timmy doesn't seem to process what I'm doing. Instead, he barrels on with his accusations. *"You were on a date!"*

"I wasn't on a date," I snap, my voice steadier than I feel. "I was at the courthouse. Getting a *restraining order.*"

"I can't believe you," he says, his voice now low.

I can't bear to look him in the eye, and he notices.

"Look me in the eye! Do me the courtesy of looking me in the eye!"

I glance up, and the sight of him makes my mouth tremble.

"Fuck you," he says, his voice now low. "There she is. That's who you really are."

Great. He thinks I'm laughing at him. Last time he thought that, he broke my skull.

"My mouth is trembling because I'm *scared* of you, Timmy. That's why."

He shakes his head. "I should've known you would do this," he says. "You're such an abusive cunt. *How could you?*" His voice is haunting, hollow. He freezes, his face shifting from anger to disbelief. "How could you do this to *me?*"

As he rants and rambles, my mind tries to map out escape routes.

It won't be easy to get out of here, especially with Saber.

Timmy is between me and the front door, leaving the sliding door at the front as the only option. I start mentally preparing to leap to the door, unlock it and escape.

Before I can respond, there's a knock at the door. *"POLICE!"* a voice booms.

Timmy backs down the hallway as I open the door to see four officers, including the female cop with the pink handcuffs.

I hand over the paperwork, and they serve Timmy with the TRO.

He looks stunned. "But… I live here. My stuff is here."

"You'll have one opportunity to come back with a police escort to grab essentials," one of the officers explains. "But you can't come back here alone."

"I need clothes, shoes, my medication—" He's panicking now, his voice cracking in disbelief.

"Grab what you need for right now," another officer cuts him off.

Timmy moves sluggishly, clearly reluctant, but he gathers a shirt, his flip-flops, and a few other items. Then, escorted by two of the officers, he's gone.

Heart pounding, I thank the others, and they leave.

I did it. The TRO has been served. And for now, the apartment is quiet.

––––––––

An hour later, I'm still hyper-aware of every sound. Every creak in the building feels like a harbinger of doom.

I know better than to think a piece of paper will keep Timmy away.

When the knock comes, it's softer this time. "Police," a voice calls.

I open the door to find Timmy standing with two officers.

"He's here for an escorted visit to pick up some essentials," the officer explains.

"I need to get all my stuff," Timmy argues, his face a mask of exaggerated sadness.

"No," the officer replies firmly. "This visit is to grab *essentials*—clothing, medication, chargers. Not *everything*."

"But it's all my stuff," Timmy whines, gesturing around the apartment as if he's leaving behind untold riches.

The reality? His 'stuff' amounts to a sad list:

- tattered clothing
- mattresses he's ruined by peeing on them while he was drunk
- a broken surfboard
- a couple of tools that he didn't give away to his meth friends the day before
- a small amount of medication
- the cheap TV he inherited from Skank Face.

That's it. *The totality of Timmy.*

Everything else—the appliances, furniture, and electronics—is mine.

An officer hurries him along. Reluctantly, he picks up a few more items of clothing and is escorted out again.

Then they leave.

But I have a feeling this won't be the last time I see him.

Nerves frayed, I call Jo, and update her. She's kind and supportive, and very relieved to hear the TRO has been served.

We talk through next steps—how I'm going to leave this apartment, what I need to do in preparation for the permanent restraining order hearing, and so on.

It's nice to hear a friendly voice on the other end of the phone, a stark reminder of how I've been unable to speak often with anyone other than Timmy for the past seventeen months.

———

When darkness falls, I try to relax, forcing myself to watch TV. I'm feeling drained, exhausted, and yet still on edge, and sleep doesn't come easily.

I drift off eventually, only to be woken around 230AM by an intense, gnawing feeling of unease.

I feel like Timmy is near.

By 330AM, my worst fear materializes.

The door beeps as he enters the code. He shouldn't be able to get in, because I've locked the bottom lock, and he doesn't have a key.

But then I hear the unmistakable swoosh of the door opening.

My blood turns to ice. *Timmy is inside.*

His eyes lock with mine. I see something in them that I can't quite put my finger on.

Hands shaking, and heart about to bounce out of my chest, I dial 911.

"Please, Margaux," he says, his voice low and shaky. "I just need to sleep in the back room. The meth heads on the beach told me they're going to snap my neck the moment I fall asleep."

His words are desperate, but I'm not falling for it. He's told me time and again how much nicer the meth heads are than me.

If they're turning on him, that's not my problem.

I refuse to be his caregiver and guardian any longer.

He can call his daddy to come and save him.

"I can't help you, Timmy," I say, as a dispatcher answers and I request police. My hands are trembling so badly I nearly drop the phone.

The officers arrive quickly, but by the time they get here, Timmy is long gone.

The violation is noted, and I lock every door and window with a renewed sense of urgency.

———

A few days later, I receive texts from Timmy. It's yet another TRO violation. I call the police, and they come over to take a report.

While one officer goes to his vehicle to retrieve a document, the other stands in the living room with me. Sabre keeps trying to escape, darting toward the door every time it opens. I scoop him up and shut him in the bathroom temporarily.

When the officer returns, he looks around, confused. "Wait… wasn't there a cat? I could have sworn there was a cat."

"Yes," I reply, smirking. "He's safely in the bathroom for now."

The officer with the aggressive mustache listens as I explain that Timmy somehow knew I was at the courthouse.

"Well," he says, eyeing my wrist. "Do you have an Apple Watch?"

"Yes," I reply, holding it up.

"Go into your settings," he instructs.

I do, and to my shock, I see that my watch is still tracking my location independently of my phone.

Relief washes over me—it's not some elaborate tracking device Timmy planted—it's just a setting I overlooked.

"This isn't some James Bond situation," the officer quips, breaking into laughter.

Despite everything, I find myself laughing too. It feels good to laugh, even if just for a moment.

It reminds me that I'm still here, still standing.

And I'm going to keep standing, no matter what.

CHAPTER 134
GODDAMN SUPERNOVA

DEX

She did it.

She finally fucking did it.

Disposed of that moron.

Margaux's fire had been flickering in the background for months, threatening to fade completely, but now, it's *blazing*.

Filing the TRO—and insisting it be served—proves that.

When I see her return with signed paperwork, and then watch as it's served, I feel an odd surge of pride.

Not that she needs my validation, but damn it, she deserves someone in her corner.

I send a message:

ANONYMOUS:

You did it. You got him out.

Her relief is palpable, even over the camera audio. "I did," she whispers. "God, I actually did."

And yet, even as I admire her resolve, I can't shake the gnawing unease. Timmy isn't the type to bow out gracefully—guys like him never quit anything but their jobs, the gym, or positive contributions to society.

He's almost certain to push boundaries, test limits, and attempt to worm his way back into her life if he thinks he can get away with it.

And Margaux? She'll have to fend him off, over and over again.

It doesn't take long for my fears to be confirmed.

I watch with horror from afar as he violates the TRO the day it's served, entering her apartment in the wee hours of the morning, sneaking in uninvited, claiming the meth heads are after him.

Classic Timmy—spinning tales of victimhood to wriggle out of accountability.

But Margaux doesn't fall for it this time. She calls 911 again, her voice steady despite the fear I knew she feels.

The police officers who served the TRO earlier were very clear he wasn't to return, and the audacity of Timmy's actions are staggering. The man's disregard for boundaries isn't just infuriating—it's dangerous and scary.

That's the thing about Margaux—even when she's scared, she's unflinching. Resilient. Stronger than she realizes. Watching her fight for herself, for her safety, has been humbling in a way I can't fully articulate.

I'm ready to jump through the screen, yet helpless. I should have flown over sooner, just in case. This last thread of their relationship just snapped so quickly—I thought I had more time.

Through the days that follow, Margaux holds firm. She calls the police every time he breaches the TRO. She documents everything—even the text-based violations. She doesn't let him manipulate her into backing down.

And when he tries to weasel his way into her apartment, claiming he needs essentials, she stands her ground.

When Steve the Horse Cop reaches out, pretending he's not acting on behalf of Timmy—yeah right—she does the same.

"Essentials?" I mutter to myself as I watch the scene unfold. "You mean the tattered clothes, peed-on mattress, and the broken surfboard you haven't used in years? Fuck off, Timmy." I roll my eyes.

Timmy's antics might be exhausting, but they're also revealing. He's a black hole, sucking in the light and joy of everyone around him.

And Margaux? She's a goddamn supernova, burning brighter every day she distances herself from him.

So let Last-Choice Lisa have him. They're perfect for each other—two miserable, toxic messes destined to implode. Meanwhile, Margaux will be here, shining like the unstoppable force she is.

And me?

I'll be here too, marveling at her strength, ready to step in and be there for her the way she deserves.

CHAPTER 135
AFTERMATH

MARGAUX

feel so alone. Empty. Numb. But also… free.

There's so much to process.

For the next few days, I binge-listen to podcasts and YouTube channels aimed at survivors of narcissistic and toxic relationships—*Dimming the Gaslight, Why She Stayed*, Dr. Ramani.

It's compulsive.

I need the validation, the reinforcement, to keep me grounded in my decision. Every story I hear emboldens me. It reminds me that it wasn't just me. That I wasn't deserving of Timmy's treatment.

And Timmy? Timmy was very much the problem. Him and his awful father.

I sit with my thoughts, and it feels like peeling back the layers of an onion, each one stinging more than the last.

The worst part isn't the fractured skull, or the so-called 'not real' black eyes—which are both real AF. Real as the pain that gnaws at my chest when I think of the person I was before him. The physical injuries, terrible as they were, aren't the most devastating part of all this.

No, the worst part is this idea I had of love, that I wanted and needed and craved. And which he dangled in front of me. He gave it to me, or at least the illusion of it, but never consistently, and always with strings attached.

Was it real? Did he love me at all, or was he just so obsessed with what I could provide for him that he faked it all?

The thought lodges in my throat like a stone.

Am I not worthy of love? Am I not beautiful enough, not kind enough?

His words—the biting cruelty of them—make me shrink into myself.

Maybe I'm just ordinary. Maybe a love like his is all I deserve.

I've had to weigh the highest highs against the lowest lows, and I've figured out one thing—*I don't want to die.*

I made the right decision leaving. There's no doubt about that.

But what if that was it—the highest high of love that I ever get to feel?

What if I never feel love like that again?

What if the soul-expanding, life-altering love I long for doesn't exist?

Or worse, what if it does, but I'm not enough to deserve it?

I don't know if I'm going to be able to trust anybody again who shows me what appears to be genuine love—because this whole experience has made me feel like maybe that type of love doesn't really exist.

I know people care for me. My friends, my chosen family—they love me and think highly of me in their own ways.

But the kind of adoration I dream about? It feels fake, like a shot of artificial sugar that spurs a dopamine rush. Sweet, but hollow.

And I want real.

But maybe real means I'm just… mediocre. Maybe real means settling for a man who spends his days drooling into his beer while yelling at extremist news.

Maybe that's my fate.

I'm at war with myself. One part of me believes in my worth. The other whispers doubts, feeding on the lies Timmy planted in me.

I blame my mother.

I blame Timmy.

I blame the universe. And yet, I feel like the universe is guiding me in the right direction. Slowly, though. *Too* slowly. I crave instant progress, but life doesn't work that way.

I want an infomercial with a shortcut to cure my life, to wipe away these feelings. But it doesn't exist.

The only way out is through.

Feeling every emotion, confronting every memory, no matter how raw. And it's agonizing. But it's the only way I'll make it through this.

I'm proud of myself for leaving, but Timmy's father's voice echoes in my head.

"He's a really nice guy."

"You're a liar."

"You're a whole volcano of pain."

It's infuriating. It hurts. And it's *wrong*.

I rage, because even if I had pulled Timmy's hair—so what?

I didn't fracture his skull.

I didn't give him black eyes or lower his self-esteem.

I didn't chip away at his sense of self until he doubted his worth. I boosted him up.

No—I gave him a life he could never have achieved on his own. I did it because I loved him.

And what did I get in return? A torrent of abuse. A chorus of *'You're a cunt'* and other insults and blame from him and his enablers.

All I can believe is that his father treated his mother the same way, and Timmy learned by example. I feel pity for her. She seems kind, just beaten down by the men in her life—the one she married and some of the ones she raised.

And I'm resentful. Resentful that no one ever said, *"Timmy, you're fucking up. This isn't how you treat a woman."*

Instead, they coddled him.

Poor, sweet Timmy. So misunderstood.

Never mind that he's had six restraining orders filed against him. *Six*. I can understand one in extenuating circumstances, maybe even two—maybe. But six? That's not bad luck. That's a pattern.

Bruh, that's on you.

And yet, through all this, there have been glimmers of light.

Friends—people who I didn't necessarily expect—who stepped in and stood with me and held space for me and were just *there*.

I'm sure I drove them all nuts at times—for not just leaving.

But at the same time, they understood, and they all played a part in helping me to leave. Alice, Josephine, Stacey and so many more—reaching out when I needed it most.

I'm forever grateful.

I don't know who sent those anonymous messages of encouragement, but they buoyed me. Someone out there saw my struggle and cared enough to reach out.

Was it a friend?

A stranger?

I don't know, but their words carried me forward when I wanted to collapse.

They reminded me that I'm not alone. That I'm worthy of more.

I've started journaling again. Every page feels like a battle, forcing me to confront the memories, the lies, the manipulation.

But it's helping.

Slowly.

I'm stitching myself back together, piece by painful piece.

One day, I'll be whole again.

And when that day comes, Timmy's voice will be nothing more than a distant echo, lost in the void of the sad excuse for a man that he's always been.

A monster who couldn't destroy me, no matter how hard he tried.

CHAPTER 136
TIMING IS EVERYTHING

DEX

'm sure she's hurting. I'm sure she still thinks about him.

Because, unlike him, she has a heart, and she poured it into this absolute trash bag of society.

I want to comfort and console her, but if I do it too quickly, she might repel my advances. And she'd be right to do so, honestly.

And it's all so fresh, I can imagine him strategically placing an email or text or some other gesture right in her path that throws her and sucks her back in.

Forget a fucking Hoover, he's a Roomba.

He's running around on autopilot fucking with people's emotions.

But he's the filth that the Roomba cleans up.

I don't know where I'm going with this fucking analogy, other than to say he's despicable and she deserves so much better than him.

So I'm going to hang out for a minute, until I sense she's ready.

As hard as it is to hang back and not jump right in, she has to fix this for herself.

There's no other way.

CHAPTER 137
DRAGONFLIES

MARGAUX

TWO WEEKS LATER

What is grief when you can't see the body?

What is grief when you can see the body is still living, repeating their behavior on someone else?

It hurts, seeing them move along, and inflict the same pain on another person, reaching out to triangulate with everyone they've ever known.

Because, for some their wounds have been dulled, their scars healed almost—if not totally.

But he'll rip them open again.

I'm sure of it.

It's not my place to point it out.

I have to live here in silence, with my altered DNA.

Because I fell for a cute boy full of lies.

Who wanted nothing other than to hurt me and to blame me for everything he thinks everyone ever did him wrong by.

—————

I'm so much stronger now. That's the mantra I tell myself as I pack my belongings.

I've learned to value myself, to set boundaries about how I expect to be treated. There's still plenty of self-work to do, and it's a hard-earned realization, but it's here—and I'm clinging to it like a life raft.

Soon, I'll be out of this apartment—out of the suffocating space where the beep of the door and the swoosh of it opening became the soundtrack of my nightmares.

It's sad it took this long to get to this point, but I'm here.

I walk out to the dumpster, my arms full of things that hold memories I no longer want. With every cathartic clang as they hit the metal, I feel a little lighter.

Dr. Ramani's podcast plays in my ears, drowning out my negative thoughts, her voice a steady reminder of what I've endured and why I'll never go back.

On my way back to the apartment, something magical happens. A swarm of dragonflies surrounds me, darting and swirling like they're performing just for me. Normally, the sudden flurry of movement would startle me, but today?

Today, I laugh.

It's like the universe is giving me a sign.

I'm free.

Packing my life into four suitcases and a cat carrier feels strangely liberating. I can go anywhere I want now.

The weight of Timmy's chaos is no longer dragging me down.

I'm relieved, in ways I hadn't even realized were possible. No more beeps, no more swooshing doors, no more smashed glass or angry accusations.

The thought makes me smile.

I won't be on his home turf anymore.

I won't be living right next to people doing meth who he's talked badly about me to.

He won't be able to pop up in the window.

Life is back on my terms.

I'm living for me, not somebody that doesn't deserve my time.

It feels like a parasite has been removed. Extracted.

I'm surrounded by strangers and yet I already feel much safer than I did in my own home.

I have a life that many others would envy now.

I can go where I want, whenever I want. As long as my sweet cat is taken care of, of course.

The cat I didn't let him throw in the ocean.

The cat who he tried to take on a 2AM walk over to his meth head friends.

Sabre watches me from the bed, his green eyes wide and curious. I crouch down to scratch behind his ears. "We're almost out of here, buddy. Just a little longer, and we'll be free."

I feel a twinge of guilt looking at him. Sabre didn't ask for any of this. He didn't deserve the danger I put him in by staying with Timmy as long as I did. If something had happened… The thought makes my stomach churn, but I push it aside.

I can't change the past. I can only move forward.

And if I do ever end up in another relationship, one thing is for sure—I need to be with someone who needs absolutely nothing from me.

As if on cue, my phone buzzes. The screen lights up with a name I haven't seen in a while. My heart skips. *Dex.*

The man I've thought about far too often, even when I shouldn't have. Especially when I shouldn't have.

I've been far too embarrassed to reach out to him, for one thing. But I've also been defensive—protective of Timmy—and I know Dex would have pushed me to end things long ago.

More than anything, it's embarrassing being in a cycle of abuse. Every time the cycle begins again, hope rises—then it deflates like a sad balloon… and that's, well… mortifying.

Because every time you forgive them, you really believe in their will to change. That they mean the promises they make.

It's exhausting, and I feel like an idiot for giving Timmy so many chances despite the growing evidence that he is an evil person, and the only outcome of staying with him—as my sister said—would have been my funeral.

But I can't think of that.

I answer the phone just before it goes to voicemail. "Hello?" My voice comes out shaky, a reminder that I haven't spoken out loud much lately.

I've been sheltered in my apartment, scared and frantic.

"Hey, Margaux," Dex says, his voice warm and familiar. It's deeper than I remember, like it's been steeped in late nights and hard whiskey. "I just wanted to check in. How are you holding up?"

The question is simple, but it unravels me. I start to cry, tears streaming down my face before I can stop them. "I'm… I'm okay," I manage between sobs.

There's a pause on the other end, and then he speaks again. "It's okay to not be okay, you know, Margaux. You've been through a lot."

He must have been keeping track of my public social media meltdown. *Great.*

Blood rushes to my cheeks.

But I quickly get over my embarrassment. Dex listens as I unload everything—the restraining order, the move, the fear, the guilt.

I cry as I speak. He doesn't interrupt, doesn't try to fix it. He just listens. He's just *there* for me.

"I should've called you sooner," I say, wiping my face. "But I didn't want to burden you."

"Burden me?" he says, and I can hear the smile in his voice. "Margaux, you could never be a burden. Besides, I'm here, aren't I?"

His words are a balm, soothing the raw edges of my emotions.

And there's a softness to him now, a side I didn't know existed.

Dex has always been confident, sharp, and—let's be honest—devastatingly hot. But this? This patience, this gentleness? It's enough to undo me all over again.

"Let me help," he says. "I'll fly out, help you move the last of your things."

"No, Dex, that's too much. You don't have to—"

"I'm not asking," he interrupts, his tone firm but kind. "I'm coming. And when you're ready, you can stay at my spare apartment back in California. No strings, no expectations. Just… a place where you can breathe."

I'm crying again, but this time it's from relief. "Thank you," I whisper.

"You don't have to thank me," he says softly. "Just promise me one thing."

"What?"

"Let me be there for you," his tone is gravely, soothing. Hot as hell. "No shutting me out this time."

I can hear the sincerity in his voice, and it makes my chest ache. "I promise."

After we hang up, he sends me his flight confirmation, and I find myself counting down the hours until I see him.

Until I'm in the presence of someone who doesn't need anything from me, who doesn't expect me to shrink myself to fit their world.

Dex is more than just a safety net. He's a reminder that there are good people out there.

That I deserve to surround myself with better people.

And for the first time in a long time, I believe it.

CHAPTER 138
A FRIENDLY FACE

Dex arrives at Sunset Cay just after noon, his presence impossible to miss. He strides out of the airport with a leather jacket slung over his shoulder, tattoos curling up his arms and disappearing under the fabric. His long brown hair is tied back in a messy man bun, and his sharp green-and-hazel eyes scan the arrivals area until they land on me.

My breath catches. He's even hotter than I remembered—or imagined. His outdated social media photos don't do him justice. He radiates a quiet confidence, and an intensity that makes my pulse quicken.

"Margaux," he says, his voice low and warm, and suddenly, every feeling I've been trying to suppress comes rushing back.

"Dex," I manage, my voice small and shaky.

He pulls me into a hug—brief but firm, grounding. "It's so good to see you," he says, pulling back to look at me. His gaze is filled with concern, and I can't help but avert mine, afraid of what he might see if he looks too closely.

We don't say much as we drive back to the apartment. Dex doesn't push, doesn't ask questions I'm not ready to answer. He's just here. Solid. A quiet, protective presence that feels like a shield against the lingering chaos.

Later, Dex checks into a hotel nearby, giving me space without even needing to be asked. It's considerate, just like him.

But as the evening wears on, the fear creeps back in. I haven't received official word that Timmy has left the Cay yet, and every creak of the apartment feels like a harbinger of his return.

I text Dex.

ME:

Can you come stay in the spare room?

His reply is immediate.

DEX:

Of course. Be there in ten.

When he arrives, he's carrying his duffel bag and wearing a loose tank top that shows off even more tattoos. He doesn't comment on the nervous energy radiating from me. He just gives me a small smile and heads to the spare room without hesitation.

"I'll be right here if you need anything," he says, and the reassurance in his voice feels like a warm blanket.

For days, I avoid looking directly at Dex for too long. His intense, searching gaze is unnerving, like he can see through all the walls I've carefully built around myself—every time he's glanced at me, I've looked away.

Scared of what I'll find if I look too deeply, because I trusted the kindness in Timmy's eyes, and look where that got me.

But tonight, as we sit on the mattress that serves as my bed and couch, surrounded by the remnants of my old life—items to be packed, donated, or trashed—I finally meet his eyes. I see him fully for the first time, and I'm ready for him to see me—all of me—no matter what that means.

Even if he can't handle my darkness, I'm willing to risk it all.

His gaze doesn't waver, either. It's steady, calm, but full of something I can't quite name.

Not pity.

Not judgment.

Just… *understanding.*

I swallow hard. "I need to tell you everything," I say, my voice barely above a whisper.

"Okay," he says simply, leaning forward to rest his elbows on his knees. "I'm here. Take your time."

The words pour out of me, more descriptive than before, seventeen months of pain and fear spilling into the quiet space between us.

I tell him about the insults, the violence, the isolation.

Every dark detail that I've kept locked away.

There are moments when I falter, when the shame threatens to choke me. "I'm sorry I keep talking about it," I say, tears streaming down my face.

"Don't be sorry," he replies, his voice firm but gentle. "You're perfect just the way you are. You can tell me anything, and I'll always be here to listen."

His words wrap around me like armor, shielding me from the weight of my own memories.

The next morning, I'm heading to the bathroom when I catch Dex walking out of the back room, a towel slung low around his hips. His torso is a masterpiece—defined muscles, tattoos that tell stories I'd love to know. My face flushes, and I immediately look away.

"Morning," he says, a small smirk tugging at his lips as he adjusts the towel.

"Morning," I mumble, rushing past him before I embarrass myself further.

The heat in my cheeks lingers for hours.

We spend the next few days tackling the apartment. Dex doesn't complain once, even when we're hauling heavy boxes or sorting through piles of junk. His humor lightens the mood, and for the first time in months, I find myself laughing without it being tinged by nervousness.

The truck, unsurprisingly, isn't worth anything. After a few failed attempts to sell it, we end up donating it. "One less thing to worry about," Dex says, patting the hood as we walk away.

Thank god I never have to look at that ugly thing again.

The day of our flight arrives, and the apartment is empty now, stripped of everything that made it mine. As I stand in the doorway for the last time, memories flood back—both good and bad.

The nights I spent laughing with Timmy, believing in the illusion he created.

The mornings I woke up terrified, the swoosh of the door signaling another fight.

The times I doubted myself, wondering if *I* was the problem.

Tears prick my eyes, but I blink them away. I'm not that person anymore. I'm stronger now.

Dex steps up beside me, his hand brushing mine. "Ready?"

I nod, taking one last look before turning away. "Yeah. Let's go."

As we walk to the car, Sabre nestled safely in his carrier, I feel a weight lifting from my shoulders. This horrific phase of my life is over, and for the first time in a long time, I'm excited to see what comes next.

And maybe Dex will be part of my next chapter.

CHAPTER 139
BUT ARE THERE STRINGS ATTACHED?

MARGAUX

THE PAST

> FATHER: I BOUGHT YOU THE CLOTHING YOU WANTED.
> NOW, YOU NEED TO COME FOR A WALK WITH ME AND THE DOG.
> ME: BUT I DON'T FEEL LIKE IT.
> AND I HAVE HOMEWORK
> FATHER: I DID SOMETHING FOR YOU.
> NOW YOU NEED TO DO SOMETHING FOR ME.

———

THE PRESENT

Dex is warm and attentive as he helps me settle into his spare apartment.

He gives me a quick tour, pointing out the essentials—the espresso machine, the quirky light switches, the Wi-Fi password scrawled neatly on a sticky note. He even mentions a few nearby restaurants and spots he thinks I'd like.

"This place is great," I say, forcing a smile, genuinely happy but feeling overwhelmed and a little awkward about the situation.

"It's yours for as long as you need," he replies, his tone gentle but firm.

Then, just like that, he's gone.

No hovering, no unnecessary lingering. He leaves me space, and yet I feel so profoundly seen and cared for that it's unsettling.

A few hours later, there's a knock at the door. I open it to find Dex standing there, a bag in one hand and a coffee cup in the other.

"Here," he says, holding them out to me. "A bagel from that place I was telling you about. Their everything bagels are amazing, and I remember you said you liked scallion cream cheese."

I blink, stunned. "Thank you? How did you—"

"You mentioned it once a while ago," he says with a shrug, grinning. "And I filed it away. Oh, and this…" He lifts the cup. "Cold brew with a shot of espresso. No sugar, no cream. Just how you like it."

My heart races, and not entirely in a good way. He got my exact order right, and I don't even remember telling him.

"And I'm glad I did," he adds, "because I saw the way your beautiful eyes lit up when you saw both the bagel and the coffee."

I laugh. "That was because I saw *you*," I deadpan. "I… thanks," I say, taking the bag and cup.

But the truth is, my mind is spinning. I'm in fight or flight mode from this gesture, and I'm trying to figure out his angle.

"Anyway, I just stopped by to give you these," he says. "I've got to head into work for a bit, but I wanted to see you—even if just for a second."

Before I can respond, he leans in and wraps me in a quick, firm hug. His scent—clean, woodsy, with a hint of leather—lingers as he pulls back and gives me a soft, lingering kiss on the cheek that makes my pussy clench.

"Okay, gorgeous," he says with a smile. "I'll text you later to figure out our next adventure."

"Okay, bye!" my voice squeaks, and I watch him head down the driveway, his leather jacket slung over one shoulder. He stops to put on his helmet, then straddles his motorcycle and roars away, disappearing down the street.

It's such a simple act of kindness.

And I don't trust it.

"Fucking hell," I whisper to myself, staring at the bagel and coffee in my hands. "What have I gotten myself into?"

―――――

LATER IN THE WEEK

"So let me get this straight," Sophia, my new therapist, says, tapping her pen against her cheek.

I prioritized my mental health and signed up for a new provider the moment I could. We've had one intake session, and I like her already.

"You're upset because this attractive, tattooed man brought you your favorite bagel and coffee, and that he remembered your order correctly?"

I frown, hating how it sounds. "I know it seems silly…"

She holds up a hand. "I'm not judging, Margaux. I just want to understand. Your reaction is completely valid, and I want to make sure we explore it fully. No need to apologize or downplay your feelings. Let's dig into why this bothers you."

Her calm, nonjudgmental demeanor soothes me, and I nod. "It's just… with Timmy, every time he did something nice for me, there was a catch… like, he'd make me breakfast I didn't even ask for and then expect me to gush over it like he was some Michelin-star chef. Which, to be fair, he was a decent cook. Made me dinner? Wanted accolades. But it wasn't about the food—it was about what he wanted from me in return."

Sophia tilts her head, listening intently. "It sounds like his gestures weren't acts of love, but transactions. And those transactions left you anxious and wary. Am I right?"

"Exactly," I say, my voice rising with emotion. "And it wasn't just food. Cleaning the house? Oh my gosh—even if he was doing it while I worked sixteen-hour days and he didn't work at all. He'd demand a parade in his honor, and expect to be able to behave however badly he wanted—to the point I dreaded every time he cleaned. If he made me a lei or brought me a shell, it wasn't about making me happy—it was about earning points. And if I didn't react the right way, he'd sulk or pick a fight. So now, whenever anyone does something kind, I'm just waiting for the catch."

"I know your example is a joke, because you use humor to deflect. I enjoy your wit, but what did he actually do when he cleaned?"

"Well, he had a bit of a pattern. He drank when he cleaned. And he'd go and tidy some part of the house, and it'd be great at first. Super helpful to me because it's hard to find the time when working, and honestly, I'm not the best at it."

She smirks.

"But then he would come and kiss me in this weird way. It's hard to explain, but it was almost like he was drooling on me. Just this messy, sloppy kiss with lots of tongue. A weird look in his eyes. He only did this particular thing during and after cleaning… and if I'd push him away or ask him to stop he would sulk, saying he was being 'passionate'."

She smirks. "Okay, go on…"

"And then next thing he would just *have* to have a cigarette. Or he'd *have* to go pick shells. Or he'd *have* to go for a really long swim. And he'd almost inevitably end up over by the guys in the tents for hours. And if he didn't preemptively go and do those things just because, he'd start an argument as an excuse to run out the door. *Every single time.* He'd be mad about the show I was watching even when he had my headphones on, and he didn't have to hear it. Oh my gosh, he'd even put the headphones on—which are noise-canceling—and he'd start talking about what's happening in my shows that he 'hates', even when he was perfectly able to listen to music and not listen to anything in my show.'

"How did that feel?"

"Almost like he was keeping an eye on me and what I was watching, while pretending he was listening to music. It was just really… strange."

"Well, his cleaning definitely sounds upsetting based on his behavior afterward. No wonder you were worried often when he cleaned. What else made you feel this way?"

"When he'd rub my back, he was always very careful to go a few minutes over the time. So say if we agreed on fifteen-minute massages, he'd give me one for like eighteen or nineteen minutes and then proclaim, 'See what I did for you? I went *way* over, and you just stuck to the time. But I'm happy to do that because I love you.'

I'd feel instantly guilty, even though the real estate of his back is much larger, and my hands much smaller. I'd massage him to the point my hands hurt, often, and then he always wanted more later. 'Pick my back', 'give me tickles,' 'pluck the hairs.' If it wasn't for getting satisfaction from plucking those hairs, I may have completely lost my mind. That part was cathartic."

My therapist laughs. "Fair enough. There's a reason shows like *Dr Pimple Popper* are so popular."

I laugh in return. "It's funny you should say that, actually," I say. "'Pop my pimples,' he'd say. I never liked to do it, but I would because failure to do so would impact his entire mood. I even let him pop a couple of mine here and there. But I know some of this is common couple stuff. It's not the action or request for action in itself. It was the complete, sheer lack of reciprocity. The entitlement that doing something one time for me resulted in an expectation it would be done every time for him. That he was somehow entitled to more physical affection and attention focused on him nearly every time."

"And it sounds like you're not done," she says. "Tell me what else made you feel suspicious of kind gestures. You've already given me quite the list, but I have a feeling there's more. Like the boss level of the video game."

"You're so right. It's the fear of a grand gesture. He expected accolades and excessive admiration over the small things. And then when he did the odd major act—one very thoughtful thing—like helping me with my PR boxes and filming them on time-lapse... I knew he would never let me live that down. Every time we'd argue after that, he would point back to that day as evidence that he's a really nice guy. He'd say I never thanked him even though I thanked him many, many times. Even though I told him I'd told my therapist about how kind and touching of a gesture it was."

She nods. "Wow, I can imagine that type of expectation could place you immediately on eggshells. But what impact do you think it's having on you now that you're no longer in the relationship?"

"So now, I hold a perhaps unhealthy skepticism over any act of kindness. I think it will fade with time. But, for now, I'm stuck feeling like any kind gesture is a transaction or a trap. That it's laden with some objective where the person wants something in return. Or that it will somehow be used against me in the future if the person inevitably misbehaves."

She nods. "You mentioned that your father used to do something similar, but on a much smaller scale. Is that right?"

"Yeah, so I'd pester him for this or that—you know, normal teenage stuff. Track pants that were 'cool'. Driving me here or there to do stuff with friends. Makeup. He'd always make me justify it, and then follow up basically with a, 'Well, what do I get out of it?' And then when he wanted something—like for me to accompany him for a walk or whatnot—he'd say 'remember what I did for you, now you do something for me.'"

"And your mother?"

"Well, she would be crafty about it. She'd use points like these as evidence of the strength of our mother-daughter bond, and proof that we were best friends and that she needed to be able to tell me anything and everything and trust her implicitly. When she took me to Disneyland, it was really fun and I was grateful—I'll remember it forever—but it was very much a, 'Look what I can do and how amazing I am to take you here!'.

And I truly think she was amazing for doing that, but the part of being so excited to see it through my eyes didn't ring particularly true. I just think she wanted to be told she was an amazing mother. That she could have gone anywhere in the world on vacation, but she selflessly took her daughter to a theme park."

"And Dex's gesture feels like it has a catch?" she asks gently.

I hesitate. "No... but my brain keeps telling me there *must* be one. Because why would anyone just... do something nice for me? Without expecting something in return?"

Sophia nods, her expression thoughtful. "That's a conditioned response, Margaux. Timmy—and others in your life—taught you to associate kindness with obligation. You've had a life-long struggle to accept things—or even help. But here's the thing—not everyone operates like that. Some people, like Dex, simply enjoy making others happy. No strings attached."

Her words settle over me like a hug, warm and reassuring. "You really think so?" I ask, my voice small.

"I do," she says. "But what matters most is whether *you* can start believing that, too."

"I've never thought about it that way. But... holy shit, I think you're onto something."

She smiles. "I think *you're* the one that's onto something. I'm merely here to help you find your way."

———

Later, as I sip on a refreshing glass of sparkling water, I replay the moment in my mind. Dex's smile, his quiet confidence, the way he remembered my favorite things without me even realizing it.

Maybe he *is* different.

But even if he is, I'm terrified. Terrified of letting someone in, of opening myself up only to be hurt again.

I glance at Sabre, who's curled up on the couch beside me, and stroke his soft fur.

"Baby steps," I whisper. "We'll figure this out. One day at a time."

CHAPTER 140
THE WRONG TARGET

MARGAUX

The next day, I'm hanging out with Dex. He wanted to take me around the neighborhood and he's brought me to a cute local bar.

I mention the anonymous messages to Dex casually, thinking they were nothing more than the random kindness of a stranger.

He shifts in his seat, his face turning a shade darker. For a moment, I wonder if he's blushing.

"It was me," he admits, his voice low, almost sheepish. "I sent the messages."

"What?" I blink, confused. "*You* sent them? *Why?*"

"I was… monitoring the situation from afar," he says carefully. "Making sure you were safe."

My stomach drops. "What do you mean, 'monitoring the situation'? Were you spying on me?"

He hesitates, then nods. "Well, yeah. I was worried about you. So I hacked into some of your stuff—just to keep an eye on things."

My heart starts pounding. "You *what*?"

"I didn't mean to—"

"Were there *cameras*?" My voice is trembling now.

He glances down, guilt written all over his face. "There were cameras," he admits quietly.

A wave of fury and embarrassment crashes over me.

My prior relationship was already a humiliating mess—the idea of someone watching it unfold, analyzing my every moment, makes my skin crawl.

On instinct, I leap out of my seat and run from the bar.

I hear footsteps behind me, and Dex grabs me gently by my arm.

"Margaux, let me explain," he pleads.

"You broke my trust, Dex!" I scream, my voice raw with emotion. "How could you do this to me? You, of all people!"

His expression crumples, regret etched in every line of his face. "Margaux, I'm so sorry. I was trying to protect you."

"*Protect* me? You violated my privacy in the worst way imaginable! You're a fucking *stalker!*"

Tears stream down my face. I can barely see him through the haze of my rage and hurt. "Get away from me!" I shriek, pointing at the door. "Get away from me and don't come back!"

"Margaux..." he tries again, his voice pleading.

"Get away!" I scream again, my voice cracking, unwilling to meet his gaze.

He stares at me for a moment, his face a picture of devastation, before he finally turns and leaves. If heartbreak was a face, it would be his. The sound of his footsteps as he walks away feels deafening.

But I don't have time to pity him.

He nosed around in my personal business. *What the fuck was he trying to do?*

He said he was trying to protect me, but now I feel a million times worse.

In his own way, Timmy loved me, but now he's gone.

He used to do horrible things to me.

Hell, he fractured my skull after all.

But at least he didn't pretend to be my protector—my family—and then betray me.

Well, fuck, I guess in a sense he did that too!

Jesus christ! I can't seem to escape these horrible men!

They say they're looking out for me, but they're just fucking me over left and right!

How dare Dex go through all my private information, digging into police and therapy files and god knows what else.

I can't believe this. I'm never ever going to trust another man ever again, maybe another human.

I've had enough. This is all too much.

Because I can't take this pain. This betrayal.

I just want silence. I just want peace.

And it doesn't seem like I'm going to get that. It seems like it's not my destiny.

Instead, there's just pain and suffering.

And Timmy will just come back for me anyway.

He's a psycho with a history of stalking his exes. I've read up on his behavior, and it's unlikely to stop.

I sink onto the sidewalk, my body wracked with sobs. A few passersby look at me awkwardly and hurry along.

My mind is a tornado of emotions—anger, betrayal, sadness, confusion.

How could Dex do this to me? How could someone I trusted so implicitly, someone who was supposed to be my safe place, violate me like this?

Timmy was awful, but at least his betrayals were blatant.

This… this is insidious.

Dex positioned himself as my protector, my anchor. And all the while, he was watching, prying, spying.

I feel like I've been stripped bare, my innermost thoughts laid out so vulnerably, never meant to be seen by another set of eyes.

Timmy violated me in so many ways.

And in an apparent effort to help me out of a terrible situation, Dex went and violated me, too!

Did he see the therapy notes where I admitted how broken I felt?

Did he read the journal entries where I wrote about him, the flickers of hope I had for someone like him?

A fresh wave of humiliation crashes over me.

God, how pathetic. How utterly stupid I've been.

Timmy destroyed my trust, and now Dex has shattered whatever fragile remnants were left.

I wipe my face, but the tears keep coming. This is my life now—an endless cycle of betrayal and heartbreak. Maybe this is all there is.

"Never again," I whisper to myself, my voice shaking. "Never again will I let anyone in."

———

I get back to the apartment and my phone rings. I know without looking that it's Dex.

"What?" I say as I answer, my voice flat.

"Margaux, please let me explain," he begs, his voice cracking. "I was trying to keep you as safe as possible. I was scared for you."

"You still looked at my innermost feelings!" I scream. "You've been manipulating me the whole time. You're no better than Timmy!"

There's silence on the other end. That was a pretty big insult.

But I feel crushed. I finally thought I found someone who I think I can trust, and he turns out to be a big fake liar, just like Timmy.

Jesus Christ.

I sigh. "I thought for once I met someone who wasn't trying to play me."

"I'm sorry you feel that way," he replies. "I never meant for you to find out"

"So you wanted to keep it a secret forever that you've been doing this?" My voice cracks at the end.

"No, no. I mean… I never wanted to use it for nefarious purposes. I just checked in on you the first time out of genuine concern, and then I had to keep looking. I became a little obsessed, I guess. I hated seeing you like that. I wanted to protect you. But way before that… I've always wanted to protect you—you must know that."

"Oh, give me a fucking break!" My voice cracks again. "I feel so fucking betrayed—by *you*, of all people. You were meant to be a safe person for me. But there's nobody safe. Nobody who wants to be in a relationship with me, anyway."

I'm bawling now, sobs wracking through the phone.

"You can trust me," Dex says, his voice low. "I haven't used those things against you. I never would."

"Well, you still looked at it," I say, my sobs slowing as my anger intensifies. "How is this any different from Timmy eavesdropping on my therapy? Leave me alone. You're a fucking hypocrite. Just like Timmy."

I hang up.

He calls back, and I send him to voicemail, fresh tears cascading from my eyes.

I feel like an idiot, once again. I'm so sick of being treated this way.

Like a fucking joke. Like someone that gets played like a fiddle.

For someone who's meant to be smart, I feel dumber than everyone else who seems to have it figured out.

The people that innately have known to set boundaries their entire life.

The people who can spot a manipulator the entire way.

Not me.

I'm so sick of being the nice one, the sweet one.

The trusting one.

When do I get to be the bad one? The one who calls the shots.

Do I get to be the manipulator, the asshole… ever?

It's not in my nature, but maybe it should be.

By the time the tears stop, I feel hollow. Empty.

But underneath the emptiness, a new resolve begins to form.

I'm done being the victim. Done being the one who gets played and betrayed.

If Dex thought he could watch over me and play the hero, he was wrong.

From now on, I'm setting boundaries that no one will cross.

Not Timmy, not Dex, not anyone.

Because if there's one thing I've learned, it's that the only person I can truly rely on is myself. And that has to be enough.

I don't need a hero.

I'll save myself.

CHAPTER 141
WHY HE DID IT

MARGAUX

'm on the phone with Alice, and for the first time in ages, it's not just messages back and forth—it's an entire video call.

Her face fills my screen, bright and animated, a reminder of what life used to feel like before everything crumbled around me.

It's refreshing, liberating even, to talk like this. No Timmy hovering in the background, no need to keep my voice down or guard my words.

But the conversation? That's another story.

"I can't believe Dex," I say, my voice tinged with frustration. "What the hell was he thinking?"

Alice tilts her head, her expression calm but curious. "Think of it this way —what was he trying to accomplish by doing it?"

"I don't know!" I throw my hands in the air. "Reading my innermost thoughts so he could be a predator, just like Timmy?"

Her brow furrows. "I understand why you'd think that. But I'm wondering if—in his case—he was just looking out for you in his own way. A creepy way—nobody's debating that—but maybe it came from a place of care. He had the chance to look at info on anyone in the world, and he chose you."

"Sounds unhealthy. Like a stalker-y obsession."

"Again, fair," Alice says, her tone measured. "But what if he legitimately cares about your wellbeing?"

"I'm sick of everyone playing devil's advocate!" I yell, the frustration bubbling over. "I'm so sick of my world being tilted on its side. There are so many lies, hidden agendas. I just want to feel validated. To feel comfortable in my own skin. I can't handle all the deception. I just want honesty and truth."

"It's going to take a minute, babe," she says gently. "You've spent basically eighteen months in a nightmare you couldn't wake up from. Give yourself some time to heal."

"I hate this healing advice!" The words burst out of me, my voice louder than intended. "Sorry, I'm not mad at you," I say quickly. "It's just that everyone's saying it. What does it even mean? I'm not supposed to date because I'm supposed to be 'healing.' But I can't afford some fancy healing retreat. I'm doing the same shit as before—just without Timmy to interrupt me. And it's lonely."

"What do you want to be doing?"

I shrug. "I've thought about taking a trip."

"So take a trip!"

"I might." I sigh, running my fingers through my hair. "But I don't know… a trip won't solve everything. I'm listening to self-help podcasts, reading, writing. My latest book is making good progress. But what else am I supposed to do to heal? I'm too old to reinvent myself, aren't I?"

"Nope." Alice shakes her head firmly. "And nobody's asking you to reinvent yourself. This isn't about becoming a whole new Margaux. It's about figuring out who you are now, after everything you've been through. Who are you, Margaux, *in this moment*? As an individual, unattached woman. As a human being."

"But I know who I am! I'm *me*!"

"You're underestimating the shit Timmy put you through," she says, her voice soft but unwavering. "Having someone like him around you, day after day, in your ear, wears on you more than you might ever realize. It literally changes your DNA. *You're* the one he did it to, but sometimes it's easier for someone on the outside to see."

I slump back in my chair. "So what does that mean? I'm *so* frustrated. I don't know what this healing process is or how long it's supposed to take."

"Think about the progress you've made already. Are you still on eggshells all the time?"

I consider her question, and then shake my head. "Well, no. I'm still having crazy dreams, but I don't wake up screaming anymore. And I feel comfortable planning my day. I take myself out for lunch sometimes, and I'm learning not to be anxious just because I'm leaving the house. That was a big thing with Timmy—every outing was scary because of how he might act. Now I just have to worry about how *I* act. And I'm usually pretty well-behaved."

Alice laughs, and it's a warm, reassuring sound. "That you are. See? This stuff takes time. There's no timeline for grief—as cheesy as that sounds. Because that's what this is. You're grieving. You get to grieve. You get to be selfish for a bit. Take the class, listen to the podcast, watch the show."

"Oh yes. I've been binge-watching everything he would have complained about me watching. And that is a massive list, I've barely made a dent."

She grins. "See? That's self-care. You get to watch what you want without feeling guilty. You get to listen to what you want, eat what you want, wear what you want. *Be* who you want. And he no longer gets a say in how you live your life."

"Right?" I say, a faint smile tugging at my lips. "I guess I'm slowly starting to do those things without remembering how he would've made me feel for doing them. At first, that was all I could think about—how he'd react, even though he wasn't here anymore. It was like he was controlling me from afar."

"That's because he was," Alice says, her voice firm. "His claws were sunk deep into your psyche. That shit takes time to unravel, but you're already doing it."

I let out a long, deep sigh, the kind that feels like it's expelling years of tension.

Alice is right. She's always right. She's been through this herself, and she's come out better and stronger on the other side, yet still very much herself.

"Thank you," I say, my voice thick with emotion. "I'll never stop thanking you for being there for me through all this shit."

"Anytime," she replies, her smile soft and genuine. "Truly. I'm just so glad you got out."

And for the first time in a long while, I feel glad too.

Maybe healing isn't a destination, but a journey. Maybe I'm finally on my way.

And maybe Dex did some wrong things for the right reasons.

Perhaps he deserves a second chance after all.

CHAPTER 142
GREEN FLAGS ALL THE WAY

MARGAUX

Dex walks beside me, his presence steady and warm like a comforting flame that won't go out. The past few days have been a whirlwind of emotions, trying to reconcile my fury at his actions with the reality of why he did them. The old Margaux, the one buried under layers of pain and distrust, would never have entertained the possibility of forgiveness.

But now? Now I'm learning to make room for the complexities of human behavior—and the idea that maybe, just maybe, someone can care about me without ulterior motives. Even though he went about it in a pretty invasive way, Dex did have my best interests at heart.

We approach a small café, its charm understated with a cheerful striped awning and the aroma of fresh coffee wafting out the door. Dex moves quickly to grab the handle, and instinctively, I flinch. The reaction is immediate, automatic.

I blush as I realize he was merely attempting to open the door for me.

He freezes, his eyes wide with concern. "Margaux, I'm so sorry. I didn't mean to frighten you."

"No, no, you're fine." I wave him off, though my cheeks burn with embarrassment. "It's just… a habit, I guess."

Dex studies me, his green-hazel eyes softening. "You could do or say the most annoying things. Hell, you could even *hit* me—please don't, but theoretically, you *could*—and I would still never hit you. *Ever.* You could yell and scream the meanest, most vile things, and we'd work through it. But I wouldn't raise a hand to you. Not ever."

I look away, blinking back tears. The sincerity in his voice is almost too much to handle.

We settle into a small corner table inside, the kind meant for quiet conversations and stolen moments, comfortable in each other's company. I sip my dirty chai, savoring the warmth as it spreads through me, and watch Dex across the table with his plain black coffee.

"I hope you don't see me as some kind of scared shelter dog," I say, my voice nervous but teasing.

"Well," he begins with a grin, "only in the sense that you've both been through some serious trauma. But no. As much as I love dogs, I'd never compare you to one."

"A shelter *cat*, then?"

He laughs, the sound deep and easy. "No. No shelter animals. I love them, but you're much more complex and multifaceted than that."

I roll my eyes, but a smile creeps across my face despite myself.

"Doesn't it put you off?" I ask suddenly. "That I've been married several times before?"

"Not at all," Dex says, his tone steady. "We all have our pasts. Things that shape who we are today. It doesn't make you any less incredible."

"But what about me willingly being in a relationship like my last one? That I let myself be treated like that?"

"It doesn't matter," he replies. "It's not your fault you were abused. You didn't ask for or deserve that treatment. If anything, it makes me want to protect you even more."

A tear slips down my cheek, and I brush it away quickly, embarrassed.

Dex leans forward, his voice soft but firm. "From what I know, you've been way too hard on yourself for way too long. For things that were completely out of your control. None of us are perfect, Margaux. We all make mistakes. Decisions we'd change if we could. But those things don't diminish your value as a person. And I think you've believed your whole life that they do."

I smirk despite myself. "You sound like my therapist."

Dex smiles back. "She sounds like a smart lady."

"She likes you so far," I admit.

"*Very* smart lady," he repeats, grinning. "Genius, even."

"Do you have any kids?" I ask, dreading the answer.

He shakes his head. "No."

"*Secret* kids?"

He laughs softly. "No. I couldn't have a secret kid. I'd be too excited to talk about them."

I quirk a brow. "You want to be a dad?"

"Not necessarily," he shrugs. "That bird may have flown the coop. But if I was to have one, I would love it more than anything in this world."

My heart softens, any resentment toward him melting away. "Ugh. That is one of the many reasons why I love you."

He stops in his tracks. "You love me?"

"Yes," my gaze meets his. "From the moment I first saw you, I've had love for you."

He puts his hand on mine. "Same. And from the moment you turned twenty-one, it changed into something other than it originally was."

When he puts his arm around me, I don't pull away. For the first time in what feels like forever, I feel genuinely loved. Secure. Not in a hyped-up, manipulative way, but real, solid, and grounding.

"I really care about you, you know," he says, his voice low.

"I think I might finally be starting to believe you," I reply softly. "Thank you for not rushing me." It's been fast, overall, but not in the scheme of our entire friendship. Not when we've both had feelings all along.

"I'll wait as long as it takes," he says, his tone gentle but certain. "Seriously, until the end of my life and beyond—if that's what it takes to be with you, so I can make you feel loved. To make you feel safe."

"Preferably not too long," I tease. "It's hard to do much from beyond the grave."

"Oh, I'd find a way," he replies, grinning. "You can count on that."

His words linger in my mind long after our coffee cups are empty.

———

Later, as I lie in bed, I think about what Alice said during one of our conversations.

"Dex was obsessive, yes," she'd told me. "But he wasn't Timmy. He wasn't trying to manipulate you or control you. He was looking out for you the only way he knew how. If he'd intervened sooner, you probably would've pushed him away completely. And knowing you, you'd have clung to Timmy even harder just to spite him."

I'd hated hearing it, but I knew she was right. If Dex had revealed himself earlier, I wouldn't have seen his actions for what they were—protection. Care.

I would have pushed him away, never willing to see him again.

My love is a pure love. A loyal love. Once I'm in it, I'm in.

I'll never look at another human in the same way again.

Loyalty, devotion. I'm all fucking in.

I want to be with someone I can trust. Where there's no agenda other than to get to know each other. Is that so bad or wrong?

I'm worth it. I've worked hard. I'm not a bridge troll. I'm a smart, beautiful woman and I've worked really hard to get to this point.

Sure, I let an idiot nearly destroy me for 18 months. But that's a blip in the timeline of my entire life.

And I'm more than ready for the next chapter.

And now, as I replay today's conversation in my mind, I know I'm truly ready to give Dex a second chance. Not because I owe him anything, but because I'm beginning to see that maybe he really is different. Maybe he really does love me.

And maybe… I'm ready to start loving myself again, too.

CHAPTER 143
CUTTING THE CORD

When I hear Timmy has been arrested shortly after our breakup, I'm shocked—but not for the reasons one might think. His return to jail was inevitable—he's a ticking time bomb who's sure to end up in prison or dead.

But the speed of it—within a week of his move—is what catches me off guard.

The details trickle in slowly, and each revelation feels like a punch to the gut. His record stretches far beyond what I knew.

It turns out there are restraining orders filed against him in Montana too, as well as an outstanding arrest warrant from his previous visit.

Another state, another chapter of chaos he failed to mention. If these are the big lies—the glaring, documented truths he withheld—what other untruths did he spin daily? How many more pieces of his fabricated reality have I yet to uncover?

No wonder I feel so unmoored, so deeply confused. He lied about everything. Hell, he couldn't even admit he liked *cats* before he met mine. So why would I expect him to be honest about the big things—his child, his history of abuse, or the real reason for those protection orders?

He weaponizes everything.

When someone is as good as Timmy at twisting reality, at spinning every failure into someone else's fault, it's disorienting.

At first, it's hard to pinpoint the issue He was so convincing, redirecting every doubt, throwing out 'whataboutisms' until I started doubting myself instead.

Is the way I remember it really how it happened?

Because he seemed so sure, so confident in his version of events.

Now, with distance, I see it clearly—he knew exactly what he was doing.

Exploiting the natural fragility of memory to reshape the narrative.

Making me look like the crazy, desperate, toxic mess he actually was.

The amount of pain he caused me bubbles away under the surface, insidious and rotting. Therapy can help, sure, but it won't be enough for me.

I need more.

I need *vengeance*.

———

My phone buzzes, jolting me from my thoughts. I glance at the screen.

Phil.

The sight of his name sends a burst of anxiety through me. My heart races, blood pounding in my temples. My entire body feels like it's vibrating with tension.

It's as if the sight of his name on my phone screen just set me back weeks in my healing.

"Why's he calling?" I mutter. "What does he want now?"

Maybe it's to ask me not to tell the truth about his son, because he's not getting any dates, and it's making it impossible for Phil to get Timmy off his hands.

I let it go to voicemail, too anxious to answer. When the notification dings, I hesitate for a moment before pressing play with a trembling hand.

His voice is gruff, but he's clearly trying to keep it calm and fake cordial. "We're about to head to Costco," he says, as if I care. "And when we get back, I'd appreciate it if you could call me." There's a pause, the faintest edge of menace creeping into his tone. "Actually, you *will* call me back."

I shudder at the implication, my stomach turning.

The man is just as controlling as his awful son.

No wonder Timmy turned out the way he did.

I scoff at his mention of Costco. "Predictable," I mutter.

I glance at my watch. It's the 6th of the month. *Of course it is.*

Food stamp money just came in, and now Phil's dragging Timmy to the store to recoup whatever he can.

I imagine Timmy tagging along, trying to act like the dutiful son. Is he making his father pay for his contribution in other ways, just like he did with me? Is he micromanaging every step they take in the store, obsessing over which cart they grab, painstakingly massaging each onion to ensure it's 'perfect'?

The thought sends a wave of nausea through me. I don't want to dismiss his food insecurity—that's a legitimate struggle. But when it's weaponized, used as another tool of control, it becomes something else entirely.

With Phil, I bet Timmy's playing it differently. "Yes, Daddy, look at the perfect onions I curated just for you."

I used to think that kind of behavior was just Timmy being thorough, that maybe I could learn something from his attention to detail. But now I know it was just a control flex.

A power play.

And this is why I need to cut all of them off. Permanently. No second chances, no lingering connections. It's the only way to protect myself.

———

A couple of hours later, my phone buzzes again. Another voicemail.

This time, Phil's tone is venomous. "I'm calling about getting Timmy's things," he growls. "You *need* to call me back." His voice breaks at the end, the cracks in his patience starting to show.

The demand hangs in the air, heavy with entitlement. He sounds beside himself that I haven't yet returned his earlier call.

"No, Phil," I say out loud, my voice firm in the quiet of my apartment. "I don't *need* to do anything."

I sit down, my hands trembling as I call the police non-emergency line. My voice is steady as I explain the situation. The TRO is crystal clear—third parties are not allowed to contact me on Timmy's behalf.

This is a violation, plain and simple.

The dispatcher on the other end sends officers to take my report, their tone professional and reassuring. "We'll handle this," they say.

A sense of calm washes over me. Timmy and Phil may think they can still control me, manipulate me, but they're wrong. They have no power over me anymore.

They can't get to me.

And if they try? There will be consequences.

CHAPTER 144
THE DEXMATIZATION OF MARGAUX

MARGAUX

The past couple of weeks, Dex and I have been attached at the hip, and it's led me to some realizations.

Dex is funny, cute, and strong. The kind of strong man that doesn't feel threatening, but protective—like he'd never even consider using his size against me to intimidate or harm me.

And the way he laughs when I tease him? It's like he knows my jokes come from a kind, gentle place.

He doesn't get defensive or turn my humor into a weapon against me. He just laughs, his green-hazel eyes crinkling, making me feel like I'm safe here.

That's a hard feeling to trust. I've been trained by Timmy and his kind to brace for the other shoe to drop. For the sweet words to turn into venom, the kindness to reveal its hidden barbs. Part of me still waits for Dex to tell me that everything he admires about me is actually what he hates about me.

But that's just my trauma whispering in my ear. Of course, I'll stay vigilant, because I have to—I've learned too many painful lessons to ignore red flags.

But with Dex, it's different. The connection doesn't feel contrived or manufactured. It's rich, layered, and organic.

They say butterflies are your body's warning signal. With Timmy, I was radioactive—buzzing with anxiety and dopamine, swept up in a love-bombing haze that made me think he was my missing piece.

With Dex, there are no alarm bells. Just small, warm flutters of excitement. My brain is calm, my heart steady.

He has friends—plenty of them. Even some exes who he hangs out with as part of his broader friend group.

But unlike Timmy, he doesn't dangle them in front of me to make me jealous. Instead, he introduces me to them, brings me into his world, and I find that they're kind and welcoming, just like him.

And he doesn't propose within two weeks. He's not even sure if he wants to get married at all, which is fine by me. There's no rush, no pressure.

He has a job—an actual job—and he shows up for it, running his team with the kind of focus and passion that makes me admire him even more. I still don't know exactly what he does—all I know is he has a high-level security clearance and he can't talk a lot about his job—but that's okay.

I trust him.

———

After a comfortable night on the couch, snuggling against each other, I walk to the kitchen to refill my wine glass.

Dex appears next to me, and he pulls me to him.

He tilts his head and his lips brush mine, tentatively at first, as if he's gauging my response. I freeze for a moment, realizing these are the first lips to touch mine since Timmy's. The thought flickers through my mind like a shadow, but it doesn't stay. Because Dex's lips don't feel like Timmy's. They don't feel like anyone else's. They feel like warmth and safety and desire all rolled into one.

I haven't kissed anyone quite like this before. It's usually a little awkward —at least at first—although I suppose it wasn't with Timmy, either. Clearly, the quality of a first kiss isn't a strong indicator of the value of a relationship.

But the touch of his tongue on mine sends little shivers throughout my body, generating anticipation of what's to come. It feels natural, primal somehow. Electric, even. I hungrily explore his tongue with my own.

He starts to pull away, but I lean in, pressing my lips to his, feeling the way they mold perfectly against mine. Relief and yearning flood through me as his tongue grazes mine, and I let out a soft moan.

My hands find their way to the nape of his neck, my fingers tangling in his soft, sun-streaked locks. I pull him closer, deepening the kiss, hungry for him in a way that feels both primal and healing.

All thoughts of Timmy vanish. For the first time in what feels like forever, I'm not afraid. I'm not comparing. I'm just here, with Dex, and it's everything.

———

THE NEXT DAY

"I know we could've taken things further last night," Dex says, his voice low and warm. We're sitting on the couch, the soft glow of a lamp casting shadows on his chiseled features. "I know we both wanted to. But I wanted it to be on your terms. I didn't want to take advantage of you in a vulnerable moment. You've had enough of that already. And I definitely didn't want it to feel like a pity fuck. You're worth so much more than that."

His words hit me like a punch—gentle but firm, knocking the wind out of my defenses.

"I thought you didn't like me like that," I admit, my voice small. His lack of trying to get in my pants was beginning to bother me, making me feel like he wasn't interested.

"Oh no," he says, shaking his head with a soft smile. "I really, really like you. And I respect you. Sometimes that means passing up on good sex now and saving it for some mind-blowing sex later."

I laugh, the sound bubbling out before I can stop it. "I guess I'm not used to being around people who can regulate their emotions and impulses."

"Yeah," he says with a grin. "We exist."

———

STACEY:

You're sure you're ready for a relationship? This isn't too soon?

Stacey's message pings on my phone, her concern radiating from the screen. I can almost see her infamous side-eye as she types. She's ever-protective of me, and I appreciate it, even when it means she asks difficult questions.

And her question is fair.

ME:

It's not a relationship. We're just hanging out.

STACEY:

It seems to me that you're spending an awful lot of time together for two people who are just… hanging out. Are you in love or what?

I see she's typing more, so I wait for her incoming message while I ponder the answer.

STACEY:

Not that I can talk, seeing as my husband and I have been together since the night we first met.

I laugh. Stacey might be opinionated, but she's no hypocrite.

ME:

I— I wouldn't say 'in love'. I don't want to put a label on it just yet.

We have love for each other.

STACEY:

Well just be careful. I can't bear to see you hurt again. You deserve happiness and a bit of rest after all you've been through.

I can feel her trying to get into my mind, to see what's actually going on in there.

ME:

I'll be careful. I promise.

Satisfied, she leaves it at that.

———

They say comparison is the thief of joy, but in this case, contrasting Dex with Timmy gives me nothing but joy.

Dex is strong, but he doesn't use his strength to intimidate, coerce, or hurt me.

He's confident, but he doesn't use it to belittle me.

He's interested in me, but he doesn't weaponize my vulnerabilities and use things I tell him in confidence to hurt me later.

He's generous—without expecting anything in return.

He never brings up my trauma with the purpose of hurting me.

He's everything Timmy wasn't.

Dex enjoys seeing me happy, just for the sake of it. He doesn't keep a mental tally of favors or use my past against me. He has his own hobbies, his own life, and he respects mine. Sometimes we share, sometimes we don't, and that's okay.

He watches my shows without complaining, and I'm learning to enjoy football. Sometimes we're in separate rooms, but we're never far away.

I don't feel the need to look at his phone or email or track his location. Realistically, may I peek from time to time? Probably, yeah. But it's a trauma response I'm working through, and he's never given me any reason to doubt him.

I know he trusts me. I hold that like a cherished gift—like one of those fragile decorative eggs some people collect, just so much more important.

He enjoys being there for me, supporting me through the bad and the good, surprising me, and just seeing me be happy. That's all he wants.

For the first time in what feels like forever, I trust someone. *Really* trust them. It feels like a rare treasure I'm determined to protect.

I'd forgotten how good trust feels.

CHAPTER 145
NICE GUYS CAN HAVE BIG DICKS, TOO

MARGAUX

Later in the evening, we're making out on the couch. It's more than good, our tongues exploring each other while our hands roam each other's body.

But then I have a flashback, and I frown. "I'm beginning to think that's all women were put here for. To be used by men. To have our bodies trashed and desecrated for the pleasure of anyone with a dick. Until we're just shells, bashed and broken until they move onto the next one."

I'm having a bad day—nothing specific happened, just my emotions recovering, I guess, and—poor Dex—I'm taking it all out on him. *What a mood killer. Why did I just say all of that?*

But he doesn't flinch. He doesn't judge me. He just stays, steady and present. "That's where you're so wrong, Margaux," he replies, his voice calm but with an intensity that pulls my eyes to his. "And you're not wrong about much, but this is one of those times."

He uses a thumb to gently stroke an escaped tendril of my hair behind my ear, sending a little shiver through me.

"How so?" I ask, though my throat feels tight, vulnerable.

"It shouldn't be that way," he says, his eyes holding mine like he can see all the broken pieces inside me. "It should be about respect. About what you want to have happen. It should bring you pleasure. The only screams coming out of your mouth should be when I'm making you come."

My pussy clenches at the thought, a visceral response I'm too raw to hide. I swallow hard, and his lips curl slightly, like he knows exactly what effect he's having on me.

"I love the way you look at me," I say, my voice barely above a whisper. His green-hazel eyes sparkle warmly at me, and I try to smile, but my mouth twitches nervously.

He notices, of course. "You do?" he asks, tilting his head slightly. "You didn't look so sure just then."

"Well, I'd like it—love it—if it didn't make me feel so scared."

"Do I have something in my teeth?" he jokes softly, his grin teasing but never mocking.

I laugh despite myself. "No, it's just… the last time someone appeared to look at me in an adoring fashion—other than my cat when he wants a treat—was Timmy. And it's part of what made me fall for him."

His expression darkens, just a fraction. "So you don't trust my eyes because of Timmy's eyes? That doesn't seem fair." He pauses. "I'm not him."

I'm caught. "I'm sorry," I say, stepping closer to him, wrapping my arms around his neck. He doesn't flinch or pull away, just holds me like it's the most natural thing in the world. "I'm trying to make sure I don't repeat past mistakes. And I know I've gotten better about setting boundaries, but I'm still working on trusting myself to notice the red flags."

"What red flags have you noticed about me?" he asks, his tone light but curious.

"Oh, other than your awful taste in music?" I giggle, lightly punching his arm.

He grins, his face softening. "Well, you tell me if that changes." Then, with zero warning, he scoops me up and hoists me over his shoulder like I weigh nothing. I giggle uncontrollably as he carries me to the bedroom.

His hands trail down my back, strong and sure, before settling on my hips. He lifts me effortlessly, and I wrap my legs around his waist, feeling the solid strength of him against me.

I giggle as my hair flies across his back, and my pussy clenches at the easy way he lifted me.

He carries me to the bed, lowering me gently onto the mattress.

His hands are huge, and much stronger than my own. He could really hurt me if he wanted to. But he never would. He would only use them to bring me pleasure, to care for me.

His eyes meet mine, searching. "Are you sure?" he asks, his voice rough with restraint.

"You don't need to ask me that," I reply, my gaze steady. "I want you. And I don't want you to be gentle. I'm not a delicate flower."

His lips quirk into a wicked smile. "Careful what you wish for."

And then he's on me, wrapping his massive hand around the back of my neck, pulling my face to his, his mouth claiming mine with an intensity that makes my toes curl. This kiss is helping me, and I need a lot more healing.

His tongue explores mine while his other hand traces its way down my chest, and cups my breast through my shirt.

My nipples are rock hard, and only grow harder as he tugs on the delicate silver bars that run through them, sending little zaps of electricity down to my core.

I trail my hand from his neck down his muscular back and to his hip, and continue toward his thigh. He feels strong, solid under my touch. He's so much bigger than me, and his masculinity is intoxicating.

For the first time in what feels like forever, being around a man isn't scary. There's nothing I want more than to be with Dex, right here, right now.

He lets out a soft groan as my hand makes contact with his inner thigh, and trails its way across to his cock, which already strains through his pants.

I won't lie and say I hadn't thought about what it would be like, and I'm not disappointed. Even through the material, I can tell he's above average—nothing about this man is average, so no surprises there.

He groans again softly as I rub him through his pants.

His hands roam my body, pulling my shirt over my head, tugging at my jeans until we're both naked, skin to skin.

His body is a work of art, all rippling muscle and inked skin, and when I glance down, my breath catches at the sight of him.

His massive cock glimmers in the light. "Holy shit," I murmur, eyes widening as I take in the piercings. A Prince Albert *and* a Jacob's ladder. "Well, that's…" I can't find the words.

He smirks. "Not what you were expecting?"

I bite my lower lip.

"I didn't know what to expect. Definitely didn't expect all the hardware," I say, gesturing toward his piercings.

Dex chuckles, the sound low and throaty. "Nice guys can have big dicks too, you know. They don't just get handed out to the assholes. Pierced ones, as well."

I laugh, the tension easing. "Fair. And this is getting weirdly close to that one speech in *Team America: World Police.*"

"Do you want to talk about old movies, or do you want to fuck?" He leans in close, hunger in his eyes.

I bite my lower lip again as I lean down.

"Definitely want to talk about movies," I joke, reaching out to touch his cock.

He groans at my touch.

Then his gaze darkens as he trails his fingers down my body, stopping between my legs. He groans softly as he feels how wet I am, and the sound sends a fresh wave of arousal coursing through me.

"You're so fucking beautiful, Margaux," he murmurs, his voice reverent. "And so fucking ready for me."

He kisses his way down my chest, stopping at each nipple to swirl his tongue around them, sucking and tugging gently on the little silver bars. I moan, feeling the sensation all the way to my pussy, which clenches in anticipation.

His mouth continues its journey, stopping at my belly button. I moan as he swirls his tongue around the outside, and then within, exploring every part of my navel.

Then he yanks my thighs apart and licks me from my clit to my back entrance. "God, you taste good," he growls.

I moan and arch my back as his tongue attacks my clit, swirling around my rose pink bud. He sucks on my clit and my hips buck as he continues to feast on me.

"Dex," I moan, as he first points and then flattens his tongue against my entrance, and then trails it upward, back to where he started.

My hips roll as he fans his tongue over my lips and up to my clit, and he continues his assault on my swollen bud.

I can't help but tilt my head forward so I can get a better view of his expert tongue working my clit, and he returns my gaze with his gorgeous hazel-green eyes which are now darkened with lust.

My teeth clamp down on my lower lip as my orgasm builds, the coil within me tightening and tightening until it suddenly crests and takes me over.

I yell, "Oh fuck," as white stars explode in the corner of my eyes, but this time they're because of pleasure, and I wrap my thighs tightly around his head as he continues to lap at my pussy while I ride out my orgasm.

Finally, it subsides, and I push him away as the sensitivity becomes too much.

He lifts his head and smirks at me, my arousal still slick across his mouth and chin which he doesn't seem to mind at all.

When he finally enters me, it's like coming home. He puts his weight on me, and I feel dominated by his imposing figure, and I like it.

His piercings drag against my walls, hitting spots I didn't even know existed. He moves slowly at first, letting me adjust to him, but when I moan and arch my back, he picks up the pace, driving into me with a fervor that leaves me breathless.

"It's okay to be a bit rougher with me, you know. I can handle it," I pant.

I can't help but feel he might be tiptoeing and being overly gentle, as if I'm fragile. As if he might break me. And that makes me sad.

"Okay, if that's what you want, I'm into it, too," he whispers back. "But I want to make sure I don't do anything to hurt you, because that's the last thing I want to do. I want to make you feel safe and protected and worshipped like you deserve."

Good chills roll through my body. "And I want to feel safe and… ravished, please?"

He continues to thrust, harder now. "Oh, absolutely. But know there's nothing I'd do in this world to harm you, or put you in danger."

"I can feel that. I feel entirely safe around you."

He nods, and begins to thrust harder.

"But I'm totally fine with you doing dirty, dirty things to me. I want you to toss me around, throw me over your shoulder, fuck me hard. Because to me, that's good pain. That's the kind I want."

"I want to show you how it's meant to be," he growls.

"I—."

"Margaux, it's okay," he says, continuing to thrust.

"I want you to hurt me," I pant.

"You say what now?" He quirks a brow, but doesn't stop thrusting.

"I don't want all that gentle shit. I'm not a fragile piece of china that you need to handle delicately in case I shatter." I clench my pussy tighter around his cock and he lets out a soft groan. "I'm already shattered, and I've finally started to feel like I've put myself together again. I want to feel something. So stop acting like you're walking on fucking eggshells around me and fuck me properly."

He gazes into my eyes. "You're sure that's what you want?"

I return his gaze, unflinching. "Abso-fucking-lutely."

"Alright then," he says. "But I can stop at any—."

I glare at him and place a finger over his lips.

"Shut the fuck up and give it to me, Dex."

"Your wish is my command," he says, and he starts going to town, pounding into me with an intensity that makes his body slap against my pussy every time he buries himself in me all the way to his hilt.

"Fuck, Dex," I gasp, clutching at his shoulders. "Don't stop."

"Never," he growls, his hands gripping my hips as he pounds into me, each thrust sending me higher and higher. "I'll never stop. Not until you're screaming my name."

And I do. Again and again.

"That's it, Margaux, baby. Come for me," Dex growls, his thrusts becoming even more frenzied.

I come apart around his cock, my pussy contracting around his length as I shatter into a million pieces.

Dex moans my name as he follows suit, filling me with his hot seed. "Fuck, Margaux," he groans.

For a moment, we lay there panting, our bodies still connected as we catch our breath. Finally, Dex pulls out and collapses next to me on the bed.

My head nestles into the crook of his armpit where I fit perfectly.

I smile as I gaze up at him, and he smiles back.

My heart melts.

Because with Dex, it's not just about the physical. It's about everything he's giving me that I didn't know I needed.

It's about trust.

It's about healing.

It's about love.

"Well," he says, running a hand through his sweaty hair, "I think we just made up for lost time."

I can't help but laugh, my body still tingling from our intense coupling. "I'd say so," I reply, nuzzling into his chest. "But don't think you're off the hook yet, babe. We still have a lot of catching up to do."

Dex grins, his eyes twinkling with mischief. "Oh, I have no doubt we'll find ways to pass the time," he purrs, his fingers trailing a lazy pattern on my stomach. "And who knows? Maybe we'll even make it to dinner tonight."

But right now, I'm not so sure either of us is leaving this bed anytime soon.

And as for me?

I'm absolutely—without a doubt—Dexmatized.

CHAPTER 146
COCK BLOCK

DEX

Now that Margaux is safe, it's finally time for justice to take its course.

I want to kill Timmy. Every fiber of my being craves it. But death? That's too easy. Too quick. It's a mercy he doesn't deserve. *Not yet.*

He needs to be dismantled piece by piece.

A narcissist's deepest fear isn't death—it's being unmasked. Exposed for the sad, hollow shell they truly are. Timmy's built his life on lies, carefully curated to keep himself in the center of everyone's good graces. But I know the truth. I've seen the wreckage he's left in Margaux's life, and I'll make sure everyone else does too.

I start small, planting seeds that will grow into his unraveling.

First, I flood social media with posts about Timmy. Burner accounts, fake profiles, all of them loaded with receipts so he can't dispute it—screenshots of text exchanges, photos of police reports, and audio of his tantrums. Each post is tagged with his name, ensuring they reach everyone in his orbit, so that his so-called friends, his family, his potential dates—can all see him for what he truly is.

Then I hack into his personal accounts, locking him out with new passwords. I upload a fake 'confession' video where Timmy admits to all his wrongdoings, complete with tearful apologies and self-deprecating remarks about his inadequacy. It's so realistic, even *I* almost believe it.

But I'm not done.

To strangers, people who don't know him well—or the few people who still believe his lies—Timmy has crafted a persona as the good guy, even a hero in the community who helps to protect the local environment.

So I destroy it.

I leak footage of him screaming at Margaux, of him smashing plates, of him berating her for imagined slights. I post it everywhere. The local community, his surfing buddies, even the bars he frequents—none of them can look at him the same.

I lure him to a public event in Montana with his parents, with promises of the chance to win money by showing off. When he arrives, I've hired strangers to confront him one by one, listing the harm he's caused. Each confrontation is recorded and shared online.

I gather testimonies from his victims—Margaux included—and post them in public spaces. Bars, coffee shops, gyms—all plastered with the headline: *We Know What You Did, Timmy—Tick Tock!*

I lock him out of all his graphic design software, the tools he used to develop AI-generated graphics to build the meager career Margaux funded. Without them, he's nothing. No one.

Then, the petty stuff.

Posters of his face with phrases like *Have You Seen This Abuser?* go up in his neighborhood. QR codes labeled *'Curious About Timmy? Click Here'* lead to a dossier of his worst moments. His name is whispered in every corner of Sunset Cay as well as Montana, linked to scandal and shame.

I create fake dating profiles, loaded with humiliating information. He doesn't stand a chance—his matches on his real accounts get links to the same dossier before the first date.

I even sign him up for mail subscriptions—porn magazines, erectile dysfunction brochures—all sent to his parents' house. His father must love that.

I tip off the local paper about Timmy's history, ensuring his name makes the headlines for all the wrong reasons.

I anonymously have custom T-shirts and signs that say 'Ask Me About My Restraining Orders (I have 7)', along with his picture, and hang them where Timmy frequents.

I anonymously write a fictionalized version of Margaux's story, but change the names, casting Timmy as the victim. When the story becomes public, Timmy is forced to confront how it feels to be dehumanized and picked apart in front of others.

I hire actors to 'compliment' Timmy in ways that mirror his manipulative comments to Margaux when he's out trying to impress dates and strangers—things like, "You're great for a guy with so many flaws!" or "It's brave of you to still be out here after all the restraining orders."

Finally, I make sure he can't escape his shame within his surfing community. At a major surfing event, I hack the live stream and project a video compilation of Timmy's worst moments. The crowd watches in stunned silence as his true self plays out in high definition.

I sit back, watching the chaos unfold.

And just when he thinks it's over, I plant drug paraphernalia and tip off the cops. Timmy is arrested and locked up, his worst nightmare realized. A month in jail.

I savor his distress as he sits helpless, behind bars, and watch his facade begin to crack. The charm he once wielded so effortlessly fails to find an audience among the hardened faces around him.

His agitation grows with each passing day, his nerves fraying as paranoia seeps in—are his cellmates whispering about him?

He can't sleep, haunted by nightmares of betrayal and public humiliation.

Depression takes root as the weight of his tarnished reputation becomes inescapable, and he's left to stew in the silence, spiraling further into despair.

One day, during shower time, a few other inmates decide they like the look of his long hair from behind and they descend upon him, forcing themselves into him while he cries out begging them to stop. "That's what you get for raping Margaux, you piece of shit," I say out loud to myself.

By the time he's released, the once smug, self-assured Timmy is nothing but a shadow of himself—angry, broken, and consumed by the fear that the world now sees him for exactly who he is.

His life crumbles further, his reputation in more tatters than ever before.

Good luck getting a date now, Timmy.

Good luck finding a job.

Good luck escaping the shadow of your own lies.

But still—despite all of this evidence—his father stands blindly by his side, falling for Timmy's justifications, his rationalizations, his excuses. Phil clings to the idea of his son as a misunderstood victim, a man who the world just can't appreciate.

Even with the evidence laid bare, Phil refuses to see it.

"It's all lies," he says to anyone who will listen. "My boy's been set up. He's a good kid, just lost his way. These people are out to get him."

Phil defends Timmy with every ounce of misguided loyalty he has, blaming everyone else—Margaux, the cops, the system, society. It's everyone's fault but Timmy's.

And that's what keeps Timmy going. That unshakable enabler. That one person who will never stop believing in his lies, no matter how transparent they are.

It's almost sad. *Almost.*

But not enough to make me stop.

You don't get to hurt my Margaux and walk away unscathed. You don't get to move on while she's picking up the pieces.

I'll make sure of that.

A ROOM OF TRUTHS

DEX

THE NEXT DAY

t's time for the next phase of my plan. Margaux thinks I have an overnight work trip, but that was a white lie. I'm taking a personal day instead. Because I have other plans. *Plans to make things right.*

The air in the room is dense, heavy with years of pain and injustice. I lean against the doorframe, watching Phil squirm in the chair, his wrists tied firmly to the armrests. He refuses to look at the walls, his face cast downward like a scolded child.

"Look," I command, my voice a razor slicing through the silence.

He shakes his head, muttering something incoherent.

I stride forward, gripping the sides of his head and forcing it upward. His resistance is feeble. He squeezes his eyes shut, as if darkness could save him.

"I told you to *look*," I growl.

"No," he whimpers, trying to shake his head, but I hold it in place. "No," he says again.

"Alright then," I say, pulling two ophthalmic speculums from my bag that I happen to have on hand. *What can I say? My job is interesting.* "We'll do it the hard way."

Phil thrashes weakly, but it's no use. Within seconds, his eyes are pried open, wide and unable to blink.

And then he sees it.

The walls come alive with horror as he's forced to see the toll his son has taken on the world. Every wall plastered with evidence of his son's evil acts.

Mugshots of Timmy at every stage of his miserable adult life.

Police records detailing arrests for domestic violence, public intoxication, and terroristic threats. Criminal charges, police statements, court records, and outstanding child support notices.

Photos of women's faces bruised and swollen, fat lips, black eyes, children with bruises.

X-rays and scans of shattered bones and fractured skulls.

Handwritten restraining orders filled with words that sting like acid: *attacked me with deer antlers, attacked me with a hammer, strangled me, poured boiling water on me, threatened me with a chainsaw, threatened to blow fireworks up between my eyes, threatened to drive a truck into me.*

Phil's breath catches, but he stays still, as if not moving means none of this is real.

I step closer, my voice dripping with disdain. "They must've all done something to deserve it, right, Phil? Every woman. Every child. Every shattered bone and fractured skull—clearly, they earned it."

"No," Phil mumbles.

"Say it louder, Phil. Defend your son. Go on, tell me how he's really a 'nice guy.'"

His face flames with indignation. "He's a good person! He just—he's had a hard life!"

I laugh, a sharp, cruel sound. "A *hard life*? Timmy's life wasn't hard—it was easy because you *let* him make everyone *else's* life hard instead. You enabled this monster, Phil. Every time you defended him, excused him, brushed it under the rug—you made this."

I press the remote in my hand, and the screens light up. Footage of Timmy floods the room.

"I'm going to kill you, you stupid fucking cunt!"

"I'm greasing the wheels to put you in jail."

"I'm going to destroy your life."

"You won't be alive soon."

"Sure, I make some things up when I tell dad things. But I want him on my side, so I say what I have to."

Phil's breathing grows shallow, and sweat beads on his brow.

"Recognize that voice?" I ask.

"I—"

"And this?" I press another button. Surveillance footage shows Timmy stumbling through the meth encampment, laughing as he flicks a lighter at someone's tent. Another clip shows him screaming at Margaux, the veins in his neck bulging as he calls her every vile name imaginable.

Footage of him stumbling around muttering to himself and cursing at random passersby.

Phil slumps in the chair.

"Is this your 'really nice guy'?" I ask.

"But, but…"

"No fucking buts, Phil. It's time to face the fucking truth. Your son is an evil, abusive criminal."

"It's just… the alcohol.."

"Face the fucking music, Phil. It's not the alcohol, or even the copious amount of drugs he's done. It's your parenting. You created a monster, a demon that hurts women and children."

His face flames with indignation. "Well no, that's not true—"

"Oh, shut the fuck up, Phil. There are rigorous studies that show subhumans like your piece of shit excuse for a son become that way because of their value systems. And where do you think people—especially *men*—develop their value systems from?"

"I—I—"

"Oh, shut the fuck up. Stop making excuses. The reality is that you are largely responsible for all the pain and trauma and damage and loss that your son has caused. Instead of being a man and holding your son accountable, you preferred to brush his actions under the rug, choosing your own peace over protecting others from pain. You willingly stood by your son in the face of evidence of his wrongdoing, going so far as to gaslight his victims and make them feel even *worse*, questioning their own sanity."

His breathing is ragged now, and I can't tell whether it's from anger or fear and honestly, I couldn't give a flying fuck which it is.

"Your son might be a dangerous, evil mess, Phil. But *you… you* are the lowest of the low. The tree that the Timmy apple fell from. You, in your own way, abused his victims. Did you get off on that, Phil? Did you enjoy calling Margaux a 'volcano of pain' and blaming her? Did it make you feel better to abdicate your own complicity in Timmy's behavior by transferring the blame onto someone whose *skull he fucking broke*? Did you really think it was okay to blame her because after *months and months and months* of his abuse and torture she finally snapped and, what—told him he was a loser and a piece of shit? If you believe his shit—that she finally smacked him a few times, or pulled his hair or scratched him—wouldn't you have done the same fucking thing? If someone spent hour after hour telling you that you were a slut, cunt, bitch, ugly, gross, that you should have been raped, that your dead uncle doesn't matter, that you're making up health issues, removing pieces of your vehicle so you can't get away, kidnapping your friend's son, threatening to kill you constantly, telling you that you won't be alive soon, and going so far as to *rape* you and then *laugh* about it?"

"I—he—"

"You created him, Phil. You. And instead of owning up to it, you've been his accomplice. You've called his victims liars, you've made them question their sanity, and you've let Timmy go free to destroy more lives. How does it feel to know you're as guilty as he is?"

"I didn't mean—"

"You *meant* to protect yourself," I snarl, leaning in close. "It was easier for you to blame Margaux. Easier to call her vile names than to admit your son is the source of all this destruction. You're a *coward*, Phil."

He begins to shake, tears slipping from the corners of his forced-open eyes.

"You're a fucking piece of work, Phil. I'm going to leave you here to let a bit of this sink in to your thick fucking skull."

He quivers, starts to say something, and then shuts his mouth.

I cross my arms. "Take it in. Every broken bone, every tear-streaked face, every shattered life. This is your legacy. Enjoy it."

I turn the volume up, Timmy's ranting voice filling the room.

"Have a nice evening, Phil," I say. "I'd say it's been nice to meet you, but I'm not a good liar."

Phil whimpers as I walk out, slamming the door behind me.

———

When I return the next morning, Phil is broken. His shoulders slump, his head hangs low and his eyes are dull. The fight is gone from his body, replaced by a hollow emptiness.

There's no more of the bluster he usually reserves to defend his son for his heinous acts. Because Phil *loves* a good woman-blaming moment, just like his son.

Good. It's the least this piece of shit deserves after what he's assisted his son to put innocent people through.

I crouch in front of him, removing the speculums from his eyes. He blinks rapidly, the motion too little, too late.

"Have you accepted the truth?" I ask, my voice cold. "Have you finally accepted who the problem is, Phil?"

He doesn't respond.

"Say it," I demand, pulling out my phone and hitting *Record.*

Margaux needs to hear this as part of her healing, and I'm sure others do, too. It might be under duress, but after spending a night seeing and hearing my little room of harsh truths, if Phil doesn't finally accept the facts laid bare, he's even more fucked than I realized.

He shifts in his chair.

"Say it, Phil," I repeat. "*Fucking* say it. Because I don't want to have to physically hurt you, but I will if you don't say the words that Margaux and all Timmy's other victims need to hear."

"Timmy is the problem," he whispers.

"And were these situations validated or justified because 'she must have done something to upset him?' Or because 'it takes two?' That all of these relationships just happened to be toxic and the women were at fault?"

"Well…"

"Don't play with me, Phil," I growl. "I'm warning you. My dark side gets much darker than this."

He sighs. "I see it now," he says, his voice trembling. "He… he's done horrible things. Hurt so many people. I enabled it. I believed him over them because it was easier than facing the truth."

"And Margaux?"

"I'm sorry, Margaux," he says, barely audible. "I'm sorry for blaming you, for making you feel like you were the problem. You weren't. You tried to help him, and we all failed you. *I* failed you."

I stop the recording.

"Good," I say, leaning in close enough for him to feel my breath on his ear. "But sorry isn't enough, Phil. Not for Margaux, not for the others. So what do you have to say for your part in all of this? For the way you made his victims feel small? That you made them question whether they really were the ones to blame? You'll live with this guilt for the rest of your life, and that's the only justice they'll ever get."

I press 'Record' again.

"I—," he says, then he swallows. "I'm sorry. I just really loved my son and wanted to believe him and look past everything. I never intended on hurting anyone, but I see my actions have taken a toll."

"Tell Margaux specifically how sorry you are. Be specific."

"I—Margaux, I really liked you when we first met. And then Timmy told me so many things and… well, he's my son. I guess it was just easier to believe his lies and ignore the fact he's had this pattern with so many people before you. It was easier to paint you as the villain than to believe my own son was evil and that he needs to be in a mental institution or, well… prison. I'm… I'm not sorry for being a protective father, but I'm sorry for blaming you. For hurting you. For gaslighting you and magnifying my son's abuse. You were just trying to help him to be a better person. And in return, he hurt you. Mentally and physically, and he broke all your stuff."

"And? You're sorry for calling her what?"

"I'm sorry for calling you a volcano of pain, Margaux. I don't know where that even came from. It's not true, and I'm sorry."

I click 'Stop' on the recording.

I don't know whether to believe him or not, but he's said the words I needed him to, so I don't really care. Karma will take its course. At the end of the day, Phil has to live with himself.

A tear slides down his face.

I still don't quite believe his words. I still think he's a woman-hating, self-aggrandizing prick who mollycoddled his son into the evil menace to society he is today.

But I have his voice on record.

And all I really care about is giving Margaux some of the closure and validation I know she so desperately needs.

I undo the ropes restraining Phil to the chair, re-tie them and blindfold him.

He slowly rises to his feet, and I load him into my van and drive him back to his neighborhood, a few blocks away from his house.

Untying him and removing the blindfold, I let him out.

Phil stumbles out of the van, his steps shaky. Before he leaves, he turns to me.

"Thank you," he whispers. "For making me see what I didn't want to see. I think he's far beyond any help I could give him. I've raised a devil, and let him create a hell that nobody else deserves, and I can never forgive myself for that."

I say nothing, watching as he disappears into the morning light, a shadow of the man he was.

The monster he created may never be stopped, but for one brief moment, Phil had to face the full weight of his complicity.

And that's a start.

CHAPTER 148
THE PERFECT DAY

DEX

LATER IN THE EVENING

The room is dark, illuminated only by the flicker of a single overhead bulb swinging slightly with the breeze from the old ceiling fan. The shadows cast along the concrete walls feel alive, restless, as though they share my anticipation.

Timmy deserves this.

Every broken piece of Margaux's spirit, every tear she shed, every time she flinched at the sound of a raised voice—he's going to answer for all of it. Not quickly. Not easily. Not mercifully.

I pull a thick notebook from the table, its pages filled with my scrawled notes, diagrams, and lists. Tools, timing, contingencies. Everything is carefully planned. A sick sort of satisfaction rolls through me as I flip to the next page and see my collection of 'reminders.' Reminders of why I'm doing this. Photos of Margaux's bruised arms and black eyes. Screenshots of his vile text messages. A grainy image from the courthouse showing her leaving, holding back tears.

He's going to beg before I'm done. Not just for his life, but for her forgiveness. And I'll record every pathetic second of it.

I step into the corner, where my arsenal is laid out meticulously. Each item serves a purpose, a twisted piece of the justice puzzle. The ti leaf leis and string of shells, symbols of the manipulative 'thoughtful' gestures Timmy used to keep Margaux under his thumb, now dangle like trophies.

The jagged lid of a smashed toilet tank leans against the wall—a small, dirty reminder of the mundane things he used to destroy her sanity.

A soft lilac hammer, absurd in its pastel brightness, sits next to a box of deer antlers.

In the far corner of the room sits the pièce de résistance: a wood chipper. Its metal teeth gleam even in the dim light, a predator waiting for its prey.

Timmy is dragged into the room by two of my most trusted associates, his wrists bound, his face pale and sweaty. His eyes dart around, taking in the implements of his demise. He freezes when his gaze lands on the wood chipper.

"Please," he stammers. "What do you want from me? I'll do anything."

I crouch in front of him, forcing him to meet my eyes. "What I want is simple," I say, my voice low and calm. "You're going to confess. To everything. You're going to apologize to Margaux for every single thing you've done. And you're going to mean it."

"I—I didn't do anything," he whimpers, the tremor in his voice betraying his terror.

I laugh, cold and humorless. "Oh, Timmy. That's not how this works." I gesture to the table, where a recorder sits blinking red. "Let's start with the truth."

I move behind him and fasten a lei around his neck, pulling it just tight enough to make him wheeze. "Remember these? Margaux loved them. Or, she used to. Before you turned every kind gesture into a leash."

I release him and pick up the hammer. "This one's fun. Pretty, isn't it?" I swing it lightly, letting it tap his shoulder. He flinches as though I'd hit him with full force. "We'll get to it."

I walk over to the table and pull out a large pot of steaming ramen water. "Hungry? You always loved ramen." I toss a ladle of the boiling liquid onto his thigh. He screams, writhing against his restraints. The sound is music to my ears.

"Confess, Timmy," I say, tilting the pot toward him. "It'll hurt less."

His voice cracks as he begins to mumble incoherent apologies. "I'm sorry... I didn't mean to... Please, don't—"

"Not good enough." I pick up a grater, running its jagged edges across his arm with enough pressure to leave angry red lines. He winces as blood starts to pool in his abrasions. "This is for lying to the police about Margaux scratching you. Try again."

He breaks earlier than I expected. "Okay, okay!" he yells. "I'll do it! I did all those things to Margaux! I abused her and I hurt her. I lied to her. I'm *sorry!*"

His words are desperate, fake.

"Can I go now?" he pleads.

I quirk a brow and smirk. "Did you really think I was going to let you off that easily?"

His eyes grow wide as he realizes I'm far from done with him.

That he's not going to make it out of this room alive.

"Get comfy," I say. "You're going to be here for a while."

He lets out a whimper as tears slide down his cheeks.

The session continues, a twisted symphony of his screams, my calm instructions, and the rhythmic hum of the wood chipper waiting in the wings. He cries, begs, and pleads, promising anything if I'll just stop.

But I don't.

Instead, I pick up the shiny, white toilet lid and smack it over his head. He cries out and sits, stunned, while I take its jagged edge and run it down his arm, cutting a deep gash into his badly tattooed flesh. Crimson pours from the wound, large drops landing on the floor at his feet.

I bring out a device with a sturdy metal frame and multiple prods attached to the end. The device hums to life with a low mechanical whirr, a sound that feels almost innocuous compared to what it's about to unleash. The rows of polished steel rods begin their rhythm, prodding forward and retracting in perfect synchronization. The tips gleam under the dim light, deceptively small but unyielding.

Timmy's eyes widen as the realization sinks in. "What the fuck is that?" he spits, thrashing against the restraints. His voice cracks, the cocky defiance slipping as fear tightens its grip on him.

"It's something special, just for you," I say, my voice cold, detached. "Think of it as... poetic justice."

I position the device near his exposed arms first, the rods set to randomize their poking pattern. With a single press of a button, the motion intensifies. The first few pokes are almost laughably gentle, but then the rods begin to land harder, faster. The tips press into his skin, leaving faint red marks that quickly deepen into bruises.

Timmy flinches, gritting his teeth, but the composure doesn't last long. "Stop! Fuck, that hurts!" he yells, his voice high-pitched, panicked.

"Does it?" I tilt my head, feigning curiosity. "Good. Imagine what Margaux felt every time you chipped away at her, one cruel comment at a time. One lie. One bruise—hidden or otherwise."

The rods continue their relentless assault, targeting his biceps, forearms, and ribs. His skin mottles with deep purple bruises, each poke igniting a new jolt of pain. He writhes against the bindings, sweat dripping from his temple, but there's no escape.

"You're fucking insane!" he screams, his voice hoarse, cracking with desperation. *"Let me go, you psychopath!"*

I lean in close, my voice barely above a whisper. "You think *I'm* insane? You've barely scratched the surface, Timmy."

The device shifts to his thighs, and the repeated jabs force his legs to twitch involuntarily. He lets out a guttural yell, his bravado completely gone. Tears streak down his face now, pooling at the edges of his quivering lips.

"You don't get to cry," I snap, my voice suddenly sharp. "Margaux cried enough for a lifetime because of you."

As the machine continues, a strange sensation washes over me—a mix of satisfaction and hollowness. The satisfaction comes from seeing him unravel, watching as the mask he wore so confidently shatters piece by piece. But the hollowness? That's harder to explain. Maybe it's because I know this will never undo what he did to Margaux. No amount of pain I inflict on him can truly erase hers.

I step back, watching as Timmy's entire body trembles, his skin blotched and swollen. He's sobbing now, broken in a way I once thought impossible for someone as narcissistic as him.

"I'll do anything," he pleads, his voice barely audible. "I'm sorry. Please stop. *Please.*"

The apology is hollow, forced, a pathetic attempt to save himself. I know it's meaningless. But I record it anyway, every word, every broken sob. Margaux deserves to hear him grovel, even if it's a farce.

My hand hovers over the control panel. The machine slows, then halts, the rods retracting one final time. Timmy's head hangs forward, his body shaking with silent sobs. I crouch down to meet his eye level, forcing him to look at me.

"You're nothing," I tell him, my voice steady, quiet. "And you're going to feel every ounce of pain you put Margaux through before I'm done."

He stares at me, his face a canvas of terror, pain, and humiliation. For a brief moment, I wonder if he regrets everything, anything. But I dismiss the thought just as quickly as it comes. People like Timmy don't regret—they rationalize, justify, excuse.

And that's why this isn't over. *Not yet.*

Keeping his hands restrained, I drag him from the chair to the shiny metal table in the center of the room. It gleams under the harsh overhead light, a sterile contrast to the dark intentions I've brought here. He stumbles, his bound feet clumsy as he struggles against me, muttering incoherent protests.

"Please, no—what are you doing?!" His voice cracks, raw with desperation, but I ignore him.

I position him on his back, forcing his head to dangle off the end of the table, lower than his feet. The blood rushes to his face, turning it blotchy and red, making the panic in his eyes stand out stark against his flushed skin.

"Stop! You can't do this!" he screams, jerking his body uselessly as I press his shoulders down. He can't move. He's powerless.

"Quiet, Timmy," I say, my voice calm, almost detached. "We're just getting started."

I grab a dark cloth from the table nearby and slowly place it over his face, ensuring it covers his mouth and nose completely. His muffled pleas grow more frantic, his chest heaving beneath the restraints as he fights to suck in air. The fabric muffles his voice, turning his words into unintelligible whimpers, but the terror in his tone is unmistakable.

"This," I say, leaning closer so he can hear me over his muffled gasps, "is for waterboarding Margaux's laptop. Tit for tat, Timmy. It's only fair."

His entire body thrashes as the first drops of water hit the cloth, soaking it. His feet kick uselessly against the table's edge, and his hands jerk in their restraints. The water seeps through the fabric, cutting off his air supply in terrifying increments. His body convulses, his instincts screaming at him to breathe, but every attempt is met with the suffocating weight of water.

His muffled screams turn into wet, gurgling noises, his chest bucking upward in a futile attempt to fill his lungs with air. The disorientation in his eyes is raw, animalistic—pure survival. His head jerks violently from side to side, trying to escape the torrent, but there's nowhere to go.

And me? I feel... steady. *Too* steady.

There's no rush of satisfaction, no sense of justice being served. Only a cold, calculated focus. Every time I pour, I watch him struggle, his body betraying him as panic overtakes him. He sputters, chokes, convulses. It's a grotesque display, and part of me thinks it should feel wrong, should feel like it's too much.

But then I think of Margaux. I think of her sitting in her hotel room, tears streaming down her face as she picked up the shattered pieces of her life and her laptop. How she sobbed over the years of work he destroyed, knowing he'd done it just to hurt her.

And I pour again.

"You think *this* feels bad, Timmy?" I say, my voice low, deliberate. "Imagine every tear Margaux cried over what you did to her. Every ounce of pain you caused her. Multiply it by a thousand, and you might begin to understand."

His body slows, exhaustion setting in. His movements become jerky, weaker, but the terror in his eyes remains. He's drenched, his skin pale and clammy now, his breaths coming in shallow, ragged gasps whenever I pause long enough to let him recover.

A toaster oven dings in the corner. "Ah, I guess we're onto the next stage," I say. "Shame, I was enjoying that." I pull the cloth off his face, letting him cough and sputter, his chest heaving like bellows. His eyes dart wildly, filled with both terror and the faint, fragile hope that it's over.

But it's nowhere near over.

"Look at me, Timmy," I command, gripping his chin and forcing his gaze to mine. "This? This is mercy. Because if I wanted to, I could keep this up until you stop breathing entirely."

His lips tremble, and his body shivers uncontrollably. He's broken, reduced to a quivering, gasping mess on the table.

And me? I feel nothing but cold determination.

"You'll never touch her again," I tell him, my voice sharp as steel. "You'll never hurt anyone again."

I untie Timmy and move him, as he struggles, back to the chair where I restrain him once more.

Then I walk to the toaster oven and remove two piping hot pop tarts.

The sugary glaze bubbles and sizzles, a sticky, molten layer over the pastry's jagged edges. My hands feel the heat even through the dish towel, and I can only imagine what this is going to feel like for Timmy.

I carry them over to where he's strapped to the chair, his eyes darting nervously. "Hungry?" I ask, holding them up with exaggerated cheerfulness.

For a moment, his expression flickers—hope? Confusion? But then he sees the glint in my eye, the barely contained fury behind my forced smile, and his face collapses back into abject terror.

"Wait—what are you doing? Don't—please—" he stammers, his voice trembling.

Without a word, I yank down his board shorts, exposing his limp, pale dick. He flinches, trying to curl away, but the restraints hold him firm. His breathing quickens, shallow and panicked, as I press one steaming pop tart against the tender underside of his cock and nestle it between his shaft and his vulnerable scrotum.

The instant the scalding pastry touches his sensitive skin, he lets out a guttural scream, thrashing against the chair. "Oh god—stop! It burns!" he howls, his voice cracking under the intensity of his pain.

The sugary glaze sticks to his flesh like molten lava, burning deeper into his skin as the intense heat spreads. His balls contract reflexively, trying to retreat from the searing contact, but there's nowhere to go. The delicate skin of his scrotum flushes an angry, mottled red, quickly giving way to blistering patches. The underside of his dick isn't spared—angry welts rise almost instantly, the skin shiny and raw from the heat and the syrupy coating.

The sweet smell of toasted pastry mingles with the sharp, acrid scent of burning flesh, creating a nauseating combination that makes me wrinkle my nose.

Timmy's body spasms uncontrollably as he tries to twist away, his cries growing hoarse. "Please—please stop! It hurts! Oh god, it hurts!"

I step back, watching the pop tart adhere to his skin, the edges still steaming. His eyes are wide and glassy, filled with terror and disbelief as he struggles to process the blinding, unrelenting pain. Tears stream down his face, mixing with the sweat pouring off him.

"Burns, doesn't it?" I say coldly, crossing my arms. "A fitting punishment for all the pain you've caused."

I lean in close, letting my voice drop to a whisper. "But don't worry, Timmy. We're still in early stages. There's plenty more to come."

I take a bite of the other pop tart, and swipe the crumbs from my face. "Hmm," I nod. "Not bad."

"Please!" he shrieks. "Please! I apologized! I'm sorry, I'll never hurt her or anyone again! I'll do better."

Even now, in his current state, he's future faking. Promising me he can be a good person.

"Oh, Timmy," I say, shaking my head. "Now we both know *that's* not true."

I fetch a carafe from a shelf attached to the wall on the far side of the room. The weight of it feels satisfying in my hand. It's a plain, unassuming container—nothing to indicate its vile contents. I turn back to Timmy, whose eyes are already darting from me to the carafe, suspicion etched into his features.

"Thirsty?" I ask, feigning kindness.

Timmy shakes his head vigorously, panic flashing in his eyes. After the pop tart incident, he knows damn well I'm not here to provide hospitality.

"Too bad," I say, a sharp edge in my voice. "You're having this anyway."

I step closer, and his attempts to squirm away intensify. The restraints creak under his frantic movements, but he's going nowhere. Slowly, deliberately, I tilt the carafe, and a foul-smelling yellow liquid pours out in a steady stream, splashing down onto his chest and soaking his naked, welted body.

The stench hits immediately—sharp, acrid, and unmistakable. It fills the room, clinging to the air like an invisible film. Timmy's reaction is instant.

"What the fuck?" he yells, sputtering as some of the liquid splashes near his mouth. "You just poured *piss* all over me?!"

I step back, letting the now-empty carafe dangle loosely in my hand, and shrug casually. "That's for pissing all over Margaux," I say, my voice calm, almost conversational. The words hang in the air, heavy with implication.

Timmy freezes, his wide, horrified eyes locked on mine. I see it in his face —the flicker of shame that quickly gives way to terror. He knows this is more than just symbolic. He knows that I know. The things he did to Margaux, the threats he made—the ways he tried to break her spirit—are etched in my memory, and I intend to pay them back tenfold.

The sticky liquid clings to his skin, and he shivers, a combination of disgust, fear, and the cold air hitting the dampness. He grimaces as the smell intensifies, as if the weight of his own foul deeds has been physically poured back onto him.

"You're disgusting," he spits, trying to muster anger, but his voice trembles, betraying his fear.

"No, Timmy," I reply, stepping closer until I'm looming over him. "*You're* disgusting. This is *nothing* compared to what you deserve."

He cringes, his face crumpling into a pitiful mask of dread. Deep down, he knows this isn't the worst of it. Not even close. He knows this is just a warm-up. And he knows that I know every terrible thing he's ever done to Margaux—the acts he tried to downplay, the ones he thought he'd gotten away with.

Timmy shifts uncomfortably in the chair, his body writhing against the restraints. The urine dries unevenly, squelching between his skin and the chair, and he grimaces at the sensation. The air between us is charged, thick with unspoken threats and Timmy's growing realization of just how far I'm willing to go.

"There are plenty more steps to go here, Timmy," I say, my voice low and cold. "And by the end of it, you're going to wish you'd never laid a finger on her."

His head drops, and for the first time, I see the fight leave him. Fear has taken hold, and he's beginning to understand there's no escape.

Good. This is where he belongs—powerless, humiliated, drowning in the consequences of his own actions. And I'm nowhere near done.

I step back and assess him as a hairstylist might evaluate a client. "Hmm..."

He flinches as he watches me retrieve another implement from my table of devices.

I stand over Timmy, his head restrained in a makeshift clamp I rigged to the chair. He's still trying to wriggle out of his ties, twisting his body and bucking against the straps that bind him, but it's futile. He's not going anywhere.

I run my hand through his greasy hair, fingers curling around a thick lock. He flinches at the contact, his shoulders tensing beneath the straps.

"Oh relax," I say coldly, though the command is more for me than him. My heart pounds in my chest as I grip tighter. "This is just a haircut. You'll thank me for it later."

Timmy's voice is hoarse, trembling. "Man, you don't have to do this. We can talk. I'll apologize to Margaux. I'll do anything. Please."

"Too late for that," I say, my voice devoid of sympathy. "You didn't just hurt her. You *destroyed* her. And now it's your turn."

With a sharp yank, I rip the first chunk of hair from his scalp. Timmy screams, the sound raw and guttural. Blood seeps from the exposed follicles, dotting his pale skin with red. The sight of it ignites something primal in me —a grim satisfaction.

He thrashes harder, his cries echoing off the walls. "Stop! Please! Oh god, it hurts! It fucking hurts!"

"That's the idea," I say, grabbing another handful and pulling just as forcefully. The hair comes out with a sickening tear, leaving behind an uneven patch of raw, reddened scalp. Timmy's sobs become louder, more desperate.

"Please!" he wails, tears streaming down his face. "I'll do anything! I'll—"

"You'll shut the fuck up," I snap, cutting him off. My voice is steady, but inside, I'm buzzing. Anger, adrenaline, justice—it all swirls together in a chaotic storm. "Do you think Margaux begged? Do you think she cried when you tore her down piece by piece? Did you stop then?"

Timmy whimpers, his head jerking away from my hand, but there's nowhere for him to go. I grab another chunk, yanking harder this time, and his body spasms with the force of his scream.

The room fills with the metallic tang of blood and the acrid stench of sweat. Tufts of hair fall to the floor around us like a grotesque halo, dark against the concrete. With each pull, Timmy's scalp becomes more exposed, a patchwork of blood and skin that glistens under the harsh overhead light, revealing the full extent of his balding scalp.

"You're pathetic," I mutter, grabbing the last remaining section of hair. "You always were."

"No! No, no, no!" Timmy's voice cracks as I pull, his raw cries descending into incoherent babbling.

When it's done, I step back to admire my work. His head is a mottled mess—bleeding, inflamed, and completely bald. He looks up at me, his tear-streaked face contorted with pain and humiliation.

I grab a hand mirror from the table and hold it in front of him. "Take a good look, Timmy," I say, my voice dripping with contempt. "That's what the truth looks like. Ugly. Raw. Bare. *Just like you.*"

He stares at his reflection, sobbing uncontrollably, his body shaking with each ragged breath. "Why?" he whispers, his voice barely audible. "Why are you doing this?"

I lean in close, so he can't look away. "Because you need to feel what you made *her* feel," I say, my tone ice cold. "This particular step is for lying to the cops and saying she pulled your hair," I explain. "But beyond that, you stripped her of everything. Her confidence. Her dignity. Her joy. Now it's *your* turn."

I knock on the door, and my two associates re-enter the room.

"Time for a little road trip," I explain to Timmy as they remove his restraints and lead him into a neighboring room, securing him to a metal chair.

I grab my phone and cue up the playlist I've prepared. With a tap, Machine Gun Kelly's '*Ay!*' blasts through the speaker, the repetitive beat and lyrics filling the room like an assault on the senses.

Timmy flinches, his face twisting in disgust. *"What the fuck is this?"* he shouts over the noise, but I don't answer. Instead, I give him a wink and a pat on the shoulder before stepping out, locking the door behind me.

From the control room, I watch the camera feed. Timmy's head snaps toward the door as it opens again, and a wiry man with sunken cheeks and jittery movements steps in. The meth addict's eyes are wild, darting around the room like a cornered animal.

"Enjoy the company," I murmur to myself, settling into a chair to watch.

At first, the man circles Timmy like a wary predator. Timmy tries to assert dominance, barking orders at the man, but it's clear he has no idea who he's dealing with. The addict is already agitated, his movements erratic. It doesn't take long for the tension to snap.

The first punch lands squarely on Timmy's cheek, the crack of knuckles against bone loud even over the music. Timmy howls in pain, his head snapping to the side. Blood dribbles from his split lip as he spits a curse at the man.

I watch, unblinking, as the addict goes into a frenzy. His fists rain down on Timmy, who's struggling futilely against the restraints. A sick sense of satisfaction blooms in my chest as Timmy's face swells, his left eye darkening into a grotesque bruise. By the time the addict grabs a loose metal pipe and swings it against Timmy's head, the once-cocky bastard is reduced to a sobbing, incoherent mess.

"Not so tough now, are you?" I mutter, watching Timmy slump in the chair, barely conscious. The addict paces the room, muttering to himself, occasionally throwing another jab at Timmy for good measure.

By morning, the music is still blaring, and the addict is curled up in the corner, twitching but spent. Timmy's head hangs low, blood dripping from his swollen face onto his lap. His black eyes are nearly swollen shut, his lip split in multiple places, and there's a nasty gash on his scalp that's caked in dried blood.

I enter the room with my associates, the music cutting off abruptly. The silence is deafening, broken only by Timmy's shallow, ragged breaths. He lifts his head weakly, squinting at me with one barely open eye.

"Look at you," I say, crouching in front of him, a mocking smile tugging at my lips. "Black eyes, a fat lip, maybe even a fractured skull. But don't worry, Timmy. They're not real black eyes."

His gaze flickers with confusion and anger, but he's too broken to argue.

I stand, looking down at the pitiful shell of a man in front of me.

My associates bring Timmy back to the main room and re-secure him to the chair in the center of the room.

The needle gun is deceptively simple, just a handheld device with a small chamber full of thin, sharp metal needles. When triggered, it delivers rapid-fire pokes—like hundreds of tiny wasp stings—one after another. It's not a tool meant to kill, but to break someone down piece by piece. And that's exactly what I need right now.

I pick it up and feel the weight in my hand. It's lighter than I expected, but there's a heft to its purpose that resonates through me. This isn't just about pain—it's about control, about leveling the scales after everything he's done to Margaux.

Timmy sits, still strapped to the chair in the center of the room, sweat dripping down his face despite the cool air. His chest rises and falls in shallow, rapid breaths, and his eyes are wide, darting between me and the needle gun. He doesn't know what it is yet, but he knows it's not good.

"What... what is that?" His voice cracks, a mix of fear and defiance. He struggles against his restraints, testing the limits, but there's no give. His fear is palpable, an almost electric current in the room.

"It's nothing you haven't earned," I say calmly, walking toward him. I let him see the device in my hand, running a finger along the smooth metal edge. "Think of it as... a reminder. Every little jab, every little bruise—those are for Margaux. For every moment you made her question herself, every time you tore her down. Every time you needled her just to get a rise out of her and then blame her for reacting like a human."

I press the tip of the gun against his arm, letting him feel the cold metal. He flinches, his breath hitching. "Please," he stammers, his voice shaking now. "You don't have to do this."

"Oh, but I do." I press the trigger.

The first burst of needles punctures his skin, and Timmy screams, his body jerking violently against the restraints. Tiny red dots bloom across his forearm like a field of angry roses. He thrashes, but the chair holds him steady.

"Stop! Please, stop!" he howls, tears streaming down his face. The sound is guttural, raw, filled with a desperation I didn't think he was capable of.

But I don't stop. I move the gun to his other arm, then his shoulders, his thighs, his calves. Every inch of exposed skin becomes a canvas for his suffering. The room fills with the rhythmic hum of the needle gun and his screams, a twisted symphony of pain and retribution.

His reactions are visceral—his face contorts in agony, veins standing out on his neck as he tries to squirm away. His eyes are bloodshot, his throat raw from screaming. He begs, pleads, curses me, cycling through every stage of desperation.

And me? I'm calm. Detached, almost. Each burst of needles is a release, a catharsis. For every bruise that blooms on his skin, I imagine the emotional scars he left on Margaux. This is justice, not cruelty. Or at least, that's what I tell myself.

When I finally stop, his body sags in the chair, trembling uncontrollably. His skin is a patchwork of red and purple, tiny puncture wounds peppering his arms, legs, and torso. His breathing is shallow, his head lolling to the side as if even holding it up is too much effort.

I crouch down, gripping his chin and forcing him to meet my gaze. His eyes are glassy, unfocused, but there's still a flicker of something there—fear, anger, humiliation.

"Now you know," I say, my voice low and steady. "Now you know what it's like to be poked and prodded, to feel like every part of you is under attack. But don't worry, Timmy. We're nearly at the end. Only a few more stages to go now."

I let go of his chin, standing up and turning away. Behind me, he sputters, his voice weak but full of venom. "You're a monster," he rasps.

I pause, glancing back at him. "Maybe," I admit. "But I'm a monster with a purpose. And you? You're the parasite no one will miss."

I walk back to my table and grab another item. I hold the firework in my hand, turning it over slowly as Timmy watches, his eyes wide with terror. He's trembling, his wrists still bound to the table, sweat dripping from his brow. The room is silent, save for the faint hum of the old lightbulb swinging overhead.

"Do you know what this is, Timmy?" I ask, my voice calm, almost conversational.

His gaze flickers between the firework and my face, panic etched into every line of his expression. "You don't have to do this," he pleads, his voice shaky. "I'll do or say whatever you want. Just please—"

"Oh, you'll say what I want," I reply, my tone sharpening. "But not because you think it'll save you. You're going to say it because you'll finally understand what it feels like to face the truth."

I kneel in front of him, holding the firework at eye level. "You've spent your whole life looking at yourself as the hero, haven't you? The misunderstood victim, the guy who just couldn't catch a break." I lean in closer, lowering my voice. "But the world sees you for what you are now. A liar. A coward. A destroyer of everything good you ever touched."

Timmy shakes his head frantically, tears welling up. "That's not true. I loved her. I—"

"You *loved* her?" I spit, slamming my fist onto the table beside him. "You tore her down, day after day, and called it love. You made her question her worth, her sanity, her very existence. And now, you're going to see what you've done."

I light the firework, letting the flare illuminate the space between us.

Timmy's eyes widen as he sees me light the fuse. His panic sets in instantly, his head jerking back and forth, his voice a mixture of pleading and screaming. "No, no, no! You don't have to do this! Please!"

The sparks dance, casting an eerie glow on Timmy's face. He flinches, squeezing his eyes shut as though bracing for impact.

"Open your eyes," I command. "Look at me."

He hesitates, his breaths shallow and rapid, before finally obeying. His gaze locks with mine, his bravado now absent.

"You've spent years making people feel small," I say. "Now, you get to feel what it's like to be powerless."

I hold the small firework steady, positioning it on a stand just inches from the bridge of his nose, and step back, watching the fuse hiss and sputter as it burns down. His thrashing becomes frantic, his face flushed with terror, veins bulging in his neck as he strains against his restraints.

The firework explodes with a deafening bang, a sudden burst of light and force that fills the room with smoke and the acrid scent of burned flesh. The sound echoes in my ears as the immediate aftermath reveals the damage.

Timmy's head jerks back violently, his screams rising to a pitch I didn't think humanly possible. Blood gushes from the center of his face, pouring from a deep, jagged wound where the firework erupted. The skin around his eyes is scorched and blackened, the heat having singed away his eyebrows and lashes.

Raw, blistering burns spread outward from the point of impact, the skin peeling and bubbling grotesquely.

One of his eyes is completely swollen shut, a purple-red mass of damaged tissue. The other is bloodshot and wide open, darting around in panic, still black from the meth head's beating, struggling to comprehend the horror of what just happened. His nose is an unrecognizable mess, the cartilage smashed and the skin shredded by the force of the blast.

"Oh what?" I sneer, thinking about all the times he diminished Margaux's pain. "It wasn't even a very big firework. I could have used a festival ball instead."

Timmy's screams turn guttural, wet with the blood pooling in his throat. He coughs and chokes, writhing in pain as tears, mingled with soot and blood, streak down his distorted face.

"No... no! NO!" he shrieks, his voice hoarse and broken. "What did you do to me?! You... you ruined me!"

"I made you wear your sins," I reply evenly, my own voice calm, almost detached. "This is what you really are, Timmy. Ugly. Destroyed. Just like the people you hurt."

His sobs grow louder, his body trembling violently in the chair. He turns his head away from the mirror, but I grab his chin, forcing him to look. "No escape, Timmy. You don't get to hide from yourself anymore."

Inside, a dark satisfaction brews. *He deserves this.* Every moment of pain, every ounce of terror. But there's also a weight that settles on me—a quiet acknowledgment of how far I've gone, of what I've become in the name of justice for Margaux.

Timmy's cries grow weaker, his body slumping in the chair, defeated and disfigured. The room smells of smoke, blood, and burned flesh, the air heavy with the consequences of my actions.

And yet, I don't feel an ounce of regret.

I grab the mirror I'd placed nearby and hold it in front of him. "Take a good look."

I force Timmy to confront his grotesque reflection, his face pale and streaked with tears. His lips quiver as he takes in the devastation on his own features—the weight of what he's become. For a moment, there's silence. Then, a sob escapes his throat, raw and guttural.

"I didn't mean—" he starts, but I cut him off.

"Don't you dare," I growl. "This isn't about what you meant. It's about what you *did*. This is the face of the man who destroyed lives, who left scars on Margaux that may never heal. This is who you are, Timmy."

I set the mirror down, my own emotions swirling. Satisfaction? Maybe. But it's not clean or pure. It's tangled with anger, exhaustion, and a sadness that even justice can't erase.

"You wanted to be seen," I whisper. "Now, you are."

With that, I leave the room, his ragged sobs trailing behind me.

When I finally step back, he's a shadow of the smug, entitled man who tormented Margaux. His face is streaked with tears, his body covered in welts and scratches, his spirit broken.

But I'm not done.

I grab a handful of shells from the table—a mix of jagged and smooth, their edges sharp enough to cut. The same shells Margaux had collected during rare moments of peace, moments Timmy had managed to ruin. They feel heavy in my hand, weighted with the significance of what they represent.

Timmy's eyes widen as he sees them, darting between the shells and my face. He shakes his head violently, his muffled protests spilling out as incoherent sounds.

"Open up," I say, my voice calm but firm. He doesn't comply, so I grab his jaw with one hand, digging my fingers into his cheeks until he has no choice but to part his lips. He's shaking now, his whole body trembling as I push the first shell into his mouth.

It scrapes against his teeth as I shove another in, then another. The jagged edges dig into his gums, drawing blood that pools and mingles with his saliva. His muffled gagging sounds fill the room, panic and pain radiating off him like heat.

"Keep going," I say, almost to myself, as I cram more in. His cheeks bulge grotesquely, and blood seeps from the corners of his mouth. Tears stream down his face, his chest heaving as he struggles to breathe around the shards pressing into his tongue and throat.

Timmy thrashes against the restraints, his muffled cries growing more frantic with each passing second. But I don't stop.

I grab a roll of duct tape and tear off a strip, pressing it over his mouth to seal the shells inside. "There," I say, stepping back to admire my work. He looks pathetic, his face a mask of pain and terror. His muffled screams are barely audible now, his eyes wild with desperation.

"This," I say, leaning in close, "is for every word you spat at her. Every insult, every lie, every cruel twist of the knife. You don't get to speak anymore, Timmy. You don't deserve to."

He jerks his head, trying to dislodge the tape, his breathing ragged and labored. Blood dribbles down his chin, staining the duct tape as his muffled sobs turn into choking sounds.

I step back, arms crossed, watching him struggle. There's no satisfaction in this—not the kind that feels good. But there's justice. Cold, unrelenting justice.

"You're quiet now," I say, my voice low. "Funny how that works. You always had so much to say when you were tearing her apart. Where's that big mouth of yours now, huh?"

I wheel over a full-length mirror and force him to look at himself again. "This is who you are, Timmy. Ugly on the outside *and* the inside. And when I'm done, the whole world will see it too."

I hit play on a projector, showing a montage of Margaux's pain—her bruises, her tears, her laughter forced through gritted teeth. This is almost over, and I need him to remember his crimes, and why we're here. But we're not quite done yet.

And there's only one thing that will hurt him more.

I show footage of his father, bound to the chair the night before, forced to face the evidence of his son's evilness. As a creative flourish, I faked a recording so his father's voice echoes in the background, calling him a disappointment. A failure.

For the first time, real fear flickers in Timmy's eyes.

But even in this moment of imagined triumph, I know it's not enough.

It will never be enough.

Dragging Timmy is easy at this point, and I move him back to the table where I secure him to the cold metal surface.

I walk to the corner of the room and pick up a chainsaw.

Timmy's eyes grow wide as I turn on the equipment, the chains whirring loudly. He moans, shaking his head, nonverbally begging me to stop.

"You were just fine threatening to chop Margaux's head off multiple times," I shrug. "Seems only fitting you get the treatment you promised her."

I aim for Timmy's right arm, the whirring chains slicing through his soft tissue, muscles and bones with ease.

He roars in pain, even around the shells, and then grows quiet as his body enters a state of shock, temporarily dulling the excruciating sensation. His breath grows shallow, and he blinks repeatedly as if trying to process what just happened.

I move around to the other side of the table. "This is also for not being able to keep your hands to yourself," I explain.

I slice off his second arm, blood spraying everywhere with each heartbeat. He screams in agony and panic, his cries quickly turning hoarse. He hyperventilates as he tries to breathe away the pain.

He screams through the tape, incoherent now, desperate for me to stop. His eyes are wide, and his head moves rapidly from side to side as he attempts to comprehend what's happening.

He shifts on the table, a feeble attempt to escape.

But Margaux was desperate for him to stop his constant attacks, and he never did—so why should I?

Moving to the end of the table, the vibrations of the chainsaw reverberate through my hands as I sever his lower limbs one by one.

His body twitches uncontrollably due to the sudden severing of nerves.

The heat and scent of blood in the room are impossible to ignore.

He gasps as his removed limbs also twitch on the floor, residual nerve activity making it look as if they're alive independent of Timmy. I laugh. *It is kind of funny.*

There's not a lot of time left.

He knows it. His eyes are flat, dead.

He sobs as he continues to bleed out, his mind struggling to process the trauma.

I almost feel pity for Timmy at this point as he continues to thrash, limbless, beaten, broken. What he's experienced today is brutal. But the crazy part is, all of these things are either actual things he did to Margaux, threatened to do, implied he could do, or symbolic representations of the psychological and emotional torment he put her through on a daily basis.

He shrieks as I take my final slice with the chainsaw and slice his dick off. It falls to the floor with a dull thud.

I turn toward the wood chipper, running my hand along its edge. My breath comes faster as I imagine the scene that will follow.

But as I reach for him, I stop. A chill runs down my spine as I realize this isn't the moment I've been waiting for. Not yet.

The room dissolves, and I'm back in my workshop, staring at the plans I've spent weeks perfecting. It's not real—not yet. But it will be.

And when it is, Timmy will wish for death long before it comes.

CHAPTER 149
THE WORLD DIDN'T LOSE A HERO

DEX

The cabin smells of damp wood and something metallic.

I push the door open cautiously, my gloves already on, my bag of tools slung over my shoulder. The plan is meticulous. Today is the day Timmy meets his end, piece by piece, and I'll make sure it's as slow and painful as he deserves.

But as I step inside, my stomach drops. A faint tang of gunpowder lingers in the air, sharp and unmistakable.

The sight before me drains all the adrenaline from my veins.

Timmy is slumped in a chair, his head lolled to one side, a clean gunshot wound marking the center of his forehead. Blood and brain matter spatter the wall behind him in a grotesque pattern. His lifeless eyes stare straight ahead, wide with the shock of his final moment. His body looks limp, like a marionette with its strings cut.

Phil lies crumpled on the floor nearby, a revolver still clutched in his hand. A matching wound gapes in his temple, surrounded by dried blood. The gun lies just beneath his chin, a clear indicator of how he ended things.

I freeze, my pulse pounding in my ears.

What the fuck?

I take a step closer, my boots crunching on broken glass scattered across the floor. The scene is gruesome, but it's not what hits me hardest. It's the simplicity of it all.

Phil got to him first.

I stare at the tableau, a mix of disbelief and rage bubbling inside me. After all my planning, my careful setup, my months of tracking Timmy's every move, Phil beats me to the punch—and this is what he does? A single bullet?

How fucking uninspired.

I crouch down beside Timmy, studying his lifeless form. The bullet wound is clean—too clean. It's possible he didn't even see it coming. There's no fear, no suffering, no chance for him to face what he's done. Just a quick end, served by the man who raised him into a monster.

I glance over at Phil's body. His face is slack, almost peaceful, as if he found some kind of solace in ending both their lives. The sight of him makes my blood boil.

"You fucking coward," I mutter under my breath.

This wasn't justice. It was an escape.

I drop my bag to the floor with a heavy thud, my jaw clenching. I had plans for Timmy. *Big plans.* Plans that would have made him suffer for every ounce of pain he inflicted on Margaux.

But now? It's gone. All of it.

The sharp wail of sirens in the distance pulls me from my thoughts. My head snaps up, and my heart sinks as realization sets in.

Shit. I look guilty as hell.

I glance down at the bag of tools at my feet—chains, duct tape, gloves, a hammer—and then back at the two bodies. The cops won't believe I just happened upon this scene.

The sirens grow louder. Red and blue lights flicker through the dirty windows, illuminating the blood-streaked walls.

Oh, fuck.

"Hands up!" a voice booms. "Get on your knees! Drop your weapon!"

———

LATER

The holding cell reeks of piss and regret. The fluorescent lights hum overhead, casting a sickly yellow glow over everything.

I sit on the cold bench, arms crossed, my thoughts racing.

Phil. That spineless bastard. He didn't just rob me of my moment—he left me holding the fucking bag.

The detectives hauled me in without hesitation, their smug faces practically screaming *open-and-shut case*. My 'murder kit' was all the evidence they needed, along with my connection to Margaux and her well-documented history with Timmy.

"You couldn't have made this easier for us if you tried," one of them sneered as they cuffed me.

There are definitely many things I've done that could have landed me in jail. I'm sure every time I've hurt someone before, it's left some kind of indelible scar.

But I'm not about to open up the therapy door and let someone in to see that side of me. I'll shove it down and worry about the consequences later.

For now, I'm trapped in a box surrounded by metal bars, with a stinky alcoholic named Larry who was locked up for public intoxication, and a twink named Jethro who claims to have performed a lewd act in public. Which he recorded on a TikTok Live. *Idiot.*

My crime? Homicide. But I didn't fucking do it!

What are the chances someone would get to Timmy before I did?

After all my plotting and planning, someone else took the lead and got there first.

What kind of defense is that, though? "I was going to kill him but someone already did it." I'm sure there's an intent to kill crime they could charge me with.

Fuck.

So I stay silent. The detectives occasionally call me into a room and try to have a conversation, but I only reply with, "Lawyer".

And my lawyer, Mike Larsen, isn't returning my calls. *Fucker.* He's probably swanning off on some vacation using the retainer money me and plenty of other people pour into his bank account month after month. Maybe I picked the wrong profession. Being a defense lawyer to assholes like me seems more lucrative.

A FEW HOURS LATER

Mike walks into the interrogation room like he owns the place, his pinstripe suit immaculate, his briefcase gleaming under the harsh lights. "Sorry for the delay," he says, sliding into the chair across from me. "Family obligations."

"No problem," I mutter. "Thanks for coming."

He continues. "Wife dragged me out to a cocktail party, some charity event she helped organize. They work to give homeless people teeth or something like that. You know how it is."

I quirk a brow, disinterested and slightly confused. "Great. Can you get me out of here now?"

He smirks. "Let's see what we're working with." He adjusts his cufflinks and leans in. "So, what the hell happened? Start from the top."

I give him the rundown, starting with my intent to kill Timmy and ending with the tragic realization that Phil had beaten me to it.

Mike whistles low. "That's... a unique one, even for me. Let me guess— you didn't kill anyone, but the cops found you at the scene with a bag full of tools that scream 'premeditated murder,' connected the dots to Margaux, and assumed you killed them both out of revenge?"

I nod. "Pretty much."

"And you have no witnesses, no alibi, nothing to prove you didn't do it?"

"Nothing but the truth," I say bitterly.

Mike shakes his head, a faint smirk tugging at his lips. "Well, you're honest, I'll give you that. Alright, let's focus on shifting suspicion back onto Phil. He's the one who actually did it, right?"

"Has to be," I say. "The guy's been enabling Timmy his entire life. He probably snapped."

"Wow, filicide—or in this case, Philicide," Mike lets out a low whistle. "We don't see that often, but when we do, it tends to be a crime of passion. He must have pissed his dad off real bad for him to kill his own flesh and blood."

"I know. It's horrible. But this guy deserved to die. He was a piece of shit, abusing his fiancée. Cheating on her, accusing her of doing all the horrible things he was actually doing to her. Financially exploitative. And so cunning and manipulative... like a derelict loser hiding behind a charming facade. He had to go."

"Well, it sounds like the world didn't lose a hero."

"That's an understatement."

"Now we've just got to figure out how to get you out of this." He pauses for a moment, and then nods. "Alright. Leave it to me. We'll make sure the cops know you were just... unlucky enough to stumble onto the scene. It shouldn't be too difficult to establish that Phil was the shooter, seeing the gun was in his hand when you got there, and I'm sure his actions will be backed up by gunshot residue. If we can prove that, we can cast enough doubt on your involvement."

"Whatever it takes, man. I would happily have gone down for this crime if I actually did it. But I didn't."

"Then we'll get you off," he promises. "That's my job. As long as you're honest with me, we have a great chance of making this all go away."

I nod. "I will be."

"Good. Then we've got a chance. But next time, Dex?" He leans forward, fixing me with a sharp look. "Leave the murder kits at home."

I glare at him. "Noted."

For now, all I can do is trust him to work his magic. But one thing is certain—Phil may have stolen my thunder, but I'll be damned if I let him take my freedom, too.

As I sit in the cell overnight, I can't help but feel cheated. I was supposed to be the one to end Timmy's reign of terror. I was supposed to be the one to deliver justice for Margaux.

But instead, I'm stuck here while Phil gets to die the hero—or at least the martyr.

I stare at the cold, gray walls and take a deep breath.

At least Timmy's gone.

At least Margaux is safe.

But damn, I wanted to see the fear in his eyes when he realized what was coming—I wanted him to know what true helplessness felt like.

And now, thanks to his father, I'll never get that satisfaction.

CHAPTER 150
MINE

MARGAUX

immy is dead.

The words don't feel real. They float in the air like smoke, curling into my mind but refusing to settle.

I first hear about it on the news. I'm curled up on the couch, a glass of rosé in my hands, when the anchor's voice cuts through the room.

"This just in—a murder-suicide has left two individuals dead in a cabin in Montana. The victims have been identified as Timothy O'Malley and his father, Philip O'Malley."

I leap to my feet, glass in hand, getting as close as possible to the TV, as if that might give me additional information.

The anchor continues. "Authorities are currently investigating the involvement of Dexter Barrett, who is already in custody."

Dex's mugshot flashes on the screen, and my world stops.

I gasp, the wine glass slipping from my hands. The glass crashes to the floor, shattering into a hundred jagged pieces. I barely notice. My heart feels like it's doing the same thing in my chest.

"No," I whisper. My voice is barely audible over the pounding in my ears. "No, no, no..."

I stagger back, my legs buckling as I sink to the floor. My body feels disconnected from my mind, like I'm watching myself from above, a broken puppet with severed strings.

————

The night stretches on endlessly.

I can't sit still. My thoughts race, each one colliding into the next until they're an unrelenting tangle of confusion and fear. I pace the living room, my feet crunching over the shards of glass I still haven't cleaned up.

Timmy is dead.

Dex is in jail.

Do I finally get to be free of Timmy, only to have Dex ripped away from me?

The thought is unbearable.

Timmy, the man who tormented me, who broke me down piece by piece until I was a shadow of myself—he's gone. *Forever.*

And yet... the relief I thought I'd feel is tangled with something darker. He deserved to suffer for what he did to me, but I never imagined it would end like this.

And Dex. *Oh god, Dex.* My anchor, my protector, my safe harbor in a storm. The man who put me back together when I thought I was beyond repair. He's gone too, locked away for a crime I can't even begin to comprehend.

I feel like I'm drowning, pulled under by conflicting waves of emotion. Relief, guilt, anger, fear—it all swirls inside me, leaving me breathless.

————

The hours crawl by.

I stare at my phone, willing it to ring, praying for some kind of answer, some clarity. I want to scream, to cry, to throw something, but I'm frozen, trapped in this limbo of not knowing.

What happened? Did Dex really kill him?

My heart tells me no. Dex wouldn't... *would he?*

But my head is less sure. I know how fiercely protective he is of me, how much he despised Timmy for everything he put me through. I saw the darkness in his eyes when he talked about wanting to make things right, about making Timmy pay.

Still, the Dex I know—the Dex I love—isn't a murderer.

Is he?

I collapse onto the couch, burying my face in my hands. Hot tears spill down my cheeks, and I let them fall. There's no one here to see me break down, no one to hold me and tell me it's going to be okay.

Dex was that person for me.

And now he's gone, too.

As the first rays of sunlight creep through the blinds, I make a decision.

I can't just sit here, paralyzed by fear and uncertainty. I need answers. I need to know what happened.

I grab my laptop and start searching for something—anything—that will help me to figure out what's going on. How I can help.

Because whatever it takes, I'll fight for Dex. *Just like he fought for me.*

I won't lose him. Not like this.

Not now.

————

THE NEXT DAY

I manage to find out which jail Dex is locked up in.

A couple of calls later, and I'm able to figure out who his lawyer is.

"He's going to be let out in a couple of hours," the lawyer explains. "Just got to get a judge to sign off on the charges being dropped."

Three long hours later, I hear Dex's motorcycle before I see it, and as soon as he comes into view, I run up and into his arms. "Oh Dex," I exclaim. "I'm so glad you're okay."

"Of course I'm okay," he grins. "I get to be with *you* for the rest of my life."

My heart warms and my pussy clenches at the thought.

We spend the next few hours with Dex updating me on what he'd been keeping from me.

"I would have done it, you know," Dex says, brushing a strand of hair from my face.

"Done what?" I ask. He must be talking about one of two things. "Unloaded the dishwasher?"

"Very funny," he rolls his eyes. "Stop using humor to deflect hard things. You know exactly what I'm talking about. I actually came very close... too close..."

He closes his eyes for a moment and I pull him close. "But you didn't.

That's what matters." I pause. "Wow, you really would have done all that for me?" Reality sinks in.

"I would have," he says. "That's the problem. I'm not a good man, Margaux."

"That's where you're wrong," I say, brushing his own hair out of his eyes. "You're loving, caring, kind, protective, strong—"

"I'd do anything for you, Margaux," he says. "Anything at all. Even kill."

"I'm not finished," I put a finger up to silence him. "—and very, very sexy."

"Oh yeah?" he growls.

I bite my bottom lip, my gaze not leaving his. "Oh yeah."

"And what are you going to do about that?" he asks, grabbing me without warning and hoisting me over his shoulder as he walks us in the direction of the bedroom.

"I'd like to show, not tell," I giggle and he laughs. We close the door behind us and we both leap onto the bed.

He wraps his arms around me and I melt into him. His body is perfection, melding against my own.

Firm and warm and delicious.

He yanks off his shirt and I pull my own top over my head, and as I lean down to kiss him I run my hands over his rippling chest and abs.

He's divine.

And he's all mine.

CHAPTER 151
CLAIMED

MARGAUX

kneel on the bed, every nerve in my body alive under Dex's gaze. His green-hazel eyes are dark, molten with desire, but beneath the hunger, there's something deeper—care, reverence, and an unshakable loyalty that makes my chest ache.

"Raise your ass high up in the air, baby. Get down low on your forearms," Dex growls, his voice low, commanding, yet filled with a tenderness that only he can master.

A shiver of anticipation courses through me. Slowly, I bend forward, presenting myself to him. The position is vulnerable, intimate, and yet—with Dex—I don't feel small. I feel powerful, wanted, safe.

"Like this?" I purr, glancing back at him over my shoulder. A playful smile curls my lips as I wiggle my hips, teasing him.

Dex lets out a low groan, his hands gripping my hips with just enough pressure to make my breath hitch. "Fuck yes," he murmurs, his voice thick with approval. "You're so goddamn sexy."

He traces one finger along my slit, making me shudder. "Already so wet for me," he murmurs, his deep voice sending sparks of electricity through me.

The warmth of his breath brushes against my skin as he leans in, kissing a trail from the curve of my back to the sensitive dip just above my ass. His touch is reverent, as though I'm something precious, something he's determined to worship. I've never felt this before—not with anyone. *Not even close.*

He kneels behind me, his large hands caressing my cheeks with a slow deliberation that has my heart pounding in my chest. He uses his thumbs to spread me open further before diving in, licking a long strip from my clit to the tight ring of my back entrance.

I whimper as his lips press against my most sensitive place, his tongue darting out to taste me. A gasp escapes my lips as he drags it slowly along my slit, lingering at my clit before moving lower to explore me fully.

"Dex," I moan, unable to form coherent words. My fingers clutch the sheets as his tongue works its magic, circling and teasing in ways that make my entire body tremble. He's relentless, his hands gripping my hips to keep me steady as I writhe beneath him.

"Ohh yes!" I cry out at the sensation of his skilled tongue. He laps at me hungrily, licking and sucking my clit before dipping lower to tongue-fuck my dripping entrance. Then he swirls his tongue around my sensitive rim, giving special attention to that forbidden place.

I fist the sheets, my body trembling with pleasure as Dex devours me eagerly, like he can't get enough of my taste. "Don't stop... it feels... so good," I beg breathlessly, rocking my hips back against his face.

Dex moans against my flesh, the vibrations making my toes curl. He plunges his tongue deep inside my pussy, fucking me with it as he rubs tight circles around my clit with his thumb. I can feel myself growing wetter by the second, my body tensing as the pleasure mounts.

"Don't stop," I plead again, my voice breathy, desperate. "It feels so good... oh God..."

Dex moans against me, the vibrations making me arch my back further, pressing myself against his mouth. He's everywhere—his tongue, his fingers, his presence filling every inch of me. He's consuming me, and I love it. I've never felt so seen, so cherished, even as he takes control.

"You taste amazing," he groans, pulling back just enough to speak before diving back in, his tongue working in tandem with his fingers as they slide into my pussy, curling in just the right way to make me cry out.

The coil deep within me tightens, and I know I'm close. "Fuck Dex, I'm... I'm going to..." I pant desperately, grinding myself shamelessly against his mouth. "Make me come, please!"

"Do it," he growls, his voice rough, commanding. "Come for me, baby. Let me feel it."

With a final flick of his tongue against my clit, I shatter. A wave of pleasure crashes over me, leaving me gasping and trembling as he holds me through it, his lips never leaving my skin.

Before I can catch my breath, he's lifting me, cradling me against his chest as though I weigh nothing. His strength is intoxicating, and I cling to him, my nails digging into his shoulders as he lays me back down, positioning me on my hands and knees once more.

"I'm not done with you yet," he murmurs, his voice dripping with promise. "I'm going to show you how it's meant to be."

He moves behind me, his hands tracing the curve of my back before gripping my hips. I feel the head of his cock pressing against my entrance, and I can't help the moan that escapes my lips.

"Look at this gorgeous pussy," he growls. "You're soaking. Are you ready for me now?" he asks, his voice softer, checking in, always making sure I'm with him.

I bite my lip, blushing but loving his dirty talk. "Yes," I breathe. "Please fuck me, Dex. I need your cock inside me now… *please.*"

He pushes into me slowly, filling me inch by inch. The stretch is exquisite, and I'm overwhelmed by the feeling of him inside me, his piercings dragging within me, creating additional sensation. My walls clench around him like a vise, sucking him in deeper. He lets out a guttural groan, his hands tightening on my hips.

"You feel so fucking good," he murmurs, his voice strained with restraint. He begins to move, each thrust measured, deliberate, as though he's savoring every second.

"You like that, don't you, baby?" Dex growls, slapping my ass lightly. "Tell me how much you love it."

"I love it, Dex! I love the way you fuck me!" I cry out, my inhibitions long gone.

"That's my girl," he says as he continues to ram his cock into my tight, wet pussy that can't get enough of him.

I meet him, pushing back against him, desperate for more. "Harder," I beg, my voice breaking. "Please, Dex, I need more."

He doesn't hesitate. His pace quickens, his movements becoming rougher, more urgent. He pounds his rock-hard cock into me with a fervor I've never experienced before.

He leans over me, his chest pressing against my back as he kisses the side of my neck, his breath hot against my skin.

"You're *mine*," he growls, his voice possessive, but there's no malice in it, only a deep, unyielding need. "All mine, Margaux."

"Yes," I cry out, shockwaves of pleasure coursing through my body, trembling as another orgasm builds within me. "*Yours*, Dex. Always yours."

When I come again, it's with his name on my lips, and he follows soon after, his body tensing as he spills into me, his grip on my hips unrelenting. For a moment, neither of us moves, the room filled only with the sound of our heavy breathing.

Finally, he pulls out, collapsing beside me and pulling me into his arms. He brushes a strand of hair from my face, his gaze soft, tender.

"You're everything to me," he whispers, pressing a kiss to my forehead. "You're everything I've ever wanted."

I nestle closer, my heart full. "And you're everything to me."

———

The next few days go by in a blur.

We barely leave the bedroom. We're tangled together—his arms, his legs, his lips, and mine. It's as though the outside world has ceased to exist, and it's just the two of us in this cocoon we've created.

Dex kisses me like he's making up for lost time, like he's trying to erase every bruise Timmy left on my body and my soul.

He whispers words into my skin that sink deep into the cracks Timmy carved into me, filling them with something warm and real.

I don't think I've fully processed that Timmy—and his father—are really gone.

There's a strange hollowness where my anger, fear, and frustration used to sit. It's like my mind hasn't caught up to my reality yet. The monster who tormented me, broke me down piece by piece, is gone.

Sometimes I think about how his story ended, and it feels... unfinished. Like maybe it wasn't supposed to end that way—so suddenly, so violently.

But then I remember what he did to me.

What he could have done if I'd stayed.

And I remind myself that closure doesn't always come wrapped in a neat little bow.

CHAPTER 152
RUN, LITTLE RABBIT

DEX

By the next evening, I can feel the shift in the air between us. The tender quiet of the last few days has been healing, yes, but it's not enough. Not for her, and sure as hell not for me. There's a fire between us, something deeper, something primal, clawing to be unleashed.

I see it in Margaux's eyes, even if she doesn't yet. That unspoken need to feel alive again, to shed the shadows of fear and let herself be untamed. She's still holding back, still chained by the echoes of everything he did to her.

I know what she needs, what we both need. Something *raw*.

Something that lets her feel the thrill of being hunted and the safety of being caught.

So I stand, leather gloves flexing over my hands, my voice cutting through the stillness like a blade: "Run," I growl. "You have five minutes."

Margaux's eyes widen, her breath quickening. She's frozen for a beat, trying to read me, Her chest rises and falls with rapid breaths, her pupils dilating as my words sink in. There's no smile to soften the command, no hint of playfulness. She's searching for the playful, reassuring glance that says this is just a game. But I give her nothing.

I stand tall, leather gloves flexing, my body taut with barely restrained energy.

The forest looms behind her, dark and alive. When realization sinks in, her lips part in surprise, and she bolts.

I watch her go, her red hair catching the moonlight, her form vanishing between the trees, the faint rustle of leaves marking her path. My chest tightens, my pulse pounding in anticipation, the primal hunter in me roaring to life. This isn't just a game. It's raw, unfiltered adrenaline. It's about awakening something wild in her, something she doesn't even realize she craves.

The predator in me stirs, growling for the chase. I take a long, slow breath and slip the mask over my face, the bottom half of a skull transforming me into something primal, something monstrous, not quite human. I pull on my gloves tighter, savoring the stretch of the leather over my hands. I glance at my watch, the seconds ticking by like a countdown to chaos as I give her the time she needs to think she has a chance.

She doesn't.

This isn't just about catching her—it's about unleashing something raw, about pulling her from the shadows of fear and into the thrill of surrender.

When the timer beeps, I step into the woods. My boots crunch softly on the damp earth as I move between the towering trees. The forest is alive with sounds—the rustle of leaves, the whisper of wind through branches, the distant chirp of crickets, the creak of far-off trees—but I'm tuned to something more. I'm listening for *her*. The soft gasp of her breath, the erratic beat of her heart, the uneven rhythm of her steps as she weaves through the undergrowth, the occasional snap of a twig beneath her feet.

I move deliberately, each step calculated and silent. My boots barely disturb the forest floor as I close the distance. A faint gasp reaches my ears, and I adjust my course, veering to the left. *She's close.*

A faint crack reaches my ears. A twig. My lips curve into a wicked smile beneath the mask. She's trying to be quiet, but she doesn't know how. *Not like I do.*

I shift my weight, moving swiftly toward the sound. My breath is steady, controlled, my movements precise. Another noise—a sharp intake of breath —carries on the wind. *I'm getting closer.* I adjust my pace, keeping her in my sights without revealing myself. Let her think she's still hidden. Let the adrenaline surge through her veins.

I spot movement ahead—a flash of her pale skin in the moonlight, the sway of her gorgeous red hair as she glances over her shoulder. My pace quickens. The thrill of the chase tightens in my chest, my muscles coiled and ready to strike. She darts between trees, her breaths loud and ragged. Her panic is intoxicating.

I close the distance, and before she can react, I lunge forward, my hand shooting out and wrapping around her wrist.

She yelps as I yank her back, spinning her around, her body colliding with the rough bark of a tree. My gloved hand clamps around her throat, firm but careful, pinning her in place. Her wide eyes lock onto mine, and in the moonlight, I see everything—fear, exhilaration, and the unmistakable spark of arousal.

"Found you," I growl, my voice rough and muffled through the mask.

Her chest heaves, her breaths shallow and rapid. She struggles weakly, testing my grip, but we both know it's half-hearted. *She wants this.* I pull the zip ties from my pocket, the sound of plastic sharp and final. Her wrists are bound behind her back in seconds, the plastic biting into her soft skin. Her struggles stop. She's trembling now, her body betraying her as her nipples harden against the thin fabric of her shirt, her scent thick and intoxicating in the cool night air. I press my gloved fingers to her cheek, tilting her head to make her look at me. Her trembling lips part, a soft whimper escaping.

"Good girl," I murmur, my tone dark and approving.

I yank her pants down in one swift motion, exposing her bare pussy to the cool night air. My gloved fingers slide between her slick folds, and I curse under my breath. She's soaked. My fingers glide easily, teasing her clit, and a low moan escapes her lips.

"You're soaked. You've been waiting for this, haven't you?" I murmur, my voice dark and hungry.

Her breath catches. Her lips tremble, and she nods slightly, her gaze darting to my mask, unable to look away.

"Answer me," I command, gripping her chin and forcing her to look at me.

"Y-yes," she stammers, barely above a whisper, her voice shaky but filled with need.

I smirk beneath the mask and rip her top, the thin material shredding into tatters that I throw to the ground, baring her completely. Her soft, flushed skin glows in the moonlight, and I can't resist lifting the mask and running my tongue along the curve of her collarbone. Her breasts rise and fall with each shallow breath, her nipples hard and aching for my touch.

Lowering my mask, I take one of her nipples into my mouth, biting gently, and her moan sends a bolt of heat straight to my cock. Her back arches against the tree as I consume her with my mouth, my hands, my dominance.

"God, you're beautiful," I murmur, softer now, my voice rough with desire.

Dropping to my knees, I spread her legs. My hot breath fans against her inner thighs. Her scent is intoxicating, and she shivers as I let my tongue flick against her in one long, slow lick, tasting her sweetness. She cries out, her hips bucking, but I stand and snap my hand up to her throat once more, pinning her in place.

"What do you say?" I ask, my tone commanding.

"Thank you, daddy," she gasps, her voice trembling with need.

Her heart races, thudding so loudly I can hear it. The cool night air raises goosebumps on her skin, but heat courses through her.

"That's my girl," I growl, diving back in. My tongue works her relentlessly, teasing her clit and dipping into her entrance. Her cries grow louder, more desperate as they spill from her lips. Her thighs tremble against my face, her body growing tighter as she approaches the edge.

When she comes, it's violent and all-consuming. Her cries echo through the forest, her body convulsing against my hold.

But I don't stop. My tongue continues its relentless assault, dragging her toward another climax until she's writhing against the tree, her legs barely holding her up. "Dex," she gasps, squirming against my mouth, her clit throbbing with sensitivity from her earlier orgasm. "I—wait—too much."

I ignore her pleas, my hands gripping her hips to hold her steady. Instead, I keep licking and sucking her clit until she shatters, coming again, even stronger this time. Her body shakes uncontrollably, and she cries out as a gush of wetness spills all over my face. Finally, I pull back, my lips glistening, and I smirk. I wipe my mouth with the back of my glove. "That's my good girl."

Her chest heaves, her legs barely holding her up, her lips parted and trembling. Before she can catch her breath, I stand, unzipping my pants. My cock springs free, thick and pulsing, and her mouth waters at the sight.

"On your knees," I command, pulling her to the ground.

CHAPTER 153
THE THRILL OF SURRENDER

MARGAUX

My knees hit the soft earth, and I feel the chill of the night air against my bare skin. My wrists, bound behind me, leave me exposed and vulnerable, and my heart pounds as I look up at Dex.

His cock stands tall and proud, glistening with precum, his piercings reflecting in the moonlight. I lick my lips, my mouth watering at the sight.

"Good girl," he says, his voice rough, as if he can read my mind. "Take me."

I lean forward, letting my tongue swirl around his tip, savoring the salty taste of him as I lick a strip up his length. He groans, tangling his gloved fingers in my hair, and I take him deeper, letting him fill my mouth, my lips stretching around his girth.

"That's it," he murmurs, his voice thick with lust. "Look at you, taking me so well."

His words send a jolt of heat through me, and I moan around him, the vibrations making him shudder. His praise fuels me, and I take him deeper, my throat relaxing to accommodate him. His hips thrust gently as he guides me with his hands, his cock and its piercings sliding against my tongue, and I savor every inch.

"Fuck, you're perfect," he growls, his grip tightening in my hair. "My perfect little slut."

His praise sends a thrill through me, and I take him deeper, relaxing my throat to let him in. My knees press into the damp earth, and I feel the heat pooling between my legs, my arousal building with every sound he makes.

He pulls back suddenly, his cock glistening with my saliva, and smirks down at me.

"Enough. Turn around," he commands.

I rise on shaky legs and press my breasts against the rough bark of the tree. It scrapes against my sensitive skin, but I welcome the sensation as he positions himself behind me. His hands grip my hips tightly, hard enough to bruise, and then he's inside me, stretching me, filling me completely.

I cry out, my chest digging into the rough bark, as he begins to move, thrusting into me. His cock drags against my walls, the metal bars of his piercings adding a delicious friction that makes me see stars.

"Good girl," he growls, his voice rough. "You feel so fucking good."

"Please, Dex," I gasp, my voice trembling. "Don't stop."

He slams into me harder, his rhythm relentless. My body tightens, the wave of pleasure building again. When I come, it's explosive, my cries echoing through the forest as my pussy clenches around him. He follows moments later, spilling into me with a guttural moan.

We stay like that for a moment, our breaths mingling in the cool night air. Then he presses a kiss to my shoulder, his lips soft against my skin.

"Good girl," he whispers, his voice tender now.

"Thank you, daddy," I murmur, my heart still racing.

He uses a knife to free my wrists and pulls me into his arms, his touch gentle and comforting. He lends me his jacket, and I put it on to cover my bareness. Together, we walk back to the house, hand in hand, the night air cool against our heated skin.

In this moment, everything feels right. Wild, raw, and unforgettable.

———

I stare out the window one morning while Dex sleeps, his hand resting possessively on my hip even in his dreams.

I watch the sunlight creep across the room, and wonder if I'll ever stop looking over my shoulder, half-expecting Timmy to appear out of nowhere. The rational part of me knows it's impossible.

He's gone.

Dead.

He can't hurt me anymore.

But the trauma doesn't care about logic. It whispers to me in the quiet moments, when I'm alone with my thoughts.

What if?

What if he somehow survived?

What if he finds a way to come back?

I don't know if I'll ever stop worrying that Timmy will track me down somewhere, sometime, when I least expect it. Maybe that fear will always live in the back of my mind, a scar I carry forever.

But then there's Dex.

Dex, who pulls me back into bed when he feels me stirring too much, his strong arms wrapping around me like a shield.

Dex, who presses kisses into my hair and whispers, "I've got you, baby," in that low, gravelly voice that makes me believe him.

He's my protector now. My constant.

With him, I feel safe in a way I never thought I could again.

It's not just about his strength, though I won't pretend I don't love the way he towers over me, solid and unshakable.

It's about the way he *sees* me.

Not as someone who needs saving. *Someone worth protecting.*

And for the first time—ever—I'm starting to believe that about myself, too.

So, I let myself sink into him, into us. I let him love me, and I love him back with everything I have left.

Because maybe that's what healing looks like.

EPILOGUE

MARGAUX

SIX MONTHS LATER

"You'll never have to send another running pickle again," Dex says, a teasing smile tugging at his lips.

"Thank fucking goodness," I reply with a dramatic sigh, shaking my head. "I was really worried this whole experience was going to put me off pickles. And I love a good pickle."

"Oh, I know you do," he says, leaning in with an exaggerated wink. "Just as well I have an excellent pickle."

The absurdity of his statement sends us both into laughter—deep, gut-wrenching belly laughs that leave me wiping tears from my eyes. The kind of laugh I thought I could only have with Timmy back in the day.

But with Dex, it's different. The laughter isn't a mask for discomfort or an attempt to brush past red flags. It's genuine. Easy. Freeing.

With Dex, there's no baggage, no manipulation waiting in the wings. He doesn't make me feel like I'm walking a tightrope over a chasm of chaos. He's steady. Solid. A partner in every sense of the word.

He's not going to do anything crazy—well, only the good kind. Like putting on a mask and chasing me through the woods. Nothing that will hurt me.

And the best part? I don't have to fix him.

He doesn't need fixing.

He's perfectly imperfect.

Dex gets up every morning and goes to work, no prodding or pushing required. He handles his responsibilities with ease, whether it's paying bills or dealing with the mundane logistics of life. His credit is better than mine—a fact he teases me about endlessly—and he's always planning ahead, talking about investments, future trips, and dreams we can build together.

But it's not about the money. It's about the effort, the balance, the mutual respect. I never feel like he's taking more than he's giving, or expecting me to pour every ounce of myself into him without a second thought. He buys me gifts occasionally, little surprises that make my day brighter, but they're never transactional. They're just... kind. Thoughtful.

When we fight—and yes, we fight sometimes—it doesn't feel like the end of the world. Dex never uses his words as weapons. He doesn't storm off or turn silent to punish me. He raises his voice on occasion, but always calms down quickly, and we talk it out like adults. The air clears, and we move forward. Stronger.

For the first time in a long time, I feel like I'm in a partnership, not a parent-child dynamic. I'm not his caretaker or his therapist. I'm his equal. And that's exactly how it should be.

Do I ever think about Timmy? Occasionally.

It's not the kind of thinking that leaves me shaking or crying anymore. It's more like a fleeting memory—a shadow passing through my mind. I used to worry that some small, twisted part of me would always hold on to him, clinging to the idea of who he could have been. But I've learned to let that go.

Because the version of Timmy I loved never really existed. He was a mirage, a carefully constructed act designed to lure me in. The creative, loving, surfer boy who made me laugh until I cried? That was an act. A mask. And once I understood that, it became easier to release the truth about the love I thought I had for him.

Now, all I feel is pity and relief.

Pity for his rage and hatred of women. Pity for the people in his life who continued to enable him, turning a blind eye to his destruction. Relief that there will now be no next person who will fall for his act, walking into the storm I barely escaped.

Mostly, I pity him for himself. Because his life was miserable. He numbed himself with substances and distractions, trying to emulate the joy he didn't know how to feel.

I see that now. I see the emptiness that drove him, the hollowness he could never fill.

When we broke up, I told him I wished him the best. And I meant it. Because despite everything, I did hope he'd be one of the rare few who could turn it all around.

But now that's not an option.

And Timmy is not my problem anymore.

———

As I sit here, watching Dex putter around the kitchen, humming a tune I don't recognize, I feel something I thought was out of reach for me.

Peace.

This is the life I fought for. The love I deserve. It's not perfect—nothing ever is—but it's mine. *Ours.*

It's easy. It's fun. We laugh through the good parts, and support each other unconditionally through the hard parts.

Dex glances up and catches me staring. "What?" he asks, grinning. "Do I have something on my face?"

"No," I say, shaking my head. "I just love you."

His smile softens, and he crosses the room to pull me into his arms. "I love you too, Margaux. Always have. Always will." And in his embrace, I know I'm finally home.

"Don't forget our tattoo appointment later," he suddenly reminds me.

"How could I forget?" I grin. I'm so excited.

———

The tattoo studio smells like antiseptic and ink, a strangely comforting scent that blends with the low hum of the tattoo machines. I glance around, my nerves tingling with anticipation. The walls are lined with designs, some bold and intricate, others delicate and simple. It's a world of stories etched onto skin, and now, I'm about to add my own.

Dex stands next to me, his presence steady and grounding. He's calm, confident, like he's been planning this for ages. He catches me watching him and gives me that signature grin, the one that always makes me feel like everything is going to be okay.

"You ready for this, baby?" he asks, his green-hazel eyes sparkling with mischief and something deeper—something that makes my heart race.

"As ready as I'll ever be," I reply, trying to match his confidence, though my voice betrays the fluttering in my chest.

The tattoo artist, a burly man with a surprisingly gentle demeanor, shows us the design one more time—two small black hearts side by side—simple yet powerful. It's perfect, an understated symbol of us, of love and resilience, of the bond we've forged through fire and pain.

"It's beautiful," I say softly, my fingers brushing against the design.

Dex leans in, brushing a kiss against my temple. "Not as beautiful as you."

I roll my eyes playfully, but my heart melts at the warmth in his voice.

The artist gets to work, starting with Dex. I watch as the two hearts take shape on his forearm, each line bold and deliberate. He doesn't flinch, just sits there with calm resolve, his eyes occasionally meeting mine. There's something mesmerizing about seeing him like this—strong, steady, and completely at ease.

When it's my turn, I take a deep breath and lay my arm on the padded chair. The buzz of the needle sends a jolt through me at first, but then it settles into a dull, rhythmic sensation. As the artist works, Dex stays by my side, his hand resting on my knee, his thumb drawing soothing circles.

"You're doing amazing," he murmurs, his voice steady and reassuring. "I'm proud of you."

I glance up at him, and the tenderness in his gaze nearly undoes me. I focus on the sensation, the sting of the needle, the permanence of the ink. This is more than a tattoo—it's a declaration, a piece of him and me etched into my skin forever.

When the artist finishes, I lift my hand and study the design on my wrist. The two black hearts are simple, but their meaning runs deep. They're us— two souls intertwined, connected, unbreakable.

Dex grins, his expression a mix of pride and excitement. "Looks amazing," he says.

"You too," I reply, admiring his matching tattoo. The symbolism isn't lost on me. We're tied together now, not just in spirit, but in something tangible.

He stands and pulls me into his arms, holding me close, his lips finding mine in a kiss that's full of promise and passion. In this moment, everything feels right.

The weight of the past lifts, and all I see is our future, as bright and unbreakable as the bond we've just sealed in ink and love.

———

TWO WEEKS LATER

The sun is just beginning to dip below the horizon, casting the world in hues of amber and violet. My heart races as Dex's deep, commanding voice cuts through the stillness.

"Run, baby," he growls, his tone dripping with challenge. "You have five minutes."

My breath catches in my throat. His green-hazel eyes gleam with a primal intensity, but there's something else there—love, trust, the unshakable connection that binds us. I hesitate for a moment, searching his face for the playful reassurance that always lingers beneath his edge. It's there, subtle, but it's enough.

A slow, deliberate smirk tugs at his lips. "What are you waiting for? *Go.*"

That single word jolts me into motion. I bolt, the cool evening air whipping against my skin as I sprint into the forest. My pulse pounds in my ears, a mix of adrenaline and excitement coursing through me. This isn't fear—it's exhilaration, the wild kind that only Dex brings out in me.

This time is a little different, though. This time there are little markers Dex has left for me along the way. He wants me to solve some kind of puzzle.

The trees blur as I weave through them, my breaths coming in quick gasps. And then I see it—*the first marker*. A black leather glove, one of his favorites, hanging from a low branch. It's unmistakable, and I pause for just a moment, my fingers brushing over it.

A memory flashes through my mind—Dex slipping his gloves on before one of his brutal rides, his hands steady as he guided me onto his bike for the first time. "Trust me," he'd said, and I had. *Completely.*

I keep running, my heart hammering with anticipation. The second marker appears moments later—a small jar of sand, tied with a strip of leather. I stop again, my chest heaving, and pick it up. The grains sparkle faintly in the fading light, a reminder of the time we sat on the beach, his arm around my shoulders, as he promised me a world bigger than my fears.

Tears prick my eyes, but I don't linger. I press on, the forest growing darker, the air heavier with every step. I stumble across a third marker—a small, carved heart. His initials are etched into the wood, alongside mine. My thumb traces over the grooves, and I can almost hear his voice, low and steady, telling me I'm his.

The final marker stops me in my tracks. Two black hearts tattooed onto a piece of canvas, a perfect replica of the ones on our arms. The sight steals my breath. He's thought of everything, every piece of us, every moment that's brought us here.

"Dex," I whisper, my voice trembling, though I'm not sure if it's from the exertion or the overwhelming love swelling in my chest.

I don't have to go much farther. The clearing opens before me, bathed in the soft glow of string lights strung between the trees. My breath catches as I see him—Dex, kneeling on the forest floor, his broad shoulders straight, his gaze locked on me. In his hand, a simple, stunning ring sparkles in the light.

I take a shaky step forward, then another, until I'm standing before him, my chest rising and falling with emotion.

"I don't need to say much," he begins, his voice raw, the gravel in it only making it more real. "You know what we've been through. You know what you mean to me."

Tears spill down my cheeks as he continues, his gaze unwavering. "Margaux, I'm not perfect. I've got my demons. But I'll fight them every day to be the man you deserve. I promise to stand by you, to protect you, to love you in every way I can for the rest of my life."

My legs give out, and I sink to my knees before him. "Dex…"

"Will you marry me?" he asks, his voice trembling, just slightly, for the first time.

I don't hesitate. "Yes," I say, the word spilling from my lips with everything I have.

His grin is blinding, his hands steady as he slides the ring onto my finger. The cool metal feels like a promise, a tangible symbol of everything we've built, everything we are.

Dex pulls me into his arms, his lips finding mine in a kiss that feels like stepping into the warmth of the sun.

The world around us fades, leaving only the two of us, tangled together in the heart of the forest, forever.

And for the first time in my entire life, I know I truly belong.

• • •

Curious about what happened to Desperella? Click here for a bonus scene that spills all the tea!

Enjoyed Beautiful Terror? Sign up here to get early announcements about new releases, giveaways, bonus scenes, opportunities to join my ARC team for future releases, and more!

Heidi's other books:

Blood and Sand (Dark Why Choose Mafia Romance)

- Sea of Snakes(Book 1)
- Sea of Sinners(Book 2)
- Sea of Rage (Book 3)
- Sea of Pain(Book 4)
- Sinners, Rage & Pain: The Brixton Trilogy(Books 2, 3 and 4)
- Sea of Demons(Book 5)
- Sea of Redemption(Book 6)

Burn It All Down Duet

- Volcano of Pain

C(r)ouch Bind Set Series (rugby why choose sports romance)

- Rucked

Standalones

- Pretty Lovely Lies (FBI/mafia romance, single parent, international)
- Ruthless Choices(romantic horror)
- F*CKBOYS(dark revenge romance, second chance, enemies to lovers)

Billionaire's Takeover Collection

- Irreversible Decision
- Compelling Proposal
- Love Merger
- The Billionaire's Takeover Collection (all 3 of the above)

Novellas

- Love in a Seedy Motel Room

Sign up for my newsletter here for the latest on new releases, promos, giveaways and events!

Join me on social media:

Facebook: @heidistarkauthor
Instagram: @heidistarkauthor
TikTok: @heidistark_author
Bluesky: @heidistarkauthor

Website: https://heidistarkauthor.com

ACKNOWLEDGEMENTS

Since *Volcano of Pain* was released, so many women have reached out to me to share their stories of being in narcissistic, toxic, and otherwise abusive, relationships.

It breaks my heart to know that so many of us have gone through these experiences with our own real-life 'Timmys', and that we share this darkness.

And that's not to say women don't behave this way too. Mac and Phil from *Dimming the Gaslight* podcast are examples of men who have endured the same thing. Thank you to both of you for having me on your podcast to share my real-life story (if anyone is interested, it's episode 138).

They say it takes a village to help a person escape a situation like this. And, at the end of the day, only the person going through it can truly get themselves out of it.

Instead of naming everyone, and probably forgetting some, because I truly am blessed with an army of amazing people in my corner, I'll say this— to every single person who reached out, gently suggested, didn't judge, reminded me of who I am, reminded me that you were indeed in my corner… each and every one of you played a part, and I couldn't have done it without you. You know who you are.

To my Stabbies, you've helped to give me the confidence to share Margaux and Dex's story, and give it the justice it deserves. Your advice and humor help me every day and I can't wait to see your 2025 manifestation bingo cards fill up—you all deserve fully-marked cards.

To Isa, who rode shotgun with me on the cover design and supported me every step of the way.

To my editor, Trish, who is a joy to work with, thank you for helping me to make this book the best it can be. And thank you for your humor—your comments make me laugh so hard, and I love seeing your reactions as you go through my books.

To my beta reading team, thank you for making sure Dex sufficiently brought it, and ensuring the story puts the souls that were ripped to shreds while reading (and writing) it sufficiently back together.

An especially big thank you to Amanda B, for your eagle eyes while reading through the beta manuscript, and for your massive help with the playlist, but also for being my friend throughout this process—the amount of times I must have told you I was bawling as I wrote a chapter!

To my doctor and my therapist who helped to nudge me in the right direction, providing judgment-free care (and especially to my real-life 'Kathleen' and your parting words at the end of our final session—they changed my life and made me realize the strength I didn't know I had).

To my real-life Alice—you really were my emotional support Alice through my whole nightmare, and I 100% would not be here without you. Your humor and your ability to be blunt but compassionate changed my life, and your way of seeing the world is magical. I can't wait to write a book with you (for those who don't know, we've already started, and it's going to be a fun one!).

To my real-life Josephine, thank you for making it starkly clear that if I didn't get out of my situation, you would be watching my leg wash up on the beach on the news (and my own episode of *Dateline*). You said the things that needed to be said in order for me to understand.

To my real-life Stacey (who I met on Twitter while discussing true crime many years ago), I will never forget the day we pored over information on narcissism and found more and more evidence that this is what I was dealing with—I always love researching with you. For your regularly checking in on me because you had a nagging feeling things were still not okay—just knowing you cared was a big help. And for reading through his emails, I'm sorry for melting your brain with the lack of punctuation and all the typos. Please forgive me ;)

To my big sis, Donna, for sending me your mic drop email that I was too scared to read in full at first, but eventually did. Your words were filled with love, and everything you said was true. I know it took way longer than you would have liked, but I got there in the end, when the time was right for me.

To Fang and Diamond, for giving me all the snuggles to get through the trauma of putting this story down on paper so that I can hopefully help others. And to my co-editor, Pearl, for attaching yourself to my leg while I worked my way through the book, and reminding me to take a break to give you attention every now and then.

And to Ed. Thank you for showing me what a real man looks like, how I deserve to be treated, and for being my real-life (non-psycho version of) Dex. I love you so much.

ABOUT THE AUTHOR

Heidi Stark writes contemporary dark romance with a twist of danger, desire, and the occasional sports scandal.

Known for her badass heroines and irresistibly morally grey men, Heidi has captivated readers with 20+ titles, including the gripping *Blood and Sand* series, the fiery *Volcano of Pain*, and her highly anticipated new release, *Beautiful Terror*.

Originally hailing from the lush landscapes of New Zealand, Heidi now calls the U.S. home, where she shares her creative chaos with her feline sidekick, Fang.

When she's not crafting heart-pounding stories, Heidi is a whirlwind of energy—hitting up barre classes, devouring true crime podcasts, dabbling in roller derby, people-watching, or indulging in her guilty pleasure: reality TV binges. Always on the hunt for inspiration, she's probably plotting her next book—or her next travel adventure.

Dark, daring, and deliciously addictive—Heidi's world is one you'll never want to leave.